FIRESIDE READER

FIRESIDE READER

A Treasury of
Outstanding Short Stories
Selected by the Editors of
Reader's Digest
Condensed Books

Drawings by Joseph Papin

—

The Reader's Digest Association
Pleasantville, New York
Cape Town, Hong Kong, London, Montreal, Sydney

The following stories
appear in condensed form:
The Bottle Imp, The Real Thing,
Rip Van Winkle, A Terribly Strange Bed,
The Loss, The Country of the Blind, The Weather Breeder,
The Adventure of the Speckled Band, Running Wolf,
Red, The Birds and *Dygartsbush.*

Library of Congress Catalog Card Number: 77-76319
Printed in the United States of America
ISBN 0-89577-099-7

CONTENTS

THE BOTTLE IMP
ROBERT LOUIS STEVENSON

THERE WAS A MAN in the island of Hawaii, whom I shall call Keawe; for the truth is, he still lives, and his name must be kept secret; but the place of his birth was not far from Honaunau, where the bones of Keawe the Great lie hidden in a cave. This man was poor, brave, and active; he could read and write like a schoolmaster; he was a first-rate mariner besides, and steered a whaleboat on the Hamakua coast. At length it came in Keawe's mind to have a sight of the great world and foreign cities, and he shipped on a vessel bound to San Francisco.

This is a fine town, with rich people uncountable; and, in particular, there is one hill which is covered with palaces. Upon this hill Keawe was one day taking a walk, viewing the great houses upon either hand with pleasure. "What fine houses they are!" he was thinking. "And how happy must these people be who dwell in them, and take no care for the morrow!" The thought was in his mind when he came abreast of a house that was smaller than some others, but finished and beautified like a toy; the steps shone like silver, and the borders of the garden bloomed like garlands, and the windows were bright like diamonds. Keawe stopped and wondered at the excellence of all he saw. So stopping, he was aware of a man that looked forth upon him through a window. The man was elderly; his face was heavy with sorrow, and he sighed bitterly. And the truth of it is that as Keawe looked in upon the man, and the man looked out upon Keawe, each envied the other.

9

All of a sudden the man smiled and nodded and beckoned Keawe to enter. "This is a fine house of mine," said the man, at the door of the house. "Would you not care to view the chambers?"

So he led Keawe all over it, from the cellar to the roof, and there was nothing there that was not perfect of its kind, and Keawe was astonished.

"Truly," said Keawe, "this is a beautiful house; if I lived in the like of it, I should be laughing all day long."

"There is no reason," said the man, "why you should not have a house in all points similar to this, and finer, if you wish. You have some money, I suppose?"

"I have fifty dollars," said Keawe, "but a house like this will cost more than fifty dollars."

The man made a computation. "I am sorry you have no more," said he, "for it may cause you trouble in the future; but it shall be yours at fifty dollars."

"The house?" asked Keawe.

"No, not the house," replied the man, "but the bottle. For I must tell you that all my fortune, and this house itself, came out of a bottle not much bigger than a pint."

And he opened a tightly locked place and took out a round-bellied bottle with a long neck; the glass of it was white like milk, with changing rainbow colors in the grain. Inside, something obscurely moved, like a shadow and a fire.

"This is the bottle," said the man; and when Keawe laughed, he added, "You do not believe me? See if you can break it."

So Keawe took the bottle up and dashed it on the floor till he was weary; but it jumped on the floor like a child's ball, and was not injured.

"This is a strange thing," said Keawe. "For by the touch of it, as well as by the look, the bottle should be of glass."

"Of glass it is," replied the man, sighing more heavily than ever, "but the glass was tempered in the flames of hell. An imp lives in it, and that is the shadow we behold there moving. If any man buys this bottle, the imp is at his command; all that he desires—love, fame, money, houses like this house, aye, or a city like this city—all are his. Napoleon had this bottle, and by it he grew to be the king of the world; but he sold it at the last and fell. Captain Cook had this bottle, and by it he found his way to so many islands; but he, too, sold it, and was slain upon Hawaii. For, once it is sold, the power goes and the protection; and unless a man remain content with what he has, ill will befall him."

"And yet you talk of selling it yourself?" Keawe said.

"I have all I wish, and I am growing elderly," replied the man. "There is one thing the imp cannot do—he cannot prolong life; and it would not be fair to conceal from you there is a drawback to the bottle; for if a man die before he sells it, he must burn in hell forever."

"To be sure, that is a drawback and no mistake," cried Keawe. "I would not meddle with the thing. I can do without a house, thank God; but there is one thing I could not be doing with one particle, and that is to be damned."

"Dear me, you must not run away with things," returned the man. "All you have to do is to use the power of the imp in moderation, and then sell it to someone else, as I do to you, and finish your life in comfort."

"Well, I observe two things," said Keawe. "All the time you keep sighing like a maid in love—that is one; and for the other—you sell this bottle very cheap."

"I sigh," said the man, "because I fear my health is breaking up; and as you said yourself, to die and go to the devil is a pity for anyone. As for why I sell so cheap, there is a peculiarity about the bottle. Long ago, when the devil brought it first upon the earth, it was sold for many millions of dollars; but it cannot be sold at all unless sold at a loss. If you sell it for as much as you paid for it, back it comes to you again like a homing pigeon. It follows that the price has kept falling in these centuries, and the bottle is now remarkably cheap. I bought it myself from one of my great neighbors on this hill for ninety dollars. I could sell it for as high as eighty-nine dollars and ninety-nine cents, but not a penny dearer, or back the thing must come to me."

"How am I to know that this is all true?" asked Keawe.

"Some of it you can try at once," replied the man. "Give me your fifty dollars, take the bottle, and wish your fifty dollars back into your pocket. If that does not happen, I pledge you my honor I will call off the bargain and restore your money."

"Well, I will risk that much," said Keawe, "for that can do no harm," and he paid over his money to the man, and the man handed him the bottle.

"Imp of the bottle," said Keawe, "I want my fifty dollars back." And sure enough, he had scarce said the words before his pocket was as heavy as ever.

"To be sure, this is a wonderful bottle," said Keawe.

"And now good morning to you, my fine fellow, and the devil go with you for me," said the man.

"Hold on," said Keawe, "I don't want any more of this fun. Here, take your bottle back."

"You have bought it for less than I paid for it," replied the man, rubbing his hands. "It is yours now; and for my part, I am only concerned to see the back of you." And with that he rang for his servant and had Keawe shown out of the house.

Now, when Keawe was in the street, with the bottle under his arm, he began to think. "If all is true about this bottle, I may have made a losing bargain. But perhaps the man was only fooling me." The first thing he did was to count his money; the sum was exact—forty-nine dollars American money, and one Chile piece. "That looks like the truth," said Keawe. "Now I will try another part of town."

The streets in that area were as clean as a ship's decks, and though it was noon, there were no passersby. Keawe set the bottle in the gutter and walked away. Twice he looked back, and there was the milky, round-bellied bottle where he left it. A third time he looked back, and turned a corner; but he had scarce done so when something knocked upon his elbow, and behold! It was the long neck sticking up; and as for the round belly, it was jammed into the pocket of his pilot coat.

"And that looks like the truth," said Keawe.

The next thing he did was to buy a corkscrew in a shop, and go to a secret place in the fields. And there he tried to draw the cork, but as often as he put the screw in, out it came again, and the cork was as whole as ever.

"This is some new sort of cork," said Keawe, and all at once he began to shake and sweat, for he was afraid of that bottle.

On his way back to the pier he saw a shop where a man sold shells from the wild islands, old coined money, pictures from China and Japan, and all manner of things that sailors bring in their sea chests. And here he had an idea. So he went in and offered the bottle for a hundred dollars. The man of the shop laughed at him at first, and offered him five, but, indeed, it was a curious bottle, so prettily the colors shone under the milky white, and so strangely the shadow hovered in the midst; so after he had disputed a while, the shopman gave Keawe sixty silver dollars and set the bottle on a shelf in his window.

"I have sold that for sixty which I bought for fifty," said Keawe. "Now I shall know the truth upon another point."

So he went back on board his ship, and when he opened his chest, there was the bottle. Now Keawe had a shipmate whose name was Lopaka.

"What ails you?" said Lopaka, "that you stare in your chest?" They were alone in the ship's forecastle, and Keawe bound him to secrecy, and told all.

"This is a very strange affair," said Lopaka, "but there is one point very clear—that you are sure of the trouble, and you had better have the profit in the bargain. Make up your mind what you want with it; give the order, and if it is done as you desire, I will buy the bottle myself; for I have an idea of my own to get a schooner and go trading through the islands."

"That is not my idea," said Keawe, "but to have a beautiful house and garden on the Kona coast, where I was born, the sun shining in at the door, glass in the windows, and pictures on the walls, like the house I was in this day."

"Well," said Lopaka, "if all comes true, I will buy the bottle, as I said."

Upon that they were agreed, and it was not long before the ship returned to Honolulu, carrying Keawe and Lopaka, and the bottle. They had hardly come ashore when they met a friend upon the beach, who began at once to condole with Keawe.

"I do not know what I am to be condoled about," said Keawe.

"Is it possible you have not heard," said the friend, "your uncle—that good old man—is dead, and your cousin—that beautiful boy—was drowned at sea?"

Keawe was filled with sorrow, and, beginning to weep, he forgot about the bottle. But Lopaka was thinking to himself, and presently, when Keawe's grief was a little abated, "I have been thinking," said Lopaka, "had not your uncle lands in Hawaii, in the district of Kau?"

"No," said Keawe, "not in Kau. They are on the mountainside—a little south of Hookena."

"These lands will now be yours?" asked Lopaka.

"And so they will," said Keawe, and began again to lament for his relatives.

"No," said Lopaka, "do not lament at present. This must be the doing of the bottle. For here is the place ready for your house."

"If this be so," cried Keawe, "it is a very ill way to serve me by killing my relatives. But it may be, indeed; for it was in just such a station that I saw the house with my mind's eye."

"The house, however, is not yet built," said Lopaka.

"No, nor likely to be!" said Keawe. "For though my uncle has some coffee and bananas, it will not be more than will keep me in comfort; and the rest of that land is black lava."

"Let us go to the lawyer," said Lopaka. "I have this idea in my mind."

Now, when they came to the lawyer's, it appeared Keawe's uncle had grown monstrous rich in the last days, and there was a fund of money.

"And here is the money for the house!" cried Lopaka.

"If you are thinking of a new house," said the lawyer, "here is the card of a new architect of whom they tell me great things."

"Better and better!" cried Lopaka. "Here is all made plain for us. Let us continue to obey orders."

So they went to the architect, and he had drawings of houses on his table.

"You want something out of the ordinary?" said the architect. "How do you like this?" and he handed a drawing to Keawe.

Now, when Keawe set eyes on the drawing, he cried aloud, for it was the picture of his thought exactly drawn. So he told the architect how he would have that house furnished, and he asked the man for how much he would undertake the whole affair.

The architect made a computation, and when he had done, he named the very sum that Keawe had inherited.

"It is quite clear," thought Keawe, "that I am to have this house, whether or no. It comes from the devil, and I fear I will get little good by that; and of one thing I am sure, I will make no more wishes as long as I have this bottle. But with the house I am saddled, and I may as well take the good along with the evil."

So he made his terms with the architect, and Keawe and Lopaka took ship again and sailed to Australia; for it was concluded between them they should not interfere at all, but leave the architect and the bottle imp to build the house at their own pleasure.

When they got back, Keawe and Lopaka went down Kona way to view the house and see if all had been done according to the thought that was in Keawe's mind.

Now, the house stood on the mountainside, visible to ships. It was three stories high, with windows of glass so excellent that it was clear as water and as bright as day. All manner of furniture adorned the great chambers, and pictures hung upon the walls in golden frames. The balconies were so broad that a whole town might have lived upon them in delight.

"Well," asked Lopaka, "is it all as you designed?"

"Words cannot utter it," said Keawe. "It is better than I dreamed, and I am sick with satisfaction."

"There is but one thing to consider," said Lopaka. "All this may be quite natural, and the bottle imp have nothing whatever to do with it. If I were to buy the bottle, and got no schooner after all, I should have put my hand in the fire for nothing. I gave you my word, I know; but yet I think you would not grudge me one more proof."

"I have sworn I would take no more favors," said Keawe. "I have already gone deep enough."

"This is no favor I am thinking of," replied Lopaka. "It is only to see the imp himself. If I once saw him, I should be sure of the whole matter. So indulge me and let me see the imp; and after that I will buy it."

"Very well," replied Keawe. "I have a curiosity myself. So come, let us have one look at you, Mr. Imp."

Now, as soon as that was said, the imp looked out of the bottle, and in again, swift as a lizard; and there sat Keawe and Lopaka turned to stone. Night had come before either found a thought to say or voice to say it with; then Lopaka pushed the money over and took the bottle.

"I am a man of my word," said he, "or I would not touch this bottle. Well, I shall get my schooner and a dollar or two for my pocket; and then I will be rid of this devil as fast as I can. For to tell you the plain truth, the look of him has cast me down."

"Lopaka," said Keawe, "do not think any worse of me than you can help; I know it is night, and the roads bad, and the pass by the tombs an ill place to go by so late, but I declare, since I have seen that little face I cannot eat or sleep or pray till it is gone from me. I will give you a lantern, and any fine thing in all my house that takes your fancy; and you must be gone at once."

"Keawe," said Lopaka, "many a man would take this ill, but for my part, I am so extremely terrified myself, I have not the heart to blame you. Here I go, then; and I pray God you may be happy in your house, and I fortunate with my schooner, and both get to heaven in the end, in spite of the devil and his bottle."

So Lopaka went down the mountain, and Keawe gave glory to God that he himself was escaped out of trouble.

One day followed another, and the fame of the house went far and wide; it was called *Ka-Hale Nui*—the Great House—in all Kona; and sometimes the Bright House, for Keawe kept a Chinaman, who was all day dusting; and the glass and the fine stuffs and the pictures shone as bright as the morning. As for Keawe himself, he could not walk in the chambers without singing; and when ships sailed by, he would fly his colors on the mast that had been rigged up in his front yard.

So time went by, until one day Keawe went on a visit as far as Kailua to certain of his friends. There he was well feasted, and left as soon as he could the next morning, and rode hard all day, for he was impatient to behold his beautiful house. A little beyond Honaunau, looking far ahead, he was aware of a woman bathing in the edge of the sea. He saw her white shift flutter as she put it on, and then her red holoku; and by the time he came abreast of her she had come up from the sea, and stood by the track side in her red holoku, and her eyes shone and were kind. Now Keawe no sooner beheld her than he drew rein.

"I thought I knew everyone in this country," said he. "How comes it that I do not know you?"

"I am Kokua, daughter of Kiano," said the girl, "and I have just returned from Oahu. Who are you?"

"I will tell you who I am in a little," said Keawe, dismounting from his horse, "but not now. Tell me, first of all, one thing: are you married?"

At this Kokua laughed aloud. "It is you who asks questions," she said. "Are you married yourself?"

"Indeed, Kokua, I am not," replied Keawe, "and never thought to be until this hour. But I have met you here at the roadside, and my heart went to you as swift as a bird. And so now, if you want none of me, say so, and I will go on to my own place; but if you think me no worse than any other young man, say so, too, and I will turn aside to your father's for the night, and tomorrow I will talk with the good man."

Kokua said never a word, but she looked at the sea and laughed. "Kokua," said Keawe, "if you say nothing, I will take that for the good answer; so let us be stepping to your father's door."

She went on ahead of him, still without speech; only sometimes she glanced back and glanced away again, and she kept the strings of her hat in her mouth.

Now, when they had come to the door, Kiano came out and welcomed Keawe by name. At that the girl looked over, for the fame of the Great House had come to her ears; and, to be sure, it was a great temptation. All that evening they were very merry together; and the girl made a mark of Keawe, for she had a quick wit. The next day he had a word with Kiano, and later found the girl alone.

"Kokua," said he, "I would not tell you who I was, because I have so fine a house, and I feared you would think too much of that house and too little of the man that loves you. Now you know all, and if you wish to have seen the last of me, say so at once."

"No," said Kokua, but this time she did not laugh, nor did Keawe ask for more.

This was the wooing of Keawe; things had gone quickly. The thought of Keawe rang in the maiden's head, and for this young man that she had seen but twice she would have left father and mother and her native islands. As for Keawe himself, his horse flew up the path of the mountain, and the sound of Keawe singing to himself for pleasure echoed in the caverns of the dead. He came to the Bright House and still he was singing. He sat and ate on the broad balcony, and the Chinaman wondered at his master, to hear how he sang between mouthfuls. The sun went down into the sea, and the night came; and Keawe walked the balconies by lamplight, and the voice of his singing startled men on ships.

"Here am I now upon my high place," he said to himself. "Life may be no better; this is the mountaintop. For the first time I will bathe in my fine bath, and sleep above in the bed of my bridal chamber."

As the Chinaman walked below, he heard his master singing and rejoicing above him. Keawe went into the bathroom; and the Chinaman heard him sing as he filled the marble basin, and as he undressed; until suddenly the song ceased. The Chinaman listened and listened; he called up to Keawe to ask if all were well, and Keawe answered him, "Yes," and bade him go to bed; but there was no more singing in the Bright House; and all night long the Chinaman heard his master's feet go round and round the balconies without repose.

Now, the truth of it was this: as Keawe undressed for his bath, he spied upon his flesh a patch like a patch of lichen on a rock, and it was then that he stopped singing. For he knew the likeness of that patch, and knew that he was taken sick with leprosy.

Now, it is a sad thing for any man to fall into this sickness. And it would be a sad thing for anyone to leave a house so beautiful and depart from all his friends. But what was that to the case of the man Keawe, he who had met his love but yesterday and won her but that morning, and now saw all his hopes break, in a moment, like a piece of glass?

"Very willingly could I leave Hawaii, the home of my fathers," Keawe was thinking. "Very lightly could I leave my house and bravely go to Molokai, to Kalaupapa by the cliffs, to live with the smitten. But what sin lies upon my soul, that I should have encountered Kokua coming cool from the seawater in the evening? Kokua, the light of my life! Her may I never wed; and it is for you, O Kokua, that I pour my lamentations!"

A little beyond the midst of the night there came in his mind the recollection of that bottle. He called to memory the day when the devil had looked forth; and at the thought ice ran in his veins.

"A dreadful thing is the bottle," thought Keawe, "but what other hope have I to cure my sickness or to wed Kokua? Would I beard the devil once, only to get me a house, and not face him again to win Kokua? I must go to Honolulu," he thought, "and see Lopaka. For the best hope I have now is to find that same bottle I was so pleased to be rid of."

So he came down to Hookena, and there was all the country gathered for the steamer as usual. In the shed before the store they sat and jested and passed the news; but Keawe sat in their midst and looked out on the rain falling on the houses, and the sighs arose in his throat.

Then the steamer came, and the whaleboat carried him on board. The ship was full of *Haoles*—white people—who had been to visit the volcano; but Keawe sat apart from them in his sorrow. He walked the deck all night; and all the next day he paced to and fro like a wild animal in a menagerie.

Toward evening they passed Diamond Head and came to the pier of Honolulu. Keawe stepped out among the crowd and began to ask for Lopaka. It seemed he had become the owner of a schooner—none better in the islands—and was gone upon an adventure as far as Pola-Pola or Kahiki; so there was no help to be looked for from Lopaka. Keawe called to mind a lawyer in the town and inquired of him. They said he was grown suddenly rich and had a fine new house upon Waikiki shore; and this put a thought in Keawe's head, and he called a hack and drove to the lawyer's house.

The house was all brand-new, and the lawyer had the air of a man well pleased.

"What can I do to serve you?" said the lawyer.

"You are a friend of Lopaka's," replied Keawe, "and Lopaka purchased from me a certain piece of goods that I thought you might enable me to trace."

The lawyer's face became very dark. "I do not profess to misunderstand you, Mr. Keawe," said he, "though this is an ugly business to be meddling in. You may be sure I know nothing, but yet I have a guess, and if you would inquire in a certain quarter, I think you might have news." And he gave the name of a man which I had better not repeat. So it was for days, and Keawe went from one to another, finding everywhere new clothes and carriages, and fine new houses and men in great contentment, although, to be sure, when he hinted at his business, their faces would cloud over.

"No doubt I am upon the track," thought Keawe. "These glad faces are the faces of men who have taken their profit and got rid of the accursed little imp in safety. When I see pale cheeks and hear sighing, I shall know that I am near the bottle."

At last he was recommended to a *Haole* in Beretania Street. When he came to the door, there were the usual marks of the new house, but when the owner came, a shock of hope and fear ran through Keawe; for here was a young man, white as a corpse, and black about the eyes, with such a look in his countenance as a man may have when he is waiting for the gallows.

"Here it is, to be sure," thought Keawe, and so with this man he noway veiled his errand. "I am come to buy the bottle," said he.

At the word, the young *Haole* of Beretania Street reeled against the wall. "The bottle!" he gasped. "To buy the bottle!" Then he seemed to choke, and, seizing Keawe by the arm, carried him into a room and poured out wine in two glasses.

"Yes," said Keawe, "I am come to buy the bottle. What is the price by now?"

At that word the young man let his glass slip through his fingers and looked upon Keawe like a ghost. "The price," said he. "The price! You do not know the price?"

"Why are you so concerned?" returned Keawe. "How much did it cost you?"

The young man was as white as a sheet. "Two cents," said he.

"What?" cried Keawe. "Two cents? Why, then, you can only sell it for one. And he who buys it . . ." The words died upon Keawe's tongue; he who bought it could never sell it again, the bottle and the bottle imp must carry him to the red end of hell.

The young man of Beretania Street fell upon his knees. "For God's sake, buy it!" he cried. "You can have all my fortune in the bargain. I was mad when I bought it at that price. I had embezzled money at my store; I was lost else; I would have gone to jail."

"Poor creature," said Keawe. "You would risk your soul to avoid the proper punishment of your own disgrace; and you think I could hesitate with love in front of me. Give me the bottle, and the change which I am sure you have all ready. Here is a five-cent piece."

It was as Keawe supposed; the young man had the change ready in a drawer; the bottle changed hands, and Keawe breathed his wish to be a clean man. And, sure enough, when he got to his room and stripped himself before a glass, his flesh was whole like an infant's. And here was the strange thing: he had no sooner seen this miracle than his mind was changed within him, and he cared naught for the leprosy, and little enough for Kokua; and had but the one thought, that here he was bound to the bottle imp for eternity, and had no better hope but to be a cinder forever in the flames of hell. Away ahead of him he saw them blaze with his mind's eye, and his soul shrank, and darkness fell upon the light.

When Keawe came to himself, he was aware of the hotel band playing "Hiki-ao-ao"; that was a song he had sung with Kokua, and, at the strain, courage returned to him.

"It is done now," he thought, "and once more let me take the good along with the evil."

So it befell that he returned to Hawaii by the first steamer, and as soon as it could be managed he was wedded to Kokua, and carried her up the mountainside to the Bright House.

Now it was so with these two, that when they were together, Keawe's heart was stilled; but as soon as he was alone, he heard the flames crackle and saw the red fire burn in the bottomless pit. The girl, indeed, had come to him wholly; her heart leaped in her side at sight of him, her hand clung to his; and she was so fashioned, from the hair upon her head to the nails upon her toes, that none could see her without joy. Full of song she was, and went to and fro in the Bright House, caroling like the birds. And Keawe beheld her with delight, and then must shrink upon one side, and weep and groan to think upon the price that he had paid for her; and then he must dry his eyes, and wash his face, and go and sit with her on the broad balconies, joining in her songs, and, with a sick spirit, answering her smiles.

There came a day when her feet began to be heavy and her songs more rare; and now each would sit on opposite balconies, with the whole width of the Bright House betwixt. Keawe was so sunk in his despair he scarce observed the change, and was only glad he had more hours to sit alone and brood upon his destiny. But one day, coming softly through the house, he heard the sound of a child sobbing, and there was Kokua rolling her face upon the balcony floor, and weeping like the lost.

"You do well to weep in this house, Kokua," he said. "And yet I would give the head off my body that you, at least, might have been happy."

"Happy!" she cried. "Keawe, when you lived alone in your Bright House you were the word of the island for a happy man. Then you wedded poor Kokua; and the good God knows what is amiss in her—but from that day you have not smiled. Oh!" she cried. "What ails me, that I throw this cloud upon my husband?"

"Poor Kokua," said Keawe. "And I had thought all this while to spare you! Well, you shall know all. Then, at least, you will understand how Keawe dared hell for your possession—and how much he loves you."

With that he told her all, even from the beginning.

"You have done this for me?" she cried. "Ah, well, then what do I care!" and she clasped him and wept.

"Ah, child!" said Keawe. "And yet, when I consider the fire of hell, I care a good deal!"

"No man can be lost because he loved Kokua, and had no other fault," said she. "I tell you, Keawe, I shall save you with these hands, or perish in your company. What! You loved me and gave your soul, and you think I will not die to save you in return?"

"Ah, my dear, you might die a hundred times, and what difference would that make," he cried, "except to leave me lonely till the time comes for my damnation?"

"You know nothing," said she. "I tell you I shall save my lover. What is this you say about a cent? But all the world is not American. In England they have a piece they call a farthing, which is about half a cent. Ah, sorrow!" she cried. "That makes it scarcely better, for the buyer must be lost, and we shall find none so brave as my Keawe! But, then, there is France; they have a small coin there which they call a centime, and these go five to the cent, or thereabouts. Come, Keawe, let us go to the French islands; let us go to Tahiti, as fast as ships can bear us. There we have four centimes, three centimes, two centimes, one centime; four possible sales to come and go on; and two of us to push the bargain. Come, my Keawe! Kiss me, and banish care. Kokua will defend you."

"Gift of God!" he cried. "Be it as you will, then; take me where you please. I put my life and my salvation in your hands."

Early the next day Kokua went about her preparations. She took Keawe's sea chest and put the bottle in a corner, and then packed it with the richest of their clothes. "For," said she, "we must seem to be rich folks, or who would believe in the bottle?" All the time she was as gay as a bird; only when she looked upon Keawe the tears would spring in her eyes, and she must run and kiss him.

As for Keawe, a weight was off his soul and hope in front of him. Yet was terror still at his elbow; and ever and again, as the wind blows out a taper, hope died in him, and he saw the flames toss and red fire burn in hell.

It was given out in the country they were gone pleasuring to the States, and so they went in the *Umatilla* to San Francisco, and at San Francisco took their passage for Papeete, the chief place of the French in the south islands. Thither they came, after a pleasant voyage, on a fair day of the trade wind, and saw the white houses of the town low down along the shore among green trees, and overhead the mountains and the clouds of Tahiti, the wise island.

It was judged best to hire a house opposite the British consul's to make a great parade of money, and themselves conspicuous with carriages and horses. This it was very easy to do, so long as they had the bottle in their possession; for Kokua was more bold than Keawe and, whenever she had a mind, called on the imp for twenty or a hundred dollars. At this rate they soon grew to be remarked in the town, and the matter of much talk.

They got on well with the Tahitian language—which is indeed like the Hawaiian—and began to push the bottle. You are to consider it is not easy to persuade people you are in earnest when you offer to sell them for four centimes the spring of health and riches inexhaustible. It was necessary, besides, to explain the dangers of the bottle; and either people disbelieved the whole thing and laughed, or they thought the more of the darker part, and drew away from Keawe and Kokua as from persons who had dealings with the devil. So depression fell upon their spirits. They would sit at night in their new house and not exchange one word. Sometimes they would have the bottle out upon the floor, and sit all evening watching how the shadow hovered in the midst.

One night when Kokua awoke, Keawe was gone. She felt in the bed and his place was cold. Then fear fell upon her, and she sat up in bed. A little moonshine filtered through the shutters, and she could spy the bottle on the floor. Outside, it blew high, the great trees of the avenue cried aloud, and the fallen leaves rattled on the veranda. In the midst of this Kokua was aware of another sound; it was as sad as death, and cut her to the soul. Softly she arose and looked forth into the moonlit yard. There, under the bananas, lay Keawe, his mouth in the dust, and as he lay he moaned.

"Heaven," she thought, "how careless have I been—how weak! It is he, not I, that stands in this eternal peril; it was he, not I, that took the curse upon his soul. It is for my sake that he now beholds the flames of hell. Am I so dull of spirit that never till now I surmised my duty, or have I seen it before and turned aside? But now, at least, I say farewell to the white steps of heaven and the waiting faces of my friends. A love for a love, and let mine be equaled with Keawe's! A soul for a soul, and be it mine to perish!"

She was a deft woman with her hands, and was soon appareled. She took the change—the precious centimes they kept ever at their side; for this coin is little used, and they had made provision at a government office. When she was in the avenue, clouds came on the wind and the moon was blackened. The town slept, and she knew not whither to turn till she heard someone coughing in the shadow of the trees.

"Old man," said Kokua, "what do you here in the cold night?"

The man could scarce express himself for coughing, but she made out that he was old and poor, and a stranger in the island.

"Will you do me a service?" said Kokua. "As one stranger to another, and as an old man to a young woman, will you help a daughter of Hawaii?"

"Ah," said the old man. "So you are the witch from the Eight Islands, and even my old soul you seek to entangle. But I have heard of you, and defy your wickedness."

"Sit down here," said Kokua, "and let me tell you a tale." And she told him the story of Keawe.

"And now," said she, "what should I do? If I went to him myself and offered to buy it, he would refuse. But if you go, he will sell it eagerly. I will await you here; you will buy it for four centimes, and I will buy it again for three. And the Lord strengthen a poor girl!"

"If you meant falsely," said the old man, "I think God would strike you dead."

"He would!" cried Kokua. "Be sure He would. I could not be so treacherous!"

"Give me the four centimes and await me here," said the old man.

Now, when Kokua stood alone in the street, her spirit died. The wind roared in the trees, and it seemed to her the rushing of the flames of hell. She stood and trembled like an affrighted child.

Then she saw the old man returning, and he had the bottle in his hand.

"I have done your bidding," said he. "I left your husband weeping like a child; tonight he will sleep easy." And he held the bottle forth.

"Before you give it me," Kokua panted, "take the good with the evil—ask to be delivered from your cough."

"I am an old man," replied the other, "and too near the gate of the grave to take a favor from the devil. But what is this? Why do you not take the bottle? Do you hesitate?"

"I am only weak," cried Kokua. "Give me a moment. It is my hand that resists; my flesh shrinks back from the accursed thing. One moment only!"

The old man looked upon Kokua kindly. "Poor child!" said he. "You fear; your soul misgives you. Well, let me keep it. I am old, and can nevermore be happy in this world, and as for the next—"

"Give it me!" gasped Kokua. "There is your money. Do you think I am so base as that? Give me the bottle."

"God bless you, child," said the old man.

Kokua concealed the bottle under her holoku, said farewell to the old man, and walked off, she cared not whither. For all roads now led equally to hell. She saw the flames blaze, and she smelled the smoke, and her flesh withered on the coals, and she lay by the wayside in the dust and wept.

Near day she came to herself again, and returned to the house. It was even as the old man said—Keawe slumbered like a child. Kokua stood and gazed upon his face.

"Now, my husband," said she, "it is your turn to sleep. When you wake it will be your turn to sing and laugh. But for poor Kokua, alas! No more singing, no more delight, whether in earth or heaven." With that she lay down in the bed by his side and fell into a deep slumber.

Late in the morning her husband woke her and gave her the good news. He was silly with delight, paid no heed to her distress, and was all the while eating and talking, and planning the time of their return, and thanking her for saving him. He laughed at the old man that was fool enough to buy that bottle.

"It was hard enough to sell at four centimes," Keawe said, "and at three it will be quite impossible. Whoever has that bottle now will carry it to the pit."

"Oh my husband!" said Kokua. "Is it not a terrible thing to save oneself by the eternal ruin of another? It seems to me I could not laugh. I would be humbled. I would be filled with melancholy. I would pray for the poor holder."

Then Keawe, because he felt the truth of what she said, grew the more angry. "Highty-tighty!" cried he. "This is your affection! Your husband is just saved from eternal ruin, which he encountered for the love of you—and you can take no pleasure! Kokua, you have a disloyal heart." He went forth furious, and wandered in the town all day. He met friends, and drank with them. All the time Keawe was ill at ease, because he was taking this pastime while his wife was sad, and because he knew in his heart that she was more right than he; and the knowledge made him drink the deeper.

Now there was an old brutal *Haole* drinking with him, one that had been a boatswain of a whaler—a runaway, a convict in prisons. He had a low mind and a foul mouth; he loved to drink and to see others drunken; and he pressed the glass upon Keawe. Soon there was no more money in the company.

"Here, you!" said the boatswain. "You are rich, you have been always saying. You have a bottle or some foolishness."

"Yes," said Keawe, "I am rich; I will go back and get some money from my wife, who keeps it."

"That's a bad idea, mate," said the boatswain. "Never you trust a petticoat with dollars. They're all as false as water; keep an eye on her."

Now this word stuck in Keawe's mind; for he was muddled with what he had been drinking.

"I should not wonder but she was false, indeed," thought he. "Why else should she be so cast down at my release? But I will show her I am not the man to be fooled. I will catch her in the act."

Accordingly, when they were back in town, Keawe bade the boatswain wait for him at the corner, and went alone to his house. The night had come again, and Keawe crept round the corner, opened the back door softly, and looked in.

There was Kokua on the floor, the lamp at her side; before her was a milk-white bottle with a round belly and a long neck; and as she viewed it, Kokua wrung her hands.

A long time Keawe stood and looked in the doorway. At first he was struck stupid; and then fear fell upon him that the bargain had been made amiss and the bottle had come back to him, as it came at San Francisco. At that his knees were loosened, and the fumes of the wine departed from his head like mists off a river in the morning. And then he had another thought; and it was a strange one, that made his cheeks to burn.

"I must make sure of this," thought he.

So he closed the door and went softly round the corner again, and then came noisily in, as though he were but now returned. And, lo! By the time he opened the front door no bottle was to be seen; and Kokua sat in a chair and started up like one awakened out of sleep.

"I have been drinking all day and making merry," said Keawe. "I have been with good companions, and now I only came back for money." He went straight to the chest and took some out. But he looked, besides, in the corner where they had kept the bottle, and there was no bottle there. "It is what I feared," he thought. "It was she who bought it."

And then he came to himself and rose up; but the sweat streamed on his face as thick as the rain and as cold as the well water.

"Kokua," said he, "I said to you today what ill became me. Now I return to my jolly companions," and at that he laughed a little quietly. "I will take more pleasure in the cup if you forgive me."

She clasped his knees in a moment, she kissed his knees with flowing tears. "Oh," she cried, "I ask but a kind word!"

"Let us never think unkindly of each other," said Keawe, and was gone out of the house.

Now, it was very sure he had no mind to be drinking. His wife had given her soul for him, now he must give his for her; no other thought was in the world with him.

At the corner, there was the boatswain waiting. "My wife has the bottle," said Keawe, "and unless you help me to recover it, there can be no more money and no more liquor tonight. Here are two centimes; you just go to my wife and offer her these for the bottle. Bring it to me here, and I will buy it back from you for one; for that is the law with this bottle, that it still must be sold for a less sum. But whatever you do, never breathe a word to her that you have come from me."

"Mate, I wonder are you making a fool of me?" asked the boatswain.

"It will do you no harm if I am," returned Keawe. "And if you doubt me," he added, "you can try. As soon as you are clear of the house, wish to have your pocket full of money, or a bottle of the best rum, or what you please, and you will see the virtue of the thing."

"Very well," said the boatswain. "I will try; but if you are having your fun out of me, I will take my fun out of you with a belaying pin."

So the whaler man went off, and Keawe stood and waited, his soul bitter with despair.

It seemed a long time he had to wait before he heard the boatswain's voice singing in the darkness. It was strange how drunken it appeared upon a sudden.

Next the man himself came stumbling into the light of the lamp. He had the devil's bottle buttoned in his coat; another bottle was in his hand; and even as he came in view he raised it to his mouth and drank.

"You have it," said Keawe. "I see that."

"Hands off!" cried the boatswain, jumping back. "Take a step near me, and I'll smash your mouth. You thought you could make a cat's-paw of me, did you?"

"What do you mean?" cried Keawe.

"Mean?" cried the boatswain. "This is a pretty good bottle, this is; that's what I mean. How I got it for two centimes I can't make out; but I am sure you shan't have it for one."

"You mean you won't sell?" gasped Keawe.

"No, sir," cried the boatswain. "But I'll give you a drink of the rum, if you like."

"I tell you," said Keawe, "the man who has that bottle goes to hell."

"I reckon I'm going anyway," returned the sailor, "and this bottle's the best thing to go with I've struck yet. No, sir!" he cried again. "This is my bottle now, and you can go and fish for another."

"Can this be true?" Keawe cried. "For your own sake, I beseech you, sell it me!"

"I don't value any of your talk," replied the boatswain. "You thought I was a fool, now you see I'm not; and there's an end. If you won't have a swallow of the rum, I'll have one myself. Here's your health, and good night to you!"

So off he went down the avenue toward town, and there goes the bottle out of the story.

But Keawe ran to Kokua light as the wind; and great was their joy that night; and great, since then, has been the peace of all their days in the Bright House.

AN END TO DREAMS
STEPHEN VINCENT BENÉT

THE LAST THING Rimington remembered was the anesthetist's voice saying "Breathe in deeply" and the taste of pungent sweet. But now he was looking at his own face in a mirror; so he must be out of the ether. Only it was strange to be looking *up* at your mirrored face. He concentrated, and received an impression of a hand and a white-sleeved arm. Of course. He was lying flat on his back, and the nurse was holding the mirror over him so that he could see himself. A queer thing to do—and for a moment he felt sheer terror.

Then, slowly, with the discipline of half a lifetime, he beat the terror off. Of course it was queer. Everything was queer. He hardly recognized himself, in this shaken point of consciousness, staring at a shining glass. But it must be himself, James Rimington, since it was alive and thought. Alive—and over the worst.

He had known all along that this was a serious operation for a man of fifty. A weak person might go under. But he, James Rimington, had never been a weak person. At the very last hadn't he waited thirty-six hours, to get De Blowitz on from Baltimore? And now it was done—successfully—and so it should be. He had paid the doctors enough.

The next thing to do was—sleep. He knew that. Sleep and rest, for hours and days, till the rebellious body healed into the smoothly working, unobtrusive machine to which he was accustomed. It would be irritating—hospital slops and the long drag of convalescence. But he could do it. He would not even think of business for two weeks.

His eyelids closed obediently, but, for the moment, that was all. He was still awake and, in a sense, wide-awake, except for this curious feeling of detachment from his body. Well, that was all right, too. The effects of the anesthetic had probably not yet worn off. Soon, perhaps, after another interval of darkness, he might wake to self and pain, but he was oddly comfortable now.

He had no wish to move so much as a muscle, but it seemed to him as if he had never been able to think more clearly or dispassionately. That Mexican Power business, for instance. It suddenly spread out before him like a giant chessboard. He could put his finger instantly on the one weak place—Patterson, the young engineer. Recall Patterson immediately, and Grommett could take care of the report.

He checked himself. Breaking resolutions already. Bad. It must not occur again. But counting sheep over a fence was merely silly; and, as sleep would not come, it seemed a pity to waste this clarity of mind. That was how he had become James Rimington, by wasting nothing. Well, then, why not retrace the steps by which one had become James Rimington? They said the drowning did it; and had he not been drowning in deep, black waters? Surely that would not hurt; that would pass the time till sleep.

He called before his shut eyes the face he had just seen in the mirror. At first it seemed like the face of an utter stranger; then, suddenly, it fitted and was his own. He read it feature by feature with dispassionate interest—the strong jaw, the clamped lips, the full cheeks of fifty, the bleak, undefeated eyes. A busy man didn't get much time to look at his face. But it was there, waiting for him, all the time.

On this face there was strong writing—the years had scored with a heavy pen. Or was it only the years? Somebody had said that we all made our faces by fifty. Perhaps that was so.

As he watched it, the lines began to smooth away, the heavy cheeks grew younger. It was as if he gazed at one of those magic tricks of the camera where a seed pushes up from soil and grows into leaf and flower in a few seconds of time. But here the reel of the picture was running in reverse. The strong tree of his life grew backward into its beginnings, diminishing slowly to the first green shoot.

Yes, that was the way he had looked at nine. Good heavens, he could even remember the patch on the right elbow of that jacket! He'd been ashamed of the patch—bitterly ashamed—and tried to hide it by holding his arm close to his body all the way through morning school. But old Miss Lang had noticed—she would, darn her!—and asked him if he'd hurt himself; and there he was, red in the face, without a word to say, in front of the giggling class.

"Hey, Patches, who's your tailor?" That was at recess.

> *"What's old Patches made of?*
> *What's old Patches made of?*
> *Patches and tags and calico rags,*
> *And that's what old Patches is m-a-de of!"*

He glared furiously around the circle of taunting faces. They'd started out just funning, and then, when they saw it made him mad, they suddenly wanted to make him madder. People were like that. He wanted to fight now, but he didn't know where to start. Somebody pushed him from behind, and as he wheeled, sobbing with anger, a big boy tripped him neatly, and he stumbled, striking out blindly.

"Oh, P-a-tches—lookit how fierce he is—lookit him fight! Don't hurt me, Patches, darling!" the mocking voices squealed.

And then, like a pigtailed avenger, Elsa Mercer burst into the group. Elsa was only eight, but she could throw a ball like a boy and wasn't afraid of anything. It was she who led him away, wheezing and sobbing, and pumped cold water on his eye till he could see out of it again. But he wasn't grateful. You couldn't be grateful to a girl.

He thought it out that afternoon in the woodshed, with the twisted, conclusive logic of a boy, as he split kindling. You wore patches because you were poor. And when you were poor, people laughed at you. They didn't laugh the same way at Toby Beach, whose father owned the bank. He was fat and placid and they teased him some, but everybody liked to play in his yard because he had a pony. If you had a pony and your father owned the bank, they wouldn't laugh at you.

"I'm going to be rich, do you hear?" he said, chopping fiercely at an obdurate log. "Rich! And then let 'em ask me to ride on my pony!"

He came back to the house in his shirt sleeves.

"Why, Jimmy, where's your jacket?"

"I lost it, Mom." He looked at his shoes.

"*Lost* it! Oh, Jimmy!"

Nobody'd ever find it in the creek, with the big stone tied up in it. "Well," he said defiantly, "it wasn't much good. It was patched."

For a moment he thought he was going to be spanked hard. Well, he was ready for it. Then, unexpectedly, Mom's face got funny.

"Come here, Jimmy," she said in a different voice. "Sit down. You're a big enough boy now to understand what I say. That jacket—"

He sat rebelliously. Didn't she think he knew? Poor—poor—poor—of course they were—of course it was true—every word she said.

When she finished explaining he looked at her and said, in a strange, unboyish voice, "You've got almost two dollars in the ginger jar, Mom. I counted it the other day. I can wear my Sunday suit until there's enough."

He could see her very plainly looking at him with those bewildered eyes. Mom had always been bewildered; that was the trouble. He could visualize her still, trudging about the house, dropping one task in the middle to start another, never once cleanly finishing any single piece of work on time. Of course, she had five children to bring up, and James Rimington Senior had died when his eldest son and namesake was six. So she had worked hard. But hadn't he worked hard? And look where he was now! It just showed where you could get with system and ambition.

Mom's only ambition had been to have her children grow up decent small town citizens, and even that hadn't quite worked out with George. James Rimington smiled grimly. He was remembering a mawkish copybook sentiment, "Behind every famous man there stands a great mother!" If the fellows who wrote that sort of thing only knew!

Astonishing, though, going back for the funeral, and having so many people speak about Mom. It seemed as if she must have known three-quarters of Bladesburg, and liked them, which was stranger. But then, of course, when you lived all your life in a little town—he begged their pardons, a "thriving young metropolis"—like that— Why, they'd even taken him on a tour of the place, shown him the big new high school where Sally was head of the English department, and the Beach Memorial Hospital. And he hadn't cracked a smile.

Hospital. After he had slept he would remember something important about a hospital. But first, though his eyes were shut, he must look at the mirror again. It clouded and grew clear.

Great Scott! Was that actually he with the ridiculous pompadour, with the clothes and the mandolin of the small-town beau? It seemed incredible, yet the face was very distinct. An adolescent face, unformed and eager enough, but with certain prophecies in it. The eyes were older than the lips, the jaw already decided. He felt more comfortable, tracing these resemblances.

And there was Elsa, in the preposterous garb of the time, and yet not so preposterous when you looked at her closely. Astonishing that she should have grown up like that; she had not been considered a pretty child. But at seventeen—well, no wonder he had been a fool.

Why, there he was, actually plunking that mandolin, seated on the porch steps of the Mercer house, while Toby Beach and the rest of the crowd sang. Cold lemonade and cookies and the smell of the old wisteria vine in Mrs. Mercer's garden. They said that wisteria vine was forty years old. Sometimes they swung a hammock under it, and Elsa sat there with the light in her honey-colored hair.

That had been when he started in at the bank. Oh, now he remembered it all! He remembered Mr. Dacey's paper cuff protectors and the big iron inkwells, solid as a vault door. Some of those country banks had been through hard weather recently. When he got out of the hospital it might be amusing to find out how the Bladesburg Trust had stood the storm. He supposed, a little unwillingly, that it was all right. It had certainly been safe and stodgy enough in his time.

He saw himself, with a flushed face, arguing with Mr. Beach, and heard the older man's answer: "It's a brilliant scheme, son, but we can't touch it. We're here to serve our own folks, not the easterners. Now, you tell Jerry Grant I'll see him about that note."

Why, that very plan, modified to suit other conditions, had been the first stepping-stone of James Rimington's fortune. And Beach had thrown it in the wastebasket to spend an hour with an old windbag of a dairy farmer just because he lived in the community. Of course, he always showed clean books to the bank examiner. Who couldn't with a ten-foot margin of safety on everything you did? He could just imagine Beach and the Cuban sugar contract. On second thought he couldn't imagine him at all.

Two long, hot summers passed before the mirror—summers with the smell of ripe grain in them and long evening shadows—summers of hard work and foolish gaiety and all the sights and sounds of a little town. And always he and Elsa, Elsa and he. "They were going together"—yes, that was the country phrase. He saw his face grow thin and his eyes darken, saw moments of anguish, moments of ecstasy.

"I love you, Elsa."

"I love you, Jim."

"It's a long time before we can get married."

"I can wait."

"You know, Sally's finishing school this month and George is growing up big. Next year, maybe, things'll be better."

"It's all right, Jim."

The ceaseless grind of never having the money—the grindstone continually turning in his head. Not that anyone else in Bladesburg was very rich then. But then, nobody else was James Rimington.

"I love you so much, darling Elsa. Oh, Elsa, you know how it is!"

"Why, Jim, of course I know."

Just as well, perhaps. Those years had taught him work. And that was the great thing. That paid for having been a fool with a mandolin. If it hadn't been for Elsa he'd never have had the nerve to try for New York—never waylaid John Q. Dixon when the great man's private car was sidetracked at Bladesburg one hot afternoon.

They called old Dixon a pirate—the smart financial writers on the newspapers. Well, they were right. But he was a pirate who knew how to pick his crew. James Rimington still remembered the gray eyes under the big eyebrows the first time he had seen them. Curious eyes, looking all the way through a man, expecting to find what they almost always found. When Rimington's eyes met his there had been an instant comprehension. Not sympathy, not even respect, but comprehension, definite and complete.

Then, later, there had been that strange little talk with Mr. Beach in the bank, with the blinds drawn down and the other people gone.

"Well, Jim, I hear you've been moving in high financial circles."

"Mr. Dixon? Yes, sir. I—I just happened to run into him—he was out on the tracks, smoking—"

"Uh-huh. Well, he's a smart man, Dixon."

"Yes, sir."

A silence.

"A smart man," repeated Mr. Beach, "and crooked as a ram's horn."

A longer silence. At last Mr. Beach spoke again.

"Jim, there'll be a vacancy this fall. Assistant cashier. I'd like to give that job to a married man."

"Yes, sir."

"Yes, son. And Dacey's getting old, and I'm not so young myself. Toby, he wants to be a lawyer. I think a heap of this bank, Jim."

"So do I, sir."

He went on as if he had not heard the words. "And I think a good deal of your mother, Jim. I'd bank on her. There are only two kinds of people in the world, Jim. Straight—and crooked. At least, that's been my experience."

"Yes, sir."

"Well, Jim, think it over. But, as I say, it's a job for a married man."

As soon as he had his coat on he had gone over to tell Elsa. He stared at the hurrying figure in the mirror. What a fool! But even the fool had had some sense in his folly. Halfway over to the Mercer house his fingers had gone to his pocket and closed on John Dixon's card.

"Say you love me, Elsa. Say it."

"I love you, Jim."

"Say you'll always love me, Elsa."

"Silly! Is anything the matter?"

"No—no—no—"

He hadn't told her. And that evening, in the bare, hot room, he had lain awake and listened to George's breathing in the other bed. And, with that breathing, he had heard the whirring noise of the grindstone of poverty, grinding out years and days.

If he and Elsa married he would never get out of Bladesburg. He couldn't stop helping Mom. Elsa was too decent for that. And when that was done, there'd be children. Assistant cashier. Cashier. Vice-president at forty, if all went well. President, perhaps, at fifty, and a house like Mr. Beach's. A solid man. A settled, small-town citizen. And thirty years of rolling a stone uphill. "There goes old man Rimington. Yes, sir, it's quite a story. Why, I can remember when we used to call him Patches." No, thanks.

He wouldn't be able to send Mom a cent if he went with Dixon. Dixon paid his clever young men starvation wages at first. He wouldn't be getting back to see Elsa, either. Dixon worked his crew too hard.

Of course, he could come back to Elsa later. But even while he told himself that, he knew the truth.

He got up silently and moved with softly restless steps around the room. For a moment he picked up the coat of the suit he had worn that day. The sleeve was wearing at the right elbow. He threw it on the floor.

The mirror clouded again. James Rimington took a deep breath. Suppose you'd stayed in Bladesburg, worn the patched coat? Would you still be James Rimington?

You can buy anything there is, he thought, but you have to pay for it. Yes, that was true; that was what he had always believed. And yet—

He turned back with relief to the mirror. Now the face in it was quite familiar, the face of a young, pushing man. Time moved faster—already the young man was thirty—thirty-five—and a power, long past his first big coup. Already you could see James Rimington in every line and gesture. He remembered the Wall Street reporter who had called him "the quiet earthquake," and how the name had stuck. He saw many scenes, many faces, but the pace of the reel never halted.

He caught a flash of John Dixon and himself, staring at each other across a desk. The pirate captain was older; there was gray in the bushy brows and the eyes were tired, but they could still look through a man. "Well," he said, looking through James Rimington, "how much do you expect me to settle for, Jim?"

James Rimington heard his own voice remark, "A hundred and sixty," and hated the voice a little for not being quite composed.

The pirate leaned back in his chair. "Hundred and sixty," he drawled. "When you first came into the office, Jim, I told you something, didn't I? 'Always squeeze the shorts,' I said."

"Yes."

"Well," said John Dixon, "appears you've got a good memory." James Rimington looked away from the passionless comprehension of the eyes.

Now things began to accumulate around James Rimington. There was the house in New York and the house on Long Island, the yacht, and the guests who came and ate and drank, cadged for tips, and went away. There were the books and the pictures, the charities and the gifts, not because one was interested, but because one was not interested enough. There were women of various ages and different looks. They passed, light and hollow as figures made of pasteboard; they had no importance. Always there was the work and the growing power. And those were real.

Elsa had come to Mom's funeral, and he'd seen her afterward. The children all looked like Toby. He couldn't find Elsa in any of them, except, possibly, the youngest girl. "We all know about you, Jim." How tranquil her voice had sounded! What a power women had of blotting things out of memory! It had been a hot afternoon, with the smell of wisteria drifting in through the open window, and she had stood, for an instant, with her hand on young Toby's shoulder. Then they had taken him to see the Beach Memorial Hospital.

The thing to do now was—sleep—sleep and get well. He had bought life on his own terms and paid for it, and just now he had bought off death. But only sleep could quiet the rapid, shuttling flow of scenes in the mirror—the deepest, the darkest sleep. For now, with a tiny click, the reel spun back to its beginning, and there he was, a boy with a patch on his sleeve, just starting out for morning school.

No, no, it was too much; it was not to be borne. Of course, you made a decision and took one path out of two. That was what life was for. The children of Elsa call their father Judge Beach, but that was only litera-ture, and stupid. John Dixon's eyes were as crooked as a ram's horn. The old iron inkwell was heavy—far too heavy—but, once the doctors oper-ated, the room would be full of the smell of wisteria, and Mom wouldn't have to work so hard anymore. Get well—yes, that was the trick—and marry afterward, for it is better to marry than burn; and when a man's tired making money it's time he founded a family.

But "when a man's tired making money he's tired of life," said John Q. Dixon's scornful voice; and James Rimington sighed feebly and tried to turn in the bed.

He'd beat them yet—show them—all of them—a man of fifty was young. No dissipations—nothing but work and power—no wasted energies—all the eggs in one basket. What more could a man desire? If only that face called James Rimington would go away from the mirror; that was the only thing. He forced it away by a terrific effort of will, and subsided, shaken. Better now.

But was it better? For now a room took the place of the face—a room in a hospital, with a sick man quiet in a bed. A big room, a private room, somebody important. Look at the flowers. A nurse was moving toward the door with soft, catlike steps. He followed her.

What a lot of doctors—count all the pretty doctors—one, two, three! But why did they look so serious in this other room? Their lips moved, making sounds, but James Rimington could not hear what they said.

Ah, but he could do better! He might not hear what they said, but, in the mirror, he could see what they thought; beneath the bristling hair and hard skull of the famous surgeon, he could look into the clever brain. It was very interesting, lighted and bright, a switchboard of thoughts and emotions, pulsating like tiny lamps. There De Blowitz had told his hand to get him a cigarette, and the hand had done it—all so smoothly and surely and in the twinkling of an eye.

But what was the meaning of this? Treachery. De Blowitz was not thinking of the sick man at all. He was wondering how soon he could get back to Baltimore, and worrying about his son's marks at school. James Rimington shifted to the young doctor next him. He was thinking that it would do him a good deal of good to be associated with De Blowitz in a case like this, and wondering if his wife had bought a paper and seen his name signed under De Blowitz's in the bulletin that they had issued at two o'clock.

Desperately, James Rimington looked in the mind of the nurse. One part of it was taking instructions efficiently, but the rest speculated on a telephone call from an intern at another hospital and the price of a hat in a store on the avenue.

James Rimington longed to speak, to cry out, to deafen their ears with "Stop! Stop thinking about anything but this sick man! He must get well. He's paid you to get him well! Who cares about your wives and your children? You mustn't even think of them till he gets well!" But James Rimington was helpless. He could only look on.

He pondered frantically, trying to think of someone whose sole concern might be with the sick man. Mallinson, his secretary—oh, he knew Mallinson—Mallinson would be putting out a short line already, just in case. His servants—perfect servants—he saw to that—but you didn't make friends with your servants any more than you made friends with your forks and spoons. Sally, his nearest sister—no, if she had the news she would be thinking of Mom and the hard years. Elsa—

He saw Elsa now, in her garden, her quick hands moving, gathering flowers. Thank goodness, she was alone. He could get to her—tell her a man was very sick, a man in a hospital. He tried, with all the force of his will, to drive the message through.

A vague discomposure crossed her features; she lifted a hand to her brow. James Rimington could have shouted with relief. If he could only make her think of him—of him, not merely James Rimington—all would be well. But, briefly as it had lighted, the feebly burning lamp that had to do with James Rimington winked out. Toby Junior was going to be married in a month. Elsa was thinking of that, of the girl, of how things would be different, and yet how much there was still to know. He could not get through.

A flicker—a giddiness—and he was back in the hospital. Ah, that was better. They were all thinking about the sick man now, doctors and nurses. And not only thinking, but working. But then he realized what it was they thought.

He seemed to hear a voice say, "I simply don't understand this sudden collapse. If it were anyone else— But a man with everything to live for—"

"My young vriendt, how do we know what he has to live for?" Those were De Blowitz's gutturals. "He may have nozzing. I have seen such collapse before in men like him."

"Shall I try the oxygen, Doctor?"

"Oh, yes, try the oxygen. It will do no harm."

It couldn't be true. James Rimington couldn't be there, dying. James

Rimington was a boy in a patched coat who meant to grow up and marry Elsa and do all sorts of things.

"Try the mirror," said a distant, terrible voice, "the mirror," and, hearing it, James Rimington summoned his last ounce of spirit. But the mirror, when he looked at it, was blank and shining. There was no breath. Then darkness fell on James Rimington.

THE PATIENT MIDDLE-AGED woman who had been waiting in the chair moved a little now.

"Now?" she said in a whisper.

"Yes," said the nurse's voice. "He's just coming out, Mrs. Rimington."

The figure in the bed stirred, moaned. The woman took its hand.

"Elsa."

"Yes, Jim, right here."

"You're here? I—I tried to get to you, but I couldn't. Are we married, Elsa?"

"Thirty years, dear. Try to sleep now. Everything's all right."

"I will, but—Elsa—I dreamed I—did I ever wear a—a coat with a patch?"

"Why, Jim, don't you remember? They made fun—and then, by the end of the year, every boy in school wanted a patch, because you made them believe it helped you shooting marbles. That was like you, Jim."

"I didn't—throw it away—I kept it—and wore it—"

"Of course, dear. Now just keep quiet and try to go to sleep. Dr. Lee says you're doing splendidly—the best patient he ever had in the Beach Memorial. And I'll be here all the time—and the children and Sally are just crazy to see you—"

He looked away from her a moment, up at the ceiling. A round spot of sun lay on it, bright and shining, the size and shape of a mirror.

"But," he said, "I saw—"

Her eyes followed his. "Oh, poor darling—right in your eyes—don't worry—I'll get Miss Foster to—"

"Never mind," he said. "All right now," and, taking her hand, he knew the measure of his victory and defeat, and was at peace.

PARSON'S PLEASURE
ROALD DAHL

MR. BOGGIS WAS driving the car slowly, leaning back comfortably in the seat with one elbow resting on the sill of the open window. How beautiful the countryside, he thought; how pleasant to see a sign or two of summer once again. The primroses especially. And the hawthorn. The hawthorn was exploding white and pink and red along the hedges and the primroses were growing underneath in little clumps, and it was beautiful.

He took one hand off the wheel and lit himself a cigarette. The best thing now, he told himself, would be to make for the top of Brill Hill. He could see it about half a mile ahead. And that must be the village of Brill, that cluster of cottages among the trees right on the very summit. Excellent. Not many of his Sunday sections had a nice elevation like that to work from.

He drove up the hill and stopped the car just short of the summit on the outskirts of the village. Then he got out and looked around. Down below, the countryside was spread out before him like a huge green carpet. He could see for miles. It was perfect. He took a pad and pencil from his pocket, leaned against the back of the car, and allowed his practiced eye to travel slowly over the landscape.

He could see one medium farmhouse over on the right, back in the fields, with a track leading to it from the road. There was another, larger one beyond it. There was a house surrounded by tall elms that looked as though it might be a Queen Anne, and there were two likely farms away over on the left. Five places in all. That was about the lot in this direction.

Mr. Boggis drew a rough sketch on his pad showing the position of each so that he'd be able to find them easily when he was down below, then he got back into the car and drove up through the village to the other side of the hill. From there he spotted six more possibles—five farms and one big white Georgian house. He studied the Georgian house through his binoculars. It had a clean prosperous look, and the garden was well ordered. That was a pity. He ruled it out immediately. There was no point in calling on the prosperous.

In this square then, in this section, there were ten possibles in all. Ten was a nice number, Mr. Boggis told himself. Just the right amount for a leisurely afternoon's work. What time was it now? Twelve o'clock. He would have liked a pint of beer in the pub before he started, but on Sundays they didn't open until one. Very well, he would have it later. He glanced at the notes on his pad. He decided to take the Queen Anne first, the house with the elms. It had looked nicely dilapidated through the binoculars. The people there could probably do with some money. He was always lucky with Queen Annes, anyway. Mr. Boggis climbed back into the car, released the hand brake, and began cruising slowly down the hill without the engine.

Apart from the fact that he was at this moment disguised in the uniform of a clergyman, there was nothing very sinister about Mr. Cyril Boggis. By trade he was a dealer in antique furniture, with his own shop and showroom in the King's Road, Chelsea. His premises were not large, and generally he didn't do a great deal of business, but because he always bought cheap, very very cheap, and sold very very dear, he managed to make quite a tidy little income every year. He was a talented salesman, and when buying or selling a piece he could slide smoothly into whichever mood suited the client best. He could become grave and charming for the aged, obsequious for the rich, sober for the godly, masterful for the weak, mischievous for the widow, arch and saucy for the spinster. He was well aware of his gift, using it shamelessly on every possible occasion; and often, at the end of an unusually good performance, it was as much as he could do to prevent himself from turning aside and taking a bow or two as the thundering applause of the audience went rolling through the theater.

In spite of this rather clownish quality of his, Mr. Boggis was not a fool. In fact, it was said of him by some that he probably knew as much about French, English, and Italian furniture as anyone else in London. He also had surprisingly good taste, and he was quick to recognize and reject an ungraceful design, however genuine the article might be. His real love, naturally, was for the work of the great eighteenth-century English designers, Ince, Mayhew, Chippendale, Robert Adam, Manwaring, Inigo Jones, Hepplewhite, Kent, Johnson, George Smith, Lock, Sheraton, and the rest of them, but even with these he occasionally drew the line. He refused, for example, to allow a single piece from Chippendale's Chinese or Gothic period to come into his showroom, and the same was true of some of the heavier Italian designs of Robert Adam.

During the past few years, Mr. Boggis had achieved considerable fame among his friends in the trade by his ability to produce unusual and often quite rare items with astonishing regularity. Apparently the man had a source of supply that was almost inexhaustible, a sort of private warehouse, and it seemed that all he had to do was to drive out to it once a week and help himself. Whenever they asked him where he got the stuff, he would smile knowingly and wink and murmur something about a little secret.

The idea behind Mr. Boggis's little secret was a simple one, and it had come to him as a result of something that had happened on a certain Sunday afternoon nearly nine years before, while he was driving in the country.

He had gone out in the morning to visit his old mother, who lived in Sevenoaks, and on the way back the fan belt on his car had broken, causing the engine to overheat and the water to boil away. He had got out of the car and walked to the nearest house, a smallish farm building about fifty yards off the road, and had asked the woman who answered the door if he could please have a jug of water.

While he was waiting for her to fetch it, he happened to glance in through the door to the living room, and there, not five yards from where he was standing, he spotted something that made him so excited the sweat began to come out all over the top of his head. It was a large oak armchair of a type that he had only seen once before in his life. Each arm, as well as the panel at the back, was supported by a row of eight beautifully turned spindles. The back panel itself was decorated by an inlay of the most delicate floral design, and the head of a duck was carved to lie along half the length of either arm. Good God, he thought. This thing is late fifteenth century!

He poked his head in further through the door, and there, by heavens, was another of them on the other side of the fireplace!

He couldn't be sure, but two chairs like that must be worth at least a thousand pounds up in London. And oh, what beauties they were!

When the woman returned, Mr. Boggis introduced himself and straightaway asked if she would like to sell her chairs.

Dear me, she said. But why on earth should she want to sell her chairs?

No reason at all, except that he might be willing to give her a pretty nice price.

And how much would he give? They were definitely not for sale, but just out of curiosity, just for fun, you know, how much would he give?

Thirty-five pounds.

How much?

Thirty-five pounds.

Dear me, thirty-five pounds. Well, well, that was very interesting. She'd always thought they were valuable. They were very old. They were very comfortable too. She couldn't possibly do without them, not possibly. No, they were not for sale but thank you very much all the same.

They weren't really so very old, Mr. Boggis told her, and they wouldn't be at all easy to sell, but it just happened that he had a client who rather liked that sort of thing. Maybe he could go up another two pounds—call it thirty-seven. How about that?

They bargained for half an hour, and of course in the end Mr. Boggis got the chairs and agreed to pay her something less than a twentieth of their value.

That evening, driving back to London in his old station wagon with the two fabulous chairs tucked away snugly in the back, Mr. Boggis had suddenly been struck by what seemed to him to be a most remarkable idea.

Look here, he said. If there is good stuff in one farmhouse, then why not in others? Why shouldn't he search for it? Why shouldn't he comb the countryside? He could do it on Sundays. In that way, it wouldn't interfere with his work at all. He never knew what to do with his Sundays.

So Mr. Boggis bought maps, large-scale maps of all the counties around London, and with a fine pen he divided each of them up into a series of squares. Each of these squares covered an actual area of five miles by five, which was about as much territory, he estimated, as he could cope with on a single Sunday, were he to comb it thoroughly. He didn't want the towns and the villages. It was the comparatively isolated places, the large farmhouses and the rather dilapidated country mansions, that he was looking for; and in this way, if he did one square each Sunday, fifty-two squares a year, he would gradually cover every farm and every country house in the home counties.

But obviously there was a bit more to it than that. Countryfolk are a suspicious lot. So are the impoverished rich. You can't go about ringing their bells and expecting them to show you around their houses just for the asking, because they won't do it. That way you would never get beyond the front door. How then was he to gain admittance? Perhaps it would be best if he didn't let them know he was a dealer at all. He could be the telephone man, the plumber, the gas inspector. He could even be a clergyman. . . .

From this point on, the whole scheme began to take on a more practical aspect. Mr. Boggis ordered a large quantity of superior cards on which the following legend was engraved:

THE REVEREND
CYRIL WINNINGTON BOGGIS

President of the Society　　　　　　　　　　*In association with*
for the Preservation of　　　　　　　　　　*The Victoria and*
Rare Furniture　　　　　　　　　　　　　　*Albert Museum*

From now on, every Sunday, he was going to be a nice old parson spending his holiday traveling around on a labor of love for the "Society," compiling an inventory of the treasures that lay hidden in the country homes of England. And who in the world was going to kick him out when they heard that one?

Nobody.

And then, once he was inside, if he happened to spot something he really wanted, well—he knew a hundred different ways of dealing with that.

Rather to Mr. Boggis's surprise, the scheme worked. In fact, the friendliness with which he was received in one house after another through the countryside was, in the beginning, quite embarrassing, even to him. A slice of cold pie, a glass of port, a cup of tea, a basket of plums, even a full sit-down Sunday dinner with the family, such things were constantly being pressed upon him. Sooner or later, of course, there had been some bad moments and a number of unpleasant incidents, but then nine years is more than four hundred Sundays, and that adds up to a great quantity of houses visited. All in all, it had been an interesting, exciting, and lucrative business.

And now it was another Sunday and Mr. Boggis was operating in the county of Buckinghamshire, in one of the most northerly squares on his map, about ten miles from Oxford, and as he drove down the hill and headed for his first house, the dilapidated Queen Anne, he began to get the feeling that this was going to be one of his lucky days.

He parked the car about a hundred yards from the gates and got out to walk the rest of the way. He never liked people to see his car until after a deal was completed. A dear old clergyman and a large station wagon somehow never seemed quite right together. Also the short walk gave him time to examine the property closely from the outside and to assume the mood most likely to be suitable for the occasion.

Mr. Boggis strode briskly up the drive. He was a small fat-legged man with a belly. The face was round and rosy, quite perfect for the part, and the two large brown eyes that bulged out at you from this rosy face gave an impression of gentle imbecility. He was dressed in a black suit with the usual parson's dog collar around his neck, and on his head a soft black hat. He carried an old oak walking stick which lent him, in his opinion, a rather rustic easygoing air.

He approached the front door and rang the bell. He heard the sound of footsteps in the hall and the door opened and suddenly there stood before him, or rather above him, a gigantic woman dressed in riding breeches. Even through the smoke of her cigarette he could smell the powerful odor of stables and horse manure that clung about her.

"Yes?" she asked, looking at him suspiciously. "What is it you want?"

Mr. Boggis, who half expected her to whinny any moment, raised his hat, made a little bow, and handed her his card. "I do apologize for bothering you," he said, and then he waited, watching her face as she read the message.

"I don't understand," she said, handing back the card. "What is it you want?"

Mr. Boggis explained about the Society for the Preservation of Rare Furniture.

"This wouldn't by any chance be something to do with the Socialist Party?" she asked, staring at him fiercely from under a pair of pale bushy brows.

From then on, it was easy. A Tory in riding breeches, male or female, was always a sitting duck for Mr. Boggis. He spent two minutes delivering an impassioned eulogy on the extreme Right Wing Conservative Party, then two more denouncing the Socialists. As a clincher, he made particular reference to the bill that the Socialists had once introduced for the abolition of blood sports in the country, and went on to inform his listener that his idea of heaven—"though you better not tell the bishop, my dear"—was a place where one could hunt the fox, the stag, and the hare with large packs of tireless hounds from morn till night every day of the week, including Sundays.

Watching her as he spoke, he could see the magic beginning to do its work. The woman was grinning now, showing Mr. Boggis a set of enormous, slightly yellow teeth. "Madam," he cried, "I beg of you, *please* don't get me started on socialism." At that point, she let out a great guffaw of laughter, raised an enormous red hand, and slapped him so hard on the shoulder that he nearly went over.

"Come in!" she shouted. "I don't know what the hell you want, but come on in!"

Unfortunately, and rather surprisingly, there was nothing of any value in the whole house, and Mr. Boggis, who never wasted time on barren territory, soon made his excuses and took his leave. The whole visit had taken less than fifteen minutes, and that, he told himself as he climbed back into his car and started off for the next place, was exactly as it should be.

From now on, it was all farmhouses, and the nearest was about half a mile up the road. It was a large half-timbered brick building of considerable age, and there was a magnificent pear tree still in blossom covering almost the whole of the south wall.

Mr. Boggis knocked on the door. He waited, but no one came. He knocked again, but still there was no answer, so he wandered around the back to look for the farmer among the cowsheds. There was no one there either. He guessed that they must all still be in church, so he began peering in the windows to see if he could spot anything interesting. There was nothing in the dining room. Nothing in the library either. He tried the next window, the living room, and there, right under his nose, in the little alcove that the window made, he saw a beautiful thing, a semicircular card table in mahogany, richly veneered, and in the style of Hepplewhite, built around 1780.

"Aha," he said aloud, pressing his face hard against glass. "Well done, Boggis."

But that was not all. There was a chair there as well, a single chair, and if he were not mistaken it was of an even finer quality than the table. Another Hepplewhite, wasn't it? And oh, what a beauty! The lattices on the back were finely carved with the honeysuckle, the husk, and the paterae, the caning on the seat was original, the legs were very gracefully turned, and the two back ones had that peculiar outward splay that meant so much. It was an exquisite chair. "Before this day is done," Mr. Boggis said softly, "I shall have the pleasure of sitting down upon that lovely seat." He never bought a chair without doing this. It was a favorite test of his, and it was always an intriguing sight to see him lowering himself delicately into the seat, waiting for the "give," expertly gauging the precise but infinitesimal degree of shrinkage that the years had caused in the mortise and dovetail joints.

But there was no hurry, he told himself. He would return here later. He had the whole afternoon before him.

The next farm was situated some way back in the fields, and in order to keep his car out of sight, Mr. Boggis had to leave it on the road and walk about six hundred yards along a straight track that led directly into the backyard of the farmhouse. This place, he noticed as he approached, was a good deal smaller than the last, and he didn't hold out much hope for it. It looked rambling and dirty, and some of the sheds were clearly in bad repair.

There were three men standing in a close group in a corner of the yard, and one of them had two large black greyhounds with him, on leashes. When the men caught sight of Mr. Boggis walking forward in his black suit and parson's collar, they stopped talking and seemed suddenly to stiffen and freeze, becoming absolutely still, motionless, three faces turned toward him, watching him suspiciously as he approached.

The oldest of the three was a stumpy man with a wide frog mouth and small shifty eyes, and although Mr. Boggis didn't know it, his name was Rummins and he was the owner of the farm.

The tall youth beside him, who appeared to have something wrong with one eye, was Bert, the son of Rummins.

The shortish flat-faced man with a narrow corrugated brow and immensely broad shoulders was Claud. Claud had dropped in on Rummins in the hope of getting a piece of pork or ham out of him from the pig that had been killed the day before. Claud knew about the killing—the noise of it had carried far across the fields—and he also knew that a man should have a government permit to do that sort of thing, and that Rummins didn't have one.

"Good afternoon," Mr. Boggis said. "Isn't it a lovely day."

None of the three men moved. At that moment they were all thinking precisely the same thing—that somehow or other this clergyman, who was certainly not the local fellow, had been sent to poke his nose into their business and to report what he found to the government.

"What beautiful dogs," Mr. Boggis said. "I must say I've never been greyhound racing myself, but they tell me it's a fascinating sport."

Again the silence, and Mr. Boggis glanced quickly from Rummins to Bert, then to Claud, then back again to Rummins, and he noticed that each of them had the same peculiar expression on his face, something between a jeer and a challenge, with a contemptuous curl to the mouth, and a sneer around the nose.

"Might I inquire if you are the owner?" Mr. Boggis asked, undaunted, addressing himself to Rummins.

"What is it you want?"

"I do apologize for troubling you, especially on a Sunday."

Mr. Boggis offered his card and Rummins took it and held it up close to his face. The other two didn't move, but their eyes swiveled over to one side, trying to see.

"And what exactly might you be wanting?" Rummins asked.

For the second time that day, Mr. Boggis explained at some length the aims and ideals of the Society for the Preservation of Rare Furniture.

"We don't have any," Rummins told him when it was over. "You're wasting your time."

"Now, just a minute, sir," Mr. Boggis said, raising a finger. "The last man who said that to me was an old farmer down in Sussex, and when he finally let me into his house, d'you know what I found? A dirty-looking old chair in the corner of the kitchen, and it turned out to be worth *four hundred pounds!* I showed him how to sell it, and he bought himself a new tractor with the money."

"What on earth are you talking about?" Claud said. "There ain't no chair in the world worth four hundred pound."

"Excuse me," Mr. Boggis answered primly, "but there are plenty of chairs in England worth more than twice that figure. And you know where they are? They're tucked away in the farms and cottages all over the country, with the owners using them as steps and ladders and standing on them with hobnailed boots to reach a pot of jam out of the top cupboard or to hang a picture. This is the truth I'm telling you, my friends."

Rummins shifted uneasily on his feet. "You mean to say all you want to do is go inside and stand there in the middle of the room and look around?"

"Exactly," Mr. Boggis said. He was at last beginning to sense what the trouble might be. "I don't want to pry into your cupboards or into your larder. I just want to look at the furniture to see if you happen to have any treasures here, and then I can write about them in our Society magazine."

"You know what I think?" Rummins said, fixing him with his small wicked eyes. "I think you're after buying the stuff yourself. Why else would you be going to all this trouble?"

"Oh, dear me. I only wish I had the money. Of course, if I saw something that I took a great fancy to, and it wasn't beyond my means, I might be tempted to make an offer. But alas, that rarely happens."

"Well," Rummins said, "I don't suppose there's any harm in your taking a look around if that's all you want." He led the way across the yard to the back door of the farmhouse, and Mr. Boggis followed him; so did the son, Bert, and Claud with his two dogs. They went through the kitchen, where the only furniture was a cheap deal table with a dead chicken lying on it, and they emerged into a fairly large, exceedingly filthy living room.

And there it was! Mr. Boggis saw it at once, and he stopped dead in his tracks and gave a little shrill gasp of shock. Then he stood there for five, ten, fifteen seconds at least, staring like an idiot, unable to believe, not daring to believe what he saw before him. It *couldn't* be true, not possibly! But the longer he stared, the more true it began to seem. After all, there it was standing against the wall right in front of him, as real and as solid as the house itself. And who in the world could possibly make a mistake about a thing like that? Admittedly it was painted white, but that made not the slightest difference. Some idiot had done that. The paint could easily be stripped off. But good God! Just look at it! And in a place like this!

At that point, Mr. Boggis became aware of the three men, Rummins, Bert, and Claud, standing together in a group over by the fireplace, watching him intently. They had seen him stop and gasp and stare, and they must have seen his face turning red, or maybe it was white, but in any event they had seen enough to spoil the whole goddamn business if he didn't do something about it quick. In a flash, Mr. Boggis clapped one hand over his heart, staggered to the nearest chair, and collapsed into it, breathing heavily.

"What's the matter with you?" Claud asked.

"It's nothing," he gasped. "I'll be all right in a minute. Please—a glass of water. It's my heart."

Bert fetched him the water, handed it to him, and stayed close beside him, staring down at him with a fatuous leer on his face.

"I thought maybe you were looking at something," Rummins said. The wide frog mouth widened a fraction further into a crafty grin, showing the stubs of several broken teeth.

"No, no," Mr. Boggis said. "Oh dear me, no. It's just my heart. I'm so sorry. It happens every now and then. But it goes away quite quickly. I'll be all right in a couple of minutes."

He *must* have time to think, he told himself. More important still, he must have time to compose himself thoroughly before he said another word. Take it gently, Boggis. And whatever you do, keep calm. These people may be ignorant, but they are not stupid. They are suspicious and wary and sly. And if it is really true—no, it *can't* be, it *can't* be true. . . .

He was holding one hand up over his eyes in a gesture of pain, and now, very carefully, secretly, he made a little crack between two of the fingers and peeked through.

Sure enough, the thing was still there, and on this occasion he took a good long look at it. Yes—he had been right the first time! There wasn't the slightest doubt about it! It was really unbelievable!

What he saw was a piece of furniture that any expert would have given almost anything to acquire. To a layman, it might not have appeared particularly impressive, especially when covered over as it was with dirty white paint, but to Mr. Boggis it was a dealer's dream. He knew, as does every other dealer in Europe and America, that among the most celebrated and coveted examples of eighteenth-century English furniture in existence are the three famous pieces known as "The Chippendale Commodes." He knew their history backward—that the first was "discovered" in 1920, in a house at Moreton-on-the-Marsh, and was sold at Sotheby's the same year; that the other two turned up in the same auction rooms a year later, both coming out of Rainham Hall, Norfolk. They all fetched enormous prices. He couldn't quite remember the exact figure for the first one, or even the second, but he knew for certain that the last one to be sold had fetched thirty-nine hundred guineas. And that was in 1921! Today the same piece would surely be worth ten thousand pounds. Some man, Mr. Boggis couldn't remember his name, had made a study of these commodes fairly recently and had proved that all three must have come from the same workshop, for the veneers were all from the same log, and the same set of templates had been used in the construction of each. No invoices had been found for any of them, but all the experts were agreed that these three commodes could have been executed only by Thomas Chippendale himself, with his own hands, at the most exalted period in his career.

And here, Mr. Boggis kept telling himself as he peered cautiously through the crack in his fingers, here was the fourth Chippendale Commode! And *he* had found it! He would be rich! He would also be famous! Each of the other three was known throughout the furniture world by a special name—The Chastleton Commode, The First Rainham Commode, The Second Rainham Commode. This one would go down in history as The Boggis Commode! Just imagine the faces of the boys up there in London when they got a look at it tomorrow morning! And the luscious offers coming in from the big fellows over in the West End—Frank Partridge, Mallett, Jetley, and the rest of them! There would be a picture of it in *The Times*, and it would say, "The very fine Chippendale Commode which was recently discovered by Mr. Cyril Boggis, a London dealer. . . ." Dear God, what a stir he was going to make!

This one here, Mr. Boggis thought, was almost exactly similar to the Second Rainham Commode. (All three, the Chastleton and the two Rainhams, differed from one another in a number of small ways.) It was a most impressive handsome affair built in the French rococo style of Chippendale's Director period, a kind of large fat chest of drawers set upon four carved and fluted legs that raised it about a foot from the ground. There were six drawers in all, two long ones in the middle and two shorter ones on either side. The serpentine front was magnificently ornamented along the top and sides and bottom, and also vertically between each set of drawers, with intricate carvings of festoons and scrolls and clusters. The brass handles, although partly obscured by white paint, appeared to be superb. It was, of course, a rather heavy piece, but the design had been executed with such elegance and grace that the heaviness was in no way offensive.

"How're you feeling now?" Mr. Boggis heard someone saying.

"Thank you, thank you, I'm much better already. It passes quickly. My doctor says it's nothing to worry about really, so long as I rest for a few minutes whenever it happens. Ah yes," he said, raising himself slowly to his feet. "That's better. I'm all right now."

A trifle unsteadily, he began to move around the room examining the furniture, one piece at a time, commenting upon it briefly. He could see at once that apart from the commode it was a very poor lot.

"Nice oak table," he said. "But I'm afraid it's not old enough to be of any interest. Good comfortable chairs, but quite modern, yes, quite modern. Now this cupboard, well, it's rather attractive, but again, not valuable. This chest of drawers"—he walked casually past the Chippendale commode and gave it a little contemptuous flip with his fingers—"worth a few pounds, I daresay, but no more. A rather crude reproduction, I'm afraid. Probably made in Victorian times. Did you paint it white?"

"Yes," Rummins said. "Bert did it."

"A very wise move. It's considerably less offensive in white."

"That's a strong piece of furniture," Rummins said. "Some nice carving on it too."

"Machine-carved," Mr. Boggis answered superbly, bending down to examine the exquisite craftsmanship. "You can tell it a mile off. But still, I suppose it's quite pretty in its way. It has its points."

He began to saunter off, then he checked himself and turned slowly back again. He placed the tip of one finger against the point of his chin, laid his head over to one side, and frowned as though deep in thought.

"You know what?" he said, looking at the commode, speaking so casually that his voice kept trailing off. "I've just remembered . . . I've been wanting a set of legs something like that for a long time. I've got a rather curious table in my own little home, one of those low things that people put in front of the sofa, sort of a coffee table, and last Michaelmas, when I moved house, the foolish movers damaged the legs in the most shocking way. I'm very fond of that table. I always keep my big Bible on it, and all my sermon notes."

He paused, stroking his chin with the finger. "Now I was just thinking. These legs on your chest of drawers might be very suitable. Yes, they might indeed. They could easily be cut off and fixed onto my table."

He looked around and saw the three men standing absolutely still, watching him suspiciously, three pairs of eyes, all different but equally mistrusting, small pig eyes for Rummins, large slow eyes for Claud, and two odd eyes for Bert, one of them very queer and boiled and misty pale, with a little black dot in the center, like a fish eye on a plate.

Mr. Boggis smiled and shook his head. "Come, come, what on earth am I saying? I'm talking as though I owned the piece myself. I do apologize."

"What you mean to say is you'd like to buy it," Rummins said.

"Well . . ." Mr. Boggis glanced back at the commode, frowning. "I'm not sure. I might . . . and then again . . . on second thoughts . . . no . . . I think it might be a bit too much trouble. It's not worth it. I'd better leave it."

"How much were you thinking of offering?" Rummins asked.

"Not much, I'm afraid. You see, this is not a genuine antique. It's merely a reproduction."

"I'm not so sure about that," Rummins told him. "It's been in *here* over twenty years, and before that it was up at the manor house. I bought it there myself at auction when the old squire died. You can't tell me that thing's new."

"It's not exactly new, but it's certainly not more than about sixty years old."

"It's more than that," Rummins said. "Bert, where's that bit of paper you once found at the back of one of them drawers? That old bill."

The boy looked vacantly at his father.

Mr. Boggis opened his mouth, then quickly shut it again without uttering a sound. He was beginning literally to shake with excitement, and to calm himself he walked over to the window and stared out at a plump brown hen pecking around for stray grains of corn in the yard.

"It was in the back of that drawer underneath all them rabbit snares," Rummins was saying. "Go on and fetch it out and show it to the parson."

When Bert went forward to the commode, Mr. Boggis turned around again. He couldn't stand not watching him. He saw him pull out one of the big middle drawers, and he noticed the beautiful smooth way in which the drawer slid open. He saw Bert's hand dipping inside and rummaging around among a lot of wires and strings.

"You mean this?" Bert lifted out a piece of folded yellowing paper and carried it over to the father, who unfolded it and held it up close to his face.

"You can't tell me this writing ain't bloody old," Rummins said, and he held the paper out to Mr. Boggis, whose whole arm was shaking as he took it. It was brittle and it crackled slightly between his fingers. The writing was in a long sloping copperplate hand:

> *Edward Montagu, Esq.*   *Dr.*
> *To Thos. Chippendale*
> *A large mahogany Commode Table of exceeding fine wood, very rich carvd, set upon fluted legs, two very neat shapd long drawers in the middle part and two ditto on each side, with rich chasd Brass Handles and Ornaments, the whole compleatly finished in the most exquisite taste £87*

Mr. Boggis was holding on to himself tight and fighting to suppress the excitement that was spinning around inside him and making him dizzy. Oh, God, it was wonderful! With the invoice, the value had climbed even higher. What in heaven's name would it fetch now? Twelve thousand pounds? Fourteen? Maybe fifteen or even twenty! Who knows?

Oh, boy!

He tossed the paper contemptuously onto the table and said quietly, "It's exactly what I told you, a Victorian reproduction. This is simply the invoice that the seller—the man who made it and passed it off as an antique—gave to his client. I've seen lots of them. You'll notice that he doesn't say he made it himself. That would give the game away."

"Say what you like," Rummins announced, "but that's an old piece of paper."

"Of course it is, my dear friend. It's Victorian, late Victorian. About eighteen ninety. Sixty or seventy years old. I've seen hundreds of them. That was a time when masses of cabinetmakers did nothing else but apply themselves to faking the fine furniture of the century before."

"Listen, Parson," Rummins said, pointing at him with a thick dirty finger, "I'm not saying as how you may not know a fair bit about this furniture business, but what I *am* saying is this: How on earth can you be so mighty sure it's a fake when you haven't even seen what it looks like underneath all that paint?"

"Come here," Mr. Boggis said. "Come over here and I'll show you." He stood beside the commode and waited for them to gather around. "Now, anyone got a knife?"

Claud produced a horn-handled pocketknife, and Mr. Boggis took it and opened the smallest blade. Then, working with apparent casualness but actually with extreme care, he began chipping off the white paint from a small area on the top of the commode. The paint flaked away cleanly from the old hard varnish underneath, and when he had cleared away about three square inches, he stepped back and said, "Now, take a look at that!"

It was beautiful—a warm little patch of mahogany, glowing like a topaz, rich and dark with the true color of its two hundred years.

"What's wrong with it?" Rummins asked.

"It's processed! Anyone can see that!"

"How can you see it, mister? You tell us."

"Well, I must say that's a trifle difficult to explain. It's chiefly a matter of experience. My experience tells me that without the slightest doubt this wood has been processed with lime. That's what they use for mahogany, to give it that dark aged color. For oak, they use potash salts, and for walnut it's nitric acid, but for mahogany it's always lime."

The three men moved a little closer to peer at the wood. There was a slight stirring of interest among them now. It was always intriguing to hear about some new form of crookery or deception.

"Look closely at the grain. You see that touch of orange in among the dark red-brown. That's the sign of lime."

They leaned forward, their noses close to the wood, first Rummins, then Claud, then Bert.

"And then there's the patina," Mr. Boggis continued.

"The what?"

He explained to them the meaning of this word as applied to furniture.

"My dear friends, you've no idea the trouble these rascals will go to to imitate the hard beautiful bronzelike appearance of genuine patina. It's terrible, really terrible, and it makes me quite sick to speak of it!" He was spitting each word sharply off the tip of the tongue and making a sour mouth to show his extreme distaste. The men waited, hoping for more secrets.

"The time and trouble that some mortals will go to in order to deceive the innocent!" Mr. Boggis cried. "It's perfectly disgusting! D'you know what they did here, my friends? I can recognize it clearly. I can almost *see* them doing it, the long, complicated ritual of rubbing the wood with linseed oil, coating it over with French polish that has been cunningly colored, brushing it down with pumice stone and oil, beeswaxing it with a wax that contains dirt and dust, and finally giving it the heat treatment to crack the polish so that it looks like two-hundred-year-old varnish! It really upsets me to contemplate such knavery!"

The three men continued to gaze at the little patch of dark wood.

"Feel it!" Mr. Boggis ordered. "Put your fingers on it! There, how does it feel, warm or cold?"

"Feels cold," Rummins said.

"Exactly, my friend! It happens to be a fact that faked patina is always cold to the touch. Real patina has a curiously warm feel to it."

"This feels normal," Rummins said, ready to argue.

"No, sir, it's cold. But of course it takes an experienced and sensitive fingertip to pass a positive judgment. You couldn't really be expected to judge this any more than I could be expected to judge the quality of your barley. Everything in life, my dear sir, is experience."

The men were staring at this queer moonfaced clergyman with the bulging eyes, not quite so suspiciously now because he did seem to know a bit about his subject. But they were still a long way from trusting him.

Mr. Boggis bent down and pointed to one of the metal drawer handles on the commode. "This is another place where the fakers go to work," he said. "Old brass normally has a color and character all of its own. Did you know that?"

They stared at him, hoping for still more secrets.

"But the trouble is that they've become exceedingly skilled at matching it. In fact, it's almost impossible to tell the difference between genuine old and faked old. I don't mind admitting that it has me guessing. So there's not really any point in our scraping the paint off these handles. We wouldn't be any the wiser."

"How can you possibly make new brass look like old?" Claud said. "Brass doesn't rust, you know."

"You are quite right, my friend. But these scoundrels have their own secret methods."

"Such as what?" Claud asked. Any information of this nature was valuable, in his opinion. One never knew when it might come in handy.

"All they have to do," Mr. Boggis said, "is to place these handles overnight in a box of mahogany shavings saturated in sal ammoniac. The sal ammoniac turns the metal green, but if you rub off the green, you will find underneath it a fine soft silvery-warm luster, a luster identical to that which comes with very old brass. Oh, it is so bestial, the things they do! With iron they have another trick."

"What do they do with iron?" Claud asked, fascinated.

"Iron's easy," Mr. Boggis said. "Iron locks and plates and hinges are simply buried in common salt and they come out all rusted and pitted in no time."

"All right," Rummins said. "So you admit you can't tell about the handles. For all you know, they may be hundreds and hundreds of years old. Correct?"

"Ah," Mr. Boggis whispered, fixing Rummins with two big bulging brown eyes. "That's where you're wrong. Watch this."

From his jacket pocket, he took out a small screwdriver. At the same time, although none of them saw him do it, he also took out a little brass screw which he kept well hidden in the palm of his hand. Then he selected one of the screws in the commode—there were four to each handle—and began carefully scraping all traces of white paint from its head. When he had done this, he started slowly to unscrew it.

"If this is a genuine old brass screw from the eighteenth century," he was saying, "the spiral will be slightly uneven and you'll be able to see quite easily that it has been hand-cut with a file. But if this brasswork is faked from more recent times, Victorian or later, then obviously the screw will be of the same period. It will be a mass-produced, machine-made article. Anyone can recognize a machine-made screw. Well, we shall see."

It was not difficult, as he put his hands over the old screw and drew it out, for Mr. Boggis to substitute the new one hidden in his palm. This was another little trick of his, and through the years it had proved a most rewarding one. The pockets of his clergyman's jacket were always stocked with a quantity of cheap brass screws of various sizes.

"There you are," he said, handing the modern screw to Rummins. "Take a look at that. Notice the exact evenness of the spiral? See it? Of course you do. It's just a cheap common little screw that you yourself could buy today in any ironmonger's in the country."

The screw was handed around from the one to the other, each examining it carefully. Even Rummins was impressed now.

Mr. Boggis put the screwdriver back in his pocket together with the fine hand-cut screw that he'd taken from the commode, and then he turned and walked slowly past the three men toward the door.

"My dear friends," he said, pausing at the entrance to the kitchen, "it was so good of you to let me peep inside your little home—so kind. I do hope I haven't been a terrible old bore."

Rummins glanced up from examining the screw. "You didn't tell us what you were going to offer," he said.

"Ah," Mr. Boggis said. "That's quite right. I didn't, did I? Well, to tell you the honest truth, I think it's all a bit too much trouble. I think I'll leave it."

"How much would you give?"

"You mean that you really wish to part with it?"

"I didn't say I wished to part with it. I asked you how much."

Mr. Boggis looked across at the commode, and he laid his head first to one side, then to the other, and he frowned, and pushed out his lips, and shrugged his shoulders, and gave a little scornful wave of the hand as though to say the thing was hardly worth thinking about really, was it?

"Shall we say . . . ten pounds. I think that would be fair."

"Ten pounds!" Rummins cried. "Don't be so ridiculous, Parson, *please!*"

"It's worth more'n that for firewood!" Claud said, disgusted.

"Look here at the bill!" Rummins went on, stabbing that precious document so fiercely with his dirty forefinger that Mr. Boggis became alarmed. "It tells you exactly what it cost! Eighty-seven pounds! And that's when it was new. Now it's antique it's worth double!"

"If you'll pardon me, no, sir, it's not. It's a secondhand reproduction. But I'll tell you what, my friend—I'm being rather reckless, I can't help it—I'll go up as high as fifteen pounds. How's that?"

"Make it fifty," Rummins said.

A delicious little quiver like needles ran all the way down the back of Mr. Boggis's legs and then under the soles of his feet. He had it now. It was his. No question about that. But the habit of buying cheap, as cheap as it was humanly possible to buy, acquired by years of necessity and practice, was too strong in him now to permit him to give in so easily.

"My dear man," he whispered softly, "I only *want* the legs. Possibly I could find some use for the drawers later on, but the rest of it, the carcass itself, as your friend so rightly said, it's firewood, that's all."

"Make it thirty-five," Rummins said.

"I *couldn't*, sir, I *couldn't!* It's not worth it. And I simply mustn't allow myself to haggle like this about a price. It's all wrong. I'll make you one final offer, and then I must go. Twenty pounds."

"I'll take it," Rummins snapped. "It's yours."

"Oh dear," Mr. Boggis said, clasping his hands. "There I go again. I should never have started this in the first place."

"You can't back out now, Parson. A deal's a deal."

"Yes, yes, I know."

"How're you going to take it?"

"Well, let me see. Perhaps if I were to drive my car up into the yard, you gentlemen would be kind enough to help me load it?"

"In a car? This thing'll never go in a car! You'll need a truck for this!"

"I don't think so. Anyway, we'll see. My car's on the road. I'll be back in a jiffy. We'll manage it somehow, I'm sure."

Mr. Boggis walked out into the yard and through the gate and then down the long track that led across the field toward the road. He found himself giggling quite uncontrollably, and there was a feeling inside him as though hundreds and hundreds of tiny bubbles were rising up from his stomach and bursting merrily in the top of his head, like sparkling water. All the buttercups in the field were suddenly turning into golden sovereigns, glistening in the sunlight. The ground was littered with them, and he swung off the track onto the grass so that he could walk among them and tread on them and hear the little metallic tinkle they made as he kicked them around with his toes. He was finding it difficult to stop himself from breaking into a run. But clergymen never run; they walk slowly. Walk slowly, Boggis. Keep calm, Boggis. There's no hurry now. The commode is yours! Yours for twenty pounds, and it's worth fifteen or twenty thousand! The Boggis Commode! In ten minutes it'll be loaded into your car—it'll go in easily—and you'll be driving back to London and singing all the way! Mr. Boggis driving The Boggis Commode home in the Boggis car. Historic occasion. What *wouldn't* a newspaperman give to get a picture of that! Should he arrange it? Perhaps he should. Wait and see. Oh, glorious day! Oh, lovely sunny summer day! Oh, glory be!

Back in the farmhouse, Rummins was saying, "Fancy that old bastard giving twenty pound for a load of junk like this."

"You did very nicely, Mr. Rummins," Claud told him. "You think he'll pay you?"

"We don't put it in the car till he do."

"And what if it won't go in the car?" Claud asked. "You know what I think, Mr. Rummins? You want my honest opinion? I think the bloody thing's too big to go in the car. And then what happens? Then he's going to say to hell with it and just drive off without it and you'll never see him again. Nor the money either. He didn't seem all that keen on having it, you know."

Rummins paused to consider this new and rather alarming prospect.

"How can a thing like that possibly go in a car?" Claud went on relentlessly. "A parson never has a big car anyway. You ever seen a parson with a big car, Mr. Rummins?"

"Can't say I have."

"Exactly! And now listen to me. I've got an idea. He told us, didn't he, that it was only the legs he was wanting. Right? So all we've got to do is to cut 'em off quick right here on the spot before he comes back, then it'll be sure to go in the car. All we're doing is saving him the trouble of cutting them off himself when he gets home. How about it, Mr. Rummins?" Claud's flat bovine face glimmered with a mawkish pride.

"It's not such a bad idea at that," Rummins said, looking at the commode. "In fact it's a bloody good idea. Come on then, we'll have to hurry. You and Bert carry it out into the yard. I'll get the saw. Take the drawers out first."

Within a couple of minutes, Claud and Bert had carried the commode outside and had laid it upside down in the yard amidst the chicken droppings and cow dung and mud. In the distance, halfway across the field, they could see a small black figure striding along the path toward the road. They paused to watch. There was something rather comical about the way in which this figure was conducting itself. Every now and again it would break into a trot, then it did a kind of hop skip and jump, and once it seemed as though the sound of a cheerful song came rippling faintly to them from across the meadow.

"I reckon he's balmy," Claud said, and Bert grinned darkly, rolling his misty eye slowly around in its socket.

Rummins came waddling over from the shed, squat and froglike, carrying a long saw. Claud took the saw away from him and went to work.

"Cut 'em close," Rummins said. "Don't forget he's going to use 'em on another table."

The mahogany was hard and very dry, and as Claud worked, a fine red dust sprayed out from the edge of the saw and fell softly to the ground. One by one, the legs came off, and when they were all severed, Bert stooped down and arranged them carefully in a row.

Claud stepped back to survey the results of his labor. There was a longish pause.

"Just let me ask you one question, Mr. Rummins," he said slowly. "Even now, could *you* put that enormous thing into the back of a car?"

"Not unless it was a van."

"Correct!" Claud cried. "And parsons don't have vans, you know. All they've got usually is piddling little Morris Eights or Austin Sevens."

"The legs is all he wants," Rummins said. "If the rest of it won't go in, then he can leave it. He can't complain. He's got the legs."

"Now you know better'n that, Mr. Rummins," Claud said patiently. "You know damn well he's going to start knocking the price if he don't get every single bit of this into the car. A parson's just as cunning as the rest of 'em when it comes to money, don't you make any mistake about that. Especially this old boy. So why don't we give him his firewood now and be done with it. Where d'you keep the axe?"

"I reckon that's fair enough," Rummins said. "Bert, go fetch the axe."

Bert went into the shed and fetched a tall woodcutter's axe and gave it to Claud. Claud spat on the palms of his hands and rubbed them together. Then, with a long-armed high-swinging action, he began fiercely attacking the legless carcass of the commode.

It was hard work, and it took several minutes before he had the whole thing more or less smashed to pieces.

"I'll tell you one thing," he said, straightening up, wiping his brow. "That was a bloody good carpenter put this job together and I don't care what the parson says."

"We're just in time!" Rummins called out. "Here he comes!"

THE BRIDE COMES TO YELLOW SKY
STEPHEN CRANE

THE GREAT PULLMAN was whirling onward with such dignity of motion that a glance from the window seemed simply to prove that the plains of Texas were pouring eastward. Vast flats of green grass, dull-hued spaces of mesquite and cactus, little groups of frame houses, woods of light and tender trees, all were sweeping into the east, sweeping over the horizon, a precipice.

A newly married pair had boarded this coach at San Antonio. The man's face was reddened from many days in the wind and sun, and a direct result of his new black clothes was that his brick-colored hands were constantly performing in a most conscious fashion. From time to time he looked down respectfully at his attire. He sat with a hand on each knee, like a man waiting in a barbershop. The glances he devoted to other passengers were furtive and shy.

The bride was not pretty, nor was she very young. She wore a dress of blue cashmere, with small reservations of velvet here and there, and with steel buttons abounding. The blushes caused by the careless scrutiny of some passengers as she had entered the car were strange to see upon this plain, underclass countenance, which was drawn in placid, almost emotionless lines.

They were evidently very happy. "Ever been in a parlor car before?" he asked, smiling with delight.

"No," she answered, "I never was. It's fine, ain't it?"

"Great! And then after a while we'll go forward to the diner, and get a big layout. Finest meal in the world. Charge a dollar."

"Oh, do they?" cried the bride. "Charge a dollar? Why, that's too much—for us—ain't it, Jack?"

"Not this trip, anyhow," he answered bravely. "We're going to go the whole thing."

Later he explained to her about the trains. "You see, it's a thousand miles from one end of Texas to the other; and this train runs right across it, and never stops but four times." He had the pride of an owner. He pointed out to her the dazzling fittings of the coach; and in truth her eyes opened wider as she contemplated the sea-green figured velvet, the shining brass, silver, and glass, the wood that gleamed as darkly brilliant as the surface of a pool of oil. At one end a bronze figure sturdily held a support for a separated chamber, and at convenient places on the ceiling were frescoes in olive and silver.

To the minds of the pair, their surroundings reflected the glory of their marriage that morning in San Antonio; this was the environment of their new estate; and the man's face in particular beamed with an elation that made him appear ridiculous to the Negro porter. This individual at times surveyed them from afar with an amused and superior grin. On other occasions he bullied them with skill in ways that did not make it exactly plain to them that they were being bullied. He subtly used all the manners of the most unconquerable kind of snobbery. He oppressed them; but of this oppression they had small knowledge, and they speedily forgot that infrequently a number of travelers covered them with stares of derisive enjoyment. Historically there was supposed to be something infinitely humorous in their situation.

"We are due in Yellow Sky at three forty-two," he said, looking tenderly into her eyes.

"Oh, are we?" she said, as if she had not been aware of it. To evince surprise at her husband's statement was part of her wifely amiability. She took from a pocket a little silver watch; and as she held it before her and stared at it with a frown of attention, the new husband's face shone.

"I bought it in San Anton' from a friend of mine," he told her gleefully.

"It's seventeen minutes past twelve," she said, looking up at him with a kind of shy and clumsy coquetry. A passenger, noting this play, grew excessively sardonic, and winked at himself in one of the numerous mirrors.

At last they went to the dining car. Two rows of Negro waiters in glowing white suits surveyed their entrance with the interest, and also the equanimity, of men who had been forewarned. The pair fell to the lot of a waiter who happened to feel pleasure in steering them through their meal. He viewed them with the manner of a fatherly pilot, his countenance radiant with benevolence. The patronage, entwined with the ordinary deference, was not plain to them. And yet, as they returned to their coach, they showed in their faces a sense of escape.

To the left, miles down a long, purple slope, was a little ribbon of mist where moved the keening Rio Grande. The train was approaching it at an angle, and the apex was Yellow Sky. Presently it was apparent that as the distance from Yellow Sky grew shorter, the husband became commensurately restless. His brick-red hands were more insistent in their prominence. Occasionally he was even rather absentminded and far away when the bride leaned forward and addressed him.

As a matter of truth, Jack Potter was beginning to find the shadow of a deed weigh upon him like a leaden slab. He, the town marshal of Yellow Sky, a man known, liked, and feared in his corner, a prominent person, had gone to San Antonio to meet a girl he believed he loved, and had actually induced her to marry him, without consulting Yellow Sky for any part of the transaction. He was now bringing his bride before an innocent and unsuspecting community.

Of course people in Yellow Sky married as it pleased them, in accordance with a general custom; but such was Potter's thought of his duty to his friends, or of their idea of his duty, or of an unspoken form which does not control men in these matters, that he felt he was heinous. He had committed an extraordinary crime. Face to face with this girl in San Antonio, and spurred by his sharp impulse, he had gone headlong over all the social hedges. At San Antonio he was like a man hidden in the dark. A knife to sever any friendly duty, any form, was easy to his hand in that remote city. But the hour of Yellow Sky—the hour of daylight—was approaching.

He knew full well that his marriage was an important thing to his town. It could only be exceeded by the burning of the new hotel. His friends could not forgive him. Frequently he had reflected on the advisability of telling them by telegraph, but a new cowardice had been upon him. He feared to do it. And now the train was hurrying him toward a scene of amazement, glee, and reproach. He glanced out of the window at the line of haze swinging slowly in toward the train.

Yellow Sky had a kind of brass band, which played painfully, to the delight of the populace. He laughed without heart as he thought of it. If the citizens could dream of his prospective arrival with his bride, they would parade the band at the station and escort them, amid cheers and laughing congratulations, to his adobe home.

He resolved that he would use all the devices of speed and plainscraft in making the journey from the station to his house. Once within that safe citadel, he could issue some sort of vocal bulletin, and then not go among the citizens until they had time to wear off a little of their enthusiasm.

The bride looked anxiously at him. "What's worrying you, Jack?"

He laughed again. "I'm not worrying, girl; I'm only thinking of Yellow Sky."

She flushed in comprehension.

A sense of mutual guilt invaded their minds and developed a finer tenderness. They looked at each other with eyes softly aglow. But Potter often laughed the same nervous laugh; the flush upon the bride's face seemed quite permanent.

The traitor to the feelings of Yellow Sky narrowly watched the speeding landscape. "We're nearly there," he said.

Presently the porter came and announced the proximity of Potter's home. He held a brush in his hand, and, with all his airy superiority gone, he brushed Potter's new clothes as the latter slowly turned this way and that way. Potter fumbled out a coin and gave it to the porter, as he had seen others do. It was a heavy and muscle-bound business, as that of a man shoeing his first horse.

The porter took their bag, and as the train began to slow, they moved forward to the hooded platform of the car. Presently the two engines and their long string of coaches rushed into the station of Yellow Sky.

"They have to take water here," said Potter, from a constricted throat and in mournful cadence, as one announcing death. Before the train stopped, his eye had swept the length of the platform, and he was glad and astonished to see there was none upon it but the station agent, who, with a slightly hurried and anxious air, was walking toward the water tanks. When the train had halted, the porter alighted first, and placed in position a little temporary step.

"Come on, girl," said Potter hoarsely. As he helped her down, they each laughed on a false note. He took the bag from the Negro, and bade his wife cling to his arm. As they slunk rapidly away, his hangdog glance perceived that they were unloading the two trunks, and also that the station agent, far ahead near the baggage car, had turned and was running toward him, making gestures. He laughed, and groaned as he laughed, when he noted the first effect of his marital bliss upon Yellow Sky. He gripped his wife's arm firmly to his side, and they fled. Behind them the porter stood, chuckling fatuously.

THE CALIFORNIA EXPRESS on the Southern Railway was due at Yellow Sky in twenty-one minutes. There were six men at the bar of the Weary Gentleman saloon. One was a drummer who talked a great deal and rapidly; three were Texans who did not care to talk at that time; and two were Mexican sheepherders, who did not talk as a general practice in the Weary Gentleman saloon. The barkeeper's dog lay on the board-walk that crossed in front of the door. His head was on his paws, and he glanced drowsily here and there with the constant vigilance of a dog that is kicked on occasion. Across the sandy street were some vivid green grassplots, so wonderful in appearance, amid the sands that burned near them in a blazing sun, that they caused a doubt in the mind. They exactly resembled the grass mats used to represent lawns on the stage. At the cooler end of the railway station, a man without a coat sat in a tilted chair and smoked his pipe. The fresh-cut bank of the Rio Grande circled near the town, and there could be seen beyond it a great plum-colored plain of mesquite.

Save for the busy drummer and his companions in the saloon, Yellow Sky was dozing. The newcomer leaned gracefully upon the bar and recited many tales with the confidence of a bard who has come upon a new field.

"—and at the moment that the old man fell downstairs with the bureau in his arms, the old woman was coming up with two scuttles of coal, and of course—"

The drummer's tale was interrupted by a young man who suddenly appeared in the open door. He cried, "Scratchy Wilson's drunk and has turned loose with both hands." The two Mexicans at once set down their glasses and faded out of the rear entrance of the saloon.

The drummer, innocent and jocular, answered, "All right, old man. S'pose he has? Come in and have a drink, anyhow."

But the information had made such an obvious cleft in every skull in the room that the drummer was obliged to see its importance. All had become instantly solemn. "Say," said he, mystified, "what is this?" His three companions made the introductory gesture of eloquent speech; but the young man at the door forestalled them.

"It means, my friend," he answered as he came into the saloon, "that for the next two hours this town won't be a health resort."

The barkeeper went to the door and locked and barred it; reaching out of the window, he pulled in heavy wooden shutters and barred them. Immediately a solemn, chapellike gloom was upon the place. The drummer was looking from one to another.

"But say," he cried, "what is this, anyhow? You don't mean there is going to be a gunfight?"

"Don't know whether there'll be a fight or not," answered one man grimly; "but there'll be some shootin'—some good shootin'."

The young man who had warned them waved his hand. "Oh, there'll be a fight fast enough, if anyone wants it. Anybody can get a fight out there in the street. There's a fight just waiting."

The drummer seemed to be swayed between the interest of a foreigner and a perception of personal danger.

"What did you say his name was?" he asked.

"Scratchy Wilson," they answered in chorus.

"And will he kill anybody? What are you going to do? Does this happen often? Does he rampage around like this once a week or so? Can he break in that door?"

"No, he can't break down that door," replied the barkeeper. "He's tried it three times. But when he comes, you'd better lay down on the floor, stranger. He's dead sure to shoot at it, and a bullet may come through."

Thereafter the drummer kept a strict eye upon the door. The time had not yet been called for him to hug the floor, but, as a minor precaution, he sidled near to the wall. "Will he kill anybody?" he said again.

The men laughed low and scornfully at the question.

"He's out to shoot, and he's out for trouble. Don't see any good in experimentin' with him."

"But what do you do in a case like this? What do you do?"

A man responded, "Why, he and Jack Potter—"

"But," in chorus the other men interrupted, "Jack Potter's in San Anton'."

"Well, who is he? What's he got to do with it?"

"Oh, he's the town marshal. He goes out and fights Scratchy when he gets on one of these tears."

"Wow!" said the drummer, mopping his brow. "Nice job he's got."

The voices had toned away to mere whisperings. The drummer wished to ask further questions, which were born of an increasing anxiety and bewilderment; but when he attempted them, the men merely looked at him in irritation and motioned him to remain silent. A tense waiting hush was upon them. In the deep shadows of the room their eyes shone as they listened for sounds from the street. One man made three gestures at the barkeeper; and the latter, moving like a ghost, handed him a glass and a bottle. The man poured a full glass of whiskey and set down the bottle noiselessly. He gulped the whiskey in a swallow and turned again toward the door in immovable silence. The drummer saw that the barkeeper, without a sound, had taken a Winchester from beneath the bar. Later he saw this individual beckoning to him, so he tiptoed across the room.

"You better come with me back of the bar."

"No, thanks," said the drummer, perspiring. "I'd rather be where I can make a break for the back door."

Whereupon the man of bottles made a kindly but peremptory gesture. The drummer obeyed it, and finding himself seated on a box, with his head below the level of the bar, balm was laid upon his soul at sight of various zinc and copper fittings that bore a resemblance to armor plate. The barkeeper took a seat comfortably upon an adjacent box.

"You see," he whispered, "this here Scratchy Wilson is a wonder with a gun—a perfect wonder; and when he goes on the war trail, we hunt our holes—naturally. He's about the last one of the old gang that used to hang out along the river here. He's a terror when he's drunk. When he's sober he's all right—kind of simple—wouldn't hurt a fly— nicest fellow in town. But when he's drunk—whoo!"

There were periods of stillness. "I wish Jack Potter was back from San Anton'," said the barkeeper. "He shot Wilson up once—in the leg— and he would sail in and pull out the kinks in this thing."

Presently they heard from a distance the sound of a shot, followed by three wild yowls. It instantly removed a bond from the men in the darkened saloon. There was a shuffling of feet. They looked at each other. "Here he comes," they said.

A MAN IN A maroon-colored flannel shirt rounded a corner and walked into the middle of the main street of Yellow Sky. In either hand the man held a long, heavy, blue-black revolver. Often he yelled, and these cries rang through a semblance of a deserted village, shrilly flying over the roofs in a volume that seemed to have no relation to the ordinary vocal strength of a man. It was as if the surrounding stillness formed the arch of a tomb over him. These cries of ferocious challenge rang against walls of silence. And his boots had red tops with gilded imprints, of the kind beloved in winter by little sledding boys on the hillsides of New England.

The man's face flamed in a rage begot of whiskey. His eyes, rolling and yet keen for ambush, hunted the still doorways and windows. He walked with the creeping movement of the midnight cat. As it occurred to him, he roared menacing information. The long revolvers in his hands were as easy as straws; they were moved with an electric swiftness. The little fingers of each hand played sometimes in a musician's way. Plain from the low collar of the shirt, the cords of his neck straightened and sank, straightened and sank, as passion moved him. The only sounds were his terrible invitations. The calm adobes preserved their demeanor at the passing of this small thing in the middle of the street.

There was no offer of fight—no offer of fight. The man called to the sky. There were no attractions. He bellowed and fumed and swayed his revolvers here and everywhere.

The dog of the barkeeper of the Weary Gentleman saloon had not appreciated the advance of events. He yet lay dozing in front of his master's door. At sight of the dog, the man paused and raised his revolver humorously. At sight of the man, the dog sprang up and walked diagonally away, with a sullen head, and growling. The man yelled, and the dog broke into a gallop. As it was about to enter an alley, there was a loud noise, a whistling, and something spat the ground directly before it. The dog screamed and, wheeling in terror, galloped headlong in a new direction. Again there was a noise, a whistling, and sand was kicked viciously before it. Fear-stricken, the dog turned and flurried like an animal in a pen. The man stood laughing, his weapons at his hips.

Ultimately the man was attracted by the closed door of the Weary Gentleman saloon. He went to it and, hammering with a revolver, demanded drink.

The door remaining imperturbable, he picked a bit of paper from the walk and nailed it to the framework with a knife. He then turned his back contemptuously upon this popular resort and, walking to the opposite side of the street and spinning there on his heel quickly and lithely, fired at the bit of paper. He missed it by a half inch. He swore at himself and went away. Later he comfortably fusilladed the windows of his most intimate friend. The man was playing with this town; it was a toy for him.

But still there was no offer of fight. The name of Jack Potter, his ancient antagonist, entered his mind, and he concluded that it would be a glad thing if he should go to Potter's house and by bombardment induce him to come out and fight. He moved in the direction of his desire, chanting Apache scalp music.

When he arrived at it, Potter's house presented the same still front as had the other adobes. Taking up a strategic position, the man howled a challenge. But this house regarded him as might a great stone god. It gave no sign. After a decent wait, the man howled further challenges, mingling with them wonderful epithets.

Presently there came the spectacle of a man churning himself into deepest rage over the immobility of a house. He fumed at it as the winter wind attacks a prairie cabin in the North. To the distance there should have gone the sound of a tumult like the fighting of two hundred Mexicans. As necessity bade him, he paused for breath or to reload his revolvers.

POTTER AND HIS BRIDE walked sheepishly and with speed. Sometimes they laughed together shamefacedly and low.

"Next corner, dear," he said finally.

They put forth the efforts of a pair walking bowed against a strong wind. Potter was about to raise a finger to point the first appearance of the new home when, as they circled the corner, they came face to face with a man in a maroon-colored shirt, who was feverishly pushing cartridges into a large revolver. Upon the instant the man dropped his revolver to the ground and, like lightning, whipped another from its holster. The second weapon was aimed at the bridegroom's chest.

There was a silence. Potter's mouth seemed to be merely a grave for his tongue. He exhibited an instinct to at once loosen his arm from the woman's grip, and he dropped the bag to the sand. As for the bride, her face had gone as yellow as old cloth. She was a slave to hideous rites, gazing at the apparitional snake.

The two men faced each other at a distance of three paces. He of the revolver smiled with a new and quiet ferocity.

"Tried to sneak up on me," he said. "Tried to sneak up on me!" His eyes grew more baleful. As Potter made a slight movement, the man thrust his revolver venomously forward. "No, don't you do it, Jack Potter. Don't you move a finger toward a gun just yet. Don't you move an eyelash. The time has come for me to settle with you, and I'm goin' to do it my own way, and loaf along with no interferin'. So if you don't want a gun bent on you, just mind what I tell you."

Potter looked at his enemy. "I ain't got a gun on me, Scratchy," he said. "Honest, I ain't." He was stiffening and steadying, but yet somewhere at the back of his mind a vision of the Pullman floated: the sea-green figured velvet, the shining brass, silver, and glass, the wood that gleamed as darkly brilliant as the surface of a pool of oil—all the glory of the marriage, the environment of the new estate. "You know I fight when it comes to fighting, Scratchy Wilson; but I ain't got a gun on me. You'll have to do all the shootin' yourself."

His enemy's face went livid. He stepped forward and lashed his weapon to and fro before Potter's chest. "Don't you tell me you ain't got no gun on you, you whelp. Don't tell me no lie like that. There ain't a man in Texas ever seen you without no gun. Don't take me for no kid." His eyes blazed with light, and his throat worked like a pump.

"I ain't takin' you for no kid," answered Potter. His heels had not moved an inch backward. "I'm takin' you for a damn fool. I tell you I ain't got a gun, and I ain't. If you're goin' to shoot me up, you better begin now; you'll never get a chance like this again."

So much enforced reasoning had told on Wilson's rage; he was calmer. "If you ain't got a gun, why ain't you got a gun?" he sneered. "Been to Sunday school?"

"I ain't got a gun because I've just come from San Anton' with my wife. I'm married," said Potter. "And if I'd thought there was going to be any galoots like you prowling around when I brought my wife home, I'd had a gun, and don't you forget it."

"Married!" said Scratchy, not at all comprehending.

"Yes, married. I'm married," said Potter, distinctly.

"Married?" said Scratchy. Seemingly for the first time, he saw the drooping, drowning woman at the other man's side. "No!" he said. He was like a creature allowed a glimpse of another world. He moved a pace backward, and his arm, with the revolver, dropped to his side. "Is this the lady?" he asked.

"Yes, this is the lady," answered Potter.

There was another period of silence.

"Well," said Wilson at last, slowly, "I s'pose it's all off now."

"It's all off if you say so, Scratchy. You know I didn't make the trouble." Potter lifted his valise.

"Well, I 'low it's off, Jack," said Wilson. He was looking at the ground. "Married!" He was not a student of chivalry; it was merely that in the presence of this foreign condition he was a simple child of the earlier plains. He picked up his starboard revolver, and placing both weapons in their holsters, he went away. His feet made funnel-shaped tracks in the heavy sand.

THE MONKEY'S PAW
W. W. JACOBS

WITHOUT, THE NIGHT was cold and wet, but in the small parlor of Lakesnam Villa the blinds were drawn and the fire burned brightly. Father and son were at chess, the former, who possessed ideas about the game involving radical changes, putting his king into such sharp and unnecessary perils that it even provoked comment from the white-haired old lady knitting placidly by the fire.

"Hark at the wind," said Mr. White, who, having seen a fatal mistake after it was too late, was amiably desirous of preventing his son from seeing it.

"I'm listening," said the latter, grimly surveying the board as he stretched out his hand. "Check."

"I should hardly think that he'd come tonight," said his father, with his hand poised over the board.

"Mate," replied the son.

"That's the worst of living so far out," bawled Mr. White, with sudden and unlooked-for violence; "of all the beastly, slushy, out-of-the-way places to live in, this is the worst. Pathway's a bog, and the road's a torrent. I don't know what people are thinking about. I suppose because only two houses on the road are let, they think it doesn't matter."

"Never mind, dear," said his wife soothingly; "perhaps you'll win the next one."

Mr. White looked up sharply, just in time to intercept a knowing glance between mother and son. The words died away on his lips, and he hid a guilty grin in his thin gray beard.

"There he is," said Herbert White, as the gate banged to loudly and heavy footsteps came toward the door.

The old man rose with hospitable haste, and opening the door, was heard condoling with the new arrival. The new arrival also condoled with himself, so that Mrs. White said, "Tut, tut!" and coughed gently as her husband entered the room, followed by a tall, burly man, beady of eye and rubicund of visage.

"Sergeant Major Morris," he said, introducing him.

The sergeant major shook hands, and taking the proffered seat by the fire, watched contentedly while his host got out whisky and tumblers and stood a small copper kettle on the fire.

At the third glass his eyes got brighter, and he began to talk, the little family circle regarding with eager interest this visitor from distant parts, as he squared his broad shoulders in the chair and spoke of strange scenes and doughty deeds, of wars and plagues and strange peoples.

"Twenty-one years of it," said Mr. White, nodding at his wife and son. "When he went away he was a slip of a youth in the warehouse. Now look at him."

"He don't look to have taken much harm," said Mrs. White politely.

"I'd like to go to India myself," said the old man, "just to look round a bit, you know."

"Better where you are," said the sergeant major, shaking his head. He put down the empty glass, and sighing softly, shook it again.

"I should like to see those old temples and fakirs and jugglers," said the old man. "What was that you started telling me the other day about a monkey's paw or something, Morris?"

"Nothing," said the soldier hastily. "Leastways, nothing worth hearing."

"Monkey's paw?" said Mrs. White curiously.

"Well, it's just a bit of what you might call magic, perhaps," said the sergeant major offhandedly.

His three listeners leaned forward eagerly. The visitor absentmindedly put his empty glass to his lips and then set it down again. His host filled it for him.

"To look at," said the sergeant major, fumbling in his pocket, "it's just an ordinary little paw, dried to a mummy."

He took something out of his pocket and proffered it. Mrs. White drew back with a grimace, but her son, taking it, examined it curiously.

"And what is there special about it?" inquired Mr. White, as he took it from his son, and having examined it, placed it upon the table.

"It had a spell put on it by an old fakir," said the sergeant major, "a very holy man. He wanted to show that fate ruled people's lives, and that those who interfered with it did so to their sorrow. He put a spell on it so that three separate men could each have three wishes from it."

His manner was so impressive that his hearers were conscious that their light laughter jarred somewhat.

"Well, why don't you have three, sir?" said Herbert White cleverly.

The soldier regarded him in the way that middle age is wont to regard presumptuous youth. "I have," he said quietly, and his blotchy face whitened.

"And did you really have the three wishes granted?" asked Mrs. White.

"I did," said the sergeant major, and his glass tapped against his strong teeth.

"And has anybody else wished?" inquired the old lady.

"The first man had his three wishes, yes," was the reply. "I don't know what the first two were, but the third was for death. That's how I got the paw."

His tones were so grave that a hush fell upon the group.

"If you've had your three wishes, it's no good to you now, then, Morris," said the old man at last. "What do you keep it for?"

The soldier shook his head. "Fancy, I suppose," he said slowly. "I did have some idea of selling it, but I don't think I will. It has caused enough mischief already. Besides, people won't buy. They think it's a fairy tale, some of them, and those who do think anything of it want to try it first and pay me afterward."

"If you could have another three wishes," said the old man, eyeing him keenly, "would you have them?"

"I don't know," said the other. "I don't know."

He took the paw, and dangling it between his front finger and thumb, suddenly threw it upon the fire. White, with a slight cry, stooped down and snatched it off.

"Better let it burn," said the soldier solemnly.

"If you don't want it, Morris," said the old man, "give it to me."

"I won't," said his friend doggedly. "I threw it on the fire. If you keep it, don't blame me for what happens. Pitch it on the fire again, like a sensible man."

The other shook his head and examined his new possession closely. "How do you do it?" he inquired.

"Hold it up in your right hand and wish aloud," said the sergeant major, "but I warn you of the consequences."

"Sounds like the *Arabian Nights*," said Mrs. White, as she rose and began to set the supper. "Don't you think you might wish for four pairs of hands for me?"

Her husband drew the talisman from his pocket and then all three burst into laughter as the sergeant major, with a look of alarm on his face, caught him by the arm.

"If you must wish," he said gruffly, "wish for something sensible."

Mr. White dropped it back into his pocket, and placing chairs, motioned his friend to the table. In the business of supper the talisman was partly forgotten, and afterward the three sat listening in an enthralled fashion to a second installment of the soldier's adventures in India.

"If the tale about the monkey's paw is not more truthful than those he has been telling us," said Herbert, as the door closed behind their guest, just in time for him to catch the last train, "we shan't make much out of it."

"Did you give him anything for it, Father?" inquired Mrs. White, regarding her husband closely.

"A trifle," said he, coloring slightly. "He didn't want it, but I made him take it. And he pressed me again to throw it away."

"Likely," said Herbert, with pretended horror. "Why, we're going to be rich, and famous, and happy. Wish to be an emperor, Father, to begin with; then you can't be henpecked."

He darted around the table, pursued by the maligned Mrs. White armed with an antimacassar.

Mr. White took the paw from his pocket and eyed it dubiously. "I don't know what to wish for, and that's a fact," he said slowly. "It seems to me I've got all I want."

"If you only cleared the house, you'd be quite happy, wouldn't you?" said Herbert, with his hand on his shoulder. "Well, wish for two hundred pounds, then; that'll just do it."

His father, smiling shamefacedly at his own credulity, held up the talisman, as his son, with a solemn face somewhat marred by a wink at his mother, sat down at the piano and struck a few impressive chords.

"I wish for two hundred pounds," said the old man distinctly.

A fine crash from the piano greeted the words, interrupted by a shuddering cry from the old man. His wife and son ran toward him.

"It moved," he cried, with a glance of disgust at the object as it lay on the floor. "As I wished, it twisted in my hand like a snake."

"Well, I don't see the money," said his son, as he picked it up and placed it on the table, "and I bet I never shall."

"It must have been your fancy, Father," said his wife, regarding him anxiously.

He shook his head. "Never mind, though; there's no harm done, but it gave me a shock all the same."

They sat down by the fire again while the two men finished their pipes. Outside, the wind was higher than ever, and the old man started nervously at the sound of a door banging upstairs. A silence unusual and depressing settled upon all three, which lasted until the old couple rose to retire for the night.

"I expect you'll find the cash tied up in a big bag in the middle of your bed," said Herbert, as he bade them good night, "and something horrible squatting up on top of the wardrobe watching you as you pocket your ill-gotten gains."

IN THE BRIGHTNESS of the wintry sun next morning as it streamed over the breakfast table, Herbert laughed at his fears. There was an air of prosaic wholesomeness about the room which it had lacked on the previous night, and the dirty, shriveled little paw was pitched on the sideboard with a carelessness which betokened no great belief in its virtues.

"I suppose all old soldiers are the same," said Mrs. White. "The idea of our listening to such nonsense! How could wishes be granted in these days? And if they could, how could two hundred pounds hurt you, Father?"

"Might drop on his head from the sky," said the frivolous Herbert.

"Morris said the things happened so naturally," said his father, "that you might, if you so wished, attribute it to coincidence."

"Well, don't break into the money before I come back," said Herbert, as he rose from the table. "I'm afraid it'll turn you into a mean, avaricious man, and we shall have to disown you."

His mother laughed, and following him to the door, watched him down the road, and returning to the breakfast table, was very happy at the expense of her husband's credulity. All of which did not prevent her from scurrying to the door at the postman's knock, nor prevent her from referring somewhat shortly to retired sergeant majors of bibulous habits, when she found that the post brought a tailor's bill.

"Herbert will have some more of his funny remarks, I expect, when he comes home," she said, as they sat at dinner.

"I daresay," said Mr. White, pouring himself out some beer; "but for all that, the thing moved in my hand; that I'll swear to."

"You thought it did," said the old lady soothingly.

"I say it did," replied the other. "There was no thought about it; I had just— What's the matter?"

His wife made no reply. She was watching the mysterious movements of a man outside, who, peering in an undecided fashion at the house, appeared to be trying to make up his mind to enter. In mental connection with the two hundred pounds, she noticed that the stranger was well dressed and wore a silk hat of glossy newness. Three times he paused at the gate, and then walked on again. The fourth time he stood with his hand upon it, and then with sudden resolution flung it open and walked up the path. Mrs. White at the same moment placed her hands behind her, and hurriedly unfastening the strings of her apron, put that useful article of apparel beneath the cushion of her chair.

She brought the stranger, who seemed ill at ease, into the room. He gazed furtively at Mrs. White, and listened in a preoccupied fashion as the old lady apologized for the appearance of the room, and her husband's coat, a garment which he usually reserved for the garden. She then waited as patiently as her sex would permit for him to broach his business, but he was at first strangely silent.

"I—was asked to call," he said at last, and stooped and picked a piece of cotton from his trousers. "I come from Maw and Meggins."

The old lady started. "Is anything the matter?" she asked breathlessly. "Has anything happened to Herbert? What is it? What is it?"

Her husband interposed. "There, there, Mother," he said hastily. "Sit down, and don't jump to conclusions. You've not brought bad news, I'm sure, sir," and he eyed the other wistfully.

"I'm sorry—" began the visitor.

"Is he hurt?" demanded the mother.

The visitor bowed in assent. "Badly hurt," he said quietly, "but he is not in any pain."

"Oh, thank God!" said the old woman, clasping her hands. "Thank God for that! Thank—"

She broke off suddenly as the sinister meaning of the assurance dawned upon her and she saw the awful confirmation of her fears in the other's averted face. She caught her breath, and turning to her slower-witted husband, laid her trembling old hand upon his. There was a long silence.

"He was caught in the machinery," said the visitor at length, in a low voice.

"Caught in the machinery," repeated Mr. White, in a dazed fashion, "yes."

He sat staring blankly out at the window, and taking his wife's hand between his own, pressed it as he had been wont to do in their old courting days nearly forty years before.

"He was the only one left to us," he said, turning gently to the visitor. "It is hard."

The other coughed, and rising, walked slowly to the window. "The firm wished me to convey their sincere sympathy with you in your great loss," he said, without looking around. "I beg that you will understand I am only their servant and merely obeying orders."

There was no reply; the old woman's face was white, her eyes staring, and her breath inaudible; on the husband's face was a look such as his friend the sergeant might have carried into his first action.

"I was to say that Maw and Meggins disclaim all responsibility," continued the other. "They admit no liability at all, but in consideration of your son's services they wish to present you with a certain sum as compensation."

Mr. White dropped his wife's hand, and rising to his feet, gazed with a look of horror at his visitor. His dry lips shaped the words, "How much?"

"Two hundred pounds," was the answer.

Unconscious of his wife's shriek, the old man smiled faintly, put out his hands like a sightless man, and dropped, a senseless heap, to the floor.

IN THE HUGE NEW cemetery, some two miles distant, the old people buried their dead, and came back to a house steeped in shadow and silence. It was all over so quickly that at first they could hardly realize it, and remained in a state of expectation, as though of something else to happen—something else which was to lighten this load, too heavy for old hearts to bear. But the days passed, and expectation gave place to resignation—the hopeless resignation of the old, sometimes miscalled apathy. Sometimes they hardly exchanged a word, for now they had nothing to talk about, and their days were long to weariness.

It was about a week after that that the old man, waking suddenly in the night, stretched out his hand and found himself alone. The room was in darkness, and the sound of subdued weeping came from the window. He raised himself in bed and listened.

"Come back," he said tenderly. "You will be cold."

"It is colder for my son," said the old woman, and wept afresh.

The sound of her sobs died away on his ears. The bed was warm, and his eyes heavy with sleep. He dozed fitfully, and then slept until a sudden cry from his wife awoke him with a start.

"The monkey's paw!" she cried wildly. "The monkey's paw!"

He started up in alarm. "Where? Where is it? What's the matter?"

She came stumbling across the room toward him. "I want it," she said quietly. "You've not destroyed it?"

"It's in the parlor, on the bracket," he replied, marveling. "Why?"

She cried and laughed together, and bending over, kissed his cheek.

"I only just thought of it," she said hysterically. "Why didn't I think of it before? Why didn't you think of it?"

"Think of what?" he questioned.

"The other two wishes," she replied rapidly. "We've only had one."

"Was not that enough?" he demanded fiercely.

"No," she cried triumphantly; "we'll have one more. Go down and get it quickly, and wish our boy alive again."

The man sat up in bed and flung the bedclothes from his quaking limbs. "Good God, you are mad!" he cried, aghast.

"Get it," she panted; "get it quickly, and wish— Oh, my boy, my boy!"

Her husband struck a match and lit the candle. "Get back to bed," he said unsteadily. "You don't know what you are saying."

"We had the first wish granted," said the old woman feverishly; "why not the second?"

"A coincidence," stammered the old man.

"Go and get it and wish," cried the old woman, and dragged him toward the door.

He went down in the darkness, and felt his way to the parlor, and then to the mantelpiece. The talisman was in its place, and a horrible fear that the unspoken wish might bring his mutilated son before him ere he could escape from the room seized upon him, and he caught his breath as he found that he had lost the direction of the door. His brow cold with sweat, he felt his way around the table, and groped along the wall until he found himself in the small passage with the unwholesome thing in his hand.

Even his wife's face seemed changed as he entered the room. It was white and expectant, and to his fears seemed to have an unnatural look upon it. He was afraid of her.

"Wish!" she cried, in a strong voice.

"It is foolish and wicked," he faltered.

"Wish!" repeated his wife.

He raised his hand. "I wish my son alive again."

The talisman fell to the floor, and he regarded it shudderingly. Then he sank trembling into a chair as the old woman, with burning eyes, walked to the window and raised the blind.

He sat until he was chilled with the cold, glancing occasionally at the figure of the old woman peering through the window. The candle end, which had burned below the rim of the china candlestick, was throwing pulsating shadows on the ceiling and walls, until, with a flicker larger than the rest, it expired. The old man, with an unspeakable sense of relief at the failure of the talisman, crept back to his bed, and a minute or two afterward the old woman came silently and apathetically beside him.

Neither spoke, but both lay silently listening to the ticking of the clock. A stair creaked, and a squeaky mouse scurried noisily through the wall. The darkness was oppressive, and after lying for some time screwing up his courage, the husband took the box of matches, and striking one, went downstairs for a candle.

At the foot of the stairs the match went out, and he paused to strike another, and at the same moment a knock, so quiet and stealthy as to be scarcely audible, sounded on the front door.

The matches fell from his hand. He stood motionless, his breath suspended until the knock was repeated. Then he turned and fled swiftly back to his room, and closed the door behind him. A third knock sounded through the house.

"What's that?" cried the old woman, starting up.

"A rat," said the old man, in shaking tones, "a rat. It passed me on the stairs."

His wife sat up in bed listening. A loud knock resounded through the house.

"It's Herbert!" she screamed. "It's Herbert!"

She ran to the door, but her husband was before her, and catching her by the arm, held her tightly.

"What are you going to do?" he whispered hoarsely.

"It's my boy; it's Herbert!" she cried, struggling mechanically. "I forgot it was two miles away. What are you holding me for? Let go. I must open the door."

"For God's sake don't let it in," cried the old man, trembling.

"You're afraid of your own son," she cried, struggling. "Let me go. I'm coming, Herbert; I'm coming."

There was another knock, and another. The old woman with a sudden wrench broke free and ran from the room. Her husband followed to the landing, and called after her appealingly as she hurried downstairs. He heard the chain rattle back and the bottom bolt drawn slowly and stiffly from the socket. Then the old woman's voice, strained and panting.

"The bolt," she cried loudly. "Come down. I can't reach it."

But her husband was on his hands and knees groping wildly on the floor in search of the paw. If he could only find it before the thing outside got in. A perfect fusillade of knocks reverberated through the house, and he heard the scraping of a chair as his wife put it down in the passage against the door. He heard the creaking of the bolt as it came slowly back, and at the same moment, he found the monkey's paw, and frantically breathed his third and last wish.

The knocking ceased suddenly, although the echoes of it were still in the house. He heard the chair drawn back and the door opened. A cold wind rushed up the staircase, and a long, loud wail of disappointment and misery from his wife gave him courage to run down to her side, and then to the gate beyond. The streetlamp flickering opposite shone on a quiet and deserted road.

THE FOSTER PORTFOLIO
KURT VONNEGUT, JR.

I'M A SALESMAN of good advice for rich people. I'm a contact man for an investment counseling firm. It's a living, but not a whale of a one—or at least not now, when I'm just starting out. To qualify for the job, I had to buy a homburg, a navy-blue overcoat; a double-breasted banker's gray suit, black shoes, a regimental-stripe tie, half a dozen white shirts, half a dozen pairs of black socks, and gray gloves.

When I call on a client, I come by cab, and I am sleek and clean and foursquare. I carry myself as though I've made a quiet killing on the stock market and have come to call more as a public service than anything else. When I arrive in clean wool, with crackling certificates and confidential stock analyses in crisp manila folders, the reaction—ideally and usually—is the same accorded a minister or physician. I am in charge, and everything is going to be just fine.

I deal mostly with old ladies—the meek, who by dint of cast-iron constitutions have inherited sizable portions of the earth. I thumb through the clients' lists of securities, and relay our experts' suggestions for ways of making their portfolios—or bonanzas or piles—thrive and increase. I can speak of tens of thousands of dollars without a catch in my throat, and look at a list of securities worth more than a hundred thousand with no more fuss than a judicious "Mmmmm, uh-huh."

Since *I* don't have a portfolio, my job is a little like being a hungry delivery boy for a candy store. But I never really felt that way about it until Herbert Foster asked me to have a look at his finances.

He called one evening to say a friend had recommended me, and could I come out to talk business. I washed, shaved, dusted my shoes, put on my uniform, and made my grave arrival by cab.

People in my business—and maybe people in general—have an unsavory habit of sizing up a man's house, car, and suit, and estimating his annual income. Herbert Foster was six thousand a year, or I'd never seen it. Understand, I have nothing against people in moderate circumstances, other than the crucial fact that I can't make any money off them. It made me a little sore that Foster would take my time, when the most he had to play around with, I guessed, was no more than a few hundred dollars. Say it was a thousand: my take would be a dollar or two at best.

ANYWAY, THERE I WAS in the Fosters' jerry-built postwar colonial with expansion attic. They had taken up a local furniture store on its offer of three rooms of furniture, including ashtrays, a humidor, and pictures for the wall, all for $199.99. Hell, I was there, and I figured I might as well go through with having a look at his pathetic problem.

"Nice place you have here, Mr. Foster," I said. "And this is your charming wife?"

A skinny, shrewish-looking woman smiled up at me vacuously. She wore a faded housecoat figured with a fox-hunting scene. The print was at war with the slipcover of the chair, and I had to squint to separate her features from the clash about her. "A pleasure, Mrs. Foster," I said. She was surrounded by underwear and socks to be mended, and Herbert said her name was Alma, which seemed entirely possible.

"And this is the young master," I said. "Bright little chap. Believe he favors his father." The two-year-old wiped his grubby hands on my trousers, snuffled, and padded off toward the piano. He stationed himself at the upper end of the keyboard and hammered on the highest note for one minute, then two, then three.

"Musical—like his father," Alma said.

"You play, do you, Mr. Foster?"

"Classical," Herbert said.

I took my first good look at him. He was lightly built, with the round, freckled face and big teeth I usually associate with a show-off or wise guy. It was hard to believe that he had settled for so plain a wife, or that he could be as fond of family life as he seemed. It may have been that I only imagined a look of quiet desperation in his eyes.

"Shouldn't you be getting on to your meeting, dear?" Herbert said.

"It was called off at the last minute."

"Now, about your portfolio—" I began.

Herbert looked rattled. "How's that?"

"Your portfolio—your securities."

"Yes, well, I think we'd better talk in the bedroom. It's quieter in there."

Alma put down her sewing. "What securities?"

"The bonds, dear. The government bonds."

"Now, Herbert, you're not going to cash them in."

"No, Alma, just want to talk them over."

"I see," I said tentatively. "Uh—approximately how much in government bonds?"

"Three hundred and fifty dollars," Alma said proudly.

"Well," I said, "I don't see any need for going into the bedroom to talk. My advice, and I give it free, is to hang on to your nest egg until it matures. And now, if you'll let me phone a cab—"

"Please," Herbert said, standing in the bedroom door, "there are a couple of other things I'd like to discuss."

"What?" Alma said.

"Oh, long-range investment planning," Herbert said vaguely.

"We could use a little short-range planning for next month's grocery bill."

"Please," Herbert said to me again.

I shrugged, and followed him into the bedroom. He closed the door behind me. I sat on the edge of the bed and watched him open a little door in the wall, which bared the pipes servicing the bathroom. He slid his arm up into the wall, grunted, and pulled down an envelope.

"Oho," I said apathetically, "so that's where we've got the bonds, eh? Very clever. You needn't have gone to that trouble, Mr. Foster. I have an idea what government bonds look like."

"Alma," he called.

"Yes, Herbert."

"Will you start some coffee for us?"

"I don't drink coffee at night," I said.

"We have some from dinner," Alma said.

"I can't sleep if I touch it after supper," I said.

"Fresh—we want some fresh," Herbert said.

The chair springs creaked, and her reluctant footsteps faded into the kitchen.

"Here," said Herbert, putting the envelope in my lap. "I don't know anything about this business, and I guess I ought to have professional help."

All right, so I'd give the poor guy a professional talk about his three hundred and fifty dollars in government bonds. "They're the most conservative investment you can make. They haven't the growth characteristics of many securities, and the return isn't great, but they're very safe. By all means, hang on to them." I stood up. "And now, if you'll let me call a cab—"

"You haven't looked at them."

I sighed, and untwisted the red string holding the envelope shut. Nothing would do but that I admire the things. The bonds and a list of securities slid into my lap. I riffled through the bonds quickly, and then read the list of securities slowly.

"Well?"

I put the list down on the faded bedspread. I composed myself. "Mmmmm, uh-huh," I said. "Do you mind telling me where the securities listed here came from?"

"Grandfather left them to me two years ago. The lawyers who handled the estate have them. They sent me that list."

"Do you know what these stocks are worth?"

"They were appraised when I inherited them." He told me the figure, and, to my bewilderment, he looked sheepish, even a little unhappy.

"They've gone up a little since then."

"How much?"

"On today's market—maybe they're worth seven hundred and fifty thousand dollars, Mr. Foster. Sir."

His expression didn't change. My news moved him about as much as if I'd told him it'd been a chilly winter. He raised his eyebrows as Alma's footsteps came back into the living room. "Shhhh!"

"She doesn't know?"

"Lord, no!" He seemed to have surprised himself with his vehemence. "I mean, the time isn't ripe."

"If you'll let me have this list of securities, I'll have our New York office give you a complete analysis and recommendations," I whispered. "May I call you Herbert, sir?"

MY CLIENT, HERBERT FOSTER, hadn't had a new suit in three years; he had never owned more than one pair of shoes at a time. He worried about payments on his secondhand car, and ate tuna and cheese instead of meat, because meat was too expensive. His wife made her own clothes, and those of Herbert, Jr., and the curtains and slipcovers—all cut from the same bargain bolt.

The Fosters were going through hell, trying to choose between new tires or retreads for the car; and television was something they had to go two doors down the street to watch. Determinedly, they kept within the small salary Herbert made as a bookkeeper for a wholesale grocery house.

God knows it's no disgrace to live that way—which is better than the way I live—but it was pretty disturbing to watch, knowing Herbert had an income, after taxes, of perhaps twenty thousand a year.

I had our securities analysts look over Foster's holdings and report on the stocks' growth possibilities, prospective earnings, the effect of war and peace, inflation and deflation, and so on. The report ran to twenty pages, a record for any of my clients. Usually the reports are bound in cardboard covers. Herbert's was done up in red Leatherette.

It arrived at my place on a Saturday afternoon, and I called up Herbert to ask if I could bring it out. I had exciting news for him. My by-eye estimate of the values had been off, and his portfolio, as of that day, was worth close to eight hundred and fifty thousand.

"I've got the analysis and recommendations," I said, "and things look good, Mr. Foster—*very* good. You need a little diversification here and there, and maybe more emphasis on growth, but—"

"Just go ahead and do whatever needs to be done," he said.

"When could we talk about this? It's something we ought to go over together, certainly. Tonight would be fine with me."

"I work tonight."

"Overtime at the wholesale house?"

"Another job—in a restaurant. Work Friday, Saturday, and Sunday nights."

I winced. The man had maybe seventy-five dollars a day coming in from his securities, and he worked three nights a week to make ends meet! "Monday?"

"Play organ for choir practice at the church."

"Tuesday?"

"Volunteer fire department drill."

"Wednesday?"

"Play piano for folk dancing at the church."

"Thursday?"

"Movie night for Alma and me."

"When, then?"

"You go ahead and do whatever needs to be done."

"Don't you want to be in on what I'm doing?"

"Do I have to be?"

"I'd feel better if you were."

"All right, Tuesday noon, lunch."

"Fine with me. Maybe you'd better have a good look at this report before then, so you can have questions ready."

He sounded annoyed. "Okay, okay, okay. I'll be here tonight until nine. Drop it off before then."

"One more thing, Herbert." I'd saved the kicker for last. "I was way off about what the stocks are worth. They're now up to about eight hundred and fifty thousand dollars."

"Um."

"I said, you're about a hundred thousand dollars richer than you thought!"

"Uh-huh. Well, you just go ahead and do whatever needs to be done."

"Yes, sir." The phone was dead.

I WAS DELAYED BY OTHER business, and I didn't get out to the Fosters' until quarter of ten. Herbert was gone. Alma answered the door, and, to my surprise, she asked for the report, which I was hiding under my coat.

"Herbert said I wasn't supposed to look at it," she said, "so you don't need to worry about me peeking."

"Herbert told you about this?" I said carefully.

"Yes. He said it's confidential reports on stocks you want to sell him."

"Yes, uh-huh—well, if he said to leave it with you, here it is."

"He told me he had to promise you not to let *anybody* look at it."

"Mmm? Oh, yes, yes. Sorry, company rules."

She was a shade hostile. "I'll tell you one thing without looking at any reports, and that is he's not going to cash those bonds to buy any stocks with."

"I'd be the last one to recommend that, Mrs. Foster."

"Then why do you keep after him?"

"He may be a good customer at a later date." I looked at my hands, which I realized had become ink-stained on the earlier call. "I wonder if I might wash up?"

Reluctantly she let me in, keeping as far away from me as the modest floor plan would permit.

As I washed up, I thought of the list of securities Herbert had taken from between the plasterboard walls. Those securities meant winters in Florida, filet mignon and twelve-year-old bourbon, Jaguars, silk underwear and handmade shoes, a trip around the world. . . . Name it; Herbert Foster could have it. I sighed heavily. The soap in the Foster soap dish was mottled and dingy—a dozen little chips moistened and pressed together to make a new bar.

I thanked Alma and started to leave. On my way out, I paused by the mantel to look at a small tinted photograph. "Good picture of you," I said. A feeble effort at public relations. "I like that."

"Everybody says that. It isn't me; it's Herbert's mother."

"Amazing likeness." And it was. Herbert had married a girl just like the girl that married dear old Dad. "And this picture is his father?"

"*My* father. We don't want a picture of *his* father."

This looked like a sore point that might prove informative. "Herbert is such a wonderful person, his father must have been wonderful, too, eh?"

"He deserted his wife and child. That's how wonderful he was. You'll be smart not to mention him to Herbert."

"Sorry. Everything good about Herbert comes from his mother?"

"She was a saint. She taught Herbert to be decent and respectable and God-fearing." Alma was grim about it.

"Was she musical, too?"

"He gets that from his father. But what he does with it is something quite different. His taste in music is his mother's—the classics."

"His father was a jazzman, I take it?" I hinted.

"He preferred playing piano in dives, and breathing smoke and drinking gin, to his wife and child and home and job. Herbert's mother finally said he had to choose one life or the other."

I nodded sympathetically. Maybe Herbert looked on his fortune as filthy, untouchable, since it came from his father's side of the family. "This grandfather of Herbert's, who died two years ago—"

"He supported Herbert and his mother after his son deserted them. Herbert worshipped him." She shook her head sadly. "He was penniless when he died."

"What a shame."

"I'd so hoped he would leave us a little something, so Herbert wouldn't have to work weekends."

We were trying to talk above the clatter, tinkle, and crash of the cafeteria where Herbert ate every day. Lunch was on me—or on my expense account—and I'd picked up his check for eighty-seven cents. I said, "Now, Herbert, before we go any further, we'd better decide what you want from your investments: growth or income." It was a cliché of the counseling business. God knows what *he* wanted from the securities. It didn't seem to be what everybody else wanted—money.

"Whatever you say," Herbert said absently. He was upset about something and not paying much attention to me.

"Herbert—look, you've got to face this thing. You're a rich man. You've got to concentrate on making the most of your holdings."

"That's why I called you. I want *you* to concentrate. I want you to run things for me, so I won't have to bother with the deposits and proxies and taxes. Don't trouble me with it at all."

"Your lawyers have been banking the dividends, eh?"

"Most of them. Took out thirty-two dollars for Christmas, and gave a hundred to the church."

"So what's your balance?"

He handed me the deposit book.

"Not bad," I said. Despite his Christmas splurge and largess toward the church, he'd managed to salt away $50,227.33. "May I ask what a man with a balance like that can be blue about?"

"Got bawled out at work again."

"Buy the place and burn it down," I suggested.

"I could, couldn't I?" A wild look came into his eyes, then disappeared.

"Herbert, you can do anything your heart desires."

"Oh, I suppose so. It's all in the way you look at it."

I leaned forward. "How *do* you look at it, Herbert?"

"I think every man, for his own self-respect, should earn what he lives on."

"But, Herbert—"

"I have a wonderful wife and child, a nice house for them, and a car. And I've earned every penny of the way. I'm living up to the full measure of my responsibilities. I'm proud to say I'm everything my mother wanted me to be, and nothing my father was."

"Do you mind my asking what your father was?"

"I don't enjoy talking about him. Home and family meant nothing to him. His real love was for low-down music and honky-tonks, and for the trash in them."

"Was he a good musician, do you think?"

"Good?" For an instant there was excitement in his voice, and he tensed, as though he were going to make an important point. But he relaxed again. "Good?" he repeated, flatly this time. "Yes, in a crude way, I suppose he was passable—technically, that is."

"And that much you inherited from him."

"His wrists and hands, maybe. God help me if there's any more of him in me."

"You've got his love of music, too."

"I love music, but I'd never let it get like dope to me!" he said, with more force than seemed necessary.

"Uh-huh. Well—"

"Never!"

"Beg your pardon?"

His eyes were wide. "I said I'll never let music get like dope to me. It's important to me, but I'm master of it, and not the other way around."

Apparently it was a treacherous subject, so I switched back to the matter of his finances. "Yes, well, now about your portfolio again: just what use do you expect to make of it?"

"Use some of it for Alma's and my old age; leave most of it to the boy."

"The least you can do is take enough out of the kitty to let you out of working weekends."

He stood up suddenly. "Look. I want you to handle my securities, not my life. If you can't do one without the other, I'll find someone who can."

"Please, Herbert, Mr. Foster. I'm sorry, sir. I was only trying to get the whole picture for planning."

He sat down, red-faced. "All right then, respect my convictions. I want to make my own way. If I have to hold a second job to make ends meet, then that's my cross to bear."

"Sure, sure, certainly. And you're dead right, Herbert. I respect you for it." I thought he belonged in the bughouse for it. "You leave everything to me from now on. I'll invest those dividends and run the whole show." As I puzzled over Herbert, I glanced at a passing blonde. Herbert said something I missed. "What was that, Herbert?"

"I said, *If thy right eye offend thee, pluck it out, and cast it from thee.*"

I laughed appreciatively, then cut it short. Herbert was deadly serious. "Well, pretty soon you'll have the car paid for, and then you can take a well-earned rest on the weekends. And you'll really have something to be proud of, eh? Earned the whole car by the sweat of your brow, right down to the tip of the exhaust pipe."

"One more payment."

"*Then* by-by, restaurant."

"There'll still be Alma's birthday present to pay for. I'm getting her television."

"Going to earn that, too, are you?"

"Think how much more meaningful it will be as a gift, if I do."

"Yes, sir, and it'll give her something to do on weekends, too."

"If I have to work weekends for twenty-eight more months, God knows it's little enough to do for her."

If the stock market kept doing what it had been doing for the past three years, Herbert would be a millionaire just about the time he made the last payment on Alma's birthday present. "Fine."

"I love my family," Herbert said earnestly.

"I'm sure you do."

"And I wouldn't trade the life I've got for anything."

"I can certainly see why," I said. I had the impression that he was arguing with me, that it was important to him that I be convinced.

"When I consider what my father was, and then see the life I've made for myself, it's the biggest thrill in all my experience."

A very small thrill could qualify for the biggest in Herbert's experience, I thought. "I envy you. It must be gratifying."

"Gratifying," he repeated determinedly. "It is, it is, it is."

MY FIRM BEGAN managing Herbert's portfolio, converting some of the slower-moving securities into more lucrative ones, investing the accumulated dividends, diversifying his holdings so he'd be in better shape to weather economic shifts—and in general making his fortune altogether shipshape. A sound portfolio is a thing of beauty in its way, aside from its cash value. Putting one together is a creative act, if done right, with solid major themes of industrials, rails, and utilities, and with the lighter, more exciting themes of electronics, frozen foods, magic drugs, oil and gas, aviation, and other more speculative items. Herbert's portfolio was our masterpiece. I was thrilled and proud of what the firm had done, and not being able to show it off, even to him, was depressing.

It was too much for me, and I decided to engineer a coincidence. I would find out in which restaurant Herbert worked, and then drop in, like any other citizen, for something to eat. I would happen to have a report on his overhauled portfolio with me.

I telephoned Alma, who told me the name of the place—one I'd never heard of. Herbert hadn't wanted to talk about the place, so I gathered that it was pretty grim—as he said, his cross to bear.

It was worse than I'd expected: tough, brassy, dark, and noisy. Herbert had picked one hell of a place, indeed, to do penance for a wayward father, or to demonstrate his gratitude to his wife, or to maintain his self-respect by earning his own way—or to do whatever it was he was doing there.

I elbowed my way between bored-looking women and racetrack types to the bar. I had to shout at the bartender to be heard. When I did get through to him, he yelled back that he'd never heard of no Herbert Foster. Herbert, then, was about as minor an employee as there was in the establishment. He was probably doing something greasy in the kitchen or basement. Typical.

In the kitchen, a crone was making questionable-looking hamburgers and nipping at a quart of beer.

"I'm looking for Herbert Foster."

"Ain' no damn Herbert Foster in here."

"In the basement?"

"Ain' no damn basement."

"Ever hear of Herbert Foster?"

"Ain' never heard of no damn Herbert Foster."

"Thanks."

I sat in a booth to think it over. Herbert had apparently picked the joint out of a telephone book, and told Alma it was where he spent his weekend evenings. In a way, it made me feel better, because it began to look as though Herbert maybe had better reasons than he'd given me for letting eight hundred and fifty thousand dollars get musty. I remembered that every time I'd mentioned his giving up the weekend job, he'd reacted like a man hearing a dentist tune up his drill. I saw it now: the minute he let Alma know he was rich, he'd lose his excuse for getting away from her on weekends.

But what was it that was worth more to Herbert than eight hundred and fifty thousand? Binges? Dope? Women? I sighed, and admitted I was kidding myself, that I was no closer to the answer than I'd ever been. Moral turpitude on Herbert's part was inconceivable. Whatever he was up to, it had to be for a good cause. His mother had done such a thorough job on him, and he was so awfully ashamed of his father's failings, that I was sure he couldn't operate any other way but righteously. I gave up on the puzzle and ordered a nightcap.

And then Herbert Foster, looking drab and hunted, picked his way through the crowd. His expression was one of disapproval, of a holy man in Babylon. He was oddly stiff-necked and held his arms at his sides as he pointedly kept from brushing against anyone or from meeting any of the gazes that fell upon him. There was no question that being in the place was absolute, humiliating hell for him.

I called to him, but he paid no attention. There was no communicating with him. Herbert was in a near coma of see-no-evil, speak-no-evil, hear-no-evil.

The crowd in the rear parted for him, and I expected to see Herbert go into a dark corner for a broom or a mop. But a light flashed on at the far end of the aisle the crowd made for him, and a tiny white piano sparkled there like jewelry. The bartender set a drink on the piano and went back to his post.

Herbert dusted off the piano bench with his handkerchief and sat down gingerly. He took a cigarette from his breast pocket and lighted it. And then the cigarette started to droop slowly from his lips; and, as it drooped, Herbert hunched over the keyboard and his eyes narrowed, as though he were focusing on something beautiful on a faraway horizon.

Startlingly, Herbert Foster disappeared. In his place sat an excited stranger, his hands poised like claws. Suddenly he struck, and a spasm of dirty, low-down, gorgeous jazz shook the air—a hot, clanging wraith of the twenties.

LATE THAT NIGHT I went over my masterpiece, the portfolio of Herbert Foster, alias "Firehouse" Harris. I hadn't bothered Firehouse with it or with myself.

In a week or so there would be a juicy melon from one of his steel companies. Three of his oil stocks were paying extra dividends. The farm machinery company in which he owned five thousand shares was about to offer him rights worth three dollars apiece.

Thanks to me and my company and an economy in full bloom, Herbert was about to be several thousand dollars richer than he'd been a month before. I had a right to be proud, but my triumph—except for the commission—was gall and wormwood.

Nobody could do anything for Herbert. Herbert already had what he wanted. He had had it long before the inheritance or I intruded. He had the respectability his mother had hammered into him. But just as priceless as that was an income not quite big enough to go around. It left him no alternative but—in the holy names of wife, child, and home—to play piano in a dive, and breathe smoke, and drink gin—to be Firehouse Harris, his father's son, three nights out of seven.

THE POOR RELATION'S STORY
CHARLES DICKENS

H<small>E WAS VERY RELUCTANT</small> to take precedence of so many respected
members of the family, by beginning the round of stories they were to
relate as they sat in a goodly circle by the Christmas fire: and he modestly suggested that it would be more correct if "John our esteemed
host" (whose health he begged to drink) would have the kindness to
begin. For as to himself, he said, he was so little used to lead the way
that really— But as they all cried out here, that he must begin, and
agreed with one voice that he might, could, would, and should begin,
he left off rubbing his hands, and took his legs out from under his
armchair, and did begin.

I have no doubt (said the poor relation) that I shall surprise the
assembled members of our family, and particularly John our esteemed
host to whom we are so much indebted for the great hospitality with
which he has this day entertained us, by the confession I am going to
make. But, if you do me the honor to be surprised at anything that falls
from a person so unimportant in the family as I am, I can only say that I
shall be scrupulously accurate in all I relate.

I am not what I am supposed to be. I am quite another thing.
Perhaps before I go further I had better glance at what I *am* supposed
to be.

It is supposed, unless I mistake—the assembled members of our
family will correct me if I do, which is very likely (here the poor relation

looked mildly about him for contradiction)—that I am nobody's enemy but my own. That I never met with any particular success in anything. That I failed in business because I was unbusinesslike and credulous—in not being prepared for the interested designs of my partner. That I failed in love because I was ridiculously trustful—in thinking it impossible that Christiana could deceive me. That I failed in my expectations from my uncle Chill, on account of not being as sharp as he could have wished in worldly matters. That, through life, I have been rather put upon and disappointed in a general way. That I am at present a bachelor of between fifty-nine and sixty years of age, living on a limited income in the form of a quarterly allowance, to which I see that John our esteemed host wishes me to make no further allusion.

The supposition as to my present pursuits and habits is to the following effect.

I live in a lodging in the Clapham Road—a very clean back room, in a very respectable house—where I am expected not to be at home in the daytime, unless poorly; and which I usually leave in the morning at nine o'clock, on pretense of going to business. I take my breakfast—my roll and butter, and my half-pint of coffee—at the old-established coffee shop near Westminster Bridge; and then I go into the City—I don't know why—and sit in Garraway's Coffee House, and on 'Change, and walk about, and look into a few offices and countinghouses where some of my relations or acquaintances are so good as to tolerate me, and where I stand by the fire if the weather happens to be cold. I get through the day in this way until five o'clock, and then I dine: at a cost, on the average, of one and threepence. Having still a little money to spend on my evening's entertainment, I look into the old-established coffee shop as I go home, and take my cup of tea, and perhaps my bit of toast. So, as the large hand of the clock makes its way round to the morning hour again, I make my way round to the Clapham Road again, and go to bed when I get to my lodging—fire being expensive, and being objected to by the family on account of its giving trouble and making a dirt.

Sometimes one of my relations or acquaintances is so obliging as to ask me to dinner. These are holiday occasions, and then I generally walk in the Park. I am a solitary man, and seldom walk with anybody. Not that I am avoided because I am shabby; for I am not at all shabby, having always a very good suit of black on (or rather Oxford mixture, which has the appearance of black and wears much better); but I have got into a habit of speaking low, and being rather silent, and my spirits are not high, and I am sensible that I am not an attractive companion.

The only exception to this general rule is the child of my first cousin, Little Frank. I have a particular affection for that child, and he takes very kindly to me. He is a diffident boy by nature; and in a crowd he is soon run over, as I may say, and forgotten. He and I, however, get on exceedingly well. I have a fancy that the poor child will in time succeed to my peculiar position in the family. We talk but little; still, we understand each other. We walk about, hand in hand; and without much speaking he knows what I mean, and I know what he means.

Little Frank and I go and look at the outside of the Monument—he is very fond of the Monument—and at the Bridges, and at all the sights that are free. On two of my birthdays we have dined on *à la mode* beef, and gone at half price to the play, and been deeply interested. I was once walking with him in Lombard Street, which we often visit on account of my having mentioned to him that there are great riches there—he is very fond of Lombard Street—when a gentleman said to me as he passed by, "Sir, your little son has dropped his glove." I assure you, if you will excuse my remarking on so trivial a circumstance, this accidental mention of the child as mine brought the foolish tears into my eyes.

When Little Frank is sent to school in the country I shall be very much at a loss what to do with myself, but I have the intention of walking down there once a month and seeing him on a half holiday. I am told he will then be at play upon the Heath; and if my visits should be objected to, as unsettling the child, I can see him from a distance without his seeing me, and walk back again. His mother comes of a highly genteel family, and rather disapproves, I am aware, of our being too much together. I know that I am not calculated to improve his retiring disposition; but I think he would miss me beyond the feeling of the moment if we were wholly separated.

When I die in the Clapham Road I shall not leave much more in this world than I shall take out of it; but I happen to have a miniature of a bright-faced boy, with a curling head, and an open shirt frill waving down his bosom (my mother had it taken for me, but I can't believe that it was ever like), which will be worth nothing to sell, and which I shall beg may be given to Frank. I have written my dear boy a little letter with it, in which I have told him that I felt very sorry to part from him, though bound to confess that I knew no reason why I should remain here. I have given him some short advice, the best in my power, to take warning of the consequences of being nobody's enemy but his own; and I have endeavored to comfort him for what I fear he will consider a bereavement, by pointing out to him that I was only a superfluous something to everyone but him; and that having by some means failed to find a place in this great assembly, I am better out of it.

Such (said the poor relation, clearing his throat and beginning to speak a little louder) is the general impression about me. Now, it is a remarkable circumstance, which forms the aim and purpose of my story, that this is all wrong. This is not my life, and these are not my habits. I do not even live in the Clapham Road. Comparatively speaking, I am very seldom there. I reside, mostly, in a—I am almost ashamed to say the word, it sounds so full of pretension—in a Castle. I do not mean that it is an old baronial habitation, but still it is a building always known to everyone by the name of a Castle. In it I preserve the particulars of my history; they run thus:

It was when I first took John Spatter (who had been my clerk) into partnership, and when I was still a young man of not more than five-and-twenty, residing in the house of my uncle Chill, from whom I had considerable expectations, that I ventured to propose to Christiana. I had loved Christiana a long time. She was very beautiful, and very winning in all respects. I rather mistrusted her widowed mother, who I feared was of a plotting and mercenary turn of mind; but I thought as well of her as I could, for Christiana's sake. I never had loved anyone but Christiana, and she had been all the world, and oh far more than all the world, to me, from our childhood!

Christiana accepted me with her mother's consent, and I was rendered very happy indeed. My life at my uncle Chill's was of a spare dull kind, and my garret chamber was as dull, and bare, and cold as an upper prison room in some stern northern fortress. But, having Christiana's love, I wanted nothing upon earth. I would not have changed my lot with any human being.

Avarice was, unhappily, my uncle Chill's master vice. Though he was rich, he pinched, and scraped, and clutched, and lived miserably. As Christiana had no fortune, I was for some time a little fearful of confessing our engagement to him; but at length I wrote him a letter, saying how it all truly was. I put it into his hand one night, on going to bed.

As I came downstairs next morning, shivering in the cold December air—colder in my uncle's unwarmed house than in the street, where the winter sun did sometimes shine, and which was at all events enlivened by cheerful faces and voices passing along—I carried a heavy heart towards the long, low breakfast room in which my uncle sat. It was a large room with a small fire, and there was a great bay window in it which the rain had marked in the night as if with the tears of house-less people.

We rose so early always that at that time of the year we breakfasted by candlelight. When I went into the room my uncle was so contracted by the cold, and so huddled together in his chair behind the one dim candle, that I did not see him until I was close to the table.

As I held out my hand to him, he caught up his stick (being infirm, he always walked about the house with a stick), and made a blow at me, and said, "You fool!"

"Uncle," I returned, "I didn't expect you to be so angry as this." Nor had I expected it, though he was a hard and angry old man.

"You didn't expect!" said he; "when did you ever expect? When did you ever calculate, or look forward, you contemptible dog?"

"These are hard words, uncle!"

"Hard words? Feathers, to pelt such an idiot as you with," said he. "Here! Betsy Snap! Look at him!"

Betsy Snap was a withered, hard-favored, yellow old woman—our only domestic—always employed, at this time of the morning, in rubbing my uncle's legs. As my uncle adjured her to look at me, he put his lean grip on the crown of her head, she kneeling beside him, and turned her face towards me.

"Look at the sniveling milksop!" said my uncle. "Look at the baby! This is the gentleman who, people say, is nobody's enemy but his own. This is the gentleman who can't say no. This is the gentleman who was making such large profits in his business that he must needs take a partner, t'other day. This is the gentleman who is going to marry a wife without a penny, and who falls into the hands of Jezebels who are speculating on my death!"

I knew, now, how great my uncle's rage was; for nothing short of his being almost beside himself would have induced him to utter that concluding word, which he held in such repugnance that it was never spoken or hinted at before him on any account.

"On my death," he repeated, as if he were defying me by defying his own abhorrence of the word. "On my death—death—Death! But I'll spoil the speculation. Eat your last under this roof, you feeble wretch, and may it choke you!"

You may suppose that I had not much appetite for the breakfast to which I was bidden in these terms; but I took my accustomed seat. I saw that I was repudiated henceforth by my uncle; still I could bear that very well, possessing Christiana's heart.

He emptied his basin of bread and milk as usual, only that he took it on his knees with his chair turned away from the table where I sat. When he had done, he carefully snuffed out the candle; and the cold, slate-colored, miserable day looked in upon us.

"Now, Mr. Michael," said he, "before we part, I should like to have a word with these ladies in your presence."

"As you will, sir," I returned; "but you deceive yourself, and wrong us cruelly, if you suppose that there is any feeling at stake in this contract but pure, disinterested, faithful love."

To this, he only replied, "You lie!" and not one other word.

We went, through half-thawed snow and half-frozen rain, to the house where Christiana and her mother lived. My uncle knew them very well. They were sitting at their breakfast, and were surprised to see us at that hour.

"Your servant, ma'am," said my uncle to the mother. "You divine the purpose of my visit, I daresay, ma'am. I understand there is a world of pure, disinterested, faithful love cooped up here. I am happy to bring it all it wants, to make it complete. I bring you your son-in-law, ma'am—and you, your husband, miss. The gentleman is a perfect stranger to me, but I wish him joy of his wise bargain."

He snarled at me as he went out, and I never saw him again.

IT IS ALTOGETHER A MISTAKE (continued the poor relation) to suppose that my dear Christiana, overpersuaded and influenced by her mother, married a rich man, the dirt from whose carriage wheels is often thrown upon me as she rides by. No, no. She married me.

The way we came to be married rather sooner than we intended was this. I took a frugal lodging and was saving and planning for her sake, when, one day, she spoke to me with great earnestness, and said:

"My dear Michael, I have given you my heart. I have said that I loved you, and I have pledged myself to be your wife. I am as much yours through all changes of good and evil as if we had been married on the day when such words passed between us. I know you well, and know that if we should be separated and our union broken off, your whole life would be shadowed, and all that might, even now, be stronger in your character for the conflict with the world would then be weakened to the shadow of what it is!"

"God help me, Christiana!" said I. "You speak the truth."

"Michael!" said she, putting her hand in mine, in all maidenly devotion, "let us keep apart no longer. It is but for me to say that I can live contented upon such means as you have, and I well know you are happy. I say so from my heart. Strive no more alone; let us strive together. My dear Michael, it is not right that I should keep secret from you what you do not suspect, but what distresses my whole life. My mother—without considering that what you have lost, you have lost for me, and on the assurance of my faith—sets her heart on riches, and urges another suit upon me, to my misery. I cannot bear this, for to bear it is to be untrue to you. I would rather share your struggles than look on. I want no better home than you can give me. I know that you will aspire and labor with a higher courage if I am wholly yours, and let it be so when you will!"

I was blest indeed, that day, and a new world opened to me. We were married in a very little while, and I took my wife to our happy home. That was the beginning of the residence I have spoken of; the Castle we have ever since inhabited together dates from that time. All our children have been born in it. Our first child—now married—was a little girl, whom we called Christiana. Her son is so like Little Frank that I hardly know which is which.

THE CURRENT IMPRESSION AS TO my partner's dealings with me is also quite erroneous. He did not begin to treat me coldly, as a poor simpleton, when my uncle and I so fatally quarreled; nor did he afterwards gradually possess himself of our business and edge me out. On the contrary, he behaved to me with the utmost good faith and honor.

Matters between us took this turn: On the day of my separation from my uncle, and even before the arrival at our countinghouse of my trunks (which he sent after me, *not* carriage paid), I went down to our room of business, on our little wharf, overlooking the river; and there I told John Spatter what had happened. John did not say, in reply, that rich old relatives were palpable facts, and that love and sentiment were moonshine and fiction. He addressed me thus:

"Michael," said John, "we were at school together, and I generally had the knack of getting on better than you, and making a higher reputation."

"You had, John," I returned.

"Although," said John, "I borrowed your books and lost them; borrowed your pocket money, and never repaid it; got you to buy my damaged knives at a higher price than I had given for them new; and to own to the windows that I had broken."

"All not worth mentioning," said I, "but certainly true."

"When you were first established in this infant business, which promises to thrive so well," pursued John, "I came to you, in my search for almost any employment, and you made me your clerk."

"Still not worth mentioning, my dear John Spatter," said I; "still, equally true."

"And finding that I had a good head for business, and that I was really useful *to* the business, you did not like to retain me in that capacity, and thought it an act of justice soon to make me your partner."

"Still less worth mentioning than any of those other little circumstances you have recalled, John Spatter," said I; "for I was, and am, sensible of your merits and my deficiencies."

"Now, my good friend," said John, drawing my arm through his, as he had had a habit of doing at school, "let there, under these friendly circumstances, be a right understanding between us. You are too easy, Michael. You are nobody's enemy but your own. If I were to give you that damaging character among our connection, with a shrug, and a shake of the head, and a sigh; and if I were further to abuse the trust you place in me—"

"But you never will abuse it at all, John," I observed.

"Never!" said he; "but I am putting a case—I say, and if I were further to abuse that trust by keeping this piece of our common affairs in the dark, and this other piece in the light, and again this other piece in the twilight, and so on, I should strengthen my strength, and weaken your weakness, day by day, until at last I found myself on the highroad to fortune, and you left behind on some bare common."

"Exactly so," said I.

"To prevent this, Michael," said John Spatter, "or the remotest chance of this, there must be perfect openness between us. Nothing must be concealed, and we must have but one interest."

"My dear John Spatter," I assured him, "that is precisely what I mean."

"And when you are too easy," pursued John, his face glowing with friendship, "you must allow me to prevent that imperfection in your nature from being taken advantage of by anyone; you must not expect me to humor it—"

"My dear John Spatter," I interrupted, "I *don't* expect you to humor it. I want to correct it."

"And I, too," said John.

"Exactly so!" cried I. "We both have the same end in view; and, honorably seeking it, and fully trusting one another, and having but one interest, ours will be a prosperous and happy partnership."

"I am sure of it!" returned John Spatter. And we shook hands most affectionately.

I took John home to my Castle, and we had a very happy day. Our partnership throve well. My friend and partner supplied what I wanted, and by improving both the business and myself, amply acknowledged any little rise in life to which I had helped him.

I AM NOT (said the poor relation, looking at the fire as he slowly rubbed his hands) very rich, for I never cared to be that; but I have enough, and am above all moderate wants and anxieties. My Castle is not a splendid place, but it is very comfortable, and it has a warm and cheerful air, and is quite a picture of Home.

Our eldest girl, who is very like her mother, married John Spatter's eldest son. Our two families are closely united in other ties of attachment.

It is very pleasant of an evening, when we are all assembled together—which frequently happens—and when John Spatter and I talk over old times, and the one interest there has always been between us.

I really do not know, in my Castle, what loneliness is. Some of our children or grandchildren are always about it, and the young voices of my descendants are delightful—oh, how delightful!—to me to hear. My dearest and most devoted wife, ever faithful, ever loving, ever helpful and sustaining and consoling, is the priceless blessing of my house; from whom all its other blessings spring. We are rather a musical family, and when Christiana sees me, at any time, a little weary or depressed, she steals to the piano and sings a gentle air she used to sing when we were first betrothed. So weak a man am I that I cannot bear to hear it from any other source. They played it once at the Theatre when I was there with Little Frank; and the child said, wondering, "Cousin Michael, whose hot tears are these that have fallen on my hand?"

Such is my Castle, and such are the real particulars of my life therein preserved. I often take Little Frank home there. He is very welcome to my grandchildren, and they play together. At this time of the year— the Christmas and New Year time—I am seldom out of my Castle. For the associations of the season seem to hold me there, and the precepts of the season seem to teach me that it is well to be there.

"AND THE CASTLE IS—" observed a grave, kind voice among the company.

"Yes. My Castle," said the poor relation, shaking his head as he still looked at the fire, "is in the Air. John our esteemed host suggests its situation accurately. My Castle is in the Air! I have done. Will you be so good as to pass the story!"

THE REAL THING
HENRY JAMES

W HEN THE PORTER'S wife announced, "A gentleman—with a lady, sir,"
I had, for the wish was father to the thought, an immediate vision of
sitters. Sitters my visitors in this case proved to be, but not in the sense I
should have preferred. However, there was nothing at first to indicate
that they might not have come for a portrait. The gentleman, a man of
fifty, very tall and very straight, with a mustache slightly grizzled and a
dark gray walking coat admirably fitted, would have struck me as a
celebrity if celebrities often were striking. The lady also looked too
distinguished to be a "personality."

Neither of the pair spoke immediately—they were visibly shy. I had
seen people painfully reluctant to mention that they desired anything so
gross as to be represented on canvas; but the scruples of my new friends
appeared almost insurmountable. Yet the gentleman might have said,
"I should like a portrait of my wife," and the lady might have said, "I
should like a portrait of my husband." Perhaps they were not husband
and wife—this naturally would make the matter more delicate. Perhaps
they wished to be done together—in which case they ought to have
brought a third person to break the news.

"We come from Mr. Rivet," the lady said at last, with a dim smile.
She was as tall and straight, in her degree, as her companion, and with
ten years less to carry. She looked as sad as a woman could look whose
face was not charged with expression. She was slim and stiff, and so well

dressed, in dark blue cloth, with lappets and pockets and buttons, that it was clear she employed the same tailor as her husband. The couple had an indefinable air of prosperous thrift.

"Ah, Claude Rivet recommended me?" I inquired; and I added that it was very kind of him, though I could reflect that, as he only painted landscape, this was not a sacrifice.

The lady looked very hard at the gentleman, and the gentleman looked around the room. Then, staring at the floor a moment and stroking his mustache, he rested his pleasant eyes on me with the remark, "He said you were the right one."

"I try to be, when people want to sit."

"Yes, we should like to," said the lady anxiously.

"Do you mean together? If so, there's a higher charge for two figures than for one."

"We should like to make it pay," the husband confessed.

"That's very good of you," I returned—for I supposed he meant pay the artist.

A sense of strangeness seemed to dawn on the lady. "We mean for the illustrations—Mr. Rivet said you might put one in."

"Put one in—an illustration?" I was equally confused.

"Sketch her, you know," said the gentleman, coloring.

It was only then that I understood the service Claude Rivet had rendered me; he had told them that I worked for magazines and story-books, and consequently had frequent employment for models. These things were true, but it was not less true that I couldn't get the honors, to say nothing of the emoluments, of a great painter of portraits out of my head. My illustrations were my potboilers; I looked to a different branch of art to perpetuate my fame. There was no shame in looking to it also to make my fortune; but that fortune was by so much farther from being made from the moment my visitors wished to be "done" for nothing.

"Ah, you're—you're—" I began. I couldn't bring out the shabby word "models"; it seemed to fit the case so little.

"We haven't had much practice," said the lady.

"We've got to *do* something, and we've thought that an artist in your line might perhaps make something of us," her husband threw off. He further mentioned that they didn't know many artists and that they had gone first to Mr. Rivet, whom they had met a few years before at a place in Norfolk where he was sketching.

"We used to sketch a little ourselves," the lady hinted.

"It's very awkward, but we absolutely *must* do something," her husband went on.

"Of course, we're not so *very* young," she admitted, with a wan smile.

With the remark that I might as well know something more about them, the husband had handed me a card extracted from a neat new pocketbook and inscribed with the words MAJOR MONARCH. "I've left the army," he added, "and we've had the misfortune to lose our money. In fact, our means are dreadfully small."

"It's an awful bore," said Mrs. Monarch.

They evidently wished to be discreet—to take care not to swagger because they were gentlefolk.

"Naturally, it's more for the figure that we thought of going in," Major Monarch observed. "*She* has got the best," he continued, nodding at his wife.

I could only reply that this didn't prevent his own from being very good; which led him in turn to rejoin, "We thought that if you ever have to do people like us, we might be something like it. *She*, particularly—for a lady in a book, you know."

I was so amused by them that, to get more of it, I did my best to take their point of view; and though it was an embarrassment to find myself appraising physically, as if they were animals on hire, I looked at Mrs. Monarch judicially enough to be able to exclaim, after a moment, with conviction, "Oh, yes, a lady in a book!" She was singularly like a bad illustration.

"We'll stand up, if you like," said the major; and he raised himself before me with a really grand air. I could take his measure at a glance—he was six feet two and a perfect gentleman. It would have paid any club in process of formation to engage him at a salary to stand in the principal window.

Mrs. Monarch sat still, not from pride but from shyness, and presently her husband said to her, "Get up, my dear, and show how smart you are." She obeyed, and walked to the end of the studio. Then she came back blushing, with her fluttered eyes on her husband. She did it quite well, but I abstained from applauding. It was very odd to see such people apply for such poor pay. She looked as if she had ten thousand a year. Her husband had used the word that described her; she was, in the current London jargon, essentially and typically "smart." Her figure was conspicuously and irreproachably "good." For a woman of her age her waist was surprisingly small; her elbow, moreover, had the orthodox crook. She held her head at a conventional angle; but why did she come to *me?* She ought to have tried on jackets at a big shop. I feared my visitors were not only destitute, but "artistic"—which would be a great complication. When she sat down again, I thanked her, observing that what a draftsman most valued in his model was the faculty of keeping quiet.

"Oh, *she* can keep quiet," said Major Monarch. Then he added, jocosely, "I've always kept her quiet."

"I'm not a nasty fidget, am I?" Mrs. Monarch appealed to her husband.

He addressed his answer to me. "Perhaps it isn't out of place to mention that when I married her she was known as the Beautiful Statue."

"Oh, dear!" said Mrs. Monarch, ruefully.

"Of course, I should want a certain amount of expression," I rejoined.

"Of *course!*" they both exclaimed.

"And then I suppose you know that you'll get awfully tired."

"Oh, we *never* get tired!" they eagerly cried.

"Have you had any kind of practice?"

They hesitated—they looked at each other. "We've been photographed, *immensely*," said Mrs. Monarch.

"She means the fellows have asked us," added the major.

"We always got our photographs for nothing," smiled Mrs. Monarch.

"We might have brought some, my dear," her husband remarked.

"I'm not sure we have any left. We've given quantities away," she explained to me.

"With our autographs and that sort of thing," said the major.

"Are they to be got in the shops?" I inquired, as a pleasantry.

"Oh, yes; *hers*—they used to be."

"Not now," said Mrs. Monarch, with her eyes on the floor.

I COULD FANCY the "sort of thing" they put on the presentation copies of their photographs, and I was sure they wrote a beautiful hand. It was odd how quickly I was sure of everything that concerned them. If they were now so poor as to have to earn shillings and pence, they never had had much of a margin. Their good looks had been their capital, and they had good-humoredly made the most of this resource. I could see the sunny drawing rooms, sprinkled with periodicals she didn't read, in which Mrs. Monarch had continuously sat; I could see the wet shrubberies in which she had walked, equipped to admiration for either exercise. I could see the rich covers the major had helped to shoot, and the wonderful garments in which, late at night, he repaired to the smoking room to talk about them. I could imagine their leggings and waterproofs, their knowing tweeds and rugs, their rolls of sticks and cases of tackle and neat umbrellas; and I could evoke the exact appearance of their servants and the compact variety of their luggage on the platforms of country stations.

They gave small tips, but they were liked; they didn't do anything themselves, but they were welcome. They looked so well everywhere; they gratified the general relish for stature, complexion and "form." They knew it without fatuity or vulgarity, and they respected themselves in consequence. I could feel how, even in a dull house, they could have been counted upon for cheerfulness. At present something had happened—their little income had grown less, it had grown least. Their friends liked them, but didn't like to support them. Fortunately they had no children—I soon divined that. They would also perhaps wish our relations to be kept secret; this was why it was "for the figure"—the reproduction of the face would betray them.

I liked them—they were so simple. But they were amateurs, and the ruling passion of my life was the detestation of the amateur. Combined with this was an innate preference for the represented subject over the real one: the defect of the real one was so apt to be a lack of representation. I liked things that appeared; then one was sure. Whether they *were* or not was a subordinate and almost always a profitless question.

There were other considerations, the first of which was that I already had two or three people in use, notably a young person from Kilburn, who for a couple of years had come to me regularly for my illustrations and with whom I was still satisfied. I explained to my visitors how the case stood, but they had taken more precautions than I supposed. They had reasoned out their opportunity, for Claude Rivet had told them of the projected *édition de luxe* of one of the writers of our day who, long neglected, had had the happy fortune of seeing, late in life, the dawn and then the full light of a higher criticism. The edition in question was planned by a publisher of taste and was to be enriched with woodcuts. Major and Mrs. Monarch confessed to me that they had hoped I might be able to work *them* into my share of the enterprise. They knew I was to do the first of the books, "Rutland Ramsay," but I had to make clear to them that my participation in the rest of the affair—this first book was to be a test—was to depend on the satisfaction I should give. Therefore I was making special preparations, looking about for new people, if they should be necessary, and securing the best types. I admitted, however, that I should like to settle down to two or three good models who would do for everything.

"Should we have often to—a—put on special clothes?" Mrs. Monarch timidly demanded.

"Dear, yes—that's half the business."

"And should we be expected to supply our own costumes?"

"Oh, no; I've got a lot of things. A painter's models put on—or put off—anything he likes."

"And do you mean—a—the same?"

"The same?"

Mrs. Monarch looked at her husband again.

"Oh, she was just wondering," he explained, "if the costumes are in *general* use."

I had to confess that they were, and I mentioned further that some of them had served their time a hundred years ago, on living, world-stained men and women.

"She has got a lot of clothes at home: they might do for contemporary life," her husband continued.

"Oh, I can imagine scenes in which you'd be quite natural." And indeed, I could see the slipshod rearrangements of stale properties—the stories I tried to produce pictures for without the exasperation of reading them—whose sandy tracts the good lady might help to people. But I had to return to the fact that for this sort of work I was already equipped with people who were fully adequate.

"We only thought we might be more like *some* characters," said Mrs. Monarch mildly, getting up.

Her husband also rose; he stood looking at me with a dim wistfulness that was touching in so fine a man. "Wouldn't it be rather a pull sometimes to have—a—to have—" He hung fire; he wanted me to help him by phrasing what he meant. But I couldn't—I didn't know. So he brought it out, awkwardly, "The *real* thing; a gentleman, you know, or a lady." I admitted that there was a great deal in that. This encouraged Major Monarch to say, following up his appeal with an unacted gulp, "It's awfully hard—we've tried everything." The gulp was communicative; it proved too much for his wife.

Before I knew it Mrs. Monarch had dropped again upon a divan and burst into tears. Her husband sat down beside her, holding one of her hands. "There isn't a confounded job I haven't applied for—waited for—prayed for. You might as well ask for a peerage. I'd be *anything*— I'm strong; a messenger or a coal heaver. I'd put on a gold-laced cap and open carriage doors in front of the haberdasher's; I'd hang about a station to carry portmanteaus; I'd be a postman. But they won't *look* at you; there are thousands, as good as yourself, already on the ground. *Gentlemen*, poor beggars, who have drunk their wine, who have kept their hunters!"

I was as reassuring as I knew how to be, and my visitors were presently on their feet again while, for the experiment, we agreed on an hour. We were discussing it when the door opened and Miss Churm, one of my models, came in with a wet umbrella. Miss Churm had to take the omnibus to Maida Vale and then walk half a mile. She looked a trifle blowsy and slightly splashed. I scarcely ever saw her come in without thinking afresh how odd it was that, being so little in herself, she should yet be so much in others. She was only a freckled cockney, but she could represent everything from a fine lady to a shepherdess; she had the faculty, as she might have had a fine voice or long hair. She couldn't spell, and she loved beer, but she had two or three "points," and practice, and a knack, and mother wit, and a kind of whimsical sensibility, and a love of the theater, and seven sisters, and not an ounce of respect, especially for the *h*. The first thing my visitors saw was that her umbrella was wet, and in their spotless perfection they visibly winced at it. The rain had come on since their arrival.

"I'm all in a soak; there *was* a mess of people in the bus. I wish you lived near a stytion," said Miss Churm. I requested her to get ready as quickly as possible, and she passed into the room in which she always changed her dress. But before going out she asked me what she was to get into this time.

"It's the Russian princess, don't you know?" I answered. "The one with the 'golden eyes,' in black velvet, for the long thing in the *Cheapside* magazine."

"Golden eyes? I *say!*" cried Miss Churm, while my companions watched her with intensity as she withdrew. She always arranged herself, when she was late, before I could turn around; and I kept my visitors a little, on purpose, so they might get an idea from seeing her what would be expected of themselves. I mentioned that she was quite my notion of an excellent model—she was really very clever.

"Do you think she looks like a Russian princess?" Major Monarch asked, with lurking alarm.

"When I make her, yes."

"Oh, if you have to *make* her—" he reasoned, acutely.

"That's the most you can ask. So many are not makable."

"Well now, *here's* a lady"—and with a persuasive smile he passed his arm into his wife's—"who's already made!"

"Oh, I'm not a Russian princess," Mrs. Monarch protested, a little coldly. I could see that she had known some and didn't like them. There, immediately, was a complication of a kind that I never had to fear with Miss Churm.

This young lady came back in black velvet—the gown was rather rusty and very low on her lean shoulders—and with a Japanese fan in her red hands. I reminded her that in the scene I was doing she had to look over someone's head. "I forget whose it is, but it doesn't matter."

"I'd rather look over a stove," said Miss Churm, and she took her station near the fire. She fell into position, settled herself into a tall attitude, gave a certain backward inclination to her head and a certain forward droop to her fan, and looked, at least to my prejudiced sense, distinguished and charming, foreign and dangerous. We left her looking so, while I went downstairs with Major and Mrs. Monarch.

"I think I could come about as near it as that," said Mrs. Monarch.

"Oh, you think she's shabby, but you must allow for the alchemy of art."

They went off with an evident increase of comfort, founded on their demonstrable advantage in being the real thing. Miss Churm was very droll about them when I went back, for I told her what they wanted.

"Well, if *she* can sit, I'll tyke to bookkeeping," said my model.

"She's very ladylike," I replied, as an innocent form of aggravation. "She'll do for the fashionable novels."

"Oh yes, she'll *do* for them!" my model humorously declared. "Ain't they bad enough without her?" I had often sociably denounced them to Miss Churm.

IT WAS FOR the elucidation of a mystery in one of these works that I first tried Mrs. Monarch. Her husband came with her, to be useful if necessary—it was clear that as a general thing he would prefer to come with her. At first I wondered if this were for propriety's sake—if he were going to be jealous and meddling. But I soon saw that if he accompanied Mrs. Monarch, it was—in addition to the chance of being wanted—simply because he had nothing else to do. When she was away from him, his occupation was gone—she never *had* been away from him. I judged, rightly, that in their awkward situation their close union was their main comfort and that this union had no weak spot. It was a real marriage. Their address was humble, and I could fancy the lamentable lodgings in which the major would have been left alone. He could bear them with his wife—he couldn't bear them without her.

He had too much tact to try and make himself agreeable when he couldn't be useful; so he simply sat and waited, when I was too absorbed in my work to talk. But I liked to make him talk. To listen to him was to combine the excitement of going out with the economy of staying at home. There was only one hindrance: that I seemed not to know any of the people he and his wife had known. I think he wondered extremely whom the deuce I *did* know. He hadn't a stray sixpence of an idea to fumble for; so we didn't spin it very fine—we confined ourselves to questions of leather and even of liquor, and matters like "good trains" and the habits of small game. His lore on these subjects was astonishing.

When I wanted to use him he came alone, which was an illustration of the superior courage of women. His wife could bear her solitary second floor, and she was in general more discreet, showing by various small reserves that she was alive to the propriety of keeping our relations markedly professional—not letting them slide into sociability. She wished it to remain clear that she and the major were employed, not cultivated; she never thought me quite good enough for an equal.

She sat with great intensity, giving the whole of her mind to it, and was capable of remaining for an hour almost as motionless as if she were before a photographer's lens. I could see she had been photographed often, but somehow the very habit that made her good for that purpose unfitted her for mine. At first I was extremely pleased with her ladylike air, and it was a satisfaction, on coming to follow her lines, to see how good they were and how far they could lead the pencil. But after a few times I began to find her too insurmountably stiff; do what I would with it, my drawing looked like a photograph or a copy of a photograph. Her figure had no variety of expression—she herself had no sense of variety. She was always a lady, certainly, and into the bargain was always the same lady. She was the real thing, but always the same thing. I found myself trying to invent types that approached her own, instead of making her own transform itself—in the clever way that was not impossible, for instance, to poor Miss Churm. And she always, in my pictures, came out too tall—landing me in the dilemma of having represented a fascinating woman as seven feet high.

After I had drawn Mrs. Monarch a dozen times I perceived more clearly than before that the value of such a model as Miss Churm resided precisely in the fact that she had no positive stamp, combined, of course, with the fact that she did have a curious and inexplicable talent for imitation. Her usual appearance was like a curtain which she could draw up at request for a capital performance. This performance was simply suggestive, but it was vivid and pretty. Sometimes, even, I reproached her that the figures drawn from her were monotonously graceful. Nothing made her more angry; it was her pride to feel that she could sit for characters that had nothing in common with each other. She would accuse me at such moments of taking away her "reputytion."

Miss Churm was never in want of employment, so I had no scruple in putting her off occasionally, to try my new friends. It was amusing at first to do the real thing—it was amusing to do Major Monarch's trousers. They *were* the real thing, even if he did come out colossal. It was amusing to do his wife's back hair (it was so mathematically neat). She lent herself especially to positions in which the face was somewhat averted or blurred. When she stood erect she took naturally one of the attitudes in which court painters represent queens and princesses.

Sometimes, however, the real thing and the make-believe came into contact; by which I mean that Miss Churm, keeping an appointment or coming to make one, encountered her invidious rivals. They noticed her no more than if she had been the housemaid; not from intentional loftiness, but simply because, as yet, professionally, they didn't know how to fraternize. They couldn't talk about the omnibus—they always walked; and Miss Churm wasn't interested in good trains or cheap claret.

One day when my young lady happened to be present with my other sitters, I asked her to be so good as to lend a hand in getting tea—a service with which she was familiar and which was one that I often appealed to my models to render. The next time I saw Miss Churm after this incident she surprised me greatly by making a scene about it—she accused me of having wished to humiliate her. She had not resented the outrage at the time, but had seemed amused, enjoying the comedy of asking Mrs. Monarch whether she would have cream and sugar, and putting an exaggerated simper into the question—as if she too wished to pass for the real thing; till I was afraid my other visitors would take offense.

Oh, *they* were determined not to do this, and their touching patience was the measure of their great need. They would sit by the hour, un-complaining, till I was ready to use them; they would come back on the chance of being wanted and would walk away cheerfully if they were not. I tried to find other employment for them—I introduced them to several artists. But they didn't "take," for reasons I could appreciate, and after such disappointments they fell back upon me with a heavier weight. They did me the honor to think that it was I who was most *their* form. Besides, they had an eye to the great job I had mentioned to them. If I could work them into it, their future would be assured, for the labor would, of course, be long and the occupation steady.

One day Mrs. Monarch came without her husband—she explained his absence by his having had to go to the City. While she sat there in her usual anxious stiffness there came, at the door, a knock followed by the entrance of a young man whom I perceived to be a foreigner and who proved in fact an Italian acquainted with no English word but my name. He conveyed to me, in graceful mimicry, that he was in search of exactly the employment in which the lady before me was engaged. I was not struck with him at first, and while I continued to draw, I emitted rough sounds of discouragement and dismissal. He stood his ground, however, with a doglike fidelity in his eyes which amounted to innocent impudence—the manner of a devoted servant unjustly suspected. Suddenly I saw that this very attitude and expression made a picture, whereupon I told him to sit down and wait till I should be free. There was another picture in the way he obeyed me, and I observed as I worked that there were others still in the way he looked wonderingly, with his head thrown back, about the high studio. He might have been crossing himself in St. Peter's. Before I finished I said to myself, "The fellow's a bankrupt orange monger, but he's a treasure."

When Mrs. Monarch withdrew, he passed across the room like a flash to open the door for her, standing there with the rapt, pure gaze of the young Dante spellbound by the young Beatrice. I reflected that he had the making of a servant (and I needed one, but couldn't pay him to be only that) as well as of a model; in short, I made up my mind to adopt my bright adventurer if he would agree to officiate in the double capacity. He jumped at my offer, proved a sympathetic though desultory ministrant, and had in a wonderful degree the *sentiment de la pose*. It was uncultivated, instinctive; a part of the happy instinct which had guided him to my door and helped him to spell out my name on the card nailed to it. He had had no other introduction to me than a guess, from the shape of my high north window, seen outside, that my place was a studio and that as a studio it would contain an artist. He had wandered to England in search of fortune, like other itinerants, and had embarked, with a partner and a small green handcart, on the sale of penny ices. The ices had melted away and the partner had dissolved in their train. My young man wore tight yellow trousers with reddish stripes and his name was Oronte. He was sallow but fair, and when I put him into some old clothes of my own he looked like an Englishman. He was as good as Miss Churm, who could look, when required, like an Italian.

I THOUGHT MRS. Monarch's face slightly convulsed when, on her coming back with her husband, she found Oronte installed. It was strange to have to recognize in a scrap of a lazzarone a competitor to her magnificent major. But Oronte gave us tea, with a hundred eager confusions (he had never seen such a queer process), and I think she thought better of me for having at last an "establishment." They saw a couple of drawings that I had made of the establishment, and Mrs. Monarch hinted that it never would have struck her that he had sat for them. "Now the drawings you make from *us*, they look exactly like us," she reminded me, smiling in triumph; and I recognized that this was indeed just their defect. When I drew the Monarchs, I couldn't, somehow, get away from them—get into the character I wanted to represent; and I had not the least desire my model should be discoverable in my picture. Miss Churm never was, and Mrs. Monarch thought I hid her, very properly, because she was vulgar.

By this time I had produced a dozen drawings for "Rutland Ramsay," the first novel in the great projected series, and I had sent them in for approval. There were moments when it *was* a comfort to have the real thing under one's hand, for there were characters in "Rutland Ramsay" that were very much like it. There were people presumably as straight as the major and women of as good a fashion as Mrs. Monarch; and there was a great deal of country-house life. There were certain things I had to settle at the outset; such things, for instance, as the exact appearance of the hero, the particular bloom of the heroine. The author, of course, gave me a lead, but there was a margin for interpretation. When once I had set *them* up, I should have to stick to them—I couldn't make my young man seven feet high in one place and five feet nine in another.

After the spontaneous Oronte had been with me a month, I waked to a sense of his heroic capacity. He was only five feet seven, but the remaining inches were latent. I tried him almost secretly at first, for I was really rather afraid of the judgment my other models would pass on such a choice. If they regarded Miss Churm as little better than a snare, what would they think of a person so little the real thing as an Italian street vendor of a protagonist formed by a public school?

If I went a little in fear of them, it was not because they bullied me, but because they counted on me so intensely. I was therefore very glad when Jack Hawley came home; he was always of such good counsel. He had been absent from England for a year, and the first evening he spent in my studio we smoked cigarettes till the small hours. He wanted to see what I had been doing, but he was disappointed. That at least seemed the meaning of two or three comprehensive groans which, as he lounged on my big divan, looking at my latest drawings, issued from his lips with the smoke of the cigarette.

"You're quite off the hinge," he said. "What's the meaning of this new fad?" And he tossed me, with visible irreverence, a drawing in which I happened to have depicted both my majestic models. The two figures looked colossal, but I supposed this was *not* what he meant, inasmuch as, for aught he knew to the contrary, I might have been trying for that. I maintained that I was working exactly in the same way as when he last had done me the honor to commend me. "Well, there's a big hole somewhere," he answered. "Wait a bit and I'll discover it." I depended upon him to do so. But he produced at last nothing more luminous than "I don't know—I don't like your types." This was lame, for a critic who had never discussed with me anything but the question of execution, the direction of strokes and the mystery of values.

"In the drawings you've been looking at, I think my types are very handsome."

"Oh, they won't do!"

"I've had a couple of new models."

"I see you have. *They* won't do. They're stupid."

"You mean *I* am—for I ought to get round that."

"You *can't*—with such people."

"You've never seen them; they're awfully good," I objected.

"Not seen them? Why, all this recent work of yours drops to pieces with them. It's all I want to see of them."

I noted the warning, but I didn't turn my friends out of doors. As I look back at this phase, I have a vision of them as most of the time in my studio, seated, against the wall, on an old velvet bench to be out of the way, and looking like a pair of patient courtiers in a royal antechamber. I am convinced that during the coldest weeks of the winter they held their ground because it saved them fire. Their newness was losing its gloss, and it was impossible not to feel that they were objects of charity. Whenever Miss Churm arrived, they went away, and after I was fairly launched in "Rutland Ramsay," Miss Churm arrived pretty often. They managed to express to me tacitly that they supposed I wanted her for the lowlife of the book, and I let them suppose it. I still took an hour from them, now and again, in spite of Jack Hawley's warning; it would be time enough to dismiss them, if dismissal should be necessary, when the rigor of the season was over. Hawley had made their acquaintance—he had met them at my fireside—and thought them a ridiculous pair. Learning that he was a painter, they tried to approach him, to show him too that they were the real thing; but he looked at them, across the big room, as if they were miles away; they were a compendium of everything that he most objected to in the social system of his country. Such people as that, all convention and patent leather, with ejaculations that stopped conversation, had no business in a studio.

The main inconvenience I suffered at their hands was that, at first, I was shy of letting them discover how my artful little servant had begun to sit for me for "Rutland Ramsay." They knew that I had been odd enough to pick a foreign vagabond out of the streets, when I might have had a person with whiskers and credentials; but it was some time before they learned how high I rated his accomplishments. They found him posing more than once, but they never doubted I was doing him as an organ-grinder. There were several things they never guessed, and one of them was that for a striking scene in the novel, in which a footman briefly figured, it occurred to me to make use of Major Monarch as the menial. I kept putting this off, I didn't like to ask him to don the livery—besides the difficulty of finding a livery to fit him. At last, one day late in the winter, when I was at work on the despised Oronte and was in the glow of feeling that I was going very straight, they came in, the major and his wife, with their society laugh about nothing, like country callers who have walked across the park after church and are presently persuaded to stay to luncheon. Luncheon was over, but they could stay to tea—I knew they wanted it. The fit was on me, however, and I couldn't let my ardor cool and my work wait, with the fading daylight, while my model prepared it. So I asked Mrs. Monarch if she would mind laying it out—a request which, for an instant, brought all the blood to her face. Her eyes were on her husband's for a second, and some mute telegraphy passed between them. Their folly was over the next moment; his cheerful shrewdness put an end to it. They bustled about together and got out the cups and saucers and made the kettle boil. I know they felt as if they were waiting on my servant, and when the tea was prepared, I said, "He'll have a cup, please—he's tired." Mrs. Monarch brought him one where he stood, and he took it from her as if he had been a gentleman at a party.

Then it came over me that she had made a great effort for me—made it with a kind of nobleness—and that I owed her a compensation. But I couldn't go on doing the wrong thing to oblige them. Oh, it *was* the wrong thing, the stamp of the work for which they sat—Hawley was not the only person to say it now. I sent in a large number of the drawings I had made for "Rutland Ramsay," and I received a warning that was more to the point than Hawley's. The artistic adviser of the house for which I was working was of the opinion that many of my illustrations were not what had been looked for. Most of these illustrations were the subjects in which the Monarchs had figured. At this rate I shouldn't get the other books to do. I hurled myself in despair upon Miss Churm; I put her through all her paces. I not only adopted Oronte publicly as my hero, but one morning when the major looked in to see if I didn't require him to finish a figure for the *Cheapside*, for which he had begun to sit the week before, I told him that I had changed my mind—I would do the drawing from my man. At this my visitor turned pale and stood looking at me. "Is *he* your idea of an English gentleman?"

I was disappointed, I was nervous, I wanted to get on with my work; so I replied with irritation, "Oh, my dear Major—I can't be ruined for *you!*"

He stood another moment; then, without a word, he quitted the studio. I drew a long breath when he was gone, for I said to myself that I shouldn't see him again. I had not told him definitely that I was in danger of having my work rejected, but I was vexed at his not having felt the catastrophe in the air.

Three days later my friends reappeared together, and under the circumstances there was something tragic in the fact. It was a proof to me that they could find nothing else in life to do. They had threshed the matter out in a dismal conference—they had digested the bad news that they were not in for the series and not useful to me even for the *Cheapside*, and I could only judge at first that they had come, forgivingly, decorously, to take a last leave. This made me rejoice in secret that I had little leisure for a scene, for I had placed both my other models in position together and I was pegging away at a drawing from which I hoped to derive glory. It had been suggested by the passage in which Rutland Ramsay, drawing up a chair to Artemisia's piano stool, says extraordinary things to her while she ostensibly fingers out a difficult piece of music. I had done Miss Churm at the piano before—it was a pose in which she knew how to take on an absolutely poetic grace. I wished the two figures to "compose" together, intensely, and my little Italian had entered perfectly into my conception. The pair were vividly before me, the piano had been pulled out; it was a charming picture of blended youth and murmured love, which I had only to catch and keep. My visitors stood and looked at it, and I was friendly to them over my shoulder.

Presently I heard Mrs. Monarch's sweet voice beside, or rather above me: "I wish her hair was a little better done." I looked up and she was staring with a strange fixedness at Miss Churm, whose back was turned to her. "Do you mind my just touching it?" she went on—a question which made me spring up for an instant, as with the instinctive fear that she might do the young lady a harm. But she quieted me with a glance I shall never forget—I confess I should like to have been able to paint *that*—and went for a moment to my model. She spoke to her softly, laying a hand upon her shoulder and bending over her; and as the girl, understanding, gratefully assented, she disposed her rough curls, with a few quick passes, in such a way as to make Miss Churm's head twice as charming. It was one of the most heroic personal services I have ever seen rendered. Then Mrs. Monarch turned away with a low sigh, and, looking about her as if for something to do, stooped to the floor with a noble humility and picked up a dirty rag that had dropped out of my paint box.

The major meanwhile had also been looking for something to do, and, wandering to the other end of the studio, saw before him my breakfast things, neglected, unremoved. "I say, can't I be useful *here?*" he called out to me with an irrepressible quaver. I assented with a laugh that I fear was awkward, and for the next ten minutes, while I worked, I heard the light clatter of china and the tinkle of spoons and glass. Mrs. Monarch assisted her husband—they washed up my crockery, they put it away. They wandered off into my little scullery, and I afterward found that they had cleaned my knives and that my slender stock of plate had an unprecedented surface. When it came over me, the latent eloquence of what they were doing, I confess that my drawing was blurred for a moment—the picture swam. They had accepted their failure, but they couldn't accept their fate. They had bowed their heads in bewilderment to the perverse and cruel law in virtue of which the real thing could be so much less precious than the unreal; but they didn't want to starve. If my servants were my models, my models might be my servants. It was an intense dumb appeal for me not to turn them out.

When all this hung before me, my pencil dropped from my hand. My sitting was spoiled and I got rid of my sitters, who were rather mystified and awestruck. Then, alone with the major and his wife, I had a most uncomfortable moment. He put their prayer into a single sentence: "I say, you know—just let *us* do for you, can't you?" I couldn't—it was dreadful to see them emptying my slops; but I pretended I could, to oblige them, for about a week. Then I gave them a sum of money to go away, and I never saw them again. I obtained the remaining books, but my friend Hawley repeats that Major and Mrs. Monarch did me a permanent harm, got me into a second-rate trick. If it be true, I am content to have paid the price—for the memory.

THE HOSTAGE
C. S. FORESTER

It was in the autumn of 1944, when the Allied armies had come bursting out of the Cotentin Peninsula, flooding across France and advancing toward the frontiers of the Fatherland, that General of Infantry Friedrich von Dexter received his new orders. They were brought by motorcycle dispatch rider to the little house in the Welfenstrasse, having presumably been teletyped to Army District Headquarters from the higher command of the armed forces. Air raids on the town had been infrequent lately; and the ruins had ceased to smoke, but traffic was scanty, so that the roar of the motorcycle engine was heard by everyone, and neighbors peeped out of their windows to find out what was happening. They saw the general himself at his front door receive the envelope and sign the receipt for it, and then the motorcycle roared away again and the general went back inside his house.

Indoors, the general found it hard to read the typewritten sheet with its printed heading, for the general was not wearing his spectacles and he had to hold the message at arm's length, which was inconvenient, as the shattered windows had been boarded up, making the stuffy, old-fashioned sitting room almost dark. Aloise, his wife, stood motionless by him while he read the message, motionless because as a soldier's wife she was trying to conceal the anxiety she felt. Dexter handed it to her without a word when he had finished, and she read it with less difficulty.

"Does this mean—" she began, and then she cut the question short.

There were factory workers billeted in the house, and although they were presumably asleep, having been on the night shift, she could not risk being overheard discussing orders which had come from the Führer himself. The two old people substituted glances for words; even in that twilit room they understood each other, after forty years of married life. The general looked over at the marble clock on the mantelpiece—the gift of the 91st Infantry on the occasion of their colonel's promotion—and reached a decision.

"We have ten minutes," he said. "Let us go for a walk."

They went out into the shattered streets; there, among the hurrying pedestrians, and the cyclists bumping their way over the uneven surfaces, they could talk safely as long as they did not display any deep emotion. The general was in civilian clothes, because when he had been dismissed from his command by a frantic Führer order he had been deprived of the right to wear uniform. So he wore his battered twenty-year-old tweeds, and Aloise walked beside him in her old-fashioned coat and skirt; and they appeared, as indeed they were, survivors of a past generation—even though, thanks to his spare figure and straight back, and with his hat concealing his white hair, the general's age was not apparent.

"What does it mean, dear?" asked Aloise before they reached the first corner.

"A direct order from the Führer," said the general. "I have been appointed to the command of Fortress Montavril."

"Yes, dear. That is in France?"

"The Belgian frontier. Near the Channel coast."

"What sort of a fortress is it?"

The general looked casually around him, back over his shoulder, before he answered.

"I doubt if it is any fortress at all," he said. "I am quite sure there is none, in fact."

"But dear . . ."

The general looked over his shoulder again.

"The Führer has a new system," he said. "It began in Russia last year—no, two years ago. He designates a particular area as a fortress and he appoints a garrison and a commandant for it."

"And then, dear? And then?"

"Because it has been designated a fortress, the place is expected to hold out to the last man."

"I understand," said Aloise.

It was hard, dreadfully hard, to have to carry on this conversation in public, while trying to appear as if merely taking a casual stroll.

"There is much for you to understand, dear," said the general. "He is obsessed with this idea. And he still believes, in spite of everything, that what he wishes must come true. A place is a fortress and so it must hold out, no matter what the conditions. A barbed-wire perimeter—that is all that is necessary. Disorganized troops—worn-out guns—shortage of ammunition—to speak of them is treason."

They could not exchange a significant glance here in the street; they must stroll along looking idly about them as if talking of nothing except trivialities.

"It is hopeless, then?"

"My duty . . ." began the general, and then he paused while making the effort to marshal all the multitudinous ideas called up by that word, the most significant in the vocabulary of a soldier. "It is my duty to obey my orders, and to fight for my country, no matter what the future."

"Of course, dear."

"But . . ." The general paused again, as a soldier well might pause after saying "but" when speaking of his duty.

"But what, dear?"

"That is not all. In a siege . . ."

The general had been married forty years. During that time he had come gradually to discuss professional matters with his wife in a way that often violated the convention that a wife should confine her interests to church, children and kitchen; but it was hard to convey to her in a few words the same picture of a siege that he carried in his mind's eye, called up with the ease of long professional experience.

"In a siege, dear?"

"There comes a time when further defense is useless. When the perimeter is broken. When the enemy has captured the commanding heights. When his artillery is overwhelming. Until then the garrison has been doing what it was intended to do. It has detained a larger force in its front. It has caused more casualties than it has suffered. Probably it has blocked some important line of communication. But after that moment is reached . . ."

The general talked with the fluency he could display when discussing professional subjects—he had talked in this way to several generations of young men at the War Academy many years ago. He broke off now, for they were passing a long line of people waiting outside a shop. When they had passed it, Aloise recalled him to his explanation.

"You were talking about a siege, dear."

"Yes. So I was. After a certain point defense usually becomes futile. The besiegers have an overwhelming artillery, good points of observation, have breached the defenses. Then the losses become heavy among the defenders, with no corresponding loss to the besiegers. To hold out longer than that means a massacre; men are killed with no chance of hitting back. Sometimes it is necessary, even so."

"It is hard to see why, dear." Aloise tried to speak with a professional tone. Womanlike, her first reaction when casualties were mentioned was not to think of figures in a return, or of a commanding officer deciding that a unit was fought out, but of dead men and tortured men, of childless mothers and widowed wives—of herself when the news came about their sons. She knew that was not the way a general's wife should think at a time when professional subjects were under discussion, and she steadied her voice in consequence.

"It may happen," explained Dexter, "that the garrison may still be blocking some important line of communication. Then it may be worthwhile to incur those losses, to fight to the last man to keep that line blocked for the last few hours. It might be worth any sacrifice."

"I suppose so," agreed Aloise doubtfully.

"But that is an unusual situation," went on Dexter, "rarer than you would think."

Aloise in her heart of hearts believed that there could never be any situation worth the sacrifice of thousands of lives, but she did not say so. She waited dutifully for her husband to continue.

"Generally speaking," he said, "a neutralized garrison under final attack has no useful part to play."

Aloise could make no contribution to the conversation, and her husband, interpreting her silence as lack of full understanding, went on to produce a specific instance, even though when lecturing to budding staff officers he had been careful to warn them not to think exclusively along arithmetical lines.

"Supposing," he said, "I have twenty thousand men in my garrison. That's a likely number. For two or three weeks I detain forty thousand of the enemy in front of me. Well and good. They attack at the decisive points. If their armor is not overwhelmingly strong, I inflict heavy casualties on them. By the time they have mastered those decisive points I have lost—say five thousand men."

Aloise tried to picture five thousand dead men, and failed.

"But the enemy has lost ten thousand—twelve thousand, perhaps," went on her husband. "That is well and good, as I said. Now my guns are wearing out, my ammunition failing, and I am under constant searching bombardment. The assault is going to succeed whenever the enemy cares to make it. If I fight on, my fifteen thousand men are killed. And what does the enemy lose? One thousand? I doubt if it would be as many as that."

"I see," said Aloise, nodding her head as she walked. The general looked at his watch.

"My dear," he said, "I—I am afraid we must turn back."

Aloise glanced sharply at him, sidelong, at that break in his voice. It would have told her, even if she had not already guessed, how deep were his feelings, and how great was the strain he was enduring. After they had turned back he added a supplement to his little lecture.

"You might think," he said, "that it did not really matter. One garrison more or less— But that is not true. There is the rest of the army to think about. And there is the Germany of the future."

The general turned almost self-conscious as he entered into a discussion of the psychology of warfare. It was a very theoretical subject for a practical soldier.

"Soldiers will always fight under good officers. You can ask for extraordinary sacrifices from them." The general paused, and his faded blue eyes looked out over dreadful distant vistas of memory. "But they will not endure the thought of their lives being thrown away uselessly.

They sulk, they desert. They shirk their duty. Once let it be known that they are going to certain death to no purpose and—no garrison would ever hold out. Do you understand that, dear?"

"I understand," said Aloise.

"Already the army is not what it was."

The general looked quickly over his shoulder after he had said that. It had slipped out, and if he had been overheard, he might be a dead man that very night—and die a shameful death at that. They walked on their homeward way for some hundred yards in silence; the general was silent not merely because he was shaken by the risk he had just run, but because he found it hard to continue with what he had to say, to advance the conversation to the next stage. It may have been accidental, or it may not, that Aloise made it easy by her next question.

"And you, dear," she asked. "Have you thought about what you will do?"

"I have my orders," said Dexter. There was a grim, hard tone in his voice, and the glance that Aloise directed at him showed her that his face bore a bleak, hopeless expression.

Most people would have thought there was very little about General Friedrich von Dexter for any woman to love—a professional soldier, hard, tough, limited both in his education and outlook, and more than sixty years old. Some men might laugh at him, some even despise him, although there had been many young men who had admired him, and there had been young captains who had loved him, back in the days of that other nightmare, when his fighting spirit alone had held his regiment together in face of utter disaster at the Butte de Warlencourt. And long after that, too; only last year at Kharkov, after he had fought his way with the remnants of his army corps out of the ring of encirclement, his staff had been moved to the deepest pity and sympathy when the savage message arrived from headquarters depriving him of his command. "The weak-kneed gentleman with a von to his name" was how that message had described him. Sorrow at losing him had been the first and principal emotion of those young staff officers. The feeling that something must be desperately amiss at Führer headquarters for such a message to be sent came only secondarily—and of course could not be expressed in any spoken words.

And the hard professional soldier had read that message without allowing his expression to change in the least. He had left with only the briefest good-bys, to return home in disgrace, humiliated; only Aloise, when she welcomed him home, knew the depths of that humiliation. And she loved him; perhaps she loved him the more. An old woman of sixty, an old man of sixty-two, walking together along the shattered street in the bleak autumn sunshine, and discussing horrors, discussing the death of twenty thousand men—how could there be love there? Yet there was, just as flowers grow among the rocks.

"I have to obey," said Dexter.

"I know you must, dear," said Aloise.

Even if there were no question of duty, one obeyed orders from the Führer, or died.

"My dear," said Dexter, looking straight before him, not daring even for a moment to meet his wife's eyes; it was as if, although speaking low, he were addressing the horizon.

"Yes, dear?"

"You know there is a law of hostages?"

"Yes."

"Do you understand about it?"

"Yes."

No one in Germany could fail to understand it. The law had been promulgated that summer, although it had been in operation, to everyone's knowledge, long before. Now it had been announced in cold print. Men's families were to be held responsible for their actions. If a man were to desert, his father or his mother, his wife or his sister or his children would be killed. Not only the man who deserted, but the man who faltered in his duty, the man whose spirit failed him, the man who could not overcome his physical weaknesses, condemned in that moment those who were dearest to him to a death which might or might not be speedy. There was to be no human weakness displayed in the defense of the Third Reich and in the prolongation of the lives of the inhuman creatures who ruled it.

"You are the only one now, dear," said Dexter, still addressing the horizon.

"I know," said Aloise.

The younger Friedrich von Dexter had died at El Alamein; Lothar von Dexter at Stalingrad. Ernst was "missing, believed killed" at Rostov. There were only the two old people left. One would command at Montavril, and one would be a hostage at home.

"Did you notice in my orders who was to be my chief of staff?" asked Dexter.

"A Gruppenführer—I can't remember his name at the moment, but I did not know it. An SS officer, of course?"

"Gruppenführer Frey," said Dexter. "I don't know him either. But I know why he has been appointed."

"To spy on you?"

"To keep me up to my duty," said Dexter.

They were nearly home again now. Everything had been said except the good-by, which would have to be said immediately.

There were several good-bys of the same sort being made at that time in Germany. Hitler was recalling to service many of the generals he had previously dismissed in disgrace, and appointing them to the command of fortresses. He needed officers of high rank and authority, officers of experience, for those posts, to make sure the troops would obey. And he could rely on the law of hostages to make the generals themselves obey, however harshly he had treated them previously, and whatever their feelings toward him—about which he could have no doubt. As Dexter kissed his wife good-by before going out to the waiting car, he had the law of hostages in his mind.

ON THE SEVENTEENTH day of the siege of Montavril the Allies launched their third attack, and succeeded in breaking through the outer perimeter of the defenses and in overrunning the whole of the area beyond the canal, which the German forces had so far contrived to maintain. It was a desperate fight, in driving rain. The general himself had taken part in it. It was he personally who had saved the day. He had rallied the broken infantry, had brought up his last reserve, and had plugged the gap which yawned in the defenses between the canal and the crossroads. He himself had posted the guns, and by his own example had kept them firing. The counterattack which he had launched might even have succeeded in regaining the vital higher ground beyond the crossroads if it had not been for the shell which momentarily disabled him. It had wounded his aide-de-camp, and had torn to pieces the brigadier a few yards from him, but by some freak of ballistics the fragment which struck the general on the shin did not even break a bone. But he had been dazed and shaken by the explosion, and by the time he could stand steady on his feet again the counterattack had failed, and the battle had died away into desultory firing. The heavy rain limited visibility on all sides, turning the low fields into swamps, soaking—and perhaps in some instances even drowning—the helpless wounded who lay in the ill-defined no-man's-land around the crossroads. Perhaps the Allies would send in a flag of truce to arrange a brief armistice to attend to them.

The general left instructions on the matter with the colonel now in command of the sector before he went limping off—alone, because he left his runner to look after his aide-de-camp—to inspect the defenses along the canal bank. Here the Allies were already in touch, in a manner of speaking. With extraordinary celerity they had brought up a loud-speaker, which was braying ceaselessly across the nearly dry canal bed. It spoke almost perfect German—the sort of German one might expect from a German-American who had used the language at home in his childhood—and it was appealing to the troops to give up a hopeless struggle. The general listened to it with the division commander at his side. Normally the penalty for listening to Allied broadcasts was death, the same as for possessing an Allied leaflet, but in these circumstances the penalty could hardly be exacted—too many of the garrison were within hearing. It was good sense that the loudspeaker talked, too, pointing out that now the Allies had direct observation over the whole of the defenses, and that there was no part of the perimeter now which was not subject to enfilade. The sensible thing to do would be to surrender, said the loudspeaker, and if the mad folly of the officers prevented that, then it would be equally sensible to desert, to slip over to the Allied lines, where honorable treatment awaited anyone who accepted the invitation. The general listened, with the rain beating down on his helmet and waterproof coat.

"I am going back to headquarters now," he said to the division commander. "If they telephone for me, say that I am on my way."

"Very well, sir," said the division commander.

He was a man in his forties, white with fatigue, and with red rims to his eyes. He watched with something like envy the stiff figure of the man in his sixties, limping solitary down the muddy path; but there was pity mingled with the envy.

The briefness of Dexter's journey from his outer defenses by the canal to his headquarters in the church of Montavril demonstrated vividly the difficulties of the defense. It took Dexter not very long, even though he had to pick his way. Here was a score of dead horses, already beginning to bulge with corruption—there was no fuel with which to burn them nor labor available to bury them. The general thought bitterly of how the Allies, fully mechanized, had not a horse in their organization. They were four times stronger numerically, ten times better equipped, a hundred times stronger in the air. He exchanged a few words with the artillery commander here, a man as worn out as the division commander he had just left. Whatever compulsion was called for, those horses must be buried. The whole entrenched camp stank—the stench of modern war, foulness and corruption and high explosives. Here, where the dead had been buried, the shells of the Allies had horribly caused the earth to give up its dead. He must remember to give orders about that.

He stumbled through a filthy puddle. By his action today he had prolonged the defense by a few hours. The Allies would have to regroup and replenish with ammunition before they renewed their assault. If the counterattack had regained the crossroads, he might have gained a day—two days, even. But it had failed, and there was not a single battalion—not even a battalion as battalions were measured nowadays, with less than company strength—in reserve. Infantry, engineers and cooks were all in the front line. No; in a cellar in the village were two men under arrest. At headquarters they were waiting for him to confirm the court-martial sentences; he had postponed his decision until his return. Yet the sentences would have to be carried out. He had been remiss in even allowing that short delay. Prompt and inevitable punishment was necessary to keep the garrison fighting. But did it matter about two miserable men who had attempted to desert, when ten thousand men were going to die? Dexter shook his head, not in dissent, but rather to shake off evil thoughts, as he plunged on.

Headquarters were in the church, in the crypt below the church, for of the building itself only a fragment of one wall still stood. The rest was piled about in jagged heaps of masonry.

Dexter went in through the sandbagged and camouflaged entrance, down the stone steps, past the signalers in the outer dugout, and into the crypt, where four candles struggled to burn in the foul air, and the chairs and tables of the staff were ranged around the tomb of the saint. Gruppenführer Frey, left in charge when the general went to Canal Corner, rose to greet him.

"Congratulations, General," he said, in his shrill voice, and the general stared at him in astonishment. There was nothing in the events of the past few hours—or days—or weeks—which called for congratulation. Frey turned back to take a little box from his improvised desk, opened it, and handed something to the general with an extravagant gesture; it was something metallic, which glittered, and lay cold in the general's hand.

"The Knight's Cross of the Iron Cross!" said Frey. "The *Ritterkreuz!* What a pleasure it is to hand it to you, General. It was never better deserved."

"How did this get here?" demanded Dexter.

"The plane—you didn't see it pass over? This morning—it dropped a message packet."

"I did not see it," said Dexter. Perhaps it had flown over while he had been rallying the Landesschützen battalion at Oak Tree Corner. He had been too busy to notice the only German plane the garrison had seen since the siege began.

"Was there anything else in the message packet?" asked Dexter, sharply still.

Frey's fingers fluttered back to the desk.

"The letter from the chief of the Military Cabinet enclosing the *Ritterkreuz,*" he said. "A most flattering letter, General."

Dexter glanced through it. A flattering letter, certainly—nothing beyond flattery either. The higher command, now that Germany was falling in ruins, avoided realities and confined its attention to trivialities like Knight's Crosses.

"Anything else?"

"Personal orders for me from SS head office."

In the fantastic disorder into which Germany had fallen it was possible—it was a certainty—that an SS officer should receive orders independently of his commanding officer. Dexter could not even ask what those orders said.

"Anything else?"

"Yes. A small amount of mail for some of the units of the garrison. I have not yet decided to distribute it. As political officer I have to consider—"

"Anything for me?"

"One letter, General."

Dexter knew what it was the instant he saw it. He snatched it from Frey's hand; Frey's fingers were twitching to open it, the born spy that he was; and as political officer with Himmler's authority behind him he could have demanded that it be shown him, but he knew that—at least in an isolated garrison like this—there was a practical limit to the power delegated to him. Dexter would not have allowed him to see Aloise's letter, not for anything on earth. Dexter stood holding it, yearning inexpressibly to open it and read it, but he would not do so in Frey's presence. When he could get a moment's privacy he would read it. It would afford him a brief glimpse of another world; it would be torment as well as unmeasured happiness, he knew. He would be reminded of Aloise's steadfast love for him, the comfort of it, the security of it, even while he was here, plunged deep into hell. Hell was all around him, and he would never escape from it; the letter he held in his hand would open a chink through which for one small moment he would be able to peer into heaven.

Hell was all around him, demanding his attention.

"Have any reports come in?" he asked. He must attend to his duty before reading Aloise's letter.

Busse, the assistant chief of staff, had them ready.

"Verbal reports, sir," he said, holding his notes of the telephone conversations in his hand. "Barmers says—perhaps I had better give you his exact words, sir."

"Very well," said Dexter. Barmers was the senior medical officer in the garrison.

"He says, 'It is my duty to report to the general that I can do nothing for the wounded that are coming in. Anesthetics and dressings are completely at an end, and plasma nearly so. The regimental aid stations are asking for morphine, and I have none to give them. The newly wounded must lie in the open outside the hospital to wait their turn for operative treatment without anesthesia, and that will not be until tomorrow morning. I should not really have spared the time to make this report.' That is the end of the report, sir."

"Thank you," said Dexter.

"The adjutant of the 507th Artillery Regiment reports—"

"I saw him on my way back. I know what his report says."

Ten rounds left per gun, and very few guns serviceable.

"General Fussel asks for the return of his Ost battalion."

Fussel commanded the 816th Division on the far side of the perimeter. His division had been stripped of every available man to make the counterattack.

"I left that decision to you, sir," interposed Frey.

"The Ost battalion must stay where it is," decided Dexter.

"Fussel has no reserves at all, sir," said Busse, in gentle warning.

"I know that. Anything else?"

"The assistant quartermaster general—"

"I can guess what he has to say," said Dexter, looking around at the gloomy face of Officer Becker. "Anything else?"

"The court-martial findings, sir."

"Yes," said Dexter.

Two men waiting to be shot, two men who had been detected in the act of desertion. There could be no mercy for them if the garrison were to be held together. The sooner they were shot, the stronger the effect on the others. It was his duty not to delay. And yet—he had fought a good fight. His iron will had implemented his immense tactical experience. Under his leadership his garrison had beaten off two assaults and had at least temporarily checked the third. In the hands of a bungler the defense might well have collapsed on the third day, and now it was the seventeenth. Surely he was entitled to some reward for that, something more satisfying although less tangible than the *Ritterkreuz?* He could spare two lives. Or could he even spare ten thousand? He was suddenly aware that Frey's eyes were fixed on his face, and he hoped that his expression had revealed none of his feelings.

The squawk of the telephone came as a fortunate diversion. Any call through to the central command post must be important, as only half a dozen officers had the right of direct access; routine calls were dealt with by the staff officer in the outer room. Frey picked up the telephone, as was his natural duty as chief of staff, but Dexter bitterly attributed to him a greedy inquisitiveness even in this hour of disaster.

"Chief of staff," said Frey. "Yes, I hear. Yes. Yes."

He looked over at Dexter, the telephone still in his hand.

"Fussel," he said. "He thinks he can hear armor moving up behind the embankment at La Haye. Coordinates—"

"I know the place," said Dexter. "Tell him it makes no difference to his orders."

Fussel apparently expostulated at the far end of the wire; there was a brief argument before Frey put down the telephone again. Well might Fussel expostulate, too. If the Allies were bringing up tanks, they could burst through Fussel's sector as if it were a paper hoop. So far the garrison had seen none.

"It may be only a ruse," said Busse.

That was possible. There were plenty of ways in which the Allies might simulate the sound of tanks advancing in the shelter of the embankment. Dexter could not believe that it was only a ruse, all the same. Nor could Frey, obviously. There was a pinched look about his thin face as he stood still, fingering the telephone. But when he raised his head and met Dexter's eyes again, the pinched look was transmuted into something more vicious. Ratlike, perhaps. Frey was a cornered rat facing finality with bared teeth. He drew attention with a gesture to the letter still unopened in Dexter's hand.

"I *hope* the baroness is well," he said, his shrill voice shriller even than usual with the heightened tension. "I *hope* she is well."

There was a hysterical edge to the remark; in other circumstances the words might have been utterly casual, but now there could be no doubt about their implication. Frey was using a threat to ensure the death of ten thousand men. He was infected with the same madness that was being displayed by the whole party from the Führer downward, with the same insane lust for destruction. If the party were doomed to perish, then nothing German was to survive. The men could die, the women and children starve, the whole area of the Reich was to be left a depopulated desert in the final Götterdämmerung, without one stone left upon another in its silent villages and cities; that was the only way left for the party to assert itself, and those stony deserts the only memorial the Führer could now hope for. Frey for his own part was ensuring for himself, like some petty Attila, the company of ten thousand spirits of men when he himself should pass on to whatever he thought lay beyond the grave. That was why he was reminding Dexter about the letter, about Aloise.

Dexter's pistol was at his belt, and he was actually tempted at that moment to draw it and to kill this madman. But that would be no help to Aloise. It would not remove her from the power of the SS; rather would it—if the news reached Germany, as it might with so many informers about—rather would it ensure the worst, the torture chamber, the pincers—the—the— Dexter felt his own sanity to be on the point of breaking down, and he mastered himself by a frightful effort. He wanted to shout and storm; the steadiness of his own voice when he spoke surprised him—it was as if someone else were speaking.

"I had forgotten my letter," he said.

Of a sudden he felt intensely weary. And he was cold, too; shuddering a little. That had to be controlled in case they thought he was trembling. Another determination was forming in his mind.

"I shall go and rest," he said. "For fifteen minutes."

Frey and Busse nodded, their eyes fixed on his face, and their gaze followed him as he walked slowly and heavily over the flagstones to the corner where a suspended blanket screened his bed. He remembered to take a candle with him, and once inside the screen he set it on the bracket at the head of the bed. He would need that much light to read his letter, even though he would need no light for what he was going to do after that. He turned back from the bracket to draw the screen close, and in that moment he saw Busse's face, tortured with pity. That was the last thing he saw before he drew the blanket.

Inside the screen there was only room for the bed. He had to lie down on it to read his letter. He ought to take off his boots. Otherwise he would smear the bed with mud, and the thought disturbed his orderly mind; he remembered the general orders he had issued to the garrison on his taking command, to the effect that every man who allowed himself to be unclean would be severely punished. That had been necessary to keep the garrison up to the mark, to maintain them as disciplined soldiers to the very end. But this was the very end, for him at least. And if the bed were soon to be fouled with blood and brains, a little mud hardly mattered. He lay down and swung his muddy boots up onto the bed.

His hand holding the letter lay on his breast, and there was a moment's incredible temptation not to read it. He was so weary. The deed he had in mind to do was an easy way out for him. It would be the end of his troubles. It might well save Aloise's life, too. A bloody sacrifice might appease the madmen of the SS. And even if it did not, he would know nothing about it. He would be at peace, even if Aloise—no; he must not think along those lines.

Nor would it solve the problems of the garrison. With his death Frey would take command, and the ten thousand men were still doomed. He must not think about that either. As he could do nothing to save them, he must congratulate himself on ending his own misery and he must give no further thought to theirs. That was cowardly. The horrible system that had mastered the Reich was forcing even Friedrich von Dexter into cowardice; could there be better proof of its inherent evil?

To draw his pistol he had to lay down the letter. As his hand touched the cold butt, he withdrew it again. He must read Aloise's letter, of course. He would read it twice, and when for the second time he had read the last dear word he would draw the pistol, quickly. His mouth actually softened into something barely like a smile as he thought of Aloise's tenderness and love. He opened the letter.

My dearest—This letter brings you from your loving wife every good wish, wherever you may be, whatever may be happening, and with my good wishes my deepest love, which you know you have had during all the years of our marriage.

But, dearest, I am afraid that this letter is going to add to your unhappiness. I have bad news for you. I did not tell you about it when we were last together, because at that time you had too many troubles already and I could not add to them. I kept it a secret from you then, but now I have to tell you.

Dearest, I shall not be alive when you receive this letter. I have a cancer. Dr. Mohrenwitz had told me so, but I knew it before he told me. I made him tell me. And he told me that it is in the same place as Frau Engel had hers, and you remember what happened to her, dearest. It has not been too bad until now, but now I cannot go on. Dr. Mohrenwitz has been giving me pills to make me sleep and to ease the pain, and I have been saving them up. Tonight after I have posted this letter I am going to take them all at once. I have made all the arrangements and I know I shall die.

So, I have to say good-by to you, dearest. I have to thank you for every bit of happiness I have enjoyed during the last forty years. You have always been the best, the kindest, the tenderest of husbands to me, and I have loved you with all my heart. And I have admired you as well—I have been such a fortunate woman to have a husband I could admire as well as love—your honesty and your sincerity and your thoughtfulness.

I only wish I could have done more for you, dearest. I used to wish I could bear all your sorrow as well as my own when we lost our dear boys. But now you know that I have no more sorrow or unhappiness or pain and that while you read this letter I shall be at peace. Tonight I shall only be thinking of you, dearest, as I always have done. My last thoughts will be of you, always and ever my very dearest.

Good-by, darling, good-by

Eternally your A.

That was the letter. Dexter read it twice, as he had planned, but not twice through from beginning to end, as he had thought he would. He read it jerkily, going back to reread each line. It was hard to focus his eyes on the words; perhaps because the light of the single candle was so dim. But he finished the reading and lay still, the letter on his breast. He was conscious only of his dreadful sense of loss. A world that did not have Aloise in it was not the same world as he had lived in for all these years. It was not a world in which he wanted to live. He remembered why he had come in here. He put his hand down again on the butt of the pistol, and perhaps it was the cold contact that recalled him to other realities. Aloise was dead—was dead—was dead. She had said she would have no more sorrow or unhappiness or pain. She had not said that now she would be beyond the power of the SS, but that was equally true. Dexter stiffened as he realized that he still had a duty to do, a duty which he could now carry out.

The realization held him rigid for some seconds as he thought about the situation, and then he relaxed as his numbness vanished and his thoughts began to flow freely again. He was a man of action, bred and trained to make rapid decisions, and born with the firmness of will to execute them. There was no time to waste. He must act, and he burst instantly into harsh action. He drew his pistol as he swung his legs off the bed; he released the safety catch as he stood up. With his left hand he held aside the screening blanket, and he emerged into the crypt with his pistol pointed and ready.

They were all three of them still there, Frey and Busse and Becker; they were waiting to hear the pistol shot behind the screen, and they looked around in surprise as he came bursting out. Dexter pointed the pistol at Frey, who was the dangerous man—he could trust the other two.

"Move and you're dead!" said Dexter, his lips hardly parting sufficiently to allow the words to escape him.

"But—but—" began Frey, backing away in astonishment from the weapon.

"Stand still! Put your hands on your head!"

Perhaps some unconscious memory of the American Western films that he had seen long ago, in the days of the Weimar Republic, prompted Dexter to give that order, but he had seen long lines of Russian prisoners emerging from strong points after surrender, with their hands on their heads, too. Frey obeyed; no sound came from his lips, although they moved.

"Busse!" snapped Dexter.

"Sir!"

"Telephone to Fussel. Get through to him at once."

"Yes, sir," said Busse, advancing to the telephone.

"You're going to surrender!" said Frey, finding his shrill voice again, his body jerking with emotion while he could not gesticulate, hands on head.

"Yes," said Dexter.

He was going to save ten thousand lives for the Germany of the future.

"But your wife!" said Frey. "Remember—"

"My wife is dead."

"But *my* wife—my children—"

Frey's voice went higher still, into a scream. It all happened in a second. Frey's excitement completely overcame him, and he put his hand down to his pistol. But to draw the weapon took far too long. Western films had not taught Frey to be quick on the draw. Before he even had the holster unfastened, Dexter shot him twice, the reports resounding like cannon shots in the restricted space of the crypt, and Frey fell dying on the tomb of the saint.

"That's better," said Dexter. "Now I can speak to Fussel myself."

THAT NIGHT THE BBC broadcast the news of the surrender of Montavril. In five languages the news was broadcast over Europe. Ten thousand men came out from the shadow of imminent death into the prisoner-of-war camps of the Allies. All through the night Allied doctors toiled over the German wounded. Far away in East Prussia, in a gloomy headquarters dugout deep below the gloomy pinewoods, a frantic tyrant raved like a maniac—like the maniac that by now he was—because ten thousand men were alive whom he wished dead.

THAT NIGHT FOUR men knocked at the door of a house in the Welfenstrasse. A dignified old lady opened the door to them, and at a glance recognized their uniform.

"I was expecting you gentlemen," she said. "You want me to come with you?"

"Come," said one of the four.

The old lady's hat and coat hung in the hall ready to hand, and she put them on quickly, and walked out with the men to the waiting car. She was still alive, and she showed no signs of the cancer she had said she had. But as she had promised, her last thoughts were of the husband to whom she had written.

RIP VAN WINKLE
WASHINGTON IRVING

Whoever has made a voyage up the Hudson must remember the Kaatskill mountains. They are a dismembered branch of the great Appalachian family, and are seen away to the west of the river, swelling up to a noble height, and lording it over the surrounding country. Every change of season, every change of weather, indeed, every hour of the day, produces some change in the magical hues and shapes of these mountains, and they are regarded by all the goodwives, far and near, as perfect barometers. When the weather is fair and settled, they are clothed in blue and purple, and print their bold outlines on the clear evening sky; but sometimes, when the rest of the landscape is cloudless, they will gather a hood of gray vapors about their summits, which, in the last rays of the setting sun, will glow and light up like a crown of glory.

At the foot of these fairy mountains, the voyager may have descried the light smoke curling up from a village, whose shingle roofs gleam among the trees, just where the blue tints of the upland melt away into the fresh green of the nearer landscape. It is a little village, of great antiquity, having been founded by some of the Dutch colonists, in the early times of the province, just about the beginning of the government of the good Peter Stuyvesant (may he rest in peace!) and there were some of the houses of the original settlers standing within a few years built of small yellow bricks brought from Holland.

In that same village and in one of these very houses (which, to tell the precise truth, was sadly timeworn and weather-beaten), there lived many years since, while the country was yet a province of Great Britain, a simple good-natured fellow, of the name of Rip Van Winkle. He was a descendant of the Van Winkles who figured so gallantly in the chivalrous days of Peter Stuyvesant, and accompanied him to the siege of Fort Christina. He inherited, however, but little of the martial character of his ancestors. I have observed that he was a simple good-natured man; he was, moreover, a kind neighbor, and an obedient henpecked husband. Indeed, to the latter circumstance might be owing that meekness of spirit which gained him such universal popularity; for those men are most apt to be obsequious and conciliating abroad, who are under the discipline of shrews at home. Their tempers, doubtless, are rendered pliant and malleable in the fiery furnace of domestic tribulation, and a curtain lecture is worth all the sermons in the world for teaching the virtues of patience and long-suffering. A termagant wife may, therefore, in some respects, be considered a tolerable blessing; and if so, Rip Van Winkle was thrice blessed.

Certain it is that he was a great favorite among all the goodwives of the village, who, as usual with the amiable sex, took his part in all family squabbles; and never failed, whenever they talked those matters over in their evening gossipings, to lay all the blame on Dame Van Winkle. The children of the village, too, would shout with joy whenever he approached. He assisted at their sports, made their playthings, taught them to fly kites and shoot marbles, and told them long stories of ghosts, witches, and Indians. Whenever he went dodging about the village, he was surrounded by a troop of them hanging on his skirts, clambering on his back, and playing a thousand tricks on him with impunity; and not a dog would bark at him throughout the neighborhood.

The great error in Rip's composition was an insuperable aversion to all kinds of profitable labor. It could not be from the want of assiduity or perseverance; for he would sit on a wet rock, with a rod as long and heavy as a Tartar's lance, and fish all day without a murmur, even though he should not be encouraged by a single nibble. He would carry a fowling piece on his shoulder for hours together, trudging through woods and swamps, and uphill and downdale, to shoot a few squirrels or wild pigeons. He would never refuse to assist a neighbor even in the roughest toil, and was a foremost man at all country frolics for husking Indian corn, or building stone fences; the women of the village, too, used to employ him to run their errands, and to do such little odd jobs as their less obliging husbands would not do for them. In a word, Rip was ready to attend to anybody's business but his own; but as to doing family duty, and keeping his farm in order, he found it impossible.

In fact, he declared it was of no use to work on his farm; it was the most pestilent little piece of ground in the whole country; everything about it went wrong, and would go wrong, in spite of him. His fences were continually falling to pieces; his cow would either go astray, or get among the cabbages; weeds were sure to grow quicker in his fields than anywhere else; the rain always made a point of setting in just as he had some outdoor work to do; so that though his patrimonial estate had dwindled away under his management, acre by acre, until there was little more left than a mere patch of Indian corn and potatoes, yet it was the worst-conditioned farm in the neighborhood.

His children, too, were as ragged and wild as if they belonged to nobody. His son Rip, an urchin begotten in his own likeness, promised to inherit the habits, with the old clothes, of his father. He was generally seen trooping like a colt at his mother's heels, equipped in a pair of his father's cast-off galligaskins, which he had much ado to hold up with one hand, as a fine lady does her train in bad weather.

Rip Van Winkle, however, was one of those happy mortals, of foolish, well-oiled dispositions, who take the world easy, eat white bread or brown, whichever can be got with least thought or trouble, and would rather starve on a penny than work for a pound. If left to himself, he would have whistled life away in perfect contentment; but his wife kept continually dinning in his ears about his idleness, his carelessness, and the ruin he was bringing on his family. Morning, noon, and night, her tongue was incessantly going, and everything he said or did was sure to produce a torrent of household eloquence. Rip had but one way of replying to all lectures of the kind, and that, by frequent use, had grown into a habit. He shrugged his shoulders, shook his head, cast up his eyes, but said nothing. This, however, always provoked a fresh volley from his wife; so that he was fain to draw off his forces, and take to the outside of the house—the only side which, in truth, belongs to a hen-pecked husband.

Rip's sole domestic adherent was his dog Wolf, who was as much henpecked as his master; for Dame Van Winkle regarded them as companions in idleness, and even looked upon Wolf with an evil eye, as the cause of his master's going so often astray. True it is, in all points of spirit, befitting an honorable dog, he was as courageous an animal as ever scoured the woods—but what courage can withstand the ever-doing and all-besetting terrors of a woman's tongue? The moment Wolf entered the house, his crest fell, his tail drooped to the ground, or curled between his legs, he sneaked about with a gallows air, casting many a sidelong glance at Dame Van Winkle, and at the least flourish of a broomstick or ladle, he would fly to the door with yelping precipitation.

Times grew worse and worse with Rip Van Winkle as years of matrimony rolled on; a tart temper never mellows with age, and a sharp tongue is the only edged tool that grows keener with constant use. For a long while he used to console himself, when driven from home, by frequenting a kind of perpetual club of the sages, philosophers, and other idle personages of the village, which held its sessions on a bench before a small inn, designated by a rubicund portrait of His Majesty George the Third. Here they used to sit in the shade through a long lazy summer's day, talking listlessly over village gossip, or telling endless sleepy stories about nothing. But it would have been worth any states-man's money to have heard the profound discussions that sometimes took place, when by chance an old newspaper fell into their hands from some passing traveler. How solemnly they would listen to the contents, as drawled out by Derrick Van Brummel, the schoolmaster, a dapper learned little man, who was not to be daunted by the most gigantic word in the dictionary; and how sagely they would deliberate upon public events some months after they had taken place.

The opinions of this junto were completely controlled by Nicholas Vedder, a patriarch of the village, and landlord of the inn, at the door of which he took his seat from morning till night, just moving sufficiently to avoid the sun and keep in the shade of a large tree; so that the neighbors could tell the hour by his movements as accurately as by a sundial. It is true he was rarely heard to speak, but smoked his pipe incessantly. His adherents, however (for every great man has his adherents), perfectly understood him, and knew how to gather his opinions. When anything that was related displeased him, he was observed to smoke his pipe vehemently, and to send forth short, frequent, and angry puffs, but when pleased he would inhale the smoke slowly and tranquilly, and emit it in light and placid clouds; and sometimes, taking the pipe from his mouth, and letting the fragrant vapor curl about his nose, would gravely nod his head in token of perfect approbation.

From even this stronghold the unlucky Rip was at length routed by his termagant wife, who would suddenly break in upon the tranquillity of the assemblage and call the members all to naught; nor was that august personage, Nicholas Vedder himself, sacred from the daring tongue of this terrible virago, who charged him outright with encouraging her husband in habits of idleness.

Poor Rip was at last reduced almost to despair; and his only alternative, to escape from the labor of the farm and clamor of his wife, was to take gun in hand and stroll away into the woods. Here he would sometimes seat himself at the foot of a tree, and share the contents of his wallet with Wolf, with whom he sympathized as a fellow sufferer in persecution. "Poor Wolf," he would say, "thy mistress leads thee a dog's life of it; but never mind, my lad, whilst I live thou shalt never want a friend to stand by thee!" Wolf would wag his tail, look wistfully in his master's face, and if dogs can feel pity, I verily believe he reciprocated the sentiment with all his heart.

In a long ramble of the kind on a fine autumnal day, Rip had unconsciously scrambled to one of the highest parts of the Kaatskill mountains. He was after his favorite sport of squirrel shooting, and the still solitudes had echoed and reechoed with the reports of his gun. Panting and fatigued, he threw himself, late in the afternoon, on a green knoll, covered with mountain herbage, that crowned the brow of a precipice. From an opening between the trees he could overlook all the lower country for many a mile of rich woodland. He saw at a distance the lordly Hudson, far, far below him, moving on its silent but majestic course, with the reflection of a purple cloud, or the sail of a lagging bark, here and there sleeping on its glassy bosom, and at last losing itself in the blue highlands.

On the other side he looked down into a deep mountain glen, wild, lonely, and shagged, the bottom filled with fragments from the impending cliffs, and scarcely lighted by the reflected rays of the setting sun. For some time Rip lay musing on this scene; evening was gradually advancing; the mountains began to throw their long blue shadows over the valleys; he saw that it would be dark long before he could reach the village, and he heaved a heavy sigh when he thought of encountering the terrors of Dame Van Winkle.

As he was about to descend, he heard a voice from a distance, hallooing, "Rip Van Winkle! Rip Van Winkle!" He looked round, but could see nothing but a crow winging its solitary flight across the mountain. He thought his fancy must have deceived him, and turned again to descend, when he heard the same cry ring through the still evening air: "Rip Van Winkle! Rip Van Winkle!"—at the same time Wolf bristled up his back, and, giving a loud growl, skulked to his master's side, looking fearfully down into the glen. Rip now felt a vague apprehension stealing over him; he looked anxiously in the same direction, and perceived a strange figure slowly toiling up the rocks, and bending under the weight of something he carried on his back. He was surprised to see any human being in this lonely and unfrequented place; but supposing it to be someone of the neighborhood in need of his assistance, he hastened down to yield it.

On nearer approach he was still more surprised at the singularity of the stranger's appearance. He was a short, square-built old fellow, with thick bushy hair and a grizzled beard. His dress was of the antique Dutch fashion—a cloth jerkin, strapped round the waist—several pairs of breeches, the outer one of ample volume, decorated with rows of buttons down the sides, and bunches at the knees. He bore on his shoulder a stout keg, that seemed full of liquor, and made signs for Rip to approach and assist him with the load. Though rather shy and distrustful of this new acquaintance, Rip complied with his usual alacrity; and mutually relieving each other, they clambered up a narrow gully, apparently the dry bed of a mountain torrent. As they ascended, Rip every now and then heard long rolling peals, like distant thunder, that seemed to issue out of a deep ravine, or rather cleft, between lofty rocks, toward which their rugged path conducted. He paused, but supposing it to be the muttering of one of those transient thundershowers which often take place in mountain heights, he proceeded.

Passing through the ravine, they came to a hollow, like a small amphitheater, surrounded by perpendicular precipices, over the brinks of which impending trees shot their branches, so that you only caught glimpses of the azure sky and the bright evening cloud. During the whole time Rip and his companion had labored on in silence, for though the former marveled greatly what could be the object of carrying a keg of liquor up this wild mountain, yet there was something strange and incomprehensible about the unknown that inspired awe and checked familiarity.

On entering the amphitheater, new objects of wonder presented themselves. On a level spot in the center was a company of odd-looking personages playing at ninepins. They were dressed in a quaint outlandish fashion; some wore short doublets, others jerkins, with long knives in their belts, and most of them had enormous breeches, of similar style with that of the guide's. Their visages, too, were peculiar; one had a large head, broad face, and small piggish eyes; the face of another seemed to consist entirely of nose, and was surmounted by a white sugarloaf hat, set off with a little red cock's tail. They all had beards, of various shapes and colors. There was one who seemed to be the commander. He was a stout old gentleman, with a weather-beaten countenance; he wore a laced doublet, broad belt and hanger, high-crowned hat and feather, red stockings, and high-heeled shoes, with roses on them. The whole group reminded Rip of the figures in an old Flemish painting, in the parlor of Dominie Van Shaick, the village parson, and which had been brought over from Holland at the time of the settlement.

What seemed particularly odd to Rip was, that though these folks were evidently amusing themselves, yet they maintained the gravest faces, the most mysterious silence, and were, withal, the most melancholy party of pleasure he had ever witnessed. Nothing interrupted the stillness of the scene but the noise of the balls, which, whenever they were rolled, echoed along the mountains like rumbling peals of thunder.

As Rip and his companion approached them, they suddenly desisted from their play, and stared at him with such fixed, statuelike gaze, and such uncouth, lackluster countenances, that his heart turned within him, and his knees smote together. His companion now emptied the contents of the keg into large flagons, and made signs to him to wait upon the company. He obeyed with fear and trembling; they quaffed the liquor in profound silence, and then returned to their game.

By degrees Rip's awe and apprehension subsided. He even ventured, when no eye was fixed upon him, to taste the beverage, which he found had much of the flavor of excellent Hollands. He was naturally a thirsty soul, and was soon tempted to repeat the draught. One taste provoked another; and he reiterated his visits to the flagon so often, that at length his senses were overpowered, his eyes swam in his head, his head gradually declined, and he fell into a deep sleep.

On waking, he found himself on the green knoll whence he had first seen the old man of the glen. He rubbed his eyes—it was a bright sunny morning. The birds were hopping and twittering among the bushes, and the eagle was wheeling aloft, and breasting the pure mountain breeze. "Surely," thought Rip, "I have not slept here all night." He recalled the occurrences before he fell asleep. The strange man with a keg of liquor—the mountain ravine—the wild retreat among the rocks—the woebegone party at ninepins—the flagon— "Oh! that flagon! that wicked flagon!" thought Rip; "what excuse shall I make to Dame Van Winkle?"

He looked round for his gun, but in place of the clean well-oiled fowling piece, he found an old firelock lying by him, the barrel incrusted with rust, the lock falling off, and the stock worm-eaten. He now suspected that the grave roysterers of the mountain had put a trick upon him, and, having dosed him with liquor, had robbed him of his gun. Wolf, too, had disappeared, but he might have strayed away after a squirrel or partridge. He whistled after him, and shouted his name, but all in vain; the echoes repeated his whistle and shout, but no dog was to be seen.

He determined to revisit the scene of the last evening's gambol, and, if he met with any of the party, to demand his dog and gun. As he rose to walk he found himself stiff in the joints, and wanting in his usual activity. "These mountain beds do not agree with me," thought Rip; "and if this frolic should lay me up with a fit of the rheumatism, I shall have a blessed time with Dame Van Winkle." With some difficulty he got down into the glen; he found the gully up which he and his companion had ascended the preceding evening; but, to his astonishment, a mountain stream was now foaming down it—leaping from rock to rock, and filling the glen with babbling murmurs. He, however, made shift to scramble up its sides, working his toilsome way through thickets of birch, sassafras, and witch hazel, and sometimes tripped up or entangled by the wild grapevines that twisted their coils or tendrils from tree to tree, and spread a kind of network in his path.

At length he reached to where the ravine had opened through the cliffs to the amphitheater; but no traces of such opening remained. The rocks presented a high impenetrable wall, over which the torrent came tumbling in a sheet of feathery foam, and fell into a broad, deep basin, black from the shadows of the surrounding forest. Here, then, poor Rip was brought to a stand. He again called and whistled after his dog; he was only answered by the cawing of a flock of idle crows, sporting high in the air about a dry tree that overhung a sunny precipice; and who, secure in their elevation, seemed to look down and scoff at the poor man's perplexities. What was to be done?—the morning was passing away, and Rip felt famished for want of his breakfast. He grieved to give up his dog and his gun; he dreaded to meet his wife; but it would not do to starve among the mountains. He shook his head, shouldered the rusty firelock, and, with a heart full of trouble and anxiety, turned his steps homeward.

As he approached the village he met a number of people, but none whom he knew, which somewhat surprised him, for he had thought himself acquainted with everyone in the country round. Their dress, too, was of a different fashion from that to which he was accustomed. They all stared at him with equal marks of surprise, and, whenever they cast their eyes upon him, invariably stroked their chins. The constant recurrence of this gesture induced Rip, involuntarily, to do the same—when, to his astonishment, he found his beard had grown a foot long!

He had now entered the skirts of the village. A troop of strange children ran at his heels, hooting after him, and pointing at his gray beard. The dogs, too, not one of which he recognized for an old acquaintance, barked at him as he passed. The very village was altered; it was larger and more populous. There were rows of houses which he had never seen before, and those which had been his familiar haunts had disappeared. Strange names were over the doors—strange faces at the windows—everything was strange. His mind now misgave him; he began to doubt whether both he and the world around him were not bewitched. Surely this was his native village, which he had left but the day before. There stood the Kaatskill mountains—there ran the silver Hudson at a distance—there was every hill and dale precisely as it had always been. Rip was sorely perplexed. "That flagon last night," thought he, "has addled my poor head sadly!"

It was with some difficulty that he found the way to his own house, which he approached with silent awe, expecting every moment to hear the shrill voice of Dame Van Winkle. He found the house gone to decay—the roof fallen in, the windows shattered, and the doors off the hinges. A half-starved dog that looked like Wolf was skulking about it. Rip called him by name, but the cur snarled, showed his teeth, and passed on. This was an unkind cut indeed—"My very dog," sighed poor Rip, "has forgotten me!"

He entered the house, which, to tell the truth, Dame Van Winkle had always kept in neat order. It was empty, forlorn, and apparently abandoned. The desolateness overcame all his connubial fears—he called loudly for his wife and children—the lonely chambers rang for a moment with his voice, and then all again was silence.

He now hurried forth, and hastened to his old resort, the village inn—but it, too, was gone. A large, rickety, wooden building stood in its place, with great gaping windows, some of them broken and mended with old hats and petticoats, and over the door was painted, THE UNION HOTEL, BY JONATHAN DOOLITTLE. Instead of the great tree that used to shelter the quiet little Dutch inn of yore, there was now reared a tall naked pole, with something on the top that looked like a red nightcap, and from it was fluttering a flag, on which was a singular assemblage of stars and stripes—all this was strange and incomprehensible. He recognized on the sign, however, the ruby face of King George, under which he had smoked so many a peaceful pipe; but even this was singularly metamorphosed. The red coat was changed for one of blue and buff, a sword was held in the hand instead of a scepter, the head was decorated with a cocked hat, and underneath was painted in large characters, GENERAL WASHINGTON.

There was, as usual, a crowd of folks about the door, but none that Rip recollected. The very character of the people seemed changed. There was a busy, bustling, disputatious tone about it, instead of the accustomed phlegm and drowsy tranquillity. He looked in vain for the sage Nicholas Vedder, with his broad face, double chin, and fair long pipe, uttering clouds of tobacco smoke instead of idle speeches; or Van Brummel, the schoolmaster, doling forth the contents of an ancient newspaper. In place of these, a lean, bilious-looking fellow, with his pockets full of handbills, was haranguing vehemently about rights of citizens—elections—members of Congress—liberty—Bunker's Hill—heroes of seventy-six—and other words, which were a perfect Babylonish jargon to the bewildered Van Winkle.

The appearance of Rip, with his long grizzled beard, his rusty fowling piece, his uncouth dress, and an army of women and children at his heels, soon attracted the attention of the tavern politicians. They crowded round him, eyeing him from head to foot with great curiosity. The orator bustled up to him, and, drawing him partly aside, inquired "on which side he voted?" Rip stared in vacant stupidity. Another short but busy little fellow pulled him by the arm, and, rising on tiptoe, inquired in his ear, "Whether he was Federal or Democrat?" Rip was equally at a loss to comprehend the question; when a knowing, self-important old gentleman, in a sharp cocked hat, made his way through the crowd, putting them to the right and left with his elbows as he passed, and planting himself before Van Winkle, with one arm akimbo, the other resting on his cane, his keen eyes and sharp hat penetrating, as it were, into his very soul, demanded in an austere tone, "What brought him to the election with a gun on his shoulder, and a mob at his heels, and whether he meant to breed a riot in the village?"—"Alas! gentlemen," cried Rip, somewhat dismayed, "I am a poor quiet man, a native of the place, and a loyal subject of the king, God bless him!"

Here a general shout burst from the bystanders—"A tory! a tory! a spy! a refugee! hustle him! away with him!" It was with great difficulty that the self-important man in the cocked hat restored order; and, having assumed a tenfold austerity of brow, demanded again of the unknown culprit, what he came there for, and whom he was seeking? The poor man humbly assured him that he meant no harm, but merely came there in search of some of his neighbors, who used to keep about the tavern.

"Well—who are they?—name them."

Rip bethought himself a moment, and inquired, "Where's Nicholas Vedder?"

There was a silence for a little while, when an old man replied in a thin piping voice, "Nicholas Vedder, why, he is dead and gone these eighteen years! There was a wooden tombstone in the churchyard that used to tell all about him, but that's rotten and gone too."

"Where's Brom Dutcher?"

"Oh, he went off to the army in the beginning of the war; some say he was killed at the storming of Stony Point—others say he was drowned in a squall at the foot of Antony's Nose. I don't know—he never came back again."

"Where's Van Brummel, the schoolmaster?"

"He went off to the wars too, was a great militia general, and is now in Congress."

Rip's heart died away at hearing of these sad changes in his home and friends, and finding himself thus alone in the world. Every answer puzzled him too, by treating of such enormous lapses of time, and of matters which he could not understand; war—Congress—Stony Point—he had no courage to ask after any more friends, but cried out in despair, "Does nobody here know Rip Van Winkle?"

"Oh, Rip Van Winkle!" exclaimed two or three. "Oh, to be sure! that's Rip Van Winkle yonder, leaning against the tree."

Rip looked, and beheld a precise counterpart of himself, as he went up the mountain: apparently as lazy, and certainly as ragged. The poor fellow was now completely confounded. He doubted his own identity, and whether he was himself or another man. In the midst of his bewilderment, the man in the cocked hat demanded who he was, and what was his name?

"God knows," exclaimed he, at his wits' end; "I'm not myself—I'm somebody else—that's me yonder—no—that's somebody else got into my shoes—I was myself last night, but I fell asleep on the mountain, and they've changed my gun, and everything's changed, and I'm changed, and I can't tell what's my name, or who I am!"

The bystanders began now to look at each other, nod, wink significantly, and tap their fingers against their foreheads. There was a whisper, also, about securing the gun, and keeping the old fellow from doing mischief, at the very suggestion of which the self-important man in the cocked hat retired with some precipitation. At this critical moment a fresh comely woman pressed through the throng to get a peep at the gray-bearded man. She had a chubby child in her arms, which, frightened at his looks, began to cry. "Hush, Rip," cried she, "hush, you little fool; the old man won't hurt you." The name of the child, the air of the mother, the tone of her voice, all awakened a train of recollections in his mind.

"What is your name, my good woman?" asked he.

"Judith Gardenier."

"And your father's name?"

"Ah, poor man, Rip Van Winkle was his name, but it's twenty years since he went away from home with his gun, and never has been heard of since—his dog came home without him; but whether he shot himself, or was carried away by the Indians, nobody can tell. I was then but a little girl."

Rip had but one question more to ask; but he put it with a faltering voice—

"Where's your mother?"

Oh, she too had died but a short time since; she broke a blood vessel in a fit of passion at a New England pedlar.

There was a drop of comfort, at least, in this intelligence. The honest man could contain himself no longer. He caught his daughter and her child in his arms. "I am your father!" cried he. "Young Rip Van Winkle once—old Rip Van Winkle now! Does nobody know poor Rip Van Winkle?"

All stood amazed, until an old woman, tottering out from among the crowd, put her hand to her brow, and peering under it in his face for a moment, exclaimed, "Sure enough! it is Rip Van Winkle—it is himself! Welcome home again, old neighbor— Why, where have you been these twenty long years?"

Rip's story was soon told, for the whole twenty years had been to him but as one night. The neighbors stared when they heard it; some were seen to wink at each other, and put their tongues in their cheeks; and the self-important man in the cocked hat, who, when the alarm was over, had returned to the field, screwed down the corners of his mouth, and shook his head—upon which there was a general shaking of the head throughout the assemblage.

It was determined, however, to take the opinion of old Peter Vanderdonk, who was seen slowly advancing up the road. He was a descendant of the historian of that name, who wrote one of the earliest accounts of the province. Peter was the most ancient inhabitant of the village, and well versed in all the wonderful events and traditions of the neighborhood. He recollected Rip at once, and corroborated his story in the most satisfactory manner. He assured the company that it was a fact, handed down from his ancestor the historian, that the Kaatskill mountains had always been haunted by strange beings. That it was affirmed that the great Hendrick Hudson, the first discoverer of the river and country, kept a kind of vigil there every twenty years, with his crew of the *Halfmoon;* being permitted in this way to revisit the scenes of his enterprise, and keep a guardian eye upon the river, and the great city called by his name. That his father had once seen them in their old Dutch dresses playing at ninepins in a hollow of the mountain; and that he himself had heard, one summer afternoon, the sound of their balls, like distant peals of thunder.

To make a long story short, the company broke up, and returned to the more important concerns of the election. Rip's daughter took him home to live with her; she had a snug, well-furnished house, and a stout cheery farmer for a husband, whom Rip recollected for one of the urchins that used to climb upon his back. As to Rip's son and heir, who was the ditto of himself, seen leaning against the tree, he was employed to work on the farm; but evinced an hereditary disposition to attend to anything else but his business.

Rip now resumed his old walks and habits; he soon found many of his former cronies, though all rather the worse for the wear and tear of time; and preferred making friends among the rising generation, with whom he soon grew into great favor.

Having nothing to do at home, and being arrived at that happy age when a man can be idle with impunity, he took his place once more on the bench at the inn door, and was reverenced as one of the patriarchs of the village, and a chronicler of the old times "before the war." It was some time before he could get into the regular track of gossip, or could be made to comprehend the strange events that had taken place during his torpor. How that there had been a revolutionary war—that the country had thrown off the yoke of Old England—and that, instead of being a subject of His Majesty George the Third, he was now a free citizen of the United States. Rip, in fact, was no politician; the changes of states and empires made but little impression on him; but there was one species of despotism under which he had long groaned, and that was—petticoat government. Happily that was at an end; he had got his neck out of the yoke of matrimony, and could go in and out whenever he pleased without dreading the tyranny of Dame Van Winkle. Whenever her name was mentioned, however, he shook his head, shrugged his shoulders, and cast up his eyes; which might pass either for an expression of resignation to his fate, or joy at his deliverance.

He used to tell his story to every stranger that arrived at Mr. Doolittle's hotel. He was observed at first to vary on some points every time he told it, which was, doubtless, owing to his having so recently awaked. It at last settled down precisely to the tale I have related, and not a man, woman, or child in the neighborhood but knew it by heart. Some always pretended to doubt the reality of it, and insisted that Rip had been out of his head, and that this was one point on which he always remained flighty. The old Dutch inhabitants, however, almost universally gave it full credit. Even to this day they never hear a thunderstorm of a summer afternoon about the Kaatskills, but they say Hendrick Hudson and his crew are at their game of ninepins; and it is a common wish of all henpecked husbands in the neighborhood, when life hangs heavy on their hands, that they might have a quieting draught out of Rip Van Winkle's flagon.

THE GIRLS IN THEIR
SUMMER DRESSES
IRWIN SHAW

Fifth Avenue was shining in the sun when they left the Brevoort and started walking toward Washington Square. The sun was warm, even though it was November, and everything looked like Sunday morning—the buses, and the well-dressed people walking slowly in couples and the quiet buildings with the windows closed.

Michael held Frances' arm tightly as they walked downtown in the sunlight. They walked lightly, almost smiling, because they had slept late and had a good breakfast and it was Sunday. Michael unbuttoned his coat and let it flap around him in the mild wind. They walked, without saying anything, among the young and pleasant-looking people who somehow seem to make up most of the population of that section of New York City.

"Look out," Frances said, as they crossed Eighth Street. "You'll break your neck."

Michael laughed and Frances laughed with him.

"She's not so pretty, anyway," Frances said. "Anyway, not pretty enough to take a chance breaking your neck looking at her."

Michael laughed again. He laughed louder this time, but not as solidly. "She wasn't a bad-looking girl. She had a nice complexion. Country-girl complexion. How did you know I was looking at her?"

Frances cocked her head to one side and smiled at her husband under the tip-tilted brim of her hat. "Mike, darling . . ." she said.

Michael laughed, just a little laugh this time. "Okay," he said. "The evidence is in. Excuse me. It was the complexion. It's not the sort of complexion you see much in New York. Excuse me."

Frances patted his arm lightly and pulled him along a little faster toward Washington Square.

"This is a nice morning," she said. "This is a wonderful morning. When I have breakfast with you it makes me feel good all day."

"Tonic," Michael said. "Morning pickup. Rolls and coffee with Mike and you're on the alkali side, guaranteed."

"That's the story. Also, I slept all night, wound around you like a rope."

"Saturday night," he said. "I permit such liberties only when the week's work is done."

"You're getting fat," she said.

"Isn't it the truth? The lean man from Ohio."

"I love it," she said, "an extra five pounds of husband."

"I love it, too," Michael said gravely.

"I have an idea," Frances said.

"My wife has an idea. That pretty girl."

"Let's not see anybody all day," Frances said. "Let's just hang around with each other. You and me. We're always up to our neck in people, drinking their Scotch, or drinking our Scotch, we only see each other in bed . . ."

"The Great Meeting Place," Michael said. "Stay in bed long enough and everybody you ever knew will show up there."

"Wise guy," Frances said. "I'm talking serious."

"Okay, I'm listening serious."

"I want to go out with my husband all day long. I want him to talk only to me and listen only to me."

"What's to stop us?" Michael asked. "What party intends to prevent me from seeing my wife alone on Sunday? What party?"

"The Stevensons. They want us to drop by around one o'clock and they'll drive us into the country."

"The lousy Stevensons," Mike said. "Transparent. They can whistle. They can go driving in the country by themselves. My wife and I have to stay in New York and bore each other tête-à-tête."

"Is it a date?"

"It's a date."

Frances leaned over and kissed him on the tip of the ear.

"Darling," Michael said. "This is Fifth Avenue."

"Let me arrange a program," Frances said. "A planned Sunday in New York for a young couple with money to throw away."

"Go easy."

"First let's go see a football game. A professional football game," Frances said, because she knew Michael loved to watch them. "The Giants are playing. And it'll be nice to be outside all day today and get hungry and later we'll go down to Cavanagh's and get a steak as big as a blacksmith's apron, with a bottle of wine, and after that, there's a new French picture at the Filmarte that everybody says . . . Say, are you listening to me?"

"Sure," he said. He took his eyes off the hatless girl with the dark hair, cut dancer-style, like a helmet, who was walking past him with the self-conscious strength and grace dancers have. She was walking without a coat and she looked very solid and strong and her belly was flat, like a boy's, under her skirt, and her hips swung boldly because she was a dancer and also because she knew Michael was looking at her. She smiled a little to herself as she went past and Michael noticed all these things before he looked back at his wife. "Sure," he said, "we're going to watch the Giants and we're going to eat steak and we're going to see a French picture. How do you like that?"

"That's it," Frances said flatly. "That's the program for the day. Or maybe you'd just rather walk up and down Fifth Avenue."

"No," Michael said carefully. "Not at all."

"You always look at other women," Frances said. "At every damn woman in the city of New York."

"Oh, come now," Michael said, pretending to joke. "Only pretty ones. And, after all, how many pretty women *are* there in New York? Seventeen?"

"More. At least you seem to think so. Wherever you go."

"Not the truth. Occasionally, maybe, I look at a woman as she passes. In the street. I admit, perhaps in the street I look at a woman once in a while. . . ."

"Everywhere," Frances said. "Every damned place we go. Restaurants, subways, theaters, lectures, concerts."

"Now, darling," Michael said. "I look at everything. God gave me eyes and I look at women and men and subway excavations and moving pictures and the little flowers of the field. I casually inspect the universe."

"You ought to see the look in your eye," Frances said, "as you casually inspect the universe on Fifth Avenue."

"I'm a happily married man." Michael pressed her elbow tenderly, knowing what he was doing. "Example for the whole twentieth century, Mr. and Mrs. Mike Loomis."

"You mean it?"

"Frances, baby . . ."

"Are you *really* happily married?"

"Sure," Michael said, feeling the whole Sunday morning sinking like lead inside him. "Now what the hell is the sense in talking like that?"

"I would like to know." Frances walked faster now, looking straight ahead, her face showing nothing, which was the way she always managed it when she was arguing or feeling bad.

"I'm wonderfully happily married," Michael said patiently. "I am the envy of all men between the ages of fifteen and sixty in the state of New York."

"Stop kidding," Frances said.

"I have a fine home," Michael said. "I got nice books and a phonograph and nice friends. I live in a town I like the way I like and I do the work I like and I live with the woman I like. Whenever something good happens, don't I run to you? When something bad happens, don't I cry on your shoulder?"

"Yes," Frances said. "You look at every woman that passes."

"That's an exaggeration."

"Every woman." Frances took her hand off Michael's arm. "If she's not pretty you turn away fairly quickly. If she's halfway pretty you watch her for about seven steps. . . ."

"My Lord, Frances!"

"If she's pretty you practically break your neck . . ."

"Hey, let's have a drink," Michael said, stopping.

"We just had breakfast."

"Now, listen, darling," Mike said, choosing his words with care, "it's a nice day and we both feel good and there's no reason why we have to break it up. Let's have a nice Sunday."

"I could have a fine Sunday if you didn't look as though you were dying to run after every skirt on Fifth Avenue."

"Let's have a drink," Michael said.

"I don't want a drink."

"What do you want, a fight?"

"No," Frances said, so unhappily that Michael felt terribly sorry for her. "I don't want a fight. I don't know why I started this. All right, let's drop it. Let's have a good time."

They joined hands consciously and walked without talking among the baby carriages and the old Italian men in their Sunday clothes and the young women with Scotties in Washington Square Park.

"I hope it's a good game today," Frances said after a while, her tone a good imitation of the tone she had used at breakfast and at the beginning of their walk. "I like professional football games. They hit each other as though they're made out of concrete. When they tackle each other," she said, trying to make Michael laugh, "they make divots. It's very exciting."

"I want to tell you something," Michael said very seriously. "I have not touched another woman. Not once. In all the five years."

"All right," Frances said.

"You believe that, don't you?"

"All right."

They walked between the crowded benches, under the scrubby city-park trees.

"I try not to notice it," Frances said, as though she were talking to herself. "I try to make believe it doesn't mean anything. Some men're like that, I tell myself, they have to see what they're missing."

"Some women're like that, too," Michael said. "In my time I've seen a couple of ladies."

"I haven't even looked at another man," Frances said, walking straight ahead, "since the second time I went out with you."

"There's no law," Michael said.

"I feel rotten inside, in my stomach, when we pass a woman and you look at her and I see that look in your eye and that's the way you looked at me the first time, in Alice Maxwell's house. Standing there in the living room, next to the radio, with a green hat on and all those people."

"I remember the hat," Michael said.

"The same look," Frances said. "And it makes me feel bad. It makes me feel terrible."

"Sssh, please, darling, sssh. . . ."

"I think I would like a drink now," Frances said.

They walked over to a bar on Eighth Street, not saying anything, Michael automatically helping her over curbstones and guiding her past automobiles. He walked, buttoning his coat, looking thoughtfully at his neatly shined heavy brown shoes as they made the steps toward the bar. They sat near a window in the bar and the sun streamed in, and there was a small cheerful fire in the fireplace. A little Japanese waiter came over and put down some pretzels and smiled happily at them.

"What do you order after breakfast?" Michael asked.

"Brandy, I suppose," Frances said.

"Courvoisier," Michael told the waiter. "Two Courvoisier."

The waiter came with the glasses and they sat drinking the brandy in the sunlight. Michael finished half his and drank a little water.

"I look at women," he said. "Correct. I don't say it's wrong or right, I look at them. If I pass them on the street and I don't look at them, I'm fooling you, I'm fooling myself."

"You look at them as though you want them," Frances said, playing with her brandy glass. "Every one of them."

"In a way," Michael said, speaking softly and not to his wife, "in a way that's true. I don't do anything about it, but it's true."

"I know it. That's why I feel bad."

"Another brandy," Michael called. "Waiter, two more brandies."

"Why do you hurt me?" Frances asked. "What're you doing?"

Michael sighed and closed his eyes and rubbed them gently with his fingertips. "I love the way women look. One of the things I like best about New York is the battalions of women. When I first came to

New York from Ohio that was the first thing I noticed, the million wonderful women, all over the city. I walked around with my heart in my throat."

"A kid," Frances said. "That's a kid's feeling."

"Guess again," Michael said. "Guess again. I'm older now, I'm a man getting near middle age, putting on a little fat and I still love to walk along Fifth Avenue at three o'clock on the east side of the street between Fiftieth and Fifty-seventh streets, they're all out then, making believe they're shopping, in their furs and their crazy hats, everything all concentrated from all over the world into eight blocks, the best furs, the best clothes, the handsomest women, out to spend money and feeling good about it, looking coldly at you, making believe they're not looking at you as you go past."

The Japanese waiter put the two drinks down, smiling with great happiness.

"Everything is all right?" he asked.

"Everything is wonderful," Michael said.

"If it's just a couple of fur coats," Frances said, "and forty-five-dollar hats . . ."

"It's not the fur coats. Or the hats. That's just the scenery for that particular kind of woman. Understand," he said, "you don't have to listen to this."

"I want to listen."

"I like the girls in the offices. Neat, with their eyeglasses, smart, chipper, knowing what everything is about, taking care of themselves all the time." He kept his eye on the people going slowly past outside the window. "I like the girls on Forty-fourth Street at lunchtime, the actresses, all dressed up on nothing a week, talking to the good-looking boys, wearing themselves out being young and vivacious outside Sardi's, waiting for producers to look at them. I like the salesgirls in Macy's, paying attention to you first because you're a man, leaving lady customers waiting, flirting with you over socks and books and phonograph needles. I got all this stuff accumulated in me because I've been thinking about it for ten years and now you've asked for it and here it is."

"Go ahead," Frances said.

"When I think of New York City, I think of all the girls, the Jewish girls, the Italian girls, the Irish, Polack, Chinese, German, Negro, Spanish, Russian girls, all on parade in the city. I don't know whether it's something special with me or whether every man in the city walks around with the same feeling inside him, but I feel as though I'm at a picnic in this city. I like to sit near the women in the theaters, the famous beauties who've taken six hours to get ready and look it. And the young girls at the football games, with the red cheeks, and when the warm weather comes, the girls in their summer dresses . . ." He finished his drink. "That's the story. You asked for it, remember. I can't help but look at them. I can't help but want them."

"You want them," Frances repeated without expression. "You said that."

"Right," Michael said, being cruel now and not caring, because she had made him expose himself. "You brought this subject up for discussion, we will discuss it fully."

Frances finished her drink and swallowed two or three times extra. "You say you love me?"

"I love you, but I also want them. Okay."

"I'm pretty, too," Frances said. "As pretty as any of them."

"You're beautiful," Michael said, meaning it.

"I'm good for you," Frances said, pleading. "I've made a good wife, a good housekeeper, a good friend. I'd do any damn thing for you."

"I know," Michael said. He put his hand out and grasped hers.

"You'd like to be free to . . ." Frances said.

"Sssh."

"Tell the truth." She took her hand away from under his.

Michael flicked the edge of his glass with his finger. "Okay," he said gently. "Sometimes I feel I would like to be free."

"Well," Frances said defiantly, drumming on the table, "anytime you say . . ."

"Don't be foolish." Michael swung his chair around to her side of the table and patted her thigh.

She began to cry, silently, into her handkerchief, bent over just enough so that nobody else in the bar would notice. "Someday," she said, crying, "you're going to make a move . . ."

Michael didn't say anything. He sat watching the bartender slowly peel a lemon.

"Aren't you?" Frances asked harshly. "Come on, tell me. Talk. Aren't you?"

"Maybe," Michael said. He moved his chair back again. "How the hell do I know?"

"You know," Frances persisted. "Don't you know?"

"Yes," Michael said after a while. "I know."

Frances stopped crying then. Two or three snuffles into the handkerchief and she put it away and her face didn't tell anything to anybody. "At least do me one favor," she said.

"Sure."

"Stop talking about how pretty this woman is, or that one. Nice eyes, nice breasts, a pretty figure, good voice," she mimicked his voice. "Keep it to yourself. I'm not interested."

"Excuse me." Michael waved to the waiter. "I'll keep it to myself."

Frances flicked the corner of her eyes. "Another brandy," she told the waiter.

"Two," Michael said.

"Yes, ma'am, yes, sir," said the waiter, backing away.

Frances regarded him coolly across the table. "Do you want me to call the Stevensons?" she asked. "It'll be nice in the country."

"Sure," Michael said. "Call them up."

She got up from the table and walked across the room toward the telephone. Michael watched her walk, thinking, What a pretty girl, what nice legs.

THE STREET
THAT GOT MISLAID

PATRICK WADDINGTON

Marc Girondin had worked in the filing section of the city hall's engineering department for so long that the city was laid out in his mind like a map, full of names and places, intersecting streets and streets that led nowhere, blind alleys and winding lanes.

In all Montreal no one possessed such knowledge; a dozen policemen and taxi drivers together could not rival him. That is not to say that he actually knew the streets whose names he could recite like a series of incantations, for he did little walking. He knew simply of their existence, where they were, and in what relation they stood to others.

But it was enough to make him a specialist. He was undisputed expert of the filing cabinets where all the particulars of all the streets from Abbott to Zotique were indexed, back, forward and across. Those aristocrats, the engineers, the inspectors of water mains and the like, all came to him when they wanted some little particular, some detail, in a hurry. They might despise him as a lowly clerk, but they needed him all the same.

Marc much preferred his office, despite the profound lack of excitement of his work, to his room on Oven Street (running north and south from Sherbrooke East to St. Catherine), where his neighbors were noisy and sometimes violent, and his landlady consistently so. He tried to explain the meaning of his existence once to a fellow tenant,

Louis, but without much success. Louis, when he got the drift, was apt to sneer.

"So Craig latches on to Bleury and Bleury gets to be Park, so who cares? Why the excitement?"

"I will show you," said Marc. "Tell me, first, where you live."

"Are you crazy? Here on Oven Street. Where else?"

"How do you know?"

"How do I know? I'm here, ain't I? I pay my rent, don't I? I get my mail here, don't I?"

Marc shook his head patiently.

"None of that is evidence," he said. "You live here on Oven Street because it says so in my filing cabinet at city hall. The post office sends you mail because my card index tells it to. If my cards didn't say so, you wouldn't exist and Oven Street wouldn't either. That, my friend, is the triumph of bureaucracy."

Louis walked away in disgust. "Try telling that to the landlady," he muttered.

So Marc continued on his undistinguished career, his fortieth birthday came and went without remark, day after day passed uneventfully. A street was renamed, another constructed, a third widened; it all went carefully into the files, back, forward and across.

And then something happened that filled him with amazement, shocked him beyond measure, and made the world of the filing cabinets tremble to their steel bases.

One August afternoon, opening a drawer to its fullest extent, he felt something catch. Exploring farther, he discovered a card stuck at the back between the top and bottom. He drew it out and found it to be an old index card, dirty and torn, but still perfectly decipherable. It was labeled Rue de la Bouteille Verte, or Green Bottle Street.

Marc stared at it in wonder. He had never heard of the place or of anything resembling so odd a name. Undoubtedly it had been retitled in some other fashion befitting the modern tendency. He checked the listed details and ruffled confidently through the master file of street names. It was not there. He made another search, careful and protracted, through the cabinets. There was nothing. Absolutely nothing.

Once more he examined the card. There was no mistake. The date of the last regular street inspection was exactly fifteen years, five months and fourteen days ago.

As the awful truth burst upon him, Marc dropped the card in horror, then pounced on it again fearfully, glancing over his shoulder as he did so.

It was a lost, a forgotten street. For fifteen years and more it had existed in the heart of Montreal, not half a mile from city hall, and no one had known. It had simply dropped out of sight, a stone in water.

In his heart, Marc had sometimes dreamed of such a possibility. There were so many obscure places, twisting lanes and streets jumbled together as intricately as an Egyptian labyrinth. But of course it could not happen, not with the omniscient file at hand. Only it had. And it was dynamite. It would blow the office sky-high.

Vaguely, in his consternation, Marc remembered how, some time after he first started to work, his section had been moved to another floor. The old-fashioned files were discarded and all the cards made out afresh. It must have been at that time that Green Bottle Street was stuck between the upper and lower drawers.

He put the card in his pocket and went home to reflect. That night he slept badly and monstrous figures flitted through his dreams. Among them appeared a gigantic likeness of his chief going mad and forcing him into a red-hot filing cabinet.

The next day he made up his mind. Pleading illness, he took the afternoon off and with beating heart went looking for the street.

Although he knew the location perfectly, he passed it twice and had to retrace his steps. Baffled, he closed his eyes, consulted his mind's infallible map and walked directly to the entry. It was so narrow that he could touch the adjoining walls with his outstretched hands. A few feet from the sidewalk was a tall and solid wooden structure, much weather-beaten, with a simple latched door in the center. This he opened and stepped inside. Green Bottle Street lay before him.

It was perfectly real, and reassuring as well. On either side of a cobbled pavement were three small houses, six in all, each with a diminutive garden in front, spaced off by low iron palings of a kind that has disappeared except in the oldest quarters. The houses looked extremely neat and well kept and the cobbles appeared to have been recently watered and swept. Windowless brick walls of ancient warehouses encircled the six homes and joined at the farther end of the street.

At his first glance, Marc realized how it had gotten its unusual name. It was exactly like a bottle in shape.

With the sun shining on the stones and garden plots, and the blue sky overhead, the street gave him a momentary sense of well-being and peace. It was completely charming, a scene from a print of fifty years ago.

A woman who Marc guessed was some sixty years of age was watering roses in the garden of the first house to his right. She gazed at him motionless, and the water flowed from her can unheeded to the ground. He took off his hat and announced, "I'm from the city engineering department, madam."

The woman recovered herself and set her watering can down.

"So you have found out at last," she said.

At these words, Marc's reborn belief that after all he had made a harmless and ridiculous error fled precipitately. There was no mistake.

"Tell me, please," he said tonelessly.

It was a curious story. For several years, she said, the tenants of Green Bottle Street had lived in amity with each other and the landlord, who also resided in one of the little houses. The owner became so attached to them that in a gesture of goodwill he deeded them his property, together with a small sum of money, when he died.

"We paid our taxes," the woman said, "and made out a multitude of forms and answered the questions of various officials at regular intervals about our property. Then, after a while, we were sent no notices, so we paid no more taxes. No one bothered us at all. It was a long time before we understood that in some way they'd forgotten about us."

Marc nodded. Of course, if Green Bottle Street had dropped from the ken of city hall, no inspectors would go there, no census takers, no tax collectors. All would pass merrily by, directed elsewhere by the infallible filing cabinet.

"Then Michael Flanagan, who lives at number four," she went on, "a most interesting man, you must meet him—Mr. Flanagan called us together and said that if miracles happened, we should aid and abet them. It was he who had the door built and put up at the entrance to keep out passersby or officials who might come along. We used to keep it locked, but it's been so long since anyone came that we don't bother now.

"Oh, there were many little things we had to do, like getting our mail at the post office and never having anything delivered at the door. Now almost the only visits we make to the outside world are to buy our food and clothes."

"And there has never been any change here all that time?" Marc asked.

"Yes, two of our friends died, and their rooms were empty for a while. Then Jean Desselin—he's in number six and sometimes goes into the city—returned with a Mr. Plonsky, a refugee. Mr. Plonsky was very tired and worn out with his travelings and gladly moved in with us. Miss Hunter, in number three, brought home a very nice person—a distant relative, I believe. They quite understand the situation."

"And you, madam?" Marc inquired.

"My name is Sara Trusdale, and I have lived here for more than twenty years. I hope to end my days here as well."

She smiled pleasantly at him, apparently forgetting for the moment that he carried in his pocket a grenade that could blow their little world to pieces.

All of them, it seemed, had had their troubles, their losses and failures, before they found themselves in this place of refuge, this Green Bottle Street. To Marc, conscious of his own unsatisfactory existence, it sounded entrancing. He fingered the card in his pocket uncertainly.

"Mr. Plonsky and Mr. Flanagan took a great liking to each other," Miss Trusdale continued. "Both of them have been travelers and they like to talk about the things they have seen. Miss Hunter plays the piano and gives us concerts. Then there's Mr. Hazard and Mr. Desselin, who are very fond of chess and who brew wine in the cellar. For myself, I have my flowers and my books. It has been very enjoyable for all of us."

Marc and Miss Trusdale sat on her front step for a long time in silence. The sky's blue darkened, the sun disappeared behind the warehouse wall on the left.

"You remind me of my nephew," Miss Trusdale said suddenly. "He was a dear boy. I was heartbroken when he died in the influenza epidemic after the war. I'm the last of my family, you know."

Marc could not recall when he had been spoken to with such simple, if indirect, goodwill. His heart warmed to this old lady. Obscurely he felt on the verge of a great moral discovery. He took the card out of his pocket.

"I found this yesterday in the filing cabinet," he said. "No one else knows about it yet. If it should come out, there would be a great scandal, and no end of trouble for all of you as well. Newspaper reporters, tax collectors . . ."

He thought again of his landlady, his belligerent neighbors, his room that defied improvement.

"I wonder," he said slowly, "I am a good tenant, and I wonder . . ."

"Oh yes," she leaned forward eagerly, "you could have the top floor of my house. I have more space than I know what to do with. I'm sure it would suit you. You must come and see it right away."

The mind of Marc Girondin, filing clerk, was made up. With a gesture of renunciation he tore the card across and dropped the pieces in the watering can. As far as he was concerned, Green Bottle Street would remain mislaid forever.

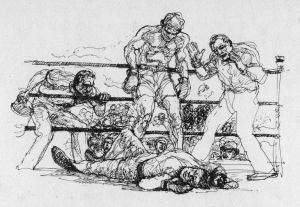

A PIECE OF STEAK

JACK LONDON

WITH THE LAST morsel of bread Tom King wiped his plate clean of the last particle of flour gravy and chewed the resulting mouthful in a slow and meditative way. When he arose from the table he was oppressed by the feeling that he was distinctly hungry. Yet he alone had eaten. The two children in the other room had been sent early to bed in order that in sleep they might forget they had gone supperless. His wife had touched nothing, and had sat silently and watched him with solicitous eyes. She was a thin, worn woman of the working class, though signs of an earlier prettiness were not wanting in her face. The flour for the gravy she had borrowed from the neighbor across the hall. The last two ha'pennies had gone to buy the bread.

He sat down by the window on a rickety chair that protested under his weight, and quite mechanically he put his pipe in his mouth and dipped into the side pocket of his coat. The absence of any tobacco made him aware of his action, and with a scowl for his forgetfulness, he put the pipe away. His movements were slow, almost hulking, as though he were burdened by the heavy weight of his muscles. He was a solid-bodied, stolid-looking man, and his appearance did not suffer from being overprepossessing. His rough clothes were old and slouchy. The uppers of his shoes were too weak to carry the heavy resoling that was itself of no recent date. And his cotton shirt, a cheap, two-shilling affair, showed a frayed collar and ineradicable paint stains.

But it was Tom King's face that advertised him unmistakably for what he was. It was the face of a typical prizefighter; of one who had put in long years of service in the squared ring and, by that means, developed and emphasized all the marks of the fighting beast. It was distinctly a lowering countenance, and that no feature of it might escape notice, it was clean-shaven. The lips were shapeless and constituted a mouth harsh to excess, that was like a gash in his face. The jaw was aggressive, brutal, heavy. The eyes, slow of movement and heavy-lidded, were almost expressionless under the shaggy, indrawn brows. Sheer animal that he was, the eyes were the most animallike feature about him. They were sleepy, lionlike—the eyes of a fighting animal. The forehead slanted quickly back to the hair, which, clipped close, showed every bump of the villainous-looking head. A nose, twice broken and molded variously by countless blows, and a cauliflower ear, permanently swollen and distorted to twice its size, completed his adornment.

Altogether, it was the face of a man to be afraid of in a dark alley or lonely place. And yet Tom King was not a criminal, nor had he ever done anything criminal. Outside of brawls, common to his walk in life, he had harmed no one. Nor had he ever been known to pick a quarrel. He was a professional, and all the fighting brutishness of him was reserved for his professional appearances. Outside the ring he was slow-going, easy-natured, and, in his younger days when money was flush, too openhanded for his own good. He bore no grudges and had few enemies. Fighting was a business with him. In the ring he struck to hurt, struck to maim, struck to destroy; but there was no animus in it. It was a plain business proposition. Audiences assembled and paid for the spectacle of men knocking each other out. The winner took the big end of the purse. When Tom King faced the Woolloomoolloo Gouger, twenty years before, he knew that the Gouger's jaw was only four months healed after having been broken in a Newcastle bout. And he had played for that jaw and broken it again in the ninth round, not because he bore the Gouger any ill will, but because that was the surest way to put the Gouger out and win the big end of the purse. Nor had the Gouger borne him any ill will for it. It was the game, and both knew the game and played it.

Tom King had never been a talker, and he sat by the window, morosely silent, staring at his hands. The veins stood out on the backs of the hands, large and swollen; and the knuckles, smashed and battered and malformed, testified to the use to which they had been put. He had never heard that a man's life was the life of his arteries, but well he knew the meaning of those big, upstanding veins. His heart had pumped too much blood through them at top pressure. They no longer did the work. He had stretched the elasticity out of them, and with their distention had passed his endurance. He tired easily now. No longer could he do a fast twenty rounds, hammer and tongs, fight, fight, fight, from gong to gong, with fierce rally on top of fierce rally, beaten to the ropes and in turn beating his opponent to the ropes, and rallying fiercest and fastest of all in that last, twentieth round, with the house on its feet and yelling, himself rushing, striking, ducking, raining showers of blows upon showers of blows and receiving showers of blows in return, and all the time the heart faithfully pumping the surging blood through the adequate veins. The veins, swollen at the time, had always shrunk down again, though not quite—each time, imperceptibly at first, remaining just a trifle larger than before. He stared at them and at his battered knuckles, and, for the moment, caught a vision of the youthful excellence of those hands before the first knuckle had been smashed on the head of Benny Jones, otherwise known as the Welsh Terror.

The impression of his hunger came back on him.

"Blimey, but couldn't I go a piece of steak!" he muttered aloud, clenching his huge fists and spitting out a smothered oath.

"I tried both Burke's an' Sawley's," his wife said half apologetically.

"An' they wouldn't?" he demanded.

"Not a ha'penny. Burke said—" She faltered.

"G'wan! Wot'd he say?"

"As how 'e was thinkin' Sandel ud do ye tonight, an' as how yer score was comfortable big as it was."

Tom King grunted, but did not reply. He was busy thinking of the bull terrier he had kept in his younger days to which he had fed steaks without end. Burke would have given him credit for a thousand steaks—then. But times had changed. Tom King was getting old; and old men, fighting before second-rate clubs, couldn't expect to run bills of any size with the tradesmen.

He had got up in the morning with a longing for a piece of steak, and the longing had not abated. He had not had a fair training for this fight. It was a drought year in Australia, times were hard and even the most irregular work was difficult to find. He had had no sparring partner and his food had not been of the best nor always sufficient. He had done a few days' navvy work when he could get it, and he had run around the Domain in the early mornings to get his legs in shape. But it was hard training without a partner and with a wife and two kiddies that must be fed. Credit with the tradesmen had undergone very slight expansion when he was matched with Sandel. The secretary of the Gayety Club had advanced him three pounds—the loser's end of the purse—and beyond that had refused to go. Now and again he had managed to borrow a few shillings from old pals, who would have lent more only that it was a drought year and they were hard put themselves. No—and there was no use in disguising the fact—his training had not been satisfactory. He should have had better food and no worries. Besides, when a man is forty it is harder to get into condition than when he is twenty.

"What time is it, Lizzie?" he asked.

His wife went across the hall to inquire and came back.

"Quarter before eight."

"They'll be startin' the first bout in a few minutes," he said. "Only a tryout. Then there's a four-round spar tween Dealer Wells an' Gridley, an' a ten-round go tween Starlight an' some sailor bloke. I don't come on for over an hour."

At the end of another silent ten minutes he rose to his feet.

"Truth is, Lizzie, I ain't had proper trainin'."

He reached for his hat and started for the door. He did not offer to kiss her—he never did on going out—but on this night she dared to kiss him, throwing her arms around him and compelling him to bend down to her face. She looked quite small against the massive bulk of the man.

"Good luck, Tom," she said. "You gotter do 'im."

"Ay, I gotter do 'im," he repeated. "That's all there is to it. I jus' gotter do 'im."

He laughed with an attempt at heartiness, while she pressed more closely against him. Across her shoulders he looked around the bare room. It was all he had in the world, with the rent overdue, and her and the kiddies. And he was leaving it to go out into the night to get meat for his mate and cubs—not like a modern workingman going to his machine grind, but in the old, primitive, royal, animal way, by fighting for it.

"I gotter do 'im," he repeated, this time a hint of desperation in his voice. "If it's a win it's thirty quid—an' I can pay all that's owin'. If it's a lose I get naught—not even a penny for me to ride home on the train. The secretary's give all that's comin' from a loser's end. Good-by, old woman. I'll come straight home if it's a win."

"An' I'll be waitin' up," she called to him along the hall.

It was a full two miles to the Gayety, and as he walked along he remembered how in his palmy days—he had once been the heavyweight champion of New South Wales—he would have ridden to the fight in a cab, and how, most likely, some heavy backer would have paid for the cab and ridden with him. There were Tommy Burns and that Yan-kee nigger, Jack Johnson—they rode about in motorcars. And he walked! And, as any man knew, a hard two miles was not the best pre-liminary to a fight. He was an old un, and the world did not wag well with old uns. He was good for nothing now except navvy work, and his broken nose and swollen ear were against him even in that. He found himself wishing that he had learned a trade. It would have been better in the long run. But no one had told him, and he knew, deep down in his heart, that he would not have listened if they had. It had been so easy. Big money—sharp, glorious fights—periods of rest and loafing in between—a following of eager flatterers, the slaps on the back, the shakes of the hand, the toffs glad to buy him a drink for the privilege of five minutes' talk—and the glory of it, the yelling houses, the whirlwind finish, the referee's "King wins!" and his name in the sporting columns next day.

Those had been times! But he realized now, in his slow, ruminating way, that it was the old uns he had been putting away. He was Youth, rising; and they were Age, sinking. No wonder it had been easy—they with their swollen veins and battered knuckles and weary in the bones of them from the long battles they had already fought. He remembered the time he put out old Stowsher Bill, at Rush-Cutters Bay, in the eighteenth round, and how old Bill had cried afterward in the dressing room like a baby. Perhaps old Bill's rent had been overdue. Perhaps he'd had at home a missus an' a couple of kiddies. And perhaps Bill, that very day of the fight, had had a hungering for a piece of steak. Bill had fought game and taken incredible punishment. He could see now, after he had gone through the mill himself, that Stowsher Bill had fought for a bigger stake, that night twenty years ago, than had young Tom King, who had fought for glory and easy money. No wonder Stowsher Bill had cried afterward in the dressing room.

Well, a man had only so many fights in him, to begin with. It was the iron law of the game. One man might have a hundred hard fights in him, another only twenty; each, according to the make of him and the quality of his fiber, had a definite number, and when he had fought them he was done. Yes, he had had more fights in him than most of them, and he had had far more than his share of the hard, grueling fights—the kind that worked the heart and lungs to bursting, that took the elastic out of the arteries and made hard knots of muscle out of youth's sleek suppleness, that wore out nerve and stamina and made brain and bones weary from excess of effort and endurance over-wrought. Yes, he had done better than all of them. There was none of his old fighting partners left. He was the last of the old guard. He had seen them all finished, and he had had a hand in finishing some of them.

They had tried him out against the old uns, and one after another he had put them away—laughing when, like old Stowsher Bill, they cried in the dressing room. And now he was an old un, and they tried out the youngsters on him. There was that bloke Sandel. He had come over from New Zealand with a record behind him. But nobody in Australia knew anything about him, so they put him up against old Tom King. If Sandel made a showing he would be given better men to fight, with bigger purses to win; so it was to be depended upon that he would put up a fierce battle. He had everything to win by it—money and glory and career; and Tom King was the grizzled old chopping block that guarded the highway to fame and fortune. And he had nothing to win except thirty quid, to pay to the landlord and the tradesmen. And, as Tom King thus ruminated, there came to his stolid vision the form of Youth, glorious Youth, rising exultant and invincible, supple of muscle and silken of skin, with heart and lungs that had never been tired and torn and that laughed at limitation of effort. Yes, Youth was the Nemesis. It destroyed the old uns and recked not that, in so doing, it destroyed itself. It enlarged its arteries and smashed its knuckles, and was in turn destroyed by Youth. For Youth was ever youthful. It was only Age that grew older.

At Castlereagh Street he turned to the left, and three blocks along came to the Gayety. A crowd of young larrikins hanging outside the door made respectful way for him, and he heard one say to another: "That's 'im! That's Tom King!"

Inside, on the way to his dressing room, he encountered the secretary, a keen-eyed, shrewd-faced young man, who shook his hand.

"How are you feelin', Tom?" he asked.

"Fit as a fiddle," King answered, knowing that he lied, and that if he had a quid he would give it right there for a good piece of steak.

When he emerged from the dressing room, his seconds behind him, and came down the aisle to the squared ring in the center of the hall, a burst of greeting and applause went up from the waiting crowd. He acknowledged salutations right and left, though few of the faces did he know. Most of them were the faces of kiddies unborn when he was winning his first laurels in the squared ring. He leaped lightly to the raised platform and ducked through the ropes to his corner, where he sat down on a folding stool. Jack Ball, the referee, came over and shook his hand. Ball was a broken-down pugilist who for over ten years had not entered the ring as a principal. King was glad that he had him for referee. They were both old uns. If he should rough it with Sandel a bit beyond the rules he knew Ball could be depended upon to pass it by.

Aspiring young heavyweights, one after another, were climbing into the ring and being presented to the audience by the referee. Also, he issued their challenges for them.

"Young Pronto," Ball announced, "from North Sydney, challenges the winner for fifty pounds side bet."

The audience applauded, and applauded again as Sandel himself sprang through the ropes and sat down in his corner. Tom King looked across the ring at him curiously, for in a few minutes they would be locked together in merciless combat, each trying with all the force of him to knock the other into unconsciousness. But little could he see, for Sandel, like himself, had trousers and sweater on. His face was strongly handsome, crowned with a curly mop of yellow hair, while his thick, muscular neck hinted at bodily magnificence.

Young Pronto went to one corner and then the other, shaking hands with the principals and dropping down out of the ring. The challenges went on. Ever Youth climbed through the ropes—Youth unknown, but insatiable—crying out to mankind that with strength and skill it would match issues with the winner. A few years before, in his own heyday of invincibleness, Tom King would have been amused and bored by these preliminaries. But now he sat fascinated, unable to shake the vision of Youth from his eyes. Always were these youngsters rising up in the boxing game, springing through the ropes and shouting their defiance; and always were the old uns going down before them. They climbed to success over the bodies of the old uns. And ever they came, more and more youngsters—Youth unquenchable and irresistible—and ever they put the old uns away, themselves becoming old uns and traveling the same downward path, while behind them, ever pressing on them, was Youth eternal—the new babies, grown lusty and dragging their elders down, with behind them more babies to the end of time—Youth that must have its will and that will never die.

King glanced over to the press box and nodded to Morgan, of the *Sportsman*, and Corbett, of the *Referee*. Then he held out his hands while Sid Sullivan and Charley Bates, his seconds, slipped on his gloves and laced them tight, closely watched by one of Sandel's seconds, who first examined critically the tapes on King's knuckles. A second of his own was in Sandel's corner, performing a like officc. Sandel's trousers were pulled off and, as he stood up, his sweater was skinned off over his head. And Tom King, looking, saw Youth incarnate, deep-chested, heavy-thewed, with muscles that slipped and slid like live things under the white satin skin. The whole body was acrawl with life, and Tom King knew that it was a life that had never oozed its freshness out through the aching pores during the long fights wherein Youth paid its toll and departed not quite so young as when it entered.

The two men advanced to meet each other and, as the gong sounded and the seconds clattered out of the ring with the folding stools, they shook hands with each other and instantly took their fighting attitudes. And instantly, like a mechanism of steel and springs balanced on a hair trigger, Sandel was in and out and in again, landing a left to the eyes, a right to the ribs, ducking a counter, dancing lightly away and dancing menacingly back again. He was swift and clever. It was a dazzling exhibition. The house yelled its approbation. But King was not dazzled. He had fought too many fights and too many youngsters. He knew the blows for what they were—too quick and too deft to be dangerous. Evidently Sandel was going to rush things from the start. It was to be expected. It was the way of Youth, expending its splendor and excellence in wild insurgence and furious onslaught, overwhelming opposition with its own unlimited glory of strength and desire.

Sandel was in and out, here, there and everywhere, light-footed and eager-hearted, a living wonder of white flesh and stinging muscle that wove itself into a dazzling fabric of attack, slipping and leaping like a flying shuttle from action to action through a thousand actions, all of them centered upon the destruction of Tom King, who stood between him and fortune. And Tom King patiently endured. He knew his business, and he knew Youth now that Youth was no longer his. There was nothing to do till the other lost some of his steam, was his thought, and he grinned to himself as he deliberately ducked so as to receive a heavy blow on the top of his head. It was a wicked thing to do, yet eminently fair according to the rules of the boxing game. A man was supposed to take care of his own knuckles, and if he insisted on hitting an opponent on the top of the head he did so at his own peril. King could have ducked lower and let the blow whiz harmlessly past, but he remembered his own early fights and how he smashed his first knuckle on the head of the Welsh Terror. He was but playing the game. That duck had accounted for one of Sandel's knuckles. Not that Sandel would mind it now. He would go on, superbly regardless, hitting as hard as ever throughout the fight. But later on, when the long ring battles had begun to tell, he would regret that knuckle and look back and remember how he smashed it on Tom King's head.

The first round was all Sandel's, and he had the house yelling with the rapidity of his whirlwind rushes. He overwhelmed King with avalanches of punches, and King did nothing. He never struck once, contenting himself with covering up, blocking and ducking and clinching to avoid punishment. He occasionally feinted, shook his head when the weight of a punch landed, and moved stolidly about, never leaping or springing or wasting an ounce of strength. Sandel must foam the froth of Youth away before discreet Age could dare to retaliate. All King's movements were slow and methodical, and his heavy-lidded, slow-moving eyes gave him the appearance of being half asleep or dazed. Yet they were eyes that saw everything, that had been trained to see everything through all his twenty years and odd in the ring. They were eyes that did not blink or waver before an impending blow, but that coolly saw and measured distance.

Seated in his corner for the minute's rest at the end of the round, he lay back with outstretched legs, his arms resting on the right angle of the ropes, his chest and abdomen heaving frankly and deeply as he gulped down the air driven by the towels of his seconds. He listened with closed eyes to the voices of the house. "Why don't yeh fight, Tom?" many were crying. "Yeh ain't afraid of 'im, are yeh?"

"Muscle-bound," he heard a man on a front seat comment. "He can't move quicker. Two to one on Sandel, in quids."

The gong struck and the two men advanced from their corners. Sandel came forward fully three-quarters of the distance, eager to begin again; but King was content to advance the shorter distance. It was in line with his policy of economy. He had not been well trained and he had not had enough to eat, and every step counted. Besides, he had already walked two miles to the ringside. It was a repetition of the first round, with Sandel attacking like a whirlwind and with the audience indignantly demanding why King did not fight. Beyond feinting and several slowly delivered and ineffectual blows he did nothing save block and stall and clinch. Sandel wanted to make the pace fast, while King, out of his wisdom, refused to accommodate him. He grinned with a certain wistful pathos in his ring-battered countenance, and went on cherishing his strength with the jealousy of which only Age is capable. Sandel was Youth, and he threw his strength away with the munificent abandon of Youth. To King belonged the ring generalship, the wisdom bred of long, aching fights. He watched with cool eyes and head, moving slowly and waiting for Sandel's froth to foam away. To the majority of the onlookers it seemed as though King was hopelessly outclassed, and they voiced their opinion in offers of three to one on Sandel. But there were wise ones, a few, who knew King of old time and who covered what they considered easy money.

The third round began as usual, one-sided, with Sandel doing all the leading and delivering all the punishment. A half minute had passed when Sandel, overconfident, left an opening. King's eyes and right arm flashed in the same instant. It was his first real blow—a hook, with the twisted arch of the arm to make it rigid, and with all the weight of the half-pivoted body behind it. It was like a sleepy-seeming lion suddenly thrusting out a lightning paw. Sandel, caught on the side of the jaw, was felled like a bullock. The audience gasped and murmured awestruck applause. The man was not muscle-bound, after all, and he could drive a blow like a trip-hammer.

Sandel was shaken. He rolled over and attempted to rise, but the sharp yells from his seconds to take the count restrained him. He knelt on one knee, ready to rise, and waited, while the referee stood over him, counting the seconds loudly in his ear. At the ninth he rose in fighting attitude, and Tom King, facing him, knew regret that the blow had not been an inch nearer the point of the jaw. That would have been a knockout, and he could have carried the thirty quid home to the missus and the kiddies.

The round continued to the end of its three minutes, Sandel for the first time respectful of his opponent and King slow of movement and sleepy-eyed as ever. As the round neared its close, King, warned of the fact by sight of the seconds crouching outside ready for the spring in through the ropes, worked the fight around to his own corner. And when the gong struck he sat down immediately on the waiting stool, while Sandel had to walk all the way across the diagonal of the square to his own corner. It was a little thing, but it was the sum of little things that counted. Sandel was compelled to walk that many more steps, to give up that much energy and to lose a part of the precious minute of rest. At the beginning of every round King loafed slowly out from his corner, forcing his opponent to advance the greater distance. The end of every round found the fight maneuvered by King into his own corner so that he could immediately sit down.

Two more rounds went by, in which King was parsimonious of effort and Sandel prodigal. The latter's attempt to force a fast pace made King uncomfortable, for a fair percentage of the multitudinous blows showered upon him went home. Yet King persisted in his dogged slowness, despite the crying of the hotheads for him to go in and fight. Again, in the sixth round, Sandel was careless, again Tom King's right flashed out to the jaw, and again Sandel took the nine seconds' count.

By the seventh round Sandel's pink of condition was gone and he settled down to what he knew was to be the hardest fight in his experience. Tom King was an old un, but a better old un than he had ever encountered—an old un who never lost his head, who was remarkably able at defense, whose blows had the impact of a knotted club and who had a knockout in either hand. Nevertheless, Tom King dared not hit often. He never forgot his battered knuckles, and knew that every hit must count if the knuckles were to last out the fight. As he sat in his corner, glancing across at his opponent, the thought came to him that the sum of his wisdom and Sandel's youth would constitute a world's champion heavyweight. But that was the trouble. Sandel would never become a world champion. He lacked the wisdom, and the only way for him to get it was to buy it with Youth; and when wisdom was his, Youth would have been spent in buying it.

King took every advantage he knew. He never missed an opportunity to clinch, and in effecting most of the clinches his shoulder drove stiffly into the other's rib. In the philosophy of the ring a shoulder was as good as a punch so far as damage was concerned, and a great deal better so far as concerned expenditure of effort. Also, in the clinches King rested his weight on his opponent and was loath to let go. This compelled the interference of the referee, who tore them apart, always assisted by Sandel, who had not yet learned to rest. He could not refrain from using those glorious flying arms and writhing muscles of his, and when the other rushed into a clinch, striking shoulder against ribs and with head resting under Sandel's left arm, Sandel almost invariably swung his right behind his own back and into the projecting face. It was a clever stroke, much admired by the audience, but it was not dangerous, and was, therefore, just that much wasted strength. But Sandel was tireless and unaware of limitations, and King grinned and doggedly endured.

Sandel developed a fierce right to the body, which made it appear that King was taking an enormous amount of punishment, and it was only the old ringsters who appreciated the deft touch of King's left glove to the other's biceps just before the impact of the blow. It was true, the blow landed each time; but each time it was robbed of its power by that touch on the biceps. In the ninth round, three times inside a minute, King's right hooked its twisted arch to the jaw; and three times Sandel's body, heavy as it was, was leveled to the mat. Each time he took the nine seconds allowed him and rose to his feet, shaken and jarred, but still strong. He had lost much of his speed and he wasted less effort. He was fighting grimly; but he continued to draw upon his chief asset, which was Youth. King's chief asset was experience. As his vitality had dimmed and his vigor abated he had replaced them with cunning, with wisdom born of the long fights and with a careful shepherding of strength. Not alone had he learned never to make a superfluous movement, but he had learned how to seduce an opponent into throwing his strength away. Again and again, by feint of foot and hand and body he continued to inveigle Sandel into leaping back or ducking. King rested, but he never permitted Sandel to rest. It was the strategy of Age.

Early in the tenth round King began stopping the other's rushes with straight lefts to the face, and Sandel, grown wary, responded by drawing the left, then by ducking it and delivering his right in a swinging hook to the side of the head. It was too high up to be vitally effective; but when first it landed King knew the old, familiar descent of the black veil of unconsciousness across his mind. For the instant, or for the slightest fraction of an instant rather, he ceased. In the one moment he saw his opponent ducking out of his field of vision and the background of white, watching faces; in the next moment he again saw his opponent and the background of faces. It was as if he had slept for a time and just opened his eyes again, and yet the interval of unconsciousness was so microscopically short that there had been no time for him to fall. The audience saw him totter and his knees give, and then saw him recover and tuck his chin deeper into the shelter of his left shoulder.

Several times Sandel repeated the blow, keeping King partially dazed, and then the latter worked out his defense, which was also a counter.

Feinting with his left he took a half step backward, at the same time uppercutting with the whole strength of his right. So accurately was it timed that it landed squarely on Sandel's face in the full, downward sweep of the duck, and Sandel lifted in the air and curled backward, striking the mat on his head and shoulders. Twice King achieved this, then turned loose and hammered his opponent to the ropes. He gave Sandel no chance to rest or to set himself, but smashed blow in upon blow till the house rose to its feet and the air was filled with an unbroken roar of applause. But Sandel's strength and endurance were superb, and he continued to stay on his feet. A knockout seemed certain, and a captain of police, appalled at the dreadful punishment, arose by the ringside to stop the fight. The gong struck for the end of the round and Sandel staggered to his corner, protesting to the captain that he was sound and strong. To prove it he threw two back air springs, and the police captain gave in.

Tom King, leaning back in his corner and breathing hard, was disappointed. If the fight had been stopped, the referee, perforce, would have rendered him the decision and the purse would have been his. Unlike Sandel, he was not fighting for glory or career, but for thirty quid. And now Sandel would recuperate in the minute of rest.

Youth will be served—this saying flashed into King's mind, and he remembered the first time he had heard it, the night when he had put away Stowsher Bill. The toff who had bought him a drink after the fight and patted him on the shoulder had used those words. Youth will be served! The toff was right. And on that night in the long ago he had been Youth. Tonight Youth sat in the opposite corner. As for himself, he had been fighting for half an hour now, and he was an old man. Had he fought like Sandel he would not have lasted fifteen minutes. But the point was that he did not recuperate. Those upstanding arteries and that sorely tried heart would not enable him to gather strength in the intervals between the rounds. And he had not had sufficient strength in him to begin with. His legs were heavy under him and beginning to cramp. He should not have walked those two miles to the fight. And there was the steak which he had got up longing for that morning. A great and terrible hatred rose up in him for the butchers who had refused him credit. It was hard for an old man to go into a fight without enough to eat. And a piece of steak was such a little thing, a few pennies at best; yet it meant thirty quid to him.

With the gong that opened the eleventh round Sandel rushed, making a show of freshness which he did not really possess. King knew it for what it was—a bluff as old as the game itself. He clinched to save himself, then, going free, allowed Sandel to get set. This was what King desired. He feinted with his left, drew the answering duck and swinging upward hook, then made the half step backward, delivered the uppercut full to the face and crumpled Sandel over to the mat. After that he never let him rest, receiving punishment himself, but inflicting far more, smashing Sandel to the ropes, hooking and driving all manner of blows into him, tearing away from his clinches or punching him out of attempted clinches, and ever, when Sandel would have fallen, catching him with one uplifting hand and with the other immediately smashing him into the ropes where he could not fall.

The house by this time had gone mad, and it was his house, nearly every voice yelling: "Go it, Tom!" "Get 'im! Get 'im!" "You've got 'im, Tom! You've got 'im!" It was to be a whirlwind finish, and that was what a ringside audience paid to see.

And Tom King, who for half an hour had conserved his strength, now expended it prodigally in the one great effort he knew he had in him. It was his one chance—now or not at all. His strength was waning fast, and his hope was that before the last of it ebbed out of him he would have beaten his opponent down for the count. And as he continued to strike and force, coolly estimating the weight of his blows and the quality of the damage wrought, he realized how hard a man Sandel was to knock out. Stamina and endurance were his to an extreme degree, and they were the virgin stamina and endurance of Youth. Sandel was certainly a coming man. He had it in him. Only out of such rugged fiber were successful fighters fashioned.

Sandel was reeling and staggering, but Tom King's legs were cramping and his knuckles going back on him. Yet he steeled himself to strike the fierce blows, every one of which brought anguish to his tortured hands. Though now he was receiving practically no punishment, he was weakening as rapidly as the other. His blows went home, but there was no longer the weight behind them, and each blow was the result of a severe effort of will. His legs were like lead, and they dragged visibly under him; while Sandel's backers, cheered by this symptom, began calling encouragement to their man.

King was spurred to a burst of effort. He delivered two blows in succession—a left, a trifle too high, to the solar plexus, and a right cross to the jaw. They were not heavy blows, yet so weak and dazed was Sandel that he went down and lay quivering. The referee stood over him, shouting the count of the fatal seconds in his ear. If before the tenth second was called he did not rise, the fight was lost. The house stood in hushed silence. King rested on trembling legs. A mortal dizziness was upon him, and before his eyes the sea of faces sagged and swayed, while to his ears, as from a remote distance, came the count of the referee. Yet he looked upon the fight as his. It was impossible that a man so punished could rise.

Only Youth could rise, and Sandel rose. At the fourth second he rolled over on his face and groped blindly for the ropes. By the seventh second he had dragged himself to his knee, where he rested, his head rolling groggily on his shoulders. As the referee cried "Nine!" Sandel stood upright, in proper stalling position, his left arm wrapped about his face, his right wrapped about his stomach. Thus were his vital points guarded, while he lurched forward toward King in the hope of effecting a clinch and gaining more time.

At the instant Sandel arose King was at him, but the two blows he delivered were muffled on the stalled arms. The next moment Sandel was in the clinch and holding on desperately while the referee strove to drag the two men apart. King helped to force himself free. He knew the rapidity with which Youth recovered and he knew that Sandel was his if he could prevent that recovery. One stiff punch would do it. Sandel was his, indubitably his. He had outgeneraled him, outfought him, outpointed him. Sandel reeled out of the clinch, balanced on the hairline between defeat or survival. One good blow would topple him over and down and out. And Tom King, in a flash of bitterness, remembered the piece of steak and wished that he had it then behind that necessary punch he must deliver. He nerved himself for the blow, but it was not heavy enough nor swift enough. Sandel swayed but did not fall, staggering back to the ropes and holding on. King staggered after him and, with a pang like that of dissolution, delivered another blow. But his body had deserted him. All that was left of him was a fighting intelligence that was dimmed and clouded from exhaustion. The blow that was aimed for the jaw struck no higher than the shoulder. He had willed the blow higher, but the tired muscles had not been able to obey. And from the impact of the blow Tom King himself reeled back and nearly fell. Once again he strove. This time his punch missed altogether, and, from absolute weakness, he fell against Sandel and clinched, holding on to him to save himself from sinking to the floor.

King did not attempt to free himself. He had shot his bolt. He was gone. And Youth had been served. Even in the clinch he could feel Sandel growing stronger against him. When the referee thrust them apart, there, before his eyes, he saw Youth recuperate. From instant to instant Sandel grew stronger. His punches, weak and futile at first, became stiff and accurate. Tom King's bleared eyes saw the gloved fist driving at his jaw and he willed to guard it by interposing his arm. He saw the danger, willed the act; but the arm was too heavy. It seemed burdened with a hundredweight of lead. It would not lift itself, and he strove to lift it with his soul. Then the gloved fist landed home. He experienced a sharp snap that was like an electric spark, and, simultaneously, the veil of blackness enveloped him.

When he opened his eyes again he was in his corner, and he heard the yelling of the audience like the roar of the surf at Bondi Beach. A wet sponge was being pressed against the base of his brain and Sid Sullivan was blowing cold water in a refreshing spray over his face and chest. His gloves had already been removed and Sandel, bending over him, was shaking his hand. He bore no ill will toward the man who had put him out, and he returned the grip with a heartiness that made his battered knuckles protest. Then Sandel stepped to the center of the ring and the audience hushed its pandemonium to hear him accept young Pronto's challenge and offer to increase the side bet to one hundred pounds. King looked on apathetically while his seconds mopped the streaming water from him, dried his face and prepared him to leave the ring. He felt hungry. It was not the ordinary, gnawing kind, but a great faintness, a palpitation at the pit of the stomach that communicated itself to all his body. He remembered back into the fight to the moment when he had Sandel tottering on the hairline balance of defeat. Ah, that piece of steak would have done it! He had lacked just that for the decisive blow, and he had lost. It was all because of the piece of steak.

His seconds were half supporting him as they helped him through the ropes. He tore free from them, ducked through the ropes unaided, and leaped heavily to the floor, following on their heels as they forced a passage for him down the crowded center aisle. Leaving the dressing room for the street, in the entrance to the hall, some young fellow spoke to him.

"W'y didn't yuh go in an' get 'im when yuh 'ad 'im?" the young fellow asked.

"Aw, go to hell!" said Tom King, and passed down the steps to the sidewalk.

The doors of the public house at the corner were swinging wide, and he saw the lights and the smiling barmaids, heard the many voices discussing the fight and the prosperous chink of money on the bar. Someone called to him to have a drink. He hesitated perceptibly, then refused and went on his way.

He had not a copper in his pocket and the two-mile walk home seemed very long. He was certainly getting old. Crossing the Domain, he sat down on a bench, unnerved by the thought of the missus sitting up for him, waiting to learn the outcome of the fight. That was harder than any knockout, and it seemed almost impossible to face.

He felt weak and sore, and the pain of his smashed knuckles warned him that, even if he could find a job at navvy work, it would be a week before he could grip a pick handle or a shovel. The hunger palpitation at the pit of the stomach was sickening. His wretchedness overwhelmed him, and into his eyes came an unwonted moisture. He covered his face with his hands, and as he cried, he remembered Stowsher Bill and how he had served him that night in the long ago. Poor old Stowsher Bill! He could understand now why Bill had cried in the dressing room.

THE SECRET INGREDIENT
PAUL GALLICO

NEXT TIME YOU are touring the château country of France and visit the string of airy castles cresting the hilltops along the placid Loire from Blois to Tours, you surely will drop down from the towered and mullioned keep of the Château Loiret, just below Chaumont-sur-Loire, to eat a meal and drink the wine at the famous Auberge Château Loiret at the foot of the castle.

There you will unquestionably partake of that superb and unrivaled specialty of the house, *Poularde Surprise Treize Minets*, and find your palate enthralled by the indefinable flavor imparted to the fowl by the mysterious ingredient which is the particular secret of M. Armand Bonneval, host and chef of the *auberge*. And like so many, many others before you, you will attempt without success to identify the famous component X which to this day has defied the most educated taste buds of all France.

You also will encounter M. Bonneval, stocky, red-faced with short-cut, upstanding, pepper-and-salt hair, youthful-looking because of the energy and kindliness in his face, and Mme. Bonneval, a woman of large heart and girth, who, as always in France, will be seated behind the desk in charge of the cashbox and the accounts.

And, either perched on the desk next to Mme. Bonneval or twining at the feet of her husband as he appears at the dining-room door to check on the effect of his cooking, you will probably observe a small black-and-white cat—not a particularly beautiful specimen, owing to the fact that she is somewhat cross-eyed, but nevertheless the beloved pet and pride and joy of monsieur and madame, your hosts.

As a matter of fact, the famous recipe is in a way associated with her, Minette being her name. But *minet* in France is also the generic nickname for cats, just as we call them puss, and thus a literal translation of the by now world-renowned dish of *Poularde Surprise Treize Minets* might be "Chicken Surprise in the style of Thirteen Cats."

However, when it comes to inquiring of M. Bonneval how this epicure's delight was named or what it is that makes his *poularde* more tasty, stimulating and unforgettable than any other in the world, and what unknown ingredient is the key to this miraculous gastronomic blend, you will, I know, run up against a stone wall.

Guarded blueprints for airplanes, battleships and submarines are traded on an international bourse, diplomatic confidences are whispered over cocktails, the secrets of the atom bomb have been bandied about; but up to this moment, not one single person in the whole world outside of M. and Mme. Bonneval has been privy to the secret of the recipe for this famous delicacy.

Permit me then:

In the days prior to the events I am about to narrate, Armand Bonneval, former assistant chef of the Café de Paris, honorably retired, *Cordon Bleu* member of the Club de Cent, and now sole owner and proprietor of the Auberge Château Loiret, was consumed with a burning ambition.

In the Guide Michelin for 1951, that tourist's and gourmet's bible, which is the automobile traveler's survey of France, the *auberge* was designated by three crossed spoons and forks, denoting a "very comfortable restaurant." This was not at all bad, particularly for a restaurant in a village as small as Loiret, where the usual indication was one crossed spoon and fork or none at all. But it did not satisfy the artistic and creative soul of M. Bonneval. In his day he had been a great cook. In his old age he longed for the tangible recognition of his genius. A higher rating would likewise make a considerable financial difference to himself and madame, his partner through forty years of unremitting toil.

The size and location of his *auberge* precluded his receiving the four or five crossed utensils reserved for the big, deluxe restaurants of Paris, Lyon, Vichy and Cannes. However, the famous Guide Michelin annual has further signs to distinguish the superior cuisines it had tested and listed in villages and towns throughout France—namely, one, two or three stars added to the spoons and forks.

Three stars, denoting one of the best tables in the nation, and worthy of a special journey of many miles, were as beyond the reach and hopes of M. Bonneval as the stars that spangled the firmament above the Loire Valley at night. There were but seven of these awarded in all France.

Nor was there any better chance of achieving two stars, indicating an "excellent cuisine: worth a detour," of which there were but fifty-one examples in all the thousands of restaurants, *auberges*, hotels and bistros throughout the land.

But M. Bonneval did yearn most mightily with his honest heart and Frenchman's pride to be awarded the addition of the single star which would announce to traveler and native alike that he set *"une bonne table dans la localité"* and that the visitor to his board would be rewarded with something special.

If his winning of the three crossed spoons and forks had already made him an important man in the district, the star would elevate him to the status of distinguished citizen. If now they just managed to make both ends meet, the added star would enable them to amass a competency toward their final days. Alas, there was nothing specific that M. Bonneval could do to achieve this ambition, for the matter was not in his hands.

As he would explain sadly to Mme. Bonneval, when sitting quietly in their apartment above the *auberge* after hours, with his beloved Minette purring in his lap, there were literally hundreds of thousands of eating places throughout France that had to be covered; the inspectors, or official tasters, of the Guide Michelin were only so many; they had but one stomach apiece, which would hold only so many cubic centimeters. Worked out mathematically, it might be years before one again appeared to sample the fare at the Auberge Loiret, and perhaps never again in their lifetime.

But even if by some chance one should appear, there was no opportunity for M. Bonneval to prepare the kind of specialty that would be likely to bowl over the taster, for the simple reason that the Guide Michelin conducted its tests and listings with scrupulous integrity and fairness. One never knew when the inspector was in one's midst. He came and went in the guise of an ordinary tourist. The Grand Lottery in Paris was not handled with more honesty and care.

"Ah, if one could but know in advance sometime," he would groan, filled with ambition and desire. "Who knows but with the star I would be able to take you to Italy on that little trip we planned so long ago."

And Mme. Bonneval would comfort him. "Never mind, Armand. I am sure you will receive your star somehow, because you deserve it. And besides, it would not be fair if you should know in advance."

One summer afternoon a letter arrived for M. Bonneval that caused him to stare as though he could not believe his eyes, and then call loudly for madame to come and read it to him again, to make sure he had not been deceived. Madame did so, with her circle of additional chins quivering a little. It was short and to the point.

My dear Bonneval:

I doubt whether you would remember me, but many years ago you had the occasion to do me a good turn when I was hungry and on my uppers, and I have never forgotten your kindness.

It so happens that I now find myself in a position to return the favor. Through my connections with the Guide Michelin, upon which I will not elaborate, I am advised that on Friday, the thirteenth of July, an inspector will be passing through Loiret-sur-Loire, and has been instructed to dine at the *auberge* to check on the quality of your meals. I know that your genius will find the best way to make use of this information. Wishing you the very best of luck, I am an old friend who must sign himself

XYZ

There it was—the bolt out of the clearest of skies. Not only was the longed-for visit to take place, but M. Bonneval was actually to have notice in advance and time to prepare one of his more superb specialties, such as duck stuffed with chopped truffles, liver pâté and champignons, with orange sauce, or his own version of coq au vin.

"I will be famous! We will grow rich!" declared M. Bonneval, feasting his eyes again on the page of the wonderful letter. But then he cried in alarm. "Great heavens! The letter is dated July eighth, but it has been delayed in transit. Friday the thirteenth, when the inspector is to come, is this very day."

It was true. The calendar on the wall displayed a large red 13. Suddenly the affair assumed an urgency that was not dispelled by the exclamation of Mme. Bonneval, who had glanced out of the window. "And that must be he, arriving this very minute!"

A large and glittery car had poked its expensive snout alongside the *auberge* and discharged one who could only have spent the major portion of his existence sampling the finest foods and wines, for he was as fat as a prize pig stuffed for exhibition. He carried the Guide Michelin in his hand, and entered the front door with a combined expression of truculence and expectancy.

At once he became identified in Bonneval's mind as M. Michelin Taster, friend, enemy, instrument upon which he would play his gastronomic symphony, critic and bearer of the laurel wreath, or rather star, that would eventually be bestowed upon him.

However, one thing was patent. There was not a moment to lose. Already flustered by the unexpected imminence of his trial, M. Bonneval rushed off to the kitchen, crying to madame as he made his exit, "I shall prepare him *le Homard dans la Lune!*" Which was not at all what he had meant either to say or to cook.

"Lobster in the Moon" was the last thing in the world he would have dreamed of making for such an important test, knowing full well that with lobster it can be this way or that way, whereas your ducks, chickens and gigots are always safe.

For the recipe is a tricky one, calling for one large lobster, *bien vivant*—in other words, a brisk and lively fellow—to be extracted, cut up, seasoned with salt and pepper, and sautéed in oil and butter, after which the oil is withdrawn and a tablespoon of finely chopped shallots or chives and a whisper of garlic is added. To give this mixture a little authority, a glass of cognac and another of white wine are now introduced, after which three tomatoes are broken into small bits with a half tablespoonful of chopped parsley and a shot of cayenne pepper, and the whole thing is cooked for twenty minutes in a casserole at a steady heat.

The lobster is then removed and stuffed into the "Moon," a hollowed-out, crisp brioche. Now comes the delicate moment. The sauce is thickened with a little cream laced with a shot of brandy and the whole thing poured over the hot, crispy, lobster-filled pastry.

A man wants to be in complete command of himself to bring off a dish like that, particularly when it meant as much as it did to M. Bonneval. That he was not, was evidenced when he almost bumped into Minette, the black-and-white cat, as he charged into the kitchen, bellowing loudly for Celeste, the kitchen maid, and Brazon, the man of all work, her lover.

This served only to unnerve him further, for it so happened that Minette had been so fortunate not long before as to encounter a gentleman friend in the park of the château who had been able to overlook the unhappy tendencies of her eyes to cross, and she was now imminently about to be blessed with the fruits of this genuine affection, and a fair packet of them, too, if one could judge from her size.

Nor was it exactly a happy moment in the life of Celeste, who, a few weeks ago, had been seized with the idea of marrying Brazon, and of course had demanded an increase in pay to support this bizarre notion—a request which M. Bonneval, backed by madame, had quite sensibly refused, since one did not say yes to such ideas the first time. As a result, Celeste was red-eyed and snuffly a good deal of the time, and not quite herself.

This was a pity, for she was to M. Bonneval what the deft instrument nurse is to the great surgeon. With paring knife and chopping bowl, a veteran of a hundred routines, she had stood at his side ready to supply in an instant what the master needed in the line of utensils, saucepans, casseroles, chopped onions, shaved carrots, bouquets of herbs, and so on.

So there was already a considerable disaster building up in M. Bonneval's kitchen, let alone its being Friday the thirteenth.

The lobster, when produced from the cold room, not only did not answer to the description of a brisk and lively fellow but, on the contrary, was practically in a state of rigor mortis. Cutting him up, hence, was no longer a culinary gesture, but an autopsy. It was Fate giving M. Bonneval one more chance to evade what it had in store for him.

Had he been in his right senses he would have dumped the crustacean corpse into the ashcan and started on something else.

But his mind was imprisoned by that inflexibility and rigidity that, in the face of a crisis, sometimes affects the best of cooks and housekeepers. M. Bonneval was bent on making Lobster in the Moon, and so he rushed onward headlong to his doom.

Almost at once there commenced such a catalogue of kitchen catastrophes as can be appreciated only by the housewife or chef who has battled the extraordinary breed of gremlins that sometimes arrive when there is a truly important dinner to be got onto the table.

While Celeste reversed her instruction and scraped a soupçon of shallot into a tablespoon of chopped garlic, instead of vice versa, Brazon announced that there appeared to have been a change in the wind, affecting the draft of the huge iron stove, plus a blockade of some sort, and he could seem to put no heat in it, and Odette, the waitress, affected by the mounting tension, upset the soup into the lap of the fat man identified in the mind of Bonneval as M. Michelin Taster. This fetched a bellow of rage from the dining room, matched only by the sound emerging from the kitchen when M. Bonneval discovered that Celeste, ruminating on the inhumanity of man, had taken his sautéing pan, which for eighteen years had known no other cleansing than with salt and a piece of bread, and washed it with kitchen soap and water.

Disaster followed upon disaster. The stove, stuffed with newspapers, straw, kindling and coke, emitted clouds of acrid smoke, one whiff of which was sufficient to affect the delicate flavors planned by M. Bonneval. The cream pitcher upset in the icebox, inundating everything therein, and at the critical moment it developed that Brazon had misplaced the key to the wine cellar.

M. Bonneval moved as one in the grip of a hideous nightmare. Matters went from bad to worse as a tin of fat caught fire, the handle of his best frying pan broke and the lamp upset. Celeste and Brazon went completely haywire, the latter breaking the eggbeater and short-circuiting the refrigerator, while the former achieved a new high in destructive confusion by putting salt in the egg whites in place of sugar, and cutting up, on the board reserved for crushing garlic, the almonds destined for the famous *Soufflé à la Curorange*.

Through all this, red-faced, sweating, the glare as of a wild animal filling his heretofore gentle eyes, struggling to retain his temper and his sanity in the face of trials that would have disjointed a saint, M. Bonneval stolidly attempted to fight his way through the morass of calamities that were engulfing him.

It was a losing battle. Friday the thirteenth was not through with him yet. For just as he was stirring the delicate *sauce vanille* intended to go with the soufflé which was browning in the oven, Mme. Bonneval, unnerved by the sounds of panic from backstage, abandoned her post next to the cashbox and invaded the kitchen. Her faith in her husband's culinary powers shaken for the first time, she committed the unpardonable crime of opening the oven door to see how the confection was coming along, just as Brazon unlatched the back entrance, permitting a swirl of cool air to tear through the kitchen and smite the soufflé where it would hurt the most.

Purple with outrage, M. Bonneval made a lunge to swing shut the oven door. It was at this precise moment that poor Minette chose to make one of her sagging promenades across the kitchen floor just in time to trip M. Bonneval and send the *sauce vanille* splashing onto the top of the range, where it made a most dreadful smell.

Something snapped inside M. Bonneval. Flesh and blood could endure no more. Tortured beyond human endurance, he hauled back his right foot and applied it to the rear end of Minette, who happened to be aimed toward the back door at the moment.

With a terrible scream of outraged indignation, the loaded Minette took off like a blimp released from its moorings, and soaring majestically up into the night, vanished from sight.

Now M. Bonneval turned upon the humans. *"Vache!"* he shouted at his wife. *"Animal!"* he bawled at Celeste. *"Crétin!"* he nominated Odette, the waitress. *"Cochon!"* he dubbed Brazon.

The reactions were immediate. Brazon resigned; Odette vanished; Celeste threw her apron over her head and had hysterics; while Mme. Bonneval swept from the kitchen, went upstairs and locked herself in her room. Bonneval himself carried in the soufflé and placed it before M. Michelin Taster, where it gave a soft sigh and collapsed flatter than an old-fashioned opera hat.

The fat man took one nibble at the edge of the thing and then let out a roar that shook the dining room. "Criminal! Assassin! Poisoner!" he shouted. "You call yourself a chef! The lobster tastes of soap, the coffee of kerosene and your soufflé is flavored with garlic! Three spoons and forks they have given you, eh?" and at this point he waved the red-covered volume of the Guide Michelin under M. Bonneval's appalled nose. "Well, when I am finished with you, you will no longer be able to swindle innocent travelers! Faker!"

And with this he tore the napkin from his collar and stalked from the room. When, a few moments later, the car thundered away from the *auberge*, it carried with it, in addition to the indignant fat man, the hopes, ambitions and large pieces of the broken heart of M. Bonneval.

M. Bonneval was of the breed that wastes no time crying over spilled cream, but faces manfully up to the blows of life and recovers quickly therefrom. But he needed the aid and companionship of his wife. Pocketing his badly damaged pride, he hurried to the door of madame's locked room, from which emerged sounds of grief, and spoke through the keyhole.

"Come now, my dear, it is all over. Nothing more can happen. I am punished for my sins. The inspector has departed to make his report, and we shall be poor again. But as long as I have you, I shall not lack the courage to make a start again—somewhere in a place where we are not known, perhaps. Come, old friend, we have been through much together. Do not take a little incident so to heart."

From within, Mme. Bonneval cried, "Little incident! You called me a cow!"

Obviously a special effort was required. M. Bonneval now addressed the door as follows: "Dear wife, I was wrong to let petty trifles exasperate me into forgetting myself. But look. Even in my anger against Fate, how careful I was in my choice of animals. For is not the cow the sweetest, the gentlest, the kindest and the most beautiful in all the kingdom? Does she not, with lavish generosity and warm heart, play mother with her milk to all mankind? Is not her glance melting, her disposition notable and her character beyond reproach? Does not her soft and expressive face invite caresses?" He ceased when he heard the key turning slowly in the lock.

Thereafter he went downstairs, soothed the waitress, apologized to Brazon and cured Celeste's hysterics with a promise of a raise in salary should the *auberge* not be forced to close.

Notwithstanding the peace declared within his domain, the heart of M. Bonneval was as heavy as a stone, for Minette had not returned. His conscience was as black as the night because of the kick he had bestowed upon her, and particularly in the light of her delicate condition. He would rather have cut off his right arm than perpetrate an indignity, much less an injury, upon his little friend. He had called and called, but there had been no sign of her.

She had every right to be angry with him—if she was still alive. How, then, to persuade her of his love for her, and his terrible contrition? Suddenly an idea smote him. Minette was mad about chicken. He would tempt her with her favorite food.

Purpose now gripped M. Bonneval, and he said to himself, "Little Minette, I shall cook you a *Poularde Surprise Royale* all for your very own. For you I will cook this as I have never cooked before, for I am very ashamed of having lost my temper and kicked you from the rear."

He set to work at once, and everything seemed to work like magic, as though Friday the thirteenth had expended its malignancy, and Fate was no longer interested in harassing M. Bonneval. The stove functioned like a charm, Brazon was as sharp as a razor, and Celeste was her old, cool, efficient self, anticipating his every wish.

With a series of deft movements he boned the chicken and then stuffed it with goose-liver pâté, truffles and a stew of giblets and kidneys made in meat stock and laced with a jigger of port wine.

Poor Minette, he thought as he added the ruby-red liquid, after what she has been through she will be in need of a little stimulant.

Working now with supreme concentration and passion, the recipe burned into his memory the way a conductor knows every note of a great symphony without the score, he set about making a sauce for the bird, using the bones of the pullet, onions, carrots, leeks, celery and a bouquet, which he fortified with a half bottle of Bollinger '43. "One gives champagne to expectant mothers," he said to himself as the yellow wine frothed into the brown gravy.

Exquisite odors began to fill the kitchen. It was art for love's sake, and like all true artists and lovers, he became inspired and began to improvise as he went along, making a daring and radical experiment with here an herb, there a spice, a bit of smoked fat, a glass of very old cognac. For if she is a little drunk she will become mellow and forgive me the more readily, he reasoned.

And then it was, as he ransacked his closet of herbs and spices, looking still further to delight the heart and appetite of Minette, that he found and added an ingredient that never before had been a part of *Poularde Surprise Royale* or any other dish.

When the bird was cooked to a turn, he performed some final rites, garnishing it with truffles and pâté de foie gras, poured the magnificent sauce over it, partitioned it, and putting one half onto a plate, went out into the night with this savory harbinger of everything good and perfect that man has learned to do with food.

"Minette! Minette!" he called, placing himself upwind, so that the evening breeze from the Loire would carry the fragrance to every corner of the courtyard where the missing Minette might be lurking. And still there came no answer.

Some time later, painfully and heartbroken and still bearing the dish, he returned to the kitchen, where, at the late hour just before midnight, he found an unaccustomed activity sparked by Mme. Bonneval. Coffee was on the fire, a soufflé was in the process of being mixed by Brazon, and the other half of the *Poularde Surprise Royale* was missing.

"Ah, there you are," madame greeted him. "What a fortunate thing you decided to cook a *poularde*. Only fifteen minutes ago there arrived a traveler, a poor fellow whose car had broken down. He was starving, and begged for a bit of something cold left over. You can imagine how agreeably surprised he was when I was able to set before him your specialty. He is drinking a bottle of the '47 Loiret Suchez with it."

M. Bonneval stared at his wife, aghast. "But, *maman!* It is impossible. I cooked this for poor little Minette, whom I kicked so bru—"

He did not finish, for the door leading from the dining room opened violently, admitting an excited bespectacled little man with a soup-strainer mustache and wearing a seedy suit, but whose eyes and expression nevertheless appeared to command authority.

He paused for a moment *en tableau*, looking from one to another in the kitchen. Then he rushed to M. Bonneval, threw his arms about him and kissed him violently on both cheeks.

"It is you!" he cried. "You are the magician who has prepared this delectable, this fabulous, this supreme dish! Chef! Genius! Master! I salute you! Not in thirty-five years have I eaten such a *Poularde Surprise Royale.* And at midnight. A veritable palace of gastronomy, a Sorbonne of cookery. Well, you shall have your reward. A star—no, no, what am I saying?—two stars!" And here he paused, and his look changed slightly to one of cunning. "Three stars if you will tell me the secret ingredient in the *poularde,* the only one I was not able to recognize."

M. Bonneval could only gape at him. Could it have been then that the other, that fat one, was not M. Michelin Taster? "I do not—understand," he stammered.

"But it is simple, dear master," the man replied. "Know then that I am Fernand Dumaire, inspector for the Guide Michelin. I was on my way here to test your cookery when that villain of a vehicle ceased to function. And then, to arrive at midnight and at once to find set before me this masterpiece! Of two stars you are certain, but as a little deal between us, I will risk the third in exchange for your secret ingredient!"

Sweat suddenly beaded the brow of M. Bonneval. "The—secret—ingredient?" he repeated.

"But of course. Naturally, I recognized the chervil and the delicate touch of burnet. It took courage to use the basil, and the idea of applying the marjoram to offset the tarragon was capital, while the amount of thyme and sage was perfectly balanced. I should judge the Oporto in the sauce was a trifle more *sec* than is usual—probably a '39—and the champagne, of course, was Bollinger '43, as anyone with half a palate would notice. But one flavor baffles and escapes me, and I, Fernand Dumaire, must know what it is. For you have changed, improved and glorified *Poularde Surprise Royale.* It has become a new creation and you shall have the honor of naming it. But first tell me the ingredient that has baffled me, in exchange for the third star. Is it a bargain?"

There was a moment of silence. Then M. Bonneval said slowly, "I cannot tell you, monsieur. I shall be content with the two stars you so generously promised me."

Mme. Bonneval stared at her husband as though he were out of his mind, but the chief taster again fell on his neck and kissed him. "You are right, my friend, and noble and honest. A great chef must never reveal his secrets. I tempted you and you resisted. Well, two stars and five spoons and forks will distinguish you so that the world will beat a path to your kitchen."

At this moment there was an interruption. There came a sweet little call from the outer darkness, and Minette loped into the room, a thin and shapely Minette, though now more cross-eyed with love than ever. She deposited a newborn kitten in the box that had been made ready at the side of the stove. She retired. She came back with another kitten, and another and another. Thirteen times she departed and returned as they watched and counted, fascinated, and the tears of joy flowed from the eyes of M. Bonneval.

When the last one had been deposited and Minette commenced nursing, M. Bonneval declared with deep feeling, "You said, monsieur, that I might name my *poularde*. Very well. I name it *Poularde Surprise Treize Minets*."

At this moment Brazon produced the *Soufflé à la Curorange* prepared from the recipe of M. Bonneval, a dream, a vision, high, potent, sturdy, uncollapsible, a beige cloud, with the interior construction apparently of reinforced steel. They joined around the table, and with a Moët and Chandon '37 they toasted the two stars of M. Bonneval and the *Poularde Surprise Treize Minets*.

SO THEN, THE next time you tour in France and drop in at the Auberge Loiret to partake of M. Bonneval's delectable Chicken à la Thirteen Kittens, do not, I beg of you, let on that I have given away his secret ingredient and the reason why he could not reveal it even for the honor and accolade of the third star.

It was simple, but a trifle unusual. As you have already suspected, for love of Minette he had seasoned the *poularde* liberally with that herb beloved of all felines, the strongly scented leaves of *Nepeta cataria*, a plant better known to one and all as catnip.

THE HAWK
LIAM O'FLAHERTY

H<small>E BREASTED THE</small> summit of the cliff and then rose in wide circles to the clouds. When their undertendrils passed about his outstretched wings, he surged straight inland. Gliding and dipping his wings at intervals, he roamed across the roof of the firmament, with his golden hawk's eyes turned down, in search of prey, toward the bright earth that lay far away below, beyond the shimmering emptiness of the vast blue sky.

Once the sunlight flashed on his gray back as he crossed an open space between two clouds. Then again he became a vague, swift shadow, rushing through the formless vapor. Suddenly his fierce heart throbbed as he saw a lark, whose dewy back was jeweled by the radiance of the morning light, come rising toward him from a green meadow. He shot forward at full speed, until he was directly over his mounting prey. Then he began to circle slowly, with his wings stiff and his round eyes dilated, as if in fright. Slight tremors passed along his skin, beneath the compact armor of his plumage—like a hunting dog that stands poised and quivering before his game.

The lark rose awkwardly at first, uttering disjointed notes as he leaped and circled to gain height. Then he broke into full-throated song and soared straight upward, drawn to heaven by the power of his glorious voice, and fluttering his wings like a butterfly.

The hawk waited until the songbird had almost reached the limit of his climb. Then he took aim and stooped. With his wings half closed, he raked like a meteor from the clouds. The lark's warbling changed to a shriek of terror as he heard the fierce rush of the charging hawk. Then he swerved aside, just in time to avoid the full force of the blow. Half stunned, he folded his wings and plunged headlong toward the earth, leaving behind a flutter of feathers that had been torn from his tail by the claws of his enemy.

When he missed his mark, the hawk at once opened wide his wings and canted them to stay his rush. He circled once more above his falling prey, took aim, and stooped again. This time the lark did nothing to avoid the kill. He died the instant he was struck; his inert wings unfolded. With his head dangling from his limp throat, through which his lovely song had just been poured, he came tumbling down, convoyed by the closely circling hawk. He struck earth on a patch of soft brown sand, beside a shining stream.

The hawk stood for a few moments over his kill, with his lewd purple tongue lolling from his open beak and his black-barred breast heaving from the effort of pursuit. Then he secured the carcass in his claws, took wing, and flew off to the cliff where his mate was hatching on a broad ledge, beneath a massive tawny-gold rock that rose, overarching, to the summit.

IT WAS A LORDLY place, at the apex of a narrow cove, and so high above the sea that the roar of the breaking waves reached there only as a gentle murmur. There was no other sound within the semicircle of towering limestone walls that rose sheer from the dark water. Two months before, a vast crowd of other birds had lived on the lower edges of the cliffs, making the cove merry with their cries as they flew out to sea and back again with fish. Then one morning the two young hawks came there from the east to mate.

For hours the rockbirds watched them in terror as the interlopers courted in the air above the cove, stooping past each other from the clouds down to the sea's edge, and then circling up again, wing to wing, winding their garland of love. At noon they saw the female draw the male into a cave, and heard his mating screech as he treaded her. Then they knew the birds of death had come to nest in their cove. So they took flight. That afternoon the mated hawks gamboled in the solitude that was now their domain, and at sundown the triumphant male brought his mate to nest on this lofty ledge, from which a pair of ravens had fled.

Now, as he dropped the dead lark beside her on the ledge, she lay there in a swoon of motherhood. Her beak rested on one of the sticks that formed her rude bed, and she looked down at the distant sea through half-closed eyes. Uttering cries of tenderness, he trailed his wings and marched around the nest on his bandy legs, pushing against her sides, caressing her back with his throat, and gently pecking at her crest. He had circled her four times before she awoke from her stupor. Then she raised her head suddenly, opened her beak, and screamed. He screamed in answer and leaped upon the carcass of the lark. Quickly he severed its head, plucked its feathers, and offered her the naked, warm meat. She opened her mouth wide, swallowed the huge morsel in one movement, and again rested her beak on the stick. Her limp body spread out once more around the pregnant eggs as she relapsed into her swoon.

His brute soul was exalted by the consciousness that he had achieved the fullness of the purpose for which nature had endowed him. Like a hound stretched out in sleep before a blazing fire, dreaming of the day's long chase, he relived the epic of his mating passion, while he strutted back and forth among the disgorged pellets and the bloody remains of eaten prey with which the rock was strewn.

Once he went to the brink of the ledge, flapped his wings against his breast, and screamed in triumph as he looked out over the majestic domain that he had conquered with his mate. Then again he continued to march, rolling from side to side in ecstasy, as he recalled his moments of tender possession and the beautiful eggs warm among the sticks.

His exaltation was suddenly broken by a sound that reached him from the summit of the cliff. He stood motionless, close to the brink, and listened with his head turned to one side. Hearing the sound again from the summit, the same tremor passed through the skin within his plumage, as when he had soared, poised, above the mounting lark. His heart also throbbed as it had done then, but not with the fierce desire to exercise his power. He knew that he had heard the sound of human voices, and he felt afraid.

He dropped from the ledge and flew, close to the face of the cliff, for a long distance toward the west. Then he circled outward, swiftly, and rose to survey the intruders. He saw them from on high. There were three humans near the brink of the cliff, a short way east of the nest. They had secured the end of a stout rope to a block of limestone. The tallest of them had tied the other end to his body, and then attached a small brown sack to his waist belt.

When the hawk saw the tall man being lowered down along the face of the cliff to a protruding ledge that was on a level with the nest, his fear increased. He knew that the men had come to steal his mate's eggs; yet he felt helpless in the presence of the one enemy that he feared by instinct. He spiraled still higher and continued to watch in agony.

The tall man reached the ledge and walked carefully to its western limit. There he signaled to his comrades, who hauled up the slack of his rope. Then he braced himself, kicked the brink of the ledge, and swung out toward the west along the blunt face of the cliff, using the taut rope as a lever. He landed on the eastern end of the ledge where the hawk's mate was sitting on her nest, on the far side of a bluff. His comrades again slackened the rope, in answer to his signal, and he began to move westward, inch by inch, crouched against the rock.

The hawk's fear vanished as he saw his enemy relentlessly move closer to the bluff. He folded his wings and dived headlong down to warn his mate. He flattened out when he came level with the ledge and screamed as he flew past her. She took no notice of the warning. He flew back and forth several times, screaming in agony, before she raised her head and answered him. Exalted by her voice, he circled far out to sea and began to climb.

Once more he rose, until the undertendrils of the clouds passed about his outstretched wings and the fierce cold of the upper firmament touched his heart. Then he fixed his golden eyes on his enemy and hovered to take aim. At this moment of supreme truth, as he stood poised, it was neither pride in his power nor the intoxication of the lust to kill that stiffened his wings and the muscles of his breast. He was drawn to battle by the wild, sad tenderness aroused in him by his mate's screech.

He folded his wings and stooped. Down he came, relentlessly, straight at the awe-inspiring man that he no longer feared. The two men on the cliff top shouted a warning when they saw him come. The tall man on the ledge raised his eyes. Then he braced himself against the cliff to receive the charge. For a moment, it was the eyes of the man that showed fear, as they looked into the golden eyes of the descending hawk. Then he threw up his arm, to protect his face, just as the hawk struck. The body of the doomed bird glanced off the thick cloth that covered the man's right arm and struck the cliff with a dull thud. It rebounded and went tumbling down.

When the man came creeping around the bluff, the mother hawk stood up in the nest and began to scream. She leaped at him and tried to claw his face. He quickly caught her, pinioned her wings, and put her in his little sack. Then he took the eggs.

Far away below, the body of the dead hawk floated, its broken wings outstretched on the foam-embroidered surface of the dark water, and drifted seaward with the ebbing tide.

THE APPRENTICE
DOROTHY CANFIELD FISHER

THE DAY HAD been one of the unbearable ones, when every sound had set her teeth on edge like chalk creaking on a blackboard, when every word her father or mother said to her or did not say to her seemed an intentional injustice. And of course it would happen, as the fitting end to such a day, that just as the sun went down back of the mountain and the long twilight began, she noticed that Rollie was not around.

Tense with exasperation at what her mother would say, she began to call him in a carefully casual tone—she would simply explode if Mother got going—"Here Rollie! He-ere boy! Want to go for a walk, Rollie?" Whistling to him cheerfully, her heart full of wrath at the way the world treated her, she made the rounds of his haunts: the corner of the woodshed, where he liked to curl up on the wool of Father's discarded old sweater; the hay barn, the cow barn, the sunny spot on the side porch. No Rollie.

Perhaps he had sneaked upstairs to lie on her bed, where he was not supposed to go. That rule was a part of Mother's fussiness. It was *her* bed, wasn't it? But was she allowed the say-so about it? Not on your life. They *said* she could have things the way she wanted in her own room, now she was in her teens, but—her heart burned at unfairness as she took the stairs stormily, two steps at a time, her pigtails flopping up and down on her back. If Rollie was there, she was just going to let him stay there, and Mother could say what she wanted to.

But he was not there. The bedspread and pillow were crumpled, but that was where she had flung herself down to cry that afternoon. But she couldn't cry. She could only lie there, her hands doubled up hard, furious that she had nothing to cry about. Not really. She was too big to cry just over Father's having said to her, severely, "I told you if I let you take the chess set, you were to put it away when you got through with it. One of the pawns was on the floor of our bedroom this morning. I stepped on it. If I'd had my shoes on I'd have broken it."

Well, he *had* told her that. And he hadn't said she mustn't ever take the set again. No, the instant she thought about that, she knew she couldn't cry about it. She could be, and was, in a rage about the way Father kept on talking, long after she'd got his point: "It's not that I care so much about the chess set. It's because if you don't learn how to take care of things, you yourself will suffer for it. You'll forget or neglect something that will be really important for *you*. We *have* to try to teach you to be responsible for what you've said you'll take care of. If we . . ." on and on.

She heard her mother coming down the hall, and hastily shut her door. She had a right to shut the door to her own room, hadn't she? She had *some* rights, she supposed, even if she was only thirteen and the youngest child. If her mother opened it to say, "What are you doing in here that you don't want me to see?" she'd say—she'd just say—

But her mother did not open the door. Her feet went steadily on along the hall, and then, carefully, slowly, down the stairs. She probably had an armful of winter things she was bringing down from the attic. She was probably thinking that a tall, thirteen-year-old daughter was big enough to help with a chore like that. But she wouldn't *say* anything. She would just get out that insulting look of a grown-up silently putting up with a crazy, unreasonable kid. She had worn that expression all day; it was too much to be endured.

Up in her bedroom behind her closed door the thirteen-year-old stamped her foot in a gust of uncontrollable rage, none the less savage and heartshaking because it was mysterious to her.

But she had not located Rollie. She would be cut into little pieces before she would let her father and mother know she had lost sight of him, forgotten about him. They would not scold her, she knew. They would do worse; they would look at her. And in their silence she would hear, droning on reproachfully, what they had said when she had been begging to keep for her own the sweet, woolly collie puppy in her arms.

How warm he had felt! Astonishing how warm and alive a puppy was compared with a doll! She had never liked her dolls much after she had held Rollie, feeling him warm against her breast, warm and wriggling, bursting with life, reaching up to lick her face. He had loved her from that first instant. As he felt her arms around him, his liquid, beautiful eyes had melted in trusting sweetness. And they did now, whenever he looked at her.

And back then, at the very minute when, as a darling baby dog, he was beginning to love her, her father and mother were saying, so cold, so reasonable—gosh, how she *hated* reasonableness!—"Now, Peg, remember that, living where we do, with sheep on the farms around us, it is a serious responsibility to have a collie dog. If you keep him, you've got to be the one to take care of him. You'll have to be the one to train him to stay at home. We're too busy with you children to start bringing up a puppy too."

Rollie, nestling in her arms, let one hind leg drop awkwardly. It must be uncomfortable. She looked down at him tenderly, tucked his leg up under him and gave him a hug. He laughed up in her face—he really did laugh, his mouth stretched wide in a cheerful grin. Now he was snug in a warm little ball.

Her parents were saying, "If you want him, you can have him. But you must be responsible for him. If he gets to running sheep, he'll just have to be shot, you know that."

They had not said, aloud, "Like the Wilsons' collie." They never mentioned that awfulness—her racing unsuspectingly down across the fields just at the horrible moment when Mr. Wilson shot their collie, caught in the very act of killing sheep. They probably thought that if they never spoke about it, she would forget it—*forget* the crack of that rifle, and the collapse of the great beautiful dog! Forget the red red blood spurting from the hole in his head. She hadn't forgotten. She never would. She knew as well as they did how important it was to train a collie puppy about sheep. They didn't have to rub it in like that. They always rubbed everything in. She had told them, fervently, indignantly, that of *course* she would take care of him, be responsible for him, teach him to stay at home. Of course. Of course. *She* understood!

And now, when he was six months old, tall, rangy, powerful, standing up far above her knee, nearly to her waist, she didn't know where he was. She composed her face to look natural and went downstairs to search the house. He was probably asleep somewhere. She looked every room over carefully. Her mother was nowhere visible. It was safe to call him again, to give the special piercing whistle which always brought him racing to her, the white-feathered plume of his tail waving in elation that she wanted him.

But he did not answer. She stood still on the front porch to think.

COULD HE HAVE gone up to their special place in the edge of the field where the three young pines, their branches growing close to the ground, made a triangular walled-in space, completely hidden from the world? Sometimes he went up there with her, and when she lay down on the dried grass to dream, he, too, lay down quietly, his head on his paws, his beautiful eyes fixed adoringly on her. It didn't seem as though he would have gone alone there. Still— She loped up the steep slope of the field rather fast, beginning to be anxious.

No, he was not there. She stood irresolutely in the roofless, green-walled triangular hideout, wondering what to do next.

Then, before she knew what thought had come into her mind, its emotional impact knocked her down. At least her knees crumpled under her. The Wilsons had, last Wednesday, brought their sheep down from the far upper pasture to the home farm! They were—she herself had seen them on her way to school, and like an idiot had not thought of Rollie—on the river meadow.

She was off like a racer at the crack of the starting pistol, her long, strong legs stretched in great leaps, her pigtails flying. She took the shortcut, regardless of the brambles. Their thorn-spiked, wiry stems tore at her flesh, but she did not care. She welcomed the pain. It was something she was doing for Rollie, for her Rollie.

She was in the pinewood now, rushing down the steep, stony path, tripping over roots, half falling, catching herself just in time, not slackening her speed. She burst out on the open knoll above the river meadow, calling wildly, "Rollie, here Rollie, here, boy! Here! Here!" She tried to whistle, but she was crying too hard to pucker her lips.

There was nobody to see or hear her. Twilight was falling over the bare, grassy knoll. The sunless evening wind slid down the mountain like an invisible river, engulfing her in cold. Her teeth began to chatter. "Here, Rollie, here, boy, here!" She strained her eyes to look down into the meadow to see if the sheep were there. She could not be sure. She stopped calling him as she would a dog, and called out his name despairingly, as if he were her child, "Rollie! Oh, *Rollie*, where are you?"

The tears ran down her cheeks in streams. She sobbed loudly, her face contorted grotesquely. "Oh, Rollie! Rollie! Rollie!" She had wanted something to cry about. Oh, how terribly now she had something to cry about.

She saw him as clearly as if he were there beside her, his muzzle and gaping mouth all smeared with the betraying blood (like the Wilsons' collie). "But he didn't *know* it was wrong!" she screamed like a wild creature. "Nobody *told* him it was wrong. It was my fault. I should have taken better care of him. I will now. I will!"

But no matter how she screamed, she could not make herself heard. In the cold, gathering darkness, she saw him stand—poor, guiltless victim of his ignorance, who should have been protected from his own nature—his beautiful soft eyes looking at her with love, his splendid plumed tail waving gently. "It was my fault. I should have *made* him stay at home. I was responsible for him. It was my fault."

But she could not make his executioners hear her. The shot rang out. Rollie sank down, his beautiful liquid eyes glazed, the blood spurting from the hole in his head—like the Wilsons' collie. She gave a wild shriek, long, soul-satisfying, frantic. It was the scream at sudden, unendurable tragedy of a mature, full-blooded woman. It drained dry the girl of thirteen. She came to herself. She was standing on the knoll, trembling and quaking with cold, the darkness closing in on her.

Her breath had given out. For once in her life she had wept all the tears there were in her body. Her hands were so stiff with cold she could scarcely close them. How her nose was running! Simply streaming down her upper lip. And she had no handkerchief. She lifted her skirt, fumbled for her slip, stooped, blew her nose on it, wiped her eyes, drew a long, quavering breath—and heard something! Far off in the distance, a faint sound, like a dog's muffled bark.

She whirled on her heels and bent her head to listen. The sound did not come from the meadow below the knoll. It came from back of her, from the Wilsons' maple grove higher up. She held her breath. Yes, it came from there. She began to run again, but now she was not sobbing. She was silent, absorbed in her effort to cover ground. If she could only live to get there, to see if it really were Rollie. She ran steadily till she came to the fence, and went over this in a great plunge. Her skirt caught on a nail. She impatiently pulled at it, not hearing or not heeding the long, sibilant tear as it came loose. She was in the dusky maple wood, stumbling over the rocks as she ran. As she tore on up the slope, she knew it was Rollie's bark.

She stopped short and leaned weakly against a tree, sick with the breathlessness of her straining lungs, sick in the reaction of relief, sick with anger at Rollie, who had been here having a wonderful time while she had been dying, just dying in terror about him.

For she could not only hear that it was Rollie's bark; she could hear, in the dog language she knew as well as he, what he was saying in those excited yips: that he had run a woodchuck into a hole in the tumbled stone wall.

The wild, joyful quality of the dog talk enraged the girl. She was trembling in exhaustion, in indignation. So that was where he had been when she was killing herself trying to take care of him. Plenty near enough to hear her calling and whistling to him, if he had paid attention. Just so set on having his foolish good time, he never thought to listen for her call.

She stooped to pick up a stout stick. She would teach him! It was time he had something to make him remember to listen. She started forward.

But she stopped, stood thinking. One of the things to remember about collies—everybody knew that—was their sensitiveness. A collie who had been beaten was never "right" again. His spirit was broken. "Anything but a broken-spirited collie," the farmers often said. They were no good after that.

She threw down her stick. Anyhow, she thought, he was too young to know, really, that he had done wrong. He was still only a puppy. Like all puppies, he got perfectly crazy over wild-animal smells. Probably he really and truly hadn't heard her calling and whistling.

All the same, all the same—she stared intently into the twilight—he couldn't be let to grow up just as he wanted to. She would have to make him understand that he mustn't go off this way by himself. He must be trained to know how to do what a good dog does—not because *she* wanted him to, but for his own sake.

She walked on now, steady, purposeful, gathering her inner strength together, Olympian in her understanding of the full meaning of the event.

When he heard his own special young god approaching, he turned delightedly and ran to meet her, panting, his tongue hanging out. His eyes shone. He jumped up on her in an ecstasy of welcome and licked her face.

But she pushed him away. Her face and voice were grave. "No, Rollie, *no!*" she said severely. "You're *bad*. You know you're not to go off in the woods without me! You are—a—*bad—dog*."

He was horrified. Stricken into misery. He stood facing her, frozen, the gladness going out of his eyes, the erect waving plume of his tail slowly lowered to slinking, guilty dejection.

"I know you were all wrapped up in that woodchuck. But that's no excuse. You *could* have heard me calling you if you'd paid attention," she went on. "You've got to learn, and I've got to teach you."

With a shudder of misery he lay down, his tail stretched out limp on the ground, his head flat on his paws, his ears drooping—ears ringing with doomsday awfulness of the voice he so loved and revered. He must have been utterly wicked. He trembled, and turned his head away from her august look of blame, groveling in remorse for whatever mysterious sin he had committed.

She sat down by him, as miserable as he. "I don't *want* to scold you. But I have to! I have to bring you up right, or you'll get shot, Rollie. You *mustn't* go away from the house without me, do you hear, *never!*"

Catching, with his sharp ears yearning for her approval, a faint overtone of relenting affection in her voice, he lifted his eyes to her, humbly, soft in imploring fondness.

"Oh, Rollie!" she said, stooping low over him. "I *do* love you. I do. But I *have* to bring you up. I'm responsible for you, don't you see?"

He did not see. Hearing sternness, or something else he did not recognize, in the beloved voice, he shut his eyes tight in sorrow, and made a little whimpering lament in his throat.

She had never heard him cry before. It was too much. She sat down by him and drew his head to her, rocking him in her arms, soothing him with inarticulate small murmurs.

He leaped in her arms and wriggled happily as he had when he was a baby; he reached up to lick her face as he had then. But he was no baby now. He was half as big as she, a great, warm, pulsing, living armful of love. She clasped him closely. Her heart was brimming full, but calmed and quiet.

It was almost dark now. "We'll be late to supper, Rollie," she said responsibly. Pushing him gently off, she stood up. "Home, Rollie, home!"

Here was a command he could understand. At once he trotted along the path toward home. His plumed tail, held high, waved cheerfully. His short dog memory had dropped into oblivion the suffering just back of him.

Her human memory was longer. His prancing gait was as carefree as a young child's. Plodding heavily like a serious adult, she trod behind him. Her very shoulders seemed bowed by what she had lived through. She felt, she thought like an old, old woman of thirty. But it was all right now. She knew she had made an impression on him.

When they came out into the open pasture, Rollie ran back to get her to play with him. He leaped around her in circles, barking in cheerful yawps, jumping up on her, inviting her to run a race with him, to throw him a stick, to come alive.

His high spirits were ridiculous. But infectious. She gave one little leap to match his. Rollie pretended that this was a threat to him, planted his forepaws low and barked loudly at her, laughing between yips. He was so funny, she thought, when he grinned that way. She laughed back, and gave another mock-threatening leap at him. Radiant that his sky was once more clear, he sprang high in an explosion of happiness, and bounded in circles around her.

Following him, not noting in the dusk where she was going, she felt the grassy slope drop steeply. Oh, yes, she knew where she was. They had come to the rolling-down hill just back of the house. All the kids rolled down there, even the little ones, because it was soft grass without a stone. She had rolled down that slope a million times—years and years ago, when she was a kid herself. It was fun. She remembered well the whirling dizziness of the descent, all the world turning over and over crazily. And the delicious giddy staggering when you first stood up, the earth still spinning under your feet.

"All right, Rollie, let's go," she cried, and flung herself down in the rolling position, her arms straight up over her head.

Rollie had never seen this skylarking before. It threw him into almost hysterical amusement. He capered around the rapidly rolling figure, half scared, mystified, enchanted.

His wild frolicsome barking might have come from her own throat, so accurately did it sound the way she felt—crazy, foolish, like a little kid no more than five years old, the age she had been when she had last rolled down that hill.

At the bottom she sprang up, on muscles as steel strong as Rollie's. She staggered a little, and laughed aloud.

The living-room windows were just before them. How yellow lighted windows looked when you were in the darkness going home. How nice and yellow. Maybe Mother had waffles for supper. She was a swell cook, Mother was, and she certainly gave her family all the breaks when it came to meals.

"Home, Rollie, home!" She burst open the door to the living room. "Hi, Mom, what you got for supper?"

From the kitchen her mother announced coolly, "I hate to break the news to you, but it's waffles."

"Oh, *Mom!* " she shouted in ecstasy.

Her mother could not see her. She did not need to. "For goodness sakes, go and wash," she called.

In the long mirror across the room she saw herself, her hair hanging wild, her long, bare legs scratched, her broadly smiling face dirt-streaked, her torn skirt dangling, her dog laughing up at her. Gosh, was it a relief to feel your own age, just exactly thirteen years old!

A SICK CALL

MORLEY CALLAGHAN

SOMETIMES FATHER MACDOWELL mumbled out loud and took a deep wheezy breath as he walked up and down the room and read his office. He was a huge old priest, white-headed except for a shiny baby-pink bald spot on the top of his head, and he was a bit deaf in one ear. His florid face had many fine red interlacing vein lines. For hours he had been hearing confessions and he was tired, for he always had to hear more confessions than any other priest at the cathedral: young girls who were in trouble, and wild but at times repentant young men, always wanted to tell their confessions to Father Macdowell, because nothing seemed to shock or excite him, or make him really angry, and he was even tender with those who thought they were most guilty.

While he was mumbling and reading and trying to keep his glasses on his nose, the house girl knocked on the door and said, "There's a young lady here to see you, Father. I think it's about a sick call."

"Did she ask for me especially?" he said in a deep voice.

"Indeed she did, Father. She said she wanted Father Macdowell and nobody else."

So he went out to the waiting room, where a girl about thirty years of age, with fine brown eyes, fine cheekbones, and rather square shoulders, was sitting daubing her eyes with a handkerchief. She was wearing a dark coat with a gray wolf collar. "Good evening, Father," she said. "My sister is sick. I wanted you to come and see her. We think she's dying."

"Be easy, child; what's the matter with her? Speak louder. I can hardly hear you."

"My sister's had pneumonia. The doctor's coming back to see her in an hour. I wanted you to anoint her, Father."

"I see. But she's not lost yet. I'll not give her extreme unction now. It may not be necessary. I'll go with you and hear her confession."

"Father, I ought to let you know, maybe. Her husband won't want to let you see her. He's not a Catholic, and my sister hasn't been to church in a long time."

"Oh, don't mind that. He'll let me see her," Father Macdowell said, and he left the room to put on his hat and coat.

WHEN HE RETURNED, the girl explained that her name was Jane Stanhope, and her sister lived only a few blocks away. "We'll walk and you tell me about your sister," he said. He put his black hat square on the top of his head, and pieces of white hair stuck out awkwardly at the sides. They went to the avenue together.

The night was mild and clear. Miss Stanhope began to walk slowly, because Father Macdowell's rolling gait didn't get him along the street very quickly. He walked as if his feet hurt him, though he wore a pair of large, soft, specially constructed shapeless shoes. "Now, my child, you go ahead and tell me about your sister," he said, breathing with difficulty, yet giving the impression that nothing could have happened to the sister which would make him feel indignant.

There wasn't much to say, Miss Stanhope replied. Her sister had married John Williams two years ago, and he was a good, hardworking fellow, only he was very bigoted and hated all church people. "My family wouldn't have anything to do with Elsa after she married him, though I kept going to see her," she said. She was talking in a loud voice to Father Macdowell so he could hear her.

"Is she happy with her husband?"

"She's been very happy, Father. I must say that."

"Where is he now?"

"He was sitting beside her bed. I ran out because I thought he was going to cry. He said if I brought a priest near the place he'd break the priest's head."

"My goodness. But never mind. Does your sister want to see me?"

"She asked me to go and get a priest, but she doesn't want John to know she did it."

TURNING INTO A side street, they stopped at the first apartment house, and the old priest followed Miss Stanhope up the stairs. His breath came with great difficulty. "Oh dear, I'm not getting any younger, not one day younger. It's a caution how a man's legs go back on him," he said. As Miss Stanhope rapped on the door, she looked pleadingly at the old priest, trying to ask him not to be offended at anything that might happen, but he was smiling and looking huge in the narrow hallway. He wiped his head with his handkerchief.

The door was opened by a young man in a white shirt with no collar, with a head of thick black wavy hair. At first he looked dazed, then his eyes got bright with excitement when he saw the priest, as though he were glad to see someone he could destroy with pent-up energy. "What do you mean, Jane?" he said. "I told you not to bring a priest around here. My wife doesn't want to see a priest."

"What's that you're saying, young man?"

"No one wants you here."

"Speak up. Don't be afraid. I'm a bit hard of hearing." Father Macdowell smiled rosily. John Williams was confused by the unexpected deafness in the priest, but he stood there, blocking the door with sullen resolution, as if waiting for the priest to try to launch a curse at him.

"Speak to him, Father," Miss Stanhope said, but the priest didn't seem to hear her; he was still smiling as he pushed past the young man, saying, "I'll go in and sit down, if you don't mind, son. I'm here on God's errand, but I don't mind saying I'm all out of breath from climbing those stairs."

John was dreadfully uneasy to see he had been brushed aside, and he followed the priest into the apartment and said loudly, "I don't want you here."

Father Macdowell said, "Eh, eh?" Then he smiled sadly. "Don't be angry with me, son," he said. "I'm too old to try and be fierce and threatening." Looking around, he said, "Where's your wife?" and he started to walk along the hall, looking for the bedroom.

John followed him and took hold of his arm. "There's no sense in your wasting your time talking to my wife, do you hear?" he said angrily.

Miss Stanhope called out suddenly, "Don't be rude, John."

"It's he that's being rude. You mind your business," John said.

"For the love of God let me sit down a moment with her, anyway. I'm tired," the priest said.

"What do you want to say to her? Say it to me, why don't you?"

THEN THEY BOTH heard someone moan softly in the adjoining room, as if the sick woman had heard them. Father Macdowell, forgetting that the young man had hold of his arm, said, "I'll go in and see her for a moment, if you don't mind," and he began to open the door.

"You're not going to be alone with her, that's all," John said, following him into the bedroom.

Lying on the bed was a white-faced, fair girl, whose skin was so delicate that her cheekbones stood out sharply. She was feverish, but her eyes rolled toward the door, and she watched them coming in. Father Macdowell took off his coat, and as he mumbled to himself he looked around the room at the mauve silk bed lamp and the light wallpaper with the tiny birds in flight. It looked like a little girl's room. "Good evening, Father," Mrs. Williams whispered. She looked scared. She didn't glance at her husband. The notion of dying had made her afraid. She loved her husband and wanted to die loving him, but she was afraid, and she looked up at the priest.

"You're going to get well, child," Father Macdowell said, smiling and patting her hand gently.

John, who was standing stiffly by the door, suddenly moved around the big priest, and he bent down over the bed and took his wife's hand and began to caress her forehead.

"Now if you don't mind, my son, I'll hear your wife's confession," the priest said.

"No, you won't," John said abruptly. "Her people didn't want her, and they left us together, and they're not going to separate us now. She's satisfied with me." He kept looking down at her face as if he could not bear to turn away.

Father Macdowell nodded his head up and down and sighed. "Poor boy," he said. "God bless you." Then he looked at Mrs. Williams, who had closed her eyes, and he saw a faint tear on her cheek. "Be sensible, my boy," he said. "You'll have to let me hear your wife's confession. Leave us alone awhile."

"I'm going to stay right here," John said, and he sat down on the end of the bed. He was working himself up and staring savagely at the priest. All of a sudden he noticed the tears on his wife's cheeks, and he muttered as though bewildered, "What's the matter, Elsa? What's the matter, darling? Are we bothering you? Just open your eyes and we'll go out of the room and leave you alone till the doctor comes." Then he turned and said to the priest, "I'm not going to leave you here with her, can't you see that? Why don't you go?"

"I could revile you, my son. I could threaten you; but I ask you, for the peace of your wife's soul, leave us alone." Father Macdowell spoke with patient tenderness. He looked very big and solid and immovable as he stood by the bed. "I liked your face as soon as I saw you," he said to John. "You're a good fellow."

John still held his wife's hand, but he ran his free hand through his thick hair and said angrily, "You don't get the point, sir. My wife and I were always left alone, and we merely want to be left alone now. Nothing is going to separate us. She's been content with me. I'm sorry, sir; you'll have to speak to her with me here, or you'll have to go."

"No, you'll have to go for a while," the priest said patiently.

THEN MRS. WILLIAMS moved her head on the pillow and said jerkily, "Pray for me, Father."

So the old priest knelt down by the bed, and with a sweet unruffled expression on his florid face he began to pray. At times his breath came with a whistling noise as though a rumbling were inside him, and at other times he sighed and was full of sorrow. He was praying that young Mrs. Williams might get better, and while he prayed he knew that her husband was more afraid of losing her to the church than losing her to death.

All the time Father Macdowell was on his knees, with his heavy prayer book in his two hands, John kept staring at him. John couldn't understand the old priest's patience and tolerance. He wanted to quarrel with him, but he kept on watching the light from overhead shining on the one baby-pink bald spot on the smooth white head, and at last he burst out, "You don't understand, sir! We've been very happy together. Neither you nor her people came near her when she was in good health, so why should you bother her now? I don't want anything to separate us now; neither does she. She came with me. You see you'd be separating us, don't you?" He was trying to talk like a reasonable man who had no prejudices.

Father Macdowell got up clumsily. His knees hurt him, for the floor was hard. He said to Mrs. Williams in quite a loud voice, "Did you really intend to give up everything for this young fellow?" and he bent down close to her so he could hear.

"Yes, Father," she whispered.

"In heaven's name, child, you couldn't have known what you were doing."

"We loved each other, Father. We've been very happy."

"All right. Supposing you were. What now? What about all eternity, child?"

"Oh, Father, I'm very sick and I'm afraid." She looked up to try to show him how scared she was, and how much she wanted him to give her peace.

He sighed and seemed distressed, and at last he said to John, "Were you married in the church?"

"No, we weren't. Look here, we're talking pretty loud and that upsets her."

"Ah, it's a crime that I'm hard of hearing, I know. Never mind, I'll go." Picking up his coat, he put it over his arm; then he sighed as if he were very tired, and he said, "I wonder if you'd just fetch me a glass of water. I'd thank you for it."

John hesitated, glancing at the tired old priest, who looked so pink and white and almost cherubic in his utter lack of guile.

"What's the matter?" Father Macdowell said.

John was ashamed of himself for appearing so sullen, so he said hastily, "Nothing's the matter. Just a moment. I won't be a moment." He hurried out of the room.

THE OLD PRIEST LOOKED DOWN at the floor and shook his head; and then, sighing and feeling uneasy, he bent over Mrs. Williams, with his good ear down to her, and he said, "I'll just ask you a few questions in a hurry, my child. You answer them quickly and I'll give you absolution." He made the sign of the cross over her and asked if she repented for having strayed from the church, and if she had often been angry, and whether she had always been faithful, and if she had ever lied or stolen—all so casually and quickly as if it hadn't occurred to him that such a young woman could have serious sins. In the same breath he muttered, "Say a good act of contrition to yourself and that will be all, my dear." He had hardly taken a minute.

When John returned to the room with the glass of water in his hand, he saw the old priest making the sign of the cross. Father Macdowell went on praying without even looking up at John. When he had finished, he turned and said, "Oh, there you are. Thanks for the water. I needed it. Well, my boy, I'm sorry if I worried you."

John hardly said anything. He looked at his wife, who had closed her eyes, and he sat down on the end of the bed. He was too disappointed to speak.

Father Macdowell, who was expecting trouble, said, "Don't be harsh, lad."

"I'm not harsh," he said mildly, looking up at the priest. "But you weren't quite fair. And it's as though she turned away from me at the last moment. I didn't think she needed you."

"God bless you, bless the both of you. She'll get better," Father Macdowell said. But he felt ill at ease as he put on his coat, and he couldn't look directly at John.

GOING ALONG THE hall, he spoke to Miss Stanhope, who wanted to apologize for her brother-in-law's attitude. "I'm sorry if it was unpleasant for you, Father," she said.

"It wasn't unpleasant," he said. "I was glad to meet John. He's a fine fellow. It's a great pity he isn't a Catholic. I don't know as I played fair with him."

As he went down the stairs, puffing and sighing, he pondered the question of whether he had played fair with the young man. But by the time he reached the street he was rejoicing amiably to think he had so successfully ministered to one who had strayed from the faith and had called out to him at the last moment. Walking along with the rolling motion as if his feet hurt him, he muttered, "Of course they were happy as they were . . . in a worldly way. I wonder if I did come between them?"

He shuffled along, feeling very tired, but he couldn't help thinking, "What beauty there was to his staunch love for her!" Then he added quickly, "But it was just a pagan beauty, of course."

As he began to wonder about the nature of this beauty, for some reason he felt inexpressibly sad.

A TERRIBLY
STRANGE BED
WILKIE COLLINS

Shortly after my education at college was finished, I happened to be staying at Paris with an English friend. We were both young men then, and lived, I am afraid, rather a wild life in the delightful city of our sojourn. One night we were idling about the neighborhood of the Palais Royal, doubtful to what amusement we should next betake ourselves. My friend proposed a visit to Frascati's, but I knew Frascati's by heart and was thoroughly tired of such a social anomaly as a respectable gambling house. "For heaven's sake," said I to my friend, "let us go somewhere where we can see a little genuine, blackguard, poverty-stricken gaming, with no false gingerbread glitter thrown over it all. Let us go to a house where they don't mind letting in a man with a ragged coat, or no coat, ragged or otherwise."

"Very well," said my friend, "we needn't go out of the Palais Royal to find the sort of company you want. Here's the place just before us—as blackguard a place, by all report, as you could possibly wish to see." In another minute we arrived at the door and entered the house.

When we got upstairs, we were admitted into the chief gambling room. We did not find many people assembled there, but they were all types—lamentably true types—of their respective classes. The quiet in the room was horrible. The thin, haggard, long-haired young man, whose sunken eyes fiercely watched the turning up of the cards, never spoke; the fat-faced, pimply player, who pricked his piece of pasteboard perseveringly—to register how often black won, and how often red—never spoke; the dirty, wrinkled old man, who had lost his last sou—and still looked on desperately, after he could play no longer—never spoke. Even the voice of the croupier sounded as if it were strangely dulled and thickened in the atmosphere of the room, and I soon found it necessary to take refuge in excitement from the depression of spirits which was fast stealing on me. Unfortunately I sought the nearest excitement, by going to the table and beginning to play. Still more unfortunately, as the event will show, I won—won at such a rate that the regular players at the table crowded round me; and, staring at my stakes with hungry, superstitious eyes, whispered to one another that the English stranger was going to break the bank.

The game was rouge et noir. I had played it in every city in Europe, but my gaming was a mere idle amusement. I never resorted to it by neccessity, because I never knew what it was to want money. In short, I had hitherto frequented gambling tables—just as I frequented ballrooms and opera houses—because they amused me and because I had nothing better to do with my leisure hours.

But on this occasion it was very different. Now, for the first time in my life, I felt what the passion for play really was. My success first bewildered and then, in the most literal meaning of the word, intoxicated me. At first, some of the men present ventured their money safely on my color, but I speedily increased my stakes to sums which they dared not risk. One after another they left off playing and breathlessly looked on at my game.

The excitement in the room rose to fever pitch. The silence was interrupted by a deep-throated chorus of oaths and exclamations in different languages every time the gold was shoveled across to my side of the table. Even the imperturbable croupier dashed his rake on the floor in astonishment at my success. But one man present preserved his self-possession; and that man was my friend. He came to my side and begged me to leave the place, satisfied with what I had already gained. I must do him the justice to say that he repeated his warnings and entreaties several times, and only went away after I had rejected his advice (I was to all intents and purposes gambling drunk) in terms which rendered it impossible for him to address me again that night.

Shortly after he had gone, a hoarse voice behind me cried, "Permit me, my dear sir! Permit me to restore to their proper place two napoleons which you have dropped. Wonderful luck, sir! I pledge you my word of honor, as an old soldier, in the course of my long experience in this sort of thing, I never saw such luck as yours! Never! Go on, sir—*sacré mille bombes!* Go on boldly and break the bank!"

I turned round and saw, nodding and smiling at me, a tall man dressed in a frogged and braided surtout.

If I had been in my senses, I should have considered him a suspicious specimen of an old soldier. He had goggling bloodshot eyes, mangy mustachios, and a broken nose. His voice betrayed a barrack-room intonation of the worst order, and he had the dirtiest pair of hands I ever saw. However, in the reckless triumph of that moment I was ready to fraternize with anybody who encouraged me in my game. I clapped the old soldier on the back and swore he was the honestest fellow in the world—the most glorious relic of the Grand Army that I had ever met with. "Go on!" cried my military friend, snapping his fingers in ecstasy. "Break the bank, my gallant English comrade, break the bank!"

And I *did* go on—went on at such a rate that in another quarter of an hour the croupier called out, "Gentlemen! The bank has discontinued for tonight." All the notes and all the gold in that "bank" now lay in a heap under my hands, waiting to pour into my pockets!

"Tie up the money in your handkerchief, my worthy sir," said the old soldier. "Your winnings are too heavy for any breeches pockets that ever were sewed. There! That's it! Shovel them in, notes and all! Now, then, sir—two tight double knots each way, with your honorable permission, and the money's safe. Feel it! Feel it, fortunate sir! Hard and round as a cannonball—*ah, bah!* If they had only fired such cannonballs at us at Austerlitz—*nom d'une pipe!* If they only had! And now, as an ex-brave of the French army, what remains for me to do? Simply this: to entreat my valued English friend to drink champagne with me, and toast the goddess Fortune in foaming goblets before we part!"

Excellent ex-brave! Champagne by all means! An English cheer for an old soldier and the goddess Fortune! Hurrah! Hurrah!

By the time the second bottle of champagne was emptied, I felt as if I had been drinking liquid fire. No excess in wine had had this effect on me before. Was it the result of a stimulant acting upon my system when I was in a highly excited state? Was my stomach in a particularly disordered condition? Or was the champagne amazingly strong?

"Ex-brave of the French army!" I cried, in a mad state of exhilaration. "You have set me on fire! Do you hear, my hero of Austerlitz? Let us have a third bottle of champagne to put the flame out!"

The old soldier rolled his goggle eyes until I expected to see them slip out of their sockets; placed his dirty forefinger by the side of his broken nose; solemnly ejaculated, "Coffee!" and immediately ran off into an inner room.

The word pronounced by the eccentric veteran seemed to have a magical effect on the rest of the company present. With one accord they all rose to depart, and when the old soldier returned, we had the room to ourselves. The silence was now deeper than ever.

A sudden change, too, had come over the ex-brave. He assumed a portentously solemn look; and when he spoke to me again, his speech was ornamented by no oaths, enforced by no finger snapping, enlivened by no apostrophes or exclamations.

"Listen, my dear sir," said he, in mysteriously confidential tones, "listen to an old soldier's advice. I have been to the mistress of the house to impress on her the necessity of making us some particularly strong and good coffee. You must drink this coffee before you think of going home. With all that money, it is a sacred duty to yourself to have your wits about you. You are known to be a winner by several gentlemen present tonight who are very worthy and excellent fellows; but they are mortal men, my dear sir, and they have their weaknesses. Need I say more? Ah, no, no, you understand me. Now, this is what you must do—send for a cabriolet when you feel quite well again—draw up all the windows when you get into it—and tell the driver to take you home through the large and well-lighted thoroughfares. Do this, and you will thank an old soldier for giving you a word of honest advice."

Just as the ex-brave ended his oration, the coffee came in, ready poured out in two cups. My attentive friend handed me one of the cups with a bow. I was parched with thirst, and drank it off at a draft. Almost instantly afterward I was seized with a fit of giddiness, and felt more completely intoxicated than ever. The room whirled round and round furiously; the old soldier seemed to be regularly bobbing up and down before me like the piston of a steam engine. I was half deafened by a violent singing in my ears; a feeling of utter helplessness overcame me. I rose from my chair, holding on by the table to keep my balance, and stammered out that I felt dreadfully unwell—so unwell that I did not know how I was to get home.

"My dear friend," answered the old soldier, "it would be madness to go home in *your* state; you might be robbed and murdered with the greatest ease. *I* am going to sleep here, *you* sleep here, too—they make up capital beds in this house—take one; sleep off the effects of the wine, and go home safely with your winnings tomorrow, in broad daylight."

I had but two ideas left: one, that I must never let go my handkerchief full of money; the other, that I must lie down somewhere immediately and fall off into a comfortable sleep. So I agreed to the proposal about the bed, and took the offered arm of the old soldier, carrying my money with my disengaged hand. Preceded by the croupier, we passed along some passages and up a flight of stairs into the bedroom which I was to occupy. The ex-brave shook me warmly by the hand, proposed that we should breakfast together, and then, followed by the croupier, left me for the night.

I ran to the washstand; drank some of the water in my jug; poured the rest out and plunged my face into it; and then sat down in a chair and tried to compose myself. I soon felt better. The giddiness left me and I began to feel a little like a reasonable being again. My first thought was of the risk of sleeping all night in a gambling house; my second, of the still greater risk of going home alone at night, through the streets of Paris, with a large sum of money about me. I had slept in worse places than this on my travels; so I determined to lock, bolt, and barricade my door, and take my chance till the next morning.

Accordingly, I secured myself against all intrusion, and then, satisfied that I had taken every precaution, pulled off my upper clothing and got into bed, with the handkerchief full of money under my pillow.

I soon felt not only that I could not go to sleep, but that I could not even close my eyes. I was wide awake and in a high fever. Every nerve in my body trembled—every one of my senses seemed to be preternaturally sharpened. I tossed and rolled, and tried every kind of position, and all to no purpose. I groaned with vexation, as I felt that I was in for a sleepless night.

What could I do? I had no book to read. And yet, unless I found some method of diverting my mind, I felt certain that I would pass the night suffering all conceivable varieties of nervous terror.

I raised myself on my elbow and looked about the room—which was brightened by a lovely moonlight pouring straight through the window—to see if it contained any pictures or ornaments that I could at all clearly distinguish. While my eyes wandered from wall to wall, I resolved to find occupation and amusement by making a mental inventory of every article of furniture I could see.

There was, first, the bed I was lying in—a four-post bed, of all things in the world to meet with in Paris! Yes, a thorough clumsy British four-poster, its top lined with chintz and fringed with a valance all round, and with the regular stifling, unwholesome curtains, which were drawn back against the posts. Then there was the marble-topped washstand, then two small chairs, with my coat and trousers flung on them. Then a large elbow chair, with my cravat and shirt collar thrown over the back. Then a chest of drawers with two of the brass handles off, and a tawdry, broken china inkstand placed on it by way of ornament for the top. Then the dressing table, adorned by a very small looking glass and a very large pincushion. Then an unusually large window. Then a dark old picture of a fellow in a high Spanish hat, crowned with a plume of towering feathers. A swarthy, sinister ruffian shading his eyes with his hand and looking intently upward—it might be at some tall gallows at which he was going to be hanged. At any rate, he had the appearance of thoroughly deserving it. I counted the feathers in the man's hat—they stood out in relief—three white, two green. I observed the crown of his hat, which was of a conical shape.

While I lingered over this intellectual employment, my thoughts began to wander. The moonlight shining into the room reminded me of a certain moonlit night in England—the night after a picnic party in a Welsh valley. Every incident of the drive homeward came back to my remembrance—though, if I had *tried* to recollect it, I could certainly have recalled little or nothing of that scene long past. Of all the wonderful faculties that help to tell us we are immortal, which speaks the sublime truth more eloquently than memory? Here was I, in a strange house of the most suspicious character, in a situation of uncertainty; nevertheless, remembering, quite involuntarily, places, people, conversations, minute circumstances of every kind, which I had thought forgotten forever. And what cause had produced this strange, mysterious effect? Nothing but some rays of moonlight shining in at my bedroom window.

I was still thinking of the picnic when, in an instant, the thread on which my memories hung snapped asunder, and I found myself, I neither knew why nor wherefore, looking hard at the picture again.

Looking for what?

Good God! The man had pulled his hat down on his brows! No! The hat itself was gone! Where was the conical crown? Where the feathers—three white, two green? Not there!

Was the bed moving?

I turned on my back and looked up. Was I mad? Drunk? Dreaming? Or was the top of the bed really moving down—sinking slowly, silently, horribly, down throughout the whole of its length and breadth—upon me, as I lay underneath?

My blood seemed to stand still. I turned my head round on the pillow, and determined to test whether the bed top was really moving or not, by keeping my eye on the man in the picture.

The next look in that direction was enough. The dull outline of the valance above me was within an inch of being parallel with his waist. Slowly—very slowly—I saw the figure, and the line of frame below the figure, vanish as the valance moved down before it.

I am, constitutionally, anything but timid. I have been on more than one occasion in peril of my life, and have not lost my self-possession for an instant; but when the conviction first settled on my mind that the bed top was really moving, I looked up shuddering, helpless, panic-stricken, beneath the hideous machinery for murder, which was advancing closer and closer to suffocate me.

Down and down, without pausing and without sounding, came the bed top, and still my panic terror seemed to bind me faster and faster to the mattress on which I lay; down and down it sank, till the dusty odor from the lining of the canopy came stealing into my nostrils.

At that final moment the instinct of self-preservation startled me out of my trance, and I moved at last. There was just room for me to roll myself sideways off the bed. As I dropped noiselessly to the floor, the edge of the murderous canopy touched me on the shoulder.

I rose instantly on my knees to watch the bed top. I was literally spellbound by it. The whole canopy came down so close that there was not room to squeeze my finger between the bed top and the bed. I felt at the sides, and discovered that what had appeared to be the ordinary light canopy of a four-post bed was in reality a thick, broad mattress, the substance of which was concealed by the valance and its fringe. I looked up and saw the four posts rising hideously bare. In the middle of the bed top was a huge wooden screw that had evidently worked it down through a hole in the ceiling. The frightful apparatus moved without making the faintest noise. Amid a dead and awful silence I beheld before me—in the nineteenth century, and in the civilized capital of France—such a machine for secret murder by suffocation as might have existed in the worst days of the Inquisition, in the lonely inns among the Harz Mountains, in the mysterious tribunals of Westphalia! As I looked, I began to recover the power of thinking, and in a moment I discovered the murderous conspiracy framed against me in all its horror.

My cup of coffee had been drugged too strongly. I had been saved from being smothered by having taken an overdose of some narcotic. How I had fretted at the fever fit which had preserved my life by keeping me awake! How recklessly I had confided myself to the two wretches who had led me into this room, determined, for the sake of my winnings, to kill me in my sleep by the surest and most horrible contrivance for secretly accomplishing my destruction! How many men, winners like me, had slept in that bed and had never been heard of more! I shuddered at the bare idea of it.

But erelong all thought was again suspended by the sight of the murderous canopy moving once more. After it had remained on the bed about ten minutes, it began to move up again. The villains who worked it from above evidently believed that their purpose was now accomplished. Slowly and silently, as it had descended, that horrible bed top rose toward its former place. When it reached the upper extremities of the four posts, it reached the ceiling too. Neither hole nor screw could be seen; the bed became in appearance an ordinary bed again even to the most suspicious eyes.

Now, for the first time, I was able to move—to rise from my knees—to dress myself—and to consider how I should escape. If I betrayed, by the smallest noise, that the attempt to suffocate me had failed, I was certain to be murdered. Had I made any noise already? I listened intently, looking toward the door.

No! Absolute silence everywhere. Besides locking and bolting my door, I had moved an old wooden chest against it, which I had found under the bed. To remove this chest without making some disturbance was impossible; and, moreover, to think of escaping through the house, now barred up for the night, was sheer insanity. Only one chance was left me—the window.

I stole to it on tiptoe and raised my hand to open it, knowing that on that action hung, by the merest hairsbreadth, my chance of safety. They keep vigilant watch in the House of Murder. If any part of the frame cracked, if the hinge creaked, I was a lost man! It must have occupied me at least five minutes, reckoning by time—five *hours*, reckoning by suspense—to open that window. I succeeded in doing it with all the dexterity of a housebreaker, and then looked down into the street. To leap the distance beneath me would be almost certain destruction! Next, I looked round at the sides of the house. Down the left side a thick water pipe passed close by the edge of the window. The moment I saw the pipe, I knew I was saved. By the practice of gymnastics I had kept up my schoolboy powers as a daring and expert climber, and knew that my head, hands, and feet would serve me faithfully in any hazards of ascent or descent.

I had already got one leg over the windowsill when I remembered the handkerchief filled with money under my pillow. I could well have afforded to leave it behind me, but I was revengefully determined that the miscreants of the gambling house should miss their plunder as well as their victim. So I went back to the bed and tied the heavy handkerchief at my back by my cravat.

Just as I had made it tight, I thought I heard a sound of breathing outside the door. The chill feeling of horror ran through me again as I listened. No! Dead silence still in the passage—I had only heard the night air blowing softly into the room. The next moment I was on the windowsill and the next I had a firm grip on the water pipe with my hands and knees.

I slid down into the street easily and quietly, and immediately set off at top speed to a branch prefecture of police, which I knew was situated in the immediate neighborhood. A subprefect, and several picked men among his subordinates, happened to be up, maturing, I believe, some scheme for discovering the perpetrator of a mysterious murder which all Paris was talking of just then. When I began my story, in a breathless hurry and in very bad French, I could see that the subprefect suspected me of being a drunken Englishman who had robbed somebody; but he soon altered his opinion, and before I had concluded, he shoved all the papers before him into a drawer, put on his hat, ordered his expert followers to get ready all sorts of tools for breaking open doors and ripping up brick flooring, and took my arm in the most friendly and familiar manner possible to lead me with him out of the house. I will venture to say that when the subprefect was a little boy, and was taken for the first time to the play, he was not half as much pleased as he was now at the job in prospect for him at the gambling house!

Sentinels were placed at the back and front of the house the moment we got to it; a tremendous battery of knocks was directed against the door; a light appeared at a window; I was told to conceal myself behind the police. Then came more knocks, and a cry of "Open in the name of the law!" At that terrible summons, bolts and locks gave way before an invisible hand; and the moment after, the subprefect was in the passage, confronting a waiter half dressed and ghastly pale. This was the short dialogue which took place:

"We want to see the Englishman who is sleeping in this house."

"He went away hours ago."

"He did no such thing. His friend went away; *he* remained. Show us to his bedroom!"

"I swear to you, Monsieur le Sous-préfet, he is not here! He—"

"I swear to you, Monsieur le Garçon, he is. He slept here—he didn't find your bed comfortable—he came to us to complain of it—here he is among my men—and here am I, ready to look for a flea or two in his bedstead. Renaudin!"—calling to one of the subordinates, and pointing to the waiter—"Collar that man and tie his hands behind him. Now, then, gentlemen, let us walk upstairs!"

Every man and woman in the house was secured—the old soldier the first. Then I identified the bed in which I had lain, and then we went into the room above.

No object that was at all extraordinary appeared in any part of it. The subprefect looked round the place, commanded everybody to be silent, stamped twice on the floor, and ordered the flooring there to be carefully taken up. This was done in no time. Lights were produced, and we saw a deep cavity between the floor of this room and the ceiling of the room beneath. Through this cavity there ran perpendicularly a case of iron thickly greased; and inside the case appeared the screw, which communicated with the bed top below. Extra lengths of screw and the works of a heavy press—constructed with infernal ingenuity so as to join the fixtures below—were next discovered and pulled out on the floor. After some difficulty the subprefect succeeded in putting the machinery together and, leaving his men to work it, descended with me to the bedroom. The smothering canopy was then lowered, but not so noiselessly as I had seen it lowered. When I mentioned this to the subprefect, his answer had a terrible significance. "My men," said he, "are working down the bed top for the first time—the men whose money you won were in better practice."

We left the house, the inmates being removed to prison, and the subprefect returned with me to my hotel to get my passport. "Do you think," I asked as I gave it to him, "that any men have really been smothered in that bed, as they tried to smother *me?*"

"I have seen dozens of drowned men laid out at the morgue," answered the subprefect, "in whose pocketbooks were found letters stating that they had committed suicide in the Seine because they had lost everything at the gaming table. Do I know how many of those men entered the same gambling house that *you* entered? Won as *you* won? Took that bed as *you* took it, slept in it, were smothered in it? And were privately thrown into the river with a letter of explanation written by the murderers? No man can say how many or how few have suffered the fate from which you have escaped. The people of the gambling house kept their bedstead machinery a secret from us. The dead kept the rest of the secret for them. Good night, or rather good morning, monsieur! Be at my office at nine o'clock. In the meantime, *au revoir!*"

The rest of my story is soon told. I was examined and reexamined; the gambling house was strictly searched from top to bottom; the prisoners were separately interrogated; and two of the less guilty among them made a confession. *I* discovered that the old soldier was the master of the gambling house—*justice* discovered that he had been drummed out of the army as a vagabond years ago; that he had been guilty of all sorts of villainies since; and that he, the croupier, another accomplice, and the woman who had made my cup of coffee were all in the secret of the bedstead. The old soldier and his two head myrmidons went to the galleys; the woman who had drugged my coffee was imprisoned; and I became, for one whole week (which is a long time), the head "lion" in Parisian society.

One good result was produced by my adventure: it cured me of ever again trying rouge et noir as an amusement. The sight of a green cloth, with packs of cards and heaps of money on it, will henceforth be forever associated in my mind with the sight of a bed canopy descending to suffocate me in the silence and darkness of the night.

THE LOSS
GILLIAN TINDALL

WHEN TOM HATCHER'S wife, Susan, died it was pretty bad for him, and yet—he realized in queer, gray moments of lucidity—not quite as bad as he had thought it might be. He had expected the pain and loneliness to be unbearable. Instead, he had had the time and the knowledge to envisage beforehand just what it would be like, so when it came, the pain was already subtly familiar.

At first, all he felt was sheer relief that it was at last over, that she was no longer suffering. Also, people were very kind. They had all been ready with cautious words of comfort and tumblers of whiskey; they had offered to help him pack up her things, invited him in for the hot meals they felt he wouldn't bother to cook himself. Some of them almost overdid it, he felt. After all, he had been to all intents living alone for the best part of two months, and for most of the year he had done the cooking, shopping, and cleaning, because of course Susan hadn't felt up to it. He was used to the routine. As a schoolmaster, his working day ended at four, and he had time to do after that what another man might not have been able to. Later, when he'd had a bite to eat while watching that news program, at the moment when the blank evening ahead might have menaced him with despair, there were always lessons to correct and tomorrow's work to think about. "Keeping busy" did help, even though it seemed a bit mechanical. There were ultimately no solutions to Susan's dying or to his missing her, any more than there had been a solution to the fact of their childlessness, which had cost them so many fruitless tests and hopes, and Susan so many tears. But they had got over it. The last five years, before the wretched kidney business started, had been really happy for both of them. And he told himself that it was possible that one day he himself would be happy again too.

When their friends had realized that the loss had not transformed him into some haggard and incompetent travesty of his former self, the pressing invitations did fall off a bit. Actually, that time, about four months after, was the worst. He began to sleep an alarming amount, as if sleep itself were a drug, and even feared for a week or two that he wasn't going to be able to hold his own at work. But he managed to get through without anybody realizing—chiefly, he thought, thanks to Jess.

Jess had been Susan's dog, bought only the year before she died, when they still clung to the idea that she was just run-down and needed the fresh air and exercise which a young dog would provide. After the first few months, however, it had been Tom who had taken the bouncing, girlish creature out for runs on Parliament Hill. Tom had never particularly liked dogs, and when he became fond of Jess it was in spite of himself. A matter of propinquity, he thought, like an unmaternal woman coming to love a child simply through the necessity of looking after it.

Jess was a golden cocker spaniel with a long plumy tail which picked up dead leaves on every outing, and huge pink-padded paws on which she liked to race through mud. She was enchantingly affectionate and maddeningly indiscriminate. She would fawn on anyone; Tom growled that she was hopeless as a watchdog. Susan had replied laughingly that they hadn't got her as a watchdog and that Jess's friendliness ought to be an example to both of them. She had said that they had both been getting too selfish and set in their ways; it was good for them to have Jess tearing around, savaging slippers, stealing chops, making shamefaced puddles, or worse, in the middle of the night when they hadn't heard her scratching and whining.

After this had happened several times they left their bedroom door open to hear better, and then of course Jess took to creeping up from her basket in the hall once they were both asleep. Once she tried to get into bed with them, as if she believed herself the size of a kitten who might easily escape detection—she was always trying to get on people's laps. Tom had taken her sternly downstairs and told her to stay there, but the next night she had been up again. Finally they compromised: Jess might creep in and sleep on the rug by the dressing table—they were prepared to pretend they didn't know she was there—but if, said Tom firmly, there were whinings or tail thumpings or other attempts to join them in bed, out she must go. He was not going to share his married life with a dog. Evidently Jess understood the situation, because the compromise worked, and she never leaped joyously onto the eiderdown till Tom was up at seven thirty and putting his dressing gown on.

When Susan was no longer there, Jess did not at once insinuate herself into the bed in her place. For a week she was clearly puzzled. She kept looking for her mistress on the side nearest the wall each morning. But because Tom hated to see the disappointment in her foolish toffee-brown eyes, he took to calling her briskly the moment he got out of bed, and urging her downstairs ahead of him. Gradually she got into the new routine. She even ceased looking around, faintly puzzled, for another person when Tom gave her her plate of food.

It was not till one night about a fortnight after Susan had died that Jess first came, while he was lying awake and wretched, and pushed her nose into his hand outstretched on the pillow. He thought afterward that she must have heard him tossing about and surmised, with some canine cunning, that this was an opportunity not to be missed. In any case, at that moment he neither knew nor cared what her motives were, but simply gathered her large, exuberant body onto the bed and buried his face in the clean, feathery undergrowth around her neck.

After that, of course, she slept on his bed every night. He still went through the ritual of making her sit on the rug and telling her to stay there. But it was well understood between them that she would climb onto the bed after he was asleep and often before. After a while he began to wait to hear the soft rustle and pad, to feel the slight lurch of the bed as she sprang delicately over his legs and settled herself comfortably within touching distance. Then, reassured by her presence, he would drift off.

On those mornings when it seemed as if he could not face shaving and breakfasting and going to school, or indeed life at all, it was for Jess that he heaved himself out of bed, since she had to be let out. It was for Jess that he went into the kitchen, and while he fed her he automatically fed himself. Then, since Jess had to have her early morning run, he got dressed anyway, and so one thing led to another and he got to school after all. One day, he had the idea of taking her with him. Why, he wondered, had he not thought of it before? She had undoubtedly been lonely in the house all day, and she had begun to make messes before he could get home. Now she came with him to school, sat behind the blackboard, and was much happier. So was he. His classes made much of her. She made much of them in return. For the first time in nearly twenty-five years of teaching he found himself becoming a character. Lovable old Mr. Hatcher with his dog. Well, well. It wasn't perhaps the image he had ever thought he would present. But it helped for the moment. Oh yes, it helped.

In the playground she would bound around retrieving a tennis ball again and again for a knot of admirers. Other boys used to gather around him telling him about their dogs, real, imaginary or longed for, the Alsatians their brothers were going to give them when they were sixteen or the champion greyhounds their uncles were breeding. He found he had joined a new club which transcended age, intelligence, or status.

One fine March day, nearly six months after Susan had died, he drove out to spend a Saturday in the Hertfordshire countryside where they had often picnicked. He took Jess for a good long walk, and sat in a cleared copse to eat his sandwiches while she chased imaginary rabbits through the stumps. Here, as everywhere, he was reminded of former occasions, when Susan had been with him, but he had become quite used to this perpetual undercurrent of memory; it no longer ruined his day for him. He took pleasure in Jess's almost hysterical appreciation of the outing, and had considerable difficulty in luring her back into the car again when it was time to turn for home.

Two days later, she went.

He had taken her out to Parliament Hill after school and had got into conversation with a neighbor, owner of a badly behaved poodle.

When they called and whistled for their respective dogs, the poodle reappeared readily enough, but there was no sign of Jess.

For ten minutes or so he did not worry. She had done this several times before, it was her way of teasing, and he kept expecting that she would be there, flying across the darkening grass from a great distance, ears and tail streaming, tongue flapping, mouth agape as if she were laughing. Not till almost half an hour had gone by did real dread strike home to him. She had never been gone nearly as long as this before.

Wretched, he made his way back home. It was not far, she would no doubt follow him in her own good time; she was hardly likely to get lost in her familiar streets, and if she did she had her collar on; someone would bring her back. But soon he was out again, tramping the hill and then the whole heath in case she had wandered farther there and lost herself among unfamiliar scrub, calling and calling on into the darkness. At one point a watchman with a flashlight joined him and stood by him a few minutes. The man listened to a description of Jess and promised to look out for her. Dogs, he said, often lost themselves on the heath; they went after something that smelled interesting, see, and then wandered in circles, but they nearly always turned up next morning looking ashamed and sorry for themselves. For a few minutes, after the man had gone on his way, Tom did feel fatuously cheered by the watchman's calm. Only gradually did he realize that the man was calm because he didn't care—why should he care? It wasn't his dog.

Lying alone in bed that night he felt cold, and tried his hardest to fix on an image of Jess, cold too, of course, but basically safe, huddled under some bush, waiting for the morning light to trot home, tail between legs. For a long time he couldn't sleep, but at last dropped off by telling himself that if he did so he would be wakened by the soft pad of Jess's feet on the stairs, the thump and lurch as she sprang onto the bed.

He woke. There was no Jess. Cold seemed to have settled in his stomach and his feet. He pulled on some warm clothes and went out into the piercing early morning. Almost no one was about on the hill. He met another watchman and gave him Jess's description too, and this one took out his notebook and wrote it down. Now Jess was officially missing. As he walked slowly home again to swallow a cup of coffee before leaving for work, he had a very complete image of Jess in last night's darkness, not huddled beneath a bush, as in his earlier fancy, but looking for her way home, running head down right into the path of a lorry.

The police would know. Run-over dogs were supposed to be reported, weren't they? He gulped his coffee and rushed to call at the police station on his way to school. The young policeman was quite kind, said no accident of any sort had been reported in the area last night, and that dogs often turned up again as right as rain. They would call him at once if any lost dog answering to Jess's description were brought in. Once again he was illogically comforted, and once again the comfort evaporated ten minutes later. He told no one at school that she was missing. His boys thought that he hadn't brought her today because they had played up a bit last week when she was there.

That evening, realizing that he had had nothing but coffee for twenty-four hours, he forced himself to swallow a can of soup before setting out again for the hill. He convinced himself that she would reappear, racing down the wind toward him just as if today were yesterday. She didn't. When darkness drove him home again he rang the vet, who said had she been coming into heat by any chance?

"I didn't see any sign of it. But it's possible, isn't it? Particularly at this time of year." It wasn't likely; her last heat had been just before Christmas. But he seized on the hope, elaborating it in his mind. Of course, Jess would be ranging north London in a ferment of desire looking for a mate. Had found one, no doubt, if not several. But when her desire was satiated she would turn for home.

"She had her collar on, of course?" said the vet. "Well then. In another day or two she may very well come trotting in as cool as you please." He saw her doing it. He saw her constantly, whenever he closed his eyes. Only it just did not happen.

On Friday, after school, he met the black poodle owner on the heath and told her what had happened. She expressed concern and wondered if perhaps Jess had gone off on her own looking for those rabbit-haunted woods where she had so enjoyed herself the weekend before.

It was a long shot, but at least to drive out there passed the time and provided the illusion of doing something. But there once again in the empty copse he felt terribly alone, and the time when Jess had been his constant companion was already, in the space of a few days, beginning to acquire for him the fabulous quality of a lost golden era, such as youth or liberty.

On Sunday he busied himself by typing out a score of neat notices on cardboard, and going around the neighborhood fixing them to posts and trees. He also had cards posted at half a dozen local newsstands. "Missing since Tuesday 7 March, cocker spaniel bitch, 18 months, light brown color . . ." He thought humbly of the times when he himself had seen such notices and had not registered any particular sympathy. He had not understood what pain such a notice represented.

The woman at one newsstand was particularly kind, creasing her face and clicking her tongue. She'd lost her doggie four years ago, she said. Those people must be really wicked, mustn't they, to do such a thing and cause such unhappiness? He murmured some vague assent, and it was only after he left that he realized she had been referring to the possibility of Jess having been stolen, for one of several purposes.

The first person to mention the word laboratory to him was Wrighty, the fat old science master at school. Wrighty had a dog himself, a wheezing dachshund of great antiquity. It transpired that Wrighty had a morbid dread of his dog being stolen and subjected to nameless experiments, and had had it tattooed with a special number on the inside leg—"so that any lab would see it, and know this is someone's pet. All they have to do is return it to a certain address and there'll be no questions asked." Wrighty represented the business of stealing pets and selling them to laboratories for vivisection as a highly organized conspiracy.

"But, good heavens," said Tom, his heart quailing, "surely any lab would know that a dog like Jess isn't likely to be an unwanted stray?"

Wrighty shook his head dubiously. These people were pretty unscrupulous. Heartless—they'd have to be, wouldn't they? If they thought they could get away with it. . . .

When Tom got home that evening, after his usual painful session of calling and whistling on the hill, he sat down and concocted a careful letter for circulation to laboratories. After describing Jess, he wrote that he was not interested in legal proceedings, that he simply wanted her back—"and so does my little boy, who is crying for her." He was normally a truthful man, but this lie seemed to flow naturally from him without making the smallest dent in his conscience. The truth, "*I* am crying for her, every night," would have been impossible to write. At school, he waited till the secretary had gone home and then worked the duplicating machine himself. He ran off four hundred copies. Then he went down to central London to an antivivisectionist league whom he had rung earlier in the day, and picked up from them a list of laboratories.

For the next week all his spare time was spent addressing envelopes. When he carted yet another basketful to the post-office box, he almost felt as if all those letters dispatched represented something achieved. Surely such endeavor should eventually produce some result?

Sooner than he expected, the replies began to come. After the first few he no longer opened them with much hope, but he still opened them. Some were mere formal notes, regretting to inform him. Others seemed to have a slightly indignant note: "Would wish to assure you that this laboratory never purchases animals from dealers. . . ." Others wrote with kindness and concern. Sometimes the letter would be from the top man himself: "Wanted to let you know without delay that we are, alas, unable to help you in your search. . . . Do hope most sincerely that it may prove fruitful . . . quite understand what you and your family must be going through." One lab even sent a multicolor ballpoint pen stamped with their name "as a small gift for your little boy. I know how hard such an experience must hit a child. . . ." The pen could write both red and blue according to how you twisted it, so he used it for marking school papers.

He ate little, moved abstractedly through the days, working the minimum, vague and testy when anyone spoke to him. He experienced pains in his stomach and supposed that these must be due to his continual tension. For he was constantly on the alert, listening. In counterbalance to his lethargic body his hearing seemed to have become abnormally acute. He heard, even from up in the bathroom, the soft chink and flap of a letter arriving, or the tiny vibration the phone made before it began to ring. And every time a dog barked, he started to his feet, listening intently.

All this awareness made him very tired. At night, his loneliness was soon blotted out in an exhausted sleep. In sleep, she was waiting for him. She leaped onto the bed and licked his face so that he started up crying, "Jess—at last—" And then he awoke. She came running up the small garden to him and he knew beyond any doubt that all the last two weeks had been a bad dream, nothing more. And then he awoke. He caressed her smooth head, played with her collar, told a friend how he had had this frightful, damn stupid dream about losing her. . . . And then he awoke.

When term ended he knew that he could have held out for only a very few more days. The world of narrowed intensity in which he was living was almost incompatible with ordinary existence. In any case, he had just inserted advertisements in several papers, both local and national—cursing himself for not having thought of this before. He needed all his time for driving out to inaccessible points on the perimeter of London, various places where a trickle of telephone callers were all sure that they had seen Jess. In response to one call he even went to see a dog in Gloucestershire. But it turned out to be brown and white, and not a bitch, anyway. By and by there were no more phone calls. But he still continued every day, driving around London, its suburbs, and the country beyond, skidding to sudden stops a few times when an arching back or a plumy tail bobbing by convinced him for half a second that it was her.

It was at the fourth or fifth of these sudden stops that a heavy lorry ran into the back of him. It had been entirely his fault. A crowd gathered and the clamorously competing sirens of police and ambulance vehicles seemed to fill the air. The steering wheel was pressed into his chest, the door had buckled in on him, and they had to cut the metal away to get him out. Quite soon he was in hospital and likely to be there, he realized, for a good long while. Really, what with the way he had been feeling, it seemed the best place for him at the moment. He even wondered, between the waves of morphine and the intermittent stabs of pain, if he had had the accident on purpose to get himself here.

Over the next six weeks his body gradually repaired itself, and after the hospital they sent him to a convalescent home for a month, near Brighton. He played chess and chatted and was gently bored and went for rather careful walks along the shore. By the time he was fit for work again, the summer term was the best part over. The head, who had visited him in Brighton, said, "Don't think of getting back into harness till September, old man—I'll make it okay with the office. Why don't you pop off abroad or somewhere on a really nice long holiday?"

As a matter of fact that was just what he intended. He'd made a good friend in the convalescent home—chap called Jo, in a wheelchair now, he'd never be able to get back into harness himself, but he was getting a pension from his firm and had just had a good fat sum in compensation. Jo was an old hand at foreign travel and was looking for someone to team up with this summer on a trip to Italy—someone to push the wheelchair and so on.

Tom agreed with alacrity to Jo's proposal. It would be grand to have a really long trip abroad without worrying too much about the expense, and to feel at the same time that he was doing someone else a good turn.

He went back home for a few days first, just to make sure everything was all right and to arrange about having letters forwarded. The house felt oddly unfamiliar. Mightn't it be better for him to get some smaller place, a flat perhaps? He might even think of teaming up with someone. . . . Maybe with Jo, if this summer's trip went well.

He was on his way out for the evening when the phone rang.

"It's about your dog," said a woman's voice. "See, we've just seen the bit in the paper, an old bit of paper that was round the shopping."

With the greatest reluctance he asked, after a pause, "Where do you live?"

"'Ounslow. Well, we found her by the edge of the M4, see, and we did put a notice in the pet shop at the time, but no one claimed her."

"When was this?"

"March. She's a brown cocker spaniel, see—just like it says."

With a sinking heart he heard himself say, "I'll be over first thing tomorrow morning. No—not first thing, because I'll have to come by public transport, I've just remembered. But I'll be there by eleven. If you'd just give me your address . . ."

A Tudor villa in a run-down residential district. Too near the motorway now, probably, for comfort; he could hear the continuous sound of the unseen traffic as he stood by the gate. A bald lawn with a broken bicycle. A heavy motorbike parked by the front door. Milk bottles on the step and a banging window. When he rang the bell, barking began, and he turned his head sharply, but it was only two collies, who rounded the corner from the back of the house and bore down on him. Behind them came a boy of about ten in shrunk jeans and heavy boots. He stopped short on seeing Tom and retreated, shouting, "Mum. *Mu-um*." He had known before she appeared that Mum would be a blowsy woman with slippers and bare legs, and he was right. "Oh come in do," she said. "Just step over—yes, that's right. Do excuse the mess, won't you, we're a bit upside down. Trev—my husband, that is, and my eldest boy—they're doing a bit of decorating, see."

The littered hall smelled strongly of dog. He felt confused. He was straining his ears for a known bark, a known scutter of feet on the floor. And yet this was not like it had been before. The intensity, the sense of personal effort and involvement, were lacking. He felt disoriented, as if he were playing a part. Playing himself, perhaps, of months ago. Was it really so long? Yes. Time had passed—in hospital, at Brighton. Nothing, it seemed, had remained exactly the same.

They went through the messy kitchen and out into a squalid back-yard. "There," said the woman, pointing, "there tied up by the fence."

The dog had been whining and snuffling as they emerged from the kitchen. Now she let forth a spate of high-pitched barking that did not stop.

"There," said the woman fatuously, "she seems to know you, doesn't she?"

"She barks at everyone like that," said a man who had just joined them from nowhere, adding dourly to Tom, "In heat, she is. Goes on like that at everyone just now. That's why she's tied up."

Brown. Indubitably the same breed as Jess. Much heavier, and in need of a bath. Fat, foolish, barking hysterically. Limping a bit, he noticed. A hind leg.

"Yeah, she was like that when we found her," said the man. "Lame, I mean. Was she before?"

"No. Mine isn't. Wasn't . . . I mean . . . ." Trying to collect his slithering thoughts, he said, "Did she have a collar on?"

"No. Reckon someone pinched it, maybe. Pinched her, perhaps, and then couldn't keep her. Wouldn't wonder—right nuisance, she is, even when she isn't in season."

Swallowing, Tom stepped forward, caressed her head. She fawned on him, trying to rub herself against him. Then she turned her attention with equal enthusiasm to the boy.

For something to say, he said, "It's funny that the police never connected her with my description. . . . You did say you'd reported her to them, didn't you?"

"That's right," said the woman. "The kid went down there to tell 'em. . . . Didn't you, Kev?"

They all looked at him. He looked away. Abruptly his mother cried, "Kev—*did you?*"

"I meant to," he said sullenly.

His mother hit out at him with perfunctory aim. He dodged and began to whine. "I did mean to, Mum. I jus' forgot. . . ."

"Forgot. I'll see you don't forget another time," said his father grimly, as if it were no surprise to him, and the whole family were simply going through some sort of charade for the visitor's benefit.

"I'm ever so sorry," said the woman, turning to Tom with fulsome insincerity. "I did think he 'ad. I *told* him to, but you know what boys are, and this one's potty on dogs."

Tom went on staring at the dog as she squirmed before them in an ecstasy of undirected anticipation. It *could* be Jess. She was the right color and size, and the changes *could* be accounted for by the lapse of time, by idiotic overfeeding, by several things. . . . He had thought once he would know Jess out of millions. He had carried an image of her in his heart for weeks; every time he had closed his eyes for a second she had been there, gamboling behind his aching lids, flying, ears flapping, down the wind on the hill. . . . But perhaps that was the trouble. He had carried this image with him for so long that the picture had begun to wear itself out, like a film incessantly being run. And he had become confused. The Jess he was now trying desperately to recall was not perhaps even the real, original Jess but Jess at second hand, the quintessential, ideal, golden Jess, the shadow he had pursued with such desire and pain. That shadow had gone, suddenly and completely, at the moment when the lorry had rammed into the back of his car. She had not accompanied him in the ambulance to hospital, had never visited him there. It was as if the accident that had miraculously spared him for a further extension of life had killed her, for good.

The noisy, indiscriminate, flesh-and-blood spaniel before him now seemed to have nothing to do with the golden shadow, or with the dead past at all. It might well be Jess, he told himself again; he didn't think so, but it was possible. . . . He simply did not know. What's more, he felt that he would never know. He knew in that moment that he wanted absolute certainty; no second best would do.

Perhaps, even if this dog were not Jess, sufficient love and effort could transform her into a living image of the original. Perhaps. But so much of his love and effort had been expended in the search for her that he felt he had not that much to offer anymore. An intensity within himself was worn out too. And, in any case, with Jess or any other dog on his hands, he would not be able to go abroad with Jo. He was particularly unwilling to let Jo down.

Turning to the boy, he said, "So you're fond of dogs? You fond of this one now? Is that why you didn't want to report her to the police?"

The child nodded wordlessly, one eye on his mother. Perhaps he was afraid of her. It wasn't a very convincing nod. But Tom decided to take it for what it was. He faced the parents squarely. "It's not my dog," he said.

Their faces fell. But they looked resigned. Perhaps they had really expected this. "Oh. Not yours, then?"

"No. Not mine." And he added, not just politely but as if apologizing for himself, "I'm sorry. . . . But there it is."

THE MOUSE
SAKI (H. H. MUNRO)

Theodoric Voler had been brought up, from infancy to the confines of middle age, by a fond mother whose chief solicitude had been to keep him screened from what she called the coarser realities of life. When she died she left Theodoric alone in a world that was as real as ever, and a good deal coarser than he considered it had any need to be. To a man of his temperament and upbringing even a simple railway journey was crammed with petty annoyances and minor discords, and as he settled himself down in a second-class compartment one September morning he was conscious of ruffled feelings and general mental discomposure. He had been staying at a country vicarage, the inmates of which had been certainly neither brutal nor bacchanalian, but their supervision of the domestic establishment had been of that lax order which invites disaster. The pony carriage that was to take him to the station had never been properly ordered, and when the moment for his departure drew near, the handyman who should have produced the required article was nowhere to be found. In this emergency Theodoric, to his mute but very intense disgust, found himself obliged to collaborate with the vicar's daughter in the task of harnessing the pony, which necessitated groping about in an ill-lighted outbuilding called a stable, and smelling very like one—except in patches where it smelled of mice. Without being actually afraid of mice, Theodoric classed them among the coarser incidents of life, and considered that Providence, with a little exercise of moral courage, might long ago have recognized that they were not indispensable, and have withdrawn them from circulation. As the train glided out of the station Theodoric's nervous imagination accused himself of exhaling a weak odor of stable yard, and possibly of displaying a moldy straw or two on his usually well-brushed garments. Fortunately the only other occupant of the compartment, a lady of about the same age as himself, seemed inclined for slumber rather than scrutiny; the train was not due to stop till the terminus was reached, in about an hour's time, and the carriage was of the old-fashioned sort that held no communication with a corridor, therefore no further traveling companions were likely to intrude on Theodoric's semiprivacy. And yet the train had scarcely attained its normal speed before he became reluctantly but vividly aware that he was not alone with the slumbering lady; he was not even alone in his own clothes. A warm, creeping movement over his flesh betrayed the unwelcome and highly resented presence, unseen but poignant, of a strayed mouse, that had evidently dashed into its present retreat during the episode of the pony harnessing. Furtive stamps and shakes and wildly directed pinches failed to dislodge the intruder, whose motto, indeed, seemed to be Excelsior; and the lawful occupant of the clothes lay back against the cushions and endeavored rapidly to evolve some means for putting an end to the dual ownership. It was unthinkable that he should continue for the space of a whole hour in the horrible position of a Rowton House for vagrant mice (already his imagination had at least doubled the numbers of the alien invasion). On the other hand, nothing less drastic than partial disrobing would ease him of his tormentor, and to undress in the presence of a lady, even for so laudable a purpose, was an idea that made his ear tips tingle in a blush of abject shame. He had never been able to bring himself even to the mild exposure of openwork socks in the presence of the fair sex. And yet—the lady in this case was to all appearances soundly and securely asleep; the mouse, on the other hand, seemed to be trying to crowd a *Wanderjahr* into a few strenuous minutes. If there is any truth in the theory of transmigration, this particular mouse must certainly have been in a former state a member of the Alpine Club. Sometimes in its eagerness it lost its footing and slipped for half an inch or so, and then, in fright, or more probably temper, it bit. Theodoric was goaded into the most audacious undertaking of his life. Crimsoning to the hue of a beetroot and keeping an agonized watch on his slumbering fellow traveler, he swiftly and noiselessly secured the ends of his railway rug to the racks on either side of the carriage, so that a substantial curtain hung athwart the compartment. In the narrow dressing room that he had thus improvised he proceeded with violent haste to extricate himself partially and the mouse entirely from the surrounding casings of tweed and half-wool. As the unraveled mouse gave a wild leap to the floor, the rug, slipping its fastening at either end, also came down with a heart-curdling flop, and almost simultaneously the awakened sleeper opened her eyes. With a movement almost quicker than the mouse's, Theodoric pounced on the rug and hauled its ample folds chin-high over his dismantled person as he collapsed into the farther corner of the carriage. The blood raced and beat in the veins of his neck and forehead, while he waited dumbly for the communication cord to be pulled. The lady, however, contented herself with a silent stare at her strangely muffled companion. How much had she seen, Theodoric queried to himself, and in any case what on earth must she think of his present posture?

"I think I have caught a chill," he ventured desperately.

"Really, I'm sorry," she replied. "I was just going to ask you if you would open this window."

"I fancy it's malaria," he added, his teeth chattering slightly, as much from fright as from a desire to support his theory.

"I've got some brandy in my holdall, if you'll kindly reach it down for me," said his companion.

"Not for worlds—I mean, I never take anything for it," he assured her earnestly.

"I suppose you caught it in the tropics?"

Theodoric, whose acquaintance with the tropics was limited to an annual present of a chest of tea from an uncle in Ceylon, felt that even the malaria was slipping from him. Would it be possible, he wondered, to disclose the real state of affairs to her in small installments?

"Are you afraid of mice?" he ventured, growing, if possible, more scarlet in the face.

"Not unless they came in quantities. Why do you ask?"

"I had one crawling inside my clothes just now," said Theodoric in a voice that hardly seemed his own. "It was a most awkward situation."

"It must have been, if you wear your clothes at all tight," she observed. "But mice have strange ideas of comfort."

"I had to get rid of it while you were asleep," he continued. Then, with a gulp, he added, "It was getting rid of it that brought me to—to this."

"Surely leaving off one small mouse wouldn't bring on a chill," she exclaimed, with a levity that Theodoric accounted abominable.

Evidently she had detected something of his predicament, and was enjoying his confusion. All the blood in his body seemed to have mobilized in one concentrated blush, and an agony of abasement, worse than a myriad mice, crept up and down over his soul. And then, as reflection began to assert itself, sheer terror took the place of humiliation. With every minute that passed the train was rushing nearer to the crowded and bustling terminus, where dozens of prying eyes would be exchanged for the one paralyzing pair that watched him from the farther corner of the carriage. There was one slender, despairing chance, which the next few minutes must decide. His fellow traveler might relapse into a blessed slumber. But as the minutes throbbed by that chance ebbed away. The furtive glance which Theodoric stole at her from time to time disclosed only an unwinking wakefulness.

"I think we must be getting near now," she presently observed.

Theodoric had already noted with growing terror the recurring stacks of small, ugly dwellings that heralded the journey's end. The words acted as a signal. Like a hunted beast breaking cover and dashing madly toward some other haven of momentary safety he threw aside his rug, and struggled frantically into his disheveled garments. He was conscious of dull suburban stations racing past the window, of a choking, hammering sensation in his throat and heart, and of an icy silence in that corner toward which he dared not look. Then as he sank back in his seat, clothed and almost delirious, the train slowed down to a final crawl, and the woman spoke.

"Would you be so kind," she asked, "as to get me a porter to put me into a cab? It's a shame to trouble you when you're feeling unwell, but being blind makes one so helpless at a railway station."

TICKETS, PLEASE
D. H. LAWRENCE

THERE IS IN THE Midlands a single-line tramway system which boldly leaves the county town and plunges off into the black, industrial countryside, uphill and downdale, through the long, ugly villages of workmen's houses, over canals and railways, past churches perched high and nobly over the smoke and shadows, through stark, grimy, cold little marketplaces, tilting away in a rush past cinemas and shops down to the hollow where the collieries are, then up again, past a little rural church, under the ash trees, on in a rush to the terminus, the last little ugly place of industry, the cold little town that shivers on the edge of the wild, gloomy country beyond. There the green and creamy-colored tramcar seems to pause and purr with curious satisfaction. But in a few minutes—the clock on the turret of the Cooperative Wholesale Society's Shops gives the time—away it starts once more on the adventure. Again there are the reckless swoops downhill, bouncing the loops; again the chilly wait in the hilltop marketplace; again the breathless slithering around the precipitous drop under the church; again the patient halts at the loops, waiting for the outcoming car; so on and on, for two long hours, till at last the city looms beyond the fat gasworks, the narrow factories draw near, we are in the sordid streets of the great town, once more we sidle to a standstill at our terminus, abashed by the great crimson and cream-colored city cars, but still perky, jaunty, somewhat daredevil, green as a jaunty sprig of parsley out of a black colliery garden.

To ride on these cars is always an adventure. Since we are in wartime, the drivers are men unfit for active service: cripples and hunchbacks. So they have the spirit of the devil in them. The ride becomes a steeple-chase. Hurray! We have leaped in a clear jump over the canal bridges—now for the four-lane corner. With a shriek and a trail of sparks we are clear again. To be sure, a tram often leaps the rails—but what matter! It sits in a ditch till other trams come to haul it out. It is quite common for a car, packed with one solid mass of living people, to come to a dead halt in the midst of unbroken blackness, the heart of nowhere on a dark night, and for the driver and the girl conductor to call, "All get off—car's on fire!" Instead, however, of rushing out in a panic, the passengers stolidly reply, "Get on—get on! We're not coming out. We're stopping where we are. Push on, George." So till flames actually appear.

The reason for this reluctance to dismount is that the nights are howlingly cold, black, and windswept, and a car is a haven of refuge. From village to village the miners travel, for a change of cinema, of girl, of pub. The trams are desperately packed. Who is going to risk himself in the black gulf outside, to wait perhaps an hour for another tram, then to see the forlorn notice DEPOT ONLY, because there is something wrong! Or to greet a unit of three bright cars all so tight with people that they sail past with a howl of derision. Trams that pass in the night.

This, the most dangerous tram service in England, as the authorities themselves declare with pride, is entirely conducted by girls, and driven by rash young men, a little crippled, or by delicate young men, who creep forward in terror. The girls are fearless young hussies. In their ugly blue uniform, skirts up to their knees, shapeless old peaked caps on their heads, they have all the sang-froid of an old noncommissioned officer. With a tram packed with howling colliers, roaring hymns downstairs and a sort of antiphony of obscenities upstairs, the lasses are perfectly at their ease. They pounce on the youths who try to evade their ticket machine. They push off the men at the end of their distance. They are not going to be done in the eye—not they. They fear nobody—and everybody fears them.

"Hello, Annie!"

"Hello, Ted!"

"Oh, mind my corn, Miss Stone. It's my belief you've got a heart of stone, for you've trod on it again."

"You should keep it in your pocket," replies Miss Stone, and she goes sturdily upstairs in her high boots.

"Tickets, please."

She is peremptory, suspicious, and ready to hit first. She can hold her own against ten thousand. The step of that tramcar is her Thermopylae.

Therefore, there is a certain wild romance aboard these cars—and in the sturdy bosom of Annie herself. The time for soft romance is in the morning, between ten o'clock and one, when things are rather slack—that is, except market day and Saturday. Thus Annie has time to look about her. Then she often hops off her car and into a shop where she has spied something, while the driver chats in the main road. There is very good feeling between the girls and the drivers. Are they not companions in peril, shipments aboard this careering vessel of a tramcar, forever rocking on the waves of a stormy land?

Then, also, during the easy hours, the inspectors are most in evidence. For some reason, everybody employed in this tram service is young; there are no gray heads. It would not do. Therefore, the inspectors are of the right age, and one, the chief, is also good-looking. See him stand on a wet, gloomy morning, in his long oilskin, his peaked cap well down over his eyes, waiting to board a car. His face is ruddy, his small brown mustache is weathered, he has a faint impudent smile. Fairly tall and agile, even in his waterproof, he springs aboard a car and greets Annie.

"Hello, Annie! Keeping the wet out?"

"Trying to."

There are only two people in the car. Inspecting is soon over. Then for a long and impudent chat on the footboard, a good, easy, twelve-mile chat.

The inspector's name is John Thomas Raynor—always called John Thomas, except sometimes, in malice, Coddy. His face sets in fury when he is addressed, from a distance, with this abbreviation. There is considerable scandal about John Thomas in a half dozen villages. He flirts with the girl conductors in the morning, and walks out with them in the dark night when they leave their tramcar at the depot. Of course, the girls quit the service frequently. Then he flirts and walks out with the newcomer, always providing she is sufficiently attractive, and that she will consent to walk. It is remarkable, however, that most of the girls are quite comely, they are all young, and this roving life aboard the car gives them a sailor's dash and recklessness. What matter how they behave when the ship is in port? Tomorrow they will be aboard again.

Annie, however, was something of a tartar, and her sharp tongue had kept John Thomas at arm's length for many months. Perhaps, therefore, she liked him all the more, for he always came up smiling, with impudence. She watched him vanquish one girl, then another. She could tell by the movement of his mouth and eyes, when he flirted with her in the morning, that he had been walking out with this lass, or the other, the night before. A fine cock of the walk he was. She could sum him up pretty well.

In this subtle antagonism they knew each other like old friends; they were as shrewd with one another almost as man and wife. But Annie had always kept him sufficiently at arm's length. Besides, she had a boy of her own.

The Statutes fair, however, came in November, at Bestwood. It happened that Annie had the Monday night off. It was a drizzling, ugly night, yet she dressed herself up and went to the fairground. She was alone, but she expected soon to find a pal of some sort.

The roundabouts were veering around and grinding out their music, the sideshows were making as much commotion as possible. In the coconut shies there were no coconuts, but artificial wartime substitutes, which the lads declared were fastened into the irons. There was a sad decline in brilliance and luxury. Nonetheless, the ground was muddy as ever, there was the same crush, the press of faces lighted up by the flares and the electric lights, the same smell of naphtha and a few fried potatoes, and of electricity.

Who should be the first to greet Miss Annie, on the show ground, but John Thomas. He had a black overcoat buttoned up to his chin, and a tweed cap pulled down over his brows; his face between was ruddy and smiling and handy as ever. She knew so well the way his mouth moved.

She was very glad to have a "boy." To be at the Statutes without a fellow was no fun. Instantly, like the gallant he was, he took her on the

Dragons, grim-toothed, roundabout switchbacks. It was not nearly so exciting as a tramcar actually. But, then, to be seated in a shaking green dragon, uplifted above the sea of bubble faces, careering in a rickety fashion in the lower heavens while John Thomas leaned over her, his cigarette in his mouth, was after all the right style. She was a plump, quick, alive little creature. So she was quite excited and happy.

John Thomas made her stay on for the next round. And therefore she could hardly for shame repulse him when he put his arm around her and drew her a little nearer to him, in a very warm and cuddly manner. Besides, he was fairly discreet; he kept his movement as hidden as possible. She looked down, and saw that his red, clean hand was out of sight of the crowd. And they knew each other so well. So they warmed up to the fair.

After the dragons they went on the horses. John Thomas paid each time, so she could but be complaisant. He, of course, sat astride on the outer horse—named Black Bess—and she sat sideways, toward him, on the inner horse—named Wildfire. But of course John Thomas was not going to sit discreetly on Black Bess, holding the brass bar. Around they spun and heaved, in the light. And around he swung on his wooden steed, flinging one leg across her mount and perilously tipping up and down across the space, half lying back, laughing at her. He was perfectly happy; she was afraid her hat was on one side, but she was excited.

He threw quoits on a table, and won for her two large, pale blue hatpins. And then, hearing the noise of the cinemas announcing another performance, they climbed the boards and went in.

Of course, during these performances pitch-darkness falls from time to time, when the machine goes wrong. Then there is a wild whooping, and a loud smacking of simulated kisses. In these moments John Thomas drew Annie toward him. After all, he had a wonderfully warm, cozy way of holding a girl with his arm, he seemed to make such a nice fit. And after all, it was pleasant to be so held, so very comforting and cozy and nice. He leaned over her and she felt his breath on her hair; she knew he wanted to kiss her on the lips. And after all, he was so warm and she fitted into him so softly. After all, she wanted him to touch her lips.

But the light sprang up; she also started electrically, and put her hat straight. He left his arm lying nonchalantly behind her. Well, it was fun, it was exciting to be at the Statutes with John Thomas.

When the cinema was over they went for a walk across the dark, damp fields. He had all the arts of lovemaking. He was especially good at holding a girl, when he sat with her on a stile in the black, drizzling darkness. He seemed to be holding her in space, against his own warmth and gratification. And his kisses were soft and slow and searching.

So Annie walked out with John Thomas, though she kept her own boy dangling in the distance. Some of the tram girls chose to be huffy. But, there, you must take things as you find them in this life.

There was no mistake about it, Annie liked John Thomas a good deal. She felt so rich and warm in herself whenever he was near. And John Thomas really liked Annie, more than usual. The soft, melting way in which she could flow into a fellow, as if she melted into his very bones, was something rare and good. He fully appreciated this.

But with a developing acquaintance there began a developing intimacy. Annie wanted to consider him a person, a man; she wanted to take an intelligent interest in him, and to have an intelligent response. She did not want a mere nocturnal presence, which was what he was so far. And she prided herself that he could not leave her.

Here she made a mistake. John Thomas intended to remain a nocturnal presence; he had no idea of becoming an all-around individual to her. When she started to take an intelligent interest in him and his life and his character, he sheered off. He hated intelligent interest. And he knew that the only way to stop it was to avoid it. The possessive female was aroused in Annie. So he left her.

It is no use saying she was not surprised. She was at first startled, thrown out of her count. For she had been so *very* sure of holding him. For a while she was staggered, and everything became uncertain to her. Then she wept with fury, indignation, desolation, and misery. Then she had a spasm of despair. And then, when he came, still impudently, onto her car, still familiar, but letting her see by the movement of his head that he had gone away to somebody else for the time being and was enjoying pastures new, then she determined to have her own back.

She had a very shrewd idea what girls John Thomas had taken out.

She went to Nora Purdy. Nora was a tall, rather pale, but well-built girl, with beautiful yellow hair. She was rather secretive.

"Hey!" said Annie, accosting her; then softly, "Who's John Thomas on with now?"

"I don't know," said Nora.

"Why tha does," said Annie, ironically lapsing into dialect. "Tha knows as well as I do."

"Well, I do, then," said Nora. "It isn't me, so don't bother."

"It's Cissy Meakin, isn't it?"

"It is, for all I know."

"Hasn't he got a face on him!" said Annie. "I don't half like his cheek. I could knock him off the footboard when he comes round at me."

"He'll get dropped on one of these days," said Nora.

"Aye, he will when somebody makes up their mind to drop it on him. I should like to see him taken down a peg or two, shouldn't you?"

"I shouldn't mind," said Nora.

"You've got quite as much cause to as I have," said Annie. "But we'll drop on him one of these days, my girl. What? Don't you want to?"

"I don't mind," said Nora.

But as a matter of fact, Nora was much more vindictive than Annie.

One by one Annie went the round of the old flames. It so happened that Cissy Meakin left the tramway service in quite a short time. Her mother made her leave. Then John Thomas was on the qui vive. He cast his eyes over his old flock. And his eyes lighted on Annie. He thought she would be safe now. Besides, he liked her.

She arranged to walk home with him on Sunday night. It so happened that her car would be in the depot at half past nine: the last car would come in at ten fifteen. So John Thomas was to wait for her there.

At the depot the girls had a little waiting room of their own. It was quite rough, but cozy, with a fire and an oven and a mirror, and table and wooden chairs. The half dozen girls who knew John Thomas only too well had arranged to take service this Sunday afternoon. So, as the cars began to come in early, the girls dropped into the waiting room. And instead of hurrying off home, they sat around the fire and had a cup of tea. Outside was the darkness and lawlessness of wartime.

John Thomas came on the car after Annie, at about a quarter to ten. He poked his head easily into the girls' waiting room.

"Prayer meeting?" he asked.

"Aye," said Laura Sharp. "Ladies only."

"That's me!" said John Thomas. It was one of his favorite exclamations.

"Shut the door, boy," said Muriel Baggaley.

"On which side of me?" said John Thomas.

"Which tha likes," said Polly Birkin.

He had come in and closed the door behind him. The girls moved in their circle, to make a place for him near the fire. He took off his greatcoat and pushed back his hat.

"Who handles the teapot?" he said.

Nora Purdy silently poured him out a cup of tea.

"Want a bit o' my bread and drippin'?" said Muriel Baggaley to him.

"Aye, give us a bit."

And he began to eat his piece of bread.

"There's no place like home, girls," he said.

They all looked at him as he uttered this piece of impudence. He seemed to be sunning himself in the presence of so many damsels.

"Especially if you're not afraid to go home in the dark," said Laura Sharp.

"Me! By myself I am."

They sat till they heard the last tram come in. In a few minutes Emma Houselay entered.

"Come on, my old duck!" cried Polly Birkin.

"It *is* perishing," said Emma, holding her fingers to the fire.

"But—*I'm afraid to—go home in—the dark*," sang Laura Sharp, the tune having got into her mind.

"Who're you going with tonight, John Thomas?" asked Muriel Baggaley coolly.

"Tonight?" said John Thomas. "Oh, I'm going home by myself tonight—all on my lonely-o."

"That's me!" said Nora Purdy, using his own ejaculation.

The girls laughed shrilly.

"Me as well, Nora," said John Thomas.

"Don't know what you mean," said Laura.

"Yes, I'm toddling," said he, rising and reaching for his overcoat.

"Nay," said Polly. "We're all here waiting for you."

"We've got to be up in good time in the morning," he said, in the benevolent official manner.

They all laughed.

"Nay," said Muriel. "Don't leave us all lonely, John Thomas. Take one!"

"I'll take the lot, if you like," he responded gallantly.

"That you won't, either," said Muriel. "Two's company; seven's too much of a good thing."

"Nay—take one," said Laura. "Fair and square, all aboveboard, and say which."

"Aye," cried Annie, speaking for the first time. "Pick, John Thomas; let's hear thee."

"Nay," he said. "I'm going home quiet tonight. Feeling good, for once."

"Whereabouts?" said Annie. "Take a good un, then. But tha's got to take one of us!"

"Nay, how can I take one?" he said, laughing uneasily. "I don't want to make enemies."

"You'd only make *one*," said Annie.

"The chosen *one*," added Laura.

"Oh, my! Who said girls!" exclaimed John Thomas, again turning, as if to escape. "Well—good night."

"Nay, you've got to make your pick," said Muriel. "Turn your face to the wall, and say which one touches you. Go on—we shall only just touch your back—one of us. Go on—turn your face to the wall, and don't look, and say which one touches you."

He was uneasy, mistrusting them. Yet he had not the courage to break away. They pushed him to a wall and stood him there with his face to it. Behind his back they all grimaced, tittering. He looked so comical. He looked around uneasily.

"Go on!" he cried.

"You're looking—you're looking!" they shouted.

He turned his head away. And suddenly, with a movement like a swift cat, Annie went forward and fetched him a box on the side of the head that sent his cap flying and himself staggering. He started around.

But at Annie's signal they all flew at him, slapping him, pinching him, pulling his hair, though more in fun than in spite or anger. He, however, saw red. His blue eyes flamed with strange fear as well as fury, and he butted through the girls to the door. It was locked. He wrenched at it. Roused, alert, the girls stood around and looked at him. He faced them, at bay. At that moment they were rather horrifying to him as they stood in their short uniforms. He was distinctly afraid.

"Come on, John Thomas! Come on! Choose!" said Annie.

"What are you after? Open the door," he said.

"We shan't—not till you've chosen!" said Muriel.

"Chosen what?" he said.

"Chosen the one you're going to marry," she replied.

He hesitated a moment.

"Open the blasted door," he said, "and get back to your senses." He spoke with official authority.

"You've got to choose!" cried the girls.

"Come on!" cried Annie, looking him in the eye. "Come on! Come on!"

He went forward, rather vaguely. She had taken off her belt, and swinging it, she fetched him a sharp blow over the head with the buckle end. He sprang and seized her. But immediately the other girls rushed upon him, pulling and tearing and beating him. Their blood was now thoroughly up. He was their sport now. They were going to have their own back, out of him. Strange, wild creatures, they hung on him and rushed at him to bear him down. His tunic was torn right up the back; Nora had hold at the back of his collar and was actually strangling him. Luckily the button burst. He struggled in a wild frenzy of fury and terror, almost mad terror. His tunic was simply torn off his back, his shirt sleeves were torn away, his arms were naked. The girls rushed at him, clenched their hands on him and pulled at him; or they rushed at him and pushed him, butted him with all their might; or they struck him wild blows. He ducked and cringed and struck sideways. They became more intense.

At last he was down. They rushed on him, kneeling on him. He had neither breath nor strength to move. His face was bleeding with a long scratch, his brow was bruised.

Annie knelt on him, the other girls knelt and hung on to him. Their faces were flushed, their hair wild, their eyes were all glittering strangely. He lay at last quite still, with face averted, as an animal lies when it is defeated and at the mercy of the captor. Sometimes his eye glanced back at the wild faces of the girls. His breast rose heavily, his wrists were torn.

"Now, then, my fellow!" gasped Annie at length. "Now then—now—"

At the sound of her terrifying, cold triumph, he suddenly started to struggle as an animal might, but the girls threw themselves upon him with unnatural strength and power, forcing him down.

"Yes—now, then!" gasped Annie at length.

And there was a dead silence, in which the thud of heartbeating was to be heard. It was a suspense of pure silence in every soul.

"Now you know where you are," said Annie.

The sight of his white, bare arm maddened the girls. He lay in a kind of trance of fear and antagonism. They felt themselves filled with supernatural strength.

Suddenly Polly started to laugh—to giggle wildly—helplessly—and Emma and Muriel joined in. But Annie and Nora and Laura remained the same, tense, watchful, with gleaming eyes. He winced away from these eyes.

"Yes," said Annie, in a curious low tone, secret and deadly. "Yes! You've got it now! You know what you've done, don't you? You know what you've done."

He made no sound nor sign, but lay with bright, averted eyes and averted, bleeding face.

"You ought to be *killed*, that's what you ought," said Annie tensely. "You ought to be *killed*." And there was a terrifying lust in her voice.

Polly was ceasing to laugh, and giving long-drawn oh-h-hs and sighs as she came to herself.

"He's got to choose," she said vaguely.

"Oh, yes, he has," said Laura, with vindictive decision.

"Do you hear—do you hear?" said Annie. And with a sharp movement that made him wince, she turned his face to her.

"Do you hear?" she repeated, shaking him.

But he was quite dumb. She fetched him a sharp slap on the face. He started, and his eyes widened. Then his face darkened with defiance, after all.

"Do you hear?" she repeated.

He only looked at her with hostile eyes.

"Speak!" she said, putting her face devilishly near his.

"What?" he said, almost overcome.

"You've got to *choose!*" she cried, as if it were some terrible menace, and as if it hurt her that she could not exact more.

"What?" he said, in fear.

"Choose your girl, Coddy. You've got to choose her now. And you'll get your neck broken if you play any more of your tricks, my boy. You're settled now."

There was a pause. Again he averted his face. He was cunning in his overthrow. He did not give in to them really—no, not if they tore him to bits.

"All right, then," he said. "I choose Annie." His voice was strange and full of malice. Annie let go of him as if he had been a hot coal.

"He's chosen Annie!" said the girls in chorus.

"Me!" cried Annie. She was still kneeling, but away from him. He was still lying prostrate, with averted face. The girls grouped uneasily around.

"Me!" repeated Annie, with a terrible, bitter accent.

Then she got up, drawing away from him with strange disgust and bitterness.

"I wouldn't touch him," she said.

But her face quivered with a kind of agony; she seemed as if she would fall. The other girls turned aside. He remained lying on the floor, with his torn clothes and bleeding, averted face.

"Oh, if he's chosen—" said Polly.

"I don't want him—he can choose again," said Annie, with the same rather bitter hopelessness.

"Get up," said Polly, lifting his shoulder. "Get up."

He rose slowly, a strange, ragged, dazed creature. The girls eyed him from a distance, curiously, furtively, dangerously.

"Who wants him?" cried Laura roughly.

"Nobody," they answered with contempt. Yet each one of them waited for him to look at her, hoped he would look at her. All except Annie, and something was broken in her.

He, however, kept his face closed and averted from them all. There was a silence of the end. He picked up the torn pieces of his tunic, without knowing what to do with them. The girls stood about uneasily, flushed, panting, tidying their hair and their dress unconsciously, and watching him. He looked at none of them. He espied his cap in a corner, and went and picked it up. He put it on his head, and one of the girls burst into a shrill, hysteric laugh at the sight he presented. He, however, took no heed, but went straight to where his overcoat hung on a peg. The girls moved away from contact with him, as if he had been an electric wire. He put on his coat and buttoned it down. Then he rolled his tunic rags into a bundle and stood before the locked door, dumbly.

"Open the door, somebody," said Laura.

"Annie's got the key," said one.

Annie silently offered the key to the girls. Nora unlocked the door.

"Tit for tat, old man," she said. "Show yourself a man, and don't bear a grudge."

But without a word or sign he had opened the door and gone, his face closed, his head dropped.

"That'll learn him," said Laura.

"Coddy!" said Nora.

"Shut up, for God's sake!" cried Annie fiercely, as if in torture.

"Well, I'm about ready to go, Polly. Look sharp!" said Muriel.

The girls were all anxious to be off. They were tidying themselves hurriedly, with mute, stupefied faces.

THE COUNTRY OF
THE BLIND
H. G. WELLS

THREE HUNDRED MILES and more from Ecuador's Chimborazo, in the wildest wastes of the Andes, there lies that mysterious mountain valley, cut off from the world of men, the Country of the Blind. Long years ago that valley lay so far open to the world that men might come at last through frightful gorges and over an icy pass into its equable meadows; and thither indeed men came, a family or so of Peruvian half-breeds fleeing the tyranny of an evil Spanish ruler. Then came the stupendous eruption of Mindobamba. Everywhere along the Pacific slopes there were swift thawings and sudden floods, and one whole side of the old Arauca crest came down in thunder and cut off the Country of the Blind forever from the exploring feet of men.

But one of these early settlers had chanced to be on the hither side of the gorges when the world had so terribly shaken itself, and, of necessity, he had to forget his wife and his child and all the possessions he had left up there, and start life over again in the lower world. This he did, and the story he told begot a legend that lingers along the length of the Andes to this day.

He told of his reason for venturing back from that fastness into which he had first been carried as a child. The valley, he said, had in it all that the heart of man could desire—sweet water, pasture, an even climate. On one side great hanging forests of pine held the avalanches high. Far overhead, on three sides, vast cliffs of gray-green rock were capped by cliffs of ice; but the glacier stream came not to the valley side but flowed away by the farther slopes. In this valley it neither rained nor snowed, but the abundant springs gave a rich green pasture. The settlers did well indeed there. Yet one thing marred their happiness. A strange disease had come upon them, and had made all the children born to them there—and several older children also—blind. It was to seek some charm or antidote against this plague of blindness that this young mountaineer had with danger and difficulty ventured down the gorge.

In those days men did not think of germs and infections but of sins; and it seemed to him that the reason for this affliction must lie in the negligence of these priestless immigrants to set up a shrine as soon as they entered the valley. Poor stray from that remoteness! I can picture him seeking to return with pious remedies against that trouble, and the infinite dismay with which he must have faced the tumbled vastness where the gorge had once come out.

As the years passed, the disease ran its course through that isolated and forgotten valley. The adults became groping and dim-sighted, and the children that were born to them saw never at all. But life was very easy in that snow-rimmed basin, lost to all the world, with no evil insects nor any beasts save the gentle descendants of llamas with which they had come. The eyes of the seeing had become clouded so gradually that they scarcely noted their loss. They guided the blind youngsters until they knew the whole valley marvelously, and when at last sight died out among them the race lived on. As generation followed generation, they forgot many things; they devised many things. In all things save sight they were strong and able, and the little community grew in numbers and in understanding.

There came a time when a child was born who was fifteen generations from that ancestor who went out of the valley to seek God's aid, and who never returned. Thereabouts it chanced that a man came into this community from the outer world. And this is the story of that man.

He was Nuñez, a mountaineer from the country near Quito, a man who had seen the world, a reader of books, an enterprising man, and he was taken on by a party of Englishmen who had come to Ecuador to climb mountains. With them he climbed here and he climbed there; then they attempted Parascotopetl, the Matterhorn of the Andes. At the foot of the last and greatest precipice they were building a night shelter amid the snow upon a little shelf of rock when they realized that Nuñez had gone from them. They shouted, and there was no reply; for the rest of that night they slept no more.

As the morning broke they saw the traces of his fall. He had slipped eastward toward the unknown side of the mountain; far below he had struck a steep slope of snow and plowed his way down it in the midst of an avalanche. His track went straight to the edge of a frightful precipice, and beyond that everything was hidden. Far, far below, and hazy with distance, they could see trees rising out of a narrow, shut-in valley. Unnerved by this disaster, they abandoned their attempt, and to this day Parascotopetl lifts an unconquered crest.

THE MAN WHO fell survived.

At the end of the slope he fell a thousand feet and came down upon a snow slope even steeper than the one above. Down this he was whirled, stunned and insensible, but without a bone broken in his body; at last he came to gentler slopes, and rolled out and lay still, buried amid a softening heap of the snow that had accompanied him. He came to himself with a dim fancy that he was ill in bed; then realized his position and worked himself loose until he saw the stars.

For a while he lay, gazing blankly at that vast pale cliff towering above. After a great interval of time he became aware that he was near the lower edge of the snow. Below, down what was now a moonlit and practicable slope, he saw the dark and broken appearance of rock-strewn turf. He struggled to his feet, aching in every joint and limb, went downward until he was on the turf, and there dropped beside a boulder and instantly fell asleep.

He was awakened by the singing of birds in the trees far below.

He sat up and perceived he was on a little alp at the foot of the vast precipice. Opposite him another wall of rock reared itself against the sky. The gorge between these precipices ran east and west and was full of the morning sunlight. He found a sort of chimney cleft dripping with water down which a desperate man might venture. He found it easier than it seemed, and came at last to another desolate alp, and then after a rock climb of no particular difficulty to a steep slope of trees. He took his bearings and turned his face into the gorge, for he saw it opened out above, upon green meadows. Among the meadows he now glimpsed quite distinctly a cluster of stone huts of unfamiliar fashion.

About midday he came at last out of the throat of the gorge into the plain. He was stiff and weary; he sat in the shadow of a rock, filled up his flask with water from a spring and drank it down, and remained for a time resting before he went on to the houses.

The whole aspect of the valley became, as he regarded it, queerer and more unfamiliar. The greater part of its surface was lush green meadow, starred with many beautiful flowers, irrigated with extraordinary care, and bearing evidence of systematic cropping. High up and ringing the valley about was a wall and what appeared to be a channel, from which came little trickles of water that fed the meadow plants. On the higher slopes above this, flocks of llamas cropped the scanty herbage.

The irrigation streams ran together into a main channel down the center of the valley, and this was enclosed on either side by a wall, which gave a singularly urban quality to this secluded place. That quality was greatly enhanced by a number of orderly paths paved with black and white stones, each with a curious little curb at the side. The houses of the village were quite unlike those of the higgledy-piggledy mountain villages he knew; they stood in a continuous row on either side of a central street of astonishing cleanliness; here and there their multicolored façades were pierced by a door. Not a solitary window broke their even frontage. They were colored with extraordinary irregularity, smeared with a sort of plaster that was sometimes gray, sometimes slate-colored or dark brown; and it was the sight of this wild plastering that first brought the word blind into Nuñez's thoughts. The good man who did that, he thought, must have been as blind as a bat.

He descended a steep place, and so came to the wall and water channel that ran about the valley. He could now see a number of men and women resting on piled heaps of grass, as if taking a siesta, and nearer the village a number of recumbent children. Closer at hand, three men carried pails on yokes along a little path that ran from the encircling wall toward the houses. They were clad in garments of llama cloth and boots and belts of leather. They followed one another slowly in single file, yawning as they walked, like men who have been up all night.

There was something so respectable in their bearing that Nuñez stood forward conspicuously and gave vent to a mighty shout that echoed around the valley.

The three men stopped and turned their faces this way and that, as though they were looking about them. Nuñez gesticulated freely, but they did not appear to see him, and after a time, directing themselves toward the mountains far away to the right, they shouted as if in answer. Nuñez bawled and gestured again, and once more the word blind came up to the top of his thoughts. "The fools must be blind," he said.

At last Nuñez crossed the stream by a little bridge and came through a gate in the wall. When he approached the three men, he was sure that this was the Country of the Blind of which the legends told. The men stood side by side with their ears directed toward him, judging him by his unfamiliar steps. They stood close together like men a little afraid, and he could see their eyelids closed and sunken. There was an expression near awe on their faces.

"A man," one said, in hardly recognizable Spanish. "A man it is—a man or a spirit—coming down from the rocks."

Nuñez advanced with confident steps. Through his thoughts ran this old proverb, as if it were a refrain:

> In the Country of the Blind the one-eyed man is king.
> In the Country of the Blind the one-eyed man is king.

Very civilly he gave them greeting. He talked to them and used his eyes.

"Where does he come from, Brother Pedro?" asked one.

"Down out of the rocks."

"Over the mountains I come," said Nuñez, "out of the country beyond there—where men can see. From near Bogotá, where there are a hundred thousand people, and where the city passes out of sight."

"Sight?" muttered Pedro. "Sight?"

"He comes," said the second blind man, "out of the rocks."

They startled him by a simultaneous movement toward him, each with a hand outstretched. He stepped back from the advance of these spread fingers.

"Come hither," said the third blind man, clutching him neatly. And they held Nuñez and felt him over.

"Carefully," he cried, as a finger poked his eye. They thought that organ, with its fluttering lids, a queer thing in him. They went over it again.

"A strange creature, Correa," said the one called Pedro. "Feel the coarseness of his hair. Like a llama's hair."

"Rough he is as the rocks that begot him," said Correa, investigating Nuñez's unshaven chin with a soft and slightly moist hand.

"Carefully," he said again.

"He speaks," said the third man. "Certainly he is a man."

"And you have come into the world?" asked Pedro.

"Out of the world. Over mountains and glaciers; right over above there, halfway to the sun."

They scarcely seemed to heed him. "Let us lead him to the elders," said Pedro, taking Nuñez by the hand.

Nuñez drew his hand away. "I can see," he said.

"See?" said Correa.

"Yes, see," said Nuñez, and stumbled against Pedro's pail.

"His senses are still imperfect," said the third blind man. "He stumbles, and talks unmeaning words. Lead him by the hand."

Nuñez was led along, laughing. It seemed they knew nothing of sight. Well, all in good time. He would teach them.

He heard people shouting, and saw a number of figures gathering together in the middle roadway of the village.

He found that it taxed his nerve and patience, that first encounter with the population of the Country of the Blind. The place seemed larger as he drew near to it, and a crowd of children and men and women (the women and girls, he was pleased to note, had some of them quite sweet faces) came about him, touching him with soft, sensitive hands, sniffing at him, and listening at every word he spoke. Some of the maidens and children, however, kept aloof, as if afraid, and indeed his voice seemed coarse and rude beside their softer notes. His three guides kept close to him, and said again and again, "A wild man out of the rocks."

"Bogotá," he said. "Bogotá. Over the mountain crests."

"A wild man—using wild words," said Pedro. "He has only the beginnings of speech."

A little boy nipped his hand. "Bogotá!" he said mockingly.

"Aye! I come from the great world—where men have eyes and see."

"He stumbled," said Correa, "stumbled twice as we came hither."

"Bring him to the elders."

They thrust him suddenly through a doorway into a room as black as pitch, save at the end there faintly glowed a fire. The crowd closed in behind him, and before he could arrest himself he had fallen headlong over the feet of a seated man. His arm, outflung, struck the face of someone else as he went down; he heard a cry of anger, and for a moment he struggled against a number of hands that clutched him. It was a one-sided fight. An inkling of the situation came to him, and he lay quiet.

"I fell down," he said. "I couldn't see in this pitchy darkness."

The voice of Correa said, "He is but newly formed. He stumbles as he walks, and mingles words that mean nothing with his speech."

"May I sit up?" Nuñez asked. "I will not struggle against you again."

They consulted and let him rise.

An older man began to question him, and Nuñez found himself trying to explain the great world out of which he had fallen, the sky and mountains and sight and suchlike marvels. And these elders who sat in darkness would believe and understand nothing he told them. They would not even understand many of his words. For fourteen generations these people had been cut off from all the seeing world; the names for all the things of sight had faded and changed; and they had ceased to concern themselves with anything beyond the rocky slopes above their circling wall. Much of their imagination had shriveled with their eyes, and they had made for themselves new imaginations with their ever more sensitive ears and fingertips.

Slowly Nuñez realized that his expectation of wonder and reverence at his origin and his gifts was not to be borne out; and after his poor attempt to explain sight to them had been set aside as the incoherent sensations of a newly made being, he subsided into listening to their instruction. And the eldest of the blind men explained to him life and philosophy and religion, how into the world (meaning their valley) had come, first, inanimate things without the gift of touch, and llamas and a few other creatures that had little sense, and then men, and at last angels, whom one could hear singing and making fluttering sounds, but whom no one could touch at all. This last puzzled Nuñez greatly until he thought of the birds.

The elder went on to tell Nuñez how time had been divided into the warm and the cold, which are the blind equivalents of day and night, and how it was good to sleep in the warm and work during the cold, so that now, but for his advent, the whole town would have been asleep. He said that for all his mental incoherence and stumbling behavior Nuñez must have courage, and do his best to learn; and at that all the people in the doorway murmured encouragingly. He said the night—for the blind call their day night—was now far gone, and it behooved everyone to go back to sleep. He asked Nuñez if he knew how to sleep, and Nuñez said he did, but that before sleep he wanted food.

They brought him food—llama's milk in a bowl, and rough salted bread—and led him into a lonely place to eat out of their hearing, and afterward to slumber until the chill of the mountain evening roused them to begin their day again. But Nuñez slumbered not at all.

Instead, he sat resting his limbs and turning the circumstances of his arrival over and over in his mind. Every now and then he laughed, sometimes with amusement, and sometimes with indignation.

"Unformed mind!" he said. "They little know they've been insulting their heaven-sent king and master. I see I must bring them to reason. Let me think—let me think."

He was still thinking when the sun set. It seemed to him that the glow upon the snowfields and glaciers that rose about the valley on every side was the most beautiful thing he had ever seen. Suddenly a wave of emotion took him, and he thanked God from the bottom of his heart that the power of sight had been given him.

He heard a voice calling to him from out of the village.

"Ya ho there, Bogotá! Come hither!"

At that he stood up smiling. He would show these people once and for all what sight would do for a man. They would not find him.

"You move not, Bogotá," said the voice.

He laughed noiselessly, and made two stealthy steps off the path.

"Trample not on the grass, Bogotá; that is not allowed."

Nuñez had scarcely heard the sound he made himself. He stopped, amazed. The owner of the voice came running up the path toward him.

He stepped back into the pathway. "Here I am," he said.

"Why did you not come when I called you?" said the blind man. "Must you be led like a child? Cannot you hear the path as you walk?"

Nuñez laughed. "I can see it," he said.

"There is no such word as see," said the blind man, after a pause. "Cease this folly, and follow the sound of my feet."

Nuñez followed, a little annoyed. "Has no one told you, 'In the Country of the Blind the one-eyed man is king'?" he asked.

"What is blind?" asked the blind man carelessly over his shoulder.

Four days passed, and the fifth found the king of the Blind still a clumsy and useless stranger among his subjects. It was, he found, much more difficult to proclaim himself than he had supposed. While he meditated his coup d'etat, he did what he was told and learned the manners and customs of the Country of the Blind.

They led a simple, laborious life, these people, with all the elements of virtue and happiness. They toiled, but not oppressively; they had food and clothing sufficient for their needs; they had days and seasons of rest; they made much of music and singing, and there was love among them, and little children.

It was marvelous with what confidence and precision they went about their ordered world. Everything, you see, had been made to fit their needs; each of the radiating paths of the valley area had a constant angle to the others, and was distinguished by a special notch upon its curbing; all obstacles and irregularities of path or meadow had long since been cleared away. Their senses had become marvelously acute; they could hear and judge the slightest gesture of a man a dozen paces away—could hear the very beating of his heart. Their sense of smell was extraordinarily fine. Intonation had long replaced expression with them, and touches gesture. Their work with hoe and spade was as free and confident as garden work can be, and they went about the tending of the llamas, who lived among the rocks above, with ease and confidence. It was only when at last Nuñez sought to assert himself that he found how easy and confident their movements could be.

He tried at first on several occasions to tell them of sight. "Look you here, you people," he said. "There are things you do not understand in me."

Once or twice, one or two of them attended to him; they sat with faces downcast and ears turned intelligently toward him, and he did his best to tell them what it was to see. Among his hearers was a girl, with eyelids less red and sunken than the others, so that one could almost fancy she was hiding eyes. She, he especially hoped to persuade. He spoke of the beauties of sight, of watching the mountains and the sunrise, but the sky and clouds and stars he described seemed to them a hideous void, a terrible blankness in the place of the smooth, cavernous roof to things in which they believed.

He gave up that aspect of the matter altogether, and tried to show them the practical value of sight. He noted certain goings and comings, but the things that really seemed to matter to these people happened inside of or behind the windowless houses—the only things they took note of to test him by—and of these he could see or tell nothing. It was after the failure of this attempt, and the ridicule they could not repress, that he resorted to force. He thought of seizing a spade and suddenly smiting one of them to earth, and so in fair combat showing the advantage of eyes. He went so far as to seize his spade, and then he discovered that it was impossible for him to hit a blind man in cold blood.

He hesitated, and found them all aware that he had snatched up the spade. They stood alert, with their heads on one side, and bent ears toward him for what he would do next. "Put that spade down," said one, and Nuñez felt a sort of helpless horror.

Then he thrust one backward against a house wall, and fled past him out of the village.

He went athwart one of their meadows, leaving a track of trampled grass, and presently sat down. Far away he saw men carrying spades and sticks come out of the street of houses and advance in a spreading line toward him. They moved slowly, speaking frequently to one another, and ever and again the whole cordon would halt and listen.

One struck his trail in the meadow grass, and came stooping and feeling his way along it. For five minutes he watched the slow extension of the cordon, and then his vague disposition to do something forthwith became frantic. He stood up, went toward the circumferential wall, and turned gripping his spade very tightly in both hands. Should he charge them?

The pulse in his ears ran to the rhythm of "In the Country of the Blind the one-eyed man is king!" He looked back at the high and unclimbable wall behind—unclimbable because of its smooth plastering though pierced with many little doors—and again at the approaching line of seekers.

"Bogotá!" called one. "Bogotá! Where are you?"

He gripped his spade still tighter, and advanced down the meadows. Directly he moved they converged upon him. I'll hit them if they touch me, he swore; by heaven, I will. I'll hit. He called aloud, "Look here, I'm going to do what I like in this valley. Do you hear? I'm going to do what I like and go where I like!"

They were moving in upon him quickly, groping, yet moving rapidly. "Get hold of him!" cried one. He found himself in the arc of a loose curve of pursuers.

"You don't understand," he cried in a voice that was meant to be great and resolute. "You are blind, and I can see. Leave me alone!"

"Bogotá! Put down that spade and come off the grass!"

The last order, grotesque in its urban familiarity, produced a gust of anger. "I'll hurt you," he said, sobbing with emotion. "By heaven, I'll hurt you. Leave me alone!"

He began to run, not knowing clearly where to run. He ran from the nearest blind man, because it was a horror to hit him. He stopped, and then made a dash for where a gap was wide. The men on either side, with a quick perception of the approach of his paces, rushed in on one another. He sprang forward, and then saw he must be caught, and *swish!* The spade had struck. He felt the soft thud of hand and arm, and the man was down with a yell of pain, and he was through.

Through! And then he was close to the street of houses again, and blind men, whirling spades and stakes, were running with a sort of reasoned swiftness hither and thither.

He heard steps behind him just in time, and found a tall man rushing forward and swiping at the sound of him. He lost his nerve, hurled his spade a yard wide at his antagonist, and whirled about and fled, panic-stricken. He ran furiously to and fro, dodging when there was no need to dodge, and in his anxiety to see on every side of him at once, stumbling. Far away in the circumferential wall a little doorway looked like heaven, and he set off in a wild rush for it. He did not even look around at his pursuers until it was gained, and he had stumbled across the bridge, clambered a little way among the rocks and lay down sobbing for breath.

And so his coup d'etat came to an end.

He stayed outside the wall of the valley of the Blind for two nights and days without food or shelter, and meditated upon the unexpected, repeating frequently, "In the Country of the Blind the one-eyed man is king." He thought chiefly of ways of conquering these people, and it grew clear that for him no practicable way was possible. He had no weapons, and now it would be hard to get one.

He tried to find food among the pine trees, to be comfortable under pine boughs while the frost fell at night, and—with less confidence—to catch a llama by artifice in order to try to kill it. But the llamas regarded him with distrustful brown eyes, and spat when he drew near. Fear came on him the second day, and fits of shivering. Finally he crawled down to the wall of the Country of the Blind, shouting until two men came out to the gate and talked to him.

"I was mad," he said. "But I was only newly made." He told them he was wiser now, and repented of all he had done. Then he wept, for he was very weak and ill, and they took that as a favorable sign.

They asked him if he still thought he could "see."

"No," he said. "That was folly. The word means nothing—less than nothing!"

They asked him what was overhead.

"About ten times ten the height of a man there is a roof above the world—of rock—and very, very smooth." He burst again into hysterical tears. "Before you ask me any more, give me some food or I shall die."

He expected dire punishments, but these blind people were capable of toleration. They regarded his rebellion as but one more proof of his general idiocy and inferiority; and after they had whipped him they appointed him to do the simplest and heaviest work they had for anyone to do. He, seeing no other way of living, did what he was told.

He was ill for some days, and they nursed him kindly. That refined his submission. And blind philosophers came and talked to him of the wicked levity of his mind, and reproved him so impressively for his doubts about the lid of rock that covered their cosmic casserole that he almost doubted whether indeed he was not the victim of hallucination in not seeing it overhead.

So Nuñez became a citizen of the Country of the Blind, and these people became individuals and familiar to him, while the world beyond the mountains became more and more remote and unreal. There was Yacob, his master, a kindly man when not annoyed; there was Pedro, Yacob's nephew; and there was Medina-saroté, who was the youngest daughter of Yacob. She was little esteemed in the world of the blind, because she had a clear-cut face, and lacked that satisfying, glossy smoothness that is the blind man's ideal of feminine beauty. Her closed eyelids were not sunken but lay as though they might open again at any moment; and she had long eyelashes, which were considered a grave disfigurement.

Nuñez thought her beautiful at first, and presently the most beautiful thing in the whole creation. There came a time when Nuñez thought that, could he win her, he would be resigned to live in the valley for all the rest of his days.

He sought opportunities of doing her little services, and soon he found that she observed him. Once at a rest-day gathering they sat side by side in the dim starlight, and the music was sweet. His hand came upon hers and he dared to clasp it. Then very tenderly she returned his pressure. And one day, as they were at their meal in the darkness, he felt her hand very softly seeking him, and as it chanced the fire leaped then and he saw the tenderness of her face.

He went to her one day when she was sitting in the summer moonlight, spinning. The light made her a thing of silver and mystery. He sat down at her feet and told her he loved her, and told her how beautiful she seemed to him. She had never before been touched by adoration, and she made him no definite answer, but it was clear his words pleased her.

After that the world beyond the mountains where men lived in sunlight seemed no more than a fairy tale he would someday pour into her ears. Very tentatively and timidly he spoke to her of sight.

Sight seemed to her the most poetical of fancies, and she listened to his description of the stars and the mountains and her own sweet beauty as though it were a guilty indulgence. She could only half understand, but she was mysteriously delighted.

His love lost its awe and took courage. Presently he was for asking Yacob and the elders for her hand in marriage, but she became fearful, and delayed. And it was one of her sisters who first told Yacob that Medina-saroté and Nuñez were in love.

There was from the first very great opposition to the marriage of Nuñez and Medina-saroté; they held Nuñez as a being apart, an idiot, an incompetent thing. Her sisters opposed it bitterly as bringing discredit on them all; and old Yacob shook his head and said the thing could not be. The young men were all angry at the idea of corrupting the race, and one went so far as to revile and strike Nuñez. He struck back. After that fight was over, no one was disposed to raise a hand against him, but they still found his marriage impossible.

Old Yacob had a tenderness for his last little daughter, and was grieved to have her weep upon his shoulder.

"You see, my dear, he's an idiot. He has delusions; he can't do anything right."

"I know," wept Medina-saroté. "But he's getting better. And he's strong, dear Father, and kind. And he loves me—and, Father, I love him."

Old Yacob was greatly distressed to find her inconsolable, and, besides, he liked Nuñez for many things. So he went and sat in the windowless council chamber with the other elders and said, at the proper time, "He's better than he was. Very likely, someday, we shall find him as sane as ourselves."

Then afterward one of the elders, the great doctor among these people, had an idea. He had an inventive mind, and the idea of curing Nuñez of his peculiarities appealed to him. One day when Yacob was present he returned to the topic of Nuñez.

"I have examined Bogotá," he said, "and the case is clearer to me. I think very probably he might be cured."

"That is what I have always hoped," said old Yacob.

"His brain is affected," said the blind doctor.

The elders murmured assent.

"Those queer things that are called the eyes, and which exist to make an agreeable soft depression in the face, are diseased, in the case of Bogotá, in such a way as to affect his brain. They are greatly distended, he has eyelashes, and his eyelids move, and consequently his brain is in a state of constant irritation and distraction."

"Yes?" said old Yacob. "Yes?"

"And I think I may say with reasonable certainty that, in order to cure him completely, all that we need do is a simple and easy surgical operation—namely, to remove these irritant bodies."

"And then he will be sane?"

"Then he will be perfectly sane, and a quite admirable citizen."

"Thank heaven for science!" said old Yacob, and went forth at once to tell Nuñez of his happy hopes.

But Nuñez's manner of receiving the good news struck him as being cold and disappointing.

"One might think," he said, "from the tone you take, that you did not care for my daughter." And he left it to Medina-saroté to persuade Nuñez to face the blind surgeons.

"You do not want me," he said, "to lose my gift of sight?"

She shook her head.

"There are the beautiful things, the far sky with its drifting down of clouds, the sunsets, and the stars. And there is you. For you alone it is good for me to have sight, to see your sweet, serene face, your dear, beautiful hands folded together. . . . It is these eyes of mine that hold me to you that these idiots seek. Instead, I must touch you, hear you, and never see you again. No; you would not have me do that?"

"I wish sometimes—you would not talk like that."

"Like what?"

"I know it's pretty—it's your imagination. I love it, but now—"

He felt cold. "Now?" he said faintly.

He was realizing things very swiftly. He felt anger at the dull course of fate, but also sympathy for her lack of understanding—a sympathy akin to pity. He could see how intensely her spirit pressed against the things she could not say. He put his arms about her, he kissed her ear, and they sat for a time in silence.

"If I were to consent to this?" he said at last, in a voice that was very gentle.

She flung her arms about him, weeping wildly. "Oh, if you would," she sobbed, "if only you would!"

FOR A WEEK before the operation that was to raise him to the level of a blind citizen, all through the warm sunlit hours, while the others slumbered happily, Nuñez sat brooding or wandered aimlessly, trying to bring his mind to bear on his dilemma. He had given his consent and still he was not sure. And at last work time was over, the sun rose in splendor over the golden crests, and his last day of vision began. He had a few minutes with Medina-saroté before she went apart to sleep.

"Tomorrow," he said, "I shall see no more."

"Dear heart!" she answered, and pressed his hands with all her strength. "They will hurt you but little," she said, "and you are going through this pain, dear lover, for *me*. . . . If a woman's heart and life can do it, I will repay you, my dearest one."

He was drenched in pity for himself and her. He held her in his arms, and looked on her sweet face for the last time. "Good-by!" he whispered. "Good-by!" And then in silence he turned away from her.

She could hear his slow, retreating footsteps, and something in the rhythm of them threw her into a passion of weeping.

He had fully meant to go to a lonely meadow, beautiful with white narcissus, and there remain until the hour of his sacrifice should come; but as he went he lifted up his eyes and saw the morning, the morning like an angel in golden armor, marching down the steeps. . . .

It seemed to him that before this splendor he, and this blind world in the valley, and his love, were no more than a pit of sin.

He did not turn aside as he had meant to do, but went on, and passed through the wall of the circumference and out upon the rocks. His eyes were always upon the sunlit ice and snow. His imagination soared over them to the things beyond.

He thought of that great free world he was parted from, the world that was his own, and of Bogotá, a place of stirring beauty, a glory by day, a luminous mystery by night. He thought of the river journey, from great Bogotá to the still vaster world beyond, through towns and villages, forest and desert places, until its banks had reached the sea—the limitless sea, with its thousands of islands, and its ships in their incessant journeyings around and about that greater world. And there, unpent by mountains, one saw the sky—an arch of immeasurable blue, a deep of deeps in which the circling stars were floating. . . .

His eyes scrutinized the great curtain of the mountains with a keener inquiry. If one went up that gully and to that chimney there, then one might come out high among those stunted pines that ran around in a sort of shelf and rose still higher and higher as it passed above the gorge. And then? Those broken rocks might be managed. Thence perhaps a climb might be found to take him up to the precipice that came below the snow. And then? Then one would be out upon the amberlit snow, and halfway up to the crest of those beautiful desolations.

He turned around then and regarded the village steadfastly. He thought of Medina-saroté, and she had become small and remote.

He turned again toward the mountain wall. Then very circumspectly he began to climb.

WHEN SUNSET CAME he was far and high. His clothes were torn, his limbs were bloodstained, he was bruised in many places, but he lay as if he were at his ease, and there was a smile on his face.

From where he rested the valley seemed dim with haze and shadow, though the mountain summits around him were things of light and fire. The rocks near at hand were drenched with subtle beauty—a vein of green mineral piercing the gray, the flash of crystal faces here and there, a minute, minutely beautiful orange lichen close beside his face. Overhead was the illimitable vastness of the sky. But he heeded these things no longer. He lay quite inactive there, smiling as if he were satisfied merely to have escaped from the valley of the Blind in which he had thought to be king.

The glow of the sunset passed, and the night came, and still he lay peacefully contented under the cold stars.

THE GIFTS OF WAR
MARGARET DRABBLE

WHEN SHE WOKE in the morning, she could tell at once, as soon as she reached consciousness, that she had some reason to feel pleased with herself, some rare cause for satisfaction. She lay there quietly for a time, enjoying the unfamiliar sensation, not bothering to place it, grateful for its vague comfortable warmth. It protected her from the disagreeable noise of her husband's snores, from the thought of getting breakfast, from the coldness of the linoleum when she finally dragged herself out of bed. She had to wake Kevin; he always overslept these days, and he took so long to get dressed and get his breakfast, she was surprised he wasn't always late for school. She never thought of making him go to bed earlier; she hadn't the heart to stop him watching the telly, and anyway she enjoyed his company, she liked having him around in the evenings, laughing in his silly seven-year-old way at jokes he didn't understand—jokes she didn't always understand herself, and which she couldn't explain when he asked her to. "You don't know *anything*, Mum," he would groan, but she didn't mind his condemnations; she didn't expect to know anything. It amused her to see him behaving like a man already, affecting superiority, harmlessly, helplessly, in an igno-rance that was as yet so much greater than her own—though she would have died rather than have allowed him to suspect her amusement, her permissiveness. She grumbled at him constantly, even while wanting to keep him there. She snapped at his endless questions, she snubbed him, she repressed him, she provoked him. And she did not suffer from doing this, because she knew that they could not hurt each other. He was a child, he wasn't a proper man yet, he couldn't inflict true pain, any more than she could truly repress him, and his teasing, obligatory conventional schoolboy complaints about her cooking and her stupidity seemed to exorcise, in a way, those other, crueler onslaughts. It was as though she said to herself, If my little boy doesn't mean it when he shouts at me, perhaps my husband doesn't either. Perhaps there's no more serious offense in my bruises and my graying hair than there is in those harmless childish moans. In the child, she found a way of accepting the man; she found a way of accepting, without too much submission, her lot.

She loved the child. She loved him with so much passion that a little of it spilled over generously onto the man who had misused her. In forgiving the child his dirty blazer and shirts and his dinner-covered tie, she forgave the man for his Friday nights and the childish vomit on the stairs and the bedroom floor. It never occurred to her that a grown man might resent more than hatred such secondhand forgiveness. She never thought of the man's emotions. She thought of her own, and her feelings for the child redeemed her from bitterness, and shed some light on the dark industrial terraces and the wastelands of the city's rubble. Her single-minded commitment was a wonder of the neighborhood. She's a sour piece, the neighbors said. She keeps herself to herself a bit too much, but you've got to hand it to her, she's been a wonderful mother to that boy. She's had a hard life, but she's been a wonderful mother to that boy. And she, tightening her woolly head scarf over her aching ears as she walked down the cold steep windy street to join the queue at the post office or the butcher's, would stiffen proudly, her hard lips secretly smiling as she claimed and accepted and nodded to her role, her place, her social dignity.

This morning, as she woke Kevin, he reminded her instantly of her cause for satisfaction, bringing to the surface the pleasant knowledge that had underlain her wakening. "Hi, Mum," he said, as he opened his eyes to her, "how old am I today?"

"Seven, of course," she said, staring dourly at him, pretending to conceal her instant knowledge of the question's meaning, assuming scorn and dismissal. "Come on, get up, child, you're going to be late, as usual."

"And how old am I tomorrow, Mum?" he asked, watching her like a hawk, waiting for that delayed, inevitable break.

"Come on, come on," she said crossly, affecting impatience, stripping the blankets off him, watching him writhe in the cold air, small and bony in his striped pajamas.

"Oh, go on, Mum," he said.

"What d'you mean, go on?" she said. "Don't be so cheeky. Come on, get a move on, you'll get no breakfast if you don't get a move on."

"Just think, Mum," he said, "how old am I tomorrow?"

"I don't know what you're talking about," she said, ripping his pajama jacket off him, wondering how long to give the game, secure in her sense of her own timing.

"Yes you do, yes you do," he yelled, his nerve beginning, very slightly, to falter. "You know what day it is tomorrow."

"Why, my goodness me," she said, judging that the moment had come, "I'd quite forgotten. Eight tomorrow. My goodness me."

And she watched him grin and wriggle, too big now for embraces, his affection clumsy and knobbly. She avoided the touch of him these days, pushing him irritably away when he leaned on her chair arm, twitching when he banged into her in the corridor or the kitchen, pulling her skirt or overall away from him when he tugged at it for attention, regretting sometimes the soft and round docile baby that he had once been, and yet proud at the same time of his gawky growing, happier, more familiar with the hostilities between them (a better cover for love) than she had been with the tender wide smiles of adoring infancy.

"What you got me for my birthday?" he asked, as he struggled out of his pajama trousers.

She turned at the door and looked back at him, and said, "What d'you mean, what've I got you? I've not got you anything. Only good boys get presents."

"I *am* good," he said. "I've been ever so good all week."

"Not that I noticed," she said, knowing that too prompt an acquiescence would ruin the dangerous pleasure of doubtful anticipation.

"Go on, tell me," he said, and she could tell from his whining plea that he was almost sure that she had got what he wanted, almost sure but not quite sure, that he was, in fact, in the grip of an exactly manipulated degree of uncertainty, a torment of hope that would last him for a whole twenty-four hours, until the next birthday morning.

"I'm telling you," she said, her hand on the door, staring at him sternly, "I'm telling you, I've not got you anything." And then, magically, delightfully, she allowed herself and him that lovely moment of grace. "I've not got you anything—*yet*," she said—portentous, conspiratorial, yet very very faintly threatening.

"You're going to get it today," he shrieked, unable to restrain himself, unable to keep the rules. And as though annoyed by his exuberance, she marched smartly out of the small back room and down the narrow stairs to the kitchen, shouting at him in an excessive parade of rigor, "Come on, get moving, get your things on, you'll be late for school, you're always late—" And she stood over him while he ate his flakes, watching each spoonful disappear, heaving a great sigh of resigned fury when he spilled on the oilcloth, catching his guilty glance as he wiped it with his sleeve, not letting him off, unwilling, unable to relax into a suspect tenderness.

He went out the back way to school. She saw him through the yard and stood in the doorway watching him disappear, as she always watched him, down the narrow alley separating the two rows of back-to-back cottages, along the ancient industrial cobbles, relics of another age. As he reached the Stephensons' door she called out to him, "Eight tomorrow, then," and smiled, and waved, and he smiled back, excited, affectionate, over the ten-yard gap, grinning, his gray knee socks pulled smartly up, his short cropped hair already standing earnestly on end, resisting the violent flattening of the brush with which she thumped him each morning. He reminded her of a bird, she didn't know why; she couldn't have said why a bird—vulnerable, clumsy, tenacious, touching. Then Bill Stephenson emerged from his back door and joined him, and they went down the alley together—excluding her, leaving her behind—kicking at pebbles and fag packets with their scuffed much polished shoes.

She went back through the yard and into the house, and made a pot of tea, and took it up to the man in bed. She dumped it down on the corner of the dressing table beside him, her lips tight, as though she dared not loosen them. Her face had only one expression, and she used it to conceal the two major emotions of her life, resentment and love. They were so violently opposed, these passions, that she could not move from one to the other. She lacked flexibility, so she inhabited a grim inexpressive no-man's-land between them, feeling in some way that she thus achieved a kind of justice.

"I'm going up town today," she said, as the man on the bed rolled over and stared at her.

He wheezed and stared.

"I'm going to get our Kevin his birthday present," she said, her voice cold and neutral, offering justice and no more.

"What'll I do about me dinner?" he said.

"I'll be back," she said. "And if I'm not, you can get your own. It won't kill you."

He mumbled and coughed, and she left the room. When she got downstairs, she began at last to enter upon the day's true enjoyment. Slowly she took possession of it, this day that she had waited for, and which could not now be taken from her. She'd left herself a cup of tea on the table, but before she sat down to drink it she got her zip plastic purse from behind the clock on the dresser and opened it and got the money out. There it was, all of it: thirty shillings, three ten-bob notes, folded up tightly in a brown envelope. Twenty-nine and eleven she needed, and a penny over. Thirty shillings, saved, unspoken for, to spend. She'd wondered from time to time if she ought to use it to buy him something useful, but she knew now that she wasn't going to. She was going to get him what he wanted—a grotesque, unjustifiable luxury, a pointless gift. It never occurred to her that the pleasure she took in doing things for Kevin was anything other than selfish. She felt vaguely guilty about it. She would have started furtively, like a miser, had anyone knocked on the door and interrupted her contemplation; she would have denied bitterly the intensity of her anticipation.

And when she put her overcoat on, and tied on her head scarf, and set off down the road, she tried to appear to the neighbors as though she wasn't going anywhere in particular. She nodded calmly, she stopped to gape at Mrs. Phillips' new baby (all frilled up, poor mite, in ribbons and pink crochet, a dreadful sight, poor little innocent, like something off an iced cake, people should know better than to do such things to their own children); she even called in at the shop for a quarter of tea as a cover for her excursion, so reluctant was she to let anyone know that she was going into town, thus unusually, on a Wednesday morning. And as she walked down the steep hillside, where the abandoned tramlines still ran, to the next fare stage of the bus, she could not have said whether she was making the extra walk to save twopence, or whether she was, more deviously, concealing her destination until the last moment from both herself and the neighborhood.

Because she hardly ever went into town these days. In the old days she had come this way often, going down the hill on the tram with her girl friends, with nothing better in mind than a bit of window-shopping and a bit of a laugh and a cup of tea—penniless then as now, but still hopeful, still endowed with the touching faith that if by some miracle she could buy a pair of nylons or a particular blue lace blouse or a new brand of lipstick, then deliverance would be granted to her in the form of money, marriage, romance, the visiting prince who would glimpse her in the crowd, glorified by that seductive blouse, and carry her off to a better world. She could remember so well how hopeful they had been. Even Betty Jones—fat, monstrous, ludicrous Betty Jones—had cherished such rosy illusions, had gazed with them in longing at garments many sizes too small and far too expensive, somehow convinced that if she could by chance or good fortune acquire one, all her flesh would melt away and reveal the lovely girl within. Time had taught Betty Jones; she shuffled now in shoes cracked and splitting beneath her own weight. Time had taught them all. The visiting prince, whom need and desire had once truly transfigured in her eyes, now lay there at home in bed, stubbly, disgusting, ill, malingering, unkind. She remembered the girl who had seen such other things in him with a contemptuous yet pitying wonder. What fools they all had been, to laugh, to giggle and point and whisper, to spend their small wages to deck themselves for such a sacrifice. When she saw the young girls today, of the age that she had been then, still pointing and giggling with the same knowing ignorance, she was filled with a bitterness so acute that her teeth set against it, and the set lines of her face stiffened to resist and endure and conceal it. Sometimes she was possessed by a rash desire to warn them, to lean forward and tap on their shoulders, to see their astonished vacant faces, topped with their mad over-perfumed mounds of sticky hair, turn upon her in alarm and disbelief. What do you think you're playing at, she would say to them, what do you think you're at? Where do you think it leads you, what do you think you're asking for? And they would blink at her, uncomprehending, like condemned cattle, the sacrificial virgins, not yet made restless by the smell of blood. I could tell you a thing or two, she wanted to say. I could tell you enough to wipe those silly grins off your faces. But she said nothing, and she could not have said that it was envy or a true charitable pity that most possessed and disturbed her when she saw such innocents.

What withheld her most from envy, pure and straight and voracious, was a sense of her own salvation. Because, amazingly, she had been saved, against all probability. Her life, which had seemed after that bridal day of white nylon net and roses to sink deeply and almost instantly into a mire of penury and beer and butchery, had been so redeemed for her by her child that she could afford to smile with a kind of superior wisdom, a higher order of knowledge, at those who had not known her trials and her comforts. They would never attain, the silly teenagers, her own level of consolation; they would never know what it was like to find in an object which had at first seemed painful, ugly, bloody and binding, which had at first appeared to her as a yet more lasting sentence, a deathblow to the panic notions of despair and flight—to find in such a thing love and identity and human warmth. When she thought of this—which she did often, though not clearly, having little else to think of—she felt as though she alone, or she one of the elected few, had been permitted to glimpse something of the very nature of the harsh, mysterious processes of human survival; and she could induce in herself a state of recognition that was almost visionary. It was all she had, and being isolated by pride from more neighborly and everyday and diminishing attempts at commiseration, she knew it. She fed off it—her maternal role, her joy, her sorrow. She gazed out of the bus window now, as the bus approached the town center and the shops, and as she thought of the gift she was going to buy him, her eyes lit on the bombed sites, and the rubble and decay of decades, and the exposed walls where dirty fading wallpapers had flapped in the wind for years, and she saw where the willow herb grew, green and purple—fields of it among the brick, on such thin soil, on the dust of broken bricks and stones, growing so tall in tenacious aspiration out of such shallow infertile ground. It was significant; she knew, as she looked at it, that it was significant. She herself had grown out of this landscape; she had nourished herself and her child upon it. She knew what it meant.

FRANCES JANET ASHTON HALL also knew what it meant, for she too had been born and bred there; although, being younger, she had not lived there for so long, and, having been born into a different class of society, she knew that she was not sentenced to it for life and was indeed upon the verge of escape, for the next autumn she was to embark upon a degree in economics at a southern university. Nevertheless, she knew what it meant. She was a postwar child, but it was not for nothing that she had witnessed since infancy the red and smoking skies of the steelworks (making arms for the Arabs, for the South Africans, for all those wicked countries)—it was not for nothing that she had seen the deep scars in the city's center, not all disguised quite comfortably as car parks. In fact, she could even claim the distinction of having lost a relative in the air raids: her great-aunt Susan, who had refused to allow herself to be evacuated to the Lake District, had perished from a stray bomb in the midst of a highly residential suburban area. Frances was not yet old enough to speculate upon the effect that this tale, oft repeated, and with lurid details, had had upon the development of her sensibility; naturally she ascribed her ardent pacifism and her strong political convictions to her own innate radical virtue, and when she did look for ulterior motives for her faith she was far more likely to relate them to her recent passion for a newfound friend, one Michael Swaines, than to any childhood neurosis.

She admired Michael. She also liked him for reasons that had nothing to do with admiration, and being an intelligent and scrupulous girl she would spend fruitless, anxious and enjoyable hours trying to disentangle and isolate her various emotions, and to assess their respective values. Being very young, she set a high value on disinterest.

Standing now, for his sake, on a windy street corner in a conspicuous position outside the biggest department store in town, carrying a banner and wearing (no less) a sandwich board, proclaiming the necessity for peace in Vietnam and calling for the banning of all armaments, nuclear or otherwise, she was carrying on a highly articulate dialogue with her own conscience, by means of which she was attempting to discover whether she was truly standing there for Michael's sake alone, or whether she would have stood there anyway, for the sake of the cause itself. What, she asked herself, if she had been solicited to make a fool of herself in this way merely by that disagreeable Nicholas, son of the head of the adult education center? Would she have been prepared to oblige? No, she certainly would not. She would have laughed the idea of sandwich boards to scorn, and would have found all sorts of convincing arguments against the kind of public display that she was now engaged in. But, on the other hand, this did not exactly invalidate her actions, for she *did* believe, with Michael, that demonstrations were necessary and useful. It was just that her natural reluctance to expose herself would have conquered her, had not Michael himself set about persuading her. So she was doing the right thing but for the wrong reason, like that man in *Murder in the Cathedral*. And perhaps it was for a *very* wrong reason, because she could not deny that she even found a sort of corrupt pleasure in doing things she didn't like doing—accosting strangers, shaking collection boxes, being stared at—when she knew that it was being appreciated by other people: a kind of yearning for disgrace and martyrdom. Like stripping in public. Though not, surely, *quite* the same, because stripping didn't do any good, whereas telling people about the dangers of total war was a useful occupation. So doing the right thing for the wrong reason could at least be said to be better than doing the wrong thing for the wrong reason, couldn't it? Though her parents, of course, said it was the wrong thing anyway, and that one shouldn't molest innocent shoppers. Oh, Lord, she thought with sudden gloom, perhaps my *only* reason for doing this is to annoy my parents; and bravely, to distract herself from the dreadful suspicion, she stepped forward and asked a scraggy thin woman in an old red velvet coat what she thought of the American policy in Vietnam.

"What's that?" said the woman crossly, annoyed at being stopped in mid stride, and when Frances repeated her question she gazed at her as though she were an idiot and walked on without replying. Frances, who was becoming used to such responses, was not as hurt as she had been at the beginning of the morning; she was even beginning to think it was quite funny. She wondered if she might knock off for a bit and go and look for Michael; he had gone into the store to try to persuade the manager of the toy department not to sell toy machine guns and toy bombs and toy battleships. She thought she would go and join him; and when a horrid man in a cloth cap spat on the pavement very near her left shoe and muttered something about bloody students ruining the city for decent folk, she made her mind up. So she ditched her sandwich board and rolled her banner up and set off through the swing doors into the cozy warmth. Although it was Easter time the weather was bitterly cold; spring seemed to reach them two months later than anywhere else in England. It was a pity, she thought, that there weren't any more Easter marches. She would have liked marching, it would have been more sociable; but Michael believed in isolated pockets of resistance. Really, what he meant was, he didn't like things that he wasn't organizing himself. She didn't blame him for that, he was a marvelous organizer. It was amazing the amount of enthusiasm he'd got up in the Students' Union for what was after all rather a dud project—no, not dud, she hadn't meant that. What she meant was that it was no fun, and anyone with a lower sense of social responsibility than herself couldn't have been expected to find it very interesting. Very nice green stockings on the stocking counter. She wondered if she could afford a pair. This thing that Michael had about children and violence, it really was very odd. He had a brother who was writing a thesis on violence on the television and she supposed it must have affected him. She admired his faith. Although at the same time she couldn't help remembering a short story by Saki that she had read years ago, called "The Toys of Peace," which had been about the impossibility of making children play with anything but soldiers, or something to that effect.

When she reached the toy department, she located Michael immediately, because she could hear his voice raised in altercation. In fact, as she approached she could see that quite a scene was going on, and if Michael hadn't looked quite so impressive when he was making a scene she would have lost nerve and fled. But as it was, she approached discreetly and hovered on the outskirts of the center of activity. Michael was arguing with a man in a black suit, some kind of manager figure, she guessed (though what managers were or did she had no idea), and a woman in an overall. The man, she could see, was beginning to lose his patience and was saying things like, "Now look here, young man, we're not here to tell our customers what they ought to do, we're here to sell them what they want," and Michael was producing his usual arguments about responsibility and education and having to make a start somewhere and why not here and now. He'd already flashed around his leaflets on violence and delinquency, and was now offering his catalogue of harmless constructive wooden playthings.

"Look," he was saying, "look how much more attractive these wooden animals are. I'm sure you'd find they'd sell just as well, and they're far more durable"—whereat the woman in an overall sniffed and said since when had salesmen dressed themselves up as university students. If he wanted to sell them toys he ought to do it in the proper way; an interjection which Michael ignored, as he proceeded to pick up off the counter in front of him a peculiarly nasty piece of clockwork, a kind of car-cum-airplane thing with real bullets, and knives in the wheels, and hidden bomb carriers and God knows what. She rather thought it was a model from some television puppet program. It was called The Desperado Destruction Machine. "I mean to say, look at this horrible thing," Michael said to the manager, pressing a knob and nearly slicing off his own finger as an extra bit of machinery jumped out at him. "Whatever do you think can happen to the minds of children who play with things like this?"

"That's a very nice model," said the manager, managing to sound personally grieved and hurt. "It's a very nice model, and you've no idea how popular it's been for the price. It's not a cheap foreign thing, that, you know. It's a really well-made toy. Look—" He grabbed it back from Michael and pulled another lever, to display the ejector-seat mechanism. The driver figure was promptly ejected with such violence that he shot right across the room, and Michael, who was quite well brought up really, dashed off to retrieve it; and by the time he got back, the situation had been increasingly complicated by the arrival of a real customer who had turned up to buy that very object. Though if it really was as popular as the manager had said, perhaps that wasn't such a coincidence. Anyway, this customer seemed very set on purchasing one, and the overalled woman detached herself from Michael's scene and started to demonstrate one for her, trying to pretend as she did so that there was no scene in progress and that nothing had been going on at all. The manager too tried to hush Michael up by engaging him in conversation and backing him away from the counter and the transaction, but Michael wasn't so easy to silence. He continued to argue in a loud voice, and stood his ground. Frances wished that he would abandon this clearly pointless attempt, and all the more as he had by now noticed her presence, and she knew that at any moment he would appeal for her support. And finally the worst happened, as she had known it might. He turned to the woman who was trying to buy The Desperado Destruction Machine and started to appeal to her, asking her if she wouldn't like to buy something less dangerous and destructive. The woman seemed confused at first, and when he asked her for whom she was buying it, she said that it was for her little boy's birthday, and she hadn't realized it was a dangerous toy; it was just something he'd set his heart on. He'd break his heart if he didn't get it, he'd seen it on the telly and he wanted one just like that. Whereupon the manager, who had quite lost his grip, intervened and started to explain to her that there was nothing dangerous about the toy at all; on the contrary, it was a well-made pure British product, with no lead paint or sharp edges, and that if Michael didn't shut up he'd call the police. Whereupon Michael said that there was no law to stop customers discussing products in shops with one another, and he was himself a bona fide customer, because look, he'd got a newly purchased pair of socks in his pocket in a store bag. The woman continued to look confused, so Frances thought that she herself ought to intervene to support Michael, who had momentarily run out of aggression. She said to the woman, in what she thought was a very friendly and reasonable tone, that nobody was trying to stop her buying her little boy a birthday present; they just wanted to point out that with all the violence in the world today anyway, it was silly to add to it by encouraging children to play at killing and exterminating and things like that, and hadn't everyone seen enough bombing, particularly here (one of Michael's favorite points, this), and why didn't she buy her boy something constructive like Meccano or a farmyard set. And as she was saying all this she glanced from time to time at the woman's face, and there was something in it, she later acknowledged, that should have warned her. She stood there, the woman, her woollen head scarf so tight around her head that it seemed to clamp her jaws together into a violently imposed silence; her face unnaturally drawn, prematurely aged; her thickly veined hands clutching a zip plastic purse and that stupid piece of clockwork machinery. And as she listened to Frances's voice droning quietly and soothingly and placatingly away, her face began to gather a glimmering of expression, from some depths of reaction too obscure to guess at. As Frances finally ran down to a polite and only very faintly hopeful inquiring standstill, she opened her mouth and spoke. She said only one word, and it was a word that Frances had never heard before, though she had seen it in print in a once banned book; and by some flash of insight, crossing the immeasurable gap of quality that separated their two lives, she knew that the woman herself had never before allowed it to pass her lips; that to her too it was a shocking syllable, portentous, unforgettable, not a familiar word casually dropped into the dividing spaces. Then the woman, having spoken, started to cry; incredibly, horribly, she started to cry. She dropped the clockwork toy onto the floor, and it fell so heavily that she could almost have been said to have thrown it down, and she stood there, staring at it, as the tears rolled down her face. Then she looked at them and walked off. Nobody followed her; they stood there and let her go. They did not know how to follow her, nor what appeasement to offer for her unknown wound. So they did nothing. But Frances knew that in their innocence they had done something dreadful to her, in the light of which those long since ended air raids and even distant Vietnam itself were an irrelevance, a triviality; but she did not know what it was, she could not know. At their feet, the Destruction Machine buzzed and whirred its way to a broken immobility, achieving a mild sensation in its death throes by shooting a large spring coil out of its complex guts; she and Michael, after lengthy apologies, had to pay for it before they were allowed to leave the store.

THE SKEDULE
H. H. WILSON

Head down, like a charging buffalo, the Royal Mail bus was hurtling along the highway which led north from Alice Springs to Darwin. Three days was fair enough to cover the nine hundred-odd miles, agreed Her Majesty's government and Big Joe Hewitt, the mail contractor. So three days it was, come high heat of summer, or the drenching deluges of the Wet. Prospectors and station folk alike could set their watches by the Royal Mail.

"No records, mind you," Big Joe would reassure his passengers, and cross his enormous forearms across a chest which did them no shame. "But I like to keep to skedule."

His American pronunciation of the word schedule was a legacy from the war years, when the Yanks had helped to build this road. It was known to impress dilatory passengers more than the softer sounding Australian pronunciation. A "skedule" could not be trifled with. A "shedule" might be. A skedule spoke of a relentless, shining efficiency. No dawdlings in bed, when a seven-o'clock breakfast was the rule; no quarreling for the last pint of tepid water from the kerosene-tin showers; no gossiping over morning or afternoon tea in the little bough shelters at the stopping places.

"Fifteen minutes," Big Joe would announce as they pulled up. And at fifteen minutes sharp the horn of the Royal Mail would sound peremptorily. Five minutes later its double tires would scrunch the gravel on the edge of the road, and woe betide any who dallied. They were forced to scamper ludicrously along beside the slowly moving leviathan, under a barrage of hostile or derisive stares from the more docile passengers. They became known as "some people," and a brand was upon their brows. Some people, it appeared, did not mind how they inconvenienced their fellows or claimed extra privileges, or thought the Royal Mail was a luxury tourist coach; or, worst crime of all, threatened the sacred skedule by their selfishness.

Big Joe looked into his rearview mirror, his eyes squinting a little and a delta of lines crinkling out from the corners. It was not unnatural perhaps that Mrs. Healley, wife of a VIP, should head the list of these unwelcome travelers. She had not wanted to travel on the Royal Mail, but the planes had been booked out. And the reluctance had been mutual. So there she was, sitting up straight, all begoggled and hooded like a spaceship passenger, her frosted face registering her displeasure as the Woodley youngsters charged past her down the aisle. "Icicle" wasn't a bad name for her, Big Joe decided privately, glancing at his watch. Jove, nearly due at the Attack Creek turnoff where he dropped the kids, home for their first-term holidays.

Yes, there it was, near the old army sign which warned against too much speed on this straight stretch. STEADY! RUBBER GROWS ON TREES—TEMPORARILY TOJO'S.

And there was the truck waiting, drawn up in the shade of a cork tree. Mum and Dad and little sister in the front, trying to preserve a dignified restraint in their joy at this homecoming. On the back were a full-blooded stockman and his three small children, all spotlessly attired in bright blue denim, and all waving and shrieking with delight.

So he gave three triumphant hoots on the big horn and slowed down. Young Tom Woodley, hanging on the step, spun out before the vehicle lumbered to a stop, and the gesticulating little group flowed over him. Angela followed more sedately, long black-stockinged legs and neat uniform looking a little prim in this vast sea of plains. Then her mother detached herself from young Tom, and with a whoop the little girl dropped her battered schoolbag and her dignity and ran toward her. Big Joe followed more leisurely, with the bag of mail. Greetings all around, a little road gossip, and the big bus moved off. The shabby station truck started up its engine in challenge. The happy group on the back shouted, laughed, cracked toy stockwhips. Some of the passengers waved back, losing for the moment that feeling of superiority which long-distance travelers feel for short-distance ones, in a kind of wistful envy.

As he pressed the accelerator, Big Joe turned to his mirror again. Yes, he thought so. Grandma was having another attempt to unload her family history, this time on the Icicle. He knew her technique. The little family brochure, open in the middle to show two uniformed soldiers, one sporting a walrus and one a toothbrush mustache. "Me husband and me son," the old lady would be saying in the firm voice of one confident that her private affairs are of absorbing interest to strangers. "One in the last war, one in this. . . ." And, if the listener did not thaw, she would add lugubriously, "Dead—both of 'em."

Big Joe studied her sympathetically. Poor old soul. Game, too. Traveling alone the three thousand miles from Melbourne to see her remaining son at Darwin, and not too sure of her welcome from a new daughter-in-law. And doing it the hard way. The only complaint she had made was a fear expressed without fail at every stop, lest her hatbox be crushed in the pile of luggage.

"It's me new hat, with the pink rose," she would apologize. "I want to look nice when I arrive . . . for my daughter-in-law."

Yes, it was hard to be old and lonely . . . and afraid. He saw, with a mixed relief, that she had turned to the two women just in front. Well, she'd find a more receptive audience there, but in return would have to listen to another and very different family saga. He knew that mother and daughter, both on the domestic staff at the Alice Springs hospital, were going north to similar positions at Katherine. "I was happy at the Alice," the mother had confided in him already. "It's Emmie, y'see. Another undesirable suitor."

He had nodded reassuringly. He knew all about Emmie. Most men on the road did. The mother had a hopeless task, he decided. But she was game all right.

Most of 'em were game. Take that middle-aged couple with the six strapping kids, all under fifteen. At least, five of 'em were strapping. The middle one, a scraggy little girl of eight, was weak-eyed and muling, like the kitten in the litter one inevitably drowns. This one had been spared somehow. Pity. The father was a little fellow. Had his home and business blown sky-high by the Japs, and they were all going back to start life over again. No more cities for them.

Or young Mrs. Percer, with the white-faced new baby and the little boy of two, going to rejoin her husband at Pine Creek. Devil of a trip for two small kiddies just out of hospital.

Quite different from those two young limbs of Satan, whose mother was taking them to join their father in the air force at Darwin. It would be the happiest moment of her life when she could turn them over to him. Still, no harm in them. Just full of the joy of living, and a boy wouldn't be a boy if he didn't have a bit of the devil in him. He looked back into his mirror with a fatherly tolerance. Then stiffened. The younger boy, aged five, was bouncing up and down on the seat, as he'd been doing for the last two hours without a break. The seven-year-old was quietly and methodically unpicking the upholstery with a penknife he had smuggled in.

Big Joe's terrible voice bellowed into the loudspeaker.

"If those two boys don't stop ruining the seats, I'll stop the bus and chuck 'em out."

There was a long moment's petrified silence. The five-year-old bouncer seemed suspended in the air before he sank slowly down into his seat, skewered by dozens of pairs of accusing eyes. He burrowed farther and farther down until only a wild tuft of hair was visible. The seven-year-old destroyer merely paused in his work and looked up with an angelic smile of innocence, sure that such a threat could not apply to him. Through the gap in his front teeth his pink tongue poked questioningly. But his tormented mother, roused from her midday torpor, woke to sudden fury, snatched the knife from him, and threw it out the window.

Big Joe laughed silently. Wonder what the young devil will be up to next? The diversion had given the passengers a topic of common interest. They straightened up from their hunched positions, grinned or frowned at the child as became their varying dispositions, began swapping stories of their own kids or their own childhood.

All but the young girl sitting alone on one of the two seats near the front. Bit of a mystery girl, he thought, frowning, for he didn't like mysteries on his bus. Getting off at Hayes' Creek. He watched her covertly amid the mild upheaval caused by his announcement.

He had noticed her when she first got on, because she wore her dark hair braided around her head, not cut short like the rest. About twenty-three or -four, he judged. Pale city face, slightly spotted now with a heat rash, and big dark eyes which, once when he caught them in his rearview mirror, were clouded with something which looked mighty like fear. Probably worked in some city office, he mused. Went to work each day on an electric train, nibbled celery and cheese sandwiches at lunchtime, saw a new movie each Friday night with the current boy friend. What was she doing up here then, getting off at Hayes' Creek, which wandered through the outermost reaches of the Never-Never?

He had looked at her left hand as she had taken off her blue cotton gloves soon after the bus had started, when the hot inland air had begun to force its way into the bus like a belated passenger. But there was no ring. What then? Governess to some outback station? Well, it was none of his business. Only there were no stations he knew of around Hayes' Creek. Only a lot of brand-new banana plantations, far from the stage of development when they could contemplate such luxuries as governesses.

She was sitting staring out the window, but he guessed she was not seeing much. She was too occupied with her own thoughts. And she was scared, too. Almost to the point of panic.

Then it was lunchtime, and he stopped with relief at the isolated shack and store at Fraser's. Here lunch was to be had in a bough shed, allegedly for coolness, but in effect only giving an advance signal to myriads of flies which now rushed from their ambush and set upon the distracted passengers.

Mrs. Healley eyed the limp spinach leaf, slice of tomato, and a piece of meat which might have come from the work-hardened shoulder of ox, sheep, goat or even buffalo, with almost equal distaste.

"This is simply disgraceful," she protested, pushing back her plate. "Not even natives should be expected to eat such stuff."

She rose and left the table in a huff. Two or three others followed suit, going surreptitiously to their bags for biscuits or fruit. The rest ate on stolidly, some even asking for a refill of the glutinous yellow substance lightheartedly masquerading under the title of "Orange Delight."

Big Joe blew his horn a second more promptly than usual. No use giving them time to get together and grouse, he thought. Get 'em going and they'll forget about the lunch. I know it's pretty awful, but it's hard enough to get anyone to take on the job up here.

Ah, two more passengers. And one well under the weather. Not the kind he cared to take. For a moment he was tempted to tell them to hitchhike a lift on the next truck. They were only going as far as Katherine. Then he looked more closely at the moderately sober one. Thought he remembered the face. Yes. Slag Slater himself. If he'd recognized him before he'd taken the money, he wouldn't have let him on. Didn't want any trouble, and once that mother set eyes on him . . .

The two men lumbered down the aisle and lurched into the back seats, one on each side. Big Joe noted that Slag arranged his companion comfortably in the corner, propped him up with a suitcase, and left him muttering away to himself like a radio someone has forgotten to turn off. Then he turned his attention to the passengers.

"Don't you look, Emmie," hissed her mother, taking her arm firmly. "It's that dreadful man . . : drunk as a—"

"Don't tell me what to do," returned her daughter promptly. "I'm over twenty-one and I guess it's a free country, isn't it?"

"Emmie, don't you dare go . . ." The worried mother wavered between command and entreaty. "I tell you he's no good, Emmie. No good."

"Emmie." The Slag settled himself comfortably in the empty back seat and patted the place beside him invitingly. "Emmie."

With a final wrench which sent her mother spinning back against the window, Emmie got up and went to him. Big Joe could see her cuddling close against Slag's arm as it lay negligently along the back of the seat. He put a fruit drop in his mouth. From the mirror, he could see the mother was sobbing, hunched up under her bleached, old-fashioned country hat. Grandma was consoling her gently.

Big Joe shrugged at himself in the mirror. Well, only two hours to Flinders' Waters and he was right on skedule. Just then, with a report like a field gun, the back tire blew out. That means a quarter of an hour at least. He cursed softly as he climbed down from his cabin, after making a brief explanation through the loudspeaker. But what with the heat and a recalcitrant tire, it turned out to be just over half an hour. Well, he told himself, easy to make that up. Blokes at the telegraph station will chiack me for running late. But I can take it. We'll be at Katherine as usual. Cut out afternoon tea if necessary.

But the outcry was too much. No, they must stop for afternoon tea. How do you expect us to continue to endure this heat and dust without a cup of tea? Besides, Mrs. Percer's baby looks very crook. Let it cool off for half an hour inside the station's creeper-shaded veranda. Sponge it down, give the mite a fresh lease of life.

Then the bouncer strayed off and could not be found. Another ten minutes of yelling and shouting. Big Joe's lips set grimly. An hour behind now. If that kid were his, he'd skin the hide off him, the young devil. Ah, there he was. Clinging grimly to some rusty parts of a jeep which he had found derelict in the scrub by the side of the road.

"Let him take them with him," he ordered the flustered mother. "Better destroying that old junk than my upholstery."

On their way again at last. Big Joe was crouching a little now over the immense wheel, like a jockey riding his steed up the straight. No stops now until Katherine, come high wind and water. But, yes, there was one stop. The girl for Hayes' Creek. He glanced back at her. She was sitting upright now, a faint color in her cheeks that was not due to the heat. Her hair was freshly done and she was wearing a yellow blouse the color of evening sunlight. Why, she looked almost pretty now. He considered her young face judicially, and as he did so, there was an apologetic knock on his cabin.

"Sorry to interrupt you," the father of the six children apologized, "but the girl getting off at Hayes' Creek—"

"What about her?" snapped Big Joe, not glancing up.

"She's getting married tonight. Told my missus at the last stop. People were dead against it, so she's come up on her own. We thought we'd take up a collection . . . give her a bit of a presentation when you stop at Hayes' Creek. It won't take more than a minute or two," he added in a placatory voice.

"I'm an hour late now," Big Joe warned him. "It had better be a pretty quick presentation."

"Oh, it will be," the man assured him, taking the note which Big Joe passed him. "Oh, thank you. . . . We thought only a token—"

"Anyone starting life at Hayes' Creek needs more than a small token." Big Joe bit off the words and crouched lower over the wheel. "Life's pretty tough out there. . . . It's still Never-Never country."

"Her husband-to-be is meeting her at the turnoff," the man continued, steadying himself against the swaying motion of the bus. "The Inland Mission clergyman is due there tonight."

Big Joe made no comment, concentrating on a difficult bend. The man still lingered.

"She hasn't seen him for over three years. . . . He went on ahead to build up the banana plantation a little."

"Beats me why city girls come up north," Big Joe growled. "They don't realize what they're letting themselves in for."

"He's meeting her at the turnoff." The man slipped the note in the hat he was carrying in his hand and made his way into the back of the bus.

Now that the news was out, the whole bus was humming with excitement. Dark looks were cast at the Icicle, who had been inclined to protest when the hat went around, but who, nevertheless, had contributed handsomely. Grandma was explaining to anyone who would listen that she must get up to the luggage van for her hatbox. The pink rose on her hat was brand-new. A bride must have a flower, even an artificial one.

The drunk had stopped his interminable crooning and turned out his pockets. The Slag and Emmie, too, had stopped their very different crooning and Slag had given generously of Emmie's last week's pay. Mrs. Percer shushed her puling infant and stared compassionately at the girl. Hope she'll have better luck than I had, she reflected without bitterness. Wouldn't be so bad if Ted didn't drink and the climate didn't get the kids down. . . . She can have that new tin of talc powder they gave me at the hospital. . . . Ted only sent me the bare fare back.

The bouncer and the destroyer heightened the atmosphere of growing excitement by counting the mileposts.

"Only four hundred and eighteen more miles to Darwin, Mum? How many to Pine Creek?"

"Hayes' Creek, not Pine Creek, darling."

"But why isn't it Pine Creek, Mum?"

"Because the plantation is at Hayes' Creek."

"But why, Mum, why . . . ?"

"Count the posts, darling. Look, there's four hundred and seventeen. Only seven more to Hayes' Creek."

Only six more. Two more. One more.

Everyone was peering out his nearest window. The drunk was pushed aside by someone who had only an aisle seat, and unceremoniously knelt upon.

"Bet you I see him first. . . ."

The bride sat stiff and embarrassed on her front seat, a shabby suitcase gripped in both hands, a piece of pale blue ribbon trailing from it, forgotten in her haste.

The bus began to slow down. There's the turnoff. Hayes' Creek turnoff. Can't see anything but a signpost. And no one there.

In a silence which was almost accusing, Big Joe climbed stiffly down from his cabin. He cast a swift look around. No one. Surely the fellow had enough decency to be on time to meet a bride who'd come three thousand miles? Well, he'd wait ten minutes for them to make the presentation. Not a second longer. Even so, he'd be an hour late at Katherine. Might make up a quarter. But no more. Hilly country was beginning and there were a few skeletons of army trucks lying at the bottom of ravines to remind one not to take the bends too quickly.

Eager hands to help down and take the suitcase and the lumpish paper parcel from her quivering hands. Little jokes to make it easier for the bride when the bridegroom tarries.

"He's takin' extra time doin' himself up. . . . Special occasion, y'know."

"Bet he's grown a beard. . . . Most fellers do in these parts."

"Is he dark or fair? Or maybe red. . . . Those red beards always get the girls in."

Then a little silence. Everybody tried not to scan the silent country-side. Away to the left where the Hayes' Creek track ran, the country rose gently, first into foothills in which were discernible the fresh green squares of plantations, and then into the towering bulk of a black mountain watching guard over them.

Big Joe spoke. "The folk on this trip want to make a little expression of their good wishes to you," he told the girl, who was making valiant efforts to appear unconcerned. "But seeing that we only knew about the wedding at the last stop, it didn't give us much time to drop into the nearest store. . . ."

There was a friendly rustle of laughter as the passengers crowded nearer, and the girl blushed red and white by turns, completely taken by surprise. While Mr. Mellows made his brief speech, one of his older daughters ran to the side of the road and gathered a little bunch of wild cotton flowers. The girl kept her eyes on the ground until he was finished, and the hand she put out to take the little purse was trembling.

"I can't thank you enough. . . ." She faced them all bravely. "I thought I'd have no one of my own folk here on my wedding day . . . and now I have over forty." There was a little silence. "Please don't wait," she went on quickly. "I know you're running late." The appeal was addressed to Big Joe personally. "Tim will be here any minute now. And thank you all, so very much."

"A few minutes more won't matter," Big Joe was surprised to find himself saying casually, as though he had a few hours up his sleeve. "I don't fancy leaving a bit of a girl here by herself. It's seven miles back to the settlement at Hayes' Creek, and when night comes on up here, it comes pretty sudden."

"Oh, please don't wait any longer." The girl's voice quivered with tears now. "Probably the jeep has broken down. Tim's always joking about it."

"While we're waitin', let's drink the bride's health." The Slag's companion, in a newly found sobriety, stood swaying on the step, miraculously holding three bottles of lukewarm beer. "Get out some glasses, someone."

Enough glasses and plastic cups and tops of thermos flasks were found to go around, and everyone had a mouthful to drink to the bride. More speeches were made, more jokes handed around. Ten minutes passed. Another ten.

"Please go now," urged the girl, almost in a sort of anguish. "You've all been so very kind. I know how tired you are. And the skedule . . ."

"Well, we'd better be making a move," admitted Joe reluctantly. "Sure this was the turnoff where he was to meet you?"

"If this is the Hayes' Creek turnoff, yes. Besides, I knew it by that funny anthill shaped like a torpedo."

Silently the passengers filed back into the bus, each making his individual good-by. When they were all settled, they looked out the windows. The girl had retreated under the shade of a cork tree, and was standing stiffly waving to them. The little red plastic purse she was holding in her hand made a splotch of bright color in the gray-green landscape.

Big Joe looked steadily into the rearview mirror above his head. All at once it seemed to him as though forty-one pairs of eyes were directed into that tiny four-by-three piece of mercury-backed glass, imploring, pleading, threatening. The accusing silence seeped through to his cabin, as though the loudspeaker system were reversed. The eye of the bouncer seemed especially accusing.

Quietly he slipped the truck into reverse gear. He noted with grim amusement the ripple of relief which washed over the tired, dusty passengers. Grandma sat back with an audible sigh of relief, wiping her eyes. The six children nearly whooped with delight and craned out the windows. Emmie gave an audible sniffle. Even the Icicle relaxed. Slowly the great vehicle reversed until it was level with the girl.

"Better hop on," Big Joe called down to her. "I'll run you along to the settlement."

"Oh no, thank you so much." The girl was scarlet with embarrassment, but behind the tears in her eyes, which had only been waiting the solace of solitude to fall, the driver thought he detected relief, too.

"Hop in," he repeated gruffly.

"But your skedule . . . ?" The girl's voice was a shamed apology.

"Can go to the devil!" It was Big Joe's ultimate gesture.

But scarcely had she got her foot on the step when a shout came ringing through the timber, followed by a tall young man dressed in army shorts, boots, hat, and nothing else. She paused, looking back over her shoulder, and a loveliness came to life in her face. The shabby suitcase slid from her hand, slithered over the gravel and came to a rest in the little gutter by the roadside.

After a few seconds, the young man lifted his head.

"Thanks," he said curtly to Big Joe, lifting one hand. His glance scuttered along the rows of friendly faces lining the bus like so many headlamps. "Thanks," he said again.

In silence they picked up the suitcase, its blue ribbon still trailing. He slung a stick through the handle and the girl took one end. The young man clutched the bulky brown paper parcel under his other arm. Farewells showered down like confetti. Good-by. Good luck. Good-by.

They set off walking down the bush track toward the knobby black mountain with the minute cleared squares of banana plantations huddled around its feet. In silence the passengers watched them, until the tiny figures were lost in the green waves of cork trees.

Big Joe glanced in his rearview mirror and started up his engine.

"WELL I'M—!"
G. E. M. SKUES

Mr. Theodore Castwell, having devoted a long, strenuous, and not unenjoyable life to hunting to their doom innumerable salmon trout and grayling in many quarters of the globe, and having gained much credit among his fellows for his many ingenious improvements in rods, flies and tackle employed for that end, in the fullness of time died and was taken to his own place.

Saint Peter looked up from a draft balance sheet at the entry of the attendant angel.

"A gentleman giving the name of Castwell. Says he is a fisherman, your Holiness, and has Fly-Fishers' Club, London, on his card."

"Hm-hm," said Saint Peter. "Fetch me the ledger with his account." Saint Peter perused it.

"Hm-hm," said Saint Peter. "Show him in."

Mr. Castwell entered cheerfully and offered a cordial right hand to Saint Peter. "As a brother of the angle—" he began.

"Hm-hm," said Saint Peter.

"I am sure I shall not appeal to you in vain for special consideration in connection with the quarters to be assigned to me here."

"Hm-hm," said Saint Peter. "I have been looking at your account from below."

"Nothing wrong with it, I hope," said Mr. Castwell.

"Hm-hm," said Saint Peter. "I have seen worse. What sort of quarters would you like?"

"Well," said Mr. Castwell. "Do you think you could manage something in the way of a country cottage of the Test Valley type, with modern conveniences and say three-quarters of a mile of one of those pleasant chalk streams, clear as crystal, which proceed from out the throne, attached?"

"Why, yes," said Saint Peter. "I think we can manage that for you. Then what about your gear? You must have left your fly rods and tackle down below. I see you prefer a light split cane of nine feet or so, with appropriate fittings. I will indent upon the Works Department for what you require, including a supply of flies. I think you will approve of our dressers' productions. Then you will want a keeper to attend you."

"Thanks awfully, your Holiness," said Mr. Castwell. "That will be first-rate. To tell you the truth, from the Revelations I read, I was inclined to fear that I might be just a teeny-weeny bit bored in heaven."

"In H—hm-hm," said Saint Peter, checking himself.

It was not long before Mr. Castwell found himself alongside an enchantingly beautiful, clear chalk stream, some fifteen yards wide, swarming with fine trout feeding greedily; and presently the attendant angel assigned to him had handed him the daintiest, most exquisite, light split-cane rod conceivable—perfectly balanced with reel and line—with a beautifully damped, tapered cast of incredible fineness and strength—and a box of flies of such marvelous tying as to be almost mistakable for the natural insects they were to simulate.

Mr. Castwell scooped up a natural fly from the water, matched it perfectly from the fly box, and knelt down to cast to a riser putting up just under a tussock ten yards or so above him. The fly lit like gossamer, six inches above the last ring, floated a moment, and went under in the next ring; and next moment the rod was making the curve of beauty. Presently, after an exciting battle, the keeper netted out a beauty of about two and a half pounds.

"Heavens," cried Mr. Castwell. "This is something like."

"I am sure his Holiness will be pleased to hear it," said the keeper.

Mr. Castwell prepared to move upstream to the next riser when he became aware that another trout had taken up the position of that which he had just landed, and was rising. "Look at that," he said, dropping instantaneously to his knee and drawing off some line. A moment later an accurate fly fell just above the neb of the fish, and instantly Mr. Castwell engaged in battle with another lusty fish. All went well, and presently the landing net received its two and a half pounds.

"A very pretty brace," said Mr. Castwell, preparing to move on to the next of the string of busy nebs which he had observed putting up around the bend. As he approached the tussock, however, he became aware that the place from which he had just extracted so satisfactory a brace was already occupied by another busy feeder.

"Well I'm damned!" cried Mr. Castwell. "Do you see that?"

"Yes, sir," said the keeper.

The chance of extracting three successive trout from the same spot was too attractive to be forgone, and once more Mr. Castwell knelt down and delivered a perfect cast to the spot. Instantly it was accepted and battle was joined. All held, and presently a third gleaming trout joined his brethren in the creel.

"Heavens!" exclaimed Mr. Castwell. "Was there ever anything like it?"

"No, sir," said the keeper.

"Look here," said he to the keeper. "I think I really must give this chap a miss and pass on to the next."

"Sorry! It can't be done, sir. His Holiness would not like it."

"Well, if that's really so," said Mr. Castwell, and knelt reluctantly to his task.

SEVERAL HOURS LATER he was still casting to the same tussock.

"How long is this confounded rise going to last?" inquired Mr. Castwell. "I suppose it will stop soon?"

"No, sir," said the keeper.

"What, isn't there a slack hour in the afternoon?"

"No afternoon, sir."

"What? Then what about the evening rise?"

"No evening, sir," said the keeper.

"Well, I shall knock off, now. I must have had about thirty brace from that corner."

"Beg pardon, sir, but his Holiness would not like that."

"What?" said Mr. Castwell. "Mayn't I even stop at night?"

"No night here, sir," said the keeper.

"Then do you mean that I have got to go on catching these damned two-and-a-half-pounders at this corner forever and ever?"

The keeper nodded.

"Hell!" said Mr. Castwell.

"Yes," said his keeper.

THE WEATHER BREEDER
MERRILL DENISON

THE FARM LAY at the eastern end of the lake, a straggling clearing which seemed to be eternally battling for its life with the poplars and birches that hemmed it in. It was a good farm; over sixty acres of stiff blue clay such as is found deposited among glacier-scoured granite hills. It had been cleared by the same pioneer who had built the log house, barns, and stable. He was a good workman; the adz work on the two-foot logs showed it; but when his wife died he sold out to old John, and left.

In spring the farm was mosquito-infested lowland, in summer something like a gigantic fireless cooker with its surrounding hills of rock. The stiff clay was hard to work, and there was no road on that side of the lake—only a trail—but old John never complained or thought his life monotonous. It was all part of the yearly fight to grow enough food to carry him and his daughter, Lize, through the winter until the fight could commence again. Year after year the same, and he was sixty, and dry and hard.

The third year at the farm he bought a secondhand threshing outfit, and one of the summer campers who owned a launch towed it across the lake for him on a raft that he and Jim, his prospective son-in-law, made out of huge driftwood cedars. The outfit was of great assistance. It saved so much time, and he was able to get his grain down to the foot of the lake before the freeze-up.

Old John was obstinate and opinionated, and also the least bit hard of hearing. Standing on the mow frame one day, bundling armfuls of dusty straw behind him, the old man paid no attention to the boys' shouted warning. The frame gave way; he slipped and fell, wrenching one knee so badly that Jim had to help him to the house. There he remained for three weeks while one after another the perfect days of late September slipped by. The boys went on threshing, and Lize cared for old John's leg and his souring mood.

It was the first time old John had ever been forced to remain indoors. He roamed between the kitchen and his bed in the back room, restless and grouchy. He growled because he could not find his pipe, got in Lize's way when she was cooking. He complained bitterly about everything; about himself, about the boys, about the weather.

Particularly about the weather.

Never had there been such a fall in Ontario—an unvarying succession of mellow, cloudless days, with a soft haze purpling the hills even at noontime. Days for pagan prayers; and each morning the old man hobbled to his window, looked out, and growled, "Grh! Another of them weather breeders."

No longer could he trust the weather; too often had his hopes, his very sustenance, been wiped out in a few hours. Late frosts, early frosts, grain burned with drought one year, scalded by sodden fields the next; a field of oats, golden ripe for reaping, pounded flat by hailstorms. To him the weather was a personality, vague and formless, but filled with trickery and deceit and low cunning, a personality with which he was engaged in a lifelong duel of wits. Bad weather he did not mind; it could not get worse. Good weather he hated; it could not get better.

Lize and the boys tried to hearten him with gossip about the work and the success of the crop. They bantered him about his gloomy weather prophecies, but every day he grew more sour. Each morning he foretold calamity; each evening a placid sunset mocked him, and the boys scoffed at his miserable forebodings. It made him bitter, and it hurt his pride to have his wisdom jeered at by youth.

At first Lize did not mind him. She was twenty, with an elusive beauty that might last two babies, certainly not three. She was happy and she had her work to do. When drying dishes she could look out of the window and see Jim, her lover, carrying hundred-pound bags of grain on his back to the water's edge. The drying waited while she watched his sturdy figure until it was hidden by a shoulder of rock near the beach. And she would turn to her dishes with a slow, happy smile. They would be married before winter; with such a crop Jim's share would give them enough to start. Young Levi passed too, sweating under his heavy load, and she was glad to see him; every bag added to the slowly mounting total she carried in her mind and heart.

But Lize's even temper had its limits. With the growing of the pile of bags down on the beach, old John's perpetual grumblings grew worse until the boys lost patience with him, and Lize grew troubled. She did not rebel; she crept within herself. When Jim stole a moment to come to the pail of drinking water standing on a bench inside the door, she would be quiet. When he tried to catch her, she would put the table between them and glance nervously over her shoulder at the door of her father's room. Jim would go back to his work hurt and disappointed.

At last the end was in sight. Early one morning Levi rowed across the lake to the summer camper's and asked him to come that afternoon with his launch and tow the big flat-bottomed punt behind it. He returned at nine o'clock, and all day the boys worked feverishly in the hot sunshine, stopping impatiently when Lize called them for dinner, gulping down their food, and hurrying back to work again. At four they looked out on the lake for the camper with his launch, the last bag under their feet, another year's battle ended in victory. Before morning their grain would be at the foot of the lake and sold, perhaps, by noon. Jim spoke. "You watch for Murl, Levi. I'm goin' up to the house."

He found Lize wiping the table when he gently opened the door. Her back was to him, and he stole up behind her and kissed her neck where the fair hair curled away from it. She was startled, and pushed him from her with nervous haste. "No, Jim, no!" she pleaded. "Paw'll hear you'n be out here raisin' ructions. Please, Jim, go on away. He's gettin' sourer'n sourer."

"It seems like you don't want me hangin' round," he complained.

"Jim!"

"And it ain't as if you hadn't promised, neither. If I hadn't been goin' with you sincet we was young ones—"

"Please, Jim," she interrupted, placing her hand soothingly on his moist arm. "Don't talk so loud. He'll hear you. And he ain't been talkin' kindly about us gettin' married this fall. Don't look at me like that, please. It ain't my fault, but we can't go agin his wishes. You said so yourself."

Jim spoke in a hot whisper. "It ain't *my* fault. I guess I done my share this summer'n last spring. I got half shares in them oats'n I'm goin' to tell him so. He ain't done no work; he ain't done nothin' but set'n growl. I'm gettin' sick o' this sort o' thing."

He strode angrily toward the door, opening it quickly. Levi was standing outside. He was on his way from the beach and had paused, puzzled by the look of the sky toward the east. It seemed heavier and darker there, but then the lower reaches of the sky are deceptive on hazy days. A dull pewter sheen comes over them and makes it difficult to know for sure if clouds or dust-screened blue is there.

"Murl's comin' round the end of Chris's Point," Levi said, stepping past Jim into the house. Jim followed him to hear the news. "He's towin' the punt an' two rowboats. We can take fifty bags at a lick. Get her down in four trips easy."

They made their plans while Lize pleaded with them to go. They were on the point of leaving when the old man opened the door of his room and stood there looking at them, a picture of abysmal gloom. His gray hair was pulled far down on his forehead, accentuating the scowl that was always there and giving him an expression of comic sorrow. He stood bent forward, leaning on a short cane, his ragged vest falling vertically from his shoulders and his braces festooned dejectedly about his knees. He hobbled toward his chair, on which the afternoon sunlight was falling. He jerked it away, as if somehow the chair had betrayed him and gone over to the enemy.

"Sure is a slick day, Mr. Hawley," Levi stammered.

The old man snarled and slumped into his chair.

"You're fools, the pack of you! Don't you know nothin'?"

"I know we got the grain down," Jim exclaimed, a hint of triumph in his voice.

"It'll all be spoiled," old John predicted with assurance. "Crazy notion draggin' a couple a tons a grain round the big lake with the squalls that's always comin' up."

Levi added to his rage. "Why, there ain't been a wind for a month, Mr. Hawley," he said.

"Ain't that what I been tellin' you all along? Jest one day like this after another," the old man shouted. "They's weather breeders, I tell you, jest one weather breeder after another. The trouble is you don't know nothin'. We ought to had a storm when the moon turned." He sneered. "There ain't been an equalnoxial this year. Do you know what that means?"

"Kinda lucky we missed her for oncet, eh?" Jim snickered.

"Missed her?" the old man roared. "We ain't missed her. She's savin' herself up, that's what she's doin'. Same haze on the hills, not a breath of air movin', jest crouchin' there, simmerin', and waitin'." He slouched down in his chair, his chin sunk upon his chest, his brooding eyes staring into the fireless stove.

Jim came, quite abruptly, to the end of his patience. "Aw, you're actin' like a cow with sore eyes in fly time," he broke out. "You old lads always figger you can tell about the weather, and I ain't never seen one of you ever get it right yet. Last fall, when we butchered that there pig and you looks at the milt, you says it was goin' to be an open winter without snow. It was the worst we seen in years. Thirty-five below down at the store, snow to your waist."

The old man rose to his feet, quivering with a mighty rage, too wrought-up to speak. He pointed his cane toward the door. Jim stood his ground defiantly, fearing that he had gone too far, perhaps.

"Well? What're you hangin' round for?" the old man quivered when he found his voice.

"I was goin' to ast you somethin'."

"About Lize, I s'pose," John spat scornfully. "Comin' round whinin' 'bout marryin' when you ain't got a cent in the world but shares in that grain down there on the beach waitin' to be spoiled. You ain't goin' to come round here throwin' no milt outen a half-starved hog up in my face and expect me to give you a thanks offerin' o' Lize."

Having avenged the insult of the pig's milt—the most respected form of divination in the backwoods—by forbidding the boy the thing that lay nearest his heart, the old man felt a little better, and a little ashamed. He jerked the chair around and sat down with his back to Jim, as if in that way he defied the boy to argue or question his decision. Besides, he did not care to meet the boy's eyes.

Jim knew that it was useless to say anything. The old man would feel differently when the grain was sold and he could be up and around again. Jim opened the door, which faced due west, and the sight of the peaceful fields and the blue lake beyond them restored something of his natural gaiety. On the beach, Levi and Murl were standing beside the launch looking anxiously toward the house. Jim closed the door and walked toward them.

The old man stared at the stove, hands folded across his belly, long legs stretched in front of him. From time to time he drew slowly on his pipe and the smoke escaped from his lips with a tiny pop. Lize returned to work with a suspicious redness about her eyes, which she wiped with her knuckles. The house was still except for the old man's heavy breathing, the frustrated hum of a bluebottle fly at the window, and the rustle of Lize at her work.

A low rumble like distant thunder broke the stillness. John raised his head and listened. The sound came again, far off and low. He shifted his chair and looked toward the half-open door, through which a bar of golden light illumined one corner of the dim interior.

"Lize, what's that noise?"

"It must be Murl draggin' the boats up, Paw."

He accepted the answer and lapsed into his morose silence.

On the beach, three young men stood close together and looked toward the east.

"What do you make of it, Jim?"

"Don't look like smoke. Lookut there, Levi. Just beyond that swale. Lookut them birches."

"See that there swirl of sand by the fence corner? There!"

"Look! There's another!"

"Look over there above the knoll. Beyond the Dyer Lake hardwoods."

"Funny, there doesn't seem to be a breath of wind. It's curiously still, isn't it?"

"But they's whitecaps out beyond Chris's Point."

"Jim, she's acomin'," in awed tones from Levi.

"Ain't nothin'," with forced assurance from Jim. "You're gettin' as bad as the old lad."

"Looks pretty black to me, boys," from Murl, a slight, dark lad with the city stamp on his khaki slacks and his white shirt. "Coming up to the house?"

"Think I'll stay here and watch a bit."

Murl left them there, two motionless figures which cast long purple shadows across the sand in the late sunlight. A great fright growing in their hearts, but each of them afraid to admit to the other the meaning of the thing they were seeing in the east. The sky was darkening with that prodigious rapidity which accompanies long-delayed storms that seem to be making up time with the remorseless haste of overdue express trains.

Inside the house the same dull fly beat against the small-paned windows through which the long rays of sun poured on the grimy, papered walls. The low rumble came again, nearer and more ominous.

"What's that?" exclaimed Murl anxiously.

"Figgered it was you druggin' your boats up," John answered indifferently.

"It's thunder, Mr. Hawley. It looked pretty threatening toward the east when I came in."

Old John raised himself slowly and hobbled into his own room, where the window looked out toward the east. He leaned his hand on the low sill. To the east and south the birch trees shone with an unreal whiteness against the black sky, as if they had been picked out with white paint. The storm was approaching with incredible speed, and yet there was no wind. Old John watched silently for a long while, enjoying the scene with morbid satisfaction. He thought of the grain down on the beach and of its inevitable ruin. It did not bother him. He spoke softly to himself with reverential rapture. "She's goin' to be a hellbender. But I knowed she'd come. I knowed it."

At the front door Lize stood, horror-stricken with the first premonition of the impending disaster that would keep her starved for Jim another winter. On the beach the two boys looked at each other and then at the pile of grain. They shook their heads and moved listlessly toward the house.

And then the wind came. A whining blast that bent the birches before it and whipped the lake into a fury of small waves. A dead poplar crashed beyond the creek, and at the edges of the field the bushes leaned far westward. A swirl of dust spun down the road, broke, and was flung toward the lake. A woodchuck scurried across the corner of the field.

Lize closed the door with difficulty and stood with her back against it. "Paw!" she cried. "It's going to be an awful storm. Somethin' terrible. Oh, Paw, ain't there nothin' we can do?"

The old man came to the door of his room, a peculiar smile playing across his face for one who has just watched ruination sweep toward him. "Nothin' but sit here and enjoy her," he answered.

She ran to him and caught his shoulders with frightened, clutching fingers. "But, Paw," she pleaded, looking at him with eyes in which sheer terror showed, "all Jim's bags down on the beach. They'll be soaked through."

"They won't be worth a red cent when this rain gets at 'em. Might as well throw 'em in the lake."

He had no sympathy. The girl guessed it, although she did not know why, and she stumbled across the room, where she looked through tear-blinded eyes toward the lake. Overhead the loose old shingles rattled in the wind. The noise of them and the sounds of the storm outside brought the old man a holy joy. They vindicated him, his age, and his experience. The righteous in an orthodox heaven, watching the torments of the damned in hell, beneath them, must have some such splendid feeling. He sat down, content, and waited for the boys.

They came in after a few minutes, wet with the first gust of rain. "Shut the door, Levi!" Jim said. "By the livin' twist she's agoin' to pour."

He looked for Lize, but she was standing in front of the window, very rigid and forbidding, fighting to control her grief. Old John watched the boys slip dejectedly into chairs. He was in the center of the room, but they ignored him and each other. "Sorta shoots the whole summer's work to hell, don't it?" Levi said.

The wind whipped around the corner of the house and moaned in the spaces between the logs and window frames. A pane of glass, insecurely held by putty long since dried and cracked, rattled pettishly against the muntins. The kitchen was in partial darkness. The leaden half-light of the storm obscured the corners and made the bowed figures vague hulks radiating gloom. There was a long silence such as comes when words seem futile or inadequate. It was broken by Lize asking in a strained voice, barely under control, "You won't make a cent outen the summer, will you, Jim?"

He shook his head despondently, and then rose, and clumsily took her in his arms. Murl, whose city life made him less of a fatalist than the backwoods people, was profoundly sorry for them, and offered to do what he could to help. "It's hard luck, Mr. Hawley," he said. "After all, yours is the greatest loss. I wish I could do something."

The old man listened and his eyes roved from one to another of the saddened group gathered in the dim shack. At last he could restrain himself no longer; the humor of the situation was too delicious. He burst into a long peal of hearty laughter. "Ha, ha! Listen to her. Comin' down like the whole Mishinog Lake was turned upside down. She's atunin'."

"Paw, stop that awful laughin'," pleaded Lize.

"You lads look good and mournful now, don't you, eh? And feel kinda mournful, too. Didn't I say all them good days was weather breeders? Didn't I say we'd missed the equalnoxials and we'd pay for it?" His voice rose in its triumphant insistence. "When you lads've farmed, like me, for forty years, you won't be so damn' cheerful when you see a spell of good weather. I was right all along, wasn't I? Eh, Jim? Didn't I tell you, Jim?"

"Shut up!" snapped Jim. "You've made life miserable for everybody in camp for most a month with your prophesyin'. You got your storm, damn it. Why can't you keep quiet and enjoy it? You're satisfied."

Levi edged toward the door. "I can't stand this," he said to Murl. "Comin' out?"

They went out together, and an angry gust of wind blew through the opened door. Jim did his awkward best to comfort Lize, but she seemed inconsolable. The old man, oblivious to anything but his startling vindication at the hands of nature, returned to the attack.

"I'll wager none of you young lads'll ever try to tell me I don't know what kind of a day it is again."

"Dry up!" ordered Jim. "Can't you see Lize is bawling her eyes out? You may think a cloudburst a fine thing, but you're the only one that does."

"But I was right, Jim—wasn't I right?"

Jim lost his temper at last. He strode toward the old man and tightened his fingers on the bony shoulders, shaking him as one shakes a dusty bag. "Great Gawd, *yes*," Jim shouted, with his face close to old John's. "You was right. A million times you was right. If you'll only keep that sour trap of your'n closed, I'll say you was always right."

The old man seemed surprised. "Ain't no need to take on so, Jim," old John placated through his chattering teeth. "Ain't no cause to get mad, Jim. As long as you know I was right, I'm satisfied."

Jim loosed his hold, but Lize, to whom this last remark seemed the crowning mark of insane cruelty, screamed at her father. "You're satisfied? And how about us? How can we get married when you says you wouldn't let us until the grain was sold and Jim had a little money? There ain't any grain to sell. How about Jim and me, I'd like to know?"

"But that don't matter, Lize," Jim added bitterly. "Your paw's havin' such a good time outen this here storm. You oughta be happy he's cheered up. He'd been hell to live with all winter if they hadn't come some kinda calamity." He took her in his arms protectingly and glared defiantly at John. "I got a mind to marry you anyways." He tried to see her face, but it was hidden against his own chest. He brushed the soft hair with his lips, and leaned forward to speak closer to her ear. "Will you, Lize?"

She shook her head. He could not tell whether the answer was yes or no.

"Lize," old John said humbly. "Don't take on so, Lize. Don't rob your old paw outen the only fun he's got this fall." Lize gave no sign she heard him, and Jim's blue eyes kept their unwavering angry stare on him. He tried again. "Lize, I didn't know you and Jim wanted to get married that bad. There ain't no reason you two shouldn't get married if you want to."

Jim snorted. "With the hull summer's crop down there soakin' on the beach with your weather breedin'? How can we get married?"

Old John ran his fingers through his gray hair apologetically. "You could live here at the house, I s'pose, Jim. Lize's got to look after one of us and there ain't no reason why she can't look after us both."

Lize slowly raised her head and looked at her father, but she could tell he was in earnest by the very shyness of him. She flung herself upon him, danced up and down in front of him, drew his face nearer to her so that she could kiss his wrinkled cheek. Her joy was so frank, so natural, and so unusual that it made the old man feel a little ashamed that he could be the cause of such emotion. But it filled him with a mighty pride as well. He was a power who could give or withhold happiness at will. And he was an unquestioned authority on the weather, an acknowledged prophet whom no one would ever doubt again.

He took Lize in his arms.

Levi found them thus when he and Murl rushed in the door, tremendously excited. "Jim! Jim!" he shouted. "It ain't hardly rained a drop. There ain't nothin' wet but the top layer, Jim. The storm's passed south o' here." He rushed out again, and Lize broke away from her father to go and see the wonder for herself.

The shadow of a great disappointment stole slowly over the old man's face. "Not rained a drop?" he quavered. "But we heard it, here on the roof."

"Must have been the shingles rattling in the wind," Murl told him over his shoulder. "We were just on the fringe of the storm."

Old John stood in the center of the deserted kitchen, trying to collect his thoughts. "I don't believe it," he muttered, and slowly turned to seek his chair. On the far wall he saw the faint pattern of the window muntins, wan shadows against feeble sunlight. But while he watched, the light strengthened, as the tattered edges of the storm were swept away, through yellow and orange, until the wall was stained the deep, rich red of the setting sun, promising a fair day tomorrow.

God might know why the old man chose the strawberries. Perhaps because they were sitting there, on the corner of the table. Whatever the reason, quite suddenly he caught the tin dish in his two hands and hurled it against the wall. "Set! You damned old weather breeder, set!" he raved, and obligingly the sun slipped behind the western hills, leaving countless trickles of deep, rich red dribbling down the wallpaper.

IN AND OUT THE HOUSES
ELIZABETH TAYLOR

Kitty Miller, wearing new red hair ribbons, bounced along the vicarage drive, skipping across ruts and jumping over puddles.

Visiting took up all her mornings during the school holidays. From kitchen to kitchen around the village she made her progress, and this morning she felt drawn toward the vicarage. Quite sure of her welcome, she tapped on the back door.

"Why, Kitty Miller!" said the vicar, opening it. He looked quite different from in church, Kitty thought. He was wearing an open-necked shirt and an old, darned cardigan. He held a tea towel to the door handle, because his fingers were sticky. He and his wife were cutting up Seville oranges for marmalade and there was a delicious, tangy smell about the kitchen.

Kitty took off her coat, and hung it on the usual peg, and fetched a knife from the dresser drawer where they were kept.

"You are on your rounds again," Mr. Edwards said. "Spreading light and succor about the parish."

Kitty glanced at him rather warily. She preferred him not to be there, disliking men about her kitchens. She reached for an orange and, watching Mrs. Edwards for a moment out of the corners of her eyes, began to slice it up.

"What's new?" asked the vicar.

"Mrs. Saddler's bad," she said accusingly. He should be at that bedside, she meant to imply, instead of making marmalade. "They were saying at the Horse and Groom that she won't last the day."

"So we are not your first call of the morning?"

She had, on her way here, slipped around the back of the pub and into the pantry, where Miss Betty Benford, eight months pregnant, was washing the floor, puffing and blowing as she splashed gray soapy water over the flagstones with a gritty rag. When this job was done—to Miss Betty's mind, not to Kitty's—they drank a cup of tea together and chatted about the baby, woman to woman. The village was short of babies, and Kitty visualized pushing this one out in its pram, taking it around with her on her visits.

In his office, the landlord had been typing the luncheon menus. The keys went down heavily; his fingers hovered and stabbed. He often made mistakes, and this morning had typed "Jam Fart and Custard." Kitty considered—and then decided against—telling the vicar this.

"They have steak-and-kidney pie on the set menu today," she said instead.

"My favorite!" groaned the vicar. "I *never* get it."

"You had it less than a fortnight ago," his wife reminded him.

"And what pudding? If it's treacle tart I shall cry bitterly."

"Jam tart," Kitty said gravely. "And custard."

"I quite like custard, too," he said simply.

"Or choice of cheese and biscuits."

"I should have cheese and biscuits," Mrs. Edwards said.

It was just the kind of conversation Kitty loved.

"Eight and sixpence," she said. "Coffee's extra."

"To be rich! To be rich!" the vicar said. "And what are *we* having, my dear? Kitty has caused the juices to run."

"Cold, of course, as it's Monday."

He shuddered and picked up another orange. "My day off, too!"

Kitty pressed her lips together primly, thinking it wrong for clergymen to have days off, especially with Mrs. Saddler lying there, dying.

They kept glancing at one another's work as they cut the oranges. Who was doing it finely enough? Only Mrs. Edwards, they all knew.

"I like it fairly chunky," the vicar said.

When the job was done, Kitty rinsed her hands at the sink and put on her coat. She had given the vicarage what time she could spare, and the morning was getting on, and all the rest of the village waiting. She was very orderly in her habits and never visited in the afternoons, for then she had her novel to write. The novel was known about in the village, and some people felt concerned, wondering if Kitty might be another child author, another little Daisy Ashford.

With the vicar's phrases of gratitude giving her momentum, Kitty tacked down the drive between the shabby laurels, and out into the lane.

"THE VICAR'S HAVING cold," she told Mrs. de Vries, who was preparing a *tajine* of chicken in a curious earthenware pot she had brought back from Morocco.

"Poor old vicar," Mrs. de Vries said absentmindedly, as she cut almonds. She had a glass of something on the drainboard and often took a sip from it. "Do run and find a drink for yourself, dear child," she said. She was one of the people who wondered about Daisy Ashford.

"I'll have a bitter lemon, if I may," Kitty said.

"Well, do, my dear. You know where to find it."

As Kitty knew everything about nearly every house in the village, she did not reply, but went with assurance to the bar in the hall. She stuck a straw in her drink, and returned to the kitchen sucking peacefully.

"Is there anything I can do?" she inquired.

"No, just tell me the news."

"Mr. Mumford typed 'Jam Fart and Custard' on the menu today."

"Oh, he didn't! Oh, dear— You've made me do the nose trick with my gin. The *pain* of it!" Mrs. de Vries snatched a handkerchief from her apron pocket and held it to her face. When she had recovered, she said, "I simply can't wait for Tom to come home, to tell him that."

Kitty looked modestly gratified. "I called at the vicarage, too."

"And what were *they* up to?"

"They are up to making marmalade."

"Poor darlings! They *do* have to scrimp and scratch. Church mice, indeed!"

"But isn't homemade marmalade nicer than shop?"

"Not all *that* much."

After a pause, Kitty said, "Mrs. Saddler's on her way out."

"Who the hell's Mrs. Saddler?"

"At the almshouse. She's dying."

"Poor old thing."

"Betty Benford is eight months gone," Kitty said, shrugging.

"I wish you'd tell me something about people I *know*," Mrs. de Vries complained, taking another sip of gin.

"Her mother plans to look after the baby while Betty goes on working. Mrs. Benford, you know."

"Not next door's daily?"

"She won't be after this month."

"Does Mrs. Glazier know?" Mrs. de Vries asked.

"Not yet," Kitty said, glancing at the clock.

"My God, she'll go up the wall," Mrs. de Vries said with relish. "She's had that old Benford for years."

"What do you call that you're cooking?"

"It's a *tajine* of chicken."

"MRS. DE VRIES is having *tajine* of chicken," Kitty said next door, five minutes later.

"And what might that be when it's at home?"

Kitty described it as best she could, and Mrs. Glazier looked huffy. "Derek wouldn't touch it," she said. "He likes good, plain English food, and no messing about."

She was rolling out pastry for that evening's steak-and-kidney pie.

"They're having that at the Horse and Groom," Kitty said.

"*And* we'll have sprouts. *And* braised celery," Mrs. Glazier added, not letting Mrs. de Vries get away with her airs and graces.

"Shall I make a pastry rose to go on the top of the pie?" Kitty offered. "Mrs. Prout showed me how to."

"No, I think we'll leave well alone."

"Do you like cooking?" Kitty asked in a conversational tone.

"I don't mind it. Why?"

"I was only thinking that then it wouldn't be so hard on you when Mrs. Benford leaves."

Mrs. Benford was upstairs. There was a droning noise of a vacuum cleaner above, in what Kitty knew to be Mrs. Glazier's bedroom.

Mrs. Glazier, with an awful fear in her heart, stared, frowning, at Kitty, who went on, "I was just telling Mrs. de Vries that after Mrs. Benford's grandchild's born, she's going to stay at home to mind it."

The fact that next door had heard this stunning news first made the blow worse, and Mrs. Glazier put a flour-covered hand to her forehead. She closed her eyes for a moment. "But why can't the girl look after the little . . . baby herself?"

Kitty took the lid off a jar marked CLOVES and looked inside, sniffing. "Her daughter earns more money at the Horse and Groom than her mother earns here," she explained.

"I suppose you told Mrs. de Vries that, too."

Kitty went to the door with dignity. "Oh, no! I never talk from house to house. My mother says I'll have to stop my visiting if I do. Oh, by the way," she called back, "you'd better keep your dog in. The de Vries's bitch is in heat."

She went home and sat down to cold lamb and bubble and squeak. "The vicar's having cold, too," she said.

"And that's *his* business," her mother said warningly.

A FEW DAYS LATER Kitty called on Mrs. Prout.

Mrs. Prout's cottage was one of Kitty's favorite visits. Many years ago, before she was married, Mrs. Prout had been a schoolteacher, and she enjoyed using her old skills to deal with Kitty. Keeping her patience pliant, she taught her visitor new card games (and they were all educational), and got her on to collecting and pressing wild flowers. She would give her pastry trimmings to cut into shapes, and showed her how to pop corn and make fudge. She was extremely kind, though firm, and Kitty respected the rules—about washing her hands and never calling on Mondays or Thursdays, because these were housecleaning days, when Mrs. Prout was far too busy to have company. They were very serious together. Mrs. Prout enjoyed being authoritative to a child again, and Kitty had a sense of orderliness that obliged her to comply.

"They sent this from the vicarage," she said, coming into the kitchen with a small pot of marmalade.

"How jolly nice!" Mrs. Prout said. She took the marmalade and tilted it slightly, and it moved. Rather sloppy. But she thought no worse of the vicar's wife for that. "That's really *jolly* nice of them," she said, going into the larder. "And they shall have some of my apple jelly in fair return. Quid pro quo, eh? And one good turn deserves another."

She came out of the larder with a different pot and held it to the light, but the content did not move when she tipped it sideways.

"What's the news?" she asked.

"Mrs. Saddler still lingers on," Kitty said. She had called at the almshouse to inquire, but the district nurse had told her to run off and mind her own business. "I looked in at the Wilsons' on my way here. Mrs. Wilson was making a cheese-and-onion pie. Of course, they're vegetarians, but I have known him to sneak a little chicken into his mouth. I was helping to hand round at the de Vries's cocktail party, and he put out his hand toward a patty. 'It's chicken,' I said to him in a low voice. 'Nary a word,' he said, and he winked at me and ate it."

"And now you *have* said a word," Mrs. Prout said briskly.

"Why, so I have," Kitty agreed, looking astonished.

Mrs. Prout cleared the kitchen table and said, "If you like, I'll show you how to make ravioli. We shall have it for our television supper."

"Make ravioli!" cried Kitty. "You can't *make* ravioli. Mrs. Glazier buys it in a tin."

"So Mrs. Glazier may. But I find time to make my own."

"I shall be fascinated," Kitty said, taking off her coat.

"Then wash your hands, and don't forget to dry them. Isn't it about time you cut your nails?" Mrs. Prout asked in her schoolmistressy voice, and Kitty, who would take anything from her, agreed. ("We all know Mrs. Prout is God," her mother sometimes said resentfully.)

"Roll up those sleeves, now. And we'll go through your multiplication tables while we work."

Mrs. Prout set out the flour bin and a dredger and a pastry cutter and the mincer. Going back and forth to the cupboard, she thought how petty she was to be pleased at knowing that by this time tomorrow most of the village would be aware that she made her own ravioli. But perhaps it was only human, she decided.

"Now this is what chefs call the *mise en place*," she explained to Kitty, when she had finished arranging the table. "Can you remember that?"

"*Mise en place*," Kitty repeated obediently.

"SHALL I HELP YOU PREPARE the *mise en place?*" Kitty inquired of Mrs. Glazier.

"Mr. Glazier wouldn't touch it. I've told you he will only eat English food."

"But you have ravioli. That's Italian."

"I just keep it as a standby," Mrs. Glazier said scornfully. She was very huffy and put out these days, especially with Mrs. de Vries next door and her getting the better of her every time. Annette de Vries was French, and didn't they all know it. Mrs. Glazier, as a result, had become violently insular.

"I can make ravioli," Kitty said, letting the *mise en place* go, for she was not absolutely certain about it. "Mrs. Prout has just been teaching me. She and Mr. Prout have television trays by the fire, and then they sit and crack walnuts and play cards, and then they have hot milk and whisky and go to bed. I think it is very nice and cozy, don't you?"

"Mr. Glazier likes a proper sit-down meal when *he* gets back. Did you happen to see Tiger anywhere down the lane?"

"No, but I expect he's next door. The de Vries's bitch is in heat. I'm just calling there, so I'll shoo him off."

She had decided to cut short this visit. Mrs. Glazier was so bad-tempered these days, and hardly put herself out at all to give a welcome, and every interesting thing Kitty told her served merely to annoy.

"And I must get on with my jugged hare," Mrs. Glazier said, making no attempt to delay the departure. "It should be marinating in the port wine by now," she added grandly. "And I must make the soup and the croutons."

"Well, then, I'll be going," Kitty said, edging toward the door.

"And apricot mousse," Mrs. Glazier called out after her, as if she were in a frenzy.

"SHALL I PREPARE your *mise en place?*" Kitty inquired of Mrs. de Vries, trying her luck again.

"My! We *are* getting professional," said Mrs. de Vries, but her mind was really on what Kitty had just been telling her. Soup and jugged hare! she was thinking. What a dreadful meal!

She was glazing a *terrine* of chicken livers and wished that all the village might see her work of art, but having Kitty there was the next best thing.

"What's that?" she asked, as Kitty put a jar on the table.

"I have to take it to the vicarage on my way home. It's some of Mrs. Prout's apple jelly."

Mrs. de Vries gave it a keen look and notched up one point to Mrs. Prout. She notched up another when she heard about the ravioli, and wondered if she had underestimated the woman.

Kitty mooched around the kitchen, peeking and prying. Mrs. de Vries was the only one in the village to possess a *mandoline* for cutting vegetables. There were a giant pestle and mortar, a wicker breadbasket, ropes of Spanish onions, and a marble cheese tray.

"You can pound the fish for me," said Mrs. de Vries.

As this was not a house where she was made to wash her hands first, Kitty immediately set to work.

Mrs. de Vries said, in a half-humorous voice, "I was just going to have pears. But if the Glaziers are going in for apricot mousse, I had better pull my socks up. That remark, of course, is strictly *entre nous.*"

"THEN MRS. DE VRIES pulled her socks up and made a big apple tart," Kitty told her mother.

"I have warned you before, Kitty. What you see going on in people's houses you keep to yourself. Or you stay out of them. Is that finally and completely understood?"

"Yes, Mother," Kitty said meekly.

"MY DEAR GIRL, I couldn't eat it. I couldn't eat another thing," said Mr. Glazier, confronted by the apricot mousse. "A three-course meal. Why, I shouldn't sleep all night if I had any more. The hare alone was ample."

"I think Mr. de Vries would do better justice to his dinner," said Mrs. Glazier bitterly. She had spent all day cooking and was exhausted. "It's not much fun slaving away and not being appreciated. And what on earth can I do with all the leftovers?"

"Finish them up tomorrow and save yourself a lot of trouble."

Glumly, Mrs. Glazier washed the dishes, and suddenly thought of the Prouts sitting peacefully beside their fire, cracking walnuts, playing cards. She felt ill-done by as she stacked the remains of dinner in the fridge, but was perfectly certain that lie as she might have to to Kitty in the morning, the whole village should not know that for the second day the Glaziers were having soup, and jugged hare, and apricot mousse.

NEXT DAY, EATING a slice of apple tart, Kitty saw Mrs. de Vries test the soup and then put the ladle back into the saucepan. "What the eye doesn't see, the heart cannot grieve over," Mrs. de Vries said cheerfully. She added salt and a turn or two of pepper. Then she took more than a sip from the glass on the drainboard.

"The vicarage can't afford drinks," Kitty said.

"They *do* confide in you."

"I said to the vicar, 'Mrs. de Vries drinks gin while she is cooking,' and he said, 'Lucky old her.'"

"There will be a lot of red faces about this village if you go on like this," said Mrs. de Vries, making her part of the prophecy come true at once. Kitty looked at her in surprise. Then she said—Mrs. de Vries's flushed face reminding her—"I think next door must be having the change of life. She is awfully grumpy these days. Nothing pleases her."

"You are too knowing for your years," Mrs. de Vries said, and she suddenly wished she had not been so unhygienic about the soup. Too late now. "How is your novel coming along?" she inquired.

"Oh, very nicely, thank you. I expect I shall finish it before I go back to school, and then it can be published for Christmas."

"We shall all look forward to that," said Mrs. de Vries, in what Kitty considered an unusual tone of voice.

"MRS. DE VRIES CUTS up her vegetables with a *mandoline*," Kitty told Mrs. Glazier some days later.

"I always knew she must be nuts," said Mrs. Glazier, thinking of the musical instrument.

Seeing Kitty dancing up the drive, she had quickly hidden the remains of a shepherd's pie at the back of a cupboard. She was more than ever ruffled this morning, because Mrs. Benford had not arrived or sent a message. She had also been getting into a frenzy with her ravioli and, in the end, had thrown the whole lot into the garbage pail. She hated waste, especially now that her housekeeping allowance always seemed to have disappeared by Wednesday, and her husband was, in his dyspeptic way, continually accusing her of extravagance.

Kitty had been hanging about outside the almshouse for a great part of the morning, and had watched Mrs. Saddler's coffin being carried across the road to the church.

"Only one wreath and two relations," she now told Mrs. Glazier. "That's what comes of being poor. What are you having for dinner tonight? I could give you a hand."

"Mr. Glazier will probably be taking me to the Horse and Groom for a change," Mrs. Glazier lied.

"They are all at sixes and sevens there. Betty Benford started her pains in the night. A fortnight early."

Then Mrs. Benford would never come again, Mrs. Glazier thought despondently. She had given a month's notice the week before, and Mrs. Glazier had received it coldly, saying, "I think I should have been informed of this before it became common gossip in the village." Mrs. Benford had seemed quite taken aback at that.

"Well, I mustn't hang around talking," Mrs. Glazier told Kitty. "There's a lot to do this morning. When do you go back to school?"

"On Thursday."

Mrs. Glazier nodded, and Kitty felt herself dismissed. She sometimes wondered why she bothered to pay this call, when everyone else made her so welcome; but coming away from the funeral she had seen Mrs. de Vries driving into town, and it was one of Mrs. Prout's housecleaning days. She had hardly liked to call at the vicarage under the circumstances of the funeral, and the Horse and Groom being at sixes and sevens had made everyone there very boring and busy.

"I hope you will enjoy your dinner," she said politely to Mrs. Glazier. "They have roast Surrey fowl and all the trimmings."

When she had gone, Mrs. Glazier took the shepherd's pie from its hiding place and began to scrape some shabby old carrots.

"KITTY, WILL YOU stop chattering and get on with your pudding," her mother said in an exasperated voice.

Kitty had been describing how skillfully the undertaker's men had lowered Mrs. Saddler's coffin into the grave, Kitty herself peering from behind the tombstone of Maria Britannia Marlowe—her favorite dead person on account of her name.

It was painful to stop talking. A pain came in her chest, severe enough to slow her breathing, and gobbling the rice pudding made it worse. As soon as her plate was cleared, she began again. "Mrs. Glazier has the change of life," she said.

"How on earth do you know about such things?" her mother asked in a faint voice.

"As *you* didn't tell me, I had to find out the hard way," Kitty said sternly.

Her mother pursed her lips to stop from laughing, and began to stack the dishes.

"How Mrs. de Vries will miss me!" Kitty said dreamily, rising to help her mother. "I shall be stuck there at school, doing boring things, and she'll be having a nice time drinking gin."

"Now *that* is enough. You are to go to your room immediately," her mother said sharply, and Kitty looked at her red face reflectively, comparing it with Mrs. de Vries's. "You will have to find some friends of your own age. You are becoming a little menace to everyone with your visiting and we have got to live in this village. Now upstairs you go, and think over what I have said."

"Very well, Mother," Kitty said meekly. If she did not have to help her mother with the washing up, she could get on with her novel all the sooner.

She went upstairs to her bedroom and spread her writing things out on the table and soon, having at once forgotten her mother's words, was lost in the joy of authorship.

Her book was all about little furry animals and their small adventures, and there was not a human being in it, except the girl, Katherine, who befriended them all.

SHE MANAGED A FEW more visits that holiday; but on Thursday she went back to school again, and then no one in the village knew what was happening anymore.

A ROSE FOR EMILY
WILLIAM FAULKNER

WHEN MISS EMILY Grierson died, our whole town went to her funeral: the men through a sort of respectful affection for a fallen monument, the women mostly out of curiosity to see the inside of her house, which no one save an old manservant—a combined gardener and cook—had seen in at least ten years.

It was a big, squarish frame house that had once been white, decorated with cupolas and spires and scrolled balconies in the heavily lightsome style of the seventies, set on what had once been our most select street. But garages and cotton gins had encroached and obliterated even the august names of that neighborhood; only Miss Emily's house was left, lifting its stubborn and coquettish decay above the cotton wagons and the gasoline pumps—an eyesore among eyesores. And now Miss Emily had gone to join the representatives of those august names where they lay in the cedar-bemused cemetery among the ranked and anonymous graves of Union and Confederate soldiers who fell at the battle of Jefferson.

Alive, Miss Emily had been a tradition, a duty, and a care; a sort of hereditary obligation upon the town, dating from that day in 1894 when Colonel Sartoris, the mayor—he who fathered the edict that no Negro woman should appear on the streets without an apron—remitted her taxes, the dispensation dating from the death of her father on into perpetuity. Not that Miss Emily would have accepted charity. Colonel Sartoris invented an involved tale to the effect that Miss Emily's father had loaned money to the town, which the town, as a matter of business, preferred this way of repaying. Only a man of Colonel Sartoris' generation and thought could have invented it, and only a woman could have believed it.

When the next generation, with its more modern ideas, became mayors and aldermen, this arrangement created some little dissatisfaction. On the first of the year they mailed her a tax notice. February came, and there was no reply. They wrote her a formal letter, asking her to call at the sheriff's office at her convenience. A week later the mayor wrote her himself, offering to call or to send his car for her, and received in reply a note on paper of an archaic shape, in a thin, flowing calligraphy in faded ink, to the effect that she no longer went out at all. The tax notice was also enclosed, without comment.

They called a special meeting of the board of aldermen. A deputation waited upon her, knocked at the door through which no visitor had passed since she ceased giving china-painting lessons eight or ten years earlier. They were admitted by the old Negro into a dim hall from which a stairway mounted into still more shadow. It smelled of dust and disuse—a close, dank smell. The Negro led them into the parlor. It was furnished in heavy, leather-covered furniture. When the Negro opened the blinds of one window, they could see that the leather was cracked; and when they sat down, a faint dust rose sluggishly about their thighs, spinning with slow motes in the single sunray. On a tarnished gilt easel before the fireplace stood a crayon portrait of Miss Emily's father.

They rose when she entered—a small, fat woman in black, with a thin gold chain descending to her waist and vanishing into her belt, leaning on an ebony cane with a tarnished gold head. Her skeleton was small and spare; perhaps that was why what would have been merely plumpness in another was obesity in her. She looked bloated, like a body long submerged in motionless water, and of that pallid hue. Her eyes, lost in the fatty ridges of her face, looked like two small pieces of coal pressed into a lump of dough as they moved from one face to another while the visitors stated their errand.

She did not ask them to sit. She just stood in the door and listened quietly until the spokesman came to a stumbling halt. Then they could hear the invisible watch ticking at the end of the gold chain.

Her voice was dry and cold. "I have no taxes in Jefferson. Colonel Sartoris explained it to me. Perhaps one of you can gain access to the city records and satisfy yourselves."

"But we have. We are the city authorities, Miss Emily. Didn't you get a notice from the sheriff, signed by him?"

"I received a paper, yes," Miss Emily said. "Perhaps he considers himself the sheriff. . . . I have no taxes in Jefferson."

"But there is nothing on the books to show that, you see. We must go by the—"

"See Colonel Sartoris. I have no taxes in Jefferson."

"But, Miss Emily—"

"See Colonel Sartoris." (Colonel Sartoris had been dead almost ten years.) "I have no taxes in Jefferson. Tobe!" The Negro appeared. "Show these gentlemen out."

SO SHE VANQUISHED them, horse and foot, just as she had vanquished their fathers thirty years before about the smell. That was two years after her father's death and a short time after her sweetheart—the one we believed would marry her—had deserted her. After her father's death she went out very little; after her sweetheart went away, people hardly saw her at all. A few of the ladies had the temerity to call, but were not received, and the only sign of life about the place was the Negro man—a young man then—going in and out with a market basket.

"Just as if a man—any man—could keep a kitchen properly," the ladies said; so they were not surprised when the smell developed. It was another link between the gross, teeming world and the high and mighty Griersons.

A neighbor, a woman, complained to the mayor, Judge Stevens, eighty years old.

"But what will you have me do about it, madam?" he said.

"Why, send her word to stop it," the woman said. "Isn't there a law?"

"I'm sure that won't be necessary," Judge Stevens said. "It's probably just a snake or a rat that nigger of hers killed in the yard. I'll speak to him about it."

The next day he received two more complaints, one from a man who came in diffident deprecation. "We really must do something about it, Judge. I'd be the last one in the world to bother Miss Emily, but we've got to do something." That night the board of aldermen met—three graybeards and one younger man, a member of the rising generation.

"It's simple enough," he said. "Send her word to have her place cleaned up. Give her a certain time to do it in, and if she don't . . ."

"Damn it, sir," Judge Stevens said, "will you accuse a lady to her face of smelling bad?"

So the next night, after midnight, four men crossed Miss Emily's lawn and slunk about the house like burglars, sniffing along the base of the brickwork and at the cellar openings while one of them performed a regular sowing motion with his hand out of a sack slung from his shoulder. They broke open the cellar door and sprinkled lime there, and in all the outbuildings. As they recrossed the lawn, a window that had been dark was lighted and Miss Emily sat in it, the light behind her, and her upright torso motionless as that of an idol. They crept quietly across the lawn and into the shadow of the locusts that lined the street. After a week or two the smell went away.

That was when people had begun to feel really sorry for her. People in our town, remembering how old lady Wyatt, her great-aunt, had gone completely crazy at last, believed that the Griersons held themselves a little too high for what they really were. None of the young men were quite good enough to Miss Emily and such. We had long thought of them as a tableau; Miss Emily a slender figure in white in the background, her father a spraddled silhouette in the foreground, his back to her and clutching a horsewhip, the two of them framed by the back-flung front door. So when she got to be thirty and was still single, we were not pleased exactly, but vindicated; even with insanity in the family she wouldn't have turned down all of her chances if they had really materialized.

When her father died, it got about that the house was all that was left to her; and in a way, people were glad. At last they could pity Miss Emily. Being left alone, and a pauper, she had become humanized. Now she too would know the old thrill and the old despair of a penny more or less.

The day after his death all the ladies prepared to call at the house and offer condolence and aid, as is our custom. Miss Emily met them at the door, dressed as usual and with no trace of grief on her face. She told them that her father was not dead. She did that for three days, with the ministers calling on her, and the doctors, trying to persuade her to let them dispose of the body. Just as they were about to resort to law and force, she broke down, and they buried her father quickly.

We did not say she was crazy then. We believed she had to do that. We remembered all the young men her father had driven away, and we knew that with nothing left, she would have to cling to that which had robbed her, as people will.

SHE WAS SICK for a long time. When we saw her again, her hair was cut short, making her look like a girl, with a vague resemblance to those angels in colored church windows—sort of tragic and serene.

The town had just let the contracts for paving the sidewalks, and in the summer after her father's death they began the work. The construction company came with niggers and mules and machinery, and a foreman named Homer Barron, a Yankee—a big, dark, ready man, with a big voice and eyes lighter than his face. The little boys would follow in groups to hear him cuss the niggers, and the niggers singing in time to the rise and fall of picks. Pretty soon he knew everybody in town. Whenever you heard a lot of laughing anywhere about the square, Homer Barron would be in the center of the group. Presently we began to see him and Miss Emily on Sunday afternoons driving in the yellow-wheeled buggy and the matched team of bays from the livery stable.

At first we were glad that Miss Emily would have an interest, because the ladies all said, "Of course a Grierson would not think seriously of a Northerner, a day laborer." But there were still others, older people, who said that even grief could not cause a real lady to forget noblesse oblige—without calling it noblesse oblige. They just said, "Poor Emily. Her kinsfolk should come to her." She had some kin in Alabama; but years ago her father had fallen out with them over the estate of old lady Wyatt, the crazy woman, and there was no communication between the two families. They had not even been represented at the funeral.

And as soon as the old people said "Poor Emily," the whispering began. "Do you suppose it's really so?" they said to one another. "Of course it is. What else could . . ." This behind their hands; rustling of craned silk and satin behind jalousies closed upon the sun of Sunday afternoon as the thin, swift clop-clop-clop of the matched team passed: "Poor Emily."

She carried her head high enough—even when we believed that she was fallen. It was as if she demanded more than ever the recognition of her dignity as the last Grierson; as if it had wanted that touch of earthiness to reaffirm her imperviousness. Like when she bought the rat poison, the arsenic. That was over a year after they had begun to say "Poor Emily," and while the two female cousins were visiting her.

"I want some poison," she said to the druggist. She was over thirty then, still a slight woman, though thinner than usual, with cold, haughty black eyes in a face the flesh of which was strained across the temples and about the eye sockets as you imagine a lighthouse keeper's face ought to look. "I want some poison," she said.

"Yes, Miss Emily. What kind? For rats and such? I'd recom—"

"I want the best you have. I don't care what kind."

The druggist named several. "They'll kill anything up to an elephant. But what you want is—"

"Arsenic," Miss Emily said. "Is that a good one?"

"Is . . . arsenic? Yes, ma'am. But what you want—"

"I want arsenic."

The druggist looked down at her. She looked back at him, erect, her face like a strained flag. "Why, of course," the druggist said. "If that's what you want. But the law requires you to tell what you are going to use it for."

Miss Emily just stared at him, her head tilted back in order to look him eye for eye, until he looked away and went and got the arsenic and wrapped it up. The Negro delivery boy brought her the package; the druggist didn't come back. When she opened the package at home, there was written on the box, under the skull and bones: "For rats."

SO THE NEXT DAY we all said, "She will kill herself"; and we said it would be the best thing. When she had first begun to be seen with Homer Barron, we had said, "She will marry him." Then we said, "She will persuade him yet," because Homer himself had remarked—he liked men, and it was known that he drank with the younger men in the Elks Club—that he was not a marrying man. Later we said "Poor Emily" behind the jalousies as they passed on Sunday afternoon in the glittering buggy, Miss Emily with her head high and Homer Barron with his hat cocked and a cigar in his teeth, reins and whip in a yellow glove.

Then some of the ladies began to say that it was a disgrace to the town and a bad example to the young people. The men did not want to interfere, but at last the ladies forced the Baptist minister—Miss Emily's people were Episcopal—to call upon her. He would never divulge what happened during that interview, but he refused to go back again. The next Sunday they again drove about the streets, and the following day the minister's wife wrote to Miss Emily's relations in Alabama.

So she had blood kin under her roof again and we sat back to watch developments. At first nothing happened. Then we were sure that they were to be married. We learned that Miss Emily had been to the jeweler's and ordered a man's toilet set in silver, with the letters H.B. on each piece. Two days later we learned that she had bought a complete outfit of men's clothing, including a nightshirt, and we said, "They are married." We were really glad. We were glad because the two female cousins were even more Grierson than Miss Emily had ever been.

So we were not surprised when Homer Barron—the streets had been finished some time since—was gone. We were a little disappointed that there was not a public blowing-off, but we believed that he had gone on to prepare for Miss Emily's coming, or to give her a chance to get rid of the cousins. (By that time it was a cabal, and we were all Miss Emily's allies to help circumvent the cousins.) Sure enough, after another week they departed. And, as we had expected all along, within three days Homer Barron was back in town. A neighbor saw the Negro man admit him at the kitchen door at dusk one evening.

And that was the last we saw of Homer Barron. And of Miss Emily for some time. The Negro man went in and out with the market basket, but the front door remained closed. Now and then we would see her at a window for a moment, as the men did that night when they sprinkled the lime, but for almost six months she did not appear on the streets. Then we knew that this was to be expected too; as if that quality of her father which had thwarted her woman's life so many times had been too virulent and too furious to die.

When we next saw Miss Emily, she had grown fat and her hair was turning gray. During the next few years it grew grayer and grayer until it attained an even pepper-and-salt iron gray, when it ceased turning. Up to the day of her death at seventy-four it was still that vigorous iron gray, like the hair of an active man.

From that time on her front door remained closed, save for a period of six or seven years, when she was about forty, during which she gave lessons in china painting. She fitted up a studio in one of the downstairs rooms, where the daughters and granddaughters of Colonel Sartoris' contemporaries were sent to her with the same regularity and in the same spirit that they were sent to church on Sundays with a twenty-five-cent piece for the collection plate. Meanwhile her taxes had been remitted.

Then the newer generation became the backbone and the spirit of the town, and the painting pupils grew up and fell away and did not send their children to her with boxes of color and tedious brushes and pictures cut from the ladies' magazines. The front door closed upon the last one and remained closed for good. When the town got free postal delivery, Miss Emily alone refused to let them fasten the metal numbers above her door and attach a mailbox to it. She would not listen to them.

Daily, monthly, yearly we watched the Negro grow grayer and more stooped, going in and out with the market basket. Each December we sent her a tax notice, which would be returned by the post office a week later, unclaimed. Now and then we would see her in one of the downstairs windows—she had evidently shut up the top floor of the house—like the carven torso of an idol in a niche, looking or not looking at us, we could never tell which. Thus she passed from generation to generation—dear, inescapable, impervious, tranquil, and perverse.

And so she died. Fell ill in the house filled with dust and shadows, with only a doddering Negro man to wait on her. We did not even know she was sick; we had long since given up trying to get any information from the Negro. He talked to no one, probably not even to her, for his voice had grown harsh and rusty, as if from disuse.

She died in one of the downstairs rooms, in a heavy walnut bed with a curtain, her gray head propped on a pillow yellow and moldy with age and lack of sunlight.

THE NEGRO MET the first of the ladies at the front door and let them in, with their hushed, sibilant voices and their quick, curious glances, and then he disappeared. He walked right through the house and out the back and was not seen again.

The two female cousins came at once. They held the funeral on the second day, with the town coming to look at Miss Emily beneath a mass of bought flowers, with the crayon face of her father musing profoundly above the bier and the ladies sibilant and macabre; and the very old men—some in their brushed Confederate uniforms—on the porch and the lawn, talking of Miss Emily as if she had been a contemporary of theirs, believing that they had danced with her and courted her perhaps, confusing time with its mathematical progression, as the old do, to whom all the past is not a diminishing road but, instead, a huge meadow which no winter ever quite touches, divided from them now by the narrow bottleneck of the most recent decade of years.

Already we knew that there was one room in that region abovestairs which no one had seen in forty years, and which would have to be forced. They waited until Miss Emily was decently in the ground before they opened it.

The violence of breaking down the door seemed to fill this room with pervading dust. A thin, acrid pall as of the tomb seemed to lie everywhere upon this room decked and furnished as for a bridal: upon the valence curtains of faded rose color, upon the rose-shaded lights, upon the dressing table, upon the delicate array of crystal and the man's toilet things backed with tarnished silver, silver so tarnished that the monogram was obscured. Among them lay a collar and tie, as if they had just been removed, which, lifted, left upon the surface a pale crescent in the dust. Upon a chair hung the suit, carefully folded; beneath it the two mute shoes and the discarded socks.

The man himself lay in the bed.

For a long while we just stood there, looking down at the profound and fleshless grin. The body had apparently once lain in the attitude of an embrace, but now the long sleep that outlasts love, that conquers even the grimace of love, had cuckolded him. What was left of him, rotted beneath what was left of the nightshirt, had become inextricable from the bed in which he lay; and upon him and upon the pillow beside him lay that even coating of the patient and biding dust.

Then we noticed that in the second pillow was the indentation of a head. One of us lifted something from it, and leaning forward, that faint and invisible dust dry and acrid in the nostrils, we saw a long strand of iron-gray hair.

THE TEST
BRENDAN GILL

B Y DECEMBER, Henry had been at school long enough to learn most of the rules. Now he was beginning to take account of the legends that lay like shadows behind the rules and lent them their particular Northway flavor. Edward Carter, who had been at Northway for three years, was his chief guide in such matters. Henry wasn't altogether sure that he liked Carter, but he was glad that he had been assigned to room with him. According to locker-room gossip, Carter held a scholarship. Partly because of this, and partly because he got high grades and disliked sports, he was regarded by the rest of the school as something of a meatball.

Henry, on the other hand, already had achieved the glory of playing on the second football team and had yet to pass his first algebra test. The disparity of their interests made it possible for them to talk as equals, with mutual wonder and respect. Henry confessed to Carter, as he could not have done to his teammates, that he hoped he wasn't too slow to make the varsity backfield. In return for this confidence, Carter revealed to Henry that he wrote the poetry signed "Q.E.D." in the school literary magazine. As time went on, he also showed Henry copies of the letters he sent to various celebrities—with no signature except "Admirer." Henry failed to understand the purpose of these letters, but he was impressed by the names of those to whom they were mailed: General Doolittle, the local mayor, Barbara Stanwyck, even President Roosevelt. "*They're* the kind of friends to have," Carter said, with a mixture of diffidence and pride.

Although Henry did not think of Carter and himself as friends, in their nightly bull sessions they had come to discuss the kind of subjects only old friends discuss—girls, for example, of whom Henry had nothing good to say; and fear, which Edward Carter admitted feeling in the most casual everyday encounters. The reason he disliked sports, he told Henry, suddenly blurting out the truth as if it were too unpleasant to hold any longer, was that he was afraid of getting hurt. Once he had broken his wrist playing football, and he never since had felt like playing football.

Henry said, "You're not *really afraid,* are you?" and blushed with embarrassment for Carter when he nodded his head. It never had occurred to Henry to worry about getting hurt. If anything, he rather looked forward to it as a test of his courage. He liked to picture himself meeting the test with Roman fortitude and assurance: dismissing the stretcher-bearers and hobbling unassisted off the field, or being spiked as he rounded third base and still managing to score the winning run. "You ought to pile into uniform someday," he said, "and come out and horse around with us. I bet you'd have a wonderful time."

Carter smiled and shook his head. "I couldn't," he said, and began to talk of some ancient, all but forgotten rule he had just unearthed.

Edward Carter knew all the rules recorded in the Northway year-book, and all the unwritten legends. Lying in bed at night, he liked to relate to Henry, on the other side of the matchboard wall that formed their cubicles, at least one legend for every rule, and sometimes to invent new ones. According to Carter, only sixth formers were allowed to walk on the Oval because, when the school was founded, the sixth form had cleared the area of loose boulders and gravel and had planted grass. But Carter's explanation of why the student body was forbidden to walk on the driveway outside the kitchen (where there was real danger of being knocked down by trucks) embraced a snowstorm, a waitress, and a Japanese chef running amok, and Henry suspected that none of it was true. He also doubted Carter's account of why the head-master's house was considered out-of-bounds. It seemed obvious to Henry that, without such a rule, Mr. Wellington would be pestered with questions night and day; but Carter furnished a second, more complicated reason. He whispered it half reluctantly over the partition, in such a way that Henry felt sure Carter believed every word he was saying.

"It's on account of Mrs. Wellington," Carter whispered. Then, after a moment's silence, "*You* know."

Henry said, "No, I don't know."

"It's on account of she's so"—Henry could hear Carter sucking in and expelling his breath in despair of finding the precise word—"so wonderful. Mr. Wellington doesn't want anybody around her. Not even the masters, not any of us. Because he's jealous of her."

Henry felt like laughing. Henry was jealous of Harvey Pierson, because Harvey played on the first team; but it was hard to imagine Mr. Wellington being jealous. He was the headmaster, after all. He had charge of the whole school. Despite his crippled left arm, he played tennis, drove a car, and got around as well as everybody else. It was true that few members of the student body ever had met Mrs. Wellington; but she was said to be a talented pianist, and probably, Henry thought, she was kept busy practicing or studying at the music school downtown.

Henry said, "What's Mr. Wellington got to be jealous about?"

Carter took a long time to answer. "She's so beautiful," he said.

Henry was surprised. Movie actresses are beautiful, and one or two girls at the Olcott School were beautiful; but it had never entered his head that Mrs. Wellington was beautiful. Carter's reactions to people and things confused Henry. With deliberate coldness he said, "I don't think she's so hot."

"Have you ever seen her?"

"Sure. I went over to the house my first week at school."

Carter was incredulous. "You went over to the house?"

"Before I'd heard about the rule. I just walked right in. She was in the living room. She was sitting at the piano, but she wasn't playing anything."

"Did you speak to her?"

"I said I was looking for Mr. Wellington, and she said she guessed I was one of the new boys."

Henry heard Carter get up from his cot. Carter walked around the partition and sat down at the foot of Henry's cot. His mouth hung open, and his eyes looked large and round in the shadows, expectant but disbelieving. "Then what did she say?" Carter asked.

"I don't remember."

Carter leaned forward. "You must remember," he said. "Henry, you have to remember."

"I guess I asked her where Mr. Wellington was, because he'd posted my name on the board, and she said he must be at his office. I said he wasn't, so she said, 'Have you tried the gym?' and I said, 'No.'" The effort of remembering bored Henry, and he closed his eyes. "I'm tired," he said. "We scrimmaged till six tonight."

"Then what did she say?"

Henry buried his face in his pillow. "She just smiled and asked me if I wouldn't like to sit down, and I said, 'No,' and then she said, 'Come back again, won't you?' and I said I would. But I never have."

"And you didn't think she was beautiful?"

"I don't know." Henry weighed his memory of Mrs. Wellington's blue eyes and smile. "She looked all right."

Carter stood up. "All right!" he said, and then walked back to his cubicle. He lay down on the cot without letting the mattress make a sound. He was still lying like that, motionless and alert, when Henry fell asleep.

ACCORDING TO ONE of the oldest legends attached to the school, the administration building had been all but finished before someone noted that the architects had left no space for stairs. This legend accounted for the fact that Mr. Wellington's office was reached by a separate flight of steps in one corner of the building. At the bottom of the steps, on a board facing the doorway, Mr. Wellington posted every day the names of the boys with whom he wished to speak.

Henry soon had got into the habit of passing the board and glancing at the names without really seeing them. Today, however, he caught sight of his own name at the head of the list. He stopped abruptly, wondering why Mr. Wellington wanted to see him. He had been summoned to the headmaster's office only twice before, once to discuss his failure to reach chapel fully dressed, once to marvel together at his interpretation of the binomial theorem. Mr. Wellington had been gentle and soft-spoken, and both interviews had ended in laughter. Henry hesitated only a moment before climbing the narrow stairs and knocking on Mr. Wellington's door.

Mr. Wellington said, "Come in."

Mr. Wellington's office was small and low-ceilinged, with a single window looking south over the Oval. A fireplace framed in Dutch tiles filled most of one wall, and this morning a sweet-smelling fire of pine logs was burning brightly on the hearth.

Mr. Wellington sat behind his desk, his face half hidden in tobacco smoke. He was tall and lean, with gray hair and horn-rimmed glasses. The metal cap of his pipe caught the light as he gestured with his fist toward a chair. "Sit down, will you?"

Mr. Wellington's left arm was crippled. Mr. Wellington had been born in England and had fought with the English army in the First World War. He had been wounded somewhere in France. He had gone to the United States after the Armistice, and while there he had been persuaded to open a small private school in a barn contributed by an interested parent. Northway had grown so rapidly since then that Mr. Wellington had never succeeded in returning home. His marriage to an American girl only half his age had come as a surprise, apparently, to the faculty and Parent-Teacher Council, but Henry's mother had understood it perfectly. "He was lonely, the poor dear," she had explained to Henry's father, while Henry had listened in silence. "He was reaching the age when it was then or never. I'm glad he did it."

Generally, Mr. Wellington kept his left hand tucked into the pocket of his tweed jacket, but now and then he lifted it onto the desk with his right hand. The hand was unmarked, but without strength or control. Mr. Wellington appeared to pay no attention to his handicap, trying neither to conceal it nor to pretend that it was normal.

Now, in his low voice, he said to Henry, "How have things been going?"

Henry said, "Fine, thank you, sir."

"Algebra picked up a little, has it?"

"I'm working on it, sir."

"I expect you are." Mr. Wellington sucked at his pipe.

Through the window, Henry could see the December wind whipping the bare elms; but the air in the room had been warmed by the fire, and he felt drowsy. It seemed a long time before Mr. Wellington spoke again.

"I have a letter here," he said. He picked up a sheet of paper and held it in his right hand for a moment, then let it fall against the surface of the desk. "Been writing many letters lately?"

"No, sir. I did write home this week, though."

"Needed a bit of money?"

"I guess so, sir."

Mr. Wellington said, "You haven't written Mrs. Wellington?"

Henry had not known what Mr. Wellington was driving at. Now he almost stammered with relief. "No, of course not, sir." He felt himself blushing because of some obscure embarrassment. "I haven't written anyone but Dad."

Mr. Wellington picked up his left hand and set it on the desk, locked both hands together. "I don't mean this week," he said. His mouth turned up in an odd, humorless grin. "I happened to see the letter this week, but it might have been written anytime in the past two months."

Henry felt his assurance ebbing. He could see that Mr. Wellington did not believe him. He said too loudly, "I didn't write the letter, sir."

"You've met Mrs. Wellington, haven't you?"

"Yes, sir."

"You went to the house and talked with her?"

"Yes, sir."

"Do you know anyone else who has done this?"

"No, sir."

"Anyone else who might have written the letter?"

Henry hesitated. Now, as if he had known it from the beginning, he knew who had written the letter. He recognized even the shape and color of the sheet of paper. Henry felt sick with fear, but he said, "No, sir, I don't."

Mr. Wellington said, "I don't much mind the letter, you know. It's perfectly harmless. In a way, I expect it's rather charming. Yes, I'm sure it is. Quite charming." His voice sharpened. "It couldn't have been anyone but you—you know it couldn't have been anyone else. I insist that you tell me the truth. I insist on it."

Henry felt his strength dissolving. His eyelids stung with the approach of tears. He said at last, "Carter wrote the letter, sir. Edward Carter wrote it."

Mr. Wellington sat for a full minute without speaking. A log broke on the hearth and sent a shower of sparks racing up the blackened bricks. Henry found that he could not look at Mr. Wellington. He sat watching the fire until Mr. Wellington said, "You'd better get out of here now. Find Carter and send him to me." As Henry got to his feet, Mr. Wellington added, "And you'd better tell him how I learned who wrote the letter."

Henry walked down the stairs and across the frozen yard to the dormitory. The last of his fear was gone, leaving him weak and cold. He found Carter sitting in the study they shared, his feet on the back of a chair, a book in his lap.

Carter said, "Hi, boy," and went on reading.

Henry said, "Mr. Wellington wants to see you."

"You're kidding."

"No, honest."

Carter looked up. "What's biting you? You act like somebody'd kicked you in the stomach."

Henry said, "He asked me about a letter. A letter to Mrs. Wellington."

Carter flushed. "Oh."

"And he wants to see you."

Carter repeated, "Oh." He got up and pulled a sweater over his head. "All right," he said, as if submitting to some unspoken command. "All right. Say me a prayer."

Henry said wonderingly, "You don't seem to care much."

"Well, I do," Carter said, making a small boy's gesture of helpless surrender. He drew in his breath. "You see, I wrote the fool letter."

"I know you did."

"You mean you saw it?"

"Yes. I recognized the paper. He asked me if I knew who'd written it."

Henry walked toward the window. He felt like crying, but he did not

358

mean to let Carter see him crying. "He asked me, and I told him. I told him."

Carter said, "Oh." He opened and shut his fists. "Well, I guess he would have found out anyhow, so it doesn't matter. It doesn't really matter."

Henry felt that he could speak only another word or two before his voice broke. He said painfully, "I'm sorry about it, Edward." He never before had called Carter by his first name. "I'm awfully sorry about it."

Carter said, "Please, Hen. Please don't talk like that." He turned hurriedly and ran out of the room, then down the dormitory stairs.

Standing at the window, Henry watched the thin figure crossing the yard. The December wind tangled Carter's long brown hair, and his body was bent nearly double as he walked. With a body like that, Henry thought, it was no wonder that Carter dreaded getting hurt, dreaded facing the test. Feeling the first tears on his cheeks and then in the corners of his mouth, Henry recalled that he had been looking forward to a test of his courage. He recalled that he had planned to meet it with Roman fortitude and assurance. Dimly he saw Carter straighten his shoulders and open the door that led upstairs to Mr. Wellington's office.

THE HAMMER OF GOD
G. K. CHESTERTON

THE LITTLE VILLAGE of Bohun Beacon was perched on a hill so steep that the tall spire of its church seemed only like the peak of a small mountain. At the foot of the church stood a smithy, generally red with fires and always littered with hammers and scraps of iron; opposite this, over a rude cross of cobbled paths, was The Blue Boar, the only inn of the place. It was upon this crossway, in the lifting of a leaden and silver daybreak, that two brothers met in the street and spoke, though one was beginning the day and the other finishing it. The Reverend and Honorable Wilfred Bohun was very devout, and was making his way to some austere exercises of prayer or contemplation at dawn. Colonel the Honorable Norman Bohun, his elder brother, was by no means devout, and was sitting in evening dress on the bench outside The Blue Boar, drinking what the philosophic observer was free to regard as his last glass on Tuesday or his first on Wednesday. The colonel was not particular.

The Bohuns were one of the very few aristocratic families really dating from the Middle Ages, and their pennon had actually seen Palestine. But it is a great mistake to suppose that such houses stand high in chivalric tradition. Few except the poor preserve traditions. Aristocrats live not in traditions but in fashions. The Bohuns had been Mohocks under Queen Anne and Mashers under Queen Victoria. But like more than one of the really ancient houses, they had rotted in the past two centuries into mere drunkards and dandy degenerates, till there had even come a whisper of insanity. Certainly there was something hardly human about the colonel's wolfish pursuit of pleasure, and his chronic resolution not to go home till morning had a touch of the hideous clarity of insomnia. He was a tall, fine animal, elderly, but with hair still startlingly yellow. He would have looked merely blond and leonine, but his blue eyes were sunk so deep in his face that they looked black. They were a little too close together. He had very long yellow mustaches; on each side of them a fold or furrow from nostril to jaw, so that a sneer seemed cut into his face. Over his evening clothes he wore a curious pale yellow coat that looked more like a very light dressing gown than an overcoat, and on the back of his head was stuck an extraordinary broad-brimmed hat of a bright green color, evidently some Oriental curiosity caught up at random. He was proud of appearing in such incongruous attires—proud of the fact that he always made them look congruous.

His brother the curate had also the yellow hair and the elegance, but he was buttoned up to the chin in black, and his face was clean-shaven, cultivated, and a little nervous. He seemed to live for nothing but his religion; but there were some who said (notably the blacksmith, who was a Presbyterian) that it was a love of Gothic architecture rather than of God, and that his haunting of the church like a ghost was only another and purer turn of the almost morbid thirst for beauty that sent his brother raging after women and wine. This charge was doubtful, while the man's practical piety was indubitable. Indeed, the charge was mostly an ignorant misunderstanding of the love of solitude and secret prayer, and was based on his being often found kneeling, not before the altar, but in peculiar places, in the crypts or gallery, or even in the belfry. He was at the moment about to enter the church through the yard of the smithy, but stopped and frowned a little as he saw his brother's cavernous eyes staring in the same direction. On the hypothesis that the colonel was interested in the church he did not waste any speculations. There only remained the blacksmith's shop, and though the blacksmith was a Puritan and none of his people, Wilfred Bohun had heard some scandals about a beautiful and rather celebrated wife. He flung a suspicious look across the shed, and the colonel, laughing, stood up to speak to him.

"Good morning, Wilfred," he said. "Like a good landlord I watch sleeplessly over my people. I am going to call on the blacksmith."

Wilfred looked at the ground and said, "The blacksmith is out. He is over at Greenford."

"I know," answered the other, with silent laughter; "that is why I am calling on him."

"Norman," said the cleric, with his eye on a pebble in the road, "are you ever afraid of thunderbolts?"

"What do you mean?" asked the colonel. "Is your hobby meteorology?"

"I mean," said Wilfred, without looking up, "do you ever think that God might strike you in the street?"

"I beg your pardon," said the colonel. "I see your hobby is folklore."

"I know your hobby is blasphemy," retorted the religious man, stung in the one live place of his nature. "But if you do not fear God, you have good reason to fear man."

The elder raised his eyebrows politely. "Fear man?" he said.

"Barnes the blacksmith is the biggest and strongest man for forty miles round," said the clergyman sternly. "I know you are no coward or weakling, but he could throw you over the wall."

This struck home, being true, and the lowering line by mouth and nostril darkened and deepened. For a moment he stood with the heavy sneer on his face. But in an instant Colonel Bohun had recovered his own cruel good humor and laughed, showing two doglike front teeth under his yellow mustache. "In that case, my dear Wilfred," he said quite carelessly, "it was wise for the last of the Bohuns to come out partially in armor."

And he took off the queer round hat covered with green, showing that it was lined within with steel. Wilfred recognized it indeed as a light Japanese or Chinese helmet torn down from a trophy that hung in the old family hall.

"It was the first hat to hand," explained his brother airily; "always the nearest hat—and the nearest woman."

"The blacksmith is away at Greenford," said Wilfred quietly; "the time of his return is unsettled."

And with that he turned and went into the church with bowed head, crossing himself like one who wishes to be quit of an unclean spirit. He was anxious to forget such grossness in the cool twilight of his tall Gothic cloisters; but on that morning it was fated that his still round of religious exercises should be everywhere arrested by small shocks. As he entered the church, hitherto always empty at that hour, a kneeling figure rose hastily to its feet and came toward the full daylight of the doorway.

When the curate saw it he stood still with surprise. For the early worshipper was none other than the village idiot, a nephew of the blacksmith, one who neither would nor could care for the church or for anything else. He was always called "Mad Joe," and seemed to have no other name; he was a dark, strong, slouching lad, with a heavy white face, dark straight hair, and a mouth always open. As he passed the priest, his mooncalf countenance gave no hint of what he had been doing or thinking. He had never been known to pray before. What sort of prayers was he saying now? Extraordinary prayers surely.

Wilfred Bohun stood rooted to the spot long enough to see the idiot go out into the sunshine, and even to see his dissolute brother hail him with a sort of avuncular jocularity. The last thing he saw was the colonel throwing pennies at the open mouth of Joe, with the serious appearance of trying to hit it.

This ugly sunlit picture of the stupidity and cruelty of the earth sent the ascetic finally to his prayers for purification and new thoughts. He went up to a pew in the gallery, which brought him under a colored window that he loved and that always quieted his spirit; a blue window with an angel carrying lilies. There he began to think less about the half-wit, with his livid face and mouth like a fish. He began to think less of his evil brother, pacing like a lean lion in his horrible hunger. He sank deeper and deeper into those cold and sweet colors of silver blossoms and sapphire sky.

In this place half an hour afterward he was found by Gibbs, the village cobbler, who had been sent for him in some haste. He got to his feet with promptitude, for he knew that no small matter would have brought Gibbs into such a place at all. The cobbler was, as in many villages, an atheist, and his appearance in church was a shade more extraordinary than Mad Joe's. It was a morning of theological enigmas.

"What is it?" asked Wilfred Bohun rather stiffly, but putting out a trembling hand for his hat.

The atheist spoke in a tone that, coming from him, was quite startlingly respectful, and even, as it were, huskily sympathetic.

"You must excuse me, sir," he said in a hoarse whisper, "but we didn't think it right not to let you know at once. I'm afraid a rather dreadful thing has happened, sir. I'm afraid your brother—"

"What devilry has he done now?" Wilfred cried.

"Why, sir," said the cobbler, coughing, "I'm afraid he's done nothing, and won't do anything. I'm afraid he's done for. You had really better come down, sir."

The curate followed the cobbler down a short winding stair, which brought them out at an entrance rather higher than the street. Bohun saw the tragedy in one glance, flat underneath him like a plan. In the yard of the smithy were standing five or six men, mostly in black, one in an inspector's uniform. They included the doctor, the Presbyterian minister, and the priest from the Roman Catholic chapel, to which the blacksmith's wife belonged. The latter was speaking to her, indeed, very rapidly, in an undertone, as she, a magnificent woman with red-gold hair, was sobbing blindly on a bench. Between these two groups, and just clear of the main heap of hammers, lay a man in evening dress, spread-eagled and flat on his face. From the height above, Wilfred could have sworn to every item of his costume and appearance, down to the Bohun rings upon his fingers; but the skull was only a hideous splash, like a star of blackness and blood.

Wilfred Bohun gave but one glance, and ran down the steps into the yard. The doctor, who was the family physician, saluted him, but he scarcely took any notice. He could only stammer out, "My brother is dead. What does it mean? What is this horrible mystery?"

There was an unhappy silence; and then the cobbler, the most outspoken man present, answered, "Plenty of horror, sir," he said, "but not much mystery."

"What do you mean?" asked Wilfred, with a white face.

"It's plain enough," answered Gibbs. "There is only one man for forty miles round that could have struck such a blow as that, and he's the man that had most reason to."

"We must not prejudge anything," put in the doctor, a tall, black-bearded man, rather nervously; "but it is competent for me to corroborate what Mr. Gibbs says about the nature of the blow, sir; it is an incredible blow. Mr. Gibbs says that only one man in this district could have done it. I should have said myself that nobody could have done it."

A shudder of superstition went through the slight figure of the curate. "I can hardly understand," he said.

"Mr. Bohun," said the doctor in a low voice, "metaphors literally fail me. It is inadequate to say that the skull was smashed to bits like an eggshell. Fragments of bone were driven into the body and the ground like bullets into a mud wall. It was the hand of a giant."

He was silent a moment, looking grimly through his glasses; then he added, "The thing has one advantage—that it clears most people of suspicion at one stroke. If you or I or any normally made man in the country were accused of this crime, we should be acquitted as an infant would be acquitted of stealing the Nelson Column."

"That's what I say," repeated the cobbler obstinately; "there's only one man that could have done it, and he's the man that would have done it. Where's Simeon Barnes, the blacksmith?"

"He's over at Greenford," faltered the curate.

"More likely over in France," muttered the cobbler.

"No, he is in neither of those places," said a small and colorless voice, which came from the little Roman priest who had joined the group. "As a matter of fact, he is coming up the road at this moment."

The little priest was not an interesting man to look at, having stubbly brown hair and a round and stolid face. But if he had been as splendid as Apollo, no one would have looked at him at that moment. Everyone turned around and peered at the pathway that wound across the plain below, along which was indeed walking, at his own huge stride and with a hammer on his shoulder, Simeon the smith. He was a bony and gigantic man, with deep, dark, sinister eyes and a dark chin beard. He was walking and talking quietly with two other men; and though he was never especially cheerful, he seemed quite at his ease.

"My God!" cried the atheistic cobbler. "And there's the hammer he did it with."

"No," said the inspector, a sensible-looking man with a sandy mustache, speaking for the first time. "There's the hammer he did it with over there by the church wall. We have left it and the body exactly as they are."

All glanced around, and the short priest went across and looked down in silence at the tool where it lay. It was one of the smallest and the lightest of the hammers and would not have caught the eye among the rest; but on the iron edge of it were blood and yellow hair.

After a silence the short priest spoke without looking up, and there was a new note in his dull voice. "Mr. Gibbs was hardly right," he said, "in saying that there is no mystery. There is at least the mystery of why so big a man should attempt so big a blow with so little a hammer."

"Oh, never mind that," cried Gibbs, in a fever. "What are we to do with Simeon Barnes?"

"Leave him alone," said the priest quietly. "He is coming here of himself. I know those two men with him. They are very good fellows from Greenford, and they have come over about the Presbyterian chapel."

Even as he spoke, the tall smith swung around the corner of the church and strode into his own yard. Then he stood there quite still, and the hammer fell from his hand. The inspector, who had preserved impenetrable propriety, immediately went up to him.

"I won't ask you, Mr. Barnes," he said, "whether you know anything about what has happened here. You are not bound to say. I hope you don't know, and that you will be able to prove it. But I must go through the form of arresting you in the king's name for the murder of Colonel Norman Bohun."

"You are not bound to say anything," said the cobbler in officious excitement. "They've got to prove everything. They haven't proved yet that it is Colonel Bohun, with the head all smashed up like that."

"That won't wash," said the doctor aside to the priest. "That's out of the detective stories. I was the colonel's medical man, and I knew his body better than he did. He had very fine hands, but quite peculiar ones. The second and third fingers were the same length. Oh, that's the colonel right enough."

As he glanced at the brained corpse upon the ground, the iron eyes of the motionless blacksmith followed them and rested there also.

"Is Colonel Bohun dead?" said the smith quite calmly. "Then he's damned."

"Don't say anything! Oh, don't say anything," cried the atheist cobbler, dancing about in an ecstasy of admiration of the English legal system. For no man is such a legalist as the good secularist.

The blacksmith turned on him over his shoulder the august face of a fanatic.

"It's well for you infidels to dodge like foxes because the world's law favors you," he said; "but God guards His own in His pocket, as you shall see this day."

Then he pointed to the colonel and said, "When did this dog die in his sins?"

"Moderate your language," said the doctor.

"Moderate the Bible's language, and I'll moderate mine. When did he die?"

"I saw him alive at six o'clock this morning," stammered Wilfred Bohun.

"God is good," said the smith. "Mr. Inspector, I have not the slightest objection to being arrested. It is you who may object to arresting me. I don't mind leaving the court without a stain on my character. You do mind, perhaps, leaving the court with a bad setback in your career."

The solid inspector for the first time looked at the blacksmith with a lively eye; as did everybody else, except the short, strange priest, who was still looking down at the little hammer that had dealt the dreadful blow.

"There are two men standing outside this shop," went on the blacksmith with ponderous lucidity, "good tradesmen in Greenford whom you all know, who will swear that they saw me from before midnight till daybreak and long after in the committee room of our Revival Mission, which sits all night, we save souls so fast. In Greenford itself twenty people could swear to me for all that time. If I were a heathen, Mr. Inspector, I would let you walk on to your downfall. But as a Christian man I feel bound to give you your chance, and ask you whether you will hear my alibi now or in court."

The inspector seemed for the first time disturbed, and said, "Of course I should be glad to clear you altogether now."

The smith walked out of his yard with the same long and easy stride and returned to his two friends from Greenford, who were indeed friends of nearly everyone present. Each of them said a few words that no one ever thought of disbelieving. When they had spoken, the innocence of Simeon stood up as solid as the great church above them.

One of those silences, which are more strange and insufferable than any speech, struck the group. Madly, in order to make conversation, the curate said to the Catholic priest, "You seem very much interested in that hammer, Father Brown."

"Yes, I am," said Father Brown. "Why is it such a small hammer?"

The doctor swung around on him.

"By George, that's true," he cried. "Who would use a little hammer, with ten larger hammers lying about?" Then he lowered his voice and said in the curate's ear, "Only the kind of person that can't lift a large hammer. It is not a question of force or courage between the sexes. It's a question of lifting power in the shoulders. A bold woman could commit ten murders with a light hammer and never turn a hair. She could not kill a beetle with a heavy one."

Wilfred Bohun was staring at him with a sort of hypnotized horror, while Father Brown listened with his head a little on one side, really interested and attentive. The doctor went on with more hissing emphasis, "Why do these idiots always assume that the only person who hates the wife's lover is the wife's husband? Nine times out of ten the person who most hates the wife's lover is the wife. Who knows what insolence or treachery he had shown her? Look there."

He made a momentary gesture toward the red-haired woman on the bench. She had lifted her head at last and the tears were drying on her splendid face. But the eyes were fixed on the corpse with an electric glare that had in it something of idiocy.

The Reverend Wilfred Bohun made a limp gesture, as if waving away all desire to know; but Father Brown, dusting off his sleeve some ashes blown from the furnace, spoke in his indifferent way.

"You are like so many doctors," he said; "your mental science is really suggestive. It is your physical science that is utterly impossible. I agree that the woman wants to kill the corespondent much more than the petitioner does. And I agree that a woman will always pick up a small hammer instead of a big one. But the difficulty is one of physical impossibility. No woman ever born could have smashed a man's skull out flat like that." Then he added reflectively, after a pause, "These people haven't grasped the whole of it. The man was actually wearing an iron helmet, and the blow scattered it like broken glass. Look at that woman. Look at her arms."

Silence held them all up again, and then the doctor said rather sulkily, "Well, I may be wrong; there are objections to everything. But I stick to the main point. No man but an idiot would pick up that little hammer if he could use a big hammer."

With that the lean and quivering hands of Wilfred Bohun went up to his head and seemed to clutch his scanty yellow hair. After an instant they dropped, and he cried, "That was the word I wanted; you have said the word."

Then he continued, mastering his discomposure, "The words you said were, 'No man but an idiot would pick up the small hammer.'"

"Yes," said the doctor. "Well?"

"Well," said the curate, "no man but an idiot did." The rest stared at him with eyes arrested and riveted, and he went on in a febrile and feminine agitation.

"I am a priest," he cried unsteadily, "and a priest should be no shedder of blood. I—I mean that he should bring no one to the gallows. And I thank God that I see the criminal clearly now—because he is a criminal who cannot be brought to the gallows."

"You will not denounce him?" inquired the doctor.

"He would not be hanged if I did denounce him," answered Wilfred, with a wild but curiously happy smile. "When I went into the church this morning I found a madman praying there—that poor Joe, who has been wrong all his life. God knows what he prayed; but with such strange folk it is not incredible to suppose that their prayers are all upside down. Very likely a lunatic would pray before killing a man. When I last saw poor Joe he was with my brother. My brother was mocking him."

"By Jove!" cried the doctor. "This is talking at last. But how do you explain—"

The Reverend Wilfred was almost trembling with the excitement of his own glimpse of the truth. "Don't you see; don't you see," he cried feverishly; "that is the only theory that covers both the queer things, that answers both the riddles. The two riddles are the little hammer and the big blow. The smith might have struck the big blow, but would not have chosen the little hammer. His wife would have chosen the little hammer, but she could not have struck the big blow. But the madman might have done both. As for the little hammer—why, he was mad and might have picked up anything. And for the big blow, have you never heard, Doctor, that a maniac in his paroxysm may have the strength of ten men?"

The doctor drew a deep breath and then said, "By golly, I believe you've got it."

Father Brown had fixed his eyes on the speaker so long and steadily as to prove that his large gray oxlike eyes were not quite so insignificant as the rest of his face. When silence had fallen he said with marked respect, "Mr. Bohun, yours is the only theory yet propounded that holds water every way and is essentially unassailable. I think, therefore, that you deserve to be told, on my positive knowledge, that it is not the true one." And with that the old little man walked away and stared again at the hammer.

"That fellow seems to know more than he ought to," whispered the doctor peevishly to Wilfred. "Those popish priests are deucedly sly."

"No, no," said Bohun, with a sort of wild fatigue. "It was the lunatic. It was the lunatic."

The group of the two clerics and the doctor had fallen away from the more official group containing the inspector and the man he had arrested. Now, however, that their own party had broken up, they heard voices from the others. Father Brown looked up quietly and then down again as he heard the blacksmith say in a loud voice, "I hope I've convinced you, Mr. Inspector. I'm a strong man, as you say, but I couldn't have flung my hammer bang here from Greenford. My hammer hasn't got wings that it should come flying half a mile over hedges and fields."

The inspector laughed amicably and said, "No, I think you can be considered out of it, though it's one of the rummiest coincidences I ever saw. I can only ask you to give us all the assistance you can in finding a man as big and strong as yourself. By George! You might be useful, if only to hold him! I suppose you yourself have no guess at the man?"

"I may have a guess," said the pale smith, "but it is not at a man." Then, seeing the scared eyes turn toward his wife on the bench, he put his huge hand on her shoulder and said, "Nor a woman either."

"What do you mean?" asked the inspector jocularly. "You don't think cows use hammers, do you?"

"I think no thing of flesh held that hammer," said the blacksmith in a stifled voice; "mortally speaking, I think the man died alone."

Wilfred made a sudden forward movement and peered at him with burning eyes.

"Do you mean to say, Barnes," came the sharp voice of the cobbler, "that the hammer jumped up of itself and knocked the man down?"

"Oh, you gentlemen may stare and snigger," cried Simeon; "you clergymen who tell us on Sunday in what a stillness the Lord smote Sennacherib. I believe that One who walks invisible in every house defended the honor of mine, and laid the defiler dead before the door of it. I believe the force in that blow was just the force there is in earthquakes, and no force less."

Wilfred said, with a voice utterly undescribable, "I told Norman myself to beware of the thunderbolt."

"That agent is outside my jurisdiction," said the inspector, with a slight smile.

"You are not outside His," answered the smith; "see you to it," and, turning his broad back, he went into the house.

The shaken Wilfred was led away by Father Brown, who had an easy and friendly way with him. "Let us get out of this horrid place, Mr. Bohun," he said. "May I look inside your church? I hear it's one of the oldest in England. We take some interest, you know," he added, with a comical grimace, "in old English churches."

Wilfred Bohun did not smile, for humor was never his strong point. But he nodded rather eagerly, being only too ready to explain the Gothic splendors to someone more likely to be sympathetic than the Presbyterian blacksmith or the atheist cobbler.

"By all means," he said; "let us go in at this side." And he led the way into the high side entrance at the top of the flight of steps. Father

Brown was mounting the first step to follow him when he felt a hand on his shoulder, and turned to behold the dark, thin figure of the doctor, his face darker yet with suspicion.

"Sir," said the physician, "you appear to know some secrets in this black business. May I ask if you are going to keep them to yourself?"

"Why, Doctor," answered the priest, smiling quite pleasantly, "there is one very good reason why a man of my trade should keep things to himself when he is not sure of them, and that is, that it is so constantly his duty to keep them to himself when he is sure of them. But if you think I have been discourteously reticent with you or anyone, I will go to the extreme limit of my custom. I will give you two very large hints."

"Well, sir?" said the doctor gloomily.

"First," said Father Brown quietly, "the thing is quite in your own province. It is a matter of physical science. The blacksmith is mistaken, not perhaps in saying that the blow was divine, but certainly in saying that it came by a miracle. It was no miracle, Doctor, except insofar as a man is himself a miracle, with his strange and wicked and yet half-heroic heart. The force that smashed that skull was a force well known to scientists—one of the most frequently debated laws of nature."

The doctor, who was looking at him with frowning intentness, only said, "And the other hint?"

"The other hint is this," said the priest. "Do you remember the blacksmith, though he believes in miracles, talking scornfully of the impossible fairy tale that his hammer had wings and flew half a mile across country?"

"Yes," said the doctor, "I remember that."

"Well," added Father Brown, with a broad smile, "that fairy tale was the nearest thing to the real truth that has been said today." And with that he turned his back and stumped up the steps after the curate.

The Reverend Wilfred, who had been waiting for him, pale and impatient, as if this little delay were the last straw for his nerves, led him immediately to his favorite corner of the church, that part of the gallery closest to the carved roof and lighted by the wonderful window with the angel. The little Latin priest explored and admired everything exhaustively, talking cheerfully but in a low voice all the time. When in the course of his investigation he found the side exit and the winding stair down which Wilfred had rushed to find his brother dead, Father Brown ran not down but up, with the agility of a monkey, and his clear voice came from an outer platform above.

"Come up here, Mr. Bohun," he called. "The air will do you good."

Bohun followed him, and came out on a kind of stone gallery or balcony outside the building, from which one could see the illimitable plain in which their small hill stood, wooded away to the purple horizon and dotted with villages and farms. Clear and square, but quite small beneath them, was the blacksmith's yard, where the inspector still stood taking notes and the corpse still lay like a smashed fly.

"Might be the map of the world, mightn't it?" said Father Brown.

"Yes," said Bohun very gravely, and nodded his head.

Immediately beneath and about them the lines of the Gothic building plunged outward into the void with a sickening swiftness akin to suicide. There is that element of titan energy in the architecture of the Middle Ages that, from whatever aspect it be seen, it always seems to be rushing away, like the strong back of some maddened horse. This church was hewn out of ancient and silent stone, bearded with old fungoids and stained with the nests of birds. And yet, when they saw it from below, it sprang like a fountain at the stars; and when they saw it, as now, from above, it poured like a cataract into a voiceless pit. For these two men on the tower were left alone with the most terrible aspect of the Gothic: the monstrous foreshortening and disproportion, the dizzy perspectives, the glimpses of great things small and small things great; a topsy-turvydom of stone in midair. Details of stone, enormous by their proximity, were relieved against a pattern of fields and farms, pygmy in their distance. A carved bird or beast at a corner seemed like some vast walking or flying dragon wasting the pastures and villages below. The whole atmosphere was dizzy and dangerous, as if men were upheld in air amid the gyrating wings of colossal genies; and the whole of that old church, as tall and rich as a cathedral, seemed to sit upon the sunlit country like a cloudburst.

"I think there is something rather dangerous about standing on these high places even to pray," said Father Brown. "Heights were made to be looked at, not to be looked from."

"Do you mean that one may fall over?" asked Wilfred.

"I mean that one's soul may fall if one's body doesn't," replied the other priest.

"I scarcely understand you," remarked Bohun indistinctly.

"Look at that blacksmith, for instance," went on Father Brown calmly; "a good man, but not a Christian—hard, imperious, unforgiving. Well, his Scotch religion was made up by men who prayed on hills and high crags, and learned to look down on the world more than to look up at heaven. Humility is the mother of giants. One sees great things from the valley, only small things from the peak."

"But he—he didn't do it," said Bohun tremulously.

"No," said the other in an odd voice; "we know he didn't do it."

After a moment he resumed, looking tranquilly out over the plain with his pale gray eyes. "I knew a man," he said, "who began by worshipping with others before the altar, but who grew fond of high and lonely places to pray from, corners or niches in the belfry or the spire. And once in one of those dizzy places, where the whole world seemed to turn under him like a wheel, his brain turned also, and he fancied he was God. So that though he was a good man, he committed a great crime."

Wilfred's face was turned away, but his bony hands turned blue and white as they tightened on the parapet of stone.

"He thought it was given to *him* to judge the world and strike down the sinner. He would never have had such a thought if he had been kneeling with other men upon a floor. But he saw all men walking about like insects. He saw one especially, strutting just below him, insolent and evident by the bright green hat—a poisonous insect."

Rooks cawed around the corners of the belfry; but there was no other sound till Father Brown went on.

"This also tempted him, that he had in his hand one of the most awful engines of nature; I mean gravitation, that mad and quickening rush by which all earth's creatures fly back to her heart when released. See, the inspector is strutting just below us in the smithy. If I were to toss a pebble over this parapet, it would be something like a bullet by the time it struck him. If I were to drop a hammer—even a small hammer—"

Wilfred Bohun threw one leg over the parapet, and Father Brown had him in a minute by the collar.

"Not by that door," he said quite gently; "that door leads to hell."

Bohun staggered back against the wall, and stared at him with frightful eyes.

"How do you know all this?" he cried. "Are you a devil?"

"I am a man," answered Father Brown gravely, "and therefore have all devils in my heart. Listen to me," he said after a short pause. "I know what you did—at least, I can guess the great part of it. When you left your brother you were racked with no unrighteous rage, to the extent even that you snatched up a small hammer, half inclined to kill him with his foulness on his mouth. Recoiling, you thrust it under your buttoned coat instead, and rushed into the church. You pray wildly in many places, under the angel window, upon the platform above, and on a higher platform still, from which you could see the colonel's Eastern hat like the back of a green beetle crawling about. Then something snapped in your soul, and you let God's thunderbolt fall."

Wilfred put a weak hand to his head, and asked in a low voice, "How did you know that his hat looked like a green beetle?"

"Oh, that," said the other, with the shadow of a smile, "that was common sense. But hear me further. I say I know all this; but no one else shall know it. The next step is for you; I shall take no more steps; I will seal this with the seal of confession. If you ask me why, there are many reasons, and only one that concerns you. I leave things to you because you have not yet gone very far wrong, as assassins go. You did not help to fix the crime on the smith when it was easy; or on his wife, when that was easy. You tried to fix it on the imbecile because you knew that he could not suffer. That was one of the gleams that it is my business to find in assassins. And now come down into the village, and go your own way as free as the wind; for I have said my last word."

They went down the winding stairs in utter silence, and came out into the sunlight by the smithy. Wilfred Bohun carefully unlatched the wooden gate of the yard, and going up to the inspector, said, "I wish to give myself up; I have killed my brother."

THE POCKETBOOK GAME
ALICE CHILDRESS

Marge ... Day's work is an education! Well, I mean workin' in different homes you learn much more than if you was steady in one place.... I tell you, it really keeps your mind sharp tryin' to watch for what folks will put over on you.

What?... No, Marge, I do not want to help shell no beans, but I'd be more than glad to stay and have supper with you, and I'll wash the dishes after. Is that all right?...

Who put anything over on who?... Oh yes! It's like this.... I been working for Mrs. E ... one day a week for several months and I notice that she has some peculiar ways. Well, there was only one thing that really bothered me and that was her pocketbook habit.... No, not those little novels.... I mean her purse—her handbag.

Marge, she's got a big old pocketbook with two long straps on it ... and whenever I'd go there, she'd be propped up in a chair with her handbag double-wrapped tight around her wrist, and from room to room she'd roam with that purse hugged to her bosom ... yes, girl! This happens every time! No, there's nobody there but me and her.... Marge, I couldn't say nothin' to her! It's her purse, ain't it? She can hold on to it if she wants to!

I held my peace for months, tryin' to figure out how I'd make my point.... Well, bless Bess! Today was the day!... Please, Marge, keep shellin' the beans so we can eat! I know you're listenin', but you listen with your ears, not your hands. . . . Well, anyway, I was almost ready to go home when she steps in the room hangin' on to her bag as usual and says, "Mildred, will you ask the super to come up and fix the kitchen faucet?" "Yes, Mrs. E . . ." I says, "as soon as I leave." "Oh, no," she says, "he may be gone by then. Please go now." "All right," I says, and out the door I went, still wearin' my Hoover apron.

I just went down the hall and stood there a few minutes . . . and then I rushed back to the door and knocked on it as hard and frantic as I could. She flung open the door sayin', "What's the matter? Did you see the super?" . . . "No," I says, gaspin' hard for breath, "I was almost downstairs when I remembered . . . I left my pocketbook!"

With that I dashed in, grabbed my purse and then went down to get the super! Later, when I was leavin' she says real timid like, "Mildred, I hope that you don't think I distrust you because . . ." I cut her off real quick. . . . "That's all right, Mrs. E . . . I understand. 'Cause if I paid anybody as little as you pay me, I'd hold my pocketbook too!"

Marge, you fool . . . look out! . . . You gonna drop the beans on the floor!

THE WEDDING GIFT

THOMAS RADDALL

Nova Scotia, in 1794. Winter. Snow on the ground. Two feet of it in the woods, less by the shore, except in drifts against Port Marriott's barns and fences; but enough to set sleigh bells ringing through the town, enough to require a multitude of paths and burrows from doors to streets, to carpet the wharves and the decks of the shipping, and to trim the ships' yards with tippets of ermine. Enough to require fires roaring in the town's chimneys, and blue woodsmoke hanging low over the rooftops in the still December air. Enough to squeal underfoot in the trodden places and to muffle the step everywhere else. Enough for the hunters, whose snowshoes now could overtake the floundering moose and caribou. Even enough for the always complaining loggers, whose ox sleds now could haul their cut from every part of the woods. But not enough, not nearly enough snow for Miss Kezia Barnes, who was going to Bristol Creek to marry Mr. Hathaway.

Kezia did not want to marry Mr. Hathaway. Indeed, she had told Mr. and Mrs. Barclay in a tearful voice that she didn't want to marry anybody. But Mr. Barclay had taken snuff and said "Ha! Humph!" in the severe tone he used when he was displeased; and Mrs. Barclay had sniffed and said it was a very good match for her, and revolved the cold blue eyes in her fat moon face, and said Kezia must not be a little fool.

There were two ways of going to Bristol Creek. One was by sea, in one of the fishing sloops. But the preacher objected to that. He was a pallid young man lately sent out from England by Lady Huntingdon's connection, and seasick five weeks on the way. He held Mr. Barclay in some awe, for Mr. Barclay had the best pew in the meetinghouse and was the chief pillar of godliness in Port Marriott. But young Mr. Mears was firm on this point. He would go by road, he said, or not at all. Mr. Barclay had retorted "Ha! Humph!" The road was twenty miles of horse path through the woods, now deep in snow. Also, the path began at Harper's farm on the far side of the harbor, and Harper had but one horse.

"I shall walk," declared the preacher calmly, "and the young woman can ride."

Kezia had prayed for snow, storms of snow, to bury the trail and keep anyone from crossing the cape to Bristol Creek. But now they were setting out from Harper's farm, with Harper's big brown horse, and all Kezia's prayers had gone for naught. Like any anxious lover, busy Mr. Hathaway had sent Black Sam overland on foot to find out what delayed his wedding, and now Sam's day-old tracks marked for Kezia the road to marriage.

She was a meek little thing, as became an orphan brought up as house help in the Barclay home; but now she looked at the preacher and saw how young and helpless he looked, so far from his native Yorkshire, and how ill-clad for this bitter transatlantic weather, and she spoke up.

"You'd better take my shawl, sir. I don't need it. I've got Miss Julia's old riding cloak. And we'll go ride and tie."

"Ride and what?" murmured Mr. Mears.

"I'll ride a mile or so, then I'll get down and tie the horse to a tree and walk on. When you come up to the horse, you mount and ride a mile or so, passing me on the way, and you tie him and walk on. Like that. Ride and tie, ride and tie. The horse gets a rest between."

Young Mr. Mears nodded and took the proffered shawl absently. It was a black thing that matched his sober broadcloth coat and small-clothes, his black woolen stockings, and his round black hat. At Mr. Barclay's suggestion he had borrowed a pair of moose-hide moccasins for the journey. As he walked, a prayer book in his coat skirts bumped the back of his legs.

At the top of the ridge above Harper's pasture, where the narrow path led off through gloomy hemlock woods, Kezia paused for a last look back across the harbor. In the morning sunlight the white roofs of the little lonely town resembled a tidal wave flung up by the sea and frozen as it broke against the dark pine forest to the west. Kezia sighed, and young Mr. Mears was surprised to see tears in her eyes.

She rode off ahead. The saddle was a man's, of course, awkward to ride modestly, woman fashion. As soon as she was out of the preacher's sight she rucked her skirts and slid a leg over to the other stirrup. That was better. There was a pleasant sensation of freedom about it, too. For a moment she forgot that she was going to Bristol Creek, in finery second-hand from the Barclay girls, in a new linen shift and drawers that she had sewn herself by the light of the kitchen candles, in white cotton stockings and a bonnet and shoes from Mr. Barclay's store, to marry Mr. Hathaway.

The Barclays had done well for her from the time when, a skinny, weeping creature of fourteen, she was taken into the Barclay household and, as Mrs. Barclay so often said, "treated more like one of my own than a bond girl from the poorhouse." She had first choice of the clothing cast off by Miss Julia and Miss Clara. She was permitted to sit in the same room, and learn what she could, when the schoolmaster came to give private lessons to the Barclay girls. She waited on table, of course, and helped in the kitchen, and made beds, and dusted and scrubbed. But then she had been taught to spin and to sew and to knit. And she was permitted, indeed encouraged, to sit with the Barclays in the meetinghouse, at the convenient end of the pew, where she could worship the Barclays' God and assist with the Barclay wraps at the beginning and end of the service. And now, to complete her rewards, she had been granted the hand of a rejected Barclay suitor.

Mr. Hathaway was Barclay's agent at Bristol Creek, where he sold rum and gunpowder and cornmeal and such things to the fishermen and hunters, and bought split cod—fresh, pickled or dry—and ran a small sawmill, and cut and shipped firewood by schooner to Port Marriott, and managed a farm, all for a salary of fifty pounds, Halifax currency, per year. Hathaway was a most capable fellow, Mr. Barclay often acknowledged. But when after fifteen capable years he came seeking a wife, and cast a sheep's eye first at Miss Julia and then at Miss Clara, Mrs.

Barclay observed with a sniff that Hathaway was looking a bit high.

So he was. The older daughter of Port Marriott's most prosperous merchant was even then receiving polite attentions from Mr. Gamage, the new collector of customs, and a connection of the Halifax Gamages, as Mrs. Barclay was fond of pointing out. And Miss Clara was going to Halifax in the spring to learn the gentle art of playing the pianoforte, and incidentally to display her charms to the naval and military young gentlemen who thronged the Halifax drawing rooms. The dear girls laughed behind their hands whenever long, solemn Mr. Hathaway came to town aboard one of the Barclay vessels and called at the big house under the elms. Mrs. Barclay bridled at Hathaway's presumption, but shrewd Mr. Barclay narrowed his little black eyes and took snuff and said "Ha! Humph!"

It was plain to Mr. Barclay that an emergency had arisen. Hathaway was a good man—in his place; and Hathaway must be kept content there, to go on making profit for Mr. Barclay at a cost of only fifty pounds a year. 'Twas a pity Hathaway couldn't satisfy himself with one of the fishermen's girls at the Creek, but there 'twas. If Hathaway had set his mind on a town miss, then a town miss he must have; but she must be the right kind, the sort who would content herself and Hathaway at Bristol Creek and not go nagging the man to remove and try his capabilities elsewhere. At once Mr. Barclay thought of Kezia—dear little Kezzie. A colorless little creature, but quiet and well-mannered and pious, and only twenty-two.

Mr. Hathaway was nearly forty and far from handsome, and he had a rather cold, seeking way about him—useful in business, of course—that rubbed women the wrong way. Privately, Mr. Barclay thought Hathaway lucky to get Kezia. But it was a nice match for the girl, better than anything she could have expected. He impressed that upon her and introduced the suitor from Bristol Creek. Mr. Hathaway spent two or three evenings courting Kezia in the kitchen—Kezia in a quite good gown of Miss Clara's, gazing out at the November moon on the snow, murmuring now and again in the tones of someone in a rather dismal trance, while the kitchen help listened behind one door and the Barclay girls giggled behind another.

The decision, reached mainly by the Barclays, was that Mr. Hathaway should come to Port Marriott aboard the packet schooner on December 23, to be married in the Barclay parlor, and then take his bride home for Christmas. But an unforeseen circumstance had changed all this. The circumstance was a ship, "from Mogador in Barbary," as Mr. Barclay wrote afterward in the salvage claim, driven off her course by gales and wrecked at the very entrance to Bristol Creek. She was a valuable wreck, laden with such queer things as goatskins in pickle, almonds, worm-seed, pomegranate skins, and gum arabic, and capable Mr. Hathaway had lost no time in salvage for the benefit of his employer.

As a result he could not come to Port Marriott for a wedding or anything else. A storm might blow up at any time and demolish this fat prize. He dispatched a note by Black Sam, urging Mr. Barclay to send Kezia and the preacher by return. It was not the orthodox note of an impatient sweetheart, but it said that he had moved into his new house by the Creek and found it "extream empty lacking a woman," and it suggested delicately that while his days were full, the nights were dull.

Kezia was no judge of distance. She rode for what she considered a reasonable time and then slid off and tied the brown horse to a maple tree beside the path. She had brought a couple of lampwicks to tie about her shoes, to keep them from coming off in the snow, and she set out afoot in the big splayed tracks of Black Sam. The soft snow came almost to her knees in places, and she lifted her skirts high. The path was no wider than the span of a man's arms, cut out with axes years before. She stumbled over a concealed stump from time to time, and the huckleberry bushes dragged at her cloak, but the effort warmed her. It had been cold, sitting on the horse with the wind blowing up her legs.

After a time the preacher overtook her, riding awkwardly and holding the reins in a nervous grip. The stirrups were too short for his long, black-stockinged legs. He called out cheerfully as he passed, "Are you all right, miss?" She nodded, standing aside with her back to a tree. When he disappeared ahead, with a last flutter of black shawl tassels in the wind, she picked up her skirts and went on. The path climbed and dropped monotonously over wooded ridges. Here and there in a hollow she heard water running, and the creak of frosty poles underfoot, and knew she was crossing a small stream, and once the trail ran across a wide swamp on half-rotten corduroy, windswept and bare of snow.

She found the horse tethered clumsily not far ahead, and the tracks of the preacher going on. She had to lead the horse to a stump so she could mount, and when she passed Mr. Mears again she called out, "Please, sir, next time leave the horse by a stump or a rock so I can get on." In his quaint old-country accent he murmured, "I'm very sorry," and gazed down at the snow. She forgot she was riding astride until she had passed him, and then she flushed, and gave the indignant horse a cut of the switch. Next time she remembered and swung her right leg back where it should be, and tucked the skirts modestly about her ankles; but young Mr. Mears looked down at the snow anyway, and after that she did not trouble to shift when she overtook him.

The ridges became steeper, and the streams roared under the ice and snow in the swales. They emerged upon the high tableland between Port Marriott and Bristol Creek, a gusty wilderness of young hardwood scrub struggling up among the gray snags of an old forest fire, and now that they were out of the gloomy softwoods they could see a stretch of sky. It was blue-gray and forbidding, and the wind whistling up from the invisible sea felt raw on the cheek. At their next meeting Kezia said, "It's going to snow."

She had no knowledge of the trail, but she guessed that they were not much more than halfway across the cape. On this high barren the track was no longer straight and clear; it meandered among the meager hardwood clumps where the path makers had not bothered to cut, and only Black Sam's footprints really marked it for her unaccustomed eyes. The preacher nodded vaguely at her remark. The woods, like everything else about his chosen mission field, were new and very interesting, and he could not understand the alarm in her voice. He looked confidently at Black Sam's tracks.

Kezia tied the horse farther on and began her spell of walking. Her shoes were solid things, the kind of shoes Mr. Barclay invoiced as "a common strong sort, for women, five shillings"; but the snow worked into them and melted and saturated the leather. Her feet were numb every time she slid down from the horse, and it took several minutes of stumbling through the snow to bring back an aching warmth. Beneath her arm she clutched the small bundle which contained all she had in the world—two flannel nightgowns, a shift of linen, three pairs of stout wool stockings—and, of course, Mr. Barclay's wedding gift for Mr. Hathaway.

Now as she plunged along she felt the first sting of snow on her face and, looking up, saw the stuff borne on the wind in small hard pellets that fell among the bare hardwoods and set up a whisper everywhere. When Mr. Mears rode up to her the snow was thick in their faces, like flung salt.

"It's a nor'easter!" she cried up to him. She knew the meaning of snow from the sea. She had been born in a fishing village down the coast.

"Yes," mumbled the preacher, and drew a fold of the shawl about his face. He disappeared. She struggled on, gasping, and after what seemed a tremendous journey came upon him standing alone and bewildered, looking off somewhere to the right.

"The horse!" he shouted. "I got off him, and before I could fasten the reins some snow fell off a branch—startled him, you know—and he ran off, over that way." He gestured with a mittened hand. "I must fetch him back," he added confusedly.

"No!" Kezia cried. "Don't you try. You'd only get lost. So would I. Oh, dear! This is awful. We'll have to go on, the best we can."

He was doubtful. The horse tracks looked very plain. But Kezia was looking at Black Sam's tracks, and tugging his arm. He gave in, and they struggled along for half an hour or so. Then the last trace of the old footprints vanished.

"What shall we do now?" the preacher asked, astonished.

"I don't know," whispered Kezia, and leaned against a dead pine stub in an attitude of weariness and indifference that dismayed him.

"We must keep moving, my dear, mustn't we? I mean, we can't stay here."

"Can't stay here," she echoed.

"Down there—a hollow, I think. I see some hemlock trees—or are they pines? I'm never quite sure. Shelter, anyway."

"Shelter," muttered Kezia.

He took her by the hand, and like a pair of lost children they dragged their steps into the deep snow of the hollow. The trees were tall spruces, a thick bunch in a ravine, where they had escaped the old fire. A stream thundered among them somewhere. There was no wind in this place, only the fine snow whirling thickly down between the trees like a sediment from the storm overhead.

"Look!" cried Mr. Mears. A hut loomed out of the whiteness before them, a small structure of moss-chinked logs with a roof of poles and birch bark. It had an abandoned look. Long streamers of moss hung out between the logs. On the roof, shreds of birch bark wavered gently in the drifting snow. The door stood half open and a thin drift of snow lay along the split-pole floor. Instinctively, Kezia went to the stone hearth. There were old ashes sodden with rain down the chimney and now frozen to a cake.

"Have you got flint and steel?" she asked. She saw in his eyes something dazed and forlorn. He shook his head, and she was filled with a sudden anger, not so much at him as at Mr. Barclay and that—that Hathaway, and all the rest of mankind. They ruled the world and made such a sorry mess of it. In a small fury she began to rummage about the hut.

There was a crude bed of poles and brushwood by the fireplace—brushwood so old that only a few brown needles clung to the twigs. A rough bench whittled from a pine log, with round birch sticks for legs. A broken earthenware pot in a corner. In another some ashwood frames such as trappers used for stretching skins. Nothing else. The single window was covered with a stretched moose bladder, cracked and dry rotten, but it still let in some daylight while keeping out the snow.

She scooped up the snow from the floor with her mittened hands, throwing it outside, and closed the door carefully, dropping the bar into place, as if she could shut out and bar the cold in such a fashion. The air inside was frigid. Their breath hung visible in the dim light from the window. Young Mr. Mears dropped on his wet knees and began to pray in a loud voice. His face was pinched with cold, and his teeth rattled as he prayed. He was a pitiable object.

"Prayers won't keep you warm," said Kezia crossly.

He looked up, amazed at the change in her. She had seemed such a meek little thing. Kezia was surprised at herself, and surprisingly she went on, "You'd far better take off those wet moccasins and stockings and shake the snow out of your clothes." She set the example, vigorously shaking out her skirts and Miss Julia's cloak, and she turned her small back on him and took off her own shoes and stockings, and pulled on dry stockings from her bundle. She threw him a pair.

"Put those on."

He looked at them and at his large feet, hopelessly.

"I'm afraid they wouldn't go on."

She tossed him one of her flannel nightgowns. "Then take off your stockings and wrap your feet and legs in that."

He obeyed, in an embarrassed silence. She rolled her eyes upward, for his modesty's sake, and saw a bundle on one of the low rafters—the late owner's bedding, stowed away from mice. She stood on the bench and pulled down three bearskins, marred with bullet holes. A rank and musty smell arose in the cold. She considered the find gravely.

"You take them," he said gallantly. "I shall be quite all right."

"You'll be dead by morning, and so shall I," she answered vigorously, "if you don't do what I say. We've got to roll up in these."

"Together?" Mr. Mears cried in horror.

"Of course! To keep each other warm. It's the only way."

She spread the skins on the floor, hair uppermost, one overlapping another, and dragged the flustered young man down beside her, clutched him in her arms, and rolled with him, over and over again, so that they became a single shapeless heap in the corner farthest from the draft between door and chimney.

"Put your arms around me," commanded the new Kezia, and he obeyed. "Now," she said, "you can pray. God helps those that help themselves."

He prayed aloud for a long time, and privately called upon heaven to witness the purity of his thoughts in this strange and shocking situation. He said "Amen" at last; and "Amen," echoed Kezia piously.

They lay silent a long time, breathing on each other's necks and hearing their own hearts—poor Mr. Mears's fluttering in an agitated way, Kezia's as steady as a clock. A delicious warmth crept over them. They relaxed in each other's arms. Outside, the storm hissed in the spruce tops and set up an occasional cold moan in the cracked clay chimney. The down-swirling snow brushed softly against the bladder pane.

"I'm warm now," murmured Kezia. "Are you?"

"Yes. How long must we stay here like this?"

"Till the storm's over, of course. Tomorrow, probably. Nor'easters usually blow themselves out in a day and a night, specially when they come up sharp, like this one. Are you hungry?"

"No."

"Abigail—that's the black cook at Barclay's—gave me bread and cheese in a handkerchief. I've got it in my bundle. Mr. Barclay thought we ought to reach Bristol Creek by suppertime, but Nabby said I must have a bite to eat on the road. She's a good kind thing, old Nabby. Sure you're not hungry?"

"Quite. I feel somewhat fatigued, but not hungry."

"Then we'll eat the bread and cheese for breakfast. Have you got a watch?"

"No, I'm sorry. They cost such a lot of money. In Lady Huntingdon's connection we—"

"Oh well, it doesn't matter. It must be about four o'clock—the light's getting dim. Of course, the dark comes very quick in a snowstorm."

"Dark," echoed young Mr. Mears drowsily. Kezia's hair, washed last night for the wedding journey, smelled pleasant so close to his face. It reminded him of something. He went to sleep dreaming of his mother, with his face snug in the curve of Kezia's neck and shoulder, and smiling, and muttering words that Kezia could not catch. After a time she kissed his cheek. It seemed a very natural thing to do.

Soon she was dozing herself, and dreaming, too; but her dreams were full of forbidding faces—Mr. Barclay's, Mrs. Barclay's, Mr. Hathaway's; especially Mr. Hathaway's. Out of a confused darkness Mr. Hathaway's hard acquisitive gaze searched her shrinking flesh like a cold wind. Then she was shuddering by the kitchen fire at Barclay's, accepting Mr. Hathaway's courtship and wishing she were dead. In the midst of that sickening wooing she wakened sharply.

It was quite dark in the hut. Mr. Mears was breathing quietly against her throat. But there was a sound of heavy steps outside, muffled in the snow and somehow felt rather than heard. She shook the young man and he wakened with a start, clutching her convulsively.

"Sh-h-h!" she warned. "Something's moving outside." She felt him stiffen.

"Bears?" he whispered.

Silly! thought Kezia. People from the old country could think of nothing but bears in the woods. Besides, bears holed up in the winter. A caribou, perhaps. More likely a moose. Caribou moved inland before this, to the wide mossy bogs up the river, away from the coastal storms. Again the sound.

"There!" hissed the preacher. Their hearts beat rapidly together. "The door—you fastened it, didn't you?"

"Yes," she said. Suddenly she knew. "Unroll, quick!" she cried. "No, not this way—your way."

They unrolled, ludicrously, and the girl scrambled up and ran across the floor in her stocking feet, and fumbled with the rotten door bar. Mr. Mears attempted to follow, but he tripped over the nightgown still wound about his feet, and fell with a crash. He was up again in a moment, catching up the clumsy wooden bench for a weapon, his bare feet slapping on the icy floor. He tried to shoulder her aside, crying, "Stand back! Leave it to me!" and waving the bench uncertainly in the darkness.

She laughed excitedly. "Silly!" she said. "It's the horse." She flung the door open. In the queer ghostly murk of a night filled with snow they beheld a large dark shape. The shape whinnied softly and thrust a long face into the doorway. Mr. Mears dropped the bench, astonished.

"He got over his fright and followed us here somehow," Kezia said, and laughed again. She put her arms about the snowy head and laid her face against it. "Good horse! Oh, good, good horse!"

"What are you going to do?" the preacher murmured over her shoulder. After the warmth of their nest in the furs they were shivering in this icy atmosphere.

"Bring him in, of course. We can't leave him out in the storm." She caught the bridle and urged the horse inside with expert clucking sounds. The animal hesitated, but fear of the storm and a desire for shelter and company decided him. In he came, tramping ponderously on the split-pole floor. The preacher closed and barred the door.

"And now?" he asked.

"Back to the furs. Quick! It's awful cold."

Rolled in the furs once more, their arms went about each other instinctively, and the young man's face found the comfortable nook against Kezia's soft throat. But sleep was difficult after that. The horse whinnied gently from time to time, and stamped about the floor. The decayed poles crackled dangerously under his hoofs whenever he moved, and Kezia trembled, thinking he might break through and frighten himself, and flounder about till he tumbled the crazy hut about their heads. She called out to him, "Steady, boy! Steady!"

It was a long night. The pole floor made its irregularities felt through the thickness of fur; and because there seemed nowhere to put their arms but about each other, the flesh became cramped, and spread its protest along the bones. They were stiff and sore when the first light of morning stained the window. They unrolled and stood up thankfully, and tramped up and down the floor, threshing their arms in an effort to fight off the gripping cold. Kezia undid her bundle in a corner and brought forth Nabby's bread and cheese, and they ate it sitting together on the edge of the brushwood bed with the skins about their shoulders. Outside, the snow had ceased.

"We must set off at once," the preacher said. "Mr. Hathaway will be anxious."

Kezia was silent. She did not move, and he looked at her curiously. She appeared very fresh, considering the hardships of the previous day and the night. He passed a hand over his cheeks and thought how unclean he must appear in her eyes, with this stubble on his pale face.

"Mr. Hathaway—" he began again.

"I'm not going to Mr. Hathaway," Kezia said quietly.

"But—the wedding!"

"There'll be no wedding. I don't want to marry Mr. Hathaway. 'Twas Mr. Hathaway's idea, and Mr. and Mrs. Barclay's. They wanted me to marry him."

"What will the Barclays say, my dear?"

She shrugged. "I've been their bond girl ever since I was fourteen, but I'm not a slave like poor black Nabby, to be handed over, body and soul, whenever it suits."

"Your soul belongs to God," said Mr. Mears devoutly.

"And my body belongs to me."

He was a little shocked at this outspokenness, but he said gently, "Of course. To give oneself in marriage without true affection would be an offense in the sight of heaven. But what will Mr. Hathaway say?"

"Well, to begin with, he'll ask where I spent the night, and I'll have to tell the truth. I'll have to say I bundled with you in a hut in the woods."

"Bundled?"

"A custom the people brought with them from Connecticut when they came to settle in Nova Scotia. Poor folk still do it. Sweethearts, I mean. It saves fire and candles when you're courting on a winter evening. It's harmless—they keep their clothes on, you see, like you and me—but Mr. Barclay and the other Methody people are terrible set against it. Mr. Barclay got old Mr. Mings—he's the Methody preacher that died last year—to make a sermon against it. Mr. Mings said bundling was an invention of the devil."

"Then if you go back to Mr. Barclay—"

"He'll ask me the same question and I'll have to give him the same answer. I couldn't tell a lie, could I?" She turned a pair of round blue eyes and met his embarrassed gaze.

"No! No, you mustn't lie. Whatever shall we do?" he murmured in a dazed voice. Again she was silent, looking modestly down her small nose.

"It's so very strange," he floundered. "This country—there are so many things I don't know, so many things to learn. You—I—we shall have to tell the truth, of course. Doubtless I can find a place in the Lord's service somewhere else, but what about you, poor girl?"

"I heard say the people at Scrod Harbor want a preacher."

"But—the tale would follow me, wouldn't it, my dear? This—er— bundling with a young woman?"

" 'Twouldn't matter if the young woman was your wife."

"Eh?" His mouth fell open. He was like an astonished child, for all his preacher's clothes and the new beard on his jaws.

"I'm a good girl," Kezia said, inspecting her foot. "I can read and write, and know all the tunes in the Psalter. And—and you need someone to look after you."

He considered the truth of that. Then he murmured uncertainly, "We'd be very poor, my dear. The connection gives some support, but, of course—"

"I've always been poor," Kezia said. She sat very still, but her cold fingers writhed in her lap.

He did something then that made her want to cry. He took hold of her hands and bowed his head and kissed them.

"It's strange—I don't even know your name, my dear."

"It's Kezia—Kezia Barnes."

He said quietly, "You're a brave girl, Kezia Barnes, and I shall try to be a good husband to you. Shall we go?"

"Hadn't you better kiss me first?" Kezia said faintly.

He put his lips awkwardly to hers; and then, as if the taste of her clean mouth itself provided strength and purpose, he kissed her again, and firmly. She threw her arms about his neck.

"Oh, Mr. Mears!"

How little he knew about everything! He hadn't even known enough to wear two or three pairs of stockings inside those roomy moccasins, nor to carry a pair of dry ones. Yesterday's wet stockings were lying like sticks on the frosty floor. She showed him how to knead the hard-frozen moccasins into softness, and she tore up one of her wedding bed shirts and wound the flannel strips about his legs and feet. It looked very queer when she had finished, and they both laughed.

They were chilled to the bone when they set off, Kezia on the horse and the preacher walking ahead, holding the reins. When they regained the slope where they had lost the path, Kezia said, "The sun rises somewhere between east and southeast, this time of year. Keep it on your left shoulder awhile. That will take us back toward Port Marriott."

When they came to the green timber she told him to shift the sun to his left eye.

"Have you changed your mind?" he asked cheerfully. The exercise had warmed him.

"No, but the sun moves across the sky."

"Ah! What a wise little head it is!"

They came over a ridge of mixed hemlock and hardwood and looked upon a long swale full of bare hackmatacks.

"Look!" the girl cried. The white slot of the axe path showed clearly in the trees at the foot of the swale, and again where it entered the dark mass of the pines beyond.

"Praise the Lord!" said Mr. Mears.

When at last they stood in the trail, Kezia slid down from the horse.

"No!" Mr. Mears protested.

"Ride and tie," she said firmly. "That's the way we came, and that's the way we'll go. Besides, I want to get warm."

He climbed up clumsily and smiled down at her.

"What shall we do when we get to Port Marriott, my dear?"

"Get the New Light preacher to marry us, and catch the packet for Scrod Harbor."

He nodded and gave a pull at his broad hatbrim. She thought of everything. A splendid helpmeet for the world's wilderness. He saw it all very humbly now as a dispensation of Providence.

Kezia watched him out of sight. Then, swiftly, she undid her bundle and took out the thing that had lain there (and on her conscience) through the night—the tinderbox—Mr. Barclay's wedding gift to Mr. Hathaway. She flung it into the woods and walked on, skirts lifted, in the track of the horse, humming a Psalm tune to the silent trees and the snow.

THE ADVENTURE OF THE SPECKLED BAND
SIR ARTHUR CONAN DOYLE

IN GLANCING OVER my notes of the seventy-odd cases in which I have during the last eight years studied the methods of my friend Sherlock Holmes, I find many tragic, some comic, a large number merely strange, but none commonplace; for, working as he did rather for the love of his art than for the acquirement of wealth, he refused to associate himself with any investigation which did not tend toward the unusual, and even the fantastic. Of all these varied cases, however, I cannot recall any which presented more singular features than that associated with the well-known Surrey family of the Roylotts of Stoke Moran. This occurred in the early days of my association with Holmes, when we were sharing rooms as bachelors, in Baker Street.

It was early in April, of the year 1883, that I woke one morning to find Sherlock Holmes standing, fully dressed, by the side of my bed. As the clock on the mantelpiece showed me that it was only a quarter past seven, I blinked up at him in some surprise, and perhaps just a little resentment.

"Very sorry to knock you up, Watson," said he, "but it's the common lot this morning. Mrs. Hudson has been knocked up, she retorted upon me, and I on you."

"What is it, then? A fire?"

"No, a client. A young lady has arrived in a considerable state of excitement, and insists upon seeing me. She is waiting now in the sitting room. Should it prove to be an interesting case, you would, I am sure, wish to follow it from the outset. I thought, at any rate, that I should give you the chance."

"My dear fellow, I would not miss it for anything." I rapidly threw on my clothes and accompanied my friend down to the sitting room. A lady dressed in black and heavily veiled, who had been sitting in the window, rose as we entered.

"Good morning, madam," said Holmes cheerily. "My name is Sherlock Holmes. This is my friend and associate, Dr. Watson. Pray draw up to the fire, and I shall order you a cup of hot coffee, for I observe that you are shivering."

"It is not cold which makes me shiver," said the woman in a low voice, changing her seat as requested.

"What, then?"

"It is fear, Mr. Holmes. Terror." She raised her veil as she spoke, and we could see that she was indeed in a pitiable state of agitation, her face all drawn and gray, with frightened eyes, like those of some hunted animal. Her features were those of a woman of thirty, but her hair was shot with premature gray, and her expression was haggard. Sherlock Holmes studied her with one of his quick, all-comprehensive glances.

"You must not fear," said he, bending forward and patting her forearm. "We shall soon set matters right. You have come in by train this morning, I see."

"Yes. But how did you know?"

"I observe the second half of a return ticket in the palm of your left glove. You must have started early, and yet you had a good drive in a dogcart, along heavy roads, before you reached the station."

The lady stared in bewilderment at my companion.

"There is no mystery, my dear madam," said he, smiling. "The left arm of your jacket is spattered with mud in no less than seven places. The marks are perfectly fresh. There is no vehicle save a dogcart which throws up mud in that way, and then only when you sit on the left-hand side of the driver."

"You are perfectly correct," said she. "I started from home before six, reached Leatherhead at twenty past, and came in by the first train to Waterloo. Sir, I can stand this strain no longer; I shall go mad if it continues. I have no one to turn to save only one, who cares for me, and he, poor fellow, can be of little aid. I have heard of you, Mr. Holmes, from Mrs. Farintosh, whom you helped in the hour of her sore need. Oh, sir, do you not think that you could help me, too? At present it is out of my power to reward you for your services, but in a month I shall be married, with the control of my own income, and then at least you shall not find me ungrateful."

Holmes turned to his desk, and unlocking it, drew out a small case-book, which he consulted. "Farintosh," said he. "Ah yes, I recall the case; it was concerned with an opal tiara. I can only say, madam, that I shall devote the same care to your case as I did to that of your friend. As to reward, my profession is its own reward; but you are at liberty to defray my expenses at the time which suits you best. And now I beg that you will lay before us everything that may help us in forming an opinion upon the matter."

"My name is Helen Stoner, and I am living with my stepfather, who is the last survivor of one of the oldest Saxon families in England, the Roylotts of Stoke Moran, on the western border of Surrey."

Holmes nodded his head. "The name is familiar to me," said he.

"The family was at one time among the richest in England. In the last century, however, four successive heirs were of a dissolute disposition, and the family ruin was completed by a gambler in the days of the Regency. Nothing was left save a few acres of ground and the two-hundred-year-old house, which is itself crushed under a heavy mortgage. The last squire dragged out his existence there, an aristocratic pauper; but his only son, my stepfather, seeing that he must adapt himself to the new conditions, obtained a medical degree and went out to Calcutta, where he established a large practice. In a fit of anger, however, caused by some robberies perpetrated in his house, he beat his native butler to death and narrowly escaped a capital sentence. As it was, he suffered a long term of imprisonment, and afterward returned to England a morose and disappointed man.

"When Dr. Roylott was in India he married my mother, Mrs. Stoner, the young widow of Major General Stoner, of the Bengal Artillery. My twin sister Julia and I were only two years old at the time of my mother's remarriage. She bequeathed a considerable sum of money—not less than a thousand pounds a year—to Dr. Roylott while we resided with him, with a provision that a certain annual sum should be allowed to each of us in the event of our marriage. Shortly after our return to England my mother died—in a railway accident near Crewe. Dr. Roylott then took us to live with him in the ancestral house at Stoke Moran. The money which my mother had left was enough for all our wants, and there seemed to be no obstacle to our happiness.

"But a terrible change came over our stepfather about this time. Instead of making friends with our neighbors, he shut himself up in his house, and seldom came out save to indulge in ferocious quarrels with whoever might cross his path. A series of disgraceful brawls took place, until at last he became the terror of the village, for he is a man of immense strength, and uncontrollable in his anger.

"Last week he hurled the local blacksmith over a parapet into a stream, and it was only by paying over all the money that I could gather that I was able to avert another public exposure. He has no friends at all save the wandering Gypsies, and he gives these vagabonds leave to encamp upon our few acres of bramble-covered land and accepts in return the hospitality of their tents, wandering away with them sometimes for weeks on end. Also, he has a passion for Indian animals. At this moment a cheetah and a baboon wander freely over his grounds, and are feared by the villagers almost as much as their master.

"You can imagine that my poor sister Julia and I had no great pleasure in our lives. She was but thirty at the time of her death, and yet her hair had already begun to whiten, even as mine has."

"Your sister is dead, then?"

"She died just two years ago, and it is of her death that I wish to speak to you. You can understand that, living the life which I have described, we were little likely to see anyone of our own age and position. However, we were occasionally allowed to pay short visits to my aunt, Miss Honoria Westphail, who lives near Harrow. Julia went there at Christmas two years ago, and met a half-pay major of marines, to whom she became engaged. My stepfather offered no objection to the marriage; but within a fortnight of the wedding day, the terrible event occurred which has deprived me of my only companion."

Sherlock Holmes had been leaning back in his chair with his eyes closed, but he half opened his lids now and glanced across at his visitor. "Pray be precise as to details," said he.

"It is easy for me to be so, for the dreadful event is seared into my memory. The manor house is, as I have said, very old, and only one wing is now inhabited. The bedrooms in this wing are on the ground floor. Of these bedrooms, the first is Dr. Roylott's, the second my sister's, and the third my own. There is no connecting door between them, but they all open out into the same corridor. Do I make myself plain?"

"Perfectly so."

"The windows of the three rooms open out upon the lawn. That fatal night Dr. Roylott had gone to his room early, though we knew that he had not retired, for my sister was troubled by the smell of the strong Indian cigars which he smokes. She left her room, therefore, and came into mine, where she sat for some time, chatting about her approaching wedding. At eleven o'clock she rose to leave me, but she paused at the door and looked back.

"'Tell me, Helen,' said she, 'have you ever heard anyone whistle in the dead of the night?'

"'Never. But why?'

"'Because during the last few nights I have always, about three in the morning, heard a low, clear whistle. I am a light sleeper, and it has awakened me. I cannot tell where it came from—perhaps from the next room, perhaps from the lawn.'

"'It must be those wretched Gypsies.'

"'Very likely. Well, it is of no great consequence.' She smiled back at me, closed my door, and a few moments later I heard her key turn in the lock."

"Indeed," said Holmes. "Was it your custom always to lock yourselves in at night?"

"Always. I think that I mentioned to you that the doctor kept a cheetah and a baboon. We had no feeling of security unless our doors were locked."

"Quite so. Pray proceed with your statement."

"I could not sleep that night. A vague feeling of impending misfortune impressed me. It was a wild night. The wind was howling, and the rain was beating against the windows. Suddenly there burst forth the wild scream of a terrified woman. I knew that it was my sister's voice. I sprang from my bed, wrapped a shawl round me, and rushed into the corridor. As I opened my door I heard a low whistle, such as my sister described, and a few moments later a clanging sound, as if a mass of metal had fallen. As I ran down the passage my sister's door slowly opened. I stared at it horror-stricken. By the light of the corridor lamp I saw my sister appear, her face blanched with terror and her hands groping for help. I threw my arms round her, but at that moment her knees gave way and she fell to the ground. She writhed in terrible pain, and her limbs were dreadfully convulsed. As I bent over her she suddenly shrieked out, in a voice which I shall never forget, 'Oh, my God! Helen! It was the band! The speckled band!' And she stabbed with her finger in the direction of the doctor's room, but a fresh convulsion choked her words. I rushed out, calling for my stepfather, and I met him hastening from his room in his dressing gown. When he reached my sister's side she was unconscious, and though he poured brandy down her throat and sent for medical aid from the village, all efforts were in vain, for she slowly sank and died without having recovered consciousness. Such was the dreadful end of my beloved sister."

"One moment," said Holmes. "Are you sure about this whistle and metallic sound? Could you swear to it?"

"That was what the county coroner asked me at the inquiry. It is my strong impression that I heard it, and yet, among the crash of the gale I may possibly have been deceived."

"Was your sister dressed?"

"No, she was in her nightdress. In her right hand was found the charred stump of a match, and in her left a matchbox."

"Showing that she had struck a light and looked about her when the alarm took place. And what conclusions did the coroner come to?"

"He investigated the case with great care, but he was unable to find any satisfactory cause of death. My evidence showed that the door had been fastened upon the inner side, and the windows were blocked by old-fashioned shutters with broad iron bars, which were secured every night. The walls and flooring were carefully sounded, and were shown to be quite solid all round. The chimney is wide, but is barred up by four large staples. It is certain, therefore, that my sister was quite alone when she met her end. Besides, there were no marks of any violence upon her."

"How about poison?"

"The doctors examined her for it, but without success."

"What do you think this unfortunate lady died of, then?"

"It is my belief that she died of pure fear, though what it was that frightened her I cannot imagine."

"Were there Gypsies in the plantation at the time?"

"Yes, there are nearly always some there."

"Ah, and what did you gather from this allusion to a band—a speckled band?"

"Sometimes I have thought that it was merely the wild talk of delirium, sometimes that it may have referred to some band of people, perhaps to these very Gypsies in the plantation. I do not know whether the spotted handkerchiefs which so many of them wear over their heads might have suggested the strange adjective which she used."

Holmes shook his head like a man who is far from being satisfied.

"These are very deep waters," said he. "Pray go on with your narrative."

"Two years have passed since then. A month ago a dear friend, whom I have known for many years, did me the honor to ask my hand in marriage. His name is Armitage—Percy Armitage. My stepfather has offered no opposition to the match, and we are to be married this spring. Two days ago some repairs were started in the west wing of the building, and my bedroom wall has been pierced, so that I have had to move into the chamber in which my sister died and to sleep in the very bed in which she slept. Imagine, then, my terror when last night, as I lay awake in the silence, I suddenly heard the low whistle which had been the herald of her own death. I lit the lamp, but nothing was to be seen in the room. I was too shaken to go to bed again, however, so I dressed, and as soon as it was daylight I slipped down, got a dogcart at the Crown Inn, and drove to Leatherhead, from whence I have come this morning with the one object of seeing you."

"You have done wisely," said my friend. "But you have not told me all. You are screening your stepfather."

"Why, what do you mean?"

For answer Holmes pushed back the frill of black lace which fringed the hand that lay upon our visitor's knee. Five little livid spots, the marks of four fingers and a thumb, were printed upon the white wrist. "You have been cruelly used," said Holmes.

The lady colored deeply and covered her injured wrist. "He is a hard man," she said, "and hardly knows his own strength."

There was a long silence, during which Holmes stared into the crackling fire.

"This is very deep business," he said at last. "We have not a moment to lose. If we were to come to Stoke Moran today, would it be possible for us to see these rooms without the knowledge of your stepfather?"

"As it happens, he is coming into town today upon some business. He will be away all day, and there will be nothing to disturb you."

"Excellent. You are not averse to this trip, Watson?"

"By no means."

"Then we shall both come. What are you going to do yourself?"

"I have one or two things which I will do, now that I am in town," said Miss Stoner. "But I shall return by the twelve-o'clock train, so as to be there in time for your coming."

"Then you may expect us early in the afternoon."

"My heart is lightened already since I have confided my trouble to you. I shall look forward to seeing you." She dropped her thick black veil over her face and glided from the room.

"And what do you think of it all, Watson?" asked Sherlock Holmes, leaning back in his chair.

"It seems to be a most dark and sinister business. If the lady is correct in saying that the flooring and walls are sound, and that the door, window, and chimney are impassable, then her sister must have been undoubtedly alone when she met her mysterious end."

"What becomes, then, of these nocturnal whistles, and what of the very peculiar words of the dying woman?"

"I cannot think."

"When you combine the whistles at night, the band of Gypsies, the fact that the doctor has an interest in preventing his stepdaughter's marriage, the dying allusion to a band, and, finally, the fact that Miss Helen Stoner heard a metallic clang, which might have been caused by one of those metal bars which secured the shutters falling back into its place, I think that there is good ground to think that the mystery may be cleared along those lines."

"I see many objections to the Gypsy theory."

"And so do I. For that reason we are going to Stoke Moran this day. I want to see whether the objections are fatal, or if they may be explained away. But what the devil . . . !"

Our door had suddenly dashed open, and a huge man framed himself in the aperture. He wore a black top hat, a long frock coat, and a pair of high gaiters, with a hunting crop swinging in his hand. So tall was he that his hat brushed the crossbar of the doorway, and his breadth seemed to span it from side to side. A large face, seared with a thousand wrinkles and marked with every evil passion, was turned from one to the other of us, while his deep-set, bile-shot eyes and his high, thin, fleshless nose gave him the resemblance to a fierce old bird of prey. "Which of you is Holmes?" asked this apparition.

"My name, sir, but you have the advantage of me."

"I am Dr. Grimesby Roylott, of Stoke Moran."

"Indeed, Doctor," said Holmes blandly. "Pray take a seat."

"I will do nothing of the kind. My stepdaughter has been here. I have traced her. What has she been saying to you?"

"It is a little cold for the time of the year," said Holmes.

"What has she been saying to you?" screamed the old man furiously.

"But I have heard that the crocuses promise well," continued my companion imperturbably.

"Ha! You put me off, do you?" Our new visitor took a step forward and shook his hunting crop. "I know you, you scoundrel! You are Holmes the meddler, the busybody!"

Holmes chuckled heartily. "Your conversation is most entertaining," said he. "When you go out, close the door, for there is a decided draft."

"I will go when I have had my say. Don't meddle with my affairs. I know that Miss Stoner has been here. I am a dangerous man to fall foul of! See here." He stepped swiftly forward, seized the poker, and bent it into a curve with his huge brown hands. "See that you keep yourself out of my grip," he snarled, and hurling the twisted poker into the fireplace, he strode out of the room.

"He seems a very amiable person," said Holmes, laughing. "Had he remained, I might have shown him that my grip was not much more feeble than his own." As he spoke he picked up the steel poker and with a sudden effort straightened it out again. "And now, Watson, we shall order breakfast, and afterward I shall walk down to Doctors' Commons, where I hope to get some data which may help us in this matter."

IT WAS NEARLY one o'clock when Sherlock Holmes returned from his excursion. He held in his hand a sheet of blue paper, scrawled over with notes and figures. "I have seen the will of the deceased wife," said he. "The total income of the investments, which at the time of the wife's death was little short of eleven hundred pounds, is now, through the fall in agricultural prices, not more than seven hundred and fifty pounds. Each daughter can claim an income of two hundred and fifty pounds, in case of marriage. It is evident, therefore, that if both girls had married, this fellow would have had a mere pittance, while even one of them would cripple him to a serious extent. My morning's work has not been wasted, since it has proved that Dr. Roylott has the very strongest motives for standing in the way of anything of the sort. And now, Watson, if you are ready, we shall call a cab and drive to Waterloo. I should be very much obliged if you would slip your revolver into your pocket. An Eley's Number Two is an excellent argument with gentlemen who can twist steel pokers into knots."

At Waterloo we caught a train for Leatherhead, where we hired a trap at the station inn and drove for four or five miles through the lovely Surrey lanes. It was a perfect day, with a bright sun and a few fleecy clouds in the heavens, and the air was full of the pleasant smell of the moist earth. My companion sat in the front of the trap, his arms folded, his chin sunk upon his breast, buried in the deepest thought. Suddenly he started, and pointed over the meadows. "Look there!"

A heavily timbered park stretched up in a gentle slope, thickening into a grove at the highest point. From amid the branches there jutted up the gray gables and high rooftree of a very old mansion.

"That be the house of Dr. Grimesby Roylott," remarked the driver. "There's the village," he continued, pointing to a cluster of roofs some distance to the left; "but if you want to get to the house, you'll find it shorter to go over this stile, and so by the footpath over the fields. There it is, where the lady is walking."

"And the lady, I fancy, is Miss Stoner," observed Holmes, shading his eyes. "Yes, I think we had better do as you suggest."

We got off, paid our fare, and the trap rattled back on its way to Leatherhead.

"Good afternoon, Miss Stoner," said Holmes, as we climbed the stile. "You see that we have been as good as our word."

Our client of the morning hurried forward to meet us. "I have been waiting so eagerly for you!" she cried. "All has turned out splendidly. Dr. Roylott has gone to town, and it is unlikely that he will be back before evening."

"We have had the pleasure of making the doctor's acquaintance," said Holmes, and in a few words he sketched out what had occurred. Miss Stoner turned white to the lips as she listened.

"Good heavens!" she cried. "He has followed me, then."

"So it appears. You must lock yourself from him tonight. If he is violent, we shall take you away to your aunt's at Harrow. Now, we must go at once to the rooms which we are to examine."

The building was of gray lichen-blotched stone, with a high central portion, and two curving wings, like the claws of a crab, thrown out on each side. In one wing the windows were broken, and blocked with wooden boards, while the roof was partly caved in, a picture of ruin. The central portion was in little better repair, but the right-hand block was comparatively modern, and the blinds in the windows, with blue smoke curling up from the chimneys, showed that this was where the family resided. Some scaffolding had been erected against the end wall, and the stonework had been broken into, but there were no signs of any workmen about. Holmes walked slowly across the ill-trimmed lawn and examined with deep attention the outsides of the windows.

"This, I take it, belongs to the room in which you used to sleep, the center one to your sister's, and the one next to the main building to Dr. Roylott's chamber?"

"Exactly so. But I am now sleeping in the middle one."

"Pending the alterations, as I understand. By the way, there does not seem to be any very pressing need for repairs at that end wall."

"There were none. I believe that it was an excuse to move me from my room."

"Ah! That is suggestive. Now, on the other side of this narrow wing runs the corridor from which these three rooms open. There are windows in it, of course?"

"Yes, but very small ones. Too narrow for anyone to pass through."

"As you both locked your doors at night, your rooms were unapproachable from that side. Now, would you have the kindness to go into your room and bar your shutters."

Miss Stoner did so, and Holmes endeavored in every way to force the shutter open, but without success. Then with his lens he tested the hinges, but they were of solid iron, built firmly into the masonry. "Hum!" said he, scratching his chin in some perplexity. "My theory presents difficulties. No one could pass these shutters if they were bolted. Well, we shall see if the inside throws any light upon the matter."

A small side door led into the corridor from which the three bedrooms opened. Holmes refused to examine the third chamber, so we passed at once to the second, that in which Miss Stoner was now sleeping, and in which her sister had met her fate. It was a homely little room, oak-paneled, with a low ceiling and a gaping fireplace, after the fashion of old country houses. A brown chest of drawers stood in one corner, a narrow white-counterpaned bed in another, and a dressing table on the left-hand side of the window. These articles, with two small wickerwork chairs, and a square of Wilton carpet in the center, made up all the furnishings in the room.

Holmes drew one of the chairs into a corner and sat silent, while his eyes traveled around, taking in every detail of the apartment. "Where does that bell communicate with?" he asked, pointing to a thick bell rope which hung down beside the bed, the tassel actually lying upon the pillow.

"It goes to the housekeeper's room."

"It looks newer than the other things?"

"Yes, it was only put there a couple of years ago."

"Your sister asked for it, I suppose?"

"No, I never heard of her using it. We always got what we wanted for ourselves."

"Indeed, it seemed unnecessary to put so nice a bellpull there. You will excuse me for a few minutes while I satisfy myself as to this floor." He knelt with his lens in his hand and examined minutely the cracks between the boards. Then he did the same with the discolored wall paneling. Next he walked over to the bed, and spent some time staring at it and running his eye up and down the wall. Finally he took the bell rope in his hand and gave it a brisk tug. "Why, it's a dummy," said he. "It is not even attached to a wire. You can see now that it is fastened to a hook just above where the little opening of the ventilator is."

"How very absurd! I never noticed that before."

"There are one or two other singular points about this room. For example, what a fool a builder must be to open a ventilator into another room, when, with the same trouble, he might have communicated with the outside air!"

"That is also quite modern," said the lady.

"Done about the same time as the bell rope," remarked Holmes.

"Yes, there were several little changes carried out about that time."

"They seem to have been of a most interesting character—dummy bell ropes, and ventilators which do not ventilate. With your permission, Miss Stoner, we shall now carry our researches into the inner apartment."

Dr. Grimesby Roylott's chamber was larger than that of his stepdaughter, but was as plainly furnished. The principal things which met the eye were a camp bed, a small wooden shelf full of technical books, an armchair beside the bed, a plain wooden chair against the wall, a round table, and a large iron safe. Holmes walked slowly around and examined each of them.

"What's in here?" he asked, tapping the safe.

"My stepfather's business papers. I saw them once."

"There isn't a cat in it, for example?"

"No. What a strange idea!"

"Well, look at this!" He took up a small saucer of milk which stood on the top of it.

"No, we don't keep a cat. But there is a cheetah and a baboon."

"Ah, yes, of course! Well, a cheetah is just a big cat, and yet a saucer of milk does not go very far in satisfying its wants." He squatted down in front of the wooden chair and examined its seat with the greatest attention. "Thank you. That is quite settled," said he, rising and putting his lens in his pocket. "Hello! Here is something interesting!"

The object which had caught his eye was a small dog lash hung on one corner of the bed. The lash, however, was curled and tied so as to make a loop of whipcord.

"What do you make of that, Watson?"

"It's a common enough lash. But I don't know why it should be tied."

"That is not quite so common, is it? Ah, me! It's a wicked world, and when a clever man turns his brain to crime it is the worst of all. I have seen enough now, Miss Stoner, and with your permission we shall walk out upon the lawn."

I had never seen my friend's face so grim, or his brow so dark, as we walked several times up and down the lawn. "It is very essential, Miss Stoner," said he, rousing himself from his reverie, "that you should absolutely follow my advice in every respect. Your life may depend upon your compliance."

"I assure you that I am in your hands."

"In the first place, my friend and I must spend the night in your room." Miss Stoner and I gazed at him in astonishment.

"I believe that that is the village inn over there?"

"Yes, that is the Crown."

"Very good. Your windows would be visible from there?"

"Certainly."

"You must confine yourself to your room, on pretense of a headache, when your stepfather comes back. Then when you hear him retire for the night, you must open the shutters of your window, undo the hasp, put your lamp there as a signal to us, and then withdraw into the room which you used to occupy. I have no doubt that, in spite of the repairs, you could manage there for one night."

"Oh, yes, easily."

"We shall spend the night in your room and investigate the cause of this noise which has disturbed you."

"I believe, Mr. Holmes, that you have already made up your mind," said Miss Stoner.

"Perhaps I have."

"Then for pity's sake tell me what was the cause of my sister's death."

"I should prefer to have clearer proofs before I speak."

"You can at least tell me whether my own thought is correct, and if she died from some sudden fright."

"No, I do not think so. I think that there was probably some more tangible cause. And now, Miss Stoner, we must leave you, for if Dr. Roylott returned and saw us, our journey would be in vain. You may rest assured that we shall soon drive away the dangers that threaten you. Good-by, and be brave."

Sherlock Holmes and I had no difficulty in engaging rooms at the Crown Inn. They were on the upper floor, and from our window we could command a view of the inhabited wing of Stoke Moran manor house.

At dusk we saw Dr. Roylott drive past, his huge form looming up beside the little figure of the lad who drove him. The boy had some slight difficulty in undoing the heavy iron gates, and we heard the hoarse roar of the doctor's voice, and saw the fury with which he shook his clenched fists at him. The trap drove on, and a few minutes later we saw a sudden light spring up among the trees as the lamp was lit in one of the sitting rooms.

"Do you know, Watson," said Holmes, as we sat together in the gathering darkness, "I have really some scruples as to taking you to-night. There is a distinct element of danger."

"Can I be of assistance?"

"Your presence might be invaluable."

"Then I shall certainly come. You speak of danger. You have evidently seen more in these rooms than was visible to me."

"No, but I fancy that I may have deduced a little more. You saw all that I did."

"I saw nothing remarkable save the bell rope, and its purpose there is more than I can imagine."

"You saw the ventilator, too?"

"Yes, but I do not think that it is such a very unusual thing to have a small opening between two rooms. It was so small that a rat could hardly pass through."

"I knew that we should find a ventilator before ever we came to Stoke Moran."

"My dear Holmes!"

"You remember in her statement Miss Stoner said that her sister could smell Dr. Roylott's cigar. That suggested at once that there must be a communication between the two rooms. It could only be a small one, or it would have been remarked upon at the coroner's inquiry. I deduced a ventilator."

"But what harm can there be in that?"

"Well, there is at least a curious coincidence of dates. A ventilator is made, a cord is hung, and a lady who sleeps in the bed dies. Does not that strike you?"

"I cannot as yet see any connection."

"Did you observe anything peculiar about that bed?"

"No."

"It was clamped to the floor. Did you ever see a bed fastened like that before?"

"I cannot say that I have."

"The lady could not move her bed. It must always be in the same relative position to the ventilator and to the rope—for so we may call it, since it was clearly never meant for a bellpull."

"Holmes," I cried, "I seem to see dimly what you are hitting at! We are only just in time to prevent some subtle and horrible crime."

"Subtle enough and horrible enough. When a doctor goes wrong, he is the first of criminals. He has nerve and he has knowledge. I think, Watson, that we shall have horrors enough before the night is over; for goodness' sake let us have a quiet pipe and turn our minds for a few hours to something more cheerful."

ABOUT NINE O'CLOCK the light among the trees was extinguished, and all was dark in the direction of the manor house. Two hours passed, and then, suddenly, just at the stroke of eleven, a single bright light shone out in front of us. "That is our signal," said Holmes, springing to his feet. "It comes from the middle window." A moment later we were out on the dark road.

Entering the grounds with little difficulty, we crossed the lawn and were about to enter through the window, when out from a clump of laurel bushes there darted what seemed to be a hideous and distorted child, who threw itself on the grass with writhing limbs, then ran swiftly into the darkness.

"My God!" I whispered. "Did you see it?"

Holmes was as startled as I. His hand closed like a vise upon my wrist; then he broke into a low laugh and put his lips to my ear. "That is the baboon," he murmured.

I had forgotten the strange pets which the doctor affected. There was a cheetah, too; perhaps we might find it upon our shoulders at any moment. I confess that I felt easier in my mind when at last I found myself inside the bedroom. My companion noiselessly closed the shutters and cast his eyes around the room. All was as we had seen it in the daytime. Then, creeping up to me, he whispered into my ear again. "The least sound would be fatal to our plans. We must sit without a light. He would see it through the ventilator."

I nodded.

"Do not fall asleep; your very life may depend upon it. Have your pistol ready in case we should need it. I will sit on the side of the bed, and you in that chair."

I took out my revolver and laid it on the table.

Holmes placed a long, thin cane upon the bed beside him. By it he laid a box of matches and the stump of a candle. Then he turned down the lamp.

How shall I ever forget that dreadful vigil? We waited in absolute darkness. I could not hear a sound, not even the drawing of a breath, and yet I knew that my companion sat open-eyed within a few feet of me. From outside came the occasional cry of a night bird, and once at our very window a long-drawn, catlike whine, which told us that the cheetah was indeed at liberty. Far away we could hear the deep tones of the parish clock, which boomed out every quarter of an hour. How long they seemed, those quarters! Twelve o'clock, and one, and two, and three, and still we sat waiting silently.

Suddenly there was the momentary gleam of a light up in the direction of the ventilator, which vanished immediately and was succeeded by a strong smell of burning oil and heated metal. Someone in the next room had lit a dark lantern. I heard a gentle sound of movement, and then all was silent once more, though the smell grew stronger. For half an hour I sat with straining ears. Then suddenly another sound became audible—a very soothing sound, like that of a small jet of steam escaping continually from a kettle. The instant that we heard it, Holmes sprang from the bed, struck a match, and lashed furiously with his cane at the bellpull.

"You see it, Watson?" he yelled. "You see it?"

But I saw nothing. At the moment when Holmes struck the light I heard a low, clear whistle, but the sudden glare flashing into my eyes made it impossible for me to tell what it was at which my friend lashed so savagely. I could, however, see that his face was deadly pale and filled with loathing.

He had ceased to strike, and was gazing up at the ventilator, when suddenly there broke from the silence of the night the most horrible cry to which I have ever listened. It swelled up louder and louder, a hoarse yell of pain and anger all mingled in the one dreadful shriek. It struck cold to our hearts, and I stood gazing at Holmes, and he at me, until the last echoes of it had died away.

"What can it mean?" I gasped.

"It means that it is all over," Holmes answered. "Take your pistol, and we shall enter Dr. Roylott's room."

With a grave face he lit the lamp and led the way down the corridor. Twice he struck at the chamber door without any reply from within. Then he turned the handle and entered, I at his heels, with the cocked pistol in my hand.

It was a singular sight which met our eyes. On the table stood a dark lantern with the shutter half open, throwing a brilliant beam of light upon the iron safe, the door of which was ajar. Beside this table, on the wooden chair, sat Dr. Grimesby Roylott, clad in a long gray dressing gown. Across his lap lay the short stock with the long lash which we had noticed during the day. His chin was cocked upward, and his eyes were fixed in a dreadful rigid stare at the ceiling. Bound tightly around his head he had a peculiar yellow band, with brownish speckles. As we entered he made neither sound nor motion.

"The band! The speckled band!" whispered Holmes.

I took a step forward. In an instant his strange headgear began to move, and there reared itself from his hair the squat diamond-shaped head and puffed neck of a loathsome serpent.

"It is a swamp adder!" cried Holmes. "The deadliest snake in India. He has died within ten seconds of being bitten." As he spoke he drew the dog whip swiftly from the dead man's lap, and throwing the noose around the reptile's neck, he drew it from its horrid perch, and, carrying it at arm's length, threw it into the iron safe, which he closed upon it. "Now let us remove Miss Stoner to some place of shelter," he said, "and let the county police know what has happened."

IT IS NOT NECESSARY that I should prolong the narrative by telling how we broke the sad news to the terrified girl, how we conveyed her to the care of her good aunt at Harrow, how the slow process of official inquiry concluded that the doctor met his fate while indiscreetly playing with a dangerous pet. The little which I had yet to learn of the case was told me by Sherlock Holmes as we traveled back next day.

"I had," said he, "come to an entirely erroneous conclusion, which shows, my dear Watson, how dangerous it always is to reason from insufficient data. The presence of the Gypsies and the word 'band' were sufficient to put me upon an entirely wrong scent. I instantly reconsidered my position, however, when it became clear to me that whatever danger threatened an occupant of the room could not come either from the window or the door. My attention was then speedily drawn to the ventilator, and to the bell rope which hung down to the bed. The discovery that this was a dummy, and that the bed was clamped to the floor, instantly gave rise to the suspicion that the rope was there as a bridge for something passing through the hole and coming to the bed. The idea of a snake occurred to me, and since the doctor was furnished with a supply of creatures from India, I felt that I was probably on the right track. The idea of using a form of poison which acted rapidly and could not possibly be discovered by any chemical test was just such a one as would occur to a clever and ruthless man who had had an Eastern training. It would be a sharp-eyed coroner indeed who could distinguish the two little dark punctures which would show where the poison fangs had done their work.

"Then I thought of the whistle. Of course, he must recall the snake before the morning light revealed it to the victim. He had trained it, probably by the use of the milk which we saw, to return to him when summoned. He would put it through the ventilator with the certainty that it would crawl down the rope and land on the bed. It might or might not bite the occupant, perhaps she might escape every night for a week, but sooner or later she must fall a victim.

"I had come to these conclusions before ever I had entered his room. An inspection of his chair showed me that he had been in the habit of standing on it, which, of course, would be necessary in order that he should reach the ventilator. The sight of the safe, the saucer of milk, and the loop of whipcord were enough to finally dispel any doubts which may have remained. The metallic clang heard by Miss Stoner was obviously caused by her stepfather hastily closing the door of his safe upon its terrible occupant. Having once made up my mind, I took steps to put the matter to the proof. I heard the creature hiss, and I instantly lit the light and attacked it."

"With the result of driving it through the ventilator."

"And also with the result of causing it to turn upon its master at the other side. Some of the blows of my cane came home, and roused its snakish temper, so that it flew upon the first person it saw. In this way I am no doubt indirectly responsible for Dr. Grimesby Roylott's death, and I cannot say that it is likely to weigh very heavily upon my conscience."

THE PIT AND
THE PENDULUM
EDGAR ALLAN POE

I WAS SICK—sick unto death with that long agony; and when they at length unbound me, and I was permitted to sit, I felt that my senses were leaving me. The sentence—the dread sentence of death—was the last of distinct accentuation which reached my ears. After that, the sound of the inquisitorial voices seemed merged in one dreamy indeterminate hum. It conveyed to my soul the idea of *revolution*—perhaps from its association in my fancy with the burr of a mill wheel. This only for a brief period; for presently I heard no more. Yet, for a while, I saw; but with how terrible an exaggeration! I saw the lips of the black-robed judges. They appeared to me white—whiter than the sheet upon which I trace these words—and thin even to grotesqueness; thin with the intensity of their expression of firmness—of immovable resolution—of stern contempt of human torture. I saw that the decrees of what to me was Fate, were still issuing from those lips. I saw them writhe with a deadly locution. I saw them fashion the syllables of my name; and I shuddered because no sound succeeded. I saw, too, for a few moments of delirious horror, the soft and nearly imperceptible waving of the sable draperies which enwrapped the walls of the apartment. And then my vision fell upon the seven tall candles upon the table. At first they wore the aspect of charity, and seemed white slender angels who would save me; but then, all at once, there came a most deadly nausea over my spirit, and I felt every fiber in my frame thrill as if I had touched the wire of a galvanic battery, while the angel forms became meaningless specters, with heads of flame, and I saw that from them there would be no help. And then there stole into my fancy, like a rich musical note, the thought of what sweet rest there must be in the grave. The thought came gently and stealthily, and it seemed long before it attained full appreciation; but just as my spirit came at length properly to feel and entertain it, the figures of the judges vanished, as if magically, from before me; the tall candles sank into nothingness; their flames went out utterly; the blackness of darkness supervened; all sensations appeared swallowed up in a mad rushing descent as of the soul into Hades. Then silence, and stillness, and night were the universe.

I had swooned; but still will not say that all of consciousness was lost. What of it there remained I will not attempt to define, or even to describe; yet all was not lost. In the deepest slumber—no! In delirium—no! In a swoon—no! In death—no! Even in the grave all *is not* lost. Else there is no immortality for man. Arousing from the most profound of slumbers, we break the gossamer web of *some* dream. Yet in a second afterward (so frail may that web have been), we remember not that we have dreamed. In the return to life from the swoon there are two stages; first, that of the sense of mental or spiritual; secondly, that of the sense of physical, existence. It seems probable that if, upon reaching the second stage, we could recall the impressions of the first, we should find these impressions eloquent in memories of the gulf beyond. And that gulf is—what? How at least shall we distinguish its shadows from those of the tomb? But if the impressions of what I have termed the first stage are not, at will, recalled, yet, after long interval, do they not come unbidden, while we marvel whence they come? He who has never swooned is not he who finds strange palaces and wildly familiar faces in coals that glow; is not he who beholds floating in midair the sad visions that the many may not view; is not he who ponders over the perfume of some novel flower—is not he whose brain grows bewildered with the meaning of some musical cadence which has never before arrested his attention.

Amid frequent and thoughtful endeavors to remember, amid earnest struggles to regather some token of the state of seeming nothingness into which my soul had lapsed, there have been moments when I have dreamed of success; there have been brief, very brief periods when I have conjured up remembrances which the lucid reason of a later epoch assures me could have had reference only to that condition of seeming unconsciousness. These shadows of memory tell, indistinctly, of tall figures that lifted and bore me in silence down—down—still down—till a hideous dizziness oppressed me at the mere idea of the interminableness of the descent. They tell also of a vague horror at my heart, on account of that heart's unnatural stillness. Then comes a sense of sudden motionlessness throughout all things; as if those who bore me (a ghastly train!) had outrun, in their descent, the limits of the limitless, and paused from the wearisomeness of their toil. After this I call to mind flatness and dampness; and then all is *madness*—the madness of a memory which busies itself among forbidden things.

Very suddenly there came back to my soul motion and sound—the tumultuous motion of the heart, and, in my ears, the sound of its beating. Then a pause in which all is blank. Then again sound, and motion, and touch—a tingling sensation pervading my frame. Then the mere consciousness of existence, without thought—a condition which lasted long. Then, very suddenly, *thought*, and shuddering terror, and earnest endeavor to comprehend my true state. Then a strong desire to lapse into insensibility. Then a rushing revival of soul and a successful effort to move. And now a full memory of the trial, of the judges, of the sable draperies, of the sentence, of the sickness, of the swoon. Then entire forgetfulness of all that followed; of all that a later day and much earnestness of endeavor have enabled me vaguely to recall.

So far, I had not opened my eyes. I felt that I lay upon my back, unbound. I reached out my hand, and it fell heavily upon something damp and hard. There I suffered it to remain for many minutes, while I strove to imagine where and *what* I could be. I longed, yet dared not to employ my vision. I dreaded the first glance at objects around me. It was not that I feared to look upon things horrible, but that I grew aghast lest there should be *nothing* to see. At length, with a wild desperation at heart, I quickly unclosed my eyes. My worst thoughts, then, were confirmed. The blackness of eternal night encompassed me. I struggled for breath. The intensity of the darkness seemed to oppress and stifle me. The atmosphere was intolerably close. I still lay quietly, and made effort to exercise my reason. I brought to mind the inquisitorial proceedings, and attempted from that point to deduce my real condition. The sentence had passed; and it appeared to me that a very long interval of time had since elapsed. Yet not for a moment did I suppose myself actually dead. Such a supposition, notwithstanding what we read in fiction, is altogether inconsistent with real existence—but where and in what state was I? The condemned to death, I knew, perished usually at the *autos-da-fé*, and one of these had been held on the very night of the day of my trial. Had I been remanded to my dungeon, to await the next sacrifice, which would not take place for many months? This I at once saw could not be. Victims had been in immediate demand. Moreover, my dungeon, as well as all the condemned cells at Toledo, had stone floors, and light was not altogether excluded.

A fearful idea now suddenly drove the blood in torrents upon my heart, and for a brief period, I once more relapsed into insensibility. Upon recovering, I at once started to my feet, trembling convulsively in every fiber. I thrust my arms wildly above and around me in all directions. I felt nothing; yet dreaded to move a step, lest I should be impeded by the walls of a *tomb*. Perspiration burst from every pore, and stood in cold big beads upon my forehead. The agony of suspense grew at length intolerable, and I cautiously moved forward, with my arms extended, and my eyes straining from their sockets, in the hope of catching some faint ray of light. I proceeded for many paces; but still all was blackness and vacancy. I breathed more freely. It seemed evident that mine was not, at least, the most hideous of fates.

And now, as I still continued to step cautiously onward, there came thronging upon my recollection a thousand vague rumors of the horrors of Toledo. Of the dungeons there had been strange things narrated—fables I had always deemed them—but yet strange, and too ghastly to repeat, save in a whisper. Was I left to perish of starvation in this subterranean world of darkness; or what fate, perhaps even more fearful, awaited me? That the result would be death, and a death of more than customary bitterness, I knew too well the character of my judges to doubt. The mode and the hour were all that occupied or distracted me.

My outstretched hands at length encountered some solid obstruction. It was a wall, seemingly of stone masonry—very smooth, slimy, and cold. I followed it up; stepping with all the careful distrust with which certain antique narratives had inspired me. This process, however, afforded me no means of ascertaining the dimensions of my dungeon; as I might make its circuit, and return to the point whence I set out, without being aware of the fact; so perfectly uniform seemed the wall. I therefore sought the knife which had been in my pocket, when led into the inquisitorial chamber; but it was gone; my clothes had been exchanged for a wrapper of coarse serge. I had thought of forcing the blade in some minute crevice of the masonry, so as to identify my point of departure. The difficulty, nevertheless, was but trivial; although, in the disorder of my fancy, it seemed at first insuperable. I tore a part of the hem from the robe and placed the fragment at full length, and at right angles to the wall. In groping my way around the prison, I could not fail to encounter this rag upon completing the circuit. So, at least I thought: but I had not counted upon the extent of the dungeon, or upon my own weakness. The ground was moist and slippery. I staggered onward for some time, when I stumbled and fell. My excessive fatigue induced me to remain prostrate; and sleep soon overtook me as I lay.

Upon awaking, and stretching forth an arm, I found beside me a loaf and a pitcher with water. I was too much exhausted to reflect upon this circumstance, but ate and drank with avidity. Shortly afterward, I resumed my tour around the prison, and with much toil, came at last upon the fragment of the serge. Up to the period when I fell I had counted fifty-two paces, and upon resuming my walk, I had counted forty-eight more—when I arrived at the rag. There were in all, then, a hundred paces; and, admitting two paces to the yard, I presumed the dungeon to be fifty yards in circuit. I had met, however, with many angles in the wall, and thus I could form no guess at the shape of the vault; for vault I could not help supposing it to be.

I had little object—certainly no hope—in these researches; but a vague curiosity prompted me to continue them. Quitting the wall, I resolved to cross the area of the enclosure. At first I proceeded with extreme caution, for the floor, although seemingly of solid material, was treacherous with slime. At length, however, I took courage, and did not hesitate to step firmly; endeavoring to cross in as direct a line as possible.

I had advanced some ten or twelve paces in this manner, when the remnant of the torn hem of my robe became entangled between my legs. I stepped on it, and fell violently on my face.

In the confusion attending my fall, I did not immediately apprehend a somewhat startling circumstance, which yet, in a few seconds afterward, and while I still lay prostrate, arrested my attention. It was this—my chin rested upon the floor of the prison, but my lips and the upper portion of my head, although seemingly at a less elevation than the chin, touched nothing. At the same time my forehead seemed bathed in a clammy vapor, and the peculiar smell of decayed fungus arose to my nostrils. I put forward my arm and shuddered to find that I had fallen at the very brink of a circular pit, whose extent, of course, I had no means of ascertaining at the moment. Groping about the masonry just below the margin, I succeeded in dislodging a small fragment, and let it fall into the abyss. For many seconds I harkened to its reverberations as it dashed against the sides of the chasm in its descent; at length there was a sudden plunge into water, succeeded by loud echoes. At the same moment there came a sound resembling the quick opening, and as rapid closing, of a door overhead, while a faint gleam of light flashed suddenly through the gloom, and as suddenly faded away.

I saw clearly the doom which had been prepared for me, and congratulated myself upon the timely accident by which I had escaped. Another step before my fall, and the world had seen me no more. And the death just avoided was of that very character which I had regarded as fabulous and frivolous in the tales respecting the Inquisition. To the victims of its tyranny, there was the choice of death with its direst physical agonies, or death with its most hideous moral horrors. I had been reserved for the latter. By long suffering my nerves had been unstrung, until I trembled at the sound of my own voice, and had become in every respect a fitting subject for the species of torture which awaited me.

Shaking in every limb, I groped my way back to the wall; resolving there to perish rather than risk the terrors of the wells, of which my imagination now pictured many in various positions about the dungeon. In other conditions of mind I might have had courage to end my misery at once by a plunge into one of these abysses; but now I was the veriest of cowards. Neither could I forget what I had read of these pits—that the *sudden* extinction of life formed no part of their most horrible plan.

Agitation of spirit kept me awake for many long hours; but at length I again slumbered. Upon arousing, I found by my side, as before, a loaf and a pitcher of water. A burning thirst consumed me, and I emptied the vessel at a draught. It must have been drugged; for scarcely had I drunk, before I became irresistibly drowsy. A deep sleep fell upon me—a sleep like that of death. How long it lasted, of course, I know not; but when, once again, I unclosed my eyes, the objects around me were visible. By a wild sulphurous luster, the origin of which I could not at first determine, I was enabled to see the extent and aspect of the prison.

In its size I had been greatly mistaken. The whole circuit of its walls did not exceed twenty-five yards. For some minutes this fact occasioned me a world of vain trouble; vain indeed! for what could be of less importance, under the terrible circumstances which environed me, than the mere dimensions of my dungeon? But my soul took a wild interest in trifles, and I busied myself in endeavors to account for the error I had committed in my measurement. The truth at length flashed upon me. In my first attempt at exploration I had counted fifty-two paces, up to the period when I fell; I must then have been within a pace or two of the fragment of serge; in fact, I had nearly performed the circuit of the vault. I then slept, and upon awaking, I must have returned upon my steps—thus supposing the circuit nearly double what it actually was. My confusion of mind prevented me from observing that I began my tour with the wall to the left, and ended it with the wall to the right.

I had been deceived, too, in respect to the shape of the enclosure. In feeling my way I had found many angles, and thus deduced an idea of great irregularity; so potent is the effect of total darkness upon one arousing from lethargy or sleep! The angles were simply those of a few slight depressions, or niches, at odd intervals. The general shape of the prison was square. What I had taken for masonry seemed now to be iron, or some other metal, in huge plates, whose sutures or joints occasioned the depression. The entire surface of this metallic enclosure was rudely daubed in all the hideous and repulsive devices to which the charnel superstition of the monks has given rise. The figures of fiends in aspects of menace, with skeleton forms, and other more really fearful images, overspread and disfigured the walls. I observed that the outlines of these monstrosities were sufficiently distinct, but that the colors seemed faded and blurred, as if from the effects of a damp atmosphere. I now noticed the floor, too, which was of stone. In the center yawned the circular pit from whose jaws I had escaped; but it was the only one in the dungeon.

All this I saw indistinctly and by much effort: for my personal condition had been greatly changed during slumber. I now lay upon my back, and at full length, on a species of low framework of wood. To this I was securely bound by a long strap resembling a surcingle. It passed in many convolutions about my limbs and body, leaving at liberty only my head, and my left arm to such extent that I could, by dint of much exertion, supply myself with food from an earthen dish which lay by my side on the floor. I saw, to my horror, that the pitcher had been removed. I say to my horror; for I was consumed with intolerable thirst. This thirst it appeared to be the design of my persecutors to stimulate: for the food in the dish was meat pungently seasoned.

Looking upward, I surveyed the ceiling of my prison. It was some thirty or forty feet overhead, and constructed much as the sidewalls. In one of its panels, a very singular figure riveted my whole attention. It was the painted figure of Time as he is commonly represented, save that, in lieu of a scythe, he held what, at a casual glance, I supposed to be the pictured image of a huge pendulum such as we see on antique clocks. There was something, however, in the appearance of this machine which caused me to regard it more attentively. While I gazed directly upward at it (for its position was immediately over my own) I fancied that I saw it in motion. In an instant afterward the fancy was confirmed. Its sweep was brief, and of course slow. I watched it for some minutes, somewhat in fear, but more in wonder. Wearied at length with observing its dull movement, I turned my eyes upon the other objects in the cell.

A slight noise attracted my notice, and, looking to the floor, I saw several enormous rats traversing it. They had issued from the well, which lay just within view to my right. Even then, while I gazed, they came up in troops, hurriedly, with ravenous eyes, allured by the scent of the meat. From this it required much effort to scare them away.

It might have been half an hour, perhaps even an hour (for I could take but imperfect note of time), before I again cast my eyes upward. What I then saw confounded and amazed me. The sweep of the pendulum had increased in extent by nearly a yard. As a natural consequence, its velocity was also much greater. But what mainly disturbed me was the idea that it had perceptibly *descended*. I now observed—with what horror it is needless to say—that its nether extremity was formed of a crescent of glittering steel, about a foot in length from horn to horn; the horns upward, and the underedge evidently as keen as that of a razor. Like a razor also, it seemed massy and heavy, tapering from the edge into a solid and broad structure above. It was appended to a weighty rod of brass, and the whole *hissed* as it swung through the air.

I could no longer doubt the doom prepared for me by monkish ingenuity in torture. My cognizance of the pit had become known to the inquisitorial agents—*the pit* whose horrors had been destined for so bold a recusant as myself—*the pit*, typical of hell, and regarded by rumor as the Ultima Thule of all their punishments. The plunge into this pit I had avoided by the merest of accidents, and I knew that surprise, or entrapment into torment, formed an important portion of all the grotesquerie of these dungeon deaths. Having failed to fall, it was no part of the demon plan to hurl me into the abyss; and thus (there being no alternative) a different and a milder destruction awaited me. Milder! I half smiled in my agony as I thought of such application of such a term.

What boots it to tell of the long, long hours of horror more than mortal, during which I counted the rushing vibrations of the steel! Inch by inch—line by line—with a descent only appreciable at intervals that seemed ages—down and still down it came! Days passed—it might have been that many days passed—ere it swept so closely over me as to fan me with its acrid breath. The odor of the sharp steel forced itself into my nostrils. I prayed—I wearied heaven with my prayer for its more speedy descent. I grew frantically mad, and struggled to force myself upward against the sweep of the fearful scimitar. And then I fell suddenly calm, and lay smiling at the glittering death, as a child at some rare bauble.

There was another interval of utter insensibility; it was brief; for, upon again lapsing into life there had been no perceptible descent in the pendulum. But it might have been long; for I knew there were demons who took note of my swoon, and who could have arrested the vibration at pleasure. Upon my recovery, too, I felt very—oh, inexpressibly sick and weak, as if through long inanition. Even amid the agonies of that period, the human nature craved food. With painful effort I outstretched my left arm as far as my bonds permitted, and took possession of the small remnant which had been spared me by the rats. As I put a portion of it within my lips, there rushed to my mind a half-formed thought of joy—of hope. Yet what business had *I* with hope? It was, as I say, a half-formed thought—man has many such which are never completed. I felt that it was of joy—of hope; but I felt also that it had perished in its formation. In vain I struggled to perfect—to regain it. Long suffering had nearly annihilated all my ordinary powers of mind. I was an imbecile—an idiot.

The vibration of the pendulum was at right angles to my length. I saw that the crescent was designed to cross the region of the heart. It would fray the serge of my robe—it would return and repeat its operations—again—and again. Notwithstanding its terrifically wide sweep (some thirty feet or more) and the hissing vigor of its descent, sufficient to sunder these very walls of iron, still the fraying of my robe would be all that, for several minutes, it would accomplish. And at this thought I paused. I dared not go farther than this reflection. I dwelt upon it with a pertinacity of attention—as if, in so dwelling, I could arrest *here* the descent of the steel. I forced myself to ponder upon the sound of the crescent as it should pass across the garment—upon the peculiar thrilling sensation which the friction of cloth produces on the nerves. I pondered upon all this frivolity until my teeth were on edge.

Down—steadily down it crept. I took a frenzied pleasure in contrasting its downward with its lateral velocity. To the right—to the left—far and wide—with the shriek of a damned spirit; to my heart with the stealthy pace of the tiger! I alternately laughed and howled as the one or the other idea grew predominant.

Down—certainly, relentlessly down! It vibrated within three inches of my bosom! I struggled violently, furiously, to free my left arm. This was free only from the elbow to the hand. I could reach the latter, from the platter beside me, to my mouth, with great effort, but no farther. Could I have broken the fastenings above the elbow, I would have seized and attempted to arrest the pendulum. I might as well have attempted to arrest an avalanche!

Down—still unceasingly—still inevitably down! I gasped and struggled at each vibration. I shrank convulsively at its every sweep. My eyes followed its outward or upward whirls with the eagerness of the most unmeaning despair; they closed themselves spasmodically at the descent, although death would have been a relief, oh! how unspeakable! Still I quivered in every nerve to think how slight a sinking of the machinery would precipitate that keen, glistening axe upon my bosom. It was *hope* that prompted the nerve to quiver—the frame to shrink. It was *hope*—the hope that triumphs on the rack—that whispers to the death-condemned even in the dungeons of the Inquisition.

I saw that some ten or twelve vibrations would bring the steel in actual contact with my robe, and with this observation there suddenly came over my spirit all the keen, collected calmness of despair. For the first time during many hours—or perhaps days—I *thought*. It now occurred to me that the bandage, or surcingle, which enveloped me, was *unique*. I was tied by no separate cord. The first stroke of the razorlike crescent athwart any portion of the band would so detach it that it might be unwound from my person by means of my left hand. But how fearful, in that case, the proximity of the steel! The result of the slightest struggle how deadly! Was it likely, moreover, that the minions of the torturer had not foreseen and provided for this possibility? Was it probable that the bandage crossed my bosom in the track of the pendulum? Dreading to find my faint and, as it seemed, my last hope frustrated, I so far elevated my head as to obtain a distinct view of my breast. The surcingle enveloped my limbs and body close in all directions—*save in the path of the destroying crescent*.

Scarcely had I dropped my head back into its original position, when there flashed upon my mind what I cannot better describe than as the unformed half of that idea of deliverance to which I have previously alluded, and of which a moiety only floated indeterminately through my brain when I raised food to my burning lips. The whole thought was now present—feeble, scarcely sane, scarcely definite—but still entire. I proceeded at once, with the nervous energy of despair, to attempt its execution.

For many hours the immediate vicinity of the low framework upon which I lay had been literally swarming with rats. They were wild, bold, ravenous; their red eyes glaring upon me as if they waited but for motionlessness on my part to make me their prey. "To what food," I thought, "have they been accustomed in the well?"

They had devoured, in spite of all my efforts to prevent them, all but a small remnant of the contents of the dish. I had fallen into an habitual seesaw, or wave of the hand about the platter: and, at length, the unconscious uniformity of the movement deprived it of effect. In their voracity the vermin frequently fastened their sharp fangs in my fingers. With the particles of the oily and spicy viand which now remained, I thoroughly rubbed the bandage wherever I could reach it; then, raising my hand from the floor, I lay breathlessly still.

At first the ravenous animals were startled and terrified at the change—at the cessation of movement. They shrank alarmedly back; many sought the well. But this was only for a moment. I had not counted in vain upon their voracity. Observing that I remained without motion, one or two of the boldest leaped upon the framework, and smelt at the surcingle. This seemed the signal for a general rush. Forth from the well they hurried in fresh troops. They clung to the wood— they overran it, and leaped in hundreds upon my person. The measured movement of the pendulum disturbed them not at all. Avoiding its strokes they busied themselves with the anointed bandage. They pressed—they swarmed upon me in ever accumulating heaps. They writhed upon my throat; their cold lips sought my own; I was half stifled by their thronging pressure; disgust, for which the world has no name, swelled my bosom, and chilled, with a heavy clamminess, my heart. Yet one minute, and I felt that the struggle would be over. Plainly I perceived the loosening of the bandage. I knew that in more than one place it must be already severed. With a more than human resolution I lay *still*.

Nor had I erred in my calculations—nor had I endured in vain. I at length felt that I was *free*. The surcingle hung in ribands from my body. But the stroke of the pendulum already pressed upon my bosom. It had divided the serge of the robe. It had cut through the linen beneath. Twice again it swung, and a sharp sense of pain shot through every nerve. But the moment of escape had arrived. At a wave of my hand my deliverers hurried tumultuously away. Wih a steady movement—cautious, sidelong, shrinking, and slow—I slid from the embrace of the bandage and beyond the reach of the scimitar. For the moment, at least, *I was free.*

Free!—and in the grasp of the Inquisition! I had scarcely stepped from my wooden bed of horror upon the stone floor of the prison, when the motion of the hellish machine ceased and I beheld it drawn up, by some invisible force, through the ceiling. This was a lesson which I took desperately to heart. My every motion was undoubtedly watched. Free!—I had but escaped death in one form of agony, to be delivered unto worse than death in some other. With that thought I rolled my eyes nervously around on the barriers of iron that hemmed me in. Something unusual—some change which, at first, I could not appreciate distinctly—it was obvious, had taken place in the apartment. For many minutes of a dreamy and trembling abstraction, I busied myself in vain, unconnected conjecture. During this period, I became aware, for the first time, of the origin of the sulphurous light which illumined the cell. It proceeded from a fissure, about half an inch in width, extending entirely around the prison at the base of the walls, which thus appeared, and were, completely separated from the floor. I endeavored, but of course in vain, to look through the aperture.

As I arose from the attempt, the mystery of the alteration in the chamber broke at once upon my understanding. I have observed that, although the outlines of the figures upon the walls were sufficiently distinct, yet the colors seemed blurred and indefinite. These colors had now assumed, and were momentarily assuming, a startling and most intense brilliancy, that gave to the spectral and fiendish portraitures an aspect that might have thrilled even firmer nerves than my own. Demon eyes, of a wild and ghastly vivacity, glared upon me in a thousand directions, where none had been visible before, and gleamed with the lurid luster of a fire that I could not force my imagination to regard as unreal.

Unreal! Even while I breathed there came to my nostrils the breath of the vapor of heated iron! A suffocating odor pervaded the prison! A deeper glow settled each moment in the eyes that glared at my agonies!

A richer tint of crimson diffused itself over the pictured horrors of blood. I panted! I gasped for breath! There could be no doubt of the design of my tormentors—oh! most unrelenting! oh! most demoniac of men! I shrank from the glowing metal to the center of the cell. Amid the thought of the fiery destruction that impended, the idea of the coolness of the well came over my soul like balm. I rushed to its deadly brink. I threw my straining vision below. The glare from the enkindled roof illumined its inmost recesses. Yet, for a wild moment, did my spirit refuse to comprehend the meaning of what I saw. At length it forced—it wrestled its way into my soul—it burned itself in upon my shuddering reason. Oh! for a voice to speak!—oh! horror—oh! any horror but this! With a shriek, I rushed from the margin, and buried my face in my hands—weeping bitterly.

The heat rapidly increased, and once again I looked up, shuddering as with a fit of the ague. There had been a second change in the cell—and now the change was obviously in the *form*. As before, it was in vain that I, at first, endeavored to appreciate or understand what was taking place. But not long was I left in doubt. The inquisitorial vengeance had been hurried by my twofold escape, and there was to be no more dallying with the King of Terrors. The room had been square. I saw that two of its iron angles were now acute—two, consequently, obtuse. The fearful difference quickly increased with a low rumbling or moaning sound. In an instant the apartment had shifted its form into that of a lozenge. But the alteration stopped not here—I neither hoped nor desired it to stop. I could have clasped the red walls to my bosom as a garment of eternal peace. "Death," I said, "any death but that of the pit!" Fool! might I have not known that *into the pit* it was the object of the burning iron to urge me? Could I resist its glow? or, if even that, could I withstand its pressure? And now, flatter and flatter grew the lozenge, with a rapidity that left me no time for contemplation. Its center, and of course, its greatest width, came just over the yawning gulf. I shrank back—but the closing walls pressed me resistlessly onward. At length for my seared and writhing body there was no longer an inch of foothold on the firm floor of the prison. I struggled no more, but the agony of my soul found vent in one loud, long, and final scream of despair. I felt that I tottered upon the brink—I averted my eyes—

There was a discordant hum of human voices! There was a loud blast as of many trumpets! There was a harsh grating as of a thousand thunders! The fiery walls rushed back! An outstretched arm caught my own as I fell, fainting, into the abyss. It was that of General Lasalle.

The French army had entered Toledo. The Inquisition was in the hands of its enemies.

THE BOY
WHO DREW CATS
LAFCADIO HEARN

A LONG, LONG time ago, in a small country village in Japan, there lived a poor farmer and his wife, who were very good people. They had a number of children and found it very hard to feed them all. The elder son was strong enough when only fourteen years old to help his father; and the little girls learned to help their mother almost as soon as they could walk.

But the youngest child, a little boy, did not seem to be fit for hard work. He was very clever—cleverer than all his brothers and sisters; but he was quite weak and small, and people said he could never grow very big. So his parents thought it would be better for him to become a priest. They took him with them to the village temple one day, and asked the good old priest who lived there if he would have their little boy for his acolyte and teach him all that a priest ought to know.

The old man spoke kindly to the lad, and asked him some hard questions. So clever were the answers that the priest agreed to take the little fellow into the temple as an acolyte, and to educate him for the priesthood.

The boy learned quickly what the old priest taught him, and was very obedient in most things. But he had one fault. He liked to draw cats during study hours, and to draw cats even where cats ought not to have been drawn at all.

Whenever he found himself alone, he drew cats. He drew them on the margins of the priest's books, and on all the screens of the temple, and on the walls, and on the pillars. Several times the priest told him this was not right; but he did not stop drawing cats. He drew them because he could not really help it. He had what is called "the genius of an *artist*," and just for that reason he was not quite fit to be an acolyte; a good acolyte should study books.

One day after he had drawn some very clever pictures of cats upon a paper screen, the old priest said to him severely, "My boy, you must go away from this temple at once. You will never make a good priest, but perhaps you will become a great artist. Now let me give you a last piece of advice, and be sure you never forget it. *Avoid large places at night— keep to small!*"

The boy did not know what the priest meant by saying, *"Avoid large places—keep to small."* He thought and thought, while he was tying up his little bundle of clothes to go away; but he could not understand those words, and he was afraid to speak to the priest anymore, except to say good-by.

He left the temple very sorrowfully, and began to wonder what he should do. If he went straight home he felt sure his father would punish him for having been disobedient to the priest, so he was afraid to go home. All at once he remembered that at the next village, twelve miles away, there was a very big temple. He had heard there were several priests at that temple, and he made up his mind to go to them and ask them to take him for their acolyte.

Now that big temple was closed up, but the boy did not know this fact. The reason it had been closed up was that a goblin had frightened the priests away and had taken possession of the place. Some brave warriors had afterward gone to the temple at night to kill the goblin, but they had never been seen alive again. Nobody had ever told these things to the boy, so he walked all the way to the village hoping to be kindly treated by the priests.

When he got to the village it was already dark, and all the people were in bed; but he saw the big temple on a hill at the other end of the principal street, and he saw there was a light in the temple. People who tell the story say the goblin used to make that light, in order to tempt lonely travelers to ask for shelter. The boy went at once to the temple, and knocked. There was no sound inside. He knocked and knocked again, but still nobody came. At last he pushed gently at the door, and was quite glad to find that it had not been fastened. So he went in, and saw a lamp burning—but no priest.

He thought some priest would be sure to come very soon, and he sat down and waited. Then he noticed that everything in the temple was gray with dust, and thickly spun over with cobwebs. So he thought to himself that the priests would certainly like to have an acolyte, to keep the place clean. He wondered why they had allowed everything to get so dusty. What most pleased him, however, were some big white screens, good to paint cats upon. Though he was tired, he looked at once for a writing box, and found one, and ground some ink, and began to paint cats.

He painted a great many cats upon the screens; and then he began to feel very, very sleepy. He was just on the point of lying down to sleep beside one of the screens when he suddenly remembered the words, *"Avoid large places—keep to small!"*

The temple was very large; he was all alone; and as he thought of these words—though he could not quite understand them—he began to feel for the first time a little afraid, and he resolved to look for a *small place* in which to sleep. He found a little cabinet with a sliding door, and went into it, and shut himself up. Then he lay down and fell fast asleep.

Very late in the night he was awakened by a most terrible noise—a noise of fighting and screaming. It was so dreadful that he was afraid even to look through a chink of the little cabinet; he lay very still, holding his breath for fright.

The light that had been in the temple went out, but the awful sounds continued, and became more awful, and all the temple shook. After a long time silence came, but the boy was still afraid to move. He did not move until the light of the morning sun shone into the cabinet through the chinks of the little door.

Then he got out of his hiding place very cautiously, and looked about. The first thing he saw was that all the floor of the temple was covered with blood. And then he saw, lying dead in the middle of it, an enormous, monstrous rat—a goblin rat—bigger than a cow!

But who or what could have killed it? There was no man or other creature to be seen. Suddenly the boy observed that the mouths of all the cats he had drawn the night before were red and wet with blood. Then he knew that the goblin had been killed by the cats which he had drawn. And then also, for the first time, he understood why the wise old priest had said to him, *"Avoid large places at night—keep to small."*

Afterward that boy became a very famous artist. Some of the cats which he drew are still shown to travelers in Japan.

THE LITTLE GOVERNESS
KATHERINE MANSFIELD

Oh, DEAR, HOW she wished that it wasn't nighttime. She'd have much rather traveled by day, much much rather. But the lady at the governess bureau had said, "You had better take an evening boat and then if you get into a compartment for 'ladies only' in the train you will be far safer than sleeping in a foreign hotel. Don't go out of the carriage; don't walk about the corridors and *be sure* to lock the lavatory door if you go there. The train arrives at Munich at eight o'clock, and Frau Arnholdt says that the Hotel Grunewald is only one minute away. A porter can take you there. She will arrive at six the same evening, so you will have a nice quiet day to rest after the journey and rub up your German. And when you want anything to eat I would advise you to pop into the nearest baker's and get a bun and some coffee. You haven't been abroad before, have you?" "No." "Well, I always tell my girls that it's better to mistrust people at first rather than trust them, and it's safer to suspect people of evil intentions rather than good ones. . . . It sounds rather hard, but we've got to be women of the world, haven't we?"

It had been nice in the ladies' cabin. The stewardess was so kind and changed her money for her and tucked up her feet. She lay on one of the hard pink-sprigged couches and watched the other passengers, friendly and natural, pinning their hats to the bolsters, taking off their boots and skirts, opening dressing cases and arranging mysterious rustling little packages, tying their heads up in veils before lying down. *Thud, thud,*

thud went the steady screw of the steamer. The stewardess pulled a green shade over the light and sat down by the stove, her skirt turned back over her knees, a long piece of knitting on her lap. On a shelf above her head there was a water bottle with a tight bunch of flowers stuck in it. "I like traveling very much," thought the little governess. She smiled and yielded to the warm rocking.

But when the boat stopped and she went up on deck, her dress basket in one hand, her rug and umbrella in the other, a cold, strange wind flew under her hat. She looked up at the masts and spars of the ship, black against a green glittering sky, and down to the dark landing stage where strange muffled figures lounged, waiting; she moved forward with the sleepy flock, all knowing where to go to and what to do except her, and she felt afraid. Just a little—just enough to wish—oh, to wish that it was daytime and that one of those women who had smiled at her in the glass, when they both did their hair in the ladies' cabin, was somewhere near now.

"Tickets, please. Show your tickets. Have your tickets ready." She went down the gangway, balancing herself carefully on her heels. Then a man in a black leather cap came forward and touched her on the arm. "Where for, miss?" He spoke English—he must be a guard or a station-master with a cap like that. She had scarcely answered when he pounced on her dress basket. "This way," he shouted, in a rude, determined voice, and elbowing his way he strode past the people. "But I don't want a porter." What a horrible man! "I don't want a porter. I want to carry it myself." She had to run to keep up with him, and her anger, far stronger than she, ran before her and snatched the bag out of the wretch's hand. He paid no attention at all, but swung on down the long dark platform and across a railway line. "He is a robber." She was sure he was a robber as she stepped between the silvery rails and felt the cinders crunch under her shoes.

On the other side—oh, thank goodness!—there was a train with MUNICH written on it. The man stopped by the huge lighted carriages. "Second class?" asked the insolent voice. "Yes, a ladies' compartment." She was quite out of breath. She opened her little purse to find something small enough to give this horrible man, while he tossed her dress basket into the rack of an empty carriage that had a ticket, DAMES

SEULES, gummed on the window. She got into the train and handed him twenty centimes. "What's this?" shouted the man, glaring at the money and then at her, holding it up to his nose, sniffing at it as though he had never in his life seen, much less held, such a sum. "It's a franc. You know that, don't you? It's a franc. That's my fare!" A franc! Did he imagine that she was going to give him a franc for playing a trick like that just because she was a girl and traveling alone at night? Never, never! She squeezed her purse in her hand and simply did not see him—she looked at a view of Saint-Malo on the wall opposite and simply did not hear him. "Ah, no. Ah, no. Four sous. You make a mistake. Here, take it. It's a franc I want." He leaped onto the step of the train and threw the money onto her lap.

Trembling with terror, she screwed herself tight, tight, and put out an icy hand and took the money—stowed it away in her hand. "That's all you're going to get," she said. For a minute or two she felt his sharp eyes pricking her all over, while he nodded slowly, pulling down his mouth: "Ve-ry well. *Trrrès bien.*" He shrugged his shoulders and disappeared into the dark.

Oh, the relief! How simply terrible that had been! As she stood up to feel if the dress basket was firm she caught sight of herself in the mirror, quite white, with big round eyes. She untied her "motor veil" and unbuttoned her green cape. "But it's all over now," she said to the mirror face, feeling in some way that it was more frightened than she.

People began to assemble on the platform. They stood together in little groups, talking; a strange light from the station lamps painted their faces almost green. A little boy in red clattered up with a huge tea wagon and leaned against it, whistling and flicking his boots with a serviette. A woman in a black alpaca apron pushed a barrow with pillows for hire. Dreamy and vacant she looked—like a woman wheeling a perambulator—up and down, up and down—with a sleeping baby inside it. Wreaths of white smoke floated up from somewhere and hung below the roof like misty vines. "How strange it all is," thought the little governess, "and the middle of the night, too." She looked out from her safe corner, frightened no longer but proud that she had not given that franc. "I can look after myself—of course I can. The great thing is not to—"

Suddenly from the corridor there came a stamping of feet and men's voices, high and broken, with snatches of loud laughter. They were coming her way. The little governess shrank into her corner as four young men in bowler hats passed, staring through the door and window. One of them, bursting with the joke, pointed to the notice DAMES SEULES, and the four bent down the better to see the one little girl in the corner. Oh dear, they were in the carriage next door. She heard them tramping about and then a sudden hush, followed by a tall thin fellow with a tiny black mustache who flung her door open. "If mademoiselle cares to come in with us," he said in French. She saw the others crowding behind him, peeping under his arm and over his shoulder, and she sat very straight and still. "If mademoiselle will do us the honor," mocked the tall man. One of them could be quiet no longer; his laughter went off in a loud crack. "Mademoiselle is serious," persisted the young man, bowing and grimacing. He took off his hat with a flourish, and she was alone again.

"*En voiture. En voi-ture!*" Someone ran up and down beside the train. "I wish it wasn't nighttime. I wish there was another woman in the carriage. I'm frightened of the men next door." The little governess looked out to see her porter coming back again—the same man making for her carriage with his arms full of luggage. But—but what *was* he doing? He put his thumbnail under the label DAMES SEULES and tore it right off and then stood aside, squinting at her while an old man wrapped in a plaid cape climbed up the high step. "But this is a ladies' compartment." "Oh, no, mademoiselle, you make a mistake. No, no, I assure you. *Merci*, monsieur." "*En voi-turre!*" A shrill whistle. The porter stepped off triumphant and the train started. For a moment or two, big tears brimmed her eyes and through them she saw the old man unwinding a scarf from his neck and untying the flaps of his jaeger cap. He looked very old. Ninety at least. He had a white mustache and big gold-rimmed spectacles with little blue eyes behind them and pink wrinkled cheeks. A nice face—and charming the way he bent forward and said in halting French, "Do I disturb you, mademoiselle? Would you rather I took all these things out of the rack and found another carriage?" What! That old man have to move all those heavy things just because she . . . "No, it's quite all right. You don't disturb me at all."

"Ah, a thousand thanks." He sat down opposite her and unbuttoned the cape of his enormous coat and flung it off his shoulders.

The train seemed glad to have left the station. With a long leap it sprang into the dark. She rubbed a place in the window with her glove, but she could see nothing—just a tree outspread like a black fan, or a scatter of lights, or the line of a hill, solemn and huge. In the carriage next door the young men started singing *"Un, deux, trois."* They sang the same song over and over at the tops of their voices.

"I never could have dared to go to sleep if I had been alone," she decided. "*I couldn't* have put my feet up or even taken off my hat." The singing gave her a queer little tremble in her stomach, and hugging herself to stop it, with her arms crossed under her cape, she felt really glad to have the old man in the carriage with her. Careful to see that he was not looking, she peeped at him through her long lashes. He sat extremely upright, the chest thrown out, the chin well in, knees pressed together, reading a German paper. That was why he spoke French so funnily. He was a German. Something in the army, she supposed—a colonel or a general—once, of course, not now; he was too old for that now. How spick-and-span he looked for an old man. He wore a pearl pin stuck in his black tie, and a ring with a dark red stone on his little finger; the tip of a white silk handkerchief showed in the pocket of his double-breasted jacket. Somehow, altogether, he was really nice to look at. Most old men were so horrid. She couldn't bear them doddery—or they had a disgusting cough or something. But not having a beard—that made all the difference—and then his cheeks were so pink and his mustache so very white.

Down went the German paper and the old man leaned forward with the same delightful courtesy: "Do you speak German, mademoiselle?" *"Ja, ein wenig, mehr als Französisch,"* said the little governess, blushing a deep pink color that spread slowly over her cheeks and made her blue eyes look almost black. *"Ach, so!"* The old man bowed graciously. "Then perhaps you would care to look at some illustrated papers." He slipped a rubber band from a little roll of them and handed them across. "Thank you very much."

She was very fond of looking at pictures, but first she would take off her hat and gloves. So she stood up, unpinned the brown straw and put it neatly in the rack beside the dress basket, stripped off her brown kid gloves, paired them in a tight roll and put them in the crown of the hat for safety, and then sat down again, more comfortably this time, her feet crossed, the papers on her lap. How kindly the old man in the corner watched her bare little hand turning over the big white pages, watched her lips moving as she pronounced the long words to herself, rested his eyes upon her hair that fairly blazed under the light. Alas! How tragic for a little governess to possess hair that made one think of tangerines and marigolds, of apricots and tortoiseshell cats and champagne! Perhaps that was what the old man was thinking as he gazed and gazed; that not even the dark ugly clothes could disguise her soft beauty. Perhaps the flush that licked his cheeks and lips was a flush of rage that anyone so young and tender should have to travel alone and unprotected through the night. Who knows he was not murmuring in his sentimental German fashion, *"Ja, es ist eine Tragödie!* Would to God I were the child's grandpapa!"

"Thank you very much. They were very interesting." She smiled prettily, handing back the papers. "But you speak German extremely well," said the old man. "You have been in Germany before, of course?" "Oh no, this is the first time"—a little pause, then—"this is the first time that I have ever been abroad at all." "Really! I am surprised. You gave me the impression, if I may say so, that you were accustomed to traveling." "Oh, well—I have been about a good deal in England, and to Scotland once." "So. I myself have been in England once, but I could not learn English." He raised one hand and shook his head, laughing. "No, it was too difficult for me. . . . ''Ow do you do. Please vich is ze vay to Leicestaire Squaare.'" She laughed too. "Foreigners always say . . ." They had quite a little talk about it. "But you will like Munich," said the old man. "Munich is a wonderful city. Museums, pictures, galleries, fine buildings and shops, concerts, theaters, restaurants—all are in Munich. I have traveled all over Europe many, many times in my life, but it is always to Munich that I return. You will enjoy yourself there." "I am not going to *stay* in Munich," said the little governess, and she added shyly, "I am going to a post as governess to a doctor's family in Augsburg."

Ah, that was it. Augsburg he knew. Augsburg—well—was not

beautiful. A solid manufacturing town. But if Germany was new to her, he hoped she would find something interesting there too. "I am sure I shall." "But what a pity not to see Munich before you go. You ought to take a little holiday on your way"—he smiled—"and store up some pleasant memories." "I am afraid I could not do *that*," said the little governess, shaking her head, suddenly important and serious. "And also, if one is alone . . ." He quite understood. He bowed, serious too. They were silent after that. The train shattered on, baring its dark, flaming breast to the hills and to the valleys. It was warm in the carriage. She seemed to lean against the dark rushing and to be carried away and away. Little sounds made themselves heard; steps in the corridor, doors opening and shutting, a murmur of voices, whistling. . . . Then the window was pricked with long needles of rain. . . . But it did not matter . . . it was outside . . . and she had her umbrella. . . . She pouted, sighed, opened and shut her hands once, and fell fast asleep.

"PARDON! PARDON!" The sliding back of the carriage door woke her with a start. What had happened? Someone had come in and gone out again. The old man sat in his corner, more upright than ever, his hands in the pockets of his coat, frowning heavily. "Ha! Ha! Ha!" came from the carriage next door. Still half asleep, she put her hands to her hair to make sure it wasn't a dream. "Disgraceful!" muttered the old man, more to himself than to her. "Common, vulgar fellows! I am afraid they disturbed you, gracious Fräulein, blundering in here like that." No, not really. She was just going to wake up, and she took out her silver watch to look at the time. Half past four. A cold blue light filled the window-panes. Now when she rubbed a place she could see bright patches of fields, a clump of white houses like mushrooms, a road "like a picture" with poplar trees on either side, a thread of river. How pretty it was! How pretty and how different! Even those pink clouds in the sky looked foreign. It was cold, but she pretended that it was far colder and rubbed her hands together and shivered, pulling at the collar of her coat because she was so happy.

The train began to slow down. The engine gave a long shrill whistle. They were coming to a town. Taller houses, pink and yellow, glided by, fast asleep behind their green eyelids, and guarded by the poplar trees that quivered in the blue air as if on tiptoe, listening. In one house a woman opened the shutters, flung a red and white mattress across the window frame, and stood staring at the train. A pale woman with black hair and a white woolen shawl over her shoulders. More women appeared at the doors and at the windows of the sleeping houses. There came a flock of sheep. The shepherd wore a blue blouse and pointed wooden shoes. Look! Look what flowers—and by the railway station too! Standard roses like bridesmaids' bouquets, white geraniums, waxy pink ones that you would *never* see out of a greenhouse at home. Slower and slower. A man with a watering can was spraying the platform. "A-a-a-ah!" Somebody came running and waving his arms. A huge fat woman waddled through the glass doors of the station with a tray of strawberries. Oh, she was thirsty! She was very thirsty! "A-a-a-ah!" The same somebody ran back again. The train stopped.

The old man pulled his coat round him and got up, smiling at her. He murmured something she didn't quite catch, but she smiled back at him as he left the carriage. While he was away the little governess looked at herself again in the glass, shook and patted herself with the precise practical care of a girl who is old enough to travel by herself and has nobody else to assure her that she is "quite all right behind." Thirsty and thirsty! The air tasted of water. She let down the window and the fat woman with the strawberries passed as if on purpose, holding up the tray to her. *"Nein, danke,"* said the little governess, looking at the big berries on their gleaming leaves. *"Wieviel?"* she asked as the fat woman moved away. "Two marks fifty, Fräulein." "Good gracious!"

She came in from the window and sat down in the corner, very sobered for a minute. Half a crown! "H-o-o-o-o-e-e-e!" shrieked the train, gathering itself together to be off again. She hoped the old man wouldn't be left behind. Oh, it was daylight—everything was lovely if only she hadn't been so thirsty. Where *was* the old man—oh, here he was. She dimpled at him as though he were an old accepted friend as he closed the door and, turning, took from under his cape a basket of the strawberries. "If Fräulein would honor me by accepting these . . ." "What, for me?" But she drew back and raised her hands as though he were about to put a wild little kitten on her lap.

"Certainly, for you," said the old man. "For myself it is twenty years since I was brave enough to eat strawberries." "Oh, thank you very much. *Danke bestens*," she stammered, *"sie sind so sehr schön!"* "Eat them and see," said the old man, looking pleased and friendly. "You won't have even one?" "No, no, no." Timidly and charmingly her hand hovered. They were so big and juicy she had to take two bites to them—the juice ran all down her fingers—and it was while she munched the berries that she first thought of the old man as a grandfather. What a perfect grandfather he would make! Just like one out of a book!

The sun came out; the pink clouds in the sky—the strawberry clouds—were eaten by the blue. "Are they good?" asked the old man. "As good as they look?"

When she had eaten them she felt she had known him for years. She told him about Frau Arnholdt and how she had got the place. Did he know the Hotel Grunewald? Frau Arnholdt would not arrive until the evening. He listened, listened until he knew as much about the affair as she did, until he said, not looking at her, but smoothing the palms of his brown suede gloves together, "I wonder if you would let me show you a little of Munich today. Nothing much—but just perhaps a picture gallery and the Englischer Garten. It seems such a pity that you should have to spend the day at the hotel, and also a little uncomfortable . . . in a strange place. *Nicht wahr?* You would be back there by the early afternoon or whenever you wish, of course, and you would give an old man a great deal of pleasure."

It was not until long after she had said yes—because the moment she had said it and he had thanked her he began telling her about his travels in Turkey and attar of roses—that she wondered whether she had done wrong. After all, she really did not know him. But he was so old and he had been so very kind—not to mention the strawberries. . . . And she couldn't have explained the reason why she said no, and it was her *last* day in a way, her last day to really enjoy herself. "Was I wrong? Was I?" A drop of sunlight fell into her hands and lay there, warm and quivering. "If I might accompany you as far as the hotel," he suggested, "and call for you again at about ten o'clock." He took out his pocket-book and handed her a card. "Herr Regierungsrat. . . ." He had a title! Well, it was *bound* to be all right!

So after that the little governess gave herself up to the excitement of being really abroad, to looking out and reading the foreign advertisement signs, to being told about the places they came to—having her attention and enjoyment looked after by the charming old grandfather—until they reached Munich and the Hauptbahnhof. "Porter! Porter!" He found her a porter, disposed of his own luggage in a few words, guided her through the bewildering crowd, out of the station, down the clean white steps into the white road to the hotel. He explained who she was to the manager, as though all this had been bound to happen, and then for one moment her little hand lost itself in the big brown suede ones. "I will call for you at ten o'clock." He was gone.

"This way, Fräulein," said a waiter, who had been dodging behind the manager's back, all eyes and ears for the strange couple. She followed him up two flights of stairs into a dark bedroom. He dashed down her dress basket and pulled up a clattering, dusty blind. Ugh! What an ugly, cold room—what enormous furniture! Fancy spending the day in here! "Is this the room Frau Arnholdt ordered?" asked the little governess. The waiter had a curious way of staring, as if there were something *funny* about her. He pursed up his lips, about to whistle, and then changed his mind. *"Gewiss,"* he said. Well, why didn't he go? Why did he stare so? *"Gehen Sie,"* said the little governess, with frigid English simplicity. His little eyes, like currants, nearly popped out of his doughy cheeks. *"Gehen Sie sofort,"* she repeated icily. At the door he turned. "And the gentleman," said he, "shall I show the gentleman upstairs when he comes?"

OVER THE WHITE streets big white clouds fringed with silver—and sunshine everywhere. Fat, fat coachmen driving fat cabs; funny women with little round hats cleaning the tramway lines; people laughing and pushing against one another; trees on both sides of the streets, and everywhere you looked almost, immense fountains; a noise of laughing from the footpaths or the middle of the streets or the open windows. And beside her, more beautifully brushed than ever, with a rolled umbrella in one hand and yellow gloves instead of brown ones, her grandfather who had asked her to spend the day. She wanted to run, she wanted to hang on his arm, she wanted to cry every minute, "Oh, I am so frightfully happy!"

He guided her across the roads, stood still while she "looked," and his kind eyes beamed on her and he said, "Just whatever you wish." She ate two white sausages and two little rolls of fresh bread at eleven o'clock in the morning and she drank some beer, which he told her wasn't intoxicating, wasn't at all like English beer, out of a glass like a flower vase. And then they took a cab and really she must have seen thousands and thousands of wonderful classical pictures in about a quarter of an hour! "I shall have to think them over when I am alone. . . ." But when they came out of the picture gallery it was raining. The grandfather unfurled his umbrella and held it over the little governess. They started to walk to the restaurant for lunch. She, very close beside him so that he should have some of the umbrella too. "It goes easier," he remarked in a detached way, "if you take my arm, Fräulein. And besides, it is the custom in Germany." So she took his arm and walked beside him while he pointed out the famous statues, so interested that he quite forgot to put down the umbrella even when the rain was long over.

After lunch they went to a café to hear a Gypsy band, but she did not like that at all. Ugh! Such horrible men were there, with heads like eggs, and cuts on their faces, so she turned her chair and cupped her burning cheeks in her hands and watched her old friend instead. . . . Then they went to the Englischer Garten.

"I wonder what the time is," asked the little governess. "My watch has stopped. I forgot to wind it in the train last night. We've seen such a lot of things that I feel it must be quite late." "Late!" He stopped in front of her, laughing and shaking his head in a way she had begun to know. "Then you have not really enjoyed yourself. Late! Why, we have not had any ice cream yet!" "Oh, but I have enjoyed myself," she cried, distressed, "more than I can possibly say. It has been wonderful! Only Frau Arnholdt is to be at the hotel at six and I ought to be there by five." "So you shall. After the ice cream I shall put you into a cab and you can go there comfortably." She was happy again. The chocolate ice cream melted—melted in little sips a long way down. The shadows of the trees danced on the tablecloths, and she sat with her back safely turned to the ornamental clock that pointed to twenty-five minutes to seven. "Really and truly," said the little governess earnestly, "this has been the happiest day of my life. I've never even imagined such a day." In spite of the ice cream her grateful baby heart glowed with love for the fairy grandfather.

So they walked out of the garden down a long alley. The day was nearly over. "You see those big buildings opposite," said the old man. "The third story—that is where I live. I and the old housekeeper who looks after me." She was very interested. "Now just before I find a cab for you, will you come and see my little 'home' and let me give you a bottle of the attar of roses I told you about in the train? For remembrance?" She would love to. "I've never seen a bachelor's flat in my life," laughed the little governess.

The passage was quite dark. "Ah, I suppose my old woman has gone out to buy me a chicken. One moment." He opened a door and stood aside for her to pass, a little shy but curious, into a strange room. She did not know quite what to say. It wasn't pretty. In a way it was very ugly—but neat and, she supposed, comfortable for such an old man. "Well, what do you think of it?" He knelt down and took from a cupboard a round tray with two pink glasses and a tall pink bottle. "Two little bedrooms beyond," he said gaily, "and a kitchen. It's enough, eh?" "Oh, quite enough." "And if ever you should be in Munich and care to spend a day or two—why there is always a little nest—a wing of a chicken, and a salad, and an old man delighted to be your host once more and many many times, dear little Fräulein!"

He took the stopper out of the bottle and poured some wine into the two pink glasses. His hand shook and the wine spilled over the tray. It was very quiet in the room. She said, "I think I ought to go now." "But you will have a tiny glass of wine with me—just one before you go?" said the old man. "No, really no. I never drink wine. I—I have promised never to touch wine or anything like that." And though he pleaded and though she felt dreadfully rude, especially when he seemed to take it to heart so, she was quite determined. "No, *really*, please." "Well, will you just sit down on the sofa for five minutes and let me drink your health?" The little governess sat down on the edge of the red velvet couch and he sat down beside her and drank her health at a gulp. "Have you really been happy today?" asked the old man, turning round, so close beside her that she felt his knee twitching against hers. Before she could answer he held her hands. "And are you going to give me one little kiss before you go?" he asked, drawing her closer still.

It was a dream! It wasn't true! It wasn't the same old man at all. Ah, how horrible! The little governess stared at him in terror. "No, no, no!" she stammered, struggling out of his hands. "One little kiss. A kiss. What is it? Just a kiss, dear little Fräulein. A kiss." He pushed his face forward, his lips smiling broadly; and how his little blue eyes gleamed behind the spectacles! "Never—never. How can you!" She sprang up, but he was too quick and he held her against the wall, pressed against her his hard old body and his twitching knee and, though she shook her head from side to side, distracted, kissed her on the mouth. On the mouth! Where not a soul who wasn't a near relation had ever kissed her before. . . .

She ran, ran down the street until she found a broad road with tramlines and a policeman standing in the middle like a clockwork doll. "I want to get a tram to the Hauptbahnhof," sobbed the little governess. "Fräulein?" She wrung her hands. "The Hauptbahnhof. There—there's one now," and while he watched, very much surprised, the little girl with her hat on one side, crying without a handkerchief, sprang onto the tram—not seeing the conductor's eyebrows, nor hearing the *hochwohlgebildete Dame* talking her over with a scandalized friend. She rocked herself and cried out loud and said, "Ah, ah!" pressing her hands to her mouth. "She has been to the dentist," shrilled a fat old woman, too stupid to be uncharitable. "*Na, sagen Sie 'mal,* what toothache! The child hasn't one left in her mouth." While the tram swung and jangled through a world full of old men with twitching knees.

WHEN THE LITTLE governess reached the hall of the Hotel Grunewald, the same waiter who had come into her room in the morning was standing by a table, polishing a tray of glasses. The sight of the little governess seemed to fill him out with some inexplicable important content. He was ready for her question; his answer came pat and suave. "Yes, Fräulein, the lady has been here. I told her that you had arrived and gone out again immediately with a gentleman. She asked me when you were coming back again—but of course I could not say. And then she went to the manager." He took up a glass from the table, held it up to the light, looked at it with one eye closed, and started polishing it with a corner of his apron. ". . ." "Pardon, Fräulein? Ach, no, Fräulein. The manager could tell her nothing—nothing." He shook his head and smiled at the brilliant glass. "Where is the lady now?" asked the little governess, shuddering so violently that she had to hold her handkerchief up to her mouth. "How should I know?" cried the waiter, and as he swooped past her to pounce upon a new arrival his heart beat so hard against his ribs that he nearly chuckled aloud. "That's it! That's it!" he thought. "That will show her." And as he swung the new arrival's box onto his shoulders—hoop!—as though he were a giant and the box a feather, he minced over again the little governess's words, *Gehen Sie. Gehen Sie sofort.* "Shall I! Shall I!" he shouted to himself.

RUNNING WOLF
ALGERNON BLACKWOOD

The man who enjoys an adventure outside the general experience of the race, and imparts it to others, must not be surprised if he is taken for either a liar or a fool, as Malcolm Hyde, hotel clerk on a holiday, discovered in due course.

When he first set eyes on Medicine Lake he was struck by its still, sparkling beauty, lying there in the vast Canadian backwoods, and by its extreme loneliness.

"It's fairly stiff with big fish," Morton of the Montreal Sporting Club had said. "Spend your holidays there—you'll have it all to yourself except for an old Indian who's got a shack there. Camp on the east side—if you'll take a tip from me." He then talked for half an hour about the wonderful sport; yet he was not otherwise very communicative. Nor had he stayed there very long. If it was such a paradise, why had he himself spent only three days there? "Ran short of grub," was the explanation offered; but to another friend he had mentioned briefly, "Flies," and to a third he gave the excuse that his half-breed took "sick," necessitating a quick return.

Hyde cared little for explanations. "Stiff with fish" was the phrase he liked. He took the Canadian Pacific train to Mattawa, laid in his outfit at Stony Creek, and set off for the fifteen-mile canoe trip without a care in the world.

Traveling light, the portages did not trouble him; the water was swift

446

and easy, the rapids negotiable. He pushed on between the immense forests, known to deer, bear, moose, and wolf, that stretched for hundreds of miles. The autumn day was calm, the water sang and sparkled, the blue sky was ablaze with light. Toward evening he passed an old beaver dam, rounded a little point, and had his first sight of Medicine Lake. He lifted his dripping paddle; the canoe shot with a silent glide into the calm water. He gave an exclamation of delight, for the loveliness caught his breath away.

The lake formed a crescent, perhaps four miles long, its width between a mile and half a mile. The slanting gold of sunset flooded it. No wind stirred its crystal surface. Towering spruce and hemlock trooped to its very edge, majestic cedars leaned down as if to drink, crimson sumacs shone in fiery patches, and maples gleamed orange and red beyond belief. The air was like wine, with the silence of a dream. It was here the red men formerly "made medicine," with all the wild ritual and tribal ceremony of an ancient day.

Hyde looked about for a good camping place before the sun sank below the forests. The Indian's shack, lying in full sunshine on the eastern shore, he found at once; but the trees lay too thick about it for comfort, nor did he wish to be so close to its inhabitant. Upon the opposite side, however, an ideal clearing offered. He paddled over quickly and examined it. The ground was hard and dry, he found, and a little brook ran tinkling down one side of it into the lake. This outlet would be a good fishing spot.

It was a perfect site, and some charred logs, with traces of former fires, proved that he was not the first to think so. Hyde was delighted. Then he recalled Morton's advice. And not Morton's only, for the storekeeper at Stony Creek had reinforced it. "Put yer tent on the east shore, I should," he had said at parting.

Hyde looked about him. He wished he had asked the storekeeper for more details. The light was fading; he must decide quickly one way or the other. "He must have had *some* reason," Hyde growled to himself. "Fellows like that usually know what they're talking about. I guess I'd better shift over to the other side—for tonight, at any rate."

He glanced across the water. No smoke rose from the Indian's shack. The man, he decided, was away. Reluctantly he paddled across the lake, and half an hour later his tent was up, firewood collected, and two small trout were already caught for supper. But the bigger fish, he knew, lay waiting for him on the other side by the little outlet, and he fell asleep at length on his bed of balsam boughs, wondering how a mere sentence could have persuaded him so easily against his own better judgment.

His morning mood was a very different one. The brilliant light, the intoxicating air were too exhilarating for the mind to harbor foolish fancies. He struck camp immediately after breakfast, paddled back across the strip of shining water, and quickly settled in upon the forbidden shore. The more he saw of the spot, the better he liked it. There was plenty of wood, running water to drink, an open space about the tent, and there were no flies. The fishing, moreover, was magnificent.

The useless hours of the early afternoon he passed dozing in the sun, or wandering through the underbrush beyond the camp. He bathed in a cool, deep pool; he reveled in the lonely little paradise. The peace and the isolation delighted him. Toward evening he strolled along the shore, looking for the first sign of a rising fish. *Plop* followed *plop* as the big fellows rose, snatched at their food, and vanished into the depths. He hurried back. Ten minutes later he had taken his rods and was gliding cautiously in the canoe through the quiet water.

So good was the sport, indeed, and so quickly did the big trout pile up in the bottom of the canoe, that despite the growing lateness, he found it hard to tear himself away. "One more," he said, "and then I really will go." He was in the act of taking his last off the hook when the deep silence of the evening was curiously disturbed. He became abruptly aware that someone watched him. He sat motionless and stared about.

Nothing stirred; the ripple on the lake had died away; the yellow sky, fast fading, threw reflections that made distances uncertain. But there was no sound, no movement; he saw no figure anywhere. Yet he knew that a pair of eyes was fixed upon him from some point in the surrounding shadows, and a wave of unreasoning terror gripped him. The nose of the canoe was against the bank. Instinctively he shoved it off and paddled into deeper water. The watcher, it came to him, was quite close to him upon that bank. But where? And who? Was it the Indian?

In deeper water, and some twenty yards from the shore, he paused and strained both sight and hearing to find some possible clue. He felt half ashamed, now that the first strange feeling had passed. But the certainty remained. Though he could discover no figure on the shore, he could have sworn in which clump of willow bushes the hidden person crouched and stared. His attention seemed drawn to that particular clump.

The water dripped slowly from his paddle, now lying across the thwarts. There was no other sound. The canvas of his tent gleamed dimly. A star or two were out. He waited. Nothing happened. Then, as suddenly as it had come, the feeling passed, and he knew that the person who had been watching him intently had gone. It was as if a current had been turned off.

He pointed the canoe in to the shore again, landed, and, paddle in hand, went over to examine the clump of willows he had singled out as the place of concealment. There was no one there, of course, nor any trace of recent human occupancy. No leaves, no branches stirred, nor was a single twig displaced. Yet, for all that, he felt positive that a little time ago someone had crouched among these very leaves and watched him. He remained absolutely convinced of that.

He returned to his little camp, more disturbed than he cared to acknowledge. He cooked his supper and hung up his catch on a string, so that no prowling animal could get at it during the night. Unconsciously he built a bigger fire than usual, and found himself peering over his pipe into the deep shadows beyond the firelight, straining his ears to catch the slightest sound.

Loneliness in a backwoods camp brings a happy sense of calm until, and unless, it comes too near. Once it has crept within short range, a curious dread may easily follow—the dread lest the loneliness suddenly be disturbed, and the solitary human feel open to attack.

For Hyde, now, this transition had been already accomplished. He sat there, with his back to the blazing logs, a very visible object in the light, while all about him the darkness of the forest lay like an impenetrable wall. He could not see a yard beyond the small circle of his campfire; the silence about him was like the silence of the dead.

Then again he became suddenly aware that the person who watched him had returned, and felt the same concentrated gaze once more fixed upon him. There was no warning; he heard no stealthy tread or snapping of dry twigs; yet the owner of those steady eyes was very close to him, probably not a dozen feet away.

A shiver ran down his spine, and for some minutes he sat straining his eyes in vain to pierce the darkness. Then, as he shifted his position to obtain another angle of vision, his heart gave two big thumps against his ribs and the hair seemed to rise on his scalp. In the darkness facing him he saw too small greenish circles that were certainly a pair of eyes, yet not the eyes of a human being. It was a pair of animal eyes that stared so fixedly at him out of the night.

At the menace of those eyes, the fears of millions of long-dead hunters since the dawn of time woke in him, hotel clerk though he was. His hand groped for a weapon, fell on the iron head of his small camp axe, and at once he was himself again, the vague, superstitious dread gone. This was a bear or wolf that smelled his catch and came to steal it. With beings of that sort he knew instinctively how to deal.

He snatched a burning log from the fire and hurled it straight at the eyes of the beast before him. The bit of pitch pine fell in a shower of sparks that lit the dry grass, flared up a moment, then died quickly down again. But in that instant of illumination he saw clearly what his unwelcome visitor was. A big timber wolf sat on its hindquarters, staring steadily at him through the firelight.

To his amazement the wolf did not turn and bolt away, but withdrew a few yards only and sat there again on its haunches, staring as before. He did not waste another good log on it, for his fear was dissipated now; he knew that wolves were harmless in the summer and autumn, and even when "packed" in winter, they would attack a man only when suffering desperate hunger. So he lay and watched the beast, threw bits of stick in its direction, even talked to it. The creature blinked its bright green eyes, but made no move.

Why then, if his fear was gone, did he think of certain things as he rolled himself in the Hudson's Bay blankets before going to sleep? The animal's refusal to turn and bolt was strange. Never before had he known a wild creature that was not afraid of fire. Why did it sit and watch him, as with purpose in its gleaming eyes? How had he felt its presence instantly? A solitary timber wolf was a timid thing, yet this one feared neither man nor fire. Now, as he lay there wrapped in his blankets inside the cozy tent, it sat outside beneath the stars, watching him, steadily watching him.

With the sunshine and the morning wind, the incident of the night before was almost forgotten. The tea and fish were delicious, his pipe had never tasted so good. The glory of this lonely lake went to his head a little; he was a hunter before the Lord, and nothing else. He tried the edge of the lake, and in the excitement of playing a big fish, knew suddenly that *it*, the wolf, was there. Hyde looked about him. The brilliant sunshine made every smallest detail clear and sharp—boulders of granite, crimson sumac, pebbles along the shore—without revealing where the watcher hid. Then, farther inshore among the tangled undergrowth, he suddenly picked up the familiar outline. The wolf was lying behind a granite boulder, so that only the head, the muzzle, and the eyes were visible. Had he not known it was a wolf, he could never have separated it from the landscape.

He looked straight at it. Their eyes met full and square. "Great Scott!" he exclaimed aloud. "Why, it's looking like a human being!" The animal rose and came down in leisurely fashion to the shore, where it stood and stared at him. Hyde was aware of a new and almost incredible sensation—that it courted recognition.

"Well! Well!" he exclaimed again, relieving his feelings by addressing it aloud. "What d'you want, anyway?"

He examined it now more carefully. It was a tremendous beast—a huge, shaggy, lean-flanked timber wolf, its wicked eyes staring straight into his own, almost with a kind of purpose in them. He saw its great jaws, its teeth, and its tongue hung out, dripping saliva a little. He wished for the first time that he had brought a rifle. And yet the idea of the beast's savagery, its fierceness, was very little in him.

With a resounding smack, Hyde brought his paddle down flat upon the water, using all his strength, till the echoes rang from one end of the lake to the other as from a pistol shot. The wolf never stirred. He shouted, but the beast remained unmoved. He blinked his eyes, speaking as to a dog, a domestic creature accustomed to human ways. It blinked its eyes in return.

At length, increasing his distance from the shore, he continued fishing, and the excitement of the marvelous sport held his attention—his surface attention, at any rate. At times he almost forgot the wolf; yet whenever he looked up, he saw it there. And worse; when he slowly paddled home again, he observed it trotting along the shore as though to keep him company. His camp was near when, to his keen relief, about half a mile from the tent, he saw the creature suddenly stop and sit down in the open. He waited a moment, then paddled on. It did not follow. It merely sat and watched him. And the absurd, yet significant, feeling came to him that the beast divined his anxiety and was now showing him, as well as it could, that it entertained no hostile intentions.

He landed; he cooked his supper in the dusk; the animal made no sign. Not far away it certainly lay and watched, but it did not advance. And Hyde, observant now in a new way, suddenly realized that his relations with the beast had progressed distinctly a stage further. He had an understanding with the wolf. He was aware of friendly thoughts toward it. He even went so far as to set out a few big fish on the spot where he had first seen it sitting the previous night. If he comes, he thought, he is welcome to them. He thought of it now as "he."

The wolf made no appearance until Hyde was in the act of entering his tent that night. As he was closing the flap, he saw the eyes near where he had placed the fish. He waited, expecting to hear sounds of munching jaws; but all was silence. Only the eyes glowed steadily out of the background of pitch-darkness. He closed the flap. He had no slightest fear. In ten minutes he was sound asleep.

He could not have slept very long, for when he woke up he could see the shine of a faint red light through the canvas; the fire had not died down completely. He rose and cautiously peeped out. The wolf was sitting by the dying embers, not two yards away from where Hyde crouched. And at these very close quarters there was something in the attitude of the big wild thing that caught his attention with a vivid thrill of startled surprise. He stared, unable to believe his eyes; for the wolf's attitude conveyed to him something familiar that at first he was unable to explain, something almost human. Then it came to him with a shock. The wolf sat beside that campfire as a man might sit.

Before he could weigh his extraordinary discovery, the animal seemed to feel his eyes fixed on it. It slowly turned and looked him in the face, and for the first time Hyde felt a superstitious fear flood through his entire being. He seemed transfixed with that nameless terror that is said to attack those who suddenly face the dead, finding themselves bereft of speech and movement. Almost at once, however, he was aware of something that ran along unaccustomed nerves and reached his feelings, even perhaps his heart, and had the effect of stilling his terror as soon as it was born. He was aware of appeal, silent, half expressed, yet vastly pathetic. He saw in the savage eyes a beseeching, even a yearning expression that changed his mood as by magic from dread to natural sympathy.

The gulf between animal and human seemed in that instant bridged. Hyde found himself nodding to the brute. Instantly the lean gray shape rose like a wraith and trotted off swiftly into the background of the night.

When Hyde woke in the morning, his first impression was that he must have dreamed the entire incident. There was a bite in the fresh autumn air; he felt brisk in mind and body. Reviewing what had happened, he saw that the fish laid out the night before had not been touched. He came to the conclusion that it was utterly vain to speculate; no possible explanation of the animal's behavior occurred to him; he was dealing with something entirely outside his experience. His fear, however, had completely left him. The odd sense of friendliness remained. The beast had a definite purpose, and he himself was included in that purpose.

It must have been a full hour after breakfast when he next saw the wolf; it was standing on the edge of the clearing, looking at him in the way now become familiar. Hyde immediately picked up his axe and advanced toward it boldly, keeping his eyes fixed straight upon its own. There was nervousness in him, but nothing betrayed it; step by step he drew nearer until some ten yards separated them. The wolf allowed him to approach without a sign of what its mood might be. Then it turned abruptly and moved slowly off, looking back first over one shoulder, exactly as a dog might do, to see if he was following.

A singular journey it was they then made together, animal and man. The trees surrounded them at once as they left the lake behind them. The beast, Hyde noticed, picked the easiest track for him to follow;

obstacles that were difficult for a man were carefully avoided with an almost uncanny skill. Deeper and deeper into the heart of the lonely forest they penetrated, cutting across the arc of the lake's crescent, it seemed to Hyde. After two miles or so, he recognized the big rocky bluff that overhung the water at its northern end. This outstanding bluff he had seen from his camp, one side of it falling sheer into the water; it was probably the spot, he imagined, where the Indians had held their medicine-making ceremonies. And it was here, close to a big spruce at the foot of the bluff, that the wolf stopped suddenly and for the first time gave audible expression to its feelings. It sat down on its haunches, lifted its muzzle with open jaws, and gave vent to a sub-dued and long-drawn howl that was more like the wail of a dog than the fierce barking cry of a wolf.

In that curious sound Hyde detected the same message that the eyes conveyed—appeal for help. While the wolf sat waiting for him, he looked about him quickly. There was young timber here; it had once been a small clearing, evidently. Axe and fire had done their work, but there was evidence to an experienced eye that it was Indians and not white men who had once been busy here. Some part of the medicine ritual, doubtless, took place in the little clearing. The end of their queer journey, Hyde felt, was close at hand.

The animal now got up and moved very slowly in the direction of a clump of low bushes. It entered these, first looking back to make sure that Hyde watched. The bushes hid it; a moment later it emerged again. Twice it performed this pantomime, each time, as it reappeared, stand-ing still and staring at the man with a distinct expression of appeal in its eyes. Hyde made up his mind quickly. Gripping his axe tightly, and ready to use it at the first hint of malice, he moved nearer to the bushes.

The wolf positively frisked about him like a happy dog, its excite-ment intense. Then, with a sudden leap, it bounded past him into the bushes and began scraping vigorously at the ground. Hyde stood and stared, amazement now banishing all his nervousness, even when the beast, in its violent scraping, touched his body with its own. No wolf, no dog certainly, used its paws in the way those paws were working. Hyde had the odd sensation that it was hands, not paws, he watched. And yet, somehow, the strange action seemed not entirely unnatural.

The wolf stopped in its task and looked up into his face. Hyde acted without hesitation then. It seemed he knew what to do, divined what was asked of him. He cut a stake and sharpened it, for the stones would blunt his axe edge. He entered the clump of bushes to complete the digging his four-legged companion had begun. The wolf sat outside the clump and watched the laborious clearing away of the hard earth with intense eagerness.

The digging continued for fully half an hour before Hyde's labor was rewarded by the discovery of a small whitish object. He picked it up and examined it—the finger bone of a man. Other discoveries then followed quickly, and soon he had collected nearly the complete skeleton. The skull he found last, and might not have found it at all but for the guidance of the wolf. It lay some few yards away from the central hole, and the wolf stood nuzzling the ground before Hyde understood that he was meant to dig in that spot. Between the beast's very paws his stake struck hard. Close beside the skull lay the rusty iron head of a toma-hawk. This confirmed him in his judgment that it was the skeleton not of a white man, but of an Indian.

During the excitement of digging, Hyde had paid little if any atten-tion to the wolf. He was aware that it sat and watched him, never moving its keen eyes from the actual operations. The further intuition that now came to him—derived, he felt positive, from his companion's dumb desire—was perhaps the cream of the entire experience to him. Gathering the bones together in his coat, he carried them, together with the tomahawk, to the foot of the big spruce where the animal had first stopped. The wolf turned its head to watch, but did not follow while he prepared the platform of boughs upon which he then laid the poor worn bones of an Indian who had been killed, doubtless, in sudden attack or ambush, and to whose remains had been denied the last grace of proper tribal burial. He wrapped the bones in bark; he laid the tomahawk beside the skull; he lit the circular fire around the pyre. The blue smoke rose upward into the clear bright sunshine of the Canadian autumn morning till it was lost among the mighty trees far overhead.

In the moment before actually lighting the little fire, he had turned to look at the wolf. It sat five yards away, gazing intently, and one of its front paws was raised a little from the ground. It made no sign of any kind. He finished the work, so absorbed that he had eyes for nothing but the ceremonial fire. It was only when the platform of boughs collapsed, laying their charred burden gently on the fragrant earth, that he turned again, to seek, perhaps, some look of satisfaction in the wolf's curiously expressive eyes. But the place he searched was empty; the wolf had gone.

He did not see it again; it gave no sign of its presence anywhere. He fished as before, sat smoking by his fire after dark, and slept peacefully in his cozy little tent. The wolf that behaved like a man had gone forever.

On the day Hyde was planning to leave, he noticed smoke rising from the shack across the lake, and paddled over to exchange a word or two with the Indian, who had evidently returned. The redskin came down to meet him as he landed. He emitted the familiar grunts at first; then bit by bit Hyde stirred his limited vocabulary into action.

"You camp there?" the man asked, pointing to the other side.

"Yes."

"Wolf come?"

"Yes."

"You see wolf?"

"Yes."

The Indian stared at him fixedly a moment. "You 'fraid wolf?" he asked after a moment's pause.

"No," replied Hyde. He knew it was useless to ask questions of his own, though he was eager for information. Then, suddenly, the Indian became comparatively voluble. There was awe in his voice and manner.

"Him no wolf. Him big medicine wolf. Him spirit wolf."

Whereupon he closed his lips tightly and said no more. His outline was still discernible on the shore an hour later, when Hyde's canoe turned the corner of the lake three miles away, and he landed to make the portages up the first rapid of his homeward stream.

IT WAS MORTON who, later, after some persuasion supplied a few details of what he called the legend. Some hundred years before, the tribe that lived in the territory beyond the lake began their annual medicine-making ceremonies on the big rocky bluff at the northern end; but no medicine could be made. The spirits, declared the chief medicine man, were offended. An investigation followed. It was discovered that a young brave had recently killed a wolf, a thing strictly forbidden, since the wolf was the totem animal of the tribe. To make matters worse, the name of the guilty man was Running Wolf. The offense being unpardonable, the man was cursed and driven from the tribe.

"Go out. Wander alone among the woods, and if we see you we slay you. Your bones shall be scattered in the forest, and your spirit shall not enter the happy hunting ground till one of another race shall find and bury them."

"Which meant," explained Morton laconically, his only comment on the story, "probably forever."

THE PEACH STONE
PAUL HORGAN

As they all knew, the drive would take them about four hours, all the way to Weed, where *she* came from. They knew the way from traveling it so often, first in the old car, and now in the new one; new to them, that is, for they'd bought it secondhand, last year, when they were down in Roswell to celebrate their tenth wedding anniversary. They still thought of themselves as a young couple, and *he* certainly did crazy things now and then, and always laughed her out of it when she was cross at the money going where it did, instead of where it ought to go. But there was so much droll orneriness in him when he did things like that that she couldn't stay mad, hadn't the heart, and the harder up they got, the more she loved him, and the little ranch he'd taken her to in the rolling plains just below the mountains.

This was a day in spring, rather hot, and the mountain was that melting blue that reminded you of something you could touch, like a china bowl. Over the sandy brown of the earth there was coming a green shadow. The air struck cool and deep in their breasts. *He* came from Texas, as a boy, and had lived here in New Mexico ever since. The word home always gave *her* a picture of unpainted, mouse-brown wooden houses in a little cluster by the rocky edge of the last mountain step—the town of Weed, where Jodey Powers met and married her ten years ago.

They were heading back that way today.

Jodey was driving, squinting at the light. It never seemed so bright as now, before noon, as they went up the valley. He had a rangy look at the wheel of the light blue Chevy—a bony man, but still fuzzed over with some look of a cub about him, perhaps the way he moved his limbs, a slight appealing clumsiness, that drew on thoughtless strength. On a rough road, he flopped and swayed at the wheel as if he were on a bony horse that galloped a little sidewise. His skin was red-brown from the sun. He had pale blue eyes, edged with dark lashes. *She* used to say he "turned them on" her, as if they were lights. He was wearing his suit, brown-striped, and a fresh blue shirt, too big at the neck. But he looked well dressed. But he would have looked that way naked, too, for he communicated his physical essence through any covering. It was what spoke out from him to anyone who encountered him. Until Cleotha married him, it had given him a time, all right, he used to reflect.

Next to him in the front seat of the sedan was Buddy, their nine-year-old boy, who turned his head to stare at them both, his father and mother.

She was in back.

On the seat beside her was a wooden box, sandpapered, but not painted. Over it lay a baby's coverlet of pale yellow flannel with cross-stitched flowers down the middle in a band of bright colors. The mother didn't touch the box except when the car lurched or the tires danced over corrugated places in the gravel highway. Then she steadied it, and kept it from creeping on the seat cushions. In the box was coffined the body of their dead child, a two-year-old girl. They were on their way to Weed to bury it there.

In the other corner of the back seat sat Miss Latcher, the teacher. They rode in silence, and Miss Latcher breathed deeply of the spring day, as they all did, and she kept summoning to her aid the fruits of her learning. She felt this was a time to be intelligent, and not to give way to feelings.

The child was burned to death yesterday, playing behind the adobe chicken house at the edge of the arroyo out back, where the fence always caught the tumbleweeds. Yesterday, in a twist of wind, a few sparks from the kitchen chimney fell in the dry tumbleweeds and set them ablaze. Jodey had always meant to clear the weeds out; never seemed to get to it; told Cleotha he'd get to it next Saturday morning, before going down to Roswell. But Saturdays went by, and the wind and the sand drove the weeds into a barrier at the fence, and they would look at it every day without noticing, so habitual had the sight become. And so for many a spring morning the little girl had played out there, behind the gray stucco house, whose adobe bricks showed through in one or two places.

The car had something loose; they believed it was the left rear fender—it chattered and wrangled over the gravel road.

Last night Cleotha stopped her weeping.

Today something happened; it came over her as they started out of the ranch lane, which curved up toward the highway. She looked as if she were trying to see something beyond the edge of Jodey's head and past the windshield.

Of course, she had sight in her eyes; she could not refuse to look at the world. As the car drove up the valley that morning, she saw in two ways—one, as she remembered the familiar sights of this region where she lived; the other, as if for the first time she were really seeing, and not simply looking. Her heart began to beat faster as they drove. It seemed to knock at her breast, as if to come forth and hurry ahead of her along the sunlighted lanes of the life after today. She remembered thinking that her head might be a little giddy, what with the sorrow in her eyes so bright and slowly shining. But it didn't matter what did it. Ready never to look at anyone or anything again, she kept still; and through the window, which had a meandering crack in it like a river on a map, all that she looked upon seemed dear to her. . . .

Jodey could only drive. He watched the road as if he expected it to rise up and smite them all over into the canyon, where the trees twinkled and flashed with bright drops of light on their new varnished leaves. Jodey watched the road and said to himself that if it thought it could turn him over or make him scrape the rocks along the near side of the hill they were going around, if it thought for one minute that he was not master of this car, this road, this journey, why, it was just crazy. The wheels spraying the gravel across the surface of the road traveled on outward from his legs; his muscles were tight and felt tired, as if he were running instead of riding. He tried to *think*, but he could not; that is, nothing came about that he would speak to her of, and he believed that she sat there, leaning forward, waiting for him to say something to her.

But this he could not do, and he speeded up a little, and his jaw made hard knots where he bit on his own rage; and he saw a lump of something coming in the road, and it aroused a positive passion in him. He aimed directly for it, and charged it fast, and hit it. The car shuddered and skidded, jolting them. Miss Latcher took a sharp breath inward, and put out her hand to touch someone, but did not reach anyone. Jodey looked for a second into the rearview mirror above him, expecting something; but his wife was looking out of the window beside her, and if he could believe his eyes, she was smiling, holding her mouth with her fingers pinched up in a little claw.

The blood came up from under his shirt, he turned dark, and a sting came across his eyes.

He couldn't explain why he had done a thing like that to her, as if it were she he was enraged with, instead of himself.

He wanted to stop the car and get out and go around to the back door on the other side, and open it, and take her hands, bring her out to stand before him in the road, and hang his arms around her until she would be locked upon him. This made a picture that he indulged like a dream, while the car ran on, and he made no change, but drove as before. . . .

The little boy, Buddy, regarded their faces, again, and again, as if to see in their eyes what had happened to them.

He felt the separateness of the three.

He was frightened by their appearance of indifference to each other. His father had a hot and drowsy look, as if he had just come out of bed. There was something in his father's face which made it impossible for Buddy to say anything. He turned around and looked at his mother, but she was gazing out the window and did not see him; and until she should see him, he had no way of speaking to her, if not with his words, then with his eyes; but if she should happen to look at him, why, he would wait to see what she looked *like*, and if she *did*, why, then he would smile at her, because he loved her; but he would have to know first if she was still his mother, and if everything was all right, and things weren't blown to smithereens—*bla-a-ash! wh-o-o-m!*—the way the dynamite did when the highway came past their ranch house, and the men worked out there for months, and whole hillsides came down at a time. All summer long, that was, always something to see. The world, the family, he, between his father and mother, had been safe.

He silently begged her to face toward him. There was no security until she should do so.

"Mumma?"

But he said it to himself, and she did not hear him this time, and it seemed intelligent to him to turn around, make a game of it (the way things often were worked out), and face the front, watch the road, delay as long as he possibly could bear to, and *then* turn around again, and *this* time, why, she would probably be looking at him all the time, and it would *be:* it would simply *be.*

So he obediently watched the road, the white gravel ribbon passing under their wheels as steadily as time.

He was a sturdy little boy, and there was a silver nap of child's dust on his face, over his plum-red cheeks. He smelled rather like a raw potato that has just been pared. The sun crowned him with a ring of light on his dark hair. . . .

What Cleotha was afraid to do was break the spell by saying anything or looking at any of them. This was *vision*, it was all she could think; never had anything looked so in all her life; everything made her heart lift, when she had believed this morning, after the night, that it would never lift again. There wasn't anything to compare her grief to. She couldn't think of anything to answer the death of her tiny child with. In her first hours of hardly believing what had happened, she had felt her own flesh and tried to imagine how it would have been if she could have borne the fire instead of the child. But all she got out of that was a longing avowal to herself of how gladly she would have borne it. Jodey had lain beside her, and she clung to his hand until she heard how he breathed off to sleep. Then she had let him go, and had wept at what seemed faithless in him. She had wanted his mind beside her then. It seemed to her that the last degree of her grief was the compassion she had had to bestow upon him while he slept.

But she had found this resource within her, and from that time on, her weeping had stopped.

It was like a wedding of pride and duty within her. There was nothing she could not find within herself, if she had to, now, she believed.

And so this morning, getting on toward noon, as they rode up the valley, climbing all the way, until they would find the road to turn off on, which would take them higher and higher before they dropped down toward Weed on the other side, she welcomed the sights of that dusty trip. Even if she had spoken her vision aloud, it would not have made sense to the others.

Look at that orchard of peach trees, she thought. I never saw such color as this year; the trees are like lamps, with the light coming from within. It must be the sunlight shining from the other side, and, of course, the petals are very thin, like the loveliest silk; so any light that shines upon them will pierce right through them and glow on this side. But they are so bright! When I was a girl at home, up to Weed, I remember we had an orchard of peach trees, but the blossoms were always a deeper pink than down here in the valley.

My! I used to catch them up by the handful, and I believed when I was a girl that if I crushed them and tied them in a handkerchief and carried the handkerchief in my bosom, I would come to smell like peach blossoms and have the same high pink in my face, and the girls I knew said that if I took a peach *stone* and held it *long enough* in my hand, it would *sprout;* and I dreamed of this one time, though, of course, I knew it was nonsense; but that was how children thought and talked in those days—we all used to pretend that *nothing* was impossible, if you simply did it hard enough and long enough.

But nobody wanted to hold a peach stone in their hand until it *sprouted*, to find out, and we used to laugh about it, but I think we believed it. I think I believed it.

It seemed to me, in between my *sensible* thoughts, a thing that any woman could probably do. It seemed to me like a parable in the Bible. I could preach you a sermon about it this day.

I believe I see a tree down there in that next orchard which is dead; it

463

has old black sprigs, and it looks twisted by rheumatism. There is one little shoot of leaves up on the top branch, and that is all. No, it is not dead, it is aged, it can no longer put forth blossoms in a swarm like pink butterflies; but there is that one little swarm of green leaves—it is just about the prettiest thing I've seen all day, and I thank God for it, for if there's anything I love, it is to see something growing. . . .

Miss Latcher had on her cloth gloves now, which she had taken from her blue cloth bag a little while back. The little winds that tracked through the moving car sought her out and chilled her nose, and the tips of her ears, and her long fingers, about which she had several times gone to visit various doctors. They had always told her not to worry, if her fingers seemed cold, and her hands moist. It was just a nervous condition, nothing to take very seriously; a good hand lotion might help the sensation, and in any case, some kind of digital exercise was a good thing—did she perhaps play the piano. It always seemed to her that doctors never *paid any attention* to her.

Her first name was Arleen, and she always considered this a very pretty name, prettier than Cleotha; and she believed that there was such a thing as an *Arleen look*, and if you wanted to know what it was, simply look at her. She had a long face, and pale hair; her skin was white, and her eyes were light blue. She was wonderfully clean, and used no cosmetics. She was a girl from "around here," but she had gone away to college, to study for her career, and what she had known as a child was displaced by what she had heard in classrooms. And she had to admit it: people *here* and *away* were not much alike. The men were different. She couldn't imagine marrying a rancher and "sacrificing" everything she had learned in college.

This poor little thing in the other corner of the car, for instance; she seemed dazed by what had happened to her—all she could do evidently was sit and stare out the window. And that man in front, simply driving, without a word. What did they have? What was their life like? They hardly had good clothes to drive to Roswell in, when they had to go to the doctor, or on some social errand.

But I must not think uncharitably, she reflected, and sat in an attitude of sustained sympathy, with her face composed in Arleenish interest and tact. The assumption of a proper aspect of grief and feeling produced the most curious effect within her, and by her attitude of concern she was suddenly reminded of the thing that always made her feel like weeping, though, of course, she never did, but when she stopped and *thought*—

Like that painting at college, in the long hallway leading from the Physical Education lecture hall to the stairway down to the girls' gym: an enormous picture depicting the Agony of the Christian Martyrs in ancient Rome. There were some days when she simply couldn't look at it; and there were others when she would pause and see those maidens with their tearful faces raised in calm prowess, and in them she would find herself—they were all Arleens; and after she would leave the picture she would proceed in her imagination to the arena, and there she would know with exquisite sorrow and pain the ordeals of two thousand years ago, instead of those of her own lifetime. She thought of the picture now, and traded its remote sorrows for those of today, until she had sincerely forgotten the mother and the father and the little brother of the dead child with whom she was riding up the spring-turning valley, where noon was warming the dust that arose from the graveled highway. It was white dust, and it settled over them in an enriching film, ever so finely. . . .

Jodey Powers had a fantastic scheme that he used to think about for taking and baling tumbleweed and make a salable fuel out of it. First, you'd compress it—probably down at the cotton compress in Roswell —where a loose bale was wheeled in under the great power drop, and when the Negro at the handle gave her a yank, down came the weight and packed the bale into a little thing, and then they let the steam exhaust go, and the press sighed once or twice and just seemed to *lie* there, while the men ran wires through the gratings of the press and tied them tight. Then up came the weight, and out came the bale.

If he did that to enough bales of tumbleweed, he believed he'd get rich. Burn? It burned like a house afire. It had oil in it, somehow, and the thing to do was to get it in shape for use as a fuel. Imagine all the tumbleweed that blew around the state of New Mexico in the fall, and sometimes all winter. In the winter, the weeds were black and brittle. They cracked when they blew against fence posts, and if one lodged there, then another one caught at its thorny lace; and next time it blew, and the sand came trailing, and the tumbleweeds rolled, they'd pile up at the same fence and build out, locked together against the wires. The wind drew through them, and the sand dropped around them. Soon there was a solid-looking but airy bank of tumbleweeds built right to the top of the fence, in a long windward slope; and the next time the wind blew, and the weeds came, they would roll up the little hill of brittle twigs and leap off the other side of the fence, for all the world like horses taking a jump, and go galloping ahead of the wind across the next pasture on the plains, a black and witchy procession.

If there was an arroyo, they gathered there. They backed up in the miniature canyons of dirt-walled watercourses, which were dry except when it rained hard up in the hills. Out behind the house, the arroyo had filled up with tumbleweeds; and in November, when it blew so hard and so cold, but without bringing any snow, some of the tumble-weeds had climbed out and scattered, and a few had tangled at the back fence, looking like rusted barbed wire. Then there came a few more; all winter the bank grew. Many times he'd planned to get out back there and clear them away, just e-e-ease them off away from the fence posts, so's not to catch the wood up, and then set a match to the whole thing, and in five minutes have it all cleared off. If he did like one thing, it was a neat place.

How Cleotha laughed at him sometimes when he said that, because she knew that as likely as not he would forget to clear the weeds away. And if he'd said it once he'd said it a thousand times, that he was going to gather up that pile of scrap iron from the front yard, and haul it to Roswell, and sell it—old car parts, and the fenders off a truck that had turned over up on the highway, which he'd salvaged with the aid of the driver.

But the rusting iron was still there, and he had actually come to have a feeling of fondness for it. If someone were to appear one night and silently make off with it, he'd be aroused the next day and demand to know who had robbed him—for it was dear junk, just through lying around and belonging to him. What was his was part of him, even that heap of fenders that rubbed off on your clothes with a rusty powder, like a caterpillar fur.

But even by thinking hard about all such matters, treading upon the fringe of what had happened yesterday, he was unable to make it all seem long ago, and a matter of custom and even of indifference. There was no getting away from it—if anybody was to blame for the terrible moments of yesterday afternoon, when the wind scattered a few sparks from the chimney of the kitchen stove, why, he was.

Jodey Powers never claimed to himself or anybody else that he was any *better* man than another. But everything he knew and hoped for, every reassurance his body had had from other people, and the children he had begotten, had made him know that he was *as good* a man as any.

And of this knowledge he was now bereft.

If he had been alone in his barrenness, he could have solaced himself with heroic stupidities. He could have produced out of himself abominations with the amplitude of Biblical despair. But he wasn't alone; there they sat, there was Buddy beside him, and Clee in back, even the teacher, Arleen—even to her he owed some return of courage.

All he could do was drive the damned car, and keep *thinking* about it.

He wished he could think of something to say, or else that Clee would.

But they continued in silence, and he believed that it was one of his making. . . .

The reverie of Arleen Latcher made her almost ill, from the sad, sweet experiences she had entered into with those people so long ago. How wonderful it was to have such a rich life, just looking up things! And the most wonderful thing of all was that even if they were beautiful, and wore semitransparent garments that fell to the ground in graceful folds, the maidens were all pure. It made her eyes swim to think how innocent they went to their death. Could anything be more beautiful, and reassuring, than this? Far, far better. Far better those hungry lions than the touch of lustful men. Her breath left her for a moment, and she closed her eyes, and what threatened her with real feeling—the presence of the Powers family in the faded blue sedan climbing through the valley sunlight toward the turnoff that led to the mountain road—was gone. Life's breath on her cheek was not so close. Oh, others had suffered. She could suffer.

All that pass by clap their hands at thee; they hiss and wag their head at the daughter of Jerusalem . . .

This image made her wince, as if she herself had been hissed and wagged at. Everything she knew made it possible for her to see herself as a proud and threatened virgin of Bible times, which were more real to her than many of the years she had lived through. Yet must not Jerusalem have sat in country like this, with its sandy hills, the frosty stars that were so bright at night, the simple Mexicans riding their burros as if to the Holy Gates? We often do not see our very selves, she would reflect, gazing ardently at the unreal creature which the name Arleen brought to life in her mind.

On her cheeks there had appeared two islands of color, as if she had a fever. What she strove to save by her anguished retreats into the memories of the last days of the Roman Empire was surely crumbling away from her. She said to herself that she must not give way to it, and that she was just wrought up; the fact that she really *didn't* feel anything—in fact, it was a pity that she *couldn't* take that little Mrs. Powers in her arms, and comfort her, just *let* her go ahead and cry, and see if it wouldn't probably help some. But Miss Latcher was aware that she felt nothing that related to the Powers family and their trouble.

Anxiously she searched her heart again, and wooed back the sacrifice of the tribe of heavenly Arleens marching so certainly toward the lions. But they did not answer her call to mind, and she folded her cloth-gloved hands and pressed them together, and begged of herself that she might think of some way to comfort Mrs. Powers; for if she could do that, it might fill her own empty heart until it became a cup that would run over. . . .

Cleotha knew Buddy wanted her to see him; but though her heart turned toward him, as it always must, no matter what he asked of her, she was this time afraid to do it, because if she ever lost the serenity of her sight now, she might never recover it this day; and the heaviest trouble was still before her.

So she contented herself with Buddy's look as it reached her from the side of her eye. She glimpsed his head and neck, like a young cat's, the wide bones behind the ears, and the smooth but visible cords of his nape, a sight of him that always made her want to laugh because it was so pathetic. When she caressed him she often fondled those strenuous hollows behind his ears. Heaven only knew, she would think, what went on within the shell of that topknot! She would pray between her words and feelings that those unseen thoughts in the boy's head were ones that would never trouble him. She was often amazed at things in him which she recognized as being like herself; and at those of Buddy's qualities which came from some alien source, she suffered pangs of doubt and fear. He was so young to be a stranger to her!

The car went around the curve that hugged the rocky fall of a hill; and on the other side of it a green quilt of alfalfa lay sparkling darkly in the light. Beyond that, to the right of the road, the land leveled out, and on a sort of platform of swept earth stood a two-room hut of adobe. It had a few stones cemented against the near corner, to give it strength. Clee had seen it a hundred times—the place where that old man Melendez lived, and where his wife had died a few years ago. He was said to be simpleminded, and claimed he was a hundred years old. In the past, riding by here, she had more or less delicately made a point of looking the other way. It often distressed her to think of such a helpless old man, too feeble to do anything but crawl out when the sun was bright and the wall was warm, and sit there, with his milky gaze resting on the hills he had known since he was born, and had never left. Somebody came to feed him once a day, and see if he was clean enough to keep his health. As long as she could remember, there'd been some kind of dog at the house. The old man had sons and grandsons and great-grandsons—you might say a whole orchard of them, sprung from this one tree that was dying, but that still held a handful of green days in its ancient veins.

Before the car had quite gone by, she had seen him. The sun was bright, and the wall must have been warm—warm enough to give his shoulders and back a reflection of the heat, which was all he could feel. He sat there on his weathered board bench, his hands on his branch of apple tree that was smooth and shiny from use as a cane. His housedoor was open, and a deep tunnel of shade lay within the sagged box of the opening. Cleotha leaned forward to see him, as if to look at him were one of her duties today. She saw his jaw moving up and down, not chewing, but just opening and closing. In the wind and flash of the car going by, she could not hear him; but from his closed eyes, and his moving mouth, and the way his head was raised, she wouldn't have been surprised if she had heard him singing. He was singing some thread of song, and it made her smile to imagine what kind of noise it made, a wisp of voice.

She was perplexed by a feeling of joyful fullness in her breast, at the sight of the very same old witless sire from whom in the past she had turned away her eyes out of delicacy and disgust.

The last thing she saw as they went by was his dog, who came around the corner of the house with a caracole. He was a mongrel puppy, partly hound—a comedian by nature. He came prancing outrageously up to the old man's knees, and invited his response, which he did not get. But as if his master were as great a wag as he, he hurled himself backward, pretending to throw himself recklessly into pieces. Everything on him flopped and was flung by his idiotic energy. It was easy to imagine, watching the puppy-fool, that the sunlight had entered him as it had entered the old man. Cleotha was reached by the hilarity of the hound, and when he tripped over himself and plowed the ground with his flapping jowls, she wanted to laugh out loud.

But they were past the place, and she winked back the merriment in her eyes, and she knew that it was something she could never have told the others about. What it stood for, in her, they would come to know in other ways, as she loved them. . . .

Jodey was glad of one thing. He had telephoned from Hondo last night, and everything was to be ready at Weed. They would drive right up the hill to the family burial ground. They wouldn't have to wait for anything. He was glad, too, that the wind wasn't blowing. It always made his heart sink when the wind rose on the plains and began to change the sky with the color of dust.

Yesterday: it was all he could see, however hard he was *thinking* about everything else.

He'd been on his horse, coming back down the pasture that rose up behind the house across the arroyo, nothing particular in mind—except to make a joke with himself about how far along the peaches would get before the frost killed them all, *snap*, in a single night, like that—when he saw the column of smoke rising from the tumbleweeds by the fence. Now who could've lighted them? he reflected, following the black smoke up on its billows into the sky. There was just enough wind idling across the long front of the hill to bend the smoke and trail it away at an angle, toward the blue.

The hillside, the fire, the wind, the column of smoke.

Oh my God! And the next minute he was tearing down the hill as fast as his horse could take him, and the fire—he could see the flames now—the fire was like a bank of yellow rags blowing violently and torn in the air, rag after rag tearing up from the ground. Cleotha was there, and in a moment, so was he, but they were too late. The baby was unconscious. They took her up and hurried to the house, the back way, where the screen door was standing open with its spring trailing on the ground. When they got inside, where it seemed so dark and cool, they held the child between them, fearing to lay her down. They called for Buddy, but he was still at school up the road, and would not be home until the orange school bus stopped by their mailbox out front at the highway after four o'clock. The fire poured in cracking tumult through the weeds. In ten minutes they were only little airy lifts of ash off the ground. Everything was black. There were three fence posts still afire; the wires were hot. The child was dead. They let her down on their large bed.

He could remember every word Clee had said to him. They were not many, and they shamed him, in his heart, because he couldn't say a thing. He comforted her, and held her while she wept. But if he had spoken then, or now, riding in the car, all he could have talked about was the image of the blowing rags of yellow fire, and blue, blue, plaster-blue sky above and beyond the mountains. But he believed that she knew why he seemed so short with her. He hoped earnestly that she knew. He might just be wrong. She might be blaming him, and keeping so still because it was more proper, now, to *be* still than full of reproaches.

But of the future he was entirely uncertain; and he drove, and came to the turnoff, and they started winding in back among the sandhills that lifted them toward the rocky slopes of the mountains. Up and up they went; the air was so clear and thin that they felt transported, and across the valleys that dropped between the grand shoulders of the pine-haired slopes, the air looked as if it were blue breath from the trees. . . .

Cleotha was blinded by a dazzling light in the distance, ahead of them, on the road.

It was a ball of diamond-brilliant light.

It danced, and shook, and quivered above the road far, far ahead. It seemed to be traveling between the pine trees on either side of the road, and somewhat above the road, and it was like nothing she had ever seen before. It was the most magic and exquisite thing she had ever seen, and wildly, even hopefully, as a child is hopeful when there is a chance and a need for something miraculous to happen, she tried to explain it to herself. It could be a star in the daytime, shaking and quivering and traveling ahead of them, as if to lead them. It was their guide. It was shaped like a small cloud, but it was made of shine, and dazzle, and quiver. She held her breath for fear it should vanish, but it did not, and she wondered if the others in the car were smitten with the glory of it as she was.

It was brighter than the sun, whiter; it challenged the daytime, and obscured everything near it by its blaze of flashing and dancing light.

It was almost as if she had approached perfect innocence through her misery, and were enabled to receive portents that might not be visible to anyone else. She closed her eyes for a moment.

But the road curved, and everything traveling on it took the curve too, and the trembling pool of diamond light ahead lost its liquid splendor, and turned into the tin signs on the back of a huge oil truck which was toiling over the mountain, trailing its links of chain behind.

When Clee looked again, the star above the road was gone. The road and the angle of the sun to the mountaintop and the two cars climbing upward had lost their harmony to produce the miracle. She saw the red oil truck, and simply saw it, and said to herself that the sun might have reflected off the big tin signs on the back of it. But she didn't believe it, for she was not thinking, but rather dreaming; fearful of awakening. . . .

The high climb up this drive always made Miss Latcher's ears pop, and she had discovered once that to swallow often prevented the disagreeable sensation. So she swallowed. Nothing happened to her ears. But she continued to swallow, and feel her ears with her cloth-covered fingers, but what really troubled her now would not be downed, and it came into her mouth as a taste; she felt giddy—that was the altitude, of course—when they got down the other side, she would be all right.

What it was was perfectly clear to her, for that was part of having an education and a trained mind—the processes of thought often went right on once you started them going.

Below the facts of this small family, in the worst trouble it had ever known, lay the fact of envy in Arleen's breast.

It made her head swim to realize this. But she envied them their entanglement with one another, and the dues they paid each other in the humility of the duty they were performing on this ride, to the family burial ground at Weed. Here she sat riding with them, to come along and be of help to them, and she was no help. She was unable to swallow the lump of desire that rose in her throat, for life's uses, even such bitter ones as that of the Powers family today. It had been filling her gradually, all the way over on the trip, this feeling of jealousy and degradation.

Now it choked her, and she knew she had tried too hard to put from her the thing that threatened her, which was the touch of life through anybody else. She said to herself that she must keep control of herself.

But Buddy turned around again, just then, slowly, as if he were a young male cat who just happened to be turning around to see what he could see, and he looked at his mother with his large eyes, so like his father's: pale petal-blue, with drops of light like the centers of cats' eyes, and dark lashes. He had a solemn look when he saw his mother's face, and he prayed her silently to acknowledge him. If she didn't, why, he was still alone. He would never again feel safe about running off to the highway to watch the scrapers work, or the huge diesel oil tankers go by, or the cars with strange license plates—of which he had already counted thirty-two different kinds, his collection, as he called it. So if she didn't see him, why, what might he find when he came back home at times like those, when he went off for a little while just to play?

They were climbing down the other side of the ridge now. In a few minutes they would be riding into Weed. The sights as they approached were like images of awakening to Cleotha. Her heart began to hurt when she saw them. She recognized the tall iron smokestack of the sawmill. It showed above the trees down on the slope ahead of them. There was a stone house which had been abandoned even when she was a girl at home here, and its windows and doors standing open always seemed to her to depict a face with an expression of dismay. The car dropped farther down—they were making that last long curve of the road to the left—and now the town stood visible, with the sunlight resting on so many of the unpainted houses and turning their weathered gray to a dark silver. Surely they must be ready for them, these houses; all had been talked over by now. They could all mention that they knew Cleotha as a little girl.

She lifted her head.

There were claims upon her.

Buddy was looking at her soberly, trying to predict to himself how she would *be*. He was ready to echo with his own small face whatever her face would show him.

Miss Latcher was watching the two of them. Her heart was racing in her breast.

The car slowed up. Now Cleotha could not look out the windows at the wandering earthen street, and the places alongside it. They would have to drive right through town, to the gently rising hill on the other side.

"Mumma?" asked the boy softly.

Cleotha winked both her eyes at him, and smiled, and leaned toward him a trifle.

And then he blushed, his eyes swam with happiness, and he smiled back at her, and his face poured forth such radiance that Miss Latcher took one look at him, and with a choke, burst into tears.

She wept into her hands, her gloves were moistened, her square shoulders rose to her ears, and she was overwhelmed by what the mother had been able to do for the boy. She shook her head and made long gasping sobs. Her sense of betrayal was not lessened by the awareness that she was weeping for herself.

Cleotha leaned across to her, and took her hand, and murmured to her. She comforted her, gently.

"Hush, honey, you'll be all right. Don't you cry, now. Don't you think about us. We're almost there, and it'll soon be over. God knows you were mighty sweet to come along and be with us. Hush, now, Arleen, you'll have Buddy crying too."

But the boy was simply watching the teacher, in whom the person he knew so well every day in school had broken up, leaving an unfamiliar likeness. It was like seeing a reflection in a pond, and then throwing a stone in. The reflection disappeared in ripples of something else.

Arleen could not stop.

The sound of her 'ooping made Jodey furious. He looked into the rearview mirror and saw his wife patting her and comforting her. Cleotha looked so white and strained that he was frightened, and he said out, without turning around, "Arleen, you cut that out, you shut up, now. I won't have you wearin' down Clee, God damn it, you quit it!"

But this rage, which arose from a sense of justice, made Arleen feel guiltier than ever; and she laid her head against the car window, and her sobs drummed her brow bitterly on the glass.

"Hush," whispered Cleotha, but she could do no more, for they were arriving at the hillside, and the car was coming to a stop. They must awaken from this journey, and come out onto the ground, and begin to toil their way up the yellow hill, where the people were waiting. Over the ground grew yellow grass that was turning to green. It was like velvet, showing dark or light, according to the breeze and the golden afternoon sunlight. It was a generous hill, curving easily and gradually as it rose. Beyond it was only the sky, for the mountains faced it from behind the road. It was called Schoolhouse Hill, and at one time the whole thing had belonged to Cleotha's father; and even before there was any schoolhouse crowning its noble swell of earth, the departed members of his family had been buried halfway up the gentle climb.

Jodey helped her out of the car, and he tried to talk to her with his holding fingers. He felt her trembling, and she shook her head at him. Then she began to walk up there, slowly. He leaned into the car, and took the covered box in his arms, and followed her. Miss Latcher was out of the car on her side, hiding from them, her back turned, while she used her handkerchief and positively clenched herself back into control of her thoughts and sobs. When she saw that they weren't waiting for her, she hurried, and in humility, reached for Buddy's hand to hold it for him as they walked. He let her have it, and he marched, watching his father, whose hair was blowing in the wind and sunshine. From behind, Jodey looked like just a kid. . . .

And now for Cleotha her visions on the journey appeared to have some value, and for a little while longer, when she needed it most, the sense of being in blind communion with life was granted her, at the little graveside where all those kind friends were gathered on the slow slope-up of the hill, on the summit of which was the schoolhouse of her girlhood.

It was afternoon, and they were all kneeling toward the upward rise, and Judge Crittenden was reading the prayer book.

Everything left them but a sense of their worship, in the present.

And a boy, a late scholar, is coming down the hill from the school, the sunlight edging him; and his wonder at what the people kneeling there are doing is, to Cleotha, the most memorable thing she is to look upon today; for she has resumed the life of her infant daughter, whom they are burying, and on whose behalf something rejoices in life anyway, as if to ask the mother whether love itself is not ever living. And she watches the boy come discreetly down the hill, trying to keep away from them, but large-eyed with a hunger *to know* which claims all acts of life, for him, and for those who will be with him later; and his respectful curiosity about those kneeling mourners, the edge of sunlight along him as he walks away from the sun and down the hill, is of all those things she saw and rejoiced in, the most beautiful; and at that, her breast is full, with the heaviness of a baby at it, and not for grief alone, but for praise.

"I believe, I believe!" her heart cries out in her, as if she were holding the peach stone of her eager girlhood in her woman's hand.

She puts her face into her hands and weeps, and they all move closer to her. Familiar as it is, the spirit has had a new discovery. . . .

Jodey then felt that she had returned to them all; and he stopped seeing, and just remembered, what happened yesterday; and his love for his wife was confirmed as something he would never be able to measure for himself or prove to her in words.

RED

W. SOMERSET MAUGHAM

THE SKIPPER THRUST his hand into one of his trouser pockets with difficulty, for he was a portly man, and pulled out a large silver watch. He looked at it and then looked again at the declining sun. The kanaka at the wheel gave him a glance, but did not speak. The skipper's eyes rested on the island they were approaching. A white line of foam marked the reef. He knew there was an opening large enough to get his ship through, and when they came a little nearer he counted on seeing it. In the lagoon the water was deep and they could anchor comfortably. The chief of the village among the coconut trees was a friend of the mate's, and it would be pleasant to go ashore for the night. The mate came forward at that minute and the skipper turned to him.

"We'll take a bottle of booze along with us and get some girls in to dance," he said.

"I don't see the opening," said the mate.

He was a kanaka, a handsome, swarthy fellow, with somewhat the look of a later Roman emperor.

"I'm dead sure there's one right here," said the captain, looking through his glasses. "Send one of the boys up the mast to have a look."

The mate called one of the crew and gave him the order, but he shouted down that he could see only the line of foam. The captain spoke Samoan like a native, and he cursed the crewman freely.

"Shall he stay up there?" asked the mate.

"What the hell good does that do?" answered the captain. "The blame fool can't see worth a cent." He looked at the slender mast with anger. "Come down," he shouted. "You're no more use than a dead dog. We'll just have to go along the reef till we find the opening."

It was a seventy-ton schooner with diesel auxiliary, and it ran, when there was no head wind, between four and five knots an hour. It had been painted white a very long time ago, but it was now dirty and dingy. It smelled strongly of oil and of the copra which was its usual cargo. They were within a hundred feet of the reef now, and the captain told the helmsman to run along it till they came to the opening. But when they had gone a couple of miles he realized that they had missed it. He came about and slowly worked back again. The white foam of the reef continued without interruption and now the sun was setting. The skipper resigned himself to waiting till next morning.

"Put her about," he said. "I can't anchor here."

They went out to sea a little and presently it was quite dark. They anchored. When the sail was furled, the ship began to roll a good deal. They said in Apia that one day she would roll right over; and the owner, a German-American who managed one of the largest stores, said that no money was big enough to induce him to go out in her.

Next morning, when the dawn crept over the tranquil sea, the opening in the reef was seen a little to the east of where they lay. The schooner entered the lagoon. There was not a ripple on the surface of the water. Down among the coral rocks you saw little colored fish swim.

When he had anchored his ship the skipper ate his breakfast and went back on deck. The sun shone from an unclouded sky, but the early morning air was cool. It was Sunday, and there was a feeling of quietness, a silence as though nature were at rest, which gave the skipper a peculiar sense of comfort. He sat, looking at the wooded coast, and felt lazy and well at ease. Presently a slow smile moved his lips and he threw the stump of his cigar into the water.

"I guess I'll go ashore," he said. "Get the boat out."

He climbed stiffly down the ladder and was rowed to a little cove. The coconut trees came down to the water's edge, not in rows, but spaced out with an ordered formality. They were like a ballet of spinsters, elderly but flippant, standing in affected attitudes with the simpering graces of a bygone age. He sauntered idly through them, along a path that led him presently to a broad creek. There was a bridge across it, but a bridge constructed of single trunks of coconut trees, a dozen of them, placed end to end and supported where they met by a forked branch driven into the bed of the creek. You walked on a smooth, round surface, narrow and slippery, and there was no support for the hand. To cross such a bridge required sure feet and a stout heart. The skipper hesitated. But he saw on the other side, nestling among the trees, a white man's house; he made up his mind and, rather gingerly, began to walk. It was with a gasp of relief that he finally set his feet on the firm ground of the other side. He had been so intent on the difficult crossing that he never noticed anyone was watching him.

"It takes a bit of nerve to cross these bridges when you're not used to them."

The captain looked up in surprise and saw a man standing in front of him. He had evidently come out of the house.

"I saw you hesitate," the man continued, with a smile on his lips, "and I was watching to see you fall in."

"Not on your life," said the captain.

"I've fallen in myself before now. I remember, one evening I came back from shooting, and I fell in, gun and all."

He was a man no longer young, with a small beard, now somewhat gray, and a thin face. He wore neither shoes nor socks. He spoke English with a slight accent.

"Are you Neilson?" asked the skipper.

"I am."

"I've heard about you. I thought you lived somewheres round here."

The skipper followed his host into the little bungalow and sat down heavily in the chair which the other motioned him to take. While Neilson went out to fetch whiskey and glasses he took a look around the room. It filled him with amazement. He had never seen so many books. The shelves reached from floor to ceiling on all four walls, and they were closely packed. There was a grand piano littered with music, and a large table on which books and magazines lay in disorder. He remembered that those who knew Neilson agreed that he was a queer fellow. He was a Swede.

"You've got one big heap of books here," he said when Neilson returned. "Have you read them all?"

"Most of them."

"I'm a bit of a reader myself. I have *The Saturday Evening Post* sent me regler."

Neilson poured his visitor a good stiff glass of whiskey and gave him a cigar. The skipper volunteered a little information.

"I never been this run before, but my people had some stuff they wanted to bring over here. Gray, d'you know him?"

"Yes, he's got a store a little way along."

"Well, there was a lot of canned stuff that he wanted over, an' he's got some copra. They thought I might just as well come over as lie idle. I run between Apia and Pago Pago mostly, but they've got smallpox there just now, and there's nothing stirring."

He took a drink of his whiskey and lit the cigar. He was a taciturn man, but there was something in Neilson that made him nervous, and his nervousness made him talk. The Swede was looking at him with an expression of faint amusement.

"This is a tidy little place you've got here."

"I've done my best with it."

"You must do pretty well with your trees. I had a bit of a plantation myself once, in Upolu it was, but I had to sell it."

He looked around the room again, where all those books gave him a feeling of something incomprehensible and hostile.

"I guess you must find it a bit lonesome here though," he said.

"I've got used to it. I've been here for twenty-five years."

The captain could think of nothing more to say, and he smoked in silence. Neilson had apparently no wish to break it. He looked at his guest with a meditative eye. The skipper was a tall man, more than six feet high, and very stout. His face was red and blotchy, with a network of little purple veins on the cheeks, and his features were sunk into its fatness. His eyes were bloodshot. But for a fringe of long curly hair, nearly white, at the back of his head, he was quite bald; and that immense, shiny surface of forehead gave him a look of peculiar imbecility. He wore a blue flannel shirt, open at the neck and showing his fat chest covered with a mat of reddish hair, and a very old pair of blue serge trousers. He sat in his chair in a heavy, ungainly attitude, his great belly thrust forward and his fat legs uncrossed. It was almost impossible to imagine that this vast creature had ever been a boy who ran about. The skipper finished his whiskey, and Neilson pushed the bottle toward him.

"Help yourself."

The skipper leaned forward and with his great hand seized it.

"And how come you in these parts anyways?" he said.

"Oh, I came out to the islands for my health. My lungs were bad and they said I hadn't a year to live. You see they were wrong."

"I meant, how come you to settle down right here?"

Neilson looked at him with an ironic twinkle in his dark eyes. Perhaps just because the skipper was so gross and dull a man the whim seized him to talk further.

"You were too busy keeping your balance to notice, when you crossed the bridge, but this spot is generally considered rather pretty."

"It's a cute little house you've got here."

"Ah, that wasn't here when I first came. There was a native hut, with its beehive roof and its pillars, overshadowed by a great tree with red flowers; and the croton bushes, their leaves yellow and red and golden, made a pied fence around it. And then all about were the coconut trees, as fanciful as women, and as vain. They stood at the water's edge and spent all day looking at their reflections. I thought it was the most beautiful spot I had ever seen. I wanted to enjoy all the loveliness of the world in the short time allotted to me before I passed into the darkness. I wasn't more than twenty-five, and though I put the best face I could on it, I didn't want to die. And somehow it seemed to me that the very beauty of this place made it easier for me to accept my fate. I felt when I came here that all my past life had fallen away, as though now at last I had achieved the reality which our doctors of philosophy—I am one myself, you know—had discussed so much. 'A year,' I cried to myself. 'I have a year. I will spend it here and then I am content to die.' We are foolish and melodramatic at twenty-five. Now drink, my friend. Don't let the nonsense I talk interfere with you."

Neilson waved his thin hand toward the bottle, and the skipper finished what remained in his glass.

"You ain't drinking nothin'," he said, reaching for the whiskey.

"I am of a sober habit." The Swede smiled. "I intoxicate myself in ways which I fancy are more subtle. But I do not see a white man often, and for once I don't think a drop of whiskey can do me any harm."

He poured himself out a little, added some soda, and took a sip.

"And presently I found out why the spot had such an unearthly loveliness. Here love had tarried for a moment like a migrant bird that happens on a ship in mid ocean and for a little while folds its tired wings. The fragrance of a beautiful passion hovered over it. It seems to me that the places where men have loved or suffered keep about them always some faint aroma of something that has not wholly died. I wish I could make myself clear." He paused. "Though I cannot imagine that if I did you would understand." He shrugged his shoulders. "But perhaps it is only that my aesthetic sense is gratified by the happy conjunction of young love and a suitable setting."

Neilson was silent for an instant and looked at the captain with eyes in which there was a sudden perplexity. "You know, I can't help thinking that I've seen you before somewhere or other," he said.

"I couldn't say as I remember you," returned the skipper. "It's thirty years since I first come to the islands. A man can't figure on remembering all the folk he meets in a while like that."

The Swede shook his head. "You know how one sometimes has the feeling that a place one has never been to before is strangely familiar. That's how I seem to see you." He gave a whimsical smile. "Thirty years you've been in the islands?"

"Every bit of thirty years."

"I wonder if you knew a man called Red?"

"Red?"

"That is the only name I've ever known him by. I never set eyes on him. And yet I seem to see him more clearly than my brothers, for instance, with whom I passed my daily life for many years. He lives in my imagination with the distinctness of a Romeo. But I daresay you have never read Shakespeare?"

"I can't say as I have," said the captain.

Neilson, smoking a cigar, leaned back in his chair and looked vacantly at the ring of smoke which floated in the still air. A smile played on his lips. The contrast between the obese man before him and the man he had in mind was pleasant.

"It appears that Red was the most comely thing you ever saw. I've talked to quite a number of people who knew him in those days, and they all agree that the first time you saw him his beauty just took your breath away. They called him Red on account of his flaming hair. It had a natural wave and he wore it long. He was tall, six feet and an inch or two—in the native house that used to stand here was the mark of his height cut with a knife on the central trunk that supported the roof— and he was made like a Greek god, broad in the shoulders and thin in the flanks. His skin was dazzling white, milky, like satin; his skin was like a woman's."

"I had kind of a white skin myself when I was a kiddie," said the skipper, with a twinkle in his bloodshot eyes.

But Neilson paid no attention to him. He was telling his story now and interruption made him impatient.

"And his face was just as beautiful as his body. He had large dark blue eyes, and unlike most red-haired people he had dark eyebrows and long dark lashes. He was twenty."

On these words the Swede stopped with a certain sense of the dramatic. He took a sip of whiskey.

"He was unique. There never was anyone more beautiful. He was a happy accident of nature.

"One day he landed at that cove into which you must have put this morning. He was an American sailor, and he had deserted from a man-of-war in Apia. He had induced some good-humored native to give him a passage on a cutter that happened to be sailing from Apia to Safoto, and he had been put ashore here in a dugout. I do not know why he deserted. Perhaps he was in trouble, or perhaps it was the South Seas and these romantic islands that got into his bones. Anyhow, he wanted to hide himself, and he thought he would be safe in this secluded nook till his ship had sailed from Samoa.

"There was a native hut at the cove and as he stood there, wondering where exactly he should turn his steps, a young girl came out and invited him to enter. He knew scarcely two words of the native tongue and she as little English. But he understood well enough what her smiles meant, and her pretty gestures, and he followed her. He sat down on a mat and she gave him slices of pineapple to eat.

"I saw the girl three years after Red first met her. You cannot imagine how exquisite she was. She was rather tall, slim, with the delicate features of her race, and large eyes like pools of still water under the palm trees; her hair, black and curling, fell down her back, and she wore a wreath of scented flowers. Her hands were lovely. They were so small, so perfectly formed, they gave your heartstrings a wrench. Her smile was so delightful that it made your knees shake. Good heavens, how can I describe her? She was too beautiful to be real.

"And these two young things, she was sixteen and he was twenty, fell in love with one another at first sight. That is the real love—the love that Adam felt for Eve when he awoke and found her in the garden gazing at him with dewy eyes, the love that draws the beasts to one another and the gods. That is the love that makes the world a miracle.

"Even now, after all these years, when I think of these two, so young, so fair, so simple, and of their love, I feel a pang. There is always pain in the contemplation of perfect beauty.

"They were children. She was good and sweet and kind. I know nothing of him, and I like to think that his soul was as comely as his body.

"Well, when Red came to the island it had recently been visited by one of those epidemics which the white man has brought to the South Seas, and one-third of the inhabitants had died. It seems that the girl had lost all her near kin and she lived now in the house of distant cousins. For a few days Red stayed there. But perhaps he felt himself too near the shore, with the possibility that white men would reveal his hiding place; perhaps the lovers could not bear that the company of others should rob them for an instant of the delight of being together.

"One morning they set out, the pair of them, and walked along a grassy path under the coconuts, till they came to the creek you see. They had to cross the bridge you crossed, and the girl laughed gleefully because he was afraid. He was obliged to take off all his clothes before he could risk it, and she carried them over for him on her head. They settled down in the empty hut that stood here. Whether the owner had died during the epidemic I do not know, but anyhow no one questioned them, and they took possession. Their furniture consisted of a couple of grass mats on which they slept, a fragment of looking glass, and a bowl or two. In this pleasant land that is enough to start house-keeping on.

"They did nothing all day long, and yet the days seemed all too short. The girl had a native name, but Red called her Sally. He picked up the language very quickly, and he used to lie on the mat for hours while she chattered gaily to him. He was a silent fellow, and smoked incessantly the cigarettes which she made him out of the pandanus leaf, and he watched her while with deft fingers she made grass mats. Sometimes he would go fishing on the reef, and bring home a basketful of colored fish. Sometimes at night he would go out with a lantern to catch lobster. There were plantains around the hut and Sally would roast them for their frugal meal. She knew how to make delicious messes from coco-nuts, and on feast days they killed a little pig and cooked it on hot stones. They bathed together in the creek, and then, cool and happy, they wandered back in the gloaming over the soft grass road, walking hand in hand. And then the night, with that great sky shining with gold, and the soft airs that blew gently through the open hut—the long night that again was all too short. The dawn crept in among the wooden pillars of the hut and looked at those lovely children sleeping in one another's arms. They opened their sleepy eyes and they smiled to welcome another day.

"The weeks lengthened into months, and a year passed. They seemed to love one another as wholeheartedly, as simply and naturally, as on that first day. If you had asked them, I have no doubt that they would have thought it impossible to suppose their love could ever cease. And yet perhaps in Red there was already a very little seed, unknown to himself and unsuspected by the girl, which would in time have grown to weariness. For one day one of the natives from the cove told them that some way down the coast, at the anchorage, was a British whal-ing ship.

"'Gee,' he said, 'I wonder if I could make a trade of some nuts and plantains for a pound or two of tobacco.'

"The pandanus cigarettes that Sally made him were strong and pleas-ant enough to smoke, but they left him unsatisfied; and he yearned on a sudden for real tobacco, hard, rank, and pungent. His mouth watered at the thought of it. One would have thought some premonition of harm would have made Sally seek to dissuade him, but it never occurred to her any power on earth could take him from her. They went up into the hills together and gathered a great basket of wild oranges; they picked plantains from around the hut, and coconuts from their trees, and breadfruit and mangoes; and they carried them down to the cove. They loaded the canoe, and Red and a native boy paddled along outside the reef.

"It was the last time she ever saw him.

"Next day the boy came back alone. He was all in tears. This is the story he told. When they reached the ship and climbed aboard, a white man took the fruit they had brought with them and one of the sailors went below and brought up tobacco. Red took some at once and lit a pipe. The boy imitated the zest with which he blew a great cloud of smoke from his mouth. Then they said something to Red and he went into the cabin. Through the open door the boy saw a bottle brought out and glasses. Red drank and smoked. The white man seemed to ask him something, for he shook his head and laughed. The man laughed too, and he filled Red's glass once more. They went on talking and drinking, and presently, growing tired of watching, the boy curled himself up on the deck and slept. He was awakened by a kick, and, jumping to his feet, he saw that the ship was slowly sailing out of the lagoon. He caught sight of Red seated at the table, with his head resting heavily on his arms, fast asleep. The boy made a movement toward him, intending to wake him, but a rough hand grabbed his arm and a man pointed to the side. The boy shouted to Red, but in a moment he was seized and flung overboard. Helpless, he swam around to his canoe, climbed in, and, sobbing all the way, paddled back to shore.

"What had happened was obvious enough. The whaler was short of hands, and the captain had asked Red to sign on; on his refusal he had made him drunk and kidnapped him.

"Sally was beside herself with grief. For three days she screamed and cried. The natives did what they could to comfort her, but she would not be comforted. And then, exhausted, she sank into a sullen apathy. She spent long days at the cove, watching the lagoon, in the vain hope that Red somehow or other would manage to escape. She sat on the white sand, hour after hour, with the tears running down her cheeks, and at night dragged herself wearily back across the creek to the little hut where she had been happy. She was convinced that Red would come back, and she wanted him to find her where he had left her. Four months later she was delivered of a stillborn child, and the old woman who had come to help her through her confinement remained with her in the hut. All joy was taken from her life, but she never lost the profound conviction that sooner or later Red would come back. Every time someone crossed this slender little bridge of coconut trees she watched. It might at last be he." Neilson stopped talking and sighed.

"And what happened to her in the end?" asked the skipper.

Neilson smiled bitterly. "Oh, three years afterward she took up with another white man."

The skipper gave a fat, cynical chuckle. "That's generally what happens to them," he said.

The Swede shot him a look of hatred. He did not know why that gross, obese man excited in him so violent a repulsion. But his thoughts wandered and he found his mind filled with memories of the past. He went back five and twenty years. It was when he first came to the island, weary of Apia, a sick man trying to resign himself to the few poor months of careful life which was all that he could count on. He was boarding with a half-caste trader who had a store a couple of miles along the coast; and one day, wandering aimlessly along the grassy paths of the coconut groves, he had come upon the hut in which Sally lived. The beauty of the spot had filled him with a rapture so great that it was almost painful, and then he saw Sally. She was the loveliest creature he had ever seen, and the sadness in those dark, magnificent eyes of hers affected him strangely. The trader told him her story and it moved him.

"Do you think he'll ever come back?" Neilson had asked.

"No fear. Why, it'll be a couple of years before the ship is paid off, and by then he'll have forgotten all about her. I bet he was pretty mad when he woke up and found he'd been shanghaied, and I shouldn't wonder but he wanted to fight somebody. But I guess in a month he was thinking it the best thing that had ever happened to him that he got away from the island."

Neilson could not get the story out of his head. Perhaps because he was sick and weakly, the radiant health of Red appealed to his imagination. He had never been passionately in love, and certainly he had never been passionately loved. The mutual attraction of those two young things gave him a singular delight. He went again to the little hut by the creek. The old crone who shared the hut with Sally invited him to come in and sit down. She gave him kava to drink and cigarettes to smoke. She was glad to have someone to chat with, and while she talked he looked at Sally.

It was not till he had seen her two or three times that he induced her to speak. Then it was only to ask him if he had seen in Apia a man called Red. Two years had passed since his disappearance, but it was plain that she still thought of him incessantly.

It did not take Neilson long to discover that he was in love with her. At first, looking upon himself as a dying man, he asked only to look at her, and occasionally hear her speak. Soon the open air, the equable temperature, the rest, the simple fare, began to have an unexpected effect on his health. He coughed less and began to put on weight; six months passed without his having a hemorrhage; and suddenly he saw the possibility that he might live. The hope dawned upon him that with great care he might arrest the course of his disease. An active life was out of the question, but he could live on the islands, and the small income he had would be ample to keep him. He could grow coconuts; that would give him an occupation; and he would send for his books and a piano; but his quick mind saw that in all this he was merely trying to conceal from himself the desire which obsessed him.

He wanted Sally. He loved not only her beauty, but that dim soul which he divined behind her suffering eyes. He would intoxicate her with his passion. In the end he would make her forget. And in an ecstasy of surrender he fancied himself giving her too the happiness which he had now so miraculously achieved.

He asked her to live with him. She refused. He had expected that and did not let it depress him. His love was irresistible. He told the old crone of his wishes, and found somewhat to his surprise that she and the neighbors, long aware of them, were strongly urging Sally to accept his offer. The trader with whom he boarded went to her and told her not to be a fool; such an opportunity would not come again, and after so long she could not still believe that Red would ever return. The girl's resistance only increased Neilson's desire, and what had been a very pure love now became an agonizing passion. He was determined that nothing should stand in his way. He gave Sally no peace. At last, worn out by his persistence, she consented. But the day after, when, exultant, he went to see her, he found that in the night she had burned down the hut in which she and Red had lived together. The old crone ran toward him, full of angry abuse of Sally, but he waved her aside; it did not matter; they would build a bungalow on the place where the hut had stood.

And so the little wooden house was built in which he had now lived for many years, and Sally became his wife. But after the first few weeks of rapture, he had known little happiness. She had yielded to him, but she had only yielded what she set no store on. He knew that she cared nothing for him. She still loved Red, and all the time she was waiting for his return. At a sign from Red, Neilson knew, she would leave him without a moment's hesitation. Anguish seized him and he battered at that impenetrable self of hers, which sullenly resisted him. He tried to melt her heart with kindness, but it remained as hard as before; he feigned indifference, but she did not notice it. Sometimes he lost his temper and abused her, and then she wept silently. His love became a prison from which he longed to escape, but he had not the strength merely to open the door and walk out into the open air. At last he became numb and hopeless. For many years now they had lived together, bound by the ties of habit and convenience, and it was with a smile that he looked back on his old passion. She was an old woman, for the women on the islands age quickly, and if he had no love for her anymore, he had tolerance. She left him alone. He was contented with his piano and his books.

His thoughts led him to a desire for words.

"When I look back now and reflect on that brief passionate love of Red and Sally, I think that perhaps they should thank the ruthless fate that separated them when their love seemed still to be at its height. They suffered, but they suffered in beauty. They were spared the real tragedy of love."

"I don't know exactly as I get you," said the skipper.

"The tragedy of love is not death or separation. How long do you think it would have been before one or other of them ceased to care? It is dreadfully bitter to look at a woman you felt you could not bear to let out of your sight, and realize that you would not mind if you never saw her again. The tragedy of love is indifference."

But while he was speaking, a very extraordinary thing happened. It was as though he saw a reflection from one of those distorting mirrors that make you extraordinarily squat or outrageously elongated, but here exactly the opposite took place, and in the obese, ugly old man he caught the shadowy glimpse of a stripling. He gave him now a quick, searching scrutiny. Why had a haphazard stroll brought the skipper just to this place? An absurd suspicion seized him. What had occurred to him was impossible, and yet it might be a fact.

"What is your name?" he asked abruptly.

The skipper gave a cunning chuckle. He looked then malicious and horribly vulgar. "It's such a damned long time since I heard my real name that I almost forget it myself. But for thirty years now in the islands they've always called me Red."

His huge form shook as he gave a low, almost silent laugh. Red was hugely amused, and from his bloodshot eyes tears ran down his cheeks.

Neilson gave a gasp, for at that moment a woman came in. She was a native, a woman of somewhat commanding presence, stout without being corpulent, dark, and with very gray hair. She wore a black Mother Hubbard, and its thinness showed her heavy breasts. The moment had come.

She made an observation to Neilson about some household matter, gave the man who was sitting in the chair by the window an indifferent glance, and went out of the room. The moment had come and gone.

Neilson for a moment could not speak. He was strangely shaken. Then he said, "I'd be very glad if you'd stay and have a bit of dinner with me. Potluck."

"I don't think I will," said Red. "I must go after this fellow Gray. I want to be back in Apia tomorrow."

"I'll send a boy along with you to show you the way."

"That'll be fine."

Red heaved himself out of his chair, while the Swede called one of the boys who worked on the plantation. He told him where the skipper wanted to go, and the boy stepped along the bridge.

"Don't fall in," said Neilson to Red.

"Not on your life."

Neilson watched him make his way across, and then sank heavily into his chair. Was that the man whom Sally had loved all these years and for whom she had waited so desperately? It was grotesque. A sudden fury seized him. He had been cheated. They had seen each other at last and had not known it. He began to laugh, mirthlessly, and his laughter grew till it became hysterical. The gods had played him a cruel trick. And he was old now.

At last Sally came in to tell him dinner was ready. He sat down in front of her and tried to eat. He wondered what she would say if he told her now that the fat old man sitting in the chair was the lover whom she remembered still with the passionate abandonment of her youth. Years ago, when he hated her because she made him so unhappy, he would have been glad to hurt her. But now he did not care.

"What did that man want?" she asked presently.

He did not answer at once. She was old too, a fat old native woman. He wondered why he had ever loved her so madly. He had laid at her feet all the treasures of his soul, and she had cared nothing for them. What waste! And now, when he looked at her, he felt only contempt. His patience was at last exhausted. He answered her question.

"He's the captain of a schooner. He's come from Apia."

"Yes."

"He brought me news from home. My eldest brother is very ill and I must go back."

"Will you be gone long?"

He shrugged his shoulders.

THE FIERY WOOING
OF MORDRED
P. G. WODEHOUSE

The Pint of Lager breathed heavily through his nose.

"Silly fathead!" he said. "Ashtrays in every nook and cranny of the room—ashtrays staring you in the eye wherever you look—and he has to go and do a fool thing like that."

He was alluding to a young gentleman with a vacant, fishlike face who, leaving the bar parlor of the Anglers' Rest a few moments before, had thrown his cigarette into the wastepaper basket, causing it to burst into a cheerful blaze. Not one of the little company of amateur fire fighters but was ruffled. A Small Bass with a high blood pressure had had to have his collar loosened, and the satin-clad bosom of Miss Postlethwaite, our emotional barmaid, was still heaving.

Only Mr. Mulliner seemed disposed to take a tolerant view of what had occurred.

"In fairness to the lad," he pointed out, sipping his hot Scotch and lemon, "we must remember that our bar parlor contains no grand piano or priceless old walnut table, which to the younger generation are the normal and natural repositories for lighted cigarette ends. Failing these, he, of course, selected the wastepaper basket. Like Mordred."

"Like who?" asked a Whisky and Splash.

"Whom," corrected Miss Postlethwaite.

The Whisky and Splash apologized.

"A nephew of mine. Mordred Mulliner, the poet."

"Mordred," murmured Miss Postlethwaite. "A sweet name."

"And one," said Mr. Mulliner, "that fitted him admirably, for he was a comely lovable sensitive youth with large, fawnlike eyes, delicately chiseled features, and excellent teeth. I mention these teeth, because it was owing to them that the train of events started which I am about to describe."

"He bit somebody?" queried Miss Postlethwaite, groping.

"No. But if he had had no teeth he would not have gone to the dentist's that day, and if he had not gone to the dentist's he would not have met Annabelle."

"Annabelle whom?"

"Who," corrected Miss Postlethwaite.

"Oh, shoot," said the Whisky and Splash.

"Annabelle Sprockett-Sprockett, the only daughter of Sir Murgatroyd and Lady Sprockett-Sprockett of Smattering Hall, Worcestershire. Impractical in many ways," said Mr. Mulliner, "Mordred never failed to visit his dentist every six months, and on the morning on which my story opens he had just seated himself in the empty waiting room and was turning the pages of a three-month-old copy of the *Tatler* when the door opened and there entered a girl at the sight of whom—or who, if our friend here prefers it—something seemed to explode on the left side of his chest like a bomb. The *Tatler* swam before his eyes, and when it solidified again he realized that love had come to him at last."

MOST OF THE Mulliners have fallen in love at first sight, but few with so good an excuse as Mordred. She was a singularly beautiful girl, and for a while it was this beauty of hers that enchained my nephew's attention to the exclusion of all else. It was only after he had sat gulping for some minutes like a dog with a chicken bone in its throat that he detected the sadness in her face. He could see now that her eyes, as she listlessly perused her four-month-old copy of *Punch*, were heavy with pain.

His heart ached for her, and as there is something about the atmosphere of a dentist's waiting room which breaks down the barriers of conventional etiquette, he was emboldened to speak.

"Courage!" he said. "It may not be so bad, after all. He may just fool about with that little mirror thing of his, and decide that there is nothing that needs to be done."

For the first time she smiled—faintly, but with sufficient breadth to give Mordred another powerful jolt.

"I'm not worrying about the dentist," she explained. "My trouble is that I live miles away in the country and only get a chance of coming to London about twice a year for about a couple of hours. I was hoping that I should be able to put in a long spell of window-shopping in Bond Street, but now I've got to wait goodness knows how long, I don't suppose I shall have time to do a thing. My train goes at one fifteen."

All the chivalry in Mordred came to the surface like a leaping trout.

"If you would care to take my place—"

"Oh, I couldn't."

"Please. I shall enjoy waiting. It will give me an opportunity of catching up with my reading."

"Well, if you really wouldn't mind—"

Considering that Mordred by this time was in the market to tackle dragons on her behalf or to climb the loftiest peak of the Alps to supply her with edelweiss, he was able to assure her that he did not mind. So in she went, flashing at him a shy glance of gratitude which nearly doubled him up, and he lit a cigarette and fell into a reverie. And presently she came out and he sprang to his feet, courteously throwing his cigarette into the wastepaper basket.

She uttered a cry. Mordred recovered the cigarette.

"Silly of me," he said, with a deprecating laugh. "I'm always doing that. Absentminded. I've burned two flats already this year."

She caught her breath.

"Burned them to the ground?"

"Well, not to the ground. They were on the top floor."

"But you burned them?"

"Oh, yes. I burned them."

"Well, well!" She seemed to muse. "Well, good-by, Mr.—"

"Mulliner. Mordred Mulliner."

"Good-by, Mr. Mulliner, and thank you so much."

"Not at all, Miss—"

"Sprockett-Sprockett."

"Not at all, Miss Sprockett-Sprockett. A pleasure."

She passed from the room, and a few minutes later he was lying back in the dentist's chair, filled with an infinite sadness. This was not due to any activity on the part of the dentist—who had just said with a rueful sigh that there didn't seem to be anything to do this time—but to the fact that his life was now a blank. He loved this beautiful girl, and he would never see her more. It was just another case of ships that pass in the waiting room.

Conceive his astonishment, therefore, when by the afternoon post next day he received a letter which ran as follows:

> Smattering Hall
> Lower Smattering-on-the-Wissel
> Worcestershire

Dear Mr. Mulliner,

My little girl has told me how very kind you were to her at the dentist's today. I cannot tell you how grateful she was. She does so love to walk down Bond Street and breathe on the jewelers' windows, and but for you she would have had to go another six months without her little treat.

I suppose you are a very busy man, like everybody in London, but if you can spare the time it would give my husband and myself so much pleasure if you could run down and stay with us for a few days—a long weekend, or even longer if you can manage it.

> With best wishes,
> Yours sincerely,
> Aurelia Sprockett-Sprockett

Mordred read this communication six times in a minute and a quarter and then seventeen times rather more slowly in order to savor any nuance of it that he might have overlooked. He took it that the girl must have got his address from the dentist's secretary on her way out, and he was doubly thrilled—first, by this evidence that one so lovely was as intelligent as she was beautiful, and secondly because the whole thing seemed to him so frightfully significant. A girl, he meant to say, does not get her mother to invite fellows for long weekends (or even longer if they can manage it) unless such fellows have made a pretty substantial hit with her. This, he contended, stood to reason.

He hastened to the nearest post office, dispatched a telegram to Lady Sprockett-Sprockett assuring her that he would be with her on the morrow, and returned to his flat to pack his effects. His heart was singing within him. Apart from anything else, the invitation could not have come at a more fortunate moment, for what with musing on his great love while smoking cigarettes he had practically gutted his little nest on the previous evening, and while it was still habitable in a sense, there was no gainsaying the fact that all those charred sofas and things struck a rather melancholy note and he would be glad to be away from it all for a few days.

It seemed to Mordred, as he traveled down on the following afternoon, that the wheels of the train, clattering over the metal, were singing "Sprockett-Sprockett"—not "Annabelle," of course, for he did not yet know her name—and it was with a whispered "Sprockett-Sprockett" on his lips that he alighted at the little station of Smattering-cum-Blimpstead-in-the-Vale, which, as his hostess' notepaper had informed him, was where you got off for the Hall. And when he perceived that the girl herself had come to meet him in a two-seater car, the whisper nearly became a shout.

For perhaps three minutes, as he sat beside her, Mordred remained in this condition of ecstatic bliss. Here he was, he reflected, and here she was—here, in fact, they both were—together, and he was just about to point out how jolly this was and—if he could work it without seeming to rush things too much—to drop a hint to the effect that he could wish this state of affairs to continue through all eternity, when the girl drew up outside a tobacconist's.

"I won't be a minute," she said. "I promised Biffy I would bring him back some cigarettes."

A cold hand seemed to lay itself on Mordred's heart.

"Biffy?"

"Captain Biffing, one of the men at the Hall. And Guffy wants some pipe cleaners."

"Guffy?"

"Jack Guffington. I expect you know his name, if you are interested in racing. He was third in last year's Grand National."

"Is he staying at the Hall, too?"

"Yes."

"You have a large house party?"

"Oh, not so very. Let me see. There's Billy Biffing, Jack Guffington, Ted Prosser, Freddie Boot—he's the tennis champion of the county— Tommy Mainprice, and—oh, yes, Algy Fripp, the big-game hunter, you know."

The hand on Mordred's heart, now definitely iced, tightened its grip. With a lover's sanguine optimism, he had supposed that this visit of his was going to be just three days of jolly sylvan solitude with Anna-belle Sprockett-Sprockett. And now it appeared that the place was un-wholesomely crowded with his fellowmen. And what fellowmen! Big-game hunters . . . tennis champions . . . chaps who rode in Grand Nationals . . . He could see them in his mind's eye—lean, wiry, riding-breeched and flannel-trousered young Apollos, any one of them cap-able of cutting out his weight in Clark Gables.

A faint hope stirred within him.

"You have also, of course, with you Mrs. Biffing, Mrs. Guffington, Mrs. Prosser, Mrs. Boot, Mrs. Mainprice and Mrs. Algernon Fripp?"

"Oh, no, they aren't married."

"None of them?"

"No."

The faint hope coughed quietly and died.

"Ah," said Mordred.

While the girl was in the shop, he remained brooding. The fact that not one of these blisters should be married filled him with an austere disapproval. If they had had the least spark of civic sense, he felt, they would have taken on the duties and responsibilities of matrimony years ago. But no. Intent upon their selfish pleasures, they had callously re-mained bachelors. It was this spirit of laissez-faire, Mordred consid-ered, that was eating like a canker into the soul of England.

He was aware of Annabelle standing beside him.

"Eh?" he said, starting.

"I was saying, have you plenty of cigarettes?"

"Plenty, thank you."

"Good. And of course there will be a box in your room. Men always like to smoke in their bedrooms, don't they? As a matter of fact, two boxes—Turkish and Virginian. Father put them there specially."

"Very kind of him," said Mordred mechanically.

He relapsed into a moody silence, and they drove off.

IT WOULD BE agreeable (said Mr. Mulliner) if, having shown you my nephew so gloomy, so apprehensive, so tortured with dark forebodings at this juncture, I were able now to state that the hearty English welcome of Sir Murgatroyd and Lady Sprockett-Sprockett on his arrival at the Hall cheered him up and put new life into him. Nothing, too, would give me greater pleasure than to say that he found, on encountering the dreaded Biffies and Guffies, that they were negligible little runts with faces incapable of inspiring affection in any good woman.

But I must adhere rigidly to the facts. Genial, even effusive, though his host and hostess showed themselves, their cordiality left him cold. And, so far from his rivals being weeds, they were one and all models of manly beauty, and the spectacle of their obvious worship of Annabelle cut my nephew like a knife.

And on top of all this there was Smattering Hall itself.

Smattering Hall destroyed Mordred's last hope. It was one of those vast edifices, so common throughout the countryside of England, whose original founders seem to have budgeted for families of twenty-five or so and a domestic staff of not less than a hundred. "Home isn't home," one can picture them saying to themselves, "unless you have plenty of elbowroom." And so this huge, majestic pile had come into being. Romantic persons, confronted with it, thought of knights in armor riding forth to the Crusades. More earthy individuals felt that it must cost a packet to keep up. Mordred's reaction on passing through the front door was a sort of sick sensation, a kind of settled despair.

How, he asked himself, even assuming that by some miracle he succeeded in fighting his way to her heart through all these Biffies and Guffies, could he ever dare to take Annabelle from a home like this? He had quite satisfactory private means, of course, and would be able, when married, to give up the bachelor flat and spread himself to something on a bigger scale—possibly, if sufficiently bijou, even a desirable residence in the Mayfair district. But after Smattering Hall, would not Annabelle feel like a sardine in the largest of London houses?

Such were the dark thoughts that raced through Mordred's brain before, during, and after dinner. At eleven o'clock he pleaded fatigue after his journey, and Sir Murgatroyd accompanied him to his room, anxious, like a good host, to see that everything was comfortable.

"Very sensible of you to turn in early," he said, in his bluff, genial way. "So many young men ruin their health with late hours. Now you, I imagine, will just get into a dressing gown and smoke a cigarette or two and have the light out by twelve. You have plenty of cigarettes? I told them to see that you were well supplied. I always think the bedroom smoke is the best one of the day. Nobody to disturb you, and all that. If you want to write letters or anything, there is lots of paper, and here is the wastepaper basket, which is always so necessary. Well, good night, my boy, good night."

The door closed, and Mordred, as foreshadowed, got into a dressing gown and lit a cigarette. But though, having done this, he made his way to the writing table, it was not with any idea of getting abreast of his correspondence. It was his purpose to compose a poem to Annabelle Sprockett-Sprockett. He had felt it seething within him all the evening, and sleep would be impossible until it was out of his system.

Hitherto, I should mention, my nephew's poetry—for he belonged to the modern fearless school—had always been stark and rhymeless and had dealt principally with corpses and the smell of cooking cabbage. But now, with the moonlight silvering the balcony outside, he found that his mind had become full of words like "love" and "dove" and "eyes" and "summer skies."

> *Blue eyes,* wrote Mordred . . .
> *Sweet lips,* wrote Mordred . . .
> *Oh, eyes like skies of summer blue . . .*
> *Oh, love . . .*
> *Oh, dove . . .*
> *Oh, lips . . .*

With a muttered ejaculation of chagrin he tore the sheet across and threw it into the wastepaper basket.

Blue eyes that burn into my soul,
Sweet lips that smile my heart away,
Pom-pom, pom-pom, pom something whole (Goal?)
And tiddly-iddly-umpty-ay (Gay? Say? Happy day?)

Blue eyes into my soul that burn,
Sweet lips that smile away my heart,
Oh, something something turn or yearn
And something something something part.

You burn into my soul, blue eyes,
You smile my heart away, sweet lips,
Short long short long of summer skies
And something something something trips. (Hips?
Ships? Pips?)

He threw the sheet into the wastepaper basket and rose with a stifled oath. The wastepaper basket was nearly full now, and still his poet's sense told him that he had not achieved perfection. He thought he saw the reason for this. You can't just sit in a chair and expect inspiration to flow—you want to walk about and clutch your hair and snap your fingers. It had been his intention to pace the room, but the moonlight pouring in through the open window called to him. He went out onto the balcony. It was but a short distance to the dim, mysterious lawn. Impulsively he dropped from the stone balustrade.

The effect was magical. Stimulated by the improved conditions, his muse gave quick service, and this time he saw at once that she had rung the bell and delivered the goods. One turn up and down the lawn, and he was reciting as follows:

"TO ANNABELLE
"Oh, lips that smile! Oh, eyes that shine
Like summer skies, or stars above!
Your beauty maddens me like wine,
Oh, umpty-pumpty-tumty love!"

And he was just wondering, for he was a severe critic of his own work, whether that last line couldn't be polished up a bit, when his eye was attracted by something that shone like summer skies or stars above, and looking more closely, he perceived that his bedroom curtains were on fire.

Now, I will not pretend that my nephew Mordred was in every respect the coolheaded man of action, but this happened to be a situation with which use had familiarized him. He knew the procedure.

"Fire!" he shouted.

A head appeared in an upstairs window. He recognized it as that of Captain Biffing.

"Eh?" said Captain Biffing.

"Fire!"

"What?"

"Fire!" vociferated Mordred. "F for Francis, I for Isabel . . ."

"Oh, fire?" said Captain Biffing. "Right ho."

And presently the house began to discharge its occupants.

In the proceedings which followed, Mordred, I fear, did not appear to the greatest advantage. This is an age of specialization, and if you take the specialist off his own particular ground he is at a loss. Mordred's genius, as we have seen, lay in the direction of starting fires. Putting them out called for quite different qualities, and these he did not possess. On the various occasions of holocausts at his series of flats, he had never attempted to play an active part, contenting himself with going downstairs and asking the janitor to step up and see what he could do about it. So now, though under the bright eyes of Annabelle Sprockett-Sprockett he would have given much to be able to dominate the scene, the truth is that the Biffies and Guffies simply played him off the stage.

His heart sank as he noted the hideous efficiency of these young men. They called for buckets. They formed a line. Freddie Boot leaped lissomely onto the balcony, and Algy Fripp, mounted on a wheelbarrow, handed up to him the necessary supplies. And after Mordred, trying to do his bit, had tripped up Jack Guffington and upset two buckets over Ted Prosser, he was advised in set terms to withdraw into the background and stay there.

It was a black ten minutes for the unfortunate young man. One glance at Sir Murgatroyd's twisted face as he watched the operations was enough to tell him how desperately anxious the fine old man was for the safety of his ancestral home and how bitter would be his resentment against the person who had endangered it. And the same applied to Lady Sprockett-Sprockett and Annabelle. Mordred could see the anxiety in their eyes, and the thought that erelong those eyes must be turned accusingly on him chilled him to the marrow.

Presently Freddie Boot emerged from the bedroom to announce that all was well.

"It's out," he said, jumping lightly down. "Anybody know whose room it was?"

Mordred felt a sickening qualm, but the splendid Mulliner courage sustained him. He stepped forward, white and tense.

"Mine," he said.

He became the instant center of attention. The six young men looked at him.

"Yours?"

"Oh, yours, was it?"

"What happened?"

"How did it start?"

"Yes, how did it start?"

"Must have started somehow, I mean," said Captain Biffing, who was a clear thinker. "I mean to say, must have, don't you know, what?"

Mordred mastered his voice.

"I was smoking, and I suppose I threw my cigarette into the waste-paper basket, and as it was full of paper—"

"Full of paper? Why was it full of paper?"

"I had been writing a poem."

There was a stir of bewilderment.

"A what?" said Ted Prosser.

"Writing a what?" said Jack Guffington.

"Writing a *poem?*" asked Captain Biffing of Tommy Mainprice.

"That's how I got the story," said Tommy Mainprice, plainly shaken.

"Chap was writing a poem," Freddie Boot informed Algy Fripp.

"You mean the chap writes poems?"

"That's right. Poems."

"Well, I'm dashed!"

"Well, I'm blowed!"

Their now unconcealed scorn was hard to bear. Mordred chafed beneath it. The word "poem" was flitting from lip to lip, and it was only too evident that, had there been an *s* in the word, those present would have hissed it. Reason told him that these men were mere clods, philistines, fatheads who would not recognize the rare and the beautiful if you handed it to them on a skewer, but that did not seem to make it any better.

He knew that he should be scorning them, but it is not easy to go about scorning people in a dressing gown, especially if you have no socks on and the night breeze is cool around the ankles. So, as I say, he chafed. And finally, when he saw the butler bend down with pursed lips to the ear of the cook, who was a little hard of hearing, and after a contemptuous glance in his direction speak into it, spacing his syllables carefully, something within him seemed to snap.

"I regret, Sir Murgatroyd," he said, "that urgent family business compels me to return to London immediately. I shall be obliged to take the first train in the morning."

Without another word he went into the house.

IN THE MATTER of camping out in devastated areas my nephew had, of course, become by this time an old hand. It was rarely nowadays that a few ashes and cinders about the place disturbed him. But when he had returned to his bedroom one look was enough to assure him that nothing practical in the way of sleep was to be achieved here. Apart from the unpleasant, acrid smell of burned poetry, the apartment, thanks to the efforts of Freddie Boot, had been converted into a kind of inland sea. The carpet was awash, and on the bed only a duck could have made itself at home.

And so it came about that some ten minutes later Mordred Mulliner lay stretched upon a high-backed couch in the library, endeavoring by means of counting sheep jumping through a gap in a hedge to lull himself into unconsciousness.

But sleep refused to come. Nor in his heart had he really thought that it would. When the human soul is on the rack, it cannot just curl up and close its eyes and expect to get its eight hours as if nothing had happened. It was all very well for Mordred to count sheep, but what did this profit him when each sheep in turn assumed the features and lineaments of Annabelle Sprockett-Sprockett and, what was more, gave him a reproachful glance as it drew itself together for the spring?

Remorse gnawed him. He was tortured by a wild regret for what might have been. He was not saying that with all these Biffies and Guffies in the field he had ever had more than a hundred-to-eight chance of winning that lovely girl, but at least his hat had been in the ring. Now it was definitely out. Dreamy Mordred may have been— romantic—impractical—but he had enough sense to see that the very worst thing you can do when you are trying to make a favorable impression on the adored object is to set fire to her childhood home, every stick and stone of which she has no doubt worshipped since they put her into rompers.

He had reached this point in his meditations, and was about to send his two hundred and thirty-second sheep at the gap, when with a suddenness which affected him much as an explosion of gelignite would have done, the lights flashed on. For an instant he lay quivering; then, cautiously poking his head around the corner of the couch, he looked to see who his visitors were.

It was a little party of three that had entered the room. First came Sir Murgatroyd, carrying a tray of sandwiches. He was followed by Lady Sprockett-Sprockett with a siphon and glasses. The rear was brought up by Annabelle, who was bearing a bottle of whisky and two dry ginger ales.

So evident was it that they were assembling here for purposes of a family council that, but for one circumstance, Mordred, to whom anything in the nature of eavesdropping was as repugnant as it has always been to all the Mulliners, would have sprung up with a polite excuse me and taken his blanket elsewhere. This circumstance was the fact that on lying down he had kicked his slippers under the couch, well out of reach. The soul of modesty, he could not affront Annabelle with the spectacle of his bare toes.

So he lay there in silence, and silence, broken only by the swishing of soda water and the *whoosh* of opened ginger ale bottles, reigned in the room beyond the couch.

Then Sir Murgatroyd spoke.

"Well, that's that," he said bleakly.

There was a gurgle as Lady Sprockett-Sprockett drank ginger ale. Then her quiet, well-bred voice broke the pause.

"Yes," she said, "it is the end."

"The end," agreed Sir Murgatroyd heavily. "No good trying to struggle on against luck like ours. Here we are and here we have got to stay, moldering on in this blasted barrack of a place which eats up every penny of my income when, but for the fussy interference of that gang of officious, ugly nitwits, there would have been nothing left of it but a pile of ashes, with a man from the insurance company standing on it with his fountain pen, writing checks. Curse those imbeciles! Did you see that young Fripp with those buckets?"

"I did, indeed," sighed Lady Sprockett-Sprockett.

"Annabelle," said Sir Murgatroyd sharply.

"Yes, Father?"

"It has seemed to me lately, watching you with a father's eye, that you have shown signs of being attracted by young Algernon Fripp. Let me tell you that if ever you allow yourself to be ensnared by his insidious wiles, or by those of William Biffing, John Guffington, Edward Prosser, Thomas Mainprice or Frederick Boot, you will do so over my dead body. After what occurred tonight, those young men shall never darken my door again. They and their buckets! To think that we could have gone and lived in London . . ."

"In a nice little flat . . ." said Lady Sprockett-Sprockett.

"Handy for my club . . ."

"Convenient for the shops . . ."

"Within a stone's throw of the theaters . . ."

"Seeing all our friends . . ."

"Had it not been," said Sir Murgatroyd, summing up, "for the pestilential activities of these Guffingtons, these Biffings, these insufferable Fripps, men who ought never to be trusted near a bucket of water when a mortgaged country house has got nicely alight. I did think," proceeded the stricken old man, helping himself to a sandwich, "that when Annabelle, with a ready intelligence which I cannot overpraise, realized this young Mulliner's splendid gifts and made us ask him down here, the happy ending was in sight. What Smattering Hall has needed for generations has been a man who throws his cigarette ends into wastepaper baskets. I was convinced that here at last was the angel of mercy we required."

"He did his best, Father."

"No man could have done more," agreed Sir Murgatroyd cordially. "The way he upset those buckets and kept getting entangled in people's legs. Very shrewd. It thrilled me to see him. I don't know when I've met a young fellow I liked and respected more. And what if he is a poet? Poets are all right. Why, dash it, I'm a poet myself. At the last dinner of the Loyal Sons of Worcestershire I composed a poem which, let me tell you, was pretty generally admired. I read it out to the boys over the port, and they cheered me to the echo. It was about a young lady of Bewdley, who sometimes behaved rather rudely—"

"Not before Mother, Father."

"Perhaps you're right. Well, I'm off to bed. Come along, Aurelia. You coming, Annabelle?"

"Not yet, Father. I want to stay and think."

"Do what?"

"Think."

"Oh, think? Well, all right."

"But, Murgatroyd," said Lady Sprockett-Sprockett, "is there no hope? After all, there are plenty of cigarettes in the house, and we could always give Mr. Mulliner another wastepaper basket. . . ."

"No good. You heard him say he was leaving by the first train tomorrow. When I think that we shall never see that splendid young man again . . . Why, hullo, hullo, hullo, what's this? Crying, Annabelle?"

"Oh, Mother!"

"My darling, what is it?"

A choking sob escaped the girl.

"Mother, I love him! Directly I saw him in the dentist's waiting room, something seemed to go all over me, and I knew that there could be no other man for me. And now—"

"Hi!" cried Mordred, popping up over the side of the couch like a jack-in-the-box.

He had listened with growing understanding to the conversation which I have related, but had shrunk from revealing his presence because, as I say, his toes were bare. But this was too much. Toes or no toes, he felt that he must be in this.

"You love me, Annabelle?" he cried.

His sudden advent had occasioned, I need scarcely say, a certain reaction in those present. Sir Murgatroyd had leaped like a jumping bean. Lady Sprockett-Sprockett had quivered like a jelly. As for Annabelle, her lovely mouth was open to the extent of perhaps three inches, and she was staring like one who sees a vision.

"You really love me, Annabelle?"

"Yes, Mordred."

"Sir Murgatroyd," said Mordred formally, "I have the honor to ask you for your daughter's hand. I am only a poor poet—"

"How poor?" asked the other keenly.

"I was referring to my art," explained Mordred. "Financially, I am nicely fixed. I could support Annabelle in modest comfort."

"Then take her, my boy, take her. You will live, of course"—the old man winced—"in London?"

"Yes. And so shall you."

Sir Murgatroyd shook his head.

"No, no, that dream is ended. It is true that in certain circumstances I had hoped to do so—for the insurance, I may mention, amounts to as much as a hundred thousand pounds—but I am resigned now to spending the rest of my life in this infernal family vault. I see no reprieve."

"I understand," said Mordred, nodding. "You mean you have no kerosene in the house?"

Sir Murgatroyd started.

"Kerosene?"

"If," said Mordred, and his voice was very gentle and winning, "there had been kerosene on the premises, I think it possible that tonight's conflagration, doubtless imperfectly quenched, might have broken out again, this time with more serious results. It is often this way with fires. You pour buckets of water on them and think they are extinguished, but all the time they have been smoldering unnoticed, to break out once more in—well, in here, for example."

"Or the billiard room," said Lady Sprockett-Sprockett.

"*And* the billiard room," corrected Sir Murgatroyd.

"And the billiard room," said Mordred. "And possibly—who knows?—in the drawing room, dining room, kitchen, servants' hall, butler's pantry, and the usual domestic offices, as well. Still, as you say you have no kerosene. . . ."

"My boy," said Sir Murgatroyd in a shaking voice, "what gave you the idea that we have no kerosene? How did you fall into this odd error? We have gallons of kerosene. The cellar is full of it."

"And Annabelle will show you the way to the cellar—in case you thought of going there," said Lady Sprockett-Sprockett. "Won't you, dear?"

"Of course, Mother. You will like the cellar, Mordred, darling. Most picturesque. Possibly, if you are interested in kerosene, you might also care to take a look at our little store of paper and shavings, too."

"My angel," said Mordred tenderly, "you think of everything."

He found his slippers, and hand in hand they passed down the stairs. Above them, they could see the head of Sir Murgatroyd as he leaned over the banisters. A box of matches fell at their feet like a father's benediction.

A SUNRISE
ON THE VELD
DORIS LESSING

Every night that winter he said aloud into the dark of the pillow: Half past four! Half past four! till he felt his brain had gripped the words and held them fast. Then he fell asleep at once, as if a shutter had fallen, and lay with his face turned to the clock so that he could see it first thing when he woke.

It was half past four to the minute, every morning. Triumphantly pressing down the alarm knob of the clock, which the dark half of his mind had outwitted, remaining vigilant all night and counting the hours as he lay relaxed in sleep, he huddled down for a last warm moment under the clothes, playing with the idea of lying abed for this once only. But he played with it for the fun of knowing that it was a weakness he could defeat without effort, just as he set the alarm each night for the delight of the moment when he woke and stretched his limbs, feeling the muscles tighten, and thought: Even my brain—even that! I can control every part of myself.

Luxury of warm rested body, with the arms and legs and fingers waiting like soldiers for a word of command! Joy of knowing that the precious hours were given to sleep voluntarily!—for he had once stayed awake three nights running, to prove that he could, and then worked all day, refusing even to admit that he was tired; and now sleep seemed to him a servant to be commanded and refused.

The boy stretched his frame full length, touching the wall at his head with his hands, and the bedfoot with his toes; then he sprang out, like a fish leaping from water. And it was cold, cold.

He always dressed rapidly, so as to try and conserve his night warmth till the sun rose two hours later; but by the time he had on his clothes his hands were numbed and he could scarcely hold his shoes. These he could not put on for fear of waking his parents, who never came to know how early he rose.

As soon as he stepped over the lintel, the flesh of his soles contracted on the chilled earth, and his legs began to ache with cold. It was night; the stars were glittering, the trees standing black and still. He looked for signs of day, for the graying of the edge of a stone, or a lightening in the sky where the sun would rise, but there was nothing yet. Alert as an animal he crept past the dangerous window, standing poised with his hand on the sill for one proudly fastidious moment, looking in at the stuffy blackness of the room where his parents lay.

Feeling for the grass edge of the path with his toes, he reached inside another window farther along the wall, where his gun had been set in readiness the night before. The steel was icy, and numbed fingers slipped along it, so that he had to hold it in the crook of his arm for safety. Then he tiptoed to the room where the dogs slept, and was fearful that they might have been tempted to go before him; but they were waiting, their haunches crouched in reluctance at the cold, but ears and swinging tails greeting the gun ecstatically. His warning undertone kept them secret and silent till the house was a hundred yards back; then they bolted off into the bush, yelping excitedly. The boy imagined his parents turning in their beds and muttering: Those dogs again! before they were dragged back in sleep; and he smiled scornfully. He always looked back over his shoulder at the house before he passed a wall of trees that shut it from sight. It looked so low and small, crouching there under a tall and brilliant sky. Then he turned his back on it, and on the frowsting sleepers, and forgot them.

He would have to hurry. Before the light grew strong he must be four miles away; and already a tint of green stood in the hollow of a leaf, and the air smelled of morning and the stars were dimming.

He slung the shoes over his shoulder—veld *skoene*, that were crinkled and hard with the dews of a hundred mornings. They would be necessary when the ground became too hot to bear. Now he felt the chilled dust push up between his toes, and he let the muscles of his feet spread and settle into the shapes of the earth; and he thought: I could walk a hundred miles on feet like these! I could walk all day, and never tire!

He was walking swiftly through the dark tunnel of foliage that in daytime was a road. The dogs were invisibly ranging the lower travel-ways of the bush, and he heard them panting. Sometimes he felt a cold muzzle on his leg before they were off again, scouting for a trail to follow. They were not trained, but free-running companions of the hunt, who often tired of the long stalk before the final shots, and went off on their own pleasure. Soon he could see them, small and wild-looking in a wild strange light, now that the bush stood trembling on the verge of color, waiting for the sun to paint earth and grass afresh.

The grass stood to his shoulders, and the trees were showering a faint silvery rain. He was soaked; his whole body was clenched in a steady shiver.

Once he bent to the road that was newly scored with animal trails, and regretfully straightened, reminding himself that the pleasure of tracking must wait till another day.

He began to run along the edge of a field, noting jerkily how it was filmed over with fresh spiderweb, so that the long reaches of great black clods seemed netted in glistening gray. He was using the steady lope he had learned by watching the natives, the run that is a dropping of the weight of the body from one foot to the next in a slow balancing movement that never tires, nor shortens the breath; and he felt the blood pulsing down his legs and along his arms, and the exultation and pride of body mounted in him till he was shutting his teeth hard against a violent desire to shout his triumph.

Soon he had left the cultivated part of the farm. Behind him the bush was low and black. In front was a long *vlei*—acres of long pale grass that sent back a hollowing gleam of light to a satiny sky. Near him thick swaths of grass were bent with the weight of water, and diamond drops sparkled on each frond.

The first bird woke at his feet and at once a flock of them sprang into the air, calling shrilly that day had come; and suddenly, behind him, the bush woke into song, and he could hear the guinea fowl calling far ahead of him. That meant they would now be sailing down from their trees into thick grass, and it was for them he had come; he was too late. But he did not mind. He forgot he had come to shoot. He set his legs wide, and balanced from foot to foot, and swung his gun up and down in both hands horizontally, in a kind of improvised exercise, and let his head sink back till it was pillowed in his neck muscles, and watched how above him small rosy clouds floated in a lake of gold.

Suddenly it all rose in him: it was unbearable. He leaped up into the air, shouting and yelling wild unrecognizable noises. Then he began to run, not carefully, as he had before, but madly, like a wild thing. He was clean crazy, yelling mad with the joy of living and a superfluity of youth. He rushed down that *vlei* under a tumult of crimson and gold, while all the birds of the world sang about him. He ran in great leaping strides, and shouted as he ran, feeling his body rise into the crisp rushing air and fall back surely onto sure feet; and thought briefly, not believing that such a thing could happen to him, that he could break his ankle any moment, in this thick tangled grass. He cleared bushes like a duiker, leaped over rocks, and finally came to a dead stop at a place where the ground fell abruptly away below him to the river. It had been a two-mile-long dash through waist-high growth, and he was breathing hoarsely and could no longer sing. But he poised on a rock and looked down at stretches of water that gleamed through stooping trees, and thought suddenly: I am fifteen! Fifteen! The words came new to him, so that he kept repeating them wonderingly, with swelling excitement; and he felt the years of his life with his hands, as it were, as if he were counting marbles, each one hard and separate and compact, each one a wonderful shining thing. That was what he was: fifteen years of this rich soil, and this slow-moving water, and air that smelled like a challenge whether it was warm and sultry at noon, or as brisk as cold water, like it was now.

There was nothing he couldn't do, nothing! A vision came to him, as he stood there, like when a child hears the word eternity and tries to understand it, and time takes possession of the mind. He felt his life ahead of him as a great and wonderful thing, something that was his; and he said aloud, with the blood rising to his head: All the great men of the world have been as I am now, and there is nothing I can't become, nothing I can't do; there is no country in the world I cannot make part of myself, if I choose. I contain the world. I can make of it what I want. If I choose, I can change everything that is going to happen; it depends on me, and what I decide now.

The urgency, and the truth and the courage of what his voice was saying exulted him so that he began to sing again, at the top of his voice, and the sound went echoing down the river gorge. He stopped for the echo, and sang again; stopped and shouted. That was what he was! He sang, if he chose; and the world had to answer him.

And for minutes he stood there, shouting and singing and waiting for the lovely eddying sound of the echo; so that his own new strong thoughts came back and washed around his head, as if someone were answering him and encouraging him; till the gorge was full of soft voices clashing back and forth from rock to rock over the river. And then it seemed as if there was a new voice. He listened, puzzled, for it was not his own. Soon he was leaning forward, all his nerves alert, quite still; somewhere close to him there was a noise that was no joyful bird, nor tinkle of falling water, nor ponderous movement of cattle.

There it was again. In the deep morning hush that held his future and his past was a sound of pain, and repeated over and over; it was a kind of shortened scream, as if someone, something, had no breath to scream. He came to himself, looked about him, and called for the dogs. They did not appear; they had gone off on their own business, and he was alone. Now he was clean sober, all the madness gone. His heart beating fast because of that frightened screaming, he stepped carefully off the rock and went toward a belt of trees. He was moving cautiously, for not so long ago he had seen a leopard in just this spot.

At the edge of the trees he stopped and peered, holding his gun ready; he advanced, looking steadily about him, his eyes narrowed. Then, all at once, in the middle of a step, he faltered, and his face was puzzled. He shook his head impatiently, as if he doubted his own sight.

There, between two trees, against a background of gaunt black rocks, was a figure from a dream, a strange beast that was horned and drunken-legged, but like something he had never even imagined. It seemed to be ragged. It looked like a small buck that had black ragged tufts of fur standing up irregularly all over it, with patches of raw flesh beneath . . . but the patches of rawness were disappearing under moving black and came again elsewhere; and all the time the creature screamed, in small gasping screams, and leaped drunkenly from side to side, as if it were blind.

Then the boy understood: it *was* a buck. He ran closer, and again stood still, stopped by a new fear. Around him the grass was whispering and alive. He looked wildly about, and then down. The ground was black with ants, great energetic ants that took no notice of him, but hurried and scurried toward that fighting shape, like glistening black water flowing through the grass.

And as he drew in his breath and pity and terror seized him, the beast fell and the screaming stopped. Now he could hear nothing but one bird singing, and the sound of the rustling, whispering ants.

He peered over at the writhing blackness that jerked convulsively with the jerking nerves. It grew quieter. There were small twitches from the mass that still looked vaguely like the shape of a small animal.

It came into his mind that he should shoot it and end its pain, and he raised the gun. Then he lowered it again. The buck could no longer feel; its fighting was a mechanical protest of the nerves. But it was not that that made him put down the gun. It was a swelling feeling of rage and misery and protest that expressed itself in the thought: If I had not come it would have died like this, so why should I interfere? All over the bush things like this happen; they happen all the time; this is how life goes on, by living things dying in anguish. He gripped the gun between his knees and felt in his own limbs the myriad swarming pain of the twitching animal that could no longer feel, and set his teeth, and said over and over again under his breath: I can't stop it. I can't stop it. There is nothing I can do.

He was glad that the buck was unconscious and had gone past suffering, so that he did not have to make a decision to kill it even when he was feeling with his whole body: This is what happens, this is how things work.

It was right—that was what he was feeling. *It was right and nothing could alter it.*

The knowledge of fatality, of what has to be, had gripped him and for the first time in his life; and he was left unable to make any movement of brain or body, except to say: Yes, yes. That is what living is. It had entered his flesh and his bones and grown into the farthest corners of his brain and would never leave him. And at that moment he could not have performed the smallest action of mercy, knowing as he did, having lived on it all his life, the vast, unalterable, cruel veld, where at any moment one might stumble over a skull or crush the skeleton of some small creature.

Suffering, sick, and angry, but also grimly satisfied with his new stoicism, he stood there leaning on his rifle, and watched the seething black mound grow smaller. At his feet, now, were ants trickling back with pink fragments in their mouths, and there was a fresh acid smell in his nostrils. He sternly controlled the uselessly convulsing muscles of his empty stomach, and reminded himself: The ants must eat too! At the same time he found that the tears were streaming down his face, and his clothes were soaked with the sweat of that other creature's pain.

The shape had grown small. Now it looked like nothing recognizable. He did not know how long it was before he saw the blackness thin, and bits of white showed through, shining in the sun—yes, there was the sun, just up, glowing over the rocks. Why, the whole thing could not have taken longer than a few minutes.

He began to swear, as if the shortness of the time was in itself unbearable, using the words he had heard his father say. He strode forward, crushing ants with each step, and brushing them off his clothes, till he stood above the skeleton, which lay sprawled under a small bush. It was clean-picked. It might have been lying there years, save that on the white bone were pink fragments of gristle. About the bones ants were ebbing away, their pincers full of meat.

The boy looked at them—big black ugly insects. A few were standing and gazing up at him with small glittering eyes.

"Go away!" he said to the ants, very coldly. "I am not for you—not just yet, at any rate. Go away." And he fancied that the ants turned and went away.

He bent over the bones and touched the sockets in the skull. That was where the eyes were, he thought incredulously, remembering the liquid dark eyes of a buck. And then he bent the slim foreleg bone, swinging it horizontally in his palm.

That morning, perhaps an hour ago, this small creature had been stepping proud and free through the bush, feeling the chill on its hide even as he himself had done, exhilarated by it. Proudly stepping the earth, tossing its horns, frisking a pretty white tail, it had sniffed the cold morning air. Walking like kings and conquerors it had moved through this free-held bush, where each blade of grass grew for it alone, and where the river ran pure sparkling water for its slaking.

And then—what had happened? Such a swift surefooted thing could surely not be trapped by a swarm of ants?

The boy bent curiously to the skeleton. Then he saw that the back leg that lay uppermost and strained out in the tension of death was snapped midway in the thigh, so that broken bones jutted over each other uselessly. So that was it! Limping into the ant masses it could not escape, once it had sensed the danger. Yes, but how had the leg been broken? Had it fallen, perhaps? Impossible; a buck was too light and graceful. Had some jealous rival horned it?

What could possibly have happened? Perhaps some natives had thrown stones at it, as they do, trying to kill it for meat, and had broken its leg. Yes, that must be it.

Even as he imagined the crowd of running, shouting natives, and the flying stones, and the leaping buck, another picture came into his mind. He saw himself, on any one of these bright ringing mornings, drunk with excitement, snapping a shot at some half-seen buck. He saw himself, with the sun lowered, wondering whether he had missed or not; and thinking at last that it was late, and he wanted his breakfast, and it was not worthwhile to track miles after an animal that would very likely get away from him in any case.

For a moment he would not face it. He was a small boy again, kicking sulkily at the skeleton, hanging his head, refusing to accept the responsibility.

Then he straightened up, and looked down at the bones with an odd expression of dismay, all the anger gone out of him. His mind went quite empty; all around him he could see trickles of ants disappearing into the grass. The whispering noise was faint and dry, like the rustling of a cast snakeskin.

At last he picked up his gun and walked homeward. He was telling himself half defiantly that he wanted his breakfast. He was telling himself that it was getting very hot, much too hot to be out roaming the bush.

Really, he was tired. He walked heavily, not looking where he put his feet. When he came within sight of his home he stopped, knitting his brows. There was something he had to think out. The death of that small animal was a thing that concerned him, and he was by no means finished with it. It lay at the back of his mind uncomfortably.

Soon, the very next morning, he would get clear of everybody and go to the bush and think about it.

THE GHOST
RICHARD HUGHES

H E KILLED ME quite easily by bumping my head on the cobbles. *Bang!*
Lord, what a fool I was! All my hate went out with that first bang; a fool
to have kicked up that fuss just because I had found him with another
woman. And now he was doing this to me—*bang!* That was the second
one, and with it *everything* went out.

My sleek young soul must have glistened somewhat in the moonlight, for I saw him look up from the body in a fixed sort of way. That
gave me an idea: I would haunt him. All my life I had been scared of
ghosts; now I was one myself, I would get a bit of my own back. *He*
never was; he said there weren't such things as ghosts. Oh, weren't
there! I'd soon teach him. John stood up, still staring in front of him; I
could see him plainly. Gradually all my hate came back. I thrust my face
close up against his, but he didn't seem to see it; he just stared. Then he
began to walk forward, as if to walk through me, and I was afeared.
Silly, for me—a spirit—to be afeared of his solid flesh; but there you
are, fear doesn't act as you would expect, ever, and I gave back before
him, then slipped aside to let him pass. Almost he was lost in the
street shadows before I recovered myself and followed him.

And yet I don't think he could have given me the slip; there was still
something between us that drew me to him—willy-nilly, you might say,
I followed him up High Street, and down Lily Lane.

Lily Lane was all shadows; but yet I could still see him as clear as if it was daylight. Then my courage came back to me; I quickened my pace till I was ahead of him—turned around, flapping my hands and making a moaning sort of noise like the ghosts did I'd read of. He began to smile a little, in a sort of satisfied way, but yet he didn't seem properly to see me. Could it be that his hard disbelief in ghosts made him so that he *couldn't see me.* *"Hoo!"* I whistled through my small teeth. *"Hoo! Murderer! Murderer!"* Someone flung up a top window. "Who's that?" she called. "What's the matter?" So other people could hear, at any rate. But I kept silent; I wouldn't give him away—not yet. And all the time he walked straight forward, smiling to himself. He never had any conscience, I said to myself. There he is with new murder on his mind, smiling as easy as if it was nothing. But there was a sort of hard look about him, *all* the same.

It was odd, my being a ghost so suddenly, when ten minutes ago I was a living woman, and now, walking on air, with the wind clear and wet between my shoulder blades. Ha-ha! I gave a regular shriek and a screech of laughter, it all felt so funny . . . surely John must have heard *that;* but no, he just turned the corner into Pole Street.

All along Pole Street the plane trees were shedding their leaves, and then I knew what I would do. I made those dead leaves rise up on their thin edges, as if the wind was doing it. All along Pole Street they followed him, pattering on the roadway with their five dry fingers. But John just stirred among them with his feet, and went on, and I followed him; for, as I said, there was still some tie between us that drew me.

Once only he turned and seemed to see me; there was a sort of recognition in his face, but no fear, only triumph. You're glad you've killed me, thought I, but I'll make you sorry!

And then all at once the fit left me. A nice sort of Christian, I, scarcely fifteen minutes dead and still thinking of revenge, instead of preparing to meet my Lord! Some sort of voice in me seemed to say, "Leave him, Millie, leave him alone *before it is too late!"* Too late? Surely I could leave him when I wanted to? Ghosts haunt as they like, don't they? I'd make just one more attempt at terrifying him, then I'd give it up and think about going to heaven.

He stopped and turned, and faced me full.

I pointed at him with both my hands.

"John!" I cried. "John! It's all very well for you to stand there and smile, and stare with your great fish eyes and think you've won, but you haven't! I'll do you, I'll finish you! I'll—"

I stopped and laughed a little. Windows shot up. "Who's that? What's the row?" and so on. They had all heard, but he only turned and walked on.

"Leave him, Millie, before it is too late," the voice said.

So that's what the voice meant: leave him before I betrayed his secret and had the crime of revenge on my soul. Very well, I would; I'd leave him. I'd go straight to heaven before any accident happened. So I stretched up my two arms, and tried to float into the air, but at once some force seized me like a great gust, and I was swept away after him down the street. There was something stirring in me that still bound me to him.

Strange that I should be so real to all those people that they thought me still a living woman, but he—who had most reason to fear me— why, it seemed doubtful whether he even saw me. And where was he going to, right up the desolate long length of Pole Street? He turned into Rope Street. I saw a blue lamp; that was the police station.

Oh, Lord, I thought, I've done it! Oh, Lord, he's going to give himself up.

"You drove him to it," the voice said. "You fool, did you think he didn't see you? What did you expect? Did you think he'd shriek, and gibber with fear at you? Did you think your John was a coward? Now his death is on your head!"

"I didn't do it, I didn't!" I cried. "I never wished him any harm, never, not *really!* I wouldn't hurt him, not for anything, I wouldn't. Oh, John, don't stare like that! There's still time . . . time!"

And all this while he stood in the door, looking at me, while the policemen came out and stood around in a ring. He couldn't escape now.

"Oh, John," I sobbed, "forgive me! I didn't mean to do it! It was jealousy, John, that did it . . . because I loved you."

Still the police took no notice of him.

"That's her," said one of them in a husky voice. "Done it with a hammer, she done it . . . brained him. But, Lord, isn't her face ghastly? Haunted, like."

"Look at her 'ead, poor girl. Looks as if she tried to do herself in with the 'ammer after."

Then the sergeant stepped forward.

"Anything you say will be taken down as evidence against you."

"John!" I cried softly, and held out my arms—for at last his face had softened.

"Holy Mary!" said one policeman, crossing himself. "She's seeing him!"

"They'll not hang her," another whispered. "Did you notice her condition, poor girl?"

THE BIRDS
DAPHNE DU MAURIER

On December the third the wind changed overnight and it was winter. Until then the autumn had been mellow, soft. The leaves had lingered on the trees, golden red, and the hedgerows were still green. The earth was rich where the plow had turned it.

Nat Hocken, because of a wartime disability, had a pension, and he also worked three days a week at the farm. They gave him the lighter jobs: hedging, thatching, repairs to the farm buildings. His was a solitary disposition; he liked best to work alone. It pleased him when he was given a bank to build up, or a gate to mend at the far end of the peninsula, where the sea surrounded the farmland on either side. At midday he would pause and eat his lunch and, sitting on the cliff's edge, would watch the birds. Autumn was best for this. In spring the birds flew inland; they knew where they were bound, the rhythm and ritual of their life brooked no delay. In autumn those that had not migrated followed a pattern of their own. Great flocks of them came to the peninsula, restless, uneasy, spending themselves in motion; now wheeling in the sky, now settling to feed on the rich new-turned soil, without hunger, without desire. Restlessness drove them to the skies again.

Black and white, jackdaw and gull, mingled in strange partnership, never satisfied, never still. Flocks of starlings, rustling like silk, flew to fresh pasture, and the smaller birds, the finches and the larks, scattered from tree to hedge as if compelled.

Nat watched them, and he watched the seabirds too. Down in the bay they waited for the tide. They had more patience. Oyster catchers, redshank, sanderling, and curlew watched by the water's edge; as the sea withdrew, leaving the strip of seaweed bare, the seabirds raced upon the beaches. Then that same impulse to flight seized upon them too. Crying, whistling, calling, they skimmed the placid sea and left the shore.

The birds had been more restless than ever this fall. Nat remarked upon it to the farmer when hedging was finished for the day. "Yes," said the farmer, "I've noticed it too. And daring, some of them. One or two gulls came so close to my head this afternoon I thought they'd knock my cap off! I have a notion the weather will change. It will be a hard winter. That's why the birds are restless."

Nat, tramping home across the fields and down the lane to his cottage, saw the birds still flocking over the western hills. No wind, and the gray sea calm and full. The farmer was right, though, and it was that night the weather turned. Nat's bedroom faced east. He woke just after two and heard the wind in the chimney, an east wind, cold and dry. A loose slate rattled on the roof, and Nat could hear the sea roaring in the bay. Even the air in the small bedroom had turned chill. Nat drew the blanket around him and leaned closer to his sleeping wife.

Then he heard the tapping on the window. He listened, and the tapping continued until, irritated by the sound, Nat got out of bed. He opened the window, and as he did so something brushed his hand, jabbing at his knuckles, grazing the skin. Then he saw the flutter of the wings and it was gone, over the roof.

It was a bird; what kind of bird he could not tell. The wind must have driven it to shelter on the sill. He shut the window and went back to bed, but, feeling his knuckles wet, put his mouth to the scratch. The bird had drawn blood. Bewildered, seeking shelter, it had stabbed at him in the darkness. Once more he settled himself to sleep.

Presently the tapping came again, this time more forceful, more insistent, and now his wife woke at the sound and, turning in the bed, said to him, "See to the window, Nat, it's rattling."

"There's some bird there trying to get in," he told her. "The wind is blowing from the east, driving the birds to shelter." He went to the window again, and when he opened it there was not one bird upon the sill but half a dozen; they flew straight into his face, attacking him. He shouted, striking out at them with his arms, scattering them; they flew over the roof and disappeared. Quickly he let the window fall and latched it.

"Did you hear that?" he said. "They went for me. Tried to peck my eyes." His wife, heavy with sleep, murmured from the bed.

"I'm not making it up," he said angrily. "I tell you the birds were on the sill, trying to get into the room." Suddenly a frightened cry came from the room across the passage, where the children slept.

"It's Jill," said his wife, sitting up. "Go and see what's the matter."

Nat lit the candle, but when he opened the bedroom door to cross the passage, the draft blew out the flame. There came a second cry of terror, this time from both children, and stumbling into their room, he felt the beating of wings about him in the darkness. The window was wide open. Through it came the birds, hitting the ceiling and the walls, swerving in mid-flight, turning on the children in their beds.

"It's all right, I'm here," shouted Nat, and the children flung themselves, screaming, upon him, while in the darkness the birds rose and dived. Swiftly he pushed the children through the door to the passage and shut it, so that he was alone in their bedroom with the birds.

Using a blanket as a weapon, he flung it to right and left about him in the air. He felt the thud of bodies, heard the fluttering of wings, but again and again they jabbed at his hands, his head, the little stabbing beaks sharp as pointed forks. He wound the blanket about his head, and beat at the birds with his bare hands. He dared not stumble to the door and open it, lest the birds should follow him. At last the fluttering and beating of the wings lessened and then ceased.

He took the blanket from his head and stared about him. The cold gray dawn and the open window had called the living birds; the dead lay on the floor. Nat gazed at the little corpses, all small birds, shocked and horrified. There must have been fifty of them. There were robins, finches, sparrows, blue tits, and larks, birds that by nature's law kept to their own flock and their own territory, and now, joining one with another, had destroyed themselves against the bedroom walls, or had been destroyed by him. Some had blood, his blood, upon their beaks.

Nat shut the window and the door of the small bedroom and went back across the passage to his own. His wife sat up in bed, one child asleep beside her, the smaller in her arms, his face bandaged. The curtains were tightly drawn across the window, the candles lit. Her face looked garish in the yellow light. She shook her head for silence.

"He's sleeping now," she whispered, looking terrified. "Something must have cut him; there was blood at the corner of his eyes. Jill said it was the birds. She said she woke up, and the birds were in the room."

"There are birds in there," he said, almost in a daze, "dead birds, nearly fifty of them. Robins, wrens, all the little birds from hereabouts. It's as though a madness seized them, with the east wind." He sat down on the bed beside his wife and held her hand. "It must be the hard weather," he said. "They aren't the birds, maybe, from here around. They've been driven down from up-country."

"But, Nat," whispered his wife, "it's only this night that the weather turned. And they can't be hungry yet. There's food for them out there in the fields."

"It's the weather," repeated Nat, his face drawn. "I tell you, it's the weather. . . . I'll go downstairs and make a cup of tea."

The sight of the kitchen reassured him. The cups and saucers, neatly stacked upon the sideboard, the table and chairs, his wife's roll of knitting on her basket chair, the children's toys in a corner cupboard. He relit the fire. The steaming kettle and the brown teapot brought comfort and security. He drank his tea, carried a cup to his wife. Then, putting on his boots, he opened the back door.

The sky was hard and leaden, and the brown hills that had gleamed in the sun the day before looked dark and bare. The east wind, like a razor, stripped the trees; and the leaves, crackling and dry, scattered in the blast. Nat stubbed the earth with his boot. It was frozen hard. He had never known a change so swift and sudden. Winter had descended in a single night.

The children were awake now. Jill was chattering upstairs, and young Johnny was crying again. Nat heard his wife's voice, soothing, comforting. When they came down, he had breakfast ready for them.

"Did you drive away the birds?" asked Jill.

"Yes, they've all gone now," said Nat. "It was the east wind brought them in. They wanted shelter."

"They tried to peck us," said Jill.

"Fright made them do that," said Nat. "They didn't know where they were in the dark bedroom."

Jill finished her breakfast and went for her coat and hood, her schoolbooks, and her satchel. "I'll walk with her to the bus," Nat said. "I don't work at the farm today." While the child was washing in the scullery he said to his wife, "Keep all the windows closed, and the doors too. Just to be on the safe side. I'll go to the farm. Find out if they heard anything in the night." Then he walked with his small daughter up the lane. She danced ahead, chasing the leaves, her face rosy under the pixie hood. All the while he searched the hedgerows for the birds, glanced to the fields beyond, looked to the small wood above the farm where the rooks and jackdaws gathered. He saw none.

At the bus stop, Jill ran to the other children, waving. She said nothing of the birds. She began to push and struggle with another little girl. The bus came ambling up the hill. Nat saw her onto it, then turned and walked back toward the farm. Jim, the cowman, was clattering in the yard.

"Boss around?" asked Nat.

"Gone to market," said Jim. "It's Tuesday, isn't it?"

Nat had forgotten it was Tuesday. He went to the back door of the farmhouse and heard Mrs. Trigg singing in the kitchen. "Are you there, missus?" he called out.

She came to the door, beaming, broad, a good-tempered woman. "Hullo, Mr. Hocken," she said. "Can you tell me where this cold is coming from? Is it Russia? I've never seen such a change. And it's going on, the radio says. Something to do with the Arctic Circle."

"We didn't turn on the radio this morning," said Nat. "Fact is, we had trouble in the night."

"Kiddies poorly?"

He tried to tell Mrs. Trigg what had happened, but he could see from her eyes that she thought his story was the result of a nightmare. "Sure they were real birds," she said, smiling, "with proper feathers and all? Not the funny-shaped kind that the men see after closing hours on a Saturday night?"

"Mrs. Trigg," he said, "there are fifty dead birds—robins, wrens, and such—lying on the floor of the children's bedroom. They went for me; they tried to go for young Johnny's eyes."

"Well there, now," she answered doubtfully. "I suppose the weather brought them. Once in the bedroom, they wouldn't know where they were. Foreign birds maybe, from that Arctic Circle. You ought to write up and ask the *Guardian*. They'd have some answer for it. Well, I must be getting on." She nodded, smiled, and went back into the kitchen.

Nat turned to the farm gate. Jim was standing there.

"Had any trouble with the birds?" asked Nat.

"Birds? What birds?"

"We got them up our place last night. Scores of them, came in the children's bedroom. Quite savage they were."

"Oh?" It took time for anything to penetrate Jim's head. "Never heard of birds acting savage," he said at length. "They get tame, like, sometimes. Come to the windows for crumbs."

Jim was no more interested than Mrs. Trigg had been. It was, Nat thought, like air raids in the war. No one down this end of the country knew what the Plymouth folk had seen and suffered. You had to endure something yourself before it touched you. He walked back along the lane and crossed the stile to his cottage. He found his wife in the kitchen with young Johnny.

"See anyone?" she asked.

"Mrs. Trigg and Jim," he answered. "I don't think they believed me. Anyway, nothing wrong up there."

"You might take the birds away," she said. "I daren't go into the room to make the beds until you do. I'm scared."

Nat went up with a sack and dropped the stiff bodies into it, one by one. Yes, there were fifty of them, all told. Just ordinary birds, nothing as large even as a thrush. Blue tits, wrens—it was incredible to think of the power of their small beaks jabbing at his face and hands the night before. He took the sack out into the garden and was faced now with a fresh problem. The ground was too hard to dig, frozen solid. It was unnatural, queer. The weather prophets must be right. The change was something connected with the Arctic Circle. He decided to take the birds to the shore and bury them.

When he reached the beach below the headland he could scarcely stand, the force of the east wind was so strong. It hurt to draw breath, and his bare hands were blue. It was low tide. He crunched his way to the softer sand and then dug a pit with his heel. He meant to drop the birds into it, but as he emptied the sack the force of the wind carried them, lifted them as though in flight again, and they were spread and scattered along the beach. There was something ugly in the sight. The tide will take them when it turns, he said to himself.

Then he saw them. The gulls. Out there, riding the seas.

What he had thought at first to be the whitecaps of the waves were gulls. Hundreds, thousands, tens of thousands . . . They rose and fell in the trough of the seas, heads to the wind, like a mighty fleet at anchor, waiting on the tide. They stretched as far as his eye could reach. Only the east wind, whipping the sea to breakers, hid them from the shore.

Nat turned and climbed the steep path home. Someone should be told of this. Something was happening, because of the east wind and the weather, that he did not understand. He wondered if he should go to the telephone box by the bus stop and ring up the police. Yet what could they do? Tens of thousands of gulls riding the sea there in the bay because of storm, because of hunger. The police would think him mad, or drunk, or take the statement from him with great calm. "Thank you. Yes, the matter has already been reported. The hard weather is driving the birds inland in great numbers."

As he drew near to the cottage, his wife came to meet him at the door. "Nat," she said excitedly, "it's on the radio. They've just read a special news bulletin about the birds. I've written it down. It's not only here, it's everywhere. In London, all over the country." Together they went into the kitchen. He read the piece of paper lying on the table.

"Statement from the Home Office at eleven a.m. today. Reports are coming in hourly about the vast quantity of birds flocking above towns, villages, and outlying districts, causing obstruction and damage and even attacking individuals. It is thought that the Arctic airstream, at present covering the British Isles, is causing birds to migrate south in immense numbers, and that intense hunger may drive these birds to attack human beings. Householders are warned to see to their windows, doors, and chimneys, and to take reasonable precautions for the safety of their children. A further statement will be issued later."

A kind of excitement seized Nat; he looked at his wife in triumph. "There you are," he said. "Let's hope they'll hear that at the farm. I've been telling myself all morning there's something wrong. And just now, down on the beach, I looked out to sea and there are gulls, thousands of them. All out there, riding on the sea, waiting."

"What are they waiting for, Nat?" she asked.

"I don't know," he said slowly. "It says here the birds are hungry." He went over to the drawer where he kept his tools.

"What are you going to do, Nat?"

"See to the windows and the chimneys, like they tell you."

"You think they would break in, with the windows shut? Those sparrows and robins and such? Why, how could they?"

He did not answer. He was not thinking of the robins and the sparrows. He was thinking of the gulls. . . . He worked upstairs the rest of the morning, boarding the windows of the bedrooms, filling up chimney bases.

When dinner was over and his wife was washing up, Nat switched on the one-o'clock news. The same announcement was repeated, but the news bulletin enlarged upon it. "The flocks of birds have caused dislocation in all areas," said the announcer, "and in London the sky was so dense at ten o'clock this morning that it seemed as if the city was covered by a vast black cloud. The birds settled on rooftops, window ledges, and chimneys. The species included blackbird, thrush, the common house sparrow, a vast quantity of pigeons and starlings, and the black-headed gull. The sight has been so unusual that traffic came to a standstill in many thoroughfares, work was abandoned in shops and offices, and the streets crowded with people standing about to watch the birds."

Various incidents were recounted, the suspected reason of cold and hunger stated again, and warnings to householders repeated. The announcer's voice was smooth. Nat had the impression that this man, in particular, treated the whole business as he would an elaborate joke. There would be others like him, hundreds of them, who did not know what it was to struggle in darkness with a flock of birds. There would be parties tonight in London, people shouting and laughing, getting drunk. "Come and watch the birds!"

Nat switched off the radio. He got up and started work on the kitchen windows.

"What, boards for down here too?" his wife said. "Why, I'll have to light up before three o'clock. I see no call for boards down here. What they ought to do is to call the army out and shoot the birds. That would soon scare them off."

"The population of London is eight million or more," said Nat. "Think of all the buildings. Do you think they've enough soldiers to go round shooting birds from every roof?"

"I don't know. But they ought to do something."

Nat thought to himself that whatever "they" decided to do in London and the big cities, it would not help the people here. Each householder must look after his own.

"How are we off for food?" he said.

"It's shopping day tomorrow, you know that. I don't keep uncooked food hanging about; it goes off. Butcher doesn't call till the day after. But I can bring back something when I go in tomorrow."

Nat did not want to scare her. He thought it possible that she might not go to town tomorrow. He looked in the larder and in the cupboard where she kept her canned goods. They would do for a couple of days. Bread was low.

"What about the baker?"

"He comes tomorrow too."

He saw she had flour. If the baker did not call, she had enough to bake one loaf.

"We'd be better off in the old days," he said, "when the women baked twice a week, and had pilchards salted, and there was food for a family to last a siege, if need be."

"I've tried the children with canned fish; they don't like it," she said.

Nat went on hammering the boards across the kitchen windows. Candles. They were low in candles too. Well, it could not be helped. They must go early to bed tonight. That was, if . . .

He got up and went out the back door and stood in the garden, looking down toward the sea. There had been no sun all day, and now, at barely three o'clock, a kind of darkness had already come. He could hear the vicious sea drumming on the rocks. He walked down the path, halfway to the beach. And then he stopped. He could see the tide had turned. The rock that had shown in midmorning was now covered, but it was not the sea that held his eyes. The gulls had risen. They were circling, thousands of them, lifting their wings against the wind. It was the gulls that made the darkening of the sky. And they were silent. They just went on soaring and circling, rising, falling, trying their strength against the wind.

Nat turned. He ran up the path, back to the cottage.

"I'm going for Jill," he said. "I'll wait for her at the bus stop."

"What's the matter?" asked his wife. "You've gone quite white."

"Keep Johnny inside," he said. "Keep the door shut. Light up now, and draw the curtains."

He looked in the toolshed outside the back door. Nothing there of much use. A spade was too heavy, and a fork no good. He took the hoe. It was the only possible tool, and light enough to carry. He started walking up the lane to the bus stop, and now and again glanced back over his shoulder.

The gulls had risen higher now, their circles were broader, wider, they were spreading out in huge formation across the sky.

At the top of the hill he waited. The east wind came whipping across the fields from the higher ground. He stamped his feet and blew upon his hands. In the distance he could see the clay hills, white and clean, against the heavy pallor of the sky. Something black rose from behind them, like a smudge at first, then widening, becoming deeper, and the smudge became a cloud, and the cloud divided again into other clouds, spreading north, east, south, and west, and they were not clouds at all; they were birds. He watched them travel across the sky, and as one section passed overhead, within two or three hundred feet of him, he knew, from their speed, they were bound inland, up-country. They were rooks, crows, jackdaws, magpies, jays, all birds that usually preyed upon the smaller species; but this afternoon they were bound on some other mission.

He went to the telephone box and lifted the receiver. The exchange would do. They would pass the message on. "I'm speaking from Highway," he said, "by the bus stop. I want to report large formations of birds traveling up-country. The gulls are also forming in the bay."

"All right," answered the voice, laconic, weary.

"You'll be sure and pass this message on to the proper quarter?"

"Yes . . . yes. . . ." Impatient now, fed up. The buzzing note resumed.

She's another, thought Nat, she doesn't care. Maybe she's had to answer calls all day. She hopes to go to the pictures tonight. She'll squeeze some fellow's hand, and point up at the sky, and say, "Look at all them birds!" She doesn't care.

The bus came lumbering up the hill. Jill climbed out, and three or four other children. The bus went on toward the town.

"Come on, now," he said to Jill's companions, "let's get home. It's cold, no hanging about. Here, you. I'll watch you across the fields. See how fast you can run." A shortcut would take them to their cottages.

"We want to play a bit in the lane," said one of them.

"No, you don't. You go off home or I'll tell your mother."

They whispered to one another, round-eyed, then scuttled off across the fields.

"We always play in the lane," Jill said, her mouth sullen.

"Not tonight, you don't," Nat said. "Come on, no dawdling."

He could see the gulls now, coming in toward the land. Still silent. Still no sound.

"Look, Dad, look at all the gulls."

Spreading out in formation across the sky, the gulls circled in bands of thousands, as though they waited for some signal.

"Do you want me to carry you, Jill? Here, come pickaback."

Jill was heavy and she kept slipping. And she was crying too. His sense of urgency, of fear, had communicated itself to the child. "I wish the gulls would go away," she said. "I don't like them."

He put her down again and started running, swinging Jill after him. As they went past the farm turning, he saw the farmer backing his car out of the garage. Nat called to him. "Can you give us a lift?"

"What's that?" Mr. Trigg turned in the driver's seat and smiled at them. "It looks as though we're in for some fun," he said. "Have you seen the gulls? Jim and I are going to take a crack at them. Everyone's gone bird crazy, talking of nothing else. I hear you were troubled in the night. Want a gun?"

"I don't want a gun," said Nat, glancing at the packed interior of the car, "but I'd be obliged if you'd run Jill home. She's scared of the birds."

"Okay," said the farmer. "I'll take her home." Jill climbed in, and, turning the car, the driver sped up the lane.

Now Nat had time to look about him. The birds were circling still above the fields. Mostly herring gulls, but the black-backed gulls among them. Usually they kept apart. Now some bond had brought them together. It was the black-backed gull that attacked the smaller birds, and even newborn lambs, so he'd heard. He remembered this now, looking above him in the sky. They were coming in toward the farm. They were circling lower in the sky, and the black-backed gulls were leading.

Nat increased his pace toward his own cottage. He saw the farmer's car turn and come back along the lane. It drew up beside him with a jerk.

"The kid has run inside," said the farmer. "Your wife was watching for her. Well, what do you make of it? They're saying in town the Russians have poisoned the birds."

"How could they do that?" asked Nat.

"Don't ask me. You know how stories get around. Will you join my shooting match?"

"No, I'll get along home. The wife will be worried else."

"My missus says if you could eat gull there'd be some sense in it," said Trigg. "We'd have roast gull, baked gull, and pickle 'em into the bargain. You wait until I let off a few barrels into the brutes. That'll scare 'em."

"Have you boarded your windows?" asked Nat.

"No. Lot of nonsense. They like to scare you on the radio."

"I'd board them now, if I were you."

"Garn. You're windy. Like to come to our place to sleep?"

"No, thanks all the same."

"All right. See you in the morning. Give you a gull breakfast."

Nat hurried on. Past the little wood, past the old barn, and then across the stile to the remaining field. As he jumped the stile he heard the whir of wings. A black-backed gull dived down at him from the sky, missed, swerved in flight, and rose to dive again. In a moment it was joined by others, six, seven, a dozen, black-backed and herring mixed.

Nat dropped his hoe. The hoe was useless. Covering his head with his arms, he ran toward the cottage. They kept coming at him, silent save for the beating wings. The terrible, fluttering wings. He could feel the blood on his hands, his wrists, his neck. Each stab of a swooping beak tore his flesh. If only he could keep them from his eyes. Nothing else mattered. With each dive they became bolder. And they had no thought for themselves. When they dived low and missed, they crashed, bruised and broken, on the ground. As Nat ran he stumbled, kicking their spent bodies in front of him.

He found the door; he hammered upon it with his bleeding hands. Because of the boarded windows no light shone. Everything was dark. "Let me in," he shouted. "It's Nat. Let me in." He shouted loud to make himself heard above the whir of the gulls' wings.

Then he saw the gannet, poised for the dive, above him in the sky. The gulls circled, retired, soared, one after another, against the wind. Only the gannet remained. One single gannet above him in the sky. The wings folded suddenly to its body. It dropped like a stone. Nat screamed, and the door opened. He stumbled across the threshold, and his wife threw her weight against the door.

They heard the thud of the gannet as it fell.

His wounds were not deep. The back of his hands had suffered most, and his wrists. Had he not worn a cap they would have reached his head. As to the gannet . . . the gannet could have split his skull.

The children were crying, of course. They had seen the blood on their father's hands. "It's all right now," he told them. "Just a few scratches. You play with Johnny, Jill. Mother will wash these cuts."

His wife was ashen. She began running water in the scullery. "I saw them when Jill ran in," she whispered. "I shut the door fast, and it jammed. I couldn't open it at once when you came." Furtively, so as not to alarm the children, they talked together as she bandaged his hands and the back of his neck.

"They're flying inland," he said, "thousands of them. Rooks, crows, all the bigger birds. They're making for the towns."

"But what can they do, Nat?"

"They'll attack. Go for everyone out in the streets. Then they'll try the windows, the chimneys."

"Why don't the authorities do something? Why don't they get the army, get machine guns, anything?"

"There's been no time. Nobody's prepared. We'll hear what they have to say on the six-o'clock news." Nat went back into the kitchen, followed by his wife. Johnny was playing quietly on the floor. Only Jill looked anxious.

"I can hear the birds," she said. "Listen, Dad."

Muffled sounds came from the windows, from the door. Wings brushing the surface, sliding, scraping, seeking a way of entry. The sound of many bodies, pressed together, shuffling on the sills. Now and again came a thud, a crash, as some bird dived and fell. "It's all right," Nat said. "I've got boards over the windows, Jill. The birds can't get in."

He went and examined all the windows. His work had been thorough. Every gap was closed. He would make extra certain, however. He found wedges, pieces of old tin, strips of wood, and fastened them at the sides to reinforce the boards. His hammering helped to deaden the sound of the birds, the shuffling, the tapping, and, more ominous—he did not want his wife or the children to hear it—the splinter of cracked glass. He went upstairs to the bedrooms and reinforced the windows there. Now he could hear the birds on the roof, the scraping of claws, a sliding, jostling sound.

He decided they must sleep in the kitchen, keep up the fire, bring down the mattresses, and lay them out on the floor. He was afraid of the bedroom chimneys. The boards he had placed at the chimney bases might give way. In the kitchen they would be safe because of the fire. If the worst happened and the birds forced an entry down the bedroom chimneys, it would be hours, days perhaps, before they could break down the doors. The birds would be imprisoned in the bedrooms. Crowded together, they would stifle and die.

He began to bring the mattresses downstairs. At sight of them his wife's eyes widened in apprehension. She thought the birds had already broken in upstairs. "All right," he said cheerfully, making a joke of it, "we'll all sleep together in the kitchen tonight. More cozy here by the fire." The children helped him rearrange the furniture, and he took the precaution of moving the sideboard across the windows as an added safeguard. The mattresses could now be laid, one beside the other, against the wall where the sideboard had stood.

We're safe enough now, he thought. We can hold out. It's just the food that worries me. Food, and coal for the fire. We've enough for two or three days, not more. By that time . . .

No use thinking ahead as far as that. And they'd be giving directions on the radio. People would be told what to do. And now he realized that it was dance music only coming over the air. Not "Children's Hour," as it should have been. He knew the reason. The usual programs had been abandoned. This only happened at exceptional times. Elections and such.

At six o'clock the records ceased. The time signal was given. No matter if it scared the children, he must hear the news. There was a pause after the pips. Then the announcer spoke. His voice was grave.

"This is London. A national emergency was proclaimed at four o'clock this afternoon. Measures are being taken to safeguard the lives and property of the population, but these are not easy to effect immediately, owing to the unparalleled nature of the present crisis. Every householder must take precautions to his own building, and where several people live together, as in apartment houses, they must unite to do the utmost they can to prevent entry. It is imperative that every individual stay indoors tonight. The birds, in vast numbers, are attacking anyone on sight, and have already begun an assault upon buildings; but these, with due care, should be impenetrable. The population is asked to remain calm and not to panic. Owing to the exceptional nature of the emergency, there will be no further broadcasts until seven a.m. tomorrow."

They played the national anthem. Nothing more happened. Nat switched off the set. "We'll have supper early," he suggested, "something for a treat. Toasted cheese, eh? Something we all like?" He winked and nodded at his wife. He wanted the look of dread to go from Jill's face. But try as they did to ignore it, they were all aware of the shuffling, the stabbing, the persistent beating and sweeping of wings.

He helped with the supper, whistling, singing, making as much clatter as he could. Presently he went up to the bedrooms and listened, and he no longer heard the jostling for place upon the roof. They've got reasoning powers, he thought. They know it's hard to break in here. They'll try elsewhere.

After supper, when they were clearing away, they heard a new sound, droning, familiar. His wife looked up, her face alight. "It's planes," she said. "They're sending out planes after the birds. That will get them."

And Jill, catching her enthusiasm, jumped up and down with Johnny. "The planes will get the birds. The planes will shoot them."

Just then they heard a crash about two miles distant, followed by a second, then a third. The droning became more distant, passed away out to sea.

"What was that?" asked Nat's wife. "Were they dropping bombs on the birds?"

"I don't know," he answered. "I don't think so."

He did not want to tell her that the sound they had heard was the crashing of aircraft. It was, he had no doubt, a venture on the part of the authorities to send out reconnaissance forces, but they might have known the venture was suicidal. What could aircraft do against birds that flung themselves to death against propeller and fuselage, but hurtle to the ground themselves? Someone high up had lost his head.

"Where have the planes gone, Dad?" asked Jill.

"Back to base," he said. "Come on, now, time to tuck down for bed."

It kept his wife occupied, undressing the children before the fire, seeing to the bedding, one thing and another, while he went around the cottage again, making sure that nothing had worked loose. There was no further drone of aircraft. Maybe they'll try spraying with gas, Nat said to himself. We'll be warned first, of course, if they do. There's one thing, the best brains of the country will be on to it tonight.

The thought reassured him. He had a picture of scientists, naturalists, all those chaps they called the back-room boys, summoned to a council; they'd be working on the problem now. They'll have to be ruthless, he thought. They'll have to risk more lives if they use gas. All the livestock too, and the soil—all contaminated. As long as everyone doesn't panic. The BBC was right to warn us of that.

Upstairs in the bedrooms all was quiet. No further scraping and stabbing at the windows. The wind hadn't dropped, though. He could still hear it roaring in the chimneys. And the sea breaking on the shore.

Then he remembered the tide. The tide would be turning. There was some law the birds obeyed, and it was all to do with the east wind and the tide.

He glanced at his watch. Nearly eight o'clock. High water must have been an hour ago. That explained the lull: the birds attacked with the incoming tide. He reckoned the time limit in his head. They had six hours to go without attack. When the tide turned again, around one twenty in the morning, the birds would come back. . . .

There were two things he could do. The first to rest, with his wife and the children, and all of them snatch what sleep they could, until the small hours. The second to go out, see how they were faring at the farm, see if the telephone was still working there, so that they might get news from the exchange.

He called softly to his wife, who had just settled the children. She came halfway up the stairs and he whispered to her. "You're not to go," she said at once. "You're not to go and leave me alone with the children. I can't stand it." Her voice rose hysterically. He hushed her, calmed her.

"All right," he said, "all right. I'll wait till morning. And we'll get the radio bulletin then too, at seven. But when the tide ebbs again, I'll try for the farm, and they may let us have bread and potatoes, and milk too."

Shaking his head for silence, he went down the stairs and opened the back door. It was pitch-dark outside. The wind was blowing harder than ever. The step was heaped with birds. There were dead birds under the windows, against the walls. These were the suicides, the divers, the ones with broken necks. Wherever he looked he saw dead birds. The living had flown seaward with the turn of the tide. The gulls would be riding the seas now, as they had done in the forenoon.

In the far distance, on a hill, something was burning. One of the aircraft that had crashed; the fire, fanned by the wind, had set light to a stack.

He looked at the bodies of the birds, and he had a notion that if he heaped them, one upon the other, on the windowsills, they would make added protection for the next attack. The bodies would have to be clawed at and dragged aside before the living birds could attack the panes. He set to work in the darkness. It was queer; he hated touching them. The bodies were still warm and bloody. He felt his stomach turn, but he went on with his work. He noticed grimly that every window-pane was shattered. Only the boards had kept the birds from breaking in. He stuffed the cracked panes with the bleeding bodies of the birds.

Then he went back into the cottage. He barricaded the kitchen door, made it doubly secure. He took off his bandages, sticky with the birds' blood, and put on fresh plaster. His wife had made him cocoa and he drank it thirstily. He was very tired. "Don't worry," he said, smiling. "We'll get through."

He lay down on his mattress and closed his eyes. He slept at once. He dreamed uneasily, because through his dreams there ran a thread of something forgotten. Some precaution that he had not taken. It was connected in some way with the burning stack upon the hill. He went on sleeping, though. It was his wife shaking his shoulder that awoke him finally.

"They've begun," she sobbed. "They've started this last hour. I can't listen to it any longer alone. There's something smelling bad too, some-thing burning."

Then he remembered. He had forgotten to make up the fire. It was smoldering, nearly out. He got up swiftly and lit the lamp. The ham-mering had started at the windows and the door, and the smell of singed feathers filled the kitchen. The birds were coming down the chimney, squeezing their way down to the kitchen range. He got sticks and paper and put them on the embers, then reached for the can of kerosene. "Stand back," he shouted to his wife. "We've got to risk this."

He threw the kerosene onto the fire. The flame roared up the pipe, and down upon the fire fell the scorched, blackened bodies of the birds. The children woke, crying. "What is it?" said Jill. "What's happened?"

Nat was raking the bodies from the chimney, clawing them out onto the floor. The flames still roared, and the danger of the chimney catch-ing fire was one he had to take. The flames would send away the living birds from the chimney top. The lower joint was the difficulty, though. This was choked with the smoldering, helpless bodies of the birds caught by fire. "Stop crying," he called to the children. "There's noth-ing to be afraid of, stop crying." He went on raking at the burning bodies as they fell into the fire.

This'll fetch them, he said to himself, the draft and the flames together. We're all right as long as the chimney doesn't catch. I ought to be shot for this. It's all my fault. Last thing, I should have made up the fire. I knew there was something.

Amid the scratching and tearing at the window boards came the sudden homely striking of the kitchen clock. Three a.m. A little more than four hours yet to go. He could not be sure of the exact time of high water. He reckoned it would not turn much before half past seven. "Light up the Primus," he said to his wife. "Make us some tea, and the kids some cocoa. No use sitting around doing nothing."

He waited by the range. The flames were dying. But no more blackened bodies fell from the chimney. He thrust his poker up as far as it could go and found nothing. The chimney was clear. He wiped the sweat from his forehead. "Jill," he said, "bring me some more sticks. We'll get a good fire going." She wouldn't come near him, though. She was staring at the singed bodies of the birds. "Never mind them," he said. "We'll put those in the passage when I've got the fire steady."

The danger of the chimney was over. It could not happen again, not if the fire was kept burning day and night.

I'll have to get more fuel from the farm tomorrow, he thought. This will never last. I'll manage, though. I can do all that with the ebb tide. It can be worked, fetching what we need, when the tide's turned.

They drank tea and cocoa and ate slices of bread with bouillon. Only half a loaf left, Nat noticed.

"Stop it," said young Johnny, pointing to the windows with his spoon. "Stop it, you old birds."

"That's right," said Nat, smiling. "We don't want the old beggars, do we? Had enough of 'em."

They began to cheer when they heard the thud of the suicide birds. "There's another, Dad," cried Jill. "He's done for."

"He's had it," said Nat. "There he goes, the blighter." This was the way to face up to it. If they could keep this up, hang on like this until seven, when the first news bulletin came through, they would not have done too badly.

"Give us a smoke," he said to his wife. "A bit of cigarette smoke will clear away the smell of the scorched feathers."

"There's only two left in the packet," she said. "I was going to buy you some from the co-op."

"I'll have one," he said. "T'other will keep for a rainy day." He sat with one arm around his wife and the other around Jill, with Johnny on his mother's lap and the blankets heaped about them on the mattress.

The tapping went on and on and a new rasping note struck Nat's ear, as though a sharper beak had come to take over from its fellows. It was not the tap of the woodpecker. That would be light and frequent. This was more serious, because if it continued long, the wood would splinter as the glass had done. Then he remembered the hawks. Could the hawks have taken over from the gulls? Were there buzzards now upon the sills, using talons as well as beaks? Hawks, buzzards, kestrels, falcons—he had forgotten the birds of prey. He had forgotten the gripping power of the birds of prey. Three hours to go, and while they waited, there was the sound of talons tearing at the splintering wood.

Nat looked about him, seeing what furniture he could destroy to fortify the door. The windows were safe because of the sideboard. He went upstairs, but when he reached the landing he heard a soft patter on the floor of the children's bedroom. The birds had broken through. . . . He put his ear to the door. No mistake. He could hear the rustle of wings and the light patter as they searched the floor. The other bedroom was still clear. He went into it and began bringing out the furniture, to pile at the head of the stairs should the door of the children's bedroom go. He could not stack the furniture against the door, because it opened inward. The only possible thing was to have it at the top of the stairs.

At five thirty he suggested breakfast—bacon and fried bread—if only to stop the growing look of panic in his wife's eyes and to calm the fretful children. She did not know about the birds upstairs. The bedroom, luckily, was not over the kitchen. So she could not hear them up there, tapping the boards. And the silly, senseless thud of the suicide birds that flew into the bedroom, smashing their heads against the walls. He knew them of old, the herring gulls. They had no brains. The blackbacks were different; they knew what they were doing. So did the buzards, the hawks . . .

He found himself watching the clock. If his theory was not correct, if the attack did not cease with the turn of the tide, he knew they were beaten. They could not continue through the long day without air, without rest, without more fuel, without . . . His mind raced. He knew they were not fully prepared to withstand a siege. It might be safer in the towns after all. If he could get a message through on the farm telephone to his cousin, only a short journey by train up-country, they might be able to hire a car. That would be quicker—hire a car during ebb tide. . . .

"The radio," said his wife. "It's nearly seven."

"Don't twist the knob," he said, impatient for the first time. "It's on the Home station where it is."

They waited. The kitchen clock struck seven. There was no sound. No chimes, no music. They waited until a quarter past, switching around the dial. The result was the same. No news bulletin.

"We've heard wrong," he said. "They won't be broadcasting until eight o'clock." They left it switched on, and Nat thought of the battery, wondered how much power was left in it. It was generally recharged when his wife went shopping in the town. If the battery failed, they would not hear the instructions.

"It's getting light," whispered his wife. "I can't see it, but I can feel it. And the birds aren't hammering so loud."

She was right. The rasping, tearing sound grew fainter every moment. The tide was turning. By eight there was no sound at all. Only the wind. The children, lulled at last by the stillness, fell asleep. At half past eight Nat switched the radio off.

"What are you doing? We'll miss the news," said his wife.

"There isn't going to be any news," said Nat. "We've got to depend upon ourselves."

He went to the door and slowly pulled away the barricades. He drew the bolts and, kicking the bodies from the step outside the door, breathed the cold air. He had six working hours before him, and he knew he must not waste his strength in any way. Food, and light, and fuel; these were the necessary things. If he could get them in sufficiency, they could endure another night.

He stepped into the garden, and as he did so he saw the living birds. The gulls had gone to ride the sea, as they had done before; they sought seafood, and the buoyancy of the tide, before they returned to the attack. Not so the land birds. They waited and watched. Nat saw them—on the hedgerows, on the soil, crowded in the trees, outside in the field—line upon line of birds, all still, doing nothing. He went to the end of his small garden. The birds did not move. They went on watching him.

He went back to the cottage. "I'm going to the farm," he said. His wife clung to him. She had seen the living birds from the open door. "Take us with you," she begged. "We can't stay here alone."

"Come on, then," he said. "Bring baskets, and Johnny's pram. We can load up the pram." They dressed against the biting wind, wore gloves and scarves. His wife put Johnny in the pram. Nat took Jill's hand.

"The birds," she whimpered, "they're out there in the fields."

"They won't hurt us," he said, "not in the light." They started walking across the field toward the stile, and the birds did not move. They waited, their heads turned to the wind.

When they reached the turning to the farm, Nat stopped and told his wife to wait in the shelter of the hedge with the two children. "I'll be back in a moment," he said.

The cows were lowing, moving restlessly in the yard, and he could see a gap in the fence where the sheep had knocked their way through, to roam unchecked in the front garden. No smoke came from the chimney. He pushed his way through the herd of bellowing cows, which turned this way and that, distressed, their udders full. He saw the car standing by the gate, not put away in the garage. The windows of the farmhouse were smashed. There were many dead gulls lying in the yard. The living birds perched on the group of trees behind the farm and on the roof of the house. They were quite still. They watched him.

Jim's body lay in the yard . . . what was left of it. When the birds had finished, the cows had trampled him. His gun was beside him. The door of the house was shut and bolted, but as the windows were smashed it was easy to lift them and climb through. Trigg's body was close to the telephone. He must have been trying to get through to the exchange when the birds came for him. The receiver was hanging loose, the instrument torn from the wall. No sign of Mrs. Trigg. She would be

543

upstairs. Was it any use going up? Sickened, Nat knew what he would find.

Thank God, he said to himself, there were no children.

He forced himself to climb the stairs, but halfway he turned and descended again. He could see her legs protruding from the open bedroom door. Beside her were the bodies of the black-backed gulls, and an umbrella, broken.

He tramped back to his wife and children. "I'm going to fill up the car with stuff," he said. "I'll put coal in it, and kerosene for the Primus. We'll take it home and return for a fresh load."

"What about the Triggs?" asked his wife.

"They must have gone to friends."

"Shall I come and help you, then?"

"No, there's a mess down there. Cows and sheep all over the place. Wait, I'll get the car. You can sit in it." Clumsily he backed the car out of the yard and into the lane. His wife and the children could not see Jim's body from there.

"Stay here," he said. "Never mind the pram. That can be fetched later. I'm going to load the car." Her eyes watched his all the time. He believed she understood; otherwise she would have suggested helping him to find the bread and groceries.

They made three journeys between their cottage and the farm before he was satisfied they had everything they needed. It was surprising, once he started thinking, how many things were necessary. He had to go around searching for timber. He wanted to renew the boards on all the windows at the cottage. Candles, kerosene, nails, canned stuff; the list was endless. Besides all that, he milked three of the cows. The rest, poor brutes, would have to go on bellowing.

On the final journey he drove the car to the bus stop, got out, and went to the telephone box. He waited a few minutes, jangling the receiver, but the line was dead. He climbed onto a bank and looked over the countryside. There was no sign of life at all, nothing in the fields but the waiting, watching birds. Some of them slept—he could see the beaks tucked into the feathers.

You'd think they'd be feeding, he said to himself, not just standing in that way. Then he remembered. They were gorged with food. They had eaten their fill during the night. That was why they did not move this morning. . . .

No smoke came from the chimneys of the cottages up the lane. He thought of the children who had run across the fields the day before. I should have taken them home with me, he thought.

He went back to the car and got into the driver's seat. "Go quickly past that second gate," whispered his wife. "The postman's lying there. I don't want Jill to see." He accelerated. The little Morris bumped and rattled along the lane. The children shrieked with laughter.

"Up-a-down, up-a-down," shouted young Johnny.

It was a quarter to one by the time they reached the cottage. Only an hour to go. "Hot up some soup for yourself and the children," said Nat. "I've no time to eat now. I've got to unload all this stuff."

He got everything inside the cottage. It could be sorted later. Give them all something to do during the long hours ahead. He went around the cottage methodically, testing every window, every door. He climbed onto the roof also, and fixed boards across every chimney except the kitchen's. The cold was so intense he could hardly bear it, but the job had to be done. He paused, his work on the bedroom chimneys finished, and looked out to sea. Something was moving out there. Something gray and white among the breakers.

"Good old navy," he said. "They never let us down. They're coming down-channel, they're turning in the bay."

He waited, straining his eyes toward the sea. He was wrong. It was not ships. The navy was not there. The gulls were rising from the sea. Then the massed flocks in the fields rose in formation from the ground and soared to the sky.

The tide had turned again.

Nat climbed down the ladder and went inside the kitchen. The family were at dinner. It was a little after two. He bolted the door, put up the barricade, and lit the lamp.

His wife had switched on the radio once again. "I've been all round the dial," she said, "foreign stations and that lot. I can't get anything."

"Maybe they have the same trouble," he said. "Maybe it's the same right through Europe."

She poured out a plateful of soup, cut him a large slice of bread, and spread dripping upon it. They ate in silence. A piece of the dripping ran down young Johnny's chin and fell onto the table. "Manners, Johnny," said Jill. "You should wipe your mouth."

The tapping began at the windows, at the door. The rustling, the jostling, the pushing for position on the sills. The first thud of the suicide gulls upon the step.

"Won't America do something?" said his wife. "They've always been our allies, haven't they?"

Nat did not answer. The boards were strong against the windows, and on the chimneys too. The cottage was filled with stores, with fuel, with all they needed for the next few days. When he had finished dinner he would put the stuff away, stack it neatly, get everything shipshape, handylike. His wife could help him, and the children too. They'd tire themselves out between now and a quarter to nine, when the tide would ebb; then he'd tuck them down on their mattresses, see that they slept good and sound until three in the morning.

He had a new scheme for the windows, which was to fix barbed wire in front of the boards. He had brought a great roll of it from the farm. The nuisance was, he'd have to work at this in the dark, when the lull came between nine and three. Pity he had not thought of it before.

The smaller birds were at the window now. He recognized the light tap-tapping of their beaks and the soft brush of their wings. The hawks ignored the windows. They concentrated their attack upon the door. Nat listened to the sound of splintering wood, and wondered how many million years of memory were stored in those little brains, behind the stabbing beaks, the piercing eyes, now giving them this instinct to destroy mankind with all the deft precision of machines.

"I'll smoke that last cigarette," he said to his wife. "Stupid of me, it was the one thing I forgot to bring back from the farm."

He reached for it, switched on the silent radio. He threw the empty packet on the fire, and watched it burn.

THE STORY OF
THE WIDOW'S SON
MARY LAVIN

THIS IS THE STORY of a widow's son, but it is a story that has two
endings.

There was once a widow, living in a small neglected village at the
foot of a steep hill. She had only one son, but he was the meaning of her
life. She lived for his sake. She wore herself out working for him. Every
day she made a hundred sacrifices in order to keep him at a good school
in the town, four miles away, because there was a better teacher there
than the village dullard that had taught herself.

She made great plans for Packy, but she did not tell him about her
plans. Instead she threatened him, day and night, that if he didn't turn
out well, she would put him to work on the roads, or in the quarry
under the hill.

But as the years went by, everyone in the village, and even Packy
himself, could tell by the way she watched him out of sight in the
morning, and watched to see him come into sight in the evening, that
he was the beat of her heart, and that her gruff words were only a cover
for her pride and her joy in him.

It was for Packy's sake that she walked for hours along the road,
letting her cow graze the long acre of the wayside grass, in order to spare
the few poor blades that pushed up through the stones in her own field.
It was for his sake she walked back and forth to the town to sell a few
cabbages as soon as ever they were fit. It was for his sake that she got up

in the cold dawning hours to gather mushrooms that would take the place of foods that had to be bought with money. She bent her back daily to make every penny she could, and as often happens, she made more by industry, out of her few bald acres, than many of the farmers around her made out of their great bearded meadows. Out of the money she made by selling eggs alone, she paid for Packy's clothes and for the greater number of his books.

When Packy was fourteen, he was in the last class in the school, and the master had great hopes of his winning a scholarship to a big college in the city. He was getting to be a tall lad, and his features were beginning to take a strong cast. His character was strengthening too, under his mother's sharp tongue. The people of the village were beginning to give him the same respect they gave to the sons of the farmers who came from their fine colleges in the summer, with blue suits and bright ties.

One day in June, when the air was so heavy the scent that rose up from the grass was imprisoned under the low clouds and hung in the air, the widow was waiting at the gate for Packy. There had been no rain for some days, and the hens and chickens were pecking irritably at the dry ground and wandering up and down the road in bewilderment.

A neighbor passed.

"Waiting for Packy?" said the neighbor pleasantly, and he stood for a minute to take off his hat and wipe the sweat of the day from his face. He was an old man.

"It's a hot day!" he said. "It will be a hard push for Packy on that battered old bike of his. I wouldn't like to have to face into four miles on a day like this!"

"Packy would travel three times that distance if there was a book at the other end of the road!" said the widow, with the pride of those who cannot read more than a line or two without wearying.

The minutes went by slowly. The widow kept looking up at the sun.

"I suppose the heat is better than the rain!" she said at last.

"The heat can do a lot of harm too, though," said the neighbor absentmindedly, as he pulled a long blade of grass from between the stones of the wall and began to chew the end of it. "You could get sunstroke on a day like this!" He looked up at the sun. "The sun is a terror," he said. "It could cause you to drop down dead like a stone!"

The widow strained out farther over the gate. She looked up the hill in the direction of the town.

"He will have a good cool breeze on his face coming down the hill, at any rate," she said.

The man looked up the hill. "That's true. On the hottest day of the year you would get a cool breeze coming down that hill on a bicycle. You would feel the air streaming past your cheeks like silk. And in the winter it's like two knives flashing to either side of you and peeling off your skin like you'd peel the bark off a willow rod." He chewed the grass meditatively. "That must be one of the steepest hills in Ireland," he said. "That hill is a hill worthy of the name of a hill." He took the grass out of his mouth. "It's my belief," he said, earnestly looking at the widow—"it's my belief that that hill is to be found marked with a name in the Ordnance Survey map!"

"If that's the case," said the widow, "Packy will be able to tell you all about it. When it isn't a book he has in his hand it's a map."

"Is that so?" said the man. "That's interesting. A map is a great thing. A map is not an ordinary thing. It isn't everyone can make out a map."

The widow wasn't listening.

"I think I see Packy!" she said, and she opened the wooden gate and stepped out into the roadway.

At the top of the hill there was a glitter of spokes as a bicycle came into sight. Then there was a flash of blue jersey as Packy came flying downward, gripping the handlebars of the bike, with his bright hair blown back from his forehead. The hill was so steep, and he came down so fast, that it seemed to the man and woman at the bottom of the hill that he was not moving at all, but that it was the bright trees and bushes, the bright ditches and wayside grasses that were streaming away to either side of him.

The hens and chickens clucked and squawked and ran along the road looking for a safe place in the ditches. They ran to either side with feminine fuss and chatter. Packy waved to his mother. He came nearer and nearer. They could see the freckles on his face.

"Shoo!" cried Packy at the squawking hens that had not yet left the roadway. They ran with their long necks straining forward.

"Shoo!" said Packy's mother, lifting her apron and flapping it in the air to frighten them out of his way.

It was only afterward, when the harm was done, that the widow began to think that it might, perhaps, have been the flapping of her own apron that frightened the old clocking hen and sent her flying out over the garden wall into the middle of the road.

The old hen appeared suddenly on top of the grassy ditch and looked with a distraught eye at the hens and chickens as they ran to right and left. Her own feathers began to stand out from her. She craned her neck forward and gave a distracted squawk and fluttered down into the middle of the hot dusty road.

Packy jammed on the brakes. The widow screamed. There was a flurry of white feathers and a spurt of blood. The bicycle swerved and fell. Packy was thrown over the handlebars.

It was such a simple accident that, although the widow screamed, and although the old man looked around to see if there was help near, neither of them thought that Packy was very badly hurt, but when they ran over and lifted his head and saw that he could not speak, they wiped the blood from his face and looked around desperately to measure the distance they would have to carry him.

It was only a few yards to the door of the cottage, but Packy was dead before they got him across the threshold.

"He's only in a weakness!" screamed the widow, and she urged the crowd that had gathered outside the door to do something for him. "Get a doctor!" she cried, pushing a young laborer toward the door. "Hurry! Hurry! The doctor will bring him around."

But the neighbors that kept coming in the door, quickly, from all sides, were crossing themselves one after another and falling on their knees as soon as they laid eyes on the boy, stretched out flat on the bed, with the dust and dirt and the sweat marks of life on his dead face.

When at last the widow was convinced that her son was dead, the other women had to hold her down. She waved her arms and cried out, and wrestled to get free. She wanted to wring the neck of every hen in the yard.

"I'll kill every one of them. What good are they to me now? All the hens in the world aren't worth one drop of human blood. That old clocking hen wasn't worth more than six shillings, at the very most. What is six shillings? Is it worth poor Packy's life?"

But after a time she stopped raving and looked from one face to another.

"Why didn't he ride over the old hen?" she asked. "Why did he try to save an old hen that wasn't worth more than six shillings? Didn't he know he was worth more to his mother than an old hen that would be going into the pot one of these days? Why did he do it? Why? Why?"

The neighbors patted her arm.

"There now!" they said. "There now!" And that was all they could think of saying, and they said it over and over again.

And years afterward, whenever the widow spoke of her son Packy to the neighbors who dropped in to keep her company for an hour or two, she always had the same question to ask—the same tireless question.

"Why did he put the price of an old clocking hen above the price of his own life?"

And the people always gave the same answer.

"There now!" they said. "There now!" And they sat as silently as the widow herself, looking into the fire.

But surely some of those neighbors must have been stirred to wonder what would have happened had Packy not yielded to his impulse of fear, and had, instead, ridden boldly over the old clocking hen? And surely some of them must have stared into the flames and pictured the scene of the accident again, altering a detail here and there as they did so, and giving the story a different end. For these people knew the widow, and they knew Packy, and when you know people well it is as easy to guess what they would say and do in certain circumstances as it is to remember what they actually did say and do in other circumstances. In fact, it is sometimes easier to invent than to remember accurately, and were this not so, two great branches of creative art would wither in an hour: the art of the storyteller and the art of the gossip. So, perhaps, if I try to tell you what I myself think might have happened had Packy killed that cackling old hen, you will not accuse me of abusing my privileges as a writer. After all, what I am about to tell you is no more of a fiction than what I have already told, and I lean no heavier now upon your credulity than, with your full consent, I did in the first instance.

And moreover, in many respects the new story is the same as the old.

It begins in the same way too. There is the widow grazing her cow by the wayside, and walking the long roads to the town, weighted down with sacks of cabbages that will pay for Packy's schooling. There she is, fussing over Packy in the morning in case he would be late for school. There she is in the evening, watching the battered clock on the dresser for the hour when he will appear on the top of the hill at his return. And there too, on a hot day in June, is the old laboring man coming up the road, and pausing to talk to her, as she stood at the door. There he is, dragging a blade of grass from between the stones of the wall and putting it between his teeth to chew, before he opens his mouth.

And when he opens his mouth at last it is to utter the same remark.

"Waiting for Packy?" said the old man, and then he took off his hat and wiped the sweat from his forehead. It will be remembered that he was an old man. "It's a hot day," he said.

"It's very hot," said the widow, looking anxiously up the hill. "It's a hot day to push a bicycle four miles along a bad road with the dust rising to choke you, and sun striking spikes off the handlebars!"

"The heat is better than the rain, all the same," said the old man.

"I suppose it is," said the widow. "All the same, there were days when Packy came home with the rain dried into his clothes so bad they stood up stiff like boards when he took them off."

"Is that so?" said the old man. "You may be sure he got a good petting on those days. There is no son like a widow's son. A ewe lamb!"

"Is it Packy?" said the widow in disgust. "Packy never got a day's petting since the day he was born. I made up my mind from the first that I'd never make a soft one out of him."

The widow looked up the hill again, and set herself to raking the gravel outside the gate as if she were in the road for no other purpose. Then she gave another look up the hill.

"Here he is now!" she said, and she rose such a cloud of dust with the rake that they could hardly see the glitter of the bicycle spokes, and the flash of blue jersey as Packy came down the hill at a breakneck speed.

Nearer and nearer he came, faster and faster, waving his hand to the widow, shouting at the hens to leave the way!

The hens ran for the ditches, stretching their necks in gawky terror.

And then, as the last hen squawked into the ditch, the way was clear for a moment before the whirling silver spokes.

Then, unexpectedly, up from nowhere it seemed, came an old clocking hen, and clucking despairingly, it stood for a moment on the top of the wall and then rose into the air with the clumsy flight of a ground fowl.

Packy stopped whistling. The widow screamed. Packy yelled and the widow flapped her apron. Then Packy swerved the bicycle, and a cloud of dust rose from the braked wheel.

For a minute it could not be seen what exactly had happened, but Packy put his foot down and dragged it along the ground in the dust till he brought the bicycle to a sharp stop. He threw the bicycle down with a clatter on the hard road and ran back. The widow could not bear to look. She threw her apron over her head.

"He's killed the clocking hen!" she said. "He's killed her! He's killed her!" And then she let the apron fall back into place, and began to run up the hill herself. The old man spat out the blade of grass that he had been chewing and ran after the woman.

"Did you kill it?" screamed the widow, and as she got near enough to see the blood and feathers she raised her arm over her head, and her fist was clenched till the knuckles shone white. Packy cowered down over the carcass of the fowl and hunched up his shoulders as if to shield himself from a blow. His legs were spattered with blood, and the brown and white feathers of the dead hen were stuck to his hands, and stuck to his clothes, and they were strewn all over the road. Some of the short white inner feathers were still swirling with the dust in the air.

"I couldn't help it, Mother. I couldn't help it. I didn't see her till it was too late!"

The widow caught up the hen and examined it all over, holding it by the bone of the breast and letting the long neck dangle. Then, catching it by the leg, she raised it suddenly above her head and brought down the bleeding body on the boy's back, in blow after blow, spattering the blood all over his face and his hands, over his clothes and over the white dust of the road around him.

"How dare you lie to me!" she screamed gaspingly between the blows. "You saw the hen. I know you saw it. You stopped whistling!

You called out! We were watching you. We saw." She turned upon the old man. "Isn't that right?" she demanded. "He saw the hen, didn't he? He saw it?"

"It looked that way," said the old man uncertainly, his eye on the dangling fowl in the widow's hand.

"There you are!" said the widow. She threw the hen down on the road. "You saw the hen in front of you on the road, as plain as you see it now," she accused, "but you wouldn't stop to save it because you were in too big a hurry home to fill your belly! Isn't that so?"

"No, Mother. No! I saw her all right, but it was too late to do anything."

"He admits now that he saw it," said the widow, turning and nodding triumphantly at the onlookers who had gathered at the sound of the shouting.

"I never denied seeing it!" said the boy, appealing to the onlookers as to his judges.

"He doesn't deny it!" screamed the widow. "He stands there as brazen as you like, and admits for all the world to hear that he saw the hen and he rode over it without a thought!"

"But what else could I do?" said the boy, throwing out his hand, appealing to the crowd now, and now appealing to the widow. "If I'd put on the brakes going down the hill at such a speed, I would have been put over the handlebars!"

"And what harm would that have done you?" screamed the widow. "I often saw you taking a toss when you were wrestling with Jimmy Mack and I heard no complaints afterward, although your elbows and knees would be running blood, and your face scraped like a gridiron!" She turned to the crowd. "That's as true as God. I often saw him come in with his nose spouting blood like a pump, and one eye closed as tight as the eye of a corpse. My hand was often stiff for a week from sopping out wet cloths to put poultices on him and try to bring his face back to rights again." She swung back to Packy again. "You're not afraid of a fall when you go climbing trees, are you? You're not afraid to go up on the roof after a cat, are you? Oh, there's more in this than you want me to know. I can see that. You killed that hen on purpose—that's what I believe! You're tired of going to school. You want to get out of going away to college. That's it! You think if you kill the few poor hens we have, there will be no money in the box when the time comes to pay for books and classes. That's it!" Packy began to redden.

"It's late in the day for me to be thinking of things like that," he said. "It's long ago I should have started those tricks if that was the way I felt. But it's not true. I want to go to college. The reason I was coming down the hill so fast was to tell you that I got the scholarship. The teacher told me as I was leaving the schoolhouse. That's why I was pedaling so hard. That's why I was whistling. That's why I was waving my hand. Didn't you see me waving my hand from once I came in sight at the top of the hill?"

The widow's hands fell to her sides. The wind of words died down within her and left her flat and limp. She didn't know what to say. She could feel the neighbors staring at her. She wished that they were gone away about their business. She wanted to throw out her arms to the boy, to drag him against her heart and hug him like a small child. But she thought of how the crowd would look at each other and nod and snigger. A ewe lamb! She didn't want to satisfy them. If she gave in to her feelings now, they would know how much she had been counting on his getting the scholarship. She wouldn't please them! She wouldn't satisfy them!

She looked at Packy, and when she saw him standing there before her, spattered with the furious feathers and crude blood of the dead hen, she felt a fierce disappointment for the boy's own disappointment, and a fierce resentment against him for killing the hen on this day of all days and spoiling the great news of his success.

Her mind was in confusion. She stared at the blood on his face, and all at once it seemed as if the blood was a bad omen of the future that was for him. Disappointment, fear, resentment, and above all defiance, raised themselves within her like screeching animals. She looked from Packy to the onlookers.

"Scholarship! Scholarship!" she sneered, putting as much derision as she could into her voice and expression.

"I suppose you think you are a great fellow now? I suppose you think you are independent now? I suppose you think you can go off with yourself now, and look down on your poor slave of a mother who scraped and sweated for you with her cabbages and her hens? I suppose you think to yourself that it doesn't matter now whether the hens are alive or dead? Is that the way? Well, let me tell you this! You're not as independent as you think. The scholarship may pay for your books and your teachers' fees, but who will pay for your clothes? Aha, you forgot that, didn't you?" She put her hands on her hips. Packy hung his head. He no longer appealed to the gawking neighbors. They might have been able to save him from blows, but he knew enough about life to know that no one could save him from shame.

The widow's heart burned at sight of his shamed face, as her heart burned with grief, but her temper too burned fiercer and fiercer, and she came to a point at which nothing could quell the blaze till it had burned itself out. "Who'll buy your suits?" she yelled. "Who'll buy your boots?" She paused to think of more humiliating accusations. "Who'll buy your breeches?" She paused again and her teeth bit against each other. What would wound deepest? What shame could she drag upon him? "Who'll buy your nightshirts, or will you sleep in your skin?"

The neighbors laughed at that, and the tension was broken. The widow herself laughed. She held her sides and laughed, and as she laughed everything seemed to take on a newer and simpler significance. Things were not as bad as they seemed a moment before. She wanted Packy to laugh too. She looked at him. But as she looked at Packy her heart turned cold with a strange new fear.

"Get into the house!" she said, giving him a push ahead of her. She wanted him safe under her own roof. She wanted to get him away from the gaping neighbors. She hated them, man, woman and child. She felt that if they had not been there, things would have been different. And she wanted to get away from the sight of the blood on the road. She wanted to mash a few potatoes and make a bit of potato cake for Packy. That would comfort him. He loved that.

Packy hardly touched the food. And even after he had washed and scrubbed himself there were stains of blood turning up in the most unexpected places: behind his ears, under his fingernails, inside the cuff of his sleeve.

"Put on your good clothes," said the widow, making a great effort to be gentle, but her manners had become as twisted and as hard as the branches of the trees across the road from her, and even the kindly offers she made sounded harsh. The boy sat on the chair in a slumped position that kept her nerves on edge, and set up a further conflict of irritation and love in her heart. She hated to see him slumping there in the chair, not asking to go outside the door, but still she was uneasy whenever he as much as looked in the direction of the door. She felt safe while he was under the roof; inside the lintel; under her eyes.

Next day she went in to wake him for school, but his room was empty; his bed had not been slept in, and when she ran out into the yard and called him everywhere there was no answer. She ran up and down. She called at the houses of the neighbors, but he was not in any house. And she thought she could hear sniggering behind her in each house that she left, as she ran to another one. He wasn't in the village nor in the town. The schoolmaster said that she should let the police have a description of him. He said he never met a boy as sensitive as Packy. A boy like that took strange notions into his head from time to time.

The police did their best, but there was no news of Packy that night. A few days later there was a letter saying that he was well. He asked his mother to notify the master that he would not be coming back, so that some other boy could claim the scholarship. He said that he would send the price of the hen as soon as he made some money.

Another letter in a few weeks said that he had got a job on a trawler and that he would not be able to write very often, but that he would put aside some of his pay every week and send it to his mother whenever he got into port. He said that he wanted to pay her back for all she had done for him. He gave no address. He kept his promise about the money, but he never gave any address when he wrote.

And so the people may have let their thoughts run on as they sat by the fire with the widow, many a night, listening to her complaining voice saying the same thing over and over. "Why did he put the price of an old hen above the price of his own life?" And it is possible that their version of the story has a certain element of truth about it too. Perhaps all our actions have this double quality about them; this possibility of alternative, and that it is only by careful watching and absolute sincerity that we follow the path that is destined for us, and, no matter how tragic that may be, it is better than the tragedy we bring upon ourselves.

THE TRAIN
FROM RHODESIA
NADINE GORDIMER

THE TRAIN CAME OUT of the red horizon and bore down toward them over the single straight track.

THE STATIONMASTER came out of his little brick station with its pointed chalet roof, feeling the creases in his serge uniform in his legs as well. A stir of preparedness rippled through the native vendors squatting in the dust; the face of a carved wooden animal, eternally surprised, stuck out of a sack. The stationmaster's barefoot children wandered over. From the gray mud huts with the untidy heads that stood within a decorated mud wall, chickens, and dogs with their skin stretched like parchment over their bones, followed the piccanins down to the track. The flushed and perspiring west cast a reflection, faint, without heat, upon the station, upon the walled kraal, upon the gray tin house of the station-master and upon the sand, that lapped all around, from sky to sky, cast little rhythmical cups of shadow, so that the sand became the sea, and closed over the children's black feet softly and without imprint.

The stationmaster's wife sat behind the mesh of her veranda. Above her head the hunk of a sheep's carcass moved slightly, dangling in a current of air.

They waited.

The train called out, along the sky; but there was no answer; and the cry hung on. I'm coming. . . . I'm coming. . . .

The engine flared out now, big, whisking a dwindling body behind it; the track flared out to let it in.

Creaking, jerking, jostling, gasping, the train filled the station.

HERE, LET ME SEE that one—the young woman curved her body farther out of the corridor window. Missus? smiled the old man, looking at the creatures he held in his hand. From a piece of string on his gray finger hung a tiny woven basket; he lifted it, questioning. No, no, she urged, leaning down toward him, across the height of the train toward the man in the piece of old rug; that one, that one, her hand commanded. It was a lion, carved out of soft dry wood that looked like sponge cake; heraldic, black and white, with impressionistic detail burned in. The old man held it up to her, still smiling, not from the heart but at the customer. Between its Vandyke teeth, in the mouth opened in an end-less roar too terrible to be heard, it had a black tongue. Look, said the young husband, if you don't mind! And around the neck of the thing, a piece of fur (rat? rabbit? meerkat?); a real mane, majestic, telling you somehow that the artist had delight in the lion.

All up and down the length of the train in the dust the artists sprang, walking bent, like performing animals, the better to exhibit the fan-tasy held toward the faces on the train. Buck, startled and stiff, staring with round black and white eyes. More lions, standing erect, grappling with strange, thin, elongated warriors who clutched spears and showed no fear in their slits of eyes. How much, they asked from the train, how much?

Give me penny, said the little ones with nothing to sell. The dogs went and sat, quite still, under the dining car, where the train breathed out the smell of meat cooking with onion.

A man passed beneath the arch of reaching arms meeting gray-black and white in the exchange of money for the staring wooden eyes, the stiff wooden legs sticking up in the air; went along under the voices and the bargaining, interrogating the wheels. Past the dogs; glancing up at the dining car, where he could stare at the faces, behind glass, drinking beer, two by two, on either side of a uniform railway vase with its pale dead flower. Right to the end, to the guard's van, where the station-master's children had just collected their mother's two loaves of bread;

to the engine itself, where the stationmaster and the driver stood talking against the steaming complaint of the resting beast.

The man called out to them, something loud and joking. They turned to laugh, in a twirl of steam. The two children careered over the sand, clutching the bread, and burst through the iron gate and up the path through the garden in which nothing grew.

Passengers drew themselves in at the corridor windows and turned into compartments to fetch money, to call someone to look. Those sitting inside looked up: suddenly different, caged faces, boxed in, cut off after the contact of outside. There was an orange a piccanin would like. . . . What about that chocolate? It wasn't very nice. . . .

A girl had collected a handful of the hard kind, that no one liked, out of the chocolate box, and was throwing them to the dogs, over at the dining car. But the hens darted in and swallowed the chocolates, incredibly quick and accurate, before they had even dropped in the dust, and the dogs, a little bewildered, looked up with their brown eyes, not expecting anything. . . .

No, leave it, said the young woman, don't take it. . . .

Too expensive, too much, she shook her head and raised her voice to the old man, giving up the lion. He held it high where she had handed it to him. No, she said, shaking her head. Three and six? insisted her husband loudly. Yes, baas! laughed the old man. *Three and six?* The young man was incredulous. Oh, leave it—she said. The young man stopped. Don't you want it? he said, keeping his face closed to the old man. No, never mind, she said, leave it. The old native kept his head on one side, looking at them sideways, holding the lion. Three and six, he murmured, as old people repeat things to themselves.

The young woman drew her head in. She went into the compartment and sat down. Out of the window, on the other side, there was nothing; sand and bush; a thorn tree. Back through the open doorway, past the figure of her husband in the corridor, there was the station, the voices, wooden animals waving, running feet. Her eye followed the funny little valance of scrolled wood that outlined the chalet roof of the station; she thought of the lion and smiled. That bit of fur around the neck. But the wooden buck, the hippos, the elephants, the baskets that already bulked out of their brown paper under the seat and on the luggage rack! How will they look at home? Where will you put them? What will they mean away from the places you found them? Away from the unreality of the last few weeks? The young man outside. But he is not part of the unreality; he is for good now. Odd . . . somewhere there was an idea that he, that living with him, was part of the holiday, the strange places.

Outside, a bell rang. The stationmaster was leaning against the end of the train, green flag rolled in readiness. A few men who had got down to stretch their legs sprang onto the train, clinging to the observation platforms, or perhaps merely standing on the iron step, holding the rail; but on the train, safe from the one dusty platform, the one tin house, the empty sand.

There was a grunt. The train jerked. Through the glass the beer drinkers looked out, as if they could not see beyond it. Behind the fly screen, the stationmaster's wife sat facing back at them beneath the darkening hunk of meat.

There was a shout. The flag drooped out. Joints not yet coordinated, the segmented body of the train heaved and bumped back against itself. It began to move; slowly the scrolled chalet moved past it, the yells of the natives, running alongside, jetted up into the air, fell back at different levels. Staring wooden faces waved drunkenly, there, then gone, questioning for the last time at the windows. Here, one and six, baas! As one automatically opens a hand to catch a thrown ball, a man fumbled wildly down his pocket, brought up the shilling and sixpence and threw them out; the old native, gasping, his skinny toes splaying the sand, flung the lion.

The piccanins were waving, the dogs stood, tails uncertain, watching the train go: past the mud huts, where a woman turned to look up from the smoke of the fire, her hand pausing on her hip.

The stationmaster went slowly in under the chalet.

The old native stood, breath blowing out the skin between his ribs, feet tense, balanced in the sand, smiling and shaking his head. In his opened palm, held in the attitude of receiving, was the retrieved shilling and sixpence.

The blind end of the train was being pulled helplessly out of the station.

THE YOUNG MAN SWUNG IN from the corridor, breathless. He was shaking his head with laughter and triumph. Here! he said, and waggled the lion at her. One and six!

What? she said.

He laughed. I was arguing with him for fun, bargaining—when the train had pulled out already, he came tearing after. . . . One and six, baas! So there's your lion.

She was holding it away from her, the head with the open jaws, the pointed teeth, the black tongue, the wonderful ruff of fur facing her. She was looking at it with an expression of not seeing, of seeing something different. Her face was drawn up, wryly, like the face of a discomforted child. Her mouth lifted nervously at the corner. Very slowly, cautious, she lifted her finger and touched the mane, where it was joined to the wood.

But how could you? she said. He was shocked by the dismay of her face.

Good Lord, he said, what's the matter?

If you wanted the thing, she said, her voice rising and breaking with the shrill impotence of anger, why didn't you buy it in the first place? If you wanted it, why didn't you pay for it? Why didn't you take it decently, when he offered it? Why did you have to wait for him to run after the train with it, and give him one and six? One and six!

She was pushing it at him, trying to force him to take the lion. He stood astonished, his hands hanging at his sides.

But you wanted it! You liked it so much?

It's a beautiful piece of work, she said fiercely, as if to protect it from him.

You liked it so much! You said yourself it was too expensive—

Oh *you*—she said, hopeless and furious. *You*— She threw the lion onto the seat.

He stood looking at her.

She sat down again in the corner and, her face slumped in her hands, stared out of the window. Everything was turning around inside her. One and six. One and six. One and six for the wood and the carving and the sinews of the legs and the switch of the tail. The mouth open like that and the teeth. The black tongue, rolling, like a wave. The mane around the neck. To give one and six for that. The heat of shame mounted through her legs and body and sounded in her ears like the sound of sand pouring. Pouring, pouring. She sat there, sick. A weariness, a tastelessness, the discovery of a void made her hands slacken their grip, atrophy emptily, as if the hour were not worth their grasp. She was feeling like this again. She had thought it was something to do with singleness, with being alone and belonging too much to oneself.

She sat there not wanting to move or speak, or to look at anything even; so that the mood should be associated with nothing, no object, word or sight that might recur and so recall the feeling again. . . . Soot blew in grittily, settled on her hands. Her back remained at exactly the same angle, turned against the young man sitting with his hands drooping between his sprawled legs, and the lion, fallen on its side in the corner.

THE TRAIN HAD CAST the station like a skin. It called out to the sky, I'm coming, I'm coming; and again, there was no answer.

DYGARTSBUSH
WALTER D. EDMONDS

JOHN BORST WAS the first settler to come into Dygartsbush after the war. He came alone in the early fall of 1784, on foot, carrying a rifle, an axe, a brush scythe, a pair of blankets and a sack of cornmeal. He found the different lots hard to recognize, for there was no sign left of the houses. Only the charred butt logs remained, surrounding a layer of dead coals that the rain had long since beaten into the earth. The fields had gone to brush; the piece where he had had his corn was covered with a scrub of berry vines, rough grass and steeplebush. But near the center of it he found a stunted, slender little group of tiny cornstalks, tasseled out, with ears that looked like buds.

Whenever the work of clearing brush seemed everlasting, he would go over and look at that corn and think how good his first crop, seven years ago, had looked. It was good land, with a southerly slope and water nearby. That was why he had come back to it. Other people were pushing westward, but the war had taught John Borst to prefer the things he knew and remembered.

After he found that his wife had been taken captive to the Indians' towns, he had joined the army. They had given him a fifty-dollar bounty and a uniform. As soon as his enlistment ended, he volunteered for the militia levies and was assigned a land bounty of two hundred acres. This he had left with Mr. Paris, of Stone Arabia, who was now with the legislature in New York City, to sell for him on a commission basis.

If he were lucky enough to sell, he would become comparatively rich; but John Borst was a methodical man who did not believe in waiting for good luck. When he had his land readied again, and his house rebuilt, it would be time enough to think of buying stock and household goods.

He needed next to nothing now. He lived on his cornmeal and the pigeons he knocked off a roosting tree at dusk each evening. All his daylight hours he spent in the field, cutting down the brush for burning. He slept in a small lean-to, and it was at nights, as he lay in his blankets and watched the fire dying, that he felt lonely. He had had no inclination to remarry, though he knew of several men whose women had been carried off by the Indians and who had taken new wives. But he had never got over his feeling that Delia would come back. He felt it more strongly here in Dygartsbush than he had in the past seven years.

At nights he would remember her in their one month of married life—the way she knelt in front of the fire and handled the pans and dishes; sitting beside him fixing his clothes after the meal; getting ready for bed when he had stepped outside the last thing. He would come in to find her in her nightdress, combing her brown hair before the hearth, and the light of the red coals showed him the shadow of her long, straight body.

He worked alone all through September. In October, when the dry winds began to parch the ground, he burned his land. Then, when he was ready to return to Fort Plain, three men turned up in Dygartsbush.

When he first sighted them, he went for his rifle. There had been cases, during the past two years, of settlers who had gone back to their farms being murdered by Indians or renegades. But the men shouted to him that they were friends, and as they came nearer, he saw that one of them was Honus Kelly.

With Kelly were two New Englanders, named Hartley and Phelps, who came to look over the land. Honus explained that he was selling some lots that touched on John's land. Hartley and Phelps liked the country and suggested to John that the four of them raise three cabins, so that in the spring they could move in.

John had not figured on building his cabin that fall, but the men had horses to skid the logs, and it seemed like a good chance to get his house built without using cash. He spent half that night deciding that he would build his new house exactly on the site of the old one. When Honus Kelly asked him why, he replied that in 1776 it had seemed to him the best site, and he had found no reason to change his mind now. In the back of his mind, however, was the thought of how it would seem to Delia when she came back. With the cabin raised, the place would look to her the way it had the day he had brought her in the first time. "My, it's a nice house, John. I think it's beautiful." He remembered her words, her fresh deep voice. That was the first time she had not sounded shy.

They built the three cabins in the next three weeks, and John helped them burn their land. Then they left to file their deeds and return to New England for their families. They would come back, they said, as soon as the roads were passable.

"Ain't you coming out with us, John?" Honus asked him.

John said no. He would stay and do finishing work on his cabin and maybe fell some timber over in the hardwood lot, so that he could put in wheat the next fall.

"Delia ought to be back next summer," Honus said understandingly. "They're going to have a treaty with the Indians this month and ask for all prisoners to get sent back. They wouldn't kill a girl like Delia. They liked her." He turned to the two New Englanders. "I'd probably have my hair hanging on an Indian post right now if it wasn't for John's wife. She helped me get away after they took us. They killed every other man but me and my brother and John here. Delia's a fine girl; she'll make a good neighbor for your families."

John flushed. Phelps, the older of the two, said it would be fine for his wife to have a woman neighbor. Especially for his mother-in-law, who didn't like the idea of their coming. He would tell his mother-in-law about Mrs. Borst.

"Tell her she's pretty," said Honus. "One of the prettiest women I ever saw."

John did not flush again. It was a fact, not flattery. The younger man, Hartley, looked around the clearing as if he were trying to imagine what an Indian raid was like. "Must've been pretty bad," he said.

Honus said, "It was bad enough." And they went off.

It seemed lonelier to John the day after they left. Then the rainy weather set in, and he hunted a deer and spent time on his new cabin. The men had had some paper, which he used in his window, and the inside of the cabin he fixed up with shelves. He went out when the snow came, and worked at what he could find around Fort Plain, and trapped a little.

In the spring he had thirty dollars left of his bounty money and thirty-five dollars' profit from trapping. He bought a mare for thirty-five dollars, a heifer in calf for twelve, and three hogs for four dollars, at a bargain. With what was left he bought his corn seed, a log chain and a plow, and hired a man to help him drive in his stock.

He was starting his planting when the Phelpses came in: Phelps, his wife, one child, and Mrs. Cutts, his mother-in-law, a thin-faced woman with a dry way of speaking.

The Hartleys came later, hardly in time to plant. Mrs. Hartley was a frightened-acting girl who seemed to take a fancy to John. She was always running over to be neighborly, offering to mend his things. Once she took them home with her when he was out. He went over next day to get them back and thank her, and looking around her cabin, he thought privately that if Mrs. Hartley put her mind to it, she would find so much work to do she would not have time to take on his. She gave him a loaf of bread, and when he got home he found that it was soggy in the middle.

But he had to admit that the sight of even Mrs. Hartley, who was a pretty-looking girl for all her sloppy ways, made him lonely. Next day, though he could have put off the trip for another week, he rode his mare to Fort Plain for flour and stopped in to see Honus Kelly. He asked Honus whether any women had been brought in from the Indian towns.

Honus thought quite a few had. "They most of them get left at Fort Stanwix." He seemed to understand how John felt. "Anyway, when Delia shows up, she'll most probably come through here. I'll tell her you're back at Dygartsbush."

"Thanks," said John. He fumbled around for a minute. "Do you think there's any chance of her coming back?"

"Sure I do. I told you before, the Indian that took her treated her real good." Honus didn't feel it was his business to tell John the old Indian planned to make a squaw of her.

"Yes, you told me that." John Borst looked out the window. "I wonder if it would do any good if I went out looking for her. They say it's safe enough traveling in the Indian country."

"You'd probably never find her that way, and she might turn up just after you left here."

"I guess that's right." Honus had told him that before too. John said good-by and went over to the store. He bought himself some flour and a bag of salt and some salt beef. He didn't know quite how it was, but when he happened to see a new bolt of dress goods, he decided to buy some. Later, he decided it was because the brown striping reminded him of the color of her hair. He told the storekeeper's wife he wanted enough for a tall girl, about so high, and he held his hand level with his cheekbones.

He started back about two hours before sunset, and it was after dark when he reached the outskirts of Dygartsbush. He could see, off on his left, the light from the Hartleys' cabin, a single small square glow, appearing and disappearing among the trees with the mare's progress. He did not see any light from the Phelpses', but he heard the child crying.

By the time he reached his own clearing, the sound of crying had died away and he was alone, with no companionship but the sound of the mare's hoofs and the motion of her walk between his legs. He rode heavily, paying no attention to the trail, and he was entirely unprepared when the mare stopped short, snorting, her head raised and ears pointed. Looking toward the far end of the clearing, he saw a light in his own window. It made a dim orange pattern on the paper panes. He could see a spark jumping from the chimney mouth, and he guessed someone had freshened a fire on the hearth.

He dismounted and got his rifle ready in his hand. Honus had told him that there were still a few Tories and Indians who had lived along the valley, who were trying to get back. Down in Fort Plain they had an organization to deal with them.

He knew how far the light reached when the door was opened. Before he came into the area he slapped the mare's flank. She stepped ahead quickly, passing the door to go around to the shed. John lay down in the grass, with his rifle pointed.

The door opened, shedding its light over the mare. A whippoorwill had started singing, but John did not hear it. A woman was standing in the door, looking out with large eyes at the mare. The woman cupped her hands on each side of her face, to act as blinders from the light, and stepped past the mare. He could see her plain now. She wore Indian clothes, moccasins and skirt and a loose overdress. He could tell by her height who she was.

He got up slowly, a little uncertain in his arms and legs, walked over to her and leaned on his rifle and looked into her face to make sure.

But he knew anyway. She stood erect, looking back at him, her hands hanging at her sides. He did not think she had changed, except for her Indian clothes and the way she wore her hair in two braids over her breast. He saw her lips part to say, "I'm back, John," but her voice was the barest whisper. He shifted a little so that her face, turning with him, came into the light, showing him again, after seven years, the curve of her cheek and the tenderness of her mouth. Then he saw that her eyes were wet. Neither of them heard the whippoorwill still calling in the young corn.

AT TIMES, JOHN BORST had the feeling that he and Delia had taken up their lives exactly where they were the night the Indians raided Dygartsbush. That night also, he had been coming home from Fort Plain with flour, almost at the same time, but afoot instead of riding his own mare.

That night might have been a dream—the burning cabins and the firing, and the rain. He had come into Hawyer's clearing just in time to see the Indians reach that place. He had seen Hawyer shot in his door and Mrs. Hawyer hauled out of the house. An Indian had her by the hair and was dragging her, the way a man might lug along a stubborn dog to put it out for the night. Then they had spotted John, half a dozen of them, and he had set out to run for the fort.

He told Delia about it the day after her return—they had not done any talking that first night. He told her how he had got fifteen men to come back with him and how they had found every house in ashes.

They had picked up the tracks at the end of his lot, followed them for half a dozen miles. Then they had come back and buried the dead. That task had taken them the rest of the day.

Delia had been crouching in front of the fire, like an Indian squaw, and while he talked she had suddenly got down on her knees, the way she used to do. Now she lifted her face, and her eyes regarded him with their old searching, level glance.

"Did you think I was dead, John?"

He thought awhile. "No. But I thought I probably wouldn't ever see you again. I joined the army. There wasn't anything left for me here, and I didn't get back for more'n a year. Then I found out that Caty Breen had got back. She's living up in Kingsland now. Honus told me about it."

"Honus was good to me, John."

"He told me how you helped him get away."

"What else did he tell you?"

John looked at her. "Why, I don't know. Just that he didn't think the Indians would hurt you any. He said the one that took you thought a lot of you. He had a comic name, High Grass, I think."

"Yes, High Grass. Gasotena."

She drew her breath slowly and became quite still. He had noticed that about her in the one day she had been home—the way she fell into a stillness. Not silence, for she always answered him at once if he said anything. He did not know how to describe it to himself. Maybe, he thought, she felt strange with him. Seven years was a long time to be away from a man; maybe a woman got to feeling different about things.

He said, "It must be queer, coming back to me after so long. Must seem like taking up with a man without getting married, almost." He tried to say it in a light, joking kind of way.

But she whirled, lifting her face and looking closely into his. "What makes you say that?" He saw her lips tremble and become still.

"I didn't mean to make you jump. I thought, maybe, there was things you'd disremembered about me. Things maybe you didn't like so well."

He could see her throat fill and empty.

"Did you think that last night?"

He felt himself coloring. "No."

"Are there things about me?"

"No," he said. "God, no." There was visible pain in her eyes. He was a fool, he thought. "Look out, Delia. That fat's catching fire."

She turned back to the cooking quickly and silently, and he looked at her. She had done up her hair in braids wound around her head, but she still wore her Indian clothing. It was good to work in, she said. Now she was still again for a long time, and he thought she had gone off into one of her spells until she began to speak. Her voice was throaty and pitched low, and she seemed to have difficulty with her words.

She said, "I used to wonder if you'd got caught. But they never brought in your scalp. I got to believe you were alive, John. Then after I'd been in the Indian town for a while I began to think I'd have to stay there all my life. It seemed as if I didn't have anything to hope for. The Indians were good to me, but it wasn't like white people being good to you. Work helped, somehow, but no work you did was for yourself. No house belongs to any one person among the Indians. Their gardens are for the whole house, all the people in it. The squaws didn't ever plant flowers by their houses. I used to think about the little dark red pinks I planted just outside the door and wonder if they ever blowed, and I used to wonder and wonder about you, what you were doing, and who you were with. When they told me about the treaty and said I could go home, I was afraid, John. I thought maybe you'd found another woman and married her."

"I saw plenty," he said. "I never had the urge to marry."

"I didn't know that. I wouldn't have blamed you, though. But I had to come back to find out. Ganowauges brought me. He knew the southern way better, and he said he'd bring me as far as Fort Plain. I asked him if we could come through here and he said we could. We got here just about dark, John. We came in the same way Gasotena took me away. We came out of the woods and I looked and saw the house, just the way it was, right in the same place. I was so frightened I could scarcely move. Ganowauges pointed to it and told me to go. I asked him if he would wait. I thought then I would go back with him if there was a woman in it. He said he'd rather wait in the woods. I went to the house, John. I had to see what she looked like."

"She wasn't there, was she?"

Delia glanced at him in a startled way, saw his eyes, and tried to smile. "No. First I thought maybe you'd taken her to Fort Plain with you. Then I went inside and I saw you'd been living alone."

"How did you know that?"

She smiled this time, to herself.

"I knew it was you too. I could tell because of the way the tooth twig was laid against the sack of gunpowder. You always laid it standing up so the brush end would dry out. It was so much the same. I just sat down and cried. I forgot all about Ganowauges. I never even thanked him. John, did you build the house right here on purpose?"

He said, "Yes."

He saw her eyelids trembling, and got up and went out to wash. When he came in again she seemed peaceful. She had laid out their food on the board table. He said, "The house isn't so well fixed. But I'll get a glass sash before winter and a chest of drawers for you to keep your clothes in. I've got a little money left."

She drew a deep breath, looking around.

"It's all ours. John, I don't care if we're poor. All I want to do is work for you, and for you to be happy, and have you care for me the way you used to. I'm older than I was, but I'm healthy and strong, still. . . ." Her voice trailed off.

He said, "You look all right." He felt strangely troubled. He could not tell why. He tried to talk about something else. "I'll have to take you over to the neighbors. They're Yankee people. But I like the Phelpses. I like Mrs. Cutts too."

"Which one is she?"

"Mrs. Phelps's mother. Hartleys are always borrowing. They mean all right. They're just shiftless." He got up. "Guess I'll begin mowing grass over in the swale this afternoon. We got to have hay for the mare and cow, next winter."

"We didn't have a cow and horse before, did we? It makes it seem more like a farm, even if we haven't got a glass window. When's the cow due?"

"They thought in September. I think maybe August. I had a chance to get her cheap," he explained. "I meant to get a window first."

"I'd rather have the cow. I used to make butter fine."

John went out, leaving her looking happy, he thought. More the way she used to be. He took his scythe and went toward the swale; but as soon as he entered the woods he made a circuit and moved along the edge of the woods until he was opposite the door. There, in crushed ferns, John found the imprint of the Indian's body. He must have lain there for quite a while. Probably he had been there when John came home from Fort Plain. He didn't like the thought of it, even though the Indian hadn't done anything.

Delia came to the door and stood for a moment, resting her weight on one hip and staring after the way John had gone. He thought he had never seen her look so pretty as she did in her Indian dress. Just why, he wasn't sure. He thought maybe it was the strangeness of it—as if she were something he didn't really have a right to. After a moment she let her head bend, and then she turned and put up her arm against the jamb of the door and rested her forehead on it. She might have been crying.

Suddenly it came to John that he was spying on his wife. His face reddened, even though he knew himself alone and unobserved; and he went back through the edge of the woods, cut across to the swale and began mowing. He prided himself on being a four-acre mower, but that afternoon he could not put his heart into it. The image of his wife leaning her head against the doorjamb kept coming before his eyes to trouble him.

SHE BECAME SUDDENLY shy of the idea of calling on the neighbors, and after twice mentioning it, John let her alone. But next day, meeting Phelps, who had come over to mow his half of the swale, John thought it only polite to mention Delia's return. Phelps thought it was almost miraculous and vowed he would tell his womenfolk that evening. John explained that Delia felt hesitant about meeting people. She had no decent clothes yet. Just the Indian things she had come home with. Phelps said he understood.

But Mrs. Cutts was a curious woman, and made a point of passing through Borst's clearing on her way home from the berry patch on Dygart's knoll. With no warning, Delia had no decent chance of getting out of her way, and when Mrs. Cutts asked if she could come in, Delia smiled uncertainly and stood aside from the door.

"It's a good thing for John you've come back, Mrs. Borst," said the old woman, sitting down. "My, the sun's hot. But I got some dandy strawberries. I'll leave you some. I've got a real likin' for John." Her keen old eyes examined Delia frankly. "Phelps—I always called him Phelps; he used to be my hired man—Phelps said you was shy about your clothes. Land sakes! If I was a part as pretty in them, I wouldn't be living with my son-in-law."

She smiled as Delia flushed.

"You ain't very talkative, are you?" she asked after a moment.

Delia got even pinker. "It's hard to be with people again—white people, I mean."

"It must have been hard," said Mrs. Cutts. "Did they burn everything you had?"

Delia nodded. "But I don't seem to mind it now. The bad part was wondering what had happened to John." She walked over to the window. "I don't like to think about it, Mrs. Cutts."

"No wonder. I expect they made a kind of slave out of you. Indians do that with their own women, I've heard tell."

"Squaws don't think they're slaves. So they didn't treat me bad by their lights. You see, I got adopted into a house."

Mrs. Cutts studied her shrewdly.

"You mean you was just like one of them?"

Delia nodded.

"I guess that's why you feel uneasy with white women. Listen, Mrs. Borst," she said. "I don't know what happened to you out there. I don't want to know unless you want to tell me. But I like John. You won't make him happy if you keep troubling yourself about what happened. It wasn't your fault, was it?"

Delia shook her head.

"You're healthy and pretty-looking, and you're still young. It's not so easy for a woman to begin over as it is for a man—I don't know why. But you can do it if you want to."

Delia swung around on the old woman, who now had stooped to pick up her berries. "Give me a dish, dearie, and I'll fill it from my pail."

But Delia made no move. She stared at Mrs. Cutts with painful intensity. "What do you think happened to me, Mrs. Cutts?"

"I don't know. It's not my business and I'm not asking. Don't you worry. My tongue's my own, and I keep it where it belongs." She gave Delia a hearty smile. "Now, where's a dish?"

Mrs. Cutts heaped the dish with the fresh berries and went out of the door. She was a dozen yards down the path before Delia thought of thanking her.

She ran after the old woman, who by then had her shawl over her head and was stumping along like a vigorous witch. Delia moved so quietly in her Indian moccasins that she startled Mrs. Cutts.

"I meant to thank you for the berries. They're lovely."

"You're real welcome to them," said Mrs. Cutts. "When you feel ready to, come over and see us."

"Thank you. I'll walk along a way with you."

"That's neighborly."

Mrs. Cutts did not speak. She thought maybe the girl would unload her trouble. She knew she had one, and the only way to get her to tell it was by keeping quiet.

But Delia walked also in silence. She was a good head taller than Mrs. Cutts. Glancing sideways, the old woman could see the thoughtfulness in her face. They reached the fork of the path without having said another word. Mrs. Cutts wasn't planning to say anything, but at the last moment she unexpectedly made up her mind.

"Delia Borst," she said, "just remember that there's some things a man is a lot happier for not knowing. It may be hard on you, but it's true."

"The man might find out sometime. Then what would he think?"

"I'd let him take his chance of it."

Delia looked over the top of Mrs. Cutts's shawl.

"But I love John," she said.

SHE MADE UP HER mind to tell him that night. But she didn't say anything until she had given him his corn bread and broth, and then she came at it roundabout.

"Mrs. Cutts stopped in this morning, John. We had a talk." Delia got the dish of berries. "She left these. I didn't like her at first, but after a while I thought she was nice. We got talking about what men think."

"Did you?"

"She said it was better for a man not to be told everything by his wife."

John said, "I guess that depends on the wife."

"That's what I said." She finished her berries and sat still, leaning slightly toward him over the table. Her hands were folded on the table edge, so that when she leaned against them she could feel the beating of her heart. She turned her eyes to her husband's. "John, I've been home most of a week, and you've never asked me what happened in Onondarha, the town I lived in."

John Borst also had become quiet. His big hands, which had been resting on the table, he put into his lap. She could imagine them holding his knees. His heavy face with its slow-moving eyes stared back at her. She had never heard his voice sound the way it did when he finally spoke to her.

"I didn't ask you because I figured you would tell me what you wanted I should know. I've wondered what happened to you sometimes. I got crazy about it sometimes. But, now you're back, I don't want you to tell me what you don't want to."

She was surprised and touched. "Mrs. Cutts almost said the same thing, John. Do you know what I said? I said I loved you. Maybe it's bad to love someone too much."

"Maybe," he said. It sounded stupid. He could see her trembling— the complete quiet of her struggle with herself.

"I've got to tell you, John. You can send me away then if you want."

"I won't never send you away."

"I won't take that for a promise," she said. "You've got to listen. I can't bear you loving me unless you know. High Grass, the Indian that took me, got me adopted into his house. The women dressed me up and showed me how to make a cake and told me to give it to the old woman of the house. I didn't know what they said; I hadn't learned Indian then. You believe that?"

His voice sounded heavy. "Yes, I believe it."

"I didn't know I was getting married. I wanted to please them. I wanted to stay alive, so I could come back to you. I didn't know till night, when he came into my place. There were thirty people in that house all round me, John."

He didn't say anything. He didn't look at her. Her voice became more urgent.

"I couldn't do anything. Anything, John. I couldn't. I didn't think I could live."

"You did, though."

"Yes, I did." She sounded suddenly calmer. "After a year, I had a baby, John. He was the only thing I loved. . . . No, I didn't love him, either. Every time I saw him I thought of you. I thought how you'd hate me."

"I don't hate you."

Her lips stayed parted. She licked them suddenly with her tongue, but even then she could not speak. After a while John got up. He turned to look out of the door.

"Where's the baby?"

"He died."

"You didn't leave him, did you?"

"No, John."

"That would have been bad. Did you have any more children?"

"No." She whispered, leaning forward over the table. "I couldn't have come back, leaving a child, could I? And I couldn't come back with one. I thought, when he died, it was like Providence telling me I could come back. I knew I had to tell you, but when I got here, I couldn't, John. Honestly, I'm sorry."

He didn't notice her.

"This High Grass," he said. "What's he doing?"

"He went off on a war party. He didn't come back. They told me he got killed."

"My God," he said. "I can't do nothing."

He turned through the door abruptly, leaving her at the table. She could hear him walking around, but she could not move. She waited like a prisoner until at last he came in. He said, "Ain't you done the dishes?" But she only shook her head and watched him. "Come on," he said. "I'll help you."

She rose slowly, reaching for the dishes blindly. "Do you want me to stay?"

He turned on her, his voice heavy with sarcasm. "Where in hell could you go to this time of night?"

AN OUTSIDER WOULD have seen nothing unusual in their relations. Delia herself sometimes almost persuaded herself that John was putting what she had told him from his mind. But, in a day or so, she would catch him watching her; and at such times something in his eyes made her feel whipped and humiliated. She accepted the feeling as part of the payment she would have to make for what had happened to her. A good woman, she thought, a Christian saint, would have died first. But Delia hadn't wanted to die; she had wanted to get back to John; now she must take the future with patience.

It was hard to be patient, living with John. Times were when she wanted to cry out, Stop looking at me that way. I'd rather you'd whip me, if you wanted. I didn't do anything bad. While they were working together in the field, it was more like old times; but in the evenings, in the intimate darkness, their reserve came between them. She felt that he thought of her as just a useful body, something one accepted as one accepted the weather. But her resentment was less against him—she remembered how he had waited seven years for her and built the cabin where she expected it to be—than against the Providence that had played tricks with her.

One way he had changed was in laying down the law about their neighbors. He said he didn't want the neighbors to think he wasn't proud to show her off, and he kept after her until she had made a dress from the calico he had brought. She could hardly bear to touch it.

They made the visits one Sunday, she in the calico that felt like a cold rag touching her limply, he with his coat brushed. They went first to the Hartley house—to get the worst part over quick, John said. Delia disliked them both, but John was pleased the way the Phelpses took to her and she to them. He would feel uneasy about leaving Delia alone when he went down to Fort Plain, if she didn't have a place she could go to. Mrs. Cutts had said they'd be glad to have Delia visit them the next time he went down.

The old woman had guessed, with one look, that something had happened between the Borsts. She took John aside as they were leaving and said, "John, I want to tell you I think she's one of the best sort of women. You can see she's honest." Then she added, "When a person's young, he or she's likely to set a lot of store in notions that don't amount to much when they get older." She gave his shoulder a sharp pat and sent him after his wife before he could think of a reply.

He walked silently and morosely until he and Delia were near home. Then he asked, "Did you tell Mrs. Cutts anything about you and that Indian?"

As she turned her head to answer, he could see that she was close to tears. "No. I didn't think anybody but you had any right to know."

Thank God, he thought, Mrs. Cutts wasn't a talkative woman. She was smart, though, and she had probably guessed. He couldn't hold it against Delia. He watched her getting supper, and then got down his rifle to oil it. He would have to go down to Fort Plain again soon, and he thought he might as well go that week. Anything to get out of the house. He glanced up, to surprise her covertly studying him from the hearth. She turned her head at once, paling slightly. She made him think of an abused dog when she did that, and he felt a senseless burst of anger.

"What do you always want to be staring at me for?"

"I didn't mean to be staring at you. I didn't want to make you mad." She watched the fire. Then, "You hate me, don't you, John?"

"No. I don't hate you. But I can't stand that way you look." He got up suddenly to replace the gun. "Don't start talking that way, either."

"I can't talk at all, can I?" She turned on her knees to face him. "John, what sense is there in us living together like this?"

"Stop it. I'm going out. When you've got the supper ready, I'll come in. I'm going to look at the heifer."

It was a feeble excuse. He felt ashamed. The heifer wasn't due for a couple of weeks yet. He tramped down to the shed and looked her over. He stayed there, fussing aimlessly about nothing, until he heard Delia's tentative call. When he entered the house, he felt an impulse to say something that would make her feel better.

"I guess I'll go down to Fort Plain tomorrow," he said. "I've got to get flour, and I might as well go sooner as later. Maybe I'll hear something about my bounty land."

Neither of them believed he would hear.

"I'm sorry I talked that way," he said.

The corners of her mouth quivered. "I know it's hard for you, John. It's hard for me. When you talk like that and look that way, you make me feel like something dirty."

He relapsed sullenly into silence.

THOUGH IT WAS RAINING, he started next morning and reached Fort Plain toward noon. He did his trading, finding that the price of salt beef had risen like everything else. Flour was pretty near prohibitive, as far as he was concerned. Then he went around to Honus Kelly's to ask whether there had been any news from Mr. Paris about his bounty land. Honus had gone out earlier that morning, he was told; no, no word had come about his land. He might find Honus down at the tavern. So John went down to the tavern. Nobody was in the place except Frank, the landlord, and a couple of women in the kitchen. John ordered some cold pork and a glass of blackstrap.

The landlord said, "Quite some rain, ain't it?"

John said it was, and asked for Honus Kelly.

"He come in this morning," the tavern keeper said casually. "He got Walrath, Pierce and the two Devendorfs, and they went off after an Indian that was in here."

John said, "That's too bad. I wanted to see him. What about the Indian?"

A stout, red-cheeked woman brought in a plate of sliced fresh ham, bread, a cold roast potato with a slice of raw onion leaning against it. The landlord leaned over it as if to smell the onion.

"Why, he acted all right when he come in here. Said he was heading south, and asked about the settlements. I said there was some people living in Dygartsbush." The landlord looked up. "Why, that's where you're settled, ain't it? I forgot. You don't come down much."

John left off eating. His big face leaned intently toward the tavern keeper's. "What was the matter with him?"

The tavern keeper poured himself a drink.

"Makes my stomach turn to think of it. He got a couple of rums inside and commenced acting big. I told him to behave himself. I said we killed fresh Indians round here, but he just slammed his hand axe down on the bar and said he'd kill me if I didn't behave myself, the lousy skunk! I didn't dast move out of the tap. So I just waited, and pretty soon he said he'd had enough, and I told him what he owed me. Then you know what he did? He hauled out a kind of funny-looking purse and held it out for me to look at. Mister, it was the skin off a human hand. Looked to me like a woman's, honest to God."

The tavern keeper looked into John's flushed face.

"Makes you feel ugly, don't it? He paid me and went right through that door, putting that purse back in his coat pocket, and he clumb the fence and went into the woods. I tell you, I went right after Honus."

"How long was it before Honus got after him?"

"'Bout an hour and a half. Honus has got the boys organized pretty well. I figure he'll pick him up before too long."

John spoke slowly, half to himself. "It's hard tracking in a rain like this one. What did the Indian look like?"

"Why," he said, "looked like any Indian. He had on an old hat and a coat he'd probably stole. Looked pretty old—he'd let his hair grow, and there was some white in it. But he was fat. He had the biggest stomach you ever saw."

"Did he say what his name was?"

"Said he was Christian boy. Called himself Joe Conjocky. Ever hear of him?"

John pulled out his purse. "What do I owe you?"

"You've hardly et."

John picked up his rifle and started. But he stopped in the doorway. "Did you tell Honus how that Indian asked about Dygartsbush?"

"Why, no. Come to think of it, I guess I didn't."

"You fool!"

JOHN WENT OUT. He didn't run, but his big legs took him swiftly along the muddy road to the barn. He saddled his mare, packed on his flour and beef and salt, and reprimed his rifle. It was still raining.

The wind brought the rain against their faces, and the mare flickered the first drops from her ears. He swung up on her and headed her home. He had a sick feeling in his insides: twenty miles, a wet trail, and the Indian had started at about ten o'clock. John figured it would be past one, now. Even if he pushed the mare, he could not expect to reach his cabin before suppertime. Delia would be coming back from the Phelpses' long before that. He felt a sudden blaze of anger. If the tavern keeper had only had the sense to tell Honus, Honus would have headed straight for Dygartsbush. But now Honus wouldn't hurry. He'd follow his usual plan of getting up with the Indian about dark and taking him by his campfire. The one sign of intelligence the fool tavern keeper had shown was to recognize the Indian as a bad one. He couldn't help it, though, after seeing that purse.

The mare came to the first ford and nearly lost her footing. John jerked her up and kicked her across. The rain fell into the gorge without much wind, but John could see the trees swaying on the rim of the rock walls. He managed to keep the mare trotting a good part of the time, sitting well forward and squinting his eyes to look into the rain.

He had told Delia to stay at the Phelpses' till he came home, but she would start out in time to get home well before him. She said a man ought not to come home from a long trip to have to wait for his food. She'd be there now, fixing the fire.

He seemed to see her kneeling in front of the fireplace, pink-cheeked. And he could see the fat figure of the Indian trotting along through the woods. Even a fat Indian could cover the ground; he'd have plenty of time to get there before dark. Delia wouldn't hear him. She wouldn't see anything, either, not even his face in the window, because the panes were made of paper. She'd only hear the door squeak on its wood hinges; and even then she'd think it was John.

"God help her," John said. He knew then that what had happened to Delia in the Indian country made no difference to him. It was what might happen to her before he could get home.

The ride became a nightmare for him. There was a lot of stony footing in the upper part of the creek section through which the mare had to take all the time she needed. On the high flats the woods thinned, and now and then he got a canter out of her. In the west the clouds showed signs of breaking, and he saw the sun once, nearly down, in a slit over the woods. Night came, however, when he was still three miles from home.

He thought he had made a mistake when he saw a light off the trail. For a minute it seemed to him that the mare must have done a lot better than he realized and that he had already reached Hartley's. Then he knew that the light was too close to the earth to come from Hartley's window. Someone was camping off the trail.

To be sure, he picked out the priming of his rifle for the second time and reprimed. Then he slid into the underbrush and began working his way up to the fire. He had not gone fifty yards before he saw that there were five men hunched around the fire. He recognized Honus Kelly's black beard.

John got to his feet and started for them, shouting Kelly's name. He saw them stop laughing and pick up their guns and roll out of the firelight, like a comical set of surprised hogs. When he got into the firelight, he couldn't see any more of them than the muzzles of their guns.

"John Borst," roared Kelly, rising up. "What are you doing here?"

"Where'd that Indian get to?" John asked.

"Oh, the Indian. How'd you know about him?"

"I've been down to Fort Plain. I heard about him in the tavern, from Frank. The fool said he didn't tell you the Indian was asking about my place."

"You didn't think he'd get away from us now, did you?" asked Honus. "The Indian's all right. He's just a piece above us."

Looking upward, John saw moccasined legs hanging beside the bole of a maple. The fat body was like a flour sack, three parts full, inside the old coat.

Honus Kelly, watching John's face, said, "Sit down. You'd better."

But John shook his head. He could hardly speak for a minute. He still wanted to get home, but he tried to be polite.

He said at last, "You boys better come back with me. It's only a short piece, and you can have a dry bed on the floor."

"No, thanks," said Honus. "We got a good place here." He saw that John was anxious to get on, so he rose to his feet and put his hand on John's shoulder and walked back with him toward the mare. "Delia and you won't be wanting a bunch like ourselves cluttering your place tonight," he said. Then he swore. "If Frank had told me about it, I'd have sent a couple of boys straight up to you. We had a time tracking him. But I always wanted to get even with that Indian. Don't you remember him? He used to hang out west of the settlement. Him and me had trouble over my trapline once or twice."

He watched while John mounted. Then he caught hold of the bridle and looked up, his eyes showing white over his beard. "You won't tell Delia?"

John shook his head.

"Best not," agreed Honus. "Well, good luck."

He slapped the mare's flank and let her go.

IT HAD STOPPED raining, but drops were still shaking off the leaves. The woods smelled of the rain, fresh and green, and the mare moved perkily. When she came into their clearing, John saw a light in the cabin window. He saw it with a quick uplifting of his heart, and he was glad now that Delia was pigheaded about being home before him. He remembered how it used to be before her return, coming home alone and fumbling his way in the dark.

He rode by to put the mare in the shed, and carried the load around to the door. It squeaked on its hinges as he pushed it open. Delia was kneeling by the fire, blowing it, her face flushed. She swung around easily. He had a quick recollection of the image he had made of the Indian entering. But her face wasn't afraid. It was only apologetic.

"I thought you weren't coming home, John. I let the fire go down. Then I heard the mare."

Her eyes were large and heavy from her effort to keep awake. He warmed himself before the sputtering fire, watching her struggle to get back her faculties. Suddenly she straightened up. "You're wet. You're hungry."

"I got delayed," he said. She went to the saddlebags, rummaging for food, and he said awkwardly, "I wanted to get some sausage, but beef was so dear I didn't have money left for it."

"Oh, John," she said. "I don't care." She started to heat water.

"There's a little tea, though, and half a dozen loaves of sugar."

"White sugar?"

"Yes. You'd better have tea with me."

"I don't need it."

He felt embarrassed and shy. He didn't know how to tell her what he wanted to. He couldn't say, I thought there was an Indian going to bust in on you and I got scared. But Honus hanged him, so it's all right. That wouldn't explain it to her at all. She was looking at him, too, in a queer, breathless, tentative way.

"You always used to like tea," he said. "You remember the first tea we had."

Her gaze was level, but her color had faded. Her voice became slow and her lips worked stiffly. "You said, 'Will you have some tea?'"

John for a moment became articulate. "No, I didn't say that."

"You did." The look in her face was suddenly pitiful.

But he shook his head at her. "I said, 'Will you have tea with me, Mrs. Borst?'"

She flushed brilliantly. "Oh, yes, John. And I said, 'I'd love to, Mr. Borst.'"

He needn't have worried about her understanding. It all passed between them, plain in their eyes. She didn't ask anything more.

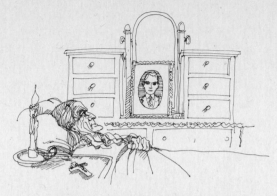

THE JILTING OF
GRANNY WEATHERALL

KATHERINE ANNE PORTER

She flicked her wrist neatly out of Doctor Harry's pudgy careful fingers and pulled the sheet up to her chin. The brat ought to be in knee breeches. Doctoring around the country with spectacles on his nose! "Get along now, take your schoolbooks and go. There's nothing wrong with me."

Doctor Harry spread a warm paw like a cushion on her forehead where the forked green vein danced and made her eyelids twitch. "Now, now, be a good girl, and we'll have you up in no time."

"That's no way to speak to a woman nearly eighty years old just because she's down. I'd have you respect your elders, young man."

"Well, Missy, excuse me." Doctor Harry patted her cheek. "But I've got to warn you, haven't I? You're a marvel, but you must be careful or you're going to be good and sorry."

"Don't tell me what I'm going to be. I'm on my feet now, morally speaking. It's Cornelia. I had to go to bed to get rid of her."

Her bones felt loose, and floated around in her skin, and Doctor Harry floated like a balloon around the foot of the bed. He floated and pulled down his waistcoat and swung his glasses on a cord. "Well, stay where you are, it certainly can't hurt you."

"Get along and doctor your sick," said Granny Weatherall. "Leave a well woman alone. I'll call for you when I want you. Where were you forty years ago when I pulled through milk leg and double pneu-

586

monia? You weren't even born. Don't let Cornelia lead you on," she shouted, because Doctor Harry appeared to float up to the ceiling and out. "I pay my own bills, and I don't throw my money away on nonsense!"

She meant to wave good-by, but it was too much trouble. Her eyes closed of themselves, it was like a dark curtain drawn around the bed. The pillow rose and floated under her, pleasant as a hammock in a light wind. She listened to the leaves rustling outside the window. No, somebody was swishing newspapers: no, Cornelia and Doctor Harry were whispering together. She leaped broad awake, thinking they whispered in her ear.

"She was never like this, *never* like this!" "Well, what can we expect?" "Yes, eighty years old. . . ."

Well, and what if she was? She still had ears. It was like Cornelia to whisper around doors. She always kept things secret in such a public way. She was always being tactful and kind. Cornelia was dutiful; that was the trouble with her. Dutiful and good: "So good and dutiful," said Granny, "that I'd like to spank her." She saw herself spanking Cornelia and making a fine job of it.

"What'd you say, Mother?"

Granny felt her face tying up in hard knots.

"Can't a body think, I'd like to know?"

"I thought you might want something."

"I do. I want a lot of things. First off, go away and don't whisper."

She lay and drowsed, hoping in her sleep that the children would keep out and let her rest a minute. It had been a long day. Not that she was tired. It was always pleasant to snatch a minute now and then. There was always so much to be done, let me see: tomorrow.

Tomorrow was far away and there was nothing to trouble about. Things were finished somehow when the time came; thank God there was always a little margin over for peace: then a person could spread out the plan of life and tuck in the edges orderly. It was good to have everything clean and folded away, with the hairbrushes and tonic bottles sitting straight on the white embroidered linen: the day started without fuss and the pantry shelves laid out with rows of jelly glasses and brown jugs and white stone-china jars with blue whirligigs and words painted on them: coffee, tea, sugar, ginger, cinnamon, allspice: and the bronze clock with the lion on top nicely dusted off. The dust that lion could collect in twenty-four hours! The box in the attic with all those letters tied up, well, she'd have to go through that tomorrow. All those letters—George's letters and John's letters and her letters to them both—lying around for the children to find afterwards made her uneasy. Yes, that would be tomorrow's business. No use to let them know how silly she had been once.

While she was rummaging around she found death in her mind and it felt clammy and unfamiliar. She had spent so much time preparing for death there was no need for bringing it up again. Let it take care of itself now. When she was sixty she had felt very old, finished, and went around making farewell trips to see her children and grandchildren, with a secret in her mind: This is the very last of your mother, children! Then she made her will and came down with a long fever. That was all just a notion like a lot of other things, but it was lucky too, for she had once for all got over the idea of dying for a long time. Now she couldn't be worried. She hoped she had better sense now. Her father had lived to be one hundred and two years old and had drunk a noggin of strong hot toddy on his last birthday. He told the reporters it was his daily habit, and he owed his long life to that. He had made quite a scandal and was very pleased about it. She believed she'd just plague Cornelia a little.

"Cornelia! Cornelia!" No footsteps, but a sudden hand on her cheek. "Bless you, where have you been?"

"Here, Mother."

"Well, Cornelia, I want a noggin of hot toddy."

"Are you cold, darling?"

"I'm chilly, Cornelia. Lying in bed stops the circulation. I must have told you that a thousand times."

Well, she could just hear Cornelia telling her husband that Mother was getting a little childish and they'd have to humor her. The thing that most annoyed her was that Cornelia thought she was deaf, dumb, and blind. Little hasty glances and tiny gestures tossed around her and over her head saying, "Don't cross her, let her have her way, she's eighty years old," and she sitting there as if she lived in a thin glass cage. Sometimes Granny almost made up her mind to pack up and move back to her own house where nobody could remind her every minute that she was old. Wait, wait, Cornelia, till your own children whisper behind your back!

In her day she had kept a better house and had got more work done. She wasn't too old yet for Lydia to be driving eighty miles for advice when one of the children jumped the track, and Jimmy still dropped in and talked things over: "Now, Mammy, you've a good business head, I want to know what you think of this? . . ." Old. Cornelia couldn't change the furniture around without asking. Little things, little things! They had been so sweet when they were little. Granny wished the old days were back again with the children young and everything to be done over. It had been a hard pull, but not too much for her. When she thought of all the food she had cooked, and all the clothes she had cut and sewed, and all the gardens she had made—well, the children showed it. There they were, made out of her, and they couldn't get away from that. Sometimes she wanted to see John again and point to them and say, Well, I didn't do so badly, did I? But that would have to wait. That was for tomorrow. She used to think of him as a man, but now all the children were older than their father, and he would be a child beside her if she saw him now. It seemed strange and there was something wrong in the idea. Why, he couldn't possibly recognize her. She had fenced in a hundred acres once, digging the post holes herself and clamping the wires with just a negro boy to help. That changed a woman. John would be looking for a young woman with the peaked Spanish comb in her hair and the painted fan. Digging post holes changed a woman. Riding country roads in the winter when women had their babies was another thing: sitting up nights with sick horses and sick negroes and sick children and hardly ever losing one. John, I hardly ever lost one of them! John would see that in a minute, that would be something he could understand, she wouldn't have to explain anything!

It made her feel like rolling up her sleeves and putting the whole place to rights again. No matter if Cornelia was determined to be every-where at once, there were a great many things left undone on this place. She would start tomorrow and do them. It was good to be strong enough for everything, even if all you made melted and changed and slipped under your hands, so that by the time you finished you almost forgot what you were working for. What was it I set out to do? she asked herself intently, but she could not remember. A fog rose over the valley, she saw it marching across the creek swallowing the trees and moving up the hill like an army of ghosts. Soon it would be at the near edge of the orchard, and then it was time to go in and light the lamps. Come in, children, don't stay out in the night air.

Lighting the lamps had been beautiful. The children huddled up to her and breathed like little calves waiting at the bars in the twilight. Their eyes followed the match and watched the flame rise and settle in a blue curve, then they moved away from her. The lamp was lit, they didn't have to be scared and hang on to Mother anymore. Never, never, never more. God, for all my life I thank Thee. Without Thee, my God, I could never have done it. Hail, Mary, full of grace.

I want you to pick all the fruit this year and see that nothing is wasted. There's always someone who can use it. Don't let good things rot for want of using. You waste life when you waste good food. Don't let things get lost. It's bitter to lose things. Now, don't let me get to thinking, not when I am tired and taking a little nap before supper. . . .

The pillow rose about her shoulders and pressed against her heart and the memory was being squeezed out of it: oh, push down the pillow, somebody: it would smother her if she tried to hold it. Such a fresh breeze blowing and such a green day with no threats in it. But he had not come, just the same. What does a woman do when she has put on the white veil and set out the white cake for a man and he doesn't come? She tried to remember. No, I swear he never harmed me but in that. He never harmed me but in that . . . and what if he did? There was the day, the day, but a whirl of dark smoke rose and covered it, crept up and over into the bright field where everything was planted so carefully in orderly rows. That was hell, she knew hell when she saw it. For sixty years she had prayed against remembering him and against losing her soul in the deep pit of hell, and now the two things were mingled in one and the thought of him was a smoky cloud from hell that moved and crept in her head when she had just got rid of Doctor Harry and was trying to rest a minute. Wounded vanity, Ellen, said a sharp voice in the top of her mind. Don't let your wounded vanity get the upper hand of you. Plenty of girls get jilted. You were jilted, weren't you? Then stand up to it. Her eyelids wavered and let in streamers of blue-gray light like tissue paper over her eyes. She must get up and pull the shades down or she'd never sleep. She was in bed again and the shades were not down. How could that happen? Better turn over, hide from the light, sleeping in the light gave you nightmares. "Mother, how do you feel now?" and a stinging wetness on her forehead. But I don't like having my face washed in cold water!

Hapsy? George? Lydia? Jimmy? No, Cornelia, and her features were swollen and full of little puddles. "They're coming, darling, they'll all be here soon." Go wash your face, child, you look funny.

Instead of obeying, Cornelia knelt down and put her head on the pillow. She seemed to be talking but there was no sound. "Well, are you tongue-tied? Whose birthday is it? Are you going to give a party?"

Cornelia's mouth moved urgently in strange shapes. "Don't do that, you bother me, daughter."

"Oh, no, Mother. Oh, no. . . ."

Nonsense. It was strange about children. They disputed your every word. "No what, Cornelia?"

"Here's Doctor Harry."

"I won't see that boy again. He just left five minutes ago."

"That was this morning, Mother. It's night now. Here's the nurse."

"This is Doctor Harry, Mrs. Weatherall. I never saw you look so young and happy!"

"Ah, I'll never be young again—but I'd be happy if they'd let me lie in peace and get rested."

She thought she spoke up loudly, but no one answered. A warm weight on her forehead, a warm bracelet on her wrist, and a breeze went on whispering, trying to tell her something. A shuffle of leaves in the everlasting hand of God, He blew on them and they danced and rattled. "Mother, don't mind, we're going to give you a little hypodermic." "Look here, daughter, how do ants get in this bed? I saw sugar ants yesterday." Did you send for Hapsy too?

It was Hapsy she really wanted. She had to go a long way back through a great many rooms to find Hapsy standing with a baby on her arm. She seemed to herself to be Hapsy also, and the baby on Hapsy's arm was Hapsy and himself and herself, all at once, and there was no surprise in the meeting. Then Hapsy melted from within and turned flimsy as gray gauze and the baby was a gauzy shadow, and Hapsy came up close and said, "I thought you'd never come," and looked at her very searchingly and said, "You haven't changed a bit!" They leaned forward to kiss, when Cornelia began whispering from a long way off, "Oh, is there anything you want to tell me? Is there anything I can do for you?"

Yes, she had changed her mind after sixty years and she would like to see George. I want you to find George. Find him and be sure to tell him I forgot him. I want him to know I had my husband just the same and my children and my house like any other woman. A good house too and a good husband that I loved and fine children out of him. Better than I hoped for even. Tell him I was given back everything he took away and more. Oh, no, oh, God, no, there was something else besides the house and the man and the children. Oh, surely they were not all? What was it? Something not given back. . . . Her breath crowded down under her ribs and grew into a monstrous frightening shape with cutting edges; it bored up into her head, and the agony was unbelievable: Yes, John, get the doctor now, no more talk, my time has come.

When this one was born it should be the last. The last. It should have been born first, for it was the one she had truly wanted. Everything came in good time. Nothing left out, left over. She was strong, in three days she would be as well as ever. Better. A woman needed milk in her to have her full health.

"Mother, do you hear me?"

"I've been telling you—"

"Mother, Father Connolly's here."

"I went to Holy Communion only last week. Tell him I'm not so sinful as all that."

"Father just wants to speak to you."

He could speak as much as he pleased. It was like him to drop in and inquire about her soul as if it were a teething baby, and then stay on for a cup of tea and a round of cards and gossip. He always had a funny story of some sort, usually about an Irishman who made his little mistakes and confessed them, and the point lay in some absurd thing he would blurt out in the confessional showing his struggles between native piety and original sin. Granny felt easy about her soul. Cornelia, where are your manners? Give Father Connolly a chair. She had her secret comfortable understanding with a few favorite saints who cleared a straight road to God for her. All as surely signed and sealed as the papers for the new Forty Acres. Forever . . . heirs and assigns forever. Since the day the wedding cake was not cut, but thrown out and wasted. The whole bottom dropped out of the world, and there she was blind and sweating with nothing under her feet and the walls falling away. His hand had caught her under the breast, she had not fallen, there was the freshly polished floor with the green rug on it, just as before. He had cursed like a sailor's parrot and said, "I'll kill him for you." Don't lay a hand on him, for my sake leave something to God. "Now, Ellen, you must believe what I tell you. . . ."

So there was nothing, nothing to worry about anymore, except sometimes in the night one of the children screamed in a nightmare, and they both hustled out shaking and hunting for the matches and calling, "There, wait a minute, here we are!" John, get the doctor now, Hapsy's time has come. But there was Hapsy standing by the bed in a white cap. "Cornelia, tell Hapsy to take off her cap. I can't see her plain."

Her eyes opened very wide and the room stood out like a picture she had seen somewhere. Dark colors with the shadows rising towards the ceiling in long angles. The tall black dresser gleamed with nothing on it but John's picture, enlarged from a little one, with John's eyes very black when they should have been blue. You never saw him, so how do you know how he looked? But the man insisted the copy was perfect, it was very rich and handsome. For a picture, yes, but it's not my husband. The table by the bed had a linen cover and a candle and a crucifix. The light was blue from Cornelia's silk lampshades. No sort of light at all, just frippery. You had to live forty years with kerosene lamps to appreciate honest electricity. She felt very strong and she saw Doctor Harry with a rosy nimbus around him.

"You look like a saint, Doctor Harry, and I vow that's as near as you'll ever come to it."

"She's saying something."

"I heard you, Cornelia. What's all this carrying-on?"

"Father Connolly's saying—"

Cornelia's voice staggered and bumped like a cart in a bad road. It rounded corners and turned back again and arrived nowhere. Granny stepped up in the cart very lightly and reached for the reins, but a man sat beside her and she knew him by his hands, driving the cart. She did not look in his face, for she knew without seeing, but looked instead down the road where the trees leaned over and bowed to each other and a thousand birds were singing a Mass. She felt like singing too, but she put her hand in the bosom of her dress and pulled out a rosary, and Father Connolly murmured Latin in a very solemn voice and tickled her feet. My God, will you stop that nonsense? I'm a married woman. What if he did run away and leave me to face the priest by myself? I found another a whole world better. I wouldn't have exchanged my husband for anybody except Saint Michael himself, and you may tell him that for me with a thank-you in the bargain.

Light flashed on her closed eyelids, and a deep roaring shook her. Cornelia, is that lightning? I hear thunder. There's going to be a storm. Close all the windows. Call the children in. . . . "Mother, here we are, all of us." "Is that you, Hapsy?" "Oh, no, I'm Lydia. We drove as fast as we could." Their faces drifted above her, drifted away. The rosary fell out of her hands and Lydia put it back. Jimmy tried to help, their hands fumbled together, and Granny closed two fingers around Jimmy's thumb. Beads wouldn't do, it must be something alive. She was so amazed her thoughts ran round and round. So, my dear Lord, this is my death and I wasn't even thinking about it. My children have come to see me die. But I can't, it's not time. Oh, I always hated surprises. I wanted to give Cornelia the amethyst set—Cornelia, you're to have the amethyst set, but Hapsy's to wear it when she wants, and, Doctor Harry, do shut up. Nobody sent for you. Oh, my dear Lord, do wait a minute. I meant to do something about the Forty Acres, Jimmy doesn't need it and Lydia will later on, with that worthless husband of hers. I meant to finish the altar cloth and send six bottles of wine to Sister Borgia for her dyspepsia. I want to send six bottles of wine to Sister Borgia, Father Connolly, now don't let me forget.

Cornelia's voice made short turns and tilted over and crashed. "Oh, Mother, oh, Mother, oh, Mother. . . ."

"I'm not going, Cornelia. I'm taken by surprise. I can't go."

You'll see Hapsy again. What about her? "I thought you'd never come." Granny made a long journey outward, looking for Hapsy. What if I don't find her? What then? Her heart sank down and down, there was no bottom to death, she couldn't come to the end of it. The blue light from Cornelia's lampshade drew into a tiny point in the center of her brain, it flickered and winked like an eye, quietly it fluttered and dwindled. Granny lay curled down within herself, amazed and watchful, staring at the point of light that was herself; her body was now only a deeper mass of shadow in an endless darkness and this darkness would curl around the light and swallow it up. God, give a sign!

For the second time there was no sign. Again no bridegroom and the priest in the house. She could not remember any other sorrow because this grief wiped them all away. Oh, no, there's nothing more cruel than this—I'll never forgive it. She stretched herself with a deep breath and blew out the light.

WINTER'S MORNING
LEN DEIGHTON

Major Richard Winter was a tall man with hard black eyes, a large nose and close-cropped hair. He hated getting out of bed, especially when assigned to dawn patrols on a cold morning. As he always said— and by now the whole officers' mess could chant it in unison—"If there must be dawn patrols in winter, let there be no Winter in the dawn patrols."

Winter believed that if they stopped flying them, the enemy would also stop. In 1914, the front-line soldiers of both armies had decided to live and let live for a few weeks. So now, during the coldest weather, some squadrons had allowed the dawn patrol to become a token couple of scouts hurrying over the frosty wire of no-man's-land after breakfast. The warm spirit of humanity that Christmas 1914 conjured had given way to the cold reality of self-preservation. Those wiser squadrons kept the major offensive patrol until last light, when the sun was mellow and the air less turbulent. At St. Antoine Farm airfield, however, dawn patrol was still a grueling obligation that none could escape.

"Oatmeal, toast, eggs and sausage, sir." Like everyone else in the mess tent—except Winter—the waiter spoke in a soft whisper that befitted the small hours. Winter preferred his normal booming voice. "Just coffee," he said. "But hot, really hot."

"Very good, Major Winter, sir."

The wind blew with enough force to make the canvas flap and roar, as though at any moment the whole tent would blow away. From outside they heard the sound of tent pegs being hammered more firmly into the hard chalky soil.

A young lieutenant sitting opposite offered his cigarette case, but Winter waved it aside in favor of a dented tin, from which he took cheap dark tobacco and a paper to fashion a misshapen cigarette. The young officer did not light one of his own, in the hope that he would be invited to share in this ritual. But Winter lit up, blew the noxious smoke across the table, coughed twice and pushed the tin back into his pocket.

Each time someone entered through the flap there was a clatter of canvas and ropes and a gust of cold air, but Winter looked in vain for a triangle of gray sky. The only light came from six acetylene lamps that were placed along the breakfast table. The pump of one of them was faulty; its light was dull and it left a smell of mold on the air. The other lamps hissed loudly and their eerie greenish light shone upon the mess silver, folded linen and empty plates. The table had been set the previous night for the regular squadron breakfast at eight a.m., and the mess servants were anxious that these three early-duty pilots shouldn't disarrange it too much.

Everyone stiffened as they heard the clang of the engine cylinder and con rod that hung outside for use as a gas warning. Winter laughed when Ginger, the tallest pilot on the squadron, emerged from the darkness rubbing his head and scowling in pain. Ginger walked over to the ancient piano and pulled back the edge of the tarpaulin that protected it from damp. He played a silly melody with one finger.

"Hot coffee, sir." The waiter emphasized the word hot, and the liquid spluttered as it poured over the metal spout. Winter clamped his cold hands around the pot like a drowning man clinging to flotsam. He twisted his head to see Ginger's watch. Six twenty-five. What a time to be having breakfast; it was still night.

Winter yawned and wrapped his ankle-length fur coat around his legs. New pilots thought that his fur overcoat had earned him his nickname of "the Bear," but that had come months before the coat.

The others kept a few seats between themselves and Winter. They spoke only when he addressed them, and then answered only in brief formalities.

"You flying with me, Lieutenant?"

The young ex-cavalry officer looked around the table. Ginger was munching his bread and jam, and gave no sign of having heard.

"Yes, sir," said the young man.

"How many hours?"

Always the same question. Everyone here was graded solely by flying time, though few cared whether the hours had been spent stunting, fighting or just hiding in the clouds. "Twenty-eight and a half, solo, sir."

"Twenty-eight *and a half.*" Winter nodded. "Twenty-eight *and a half! Solo!* Did you hear that, Lieutenant?" The question was addressed to Ginger, who was paying unusually close attention to the sugar bowl. Winter turned back to the new young pilot. "You'd better watch yourself."

Winter divided new pilots into assets and liabilities at either side of seventy hours. Assets sometimes became true friends and close comrades. Assets might even be told your misgivings. The demise of assets could spread grief through the whole mess. This boy would be dead within a month, Winter decided. He looked at him: handsome, in the pallid, aristocratic manner of such youngsters. His tender skin was chapped by the rain and there were cold sores on his lip. His blond hair was too long for Winter's taste, and his eyebrows girlish. This boy's kit had never known a quartermaster's shelf. It had come from an expensive tailor: a cavalry tunic fashionably nipped at the waist, tight trousers, and boots as supple as velvet. The ensemble was supplemented by accessories from the big department stores. His cigarette case was the sort that, it was advertised, could stop a bullet.

The young man returned Richard Winter's close examination with interest. So this rude fellow, so proud of his chauffeur's fur coat, was the famous Bear Winter who had twenty-nine enemy aircraft to his credit. He was a blotchy-faced devil, with bloodshot eyes and a fierce twitching eyebrow that he sometimes rubbed self-consciously, as if he knew that it undid his carefully contrived aplomb. The youngster wondered whether he would end up looking like this: dirty shirt, long fingernails, unshaved jaw and a cauliflower-knobbly head, shaved razor-close to avoid lice. Except for his quick eyes and occasional wry smile Winter looked like the archetypal Prussian *Schweinhund.*

Major Richard Winter had been flying in action for nearly two years without a leave. He was a natural pilot who'd flown every type of plane the makers could provide, and some enemy planes too. He could dismantle and assemble an engine as well as any squadron fitter, and as a precaution against jams he personally supervised the loading of every bullet he would use. Why must he be so rude to young pilots who hero-worshipped him, and would follow him to hell itself? And yet that too was part of the legend.

The young officer swallowed. "May I ask, sir, where you bought your magnificent fur coat?"

Winter gulped the rest of his coffee and got to his feet as he heard the first of the scouts' engines start. "Came off a mug I shot down in September," he bellowed. "It's from a fashionable shop, I'm told. Never traveled much myself, except here to France." Winter poked his fingers through four holes in the front. Did the boy go a shade paler, or had he imagined it in the glare of the gaslights? "Don't let some smart bastard get your overcoat, sonny."

"No, sir," said the boy. Behind him Ginger grinned. The Bear was behaving true to form. Ginger dug his knife into a tin of butter he'd scrounged from the kitchen and then offered it to the cavalry officer. The boy sniffed the tin doubtfully. It smelled rancid, but he scraped a little onto his bread and swamped it with jam to hide the taste.

"This your first patrol?" asked Ginger.

"No, sir. Yesterday one of the chaps took me as far as Cambrai to see the lie of the land. Before that I did a few hours around the airdrome here. These scouts are new to me."

"Did you see anything at Cambrai yesterday?"

"Antiaircraft gunfire."

Winter interrupted. "Let's see if we can't do better than that for you today, sonny." He leaned close to the boy and asked in his most winning voice, "Think you could down a couple before lunch?"

The boy didn't answer. Winter winked at Ginger and buttoned his fur coat. The other motors had started, so Winter shouted, "That's it, sonny. Don't try to be a hero. Don't try to be an ace in the first week you're out here. Just keep under my stinking armpit. Just keep close. Close, you understand? Bloody damn close." Winter flicked his cigarette end onto the canvas floor of the tent and put his heel on it. He coughed and growled, "Hurry up," although he could see that the others were waiting for him.

From the far side of the windswept tarmac, Major Winter's sergeant fitter saw a flash of greenish light as the mess tent flap opened and the duty pilots emerged. Winter came toward him out of the darkness, walking slowly because of his thick woolen underwear and thigh-length fleece boots. His hands were tucked into his sleeves for warmth, and his head was sunk into the high collar that stood up around his ears like a cowl. Exactly like a monk, thought the sergeant, not for the first time. Perhaps Winter cultivated this resemblance. He'd outlived all the pilots who had been here when he arrived, to become as high in rank as scout pilots ever became. Yet his moody introspective manner and his offhand attitude to high and low had prevented him from becoming the commanding officer. So Winter remained a taciturn misanthrope, without any close companions, except for Ginger, who had the same skills of survival and responded equally coldly to overtures of friendship from younger pilots.

The sergeant fitter—"Pops"—had been here even longer than the Bear. He'd always looked after his airplane, right from his first patrol, when Winter was the same sort of noisy friendly fool as the kid doing his first patrol this morning. Airplanes, he should have said; the Bear had written off seven of them. Pops spat as the fumes from the engine collected in his lungs. It was a bad business, watching these kids vanish one by one. Last year it had been considered lucky to touch Pops's bald head before takeoff. For twelve months the fitter had refused leave, knowing that the pilots were truly anxious about their joke. But Pops's bald head had proved as fallible as all the other talismans. One after another the faces had been replaced by similar faces until they were all the same pink-faced smiling boy.

Pops spat again, then cut the motor and climbed out of the cockpit. The other planes were also silent. From the main road came the noise of an army convoy hurrying to get to its destination before daylight made it vulnerable to attack. Any moment now artillery observers would be climbing into the balloons that enabled them to see far across no-man's-land.

"Good morning, Major."

"Morning, Pops."

"The old firm, eh, sir?"

"Yes—you, me and Ginger," said Winter, laughing in a way that he'd not done in the mess tent. "Sometimes I think we are fighting this war all on our own, Pops."

"We are," chuckled Pops. This was the way the Bear used to laugh. "The rest of them are just part-timers, sir."

"I'm afraid they are, Pops," said Winter. He climbed stiffly into the cramped cockpit and pulled the fur coat around him. There was hardly enough room to move his elbows, and the tiny seat creaked under his weight. The instruments were simple: compass, altimeter, speedometer and rev counter. The workmanship was crude and the finish was hasty, like a toy car put together by a bungling father. "Switches off," said Pops. Winter looked at the brass switches and then pressed them, as if not sure of his vision. "Switches off," he said.

"Fuel on," said Pops.

"Fuel on."

"Suck in."

"Suck in."

Pops cuddled the polished wooden prop blade to his ear. It was cold against his face. He walked it around to prime the cylinders. That was the thing Pops liked about Winter: when he said off, you knew it was off. Pops waited while Winter pulled on his close-fitting flying helmet; its fur trimmed a tonsure of leather that had faded to the color of flesh.

"Contact."

"Contact." Pops stretched high into the dark night and brought the blade down with a graceful sweep of his hands. Like brass and percussion responding to a conductor, the engine began its performance with a blinding sheet of yellow flame and a drumroll. Winter throttled back, slowing the drum and changing the shape and color of the flame to a gaseous feather of blue that danced around the exhaust pipes and made his face swell and contract as the shadows exploded and died. Winter held a blue flickering hand above his head. He felt the wheels lurch forward as the chocks were removed and he dabbed at the rudder bar so that he could see around the aircraft's nose. There was no brake or pitch adjustment and Winter let her gather speed while keeping the tail skid tight down upon the ground.

They took off in a vic three, bumping across frozen ruts in the balding field with only the glare of the exhausts to light their going. It was easy for Winter; as formation leader he relied on the others to watch his engine and formate on him accordingly. At full screaming throttle they climbed over the trees at the south end of the airfield. A gusty crosswind hit them. Winter banked a wing tip dangerously close to the treetops rather than slue into the boy's line of flight. Ginger did the same to avoid his major. The boy, unused to these heavy operational machines with high-compression engines, found his aircraft almost wrenched from his grasp. He yawed across the trees, a hundred yards from the others, before he put her nose up to regain his position in formation. Close, he must keep close. Winter spared him only a brief glance over the shoulder between searching the somber sky for the minuscule dots of other airplanes. For by now the black lid of night had tilted and an orange wedge prized open the eastern horizon. Winter led the way to the front lines, the others tight against his tail plane.

The first light of the sun revealed a land covered by a gray eiderdown of mist, except where a loose thread of river matched the silver of the sky. Over the front line they turned south. Winter glanced eastward, where the undersides of some low clouds were leaking dribbles of gold paint onto the earth. As the world awakened, stoves were lighted and villages were marked by dirty smoke that trailed southward.

Major Winter noted the north wind and glanced back to see Ginger's airplane catch the first light of the sun as it bent far enough over the horizon to reach them at fifteen thousand feet above the earth. The propeller blades made a perfect circle of yellow gauze, through which reflections from the polished metal cowling winked and wavered as the airplanes rose and sank gently on the clear morning air.

Here, on the Arras section of the front, the German and French lines could be clearly seen as careless scrawls in the livid chalk. Near the river Scarpe at Feuchy, Winter saw a constant flicker of artillery shells exploding: the morning hate. Pinheads of pink, only just visible through the mist. Counter–battery fire he guessed, from its concentration some way behind the lines.

He pulled his fur collar as high around his face as it could go, then raised his goggles. The icy wind made his eyes water, but not before he had scanned the entire horizon and banked enough to see below him. He pulled the goggles down again. It was more comfortable, but they acted like blinkers. Already ice had formed in the crevices of his eyes and he felt its pinpricks like daggers. His nose was numb and he let go of the stick to massage it.

The cavalry officer—"Willy," they called him—was staring anxiously at the other two airplanes. He probably thought that the banking search was a wing-rocking signal that the enemy was sighted. They read too many cheap magazines, these kids, but then so had Winter before his first posting out here: "Ace of the Black Cross," "Flying Dare-Devils," "True War Stories."

Well, now Winter knew true war stories. When old men decided to barter young men for pride and profit, the transaction was called war. It was another Richard Winter who had come to war. An eighteen-year-old child with a scrapbook of cuttings about Blériot and the Wright brothers, a roomful of models which his mother wasn't permitted to dust, and thirteen hours of dangerous experiments on contraptions that were bigger, but no more airworthy, than his dusty models. That Richard Winter was long since dead. Gone was the gangling boy whose only regret about the war was leaving his mongrel dog. Winter smiled as he remembered remonstrating with some pilots who were using fluffy yellow chicks for target practice on the pistol range. That was before he'd seen men burned alive, or, worse, men half burned alive.

He waved to frightened little Willy, who was desperately trying to fly skillfully enough to hold formation on his bad-tempered flight commander. Poor little swine. Two dots almost ahead of them to the southeast. Far below. Ginger had seen them already, but the boy wouldn't notice them until they were almost bumping into him. All the new kids were like that. It's not a matter of eyesight, it's a matter of knowledge. Just as a tracker on a safari knows that a wide golden blob in the shadow of a tree at midday is going to be a pride of lions resting after a meal, so in the morning an upright golden blob in the middle of a plain is a cheetah waiting to make a kill. So at five thousand feet, that near the lines, with shellfire visible, they were going to be enemy two-seaters on artillery observation duty. First he must be sure that there wasn't a flight of scouts in ambush above them. He looked at the cumulus and decided that it was too far from the two-seaters to be dangerous. Brownish-black smoke patches appeared around the planes as the antiaircraft guns went into action.

Winter raised his goggles. Already they had begun to mist up because of the perspiration generated by his excitement. He waggled his wings and began to lose height. He headed east to come around behind them from out of the sun. Ginger loosed off a short burst of fire to be sure his guns were not frozen. Winter and the boy did the same. The altitude had rendered him too deaf to hear it as more than a ticking, as of an anxious pulse.

Winter took another careful look around. Flashes of artillery shells were bursting on the ground just ahead of the enemy planes' track. The ground was still awash with blue gloom, although here and there hillocks and trees were crisply golden in the harsh oblique light of morning. The hedges and buildings threw absurdly long shadows, and a church steeple was bright yellow. Winter now saw that there were four more two-seaters about a mile away. They were beginning to turn.

Winter put down his nose and glanced in his mirror to be sure the others were close behind. The airspeed indicator showed well over a hundred miles an hour and was still rising. The airstream sang across the taut wires with a contented musical note. He held the two airplanes steady on his nose, giving the stick and rudder only the lightest of touches as the speed increased their sensitivity.

Five hundred yards: these two still hadn't seen their attackers. The silly bastards were hanging over the side, anxious not to get their map references wrong. Four hundred.

The boy saw them much later than Ginger and Winter. He stared in wonder at these foreign aeronauts. At a time when only a handful of madmen had ever tried this truly magical science, and when every flight was a pioneering experiment to discover more about this new world, he hated the idea of killing fellow enthusiasts. He would much rather have exchanged anecdotes and information with them.

Ginger and Winter had no such thoughts. Their minds were delivered to their subconscious. They were checking instruments, cocking guns and judging ever changing altitudes, range and deflection.

If that stupid kid fires too early . . . damn him, damn him! Oh, well. Ginger and Winter opened fire too. Damn, a real ace gets in close, close, close. They'd both learned that, if nothing else. Stupid boy! The artillery observation leader pulled back on the stick and turned so steeply as almost to collide with the two-seater to his left. He knew what he was doing; he was determined to make himself a maximum-deflection shot. Winter kept his guns going all the way through the turn. The tracer bullets seemed unnaturally bright because his eyes had become accustomed to the morning's gloom. Like glowworms they were eating the enemy's tail plane. This is what decided a dogfight: vertical turns, tighter and tighter still. Control stick held into the belly, with toes and eyes alert so that the airplane doesn't slide an inch out of a turn that glued him to the horizon. It was sheer flying skill. The sun—a watery blob of gold—seemed to drop through his upper wing and onto his engine. Winter could feel the rate of turn by the hardness of his seat. He pulled even harder on the stick to make the tracers crawl along the fuselage. The smell from his guns was acrid and the thin smoke and heat from the blurring breechblocks caused his target to wobble like a jelly. First the observer was hit, then the pilot, throwing up their hands like badly made marionettes. The two-seater stalled, falling suddenly like a dead leaf. Winter rolled. Two more airplanes slid across his sights. He pushed his stick forward to follow the damaged two-seater down. Hearing bullets close to his head, he saw the fabric of his upper plane prodded to tatters by invisible fingers, which continued their destruction to the point of breaking a center-section strut and throwing its splinters into his face. His reflexes took over and he went into a vertical turn tighter than any two-seater could manage. Airplanes were everywhere. Bright green and blue wings and black crosses passed across his sights, along with roundels and dark green fabric. One of them caught the light of the sun and its wings flashed with brilliant blue. All the time Winter kept half an eye upon his rearview mirror. A two-seater nosed down toward his tail, but Winter avoided him effortlessly. Ginger came under him, thumping his machine guns with one of the hammers which they all kept in their cockpits. He was red-faced with exertion as he tried to clear the stoppage by force. At this height every movement was exhausting. Ginger wiped his face with the back of his gauntlet and his goggles came unclipped and blew away in the airstream.

Winter had glimpsed Ginger for only a fraction of a second, but he'd seen enough to tell him the whole story. If it was a split round he'd never unjam it. Trees flashed under him. The combat had brought them lower and lower, as it always did.

The new boy was half a mile away and climbing. Winter knew it was his job to look after the kid, but he'd not leave Ginger with a jammed gun. A plane rushed past before he had a chance to fire. Winter saw one of the two-seaters behind Ginger. My God, they were tough, these fellows. You'd think they'd be away, with their tails between their legs. Hold on, Ginger, here I come. Dive, climb, roll; a perfect Immelmann turn. The world upside down; above him the dark earth, below him the dawn sky like a rasher of streaky bacon. Hold that. He centered the stick, keeping the enemy's huge wings centered in his sight. Fire. The guns shook the whole airframe and made a foul stink. He kicked the rudder and slid down past the enemy's tail with no more than six feet to spare. A white-faced observer was frozen in fear. Up. Up. Up. Winter leaned out of his cockpit to see below him. The new boy is in trouble. One of the two-seaters is pasting him. The poor kid is trying for the cloud bank, but that's half a mile away. Never throttle back in combat, you fool. White smoke? Radiator steam? No, worse: vaporizing petrol from a punctured tank or fractured lead. If it touches a hot pipe he'll go up like a torch. You should have kept close, sonny. What did I tell you? What do I always tell them? Winter flick-rolled and turned to cover Ginger's tail.

Woof: a flamer. The boy: will he jump or burn? The whole world was made up of jumpers or burners. There were no parachutes for pilots yet, so either way a man died. The machine was breaking up. Burning pieces of fuel-soaked wreckage fell away. It would be difficult to invent a more efficient bonfire. Take thin strips of timber, nail them into a framework, stretch fabric over it and paint it with highly inflammable dope. Into the middle of this build a metal tank for thirty gallons of high-grade fuel. Move air across it at fifty m.p.h. Winter couldn't decide whether the boy had jumped. A pity, the chaps in the mess always wanted to know that, even though few could bear to ask.

The dogfight had scattered the airplanes in every direction, but Ginger was just below him and a two-seater was approaching from the south. Ginger waved. His gun was working. Winter sideslipped down behind a two-seater and gave it a burst of fire. The gunner was probably dead, for no return fire came and the gun rocked uselessly on its mounting. The pilot turned steeply on full throttle and kept going in an effort to come around in a vertical turn to Winter's rear. But Ginger was waiting for that. They'd been through this many times. Ginger fired as the two-seater was halfway through the turn, raking it from engine to tail. The whole airplane lurched drunkenly, and then the port upper wing snapped, its main spar eaten through by Ginger's bullets. As it fell, nose down, the wings folded back along the fuselage like an umbrella being closed. The shapeless mess of broken struts and tangled steel wire fell vertically to earth, weighted by its heavy engine, which was still roaring at full throttle. It was so low that it hit the ground within seconds.

Winter throttled back and came around in a gentle turn to see the wreckage: not a movement. It was just a heap of junk in a field. Ginger was circling it too. From this height the sky was a vast bowl as smooth and shiny as Ming. They both looked around it, but the other two-seaters had gone. There were no planes in sight. Winter increased his throttle and came alongside Ginger. He pushed his goggles up. Ginger was laughing. The artillery fire had stopped, or perhaps its explosions were lost in the mist. They turned for home, scampering across the trees and hedges like two schoolboys.

Winter and Ginger came over the airfield in echelon. Eight airplanes were lined up outside the canvas hangars that lacked only bunting to be a circus. A dozen officers fell over themselves scrambling out of the mess tent. One of them waved. Winter's machine, painted bright green with wasplike white bands, was easily recognized. Winter circled the field while Ginger landed. He'd literally lived in this French field for almost a year and knew each tree, ditch and bump. He'd seen it from every possible angle. He remembered praying for a sight of it with a dead motor and a bootful of blood. Also how he'd focused on blurred blades of its cold dewy grass, following a long night unconscious after a squadron booze-up. He'd vomited, excreted, crashed and fornicated on this field. He couldn't imagine being anywhere else.

For the first time in a month the sun shone, but it gave no warmth. As he switched off his engine the petrol fumes made the trees bend and dance on the heavy vapor. Pops hurried across to him but couldn't resist a quick inspection of the tail before saluting.

"Everything in order, Herr Major?"

Winter was still a little deaf, but he guessed what the sergeant was saying. He always said the same thing. "Yes, Sergeant. The strut is damaged, but apart from that it probably just needs a few patches."

Winter unclipped his goggles, unwound his scarf and took off his leather helmet. The cordite deposits from his Spandaus had made a black band across his nose and cheeks.

"Another Englishman?" said Pops. He warmed his hands before the big Mercedes engine, which was groaning softly.

"Bristols: one forced down, one destroyed. We lost the new young officer, though." Winter was ashamed that he didn't know the boy's name, but there were so many of them. He knew he was right to remain unfriendly to all of them. Given half a chance, new kids would treat him like some sort of divinity, and that made him feel like hell when they went west.

Winter wiped the protective grease from his face. He was calm. Briefly he watched his own unshaking hand with a nod of satisfaction. He knew himself to be a nerveless and relentless killer, and like any professional assassin he took pride in seeing a victim die. Only such men could become aces.

THE LADY
ON THE GRAY

JOHN COLLIER

Ringwood was the last of an Anglo-Irish family which had played
the devil in County Clare for a matter of three centuries. At last all their
big houses were sold up, or burned down by the long-suffering Irish,
and of all their thousands of acres not a single foot remained. Ringwood, however, had a few hundred a year of his own, and if the family
estates had vanished, he at least inherited a family instinct which
prompted him to regard all Ireland as his domain and to rejoice in its
abundance of horses, foxes, salmon, game, and girls.

In pursuit of these delights, Ringwood ranged and roved from Don-
egal to Wexford through all the seasons of the year. There were not
many hunts he had not led at some time or other on a borrowed mount,
nor many bridges he had not leaned over through half a May morning,
nor many inn parlors where he had not snored away a wet winter
afternoon in front of the fire.

He had an intimate by the name of Bates, who was another of the
same breed and the same kidney. Bates was equally long and lean, and
equally hard up, and he had the same wind-flushed bony face, the same
shabby arrogance, and the same seignorial approach to the little girls in
the cottages and cowsheds.

Neither of these blades ever wrote a letter, but each generally knew
where the other was to be found. The ticket collector, respectfully blind
as he snipped Ringwood's third-class ticket in a first-class compartment,

would mention that Mr. Bates had traveled that way only last Tuesday, stopping off at Killorglin for a week or two after the snipe. The chambermaid, coy in the clammy bedroom of a fishing inn, would find time to tell Bates that Ringwood had gone on up to Lough Corrib for a go at the pike. Policemen, priests, salesmen, gamekeepers, even the tinkers on the roads, would pass on this verbal *pateran*. Then, if it seemed his friend was on to a good thing, the other would pack up his battered kit bag, put rods and guns into their cases, and drift off to join in the sport.

So it happened that one winter afternoon, when Ringwood was strolling back from a singularly blank day on the bog of Ballyneary, he was hailed by a one-eyed horse dealer of his acquaintance, who came trotting by in a gig, as people still do in Ireland. This worthy told our friend that he had just come down from Galway, where he had seen Mr. Bates, who was on his way to a village called Knockderry, and who had told him very particularly to mention it to Mr. Ringwood if he came across him.

Ringwood turned this message over in his mind, and noted that it was a very particular one, and that no mention was made as to whether it was fishing or shooting his friend was engaged in, or whether he had met with some Croesus who had a string of hunters that he was prepared to lend. "He certainly would have put a name to it if it was anything of that sort! I'll bet my life it's a pair of sisters he's got on the track of. It must be!"

At this thought, he grinned from the tip of his long nose like a fox, and he lost no time in packing his bag and setting off for this place Knockderry, which he had never visited before in all his roving up and down the country in pursuit of fur, feather, and girls.

He found it was a long way off the beaten track, and a very quiet place when he got to it. There were the usual low, bleak hills all around, and a river running along the valley, and the usual ruined tower up on a slight rise, girdled with a straggly wood and approached by the remains of an avenue.

The village itself was like many another: a few groups of shabby cottages, a decaying mill, half a dozen beer shops, and one inn at which a gentleman, hardened to rural cookery, might conceivably put up.

Ringwood's hired car deposited him there, and he strode in and found the landlady in the kitchen, and asked for his friend Mr. Bates.

"Why, sure, your honor," said the landlady, "the gentleman's staying here. At least, he is, so to speak, and then, now, he isn't."

"How's that?" said Ringwood.

"His bag's here," said the landlady, "and his things are here, and my grandest room taken up with them (though I've another every bit as good), and himself staying in the house best part of a week. But the day before yesterday he went out for a bit of a constitutional, and—would you believe it, sir?—we've seen neither hide nor hair of him since."

"He'll be back," said Ringwood. "Show me a room, and I'll stay here and wait for him."

Accordingly, he settled in, and waited all the evening, but Bates failed to appear. However, that sort of thing bothers no one in Ireland, and Ringwood's only impatience was in connection with the pair of sisters, whose acquaintance he was extremely anxious to make.

During the next day or two he employed his time in strolling up and down all the lanes and bypaths in the neighborhood, in the hope of discovering these beauties, or else some other. He was not particular as to which it should be, but on the whole he would have preferred a cottage girl, because he had no wish to waste time on elaborate approaches.

It was on the second afternoon, just as the early dusk was falling, he was about a mile outside the village and he met a straggle of muddy cows coming along the road, and a girl driving them. Our friend took a look at this girl, and stopped dead in his tracks, grinning more like a fox than ever.

This girl was still a child in her teens, and her bare legs were spattered with mud and scratched by brambles, but she was so pretty that the seignorial blood of all the Ringwoods boiled in the veins of their last descendant, and he felt an overmastering desire for a cup of milk. He therefore waited a minute or two, and then followed leisurely along the lane, meaning to turn in as soon as he saw the byre, and beg the favor of this innocent refreshment, and perhaps a little conversation into the bargain.

They say, though, that blessings never come singly, any more than misfortunes. As Ringwood followed his charmer, swearing to himself that there couldn't be such another in the whole county, he heard the fall of a horse's hoofs, and looked up, and there, approaching him at a walking pace, was a gray horse, which must have turned in from some bypath or other, because there certainly had been no horse in sight a moment before.

A gray horse is no great matter, especially when one is so urgently in need of a cup of milk, but this gray horse differed from all others of its species and color in two respects. First, it was no sort of a horse at all, neither hack nor hunter, and it picked up its feet in a queer way, and yet it had an arch to its neck and a small head and a wide nostril that were not entirely without distinction. And, second—and this distracted Ringwood from all curiosity as to breed and bloodline—this gray horse carried on its back a girl who was obviously and certainly the most beautiful girl he had ever seen in his life.

Ringwood looked at her, and as she came slowly through the dusk she raised her eyes and looked at Ringwood. He at once forgot the little girl with the cows. In fact, he forgot everything else in the world.

The horse came nearer, and still the girl looked, and Ringwood looked, and it was not a mere exchange of glances, it was wooing and a marriage, all complete and perfect in a mingling of the eyes.

Next moment, the horse had carried her past him, and, quickening its pace a little, it left him standing on the road. He could hardly run after it, or shout; in any case, he was too overcome to do anything but stand and stare.

He watched the horse and rider go on through the wintry twilight, and he saw her turn in at a broken gateway just a little way along the road. Just as she passed through, she turned her head and whistled, and Ringwood noticed that her dog had stopped by him, and was sniffing about his legs. For a moment he thought it was a smallish wolfhound, but then he saw it was just a tall, lean, hairy lurcher. He watched it run limping after her, with its tail down, and it struck him that the poor creature had had an appalling thrashing not so long ago; he had noticed the marks where the hair was thin on its ribs.

However, he had little thought to spare for the dog. As soon as he got over his first excitement, he moved on in the direction of the gateway. The girl was already out of sight when he got there, but he recognized the neglected avenue which led up to the battered tower on the shoulder of the hill.

Ringwood thought that was enough for the day, so he made his way back to the inn. Bates was still absent, but that was just as well. Ringwood wanted the evening to himself in order to work out a plan of campaign.

"That horse never cost two ten-pound notes of anybody's money," said he to himself. "So, she's not so rich. So much the better! Besides, she wasn't dressed up much; I don't know what she had on—a sort of cloak or something. Nothing out of Bond Street, anyway. And lives in that old tower! I should have thought it was all tumbled down. Still, I suppose there's a room or two left at the bottom. Poverty Hall! One of the old school, blue blood and no money, pining away in this godforsaken hole, miles away from everybody. Probably she doesn't see a man from one year's end to another. No wonder she gave me a look. God! If I was sure she was there by herself, I wouldn't need much of an introduction. Still, there might be a father or a brother or somebody. Never mind, I'll manage it."

Later, when the landlady brought in the lamp: "Tell me," said he, "who's the young lady who rides the cobby-looking, old-fashioned-looking gray?"

"A young lady, sir?" said the landlady doubtfully. "On a gray?"

"Yes," said he. "She passed me on the lane up there. She turned in on the old avenue, going up to the tower."

"Oh, Mary bless and keep you!" said the good woman. "That's the beautiful Murrough lady you must have seen."

"Murrough?" said he. "Is that the name? Well! Well! Well! That's a fine old name in the West here."

"It is so, indeed," said the landlady. "For they were kings and queens in Connaught before the Saxon came. And herself, sir, has the face of a queen, they tell me."

"They're right," said Ringwood. "Perhaps you'll bring me in the whiskey and water, Mrs. Doyle, and I shall be comfortable."

He had an impulse to ask if the beautiful Miss Murrough had anything in the shape of a father or a brother at the tower, but his principle was, "Least said, soonest mended," especially in little affairs of this sort.

So he sat by the fire, recapturing and savoring the look the girl had given him, and he decided he needed only the barest excuse to present himself at the tower.

Ringwood had never any shortage of excuses, so the next afternoon he spruced himself up and set out in the direction of the old avenue. He turned in at the gate, and went along under the forlorn and dripping trees, which were so ivied and overgrown that the darkness was already thickening under them. He looked ahead for a sight of the tower, but the avenue took a turn at the end, and it was still hidden among the clustering trees.

Just as he got to the end, he saw someone standing there, and he looked again, and it was the girl herself, standing as if she were waiting for him.

"Good afternoon, Miss Murrough," said he, as soon as he got into earshot. "Hope I'm not intruding. The fact is, I think I had the pleasure of meeting a relation of yours, down in Cork, only last month. . . ." By this time he had got close enough to see the look in her eyes again, and all the nonsense died away in his mouth, for this was something beyond any nonsense of that sort.

"I thought you would come," said she.

"My God!" said he. "I had to. Tell me—are you all by yourself here?"

"All by myself," said she, and she put out her hand as if to lead him along with her.

Ringwood, blessing his lucky stars, was about to take it, when her lean dog bounded between them and nearly knocked him over.

"Down!" cried she, lifting her hand. "Get back!" The dog cowered and whimpered, and slunk behind her, creeping almost on its belly. "He's not a dog to be trusted," she said.

"He's all right," said Ringwood. "He looks a knowing old fellow. I like a lurcher. Clever dogs. What? Are you trying to talk to me, old boy?"

Ringwood always paid a compliment to a lady's dog, and in fact the creature really was whining and whimpering in the most extraordinary fashion.

"Be quiet!" said the girl, raising her hand again, and the dog was silent. "A cur," said she to Ringwood. "Did you come here to sing the praises of a half-bred cur?" With that, she gave him her eyes again, and he forgot the wretched dog, and she gave him her hand, and this time he took it and they walked toward the tower.

Ringwood was in seventh heaven. "What luck!" thought he. "I might at this moment be fondling that little farm wench in some damp and smelly cowshed. And ten to one she'd be sniveling and crying and running home to tell her mammy. This is something different."

At that moment, the girl pushed open a heavy door, and, bidding the dog lie down, she led our friend through a wide, bare, stone-flagged hall and into a small vaulted room which certainly had no resemblance to a cowshed except perhaps it smelled a little damp and moldy, as these old stone places so often do. All the same, there were logs burning on the open hearth, and a broad, low couch before the fireplace. For the rest, the room was furnished with the greatest simplicity, and very much in the antique style. "A touch of the Cathleen ni Houlihan," thought Ringwood. "Well, well! Sitting in the Celtic twilight, dreaming of love. She certainly doesn't make much bones about it."

The girl sat down on the couch and motioned him down beside her. Neither of them said anything; there was no sound but the wind outside, and the dog scratching and whimpering timidly at the door of the chamber.

At last, the girl spoke. "You are of the Saxon," said she gravely.

"Don't hold it against me," said Ringwood. "My people came here in 1656. Of course, that's yesterday to the Gaelic League, but still I think we can say we have a stake in the country."

"Yes, through its heart," said she.

"Is it politics we're going to talk?" said he, putting an Irish turn to his tongue. "You and I, sitting here in the firelight?"

"It's love you'd rather be talking of," said she with a smile. "But you're the man to make a byword and a mockery of the poor girls of Eire."

"You misjudge me entirely," said Ringwood. "I'm the man to live alone and sorrowful, waiting for the one love, though it seemed something beyond hoping for."

"Yes," said she. "But yesterday you were looking at one of the Connell girls as she drove her kine along the lane."

"Looking at her? I'll go so far as to say I did," said he. "But when I saw you I forgot her entirely."

"That was my wish," said she, giving him both her hands. "Will you stay with me here?"

"Ah, that I will!" cried he in rapture.

"Always?" said she.

"Always," cried Ringwood. "Always and forever!" For he felt it better to be guilty of a slight exaggeration than to be lacking in courtesy to a lady. But as he spoke she fixed her eyes on him, looking so much as if she believed him that he positively believed himself.

"Ah," he cried. "You bewitch me!" And he took her in his arms.

He pressed his lips to hers, and at once he was over the brink. Usually he prided himself on being a pretty cool hand, but this was an intoxication too strong for him; his mind seemed to dissolve in sweetness and fire, and at last the fire was gone, and his senses went with it. As they failed, he heard her saying, "Forever! Forever!" and then everything was gone and he fell asleep.

He must have slept some time. It seemed he was awakened by the heavy opening and closing of a door. For a moment, he was all confused and hardly knew where he was.

The room was now quite dark, and the fire had sunk to a dim glow. He blinked, and shook his ears, trying to shake some sense into his head. Suddenly he heard Bates talking to him, muttering as if he, too, were half asleep, or half drunk more likely. "You *would* come here," said Bates. "I tried hard enough to stop you."

"Hullo!" said Ringwood, thinking he must have dozed off by the fire in the inn parlor. "Bates? God, I must have slept heavy! I feel queer. Damn it—so it was all a dream! Strike a light, old boy. It must be late. I'll yell for supper."

"Don't, for heaven's sake," said Bates, in his altered voice. "Don't yell. She'll thrash us if you do."

"What's that?" said Ringwood. "Thrash us? What the hell are you talking about?"

At that moment a log rolled on the hearth, and a little flame flickered up, and he saw his long and hairy forelegs, and he knew.

THE WIND AND
THE SNOW OF WINTER
WALTER VAN TILBURG CLARK

IT WAS NEAR SUNSET when Mike Braneen came onto the last pitch of the old wagon road which had led into Gold Rock from the east since the Comstock days. The road was just two ruts in the hard earth, with sagebrush growing between them, and was full of steep pitches and sharp turns. From the summit it descended even more steeply into Gold Rock in a series of short switchbacks down the slope of the canyon.

There was a paved highway on the other side of the pass now, but Mike never used that. Cars coming from behind made him uneasy, so that he couldn't follow his own thoughts long, but had to keep turning around every few minutes to see that his burro, Annie, was staying out on the shoulder of the road, where she would be safe. Mike didn't like cars anyway, and on the old road he could forget about them and feel more like himself. He could forget about Annie, too, except when the light, quick tapping of her hoofs behind him stopped. Even then he didn't really break his thoughts. It was more as if the tapping were another sound from his own inner machinery, and when it stopped, he stopped, too, and turned around to see what she was doing.

When he began to walk ahead again at the same slow, unvarying pace, his arms scarcely swinging at all, his body bent a little forward from the waist, he would not be aware that there had been any interruption of the memory or the story that was going on in his head. Mike did not like to have his stories interrupted except by an idea of his own, something to do with prospecting, or the arrival of his story at an actual memory which warmed him to closer recollection or led into a new and more attractive story.

An intense, golden light, almost liquid, fanned out from the peaks above him and reached eastward under the gray sky, and the snow which occasionally swarmed across this light was fine and dry. Such little squalls had been going on all day, and still there was nothing like real snow down, but only a fine powder which the wind swept along until it caught under the brush, leaving the ground bare. Yet Mike Braneen was not deceived. This was not just a flurrying day; it was the beginning of winter. If not tonight, then tomorrow, or the next day, the snow would begin which shut off the mountains, so that a man might as well be on a great plain for all he could see, perhaps even the snow which blinded a man at once and blanketed the desert in an hour. Fifty-two years in this country had made Mike Braneen sure about such things, although he didn't give much thought to them, but only to what he had to do because of them.

Three nights before, he had been awakened by a change in the wind. It was no longer a wind born in the near mountains, cold with night and altitude, but a wind from far places, full of a damp chill which got through his blankets and into his bones. The stars had still been clear and close above the dark humps of the mountains, and overhead the constellations had moved slowly in full panoply, unbroken by any invisible lower darkness; yet he had lain there half awake for a few minutes, hearing the new wind beat the brush around him, hearing Annie stirring restlessly and thumping in her hobble. He had thought drowsily, Smells like winter this time, and then, It's held off a long time this year, pretty near the end of December. Then he had gone back to sleep, mildly happy because the change meant he would be going back to Gold Rock.

Gold Rock was the other half of Mike Braneen's life. When the smell of winter came, he always started back for Gold Rock. From March or April until the smell of winter, he wandered slowly about among the mountains, anywhere between the White Pines and the Virginias, with only his burro for company. Then there would come the change, and they would head back for Gold Rock.

Mike had traveled with a good many burros during that time, eighteen or twenty, he thought, although he was not sure. He could not remember them all, but only those he had had first, when he was a young man and always thought most about seeing women when he got back to Gold Rock, or those with something queer about them, like Baldy, who'd had a great, pale patch like a bald spot on one side of his belly, or those who'd had something queer happen to them, like Maria.

He could remember just how it had been that night. He could remember it as if it were last night. It had been in Hamilton. He had felt unhappy, because he could remember Hamilton when the whole hollow was full of people and buildings, and everything was new and active. He had gone to sleep in the shell of the Wells Fargo Building, hearing an old iron shutter banging against the wall in the wind. In the morning, Maria had been gone. He had followed the scuffing track she made on account of her loose hobble, and it had led far up the old snow-gullied road to Treasure Hill and then ended at one of the black shafts that opened like mouths right at the edge of the road. A man remembered a thing like that. There weren't many burros that foolish. But burros with nothing particular about them were hard to remember—especially those he'd had in the last twenty years or so, when he had gradually stopped feeling so personal about them and had begun to call all the jennies Annie and all the burros Jack.

The clicking of the little hoofs behind him stopped, and Mike stopped, too, and turned around. Annie was pulling at a line of yellow grass along the edge of the road.

"Come on, Maria," Mike said patiently. The burro at once stopped pulling at the dead grass and came on up toward him, her small black nose working, the ends of the grass standing out on each side of it like whiskers. Mike began to climb again, ahead of her.

It was a long time since he had been caught by a winter, too. He could not remember how long. All the beginnings ran together in his mind, as if they were all the beginning of one winter so far back that he had almost forgotten it. He could still remember clearly, though, the winter he had stayed out on purpose, clear into January. He had been a young man then, thirty-five or forty or forty-five, somewhere in there. He would have to stop and try to bring back a whole string of memories about what had happened just before, in order to remember just how old he had been, and it wasn't worth the trouble. Besides, sometimes even that system didn't work. It would lead him into an old camp where he had been a number of times, and the dates would get mixed up. It was impossible to remember any other way, because all his comings and goings had been so much alike. He had been young, anyhow, and not much afraid of anything except running out of water in the wrong place; not even afraid of the winter.

He had stayed out because he'd thought he had a good thing, and he had wanted to prove it. He could remember how it felt to be out in the clear winter weather on the mountains; the piñon trees and the junipers weighted down with feathery snow, and making sharp blue shadows on the white slopes. The hills had made blue shadows on one another, too, and in the still air his pick had made the beginning of a sound like a bell's. He knew he had been young, because he could remember taking a day off now and then, just to go tramping around those hills, up and down the white and through the blue shadows, on a kind of holiday. He had pretended to his common sense that he was seriously prospecting, and had carried his hammer and even his drill along, but he had really just been gallivanting, playing colt. Maybe he had been even younger than thirty-five, though he could still be stirred a little, for that matter, by the memory of the kind of weather which had sent him gallivanting. High-blue weather, he called it.

There were two kinds of high-blue weather, besides the winter kind, which didn't set him off very often, spring and fall. In the spring it would have a soft, puffy wind and soft, puffy white clouds which made separate shadows that traveled silently across hills that looked soft, too. In the fall it would be still, and there would be no clouds at all in the blue, but there would be something in the golden air and the soft, steady sunlight on the mountains that made a man as uneasy as the spring blowing, though in a different way, more sad and not so excited. In the spring high-blue, a man had been likely to think about women he had slept with, or wanted to sleep with, or imaginary women made up with the help of newspaper pictures of actresses or young society ma-trons, or of the old oil paintings in the Lucky Boy Saloon, which showed pale, almost naked women against dark, sumptuous backgrounds—women with long hair or braided hair, calm, virtuous faces, small hands and feet, and ponderous limbs, breasts, and buttocks. In the fall high-blue, though it had been much longer since he had seen a woman or heard a woman's voice, he was more likely to think about old friends, men, or places he had heard about, or places he hadn't seen for a long time. He himself thought most often about Goldfield the way he had last seen it in the summer in 1912. That was as far south as Mike had ever been in Nevada. Since then he had never been south of Tonopah.

When the high-blue weather was past, though, and the season worked toward winter, he began to think about Gold Rock. There were only three or four winters out of the fifty-two when he hadn't gone home to Gold Rock, to his old room at Mrs. Wright's, up on Fourth Street, and to his meals in the dining room at the International House, and to the Lucky Boy, where he could talk to Tom Connover and his other friends, and play cards, or have a drink to hold in his hand while he sat and remembered.

This journey had seemed a little different from most, though. It had started the same as usual, but as he had come across the two vast valleys, and through the pass in the low range between them, he hadn't felt quite the same. He'd felt younger and more awake, it seemed to him, and yet, in a way, older, too, suddenly older. He had been sure that there was plenty of time, and yet he had been a little afraid of getting caught in the storm. He had kept looking ahead to see if the mountains on the horizon were still clearly outlined, or if they had been cut off by a lowering of the clouds. He had thought more than once how bad it would be to get caught out there when the real snow began, and he had been disturbed by the first flakes. It had seemed hard to him to have to walk so far, too. He had kept thinking about distance. Also the snowy cold had searched out the regions of his body where old injuries had healed.

He had taken off his left mitten a good many times to blow on the fingers which had been frosted the year he was sixty-three, so that now it didn't take much cold to turn them white and stiffen them. The queer tingling, partly like an itch and partly like a pain, in the patch on his back that had been burned in that old powder blast, was sharper than he could remember its ever having been before. The rheumatism in his joints, which was so old a companion that it usually made him feel no more than tight-knit and stiff, and the place where his leg had been broken and torn when that ladder broke in '97, ached and had a pulse he could count. All this made him believe that he was walking more slowly than usual, although nothing, probably not even a deliberate attempt, could actually have changed his pace. Sometimes he even thought, with a moment of fear, that he was getting tired.

On the other hand, he felt unusually clear and strong in his mind. He remembered things with a clarity which was like living them again—nearly all of them events from many years back, from the time when he had been really active and fearless and every burro had had its own name. Some of these events, like the night he had spent in Eureka with the little brown-haired girl, a night in the fall in 1888 or '89, somewhere in there, he had not once thought of for years. Now he could remember even her name. Armandy she had called herself—a funny name. They all picked names for their business, of course, romantic names like Cecily or Rosamunde or Belle or Claire, or hard names like Diamond Gert or Horseshoe Sal, or names that were pinned on them, like Indian Kate or Roman Mary; but Armandy was different.

He had been with Armandy only that one night, but he could remember her as if he were with her now. He remembered little things about her, things that made it seem good to think of being with her again. Armandy had a room upstairs in a hotel. They could hear a piano playing in a club across the street. He could hear the tune, and it was one he knew, although he didn't know its name. It was a gay tune that went on and on the same, but still it sounded sad when you heard it through the window, with the lights from the bars and hotels shining on the street, and the people coming and going through the lights, and then, beyond the lights, the darkness where the mountains were.

Armandy wore a white silk dress with a high waist and a locket on a gold chain. The dress made her look very brown and like a young girl. She used a white powder on her face that smelled like violets, but this could not hide her brownness. The locket was heart-shaped, and it opened to show a cameo of a man's hand holding a woman's hand very gently, just their fingers laid out long together, and the thumbs holding, the way they were sometimes on tombstones. There were two little gold initials on each hand, but Armandy wouldn't tell what they stood for, or even if the locket was really her own. He stood in the window, looking down at the club from which the piano music was coming, and Armandy stood beside him, with her shoulder against his arm, and a glass of wine in her hand. He could see the toe of her white satin slipper showing from under the edge of her skirt. Her big hat, loaded with black and white plumes, lay on the dresser behind them. His own leather coat, with the sheepskin lining, lay across the foot of the bed. It was a big bed, with a knobby brass foot and head. There was one oil lamp burning in the chandelier in the middle of the room. Armandy was soft-spoken, gentle, and a little fearful, always looking at him to see what he was thinking.

He stood with his arms folded. His arms felt big and strong upon his heavily muscled chest. He stood there, with his chin down into his heavy dark beard, and watched a man come riding down the middle of the street from the west. The horse was a fine black, which lifted its head and feet with pride. The man sat very straight, with a high rein, and something about his clothes and hat made him appear to be in uniform, although it wasn't a uniform he was wearing. The man also saluted friends upon the sidewalks like an officer, bending his head just slightly, and touching his hat instead of lifting it. Mike Braneen asked Armandy who the man was, and then felt angry because she could tell him, and because he was an important man who owned a mine that was in bonanza. He mocked the airs with which the man rode, and his princely greetings. He mocked the man cleverly, and Armandy laughed and repeated what he said, and made him drink a little of her wine as a reward. Mike had been drinking whiskey, and he did not like wine anyway, but this was not the moment in which to refuse such an invitation.

Old Mike remembered all this, which had been completely forgotten for years. He could not remember what he and Armandy had said, but he remembered everything else, and he felt very lonesome for Armandy, and for the room with the red figured carpet and the brass chandelier with oil lamps in it, and the open window with the long tune coming up through it, and the young summer night outside on the mountains. This loneliness was so much more intense than his familiar loneliness that it made him feel very young. Memories like this had come up again and again during these three days. It was like beginning life over again. It had tricked him into thinking, more than once, Next summer I'll make the strike, and this time I'll put it into something safe for the rest of my life, and stop this fool wandering around while I've still got some time left—a way of thinking which he had really stopped a long time before.

It was getting darker rapidly in the pass. When a gust of wind brought the snow against Mike's face so hard that he noticed the flakes felt larger, he looked up. The light was still there, although the fire was dying out of it, and the snow swarmed across it more thickly. Mike remembered God. He did not think anything exact. He did not think about his own relationship to God. He merely felt the idea as a comforting presence. He'd always had a feeling about God whenever he looked at a sunset, especially a sunset which came through under a stormy sky. It had been the strongest feeling left in him until these memories like the one about Armandy had begun. Even in this last pass his strange fear of the storm had come on him again a couple of times, but now that he had looked at the light and thought of God, it was gone. In a few minutes he would come to the summit and look down into his lighted city. He felt happily hurried by this anticipation.

He would take the burro down and stable her in John Hammersmith's shed, where he always kept her. He would spread fresh straw for her, and see that the shed was tight against the wind and snow, and get a measure of grain for her from John. Then he would go up to Mrs. Wright's house at the top of Fourth Street and leave his things in the same room he always had—the one in front, which looked down over the roofs and chimneys of his city and across at the east wall of the canyon, from which the sun rose late. He would trim his beard with Mrs. Wright's shears, and shave the upper part of his cheeks. He would bathe out of the blue bowl and pitcher, and wipe himself with the towel with yellow flowers on it, and dress in the good dark suit and the good black shoes with the gleaming box toes, and the good black hat which he had left in the chest in his room. In this way he would perform the ceremony which ended the life of the desert and began the life of Gold Rock. Then he would go down to the International House, and greet

Arthur Morris in the gleaming bar, and go into the dining room and eat the best supper they had, with fresh meat and vegetables, and new-made pie, and two cups of hot clear coffee. He would be served by the plump blond waitress who always joked with him and gave him many little extra things with his first supper, including the drink which Arthur Morris always sent in from the bar.

At this point Mike Braneen stumbled in his mind, and his anticipation wavered. He could not be sure that the plump blond waitress would serve him. For a moment he saw her in a long skirt, and the dining room of the International House, behind her, had potted palms standing in the corners, and was full of the laughter and loud, manly talk of many customers who wore high vests and mustaches and beards. These men leaned back from tables covered with empty dishes. They patted their tight vests and lighted expensive cigars. He knew all their faces. If he were to walk down the aisle between the tables on his side, they would all speak to him. But he also seemed to remember the dining room with only a few tables, with oilcloth on them instead of linen, and with moody young men sitting at them in their work clothes—strangers who worked for the highway department, or were just passing through, or talked mining in terms which he did not understand or which made him angry.

No, it would not be the plump blond waitress. He did not know who it would be. It didn't matter. After supper he would go up Canyon Street under the arcade to the Lucky Boy Saloon, and there it would be the same as ever. There would be the laurel wreaths on the frosted glass panels of the doors, and the old sign upon the window, the sign that was older than Tom Connover, almost as old as Mike Braneen himself. He would open the door and see the bottles, and the white women in the paintings, and the card table in the back corner, and the big stove and the chairs along the wall. Tom would look around from his place behind the bar.

"Well, now," he would roar, "look who's here, boys. Now will you believe it's winter?"

Some of them would be the younger men, of course, and there might even be a few strangers, but this would only add to the dignity of his reception, and there would also be his friends. There would be Henry

Bray, with the gray walrus mustache, and Mark Wilton and Pat Gallagher. They would all welcome him loudly.

"Mike, how are you anyway?" Tom would roar, leaning across the bar to shake hands with his big, heavy, soft hand with the diamond ring on it. "And what'll it be, Mike? The same?" he'd ask, as if Mike had been in there no longer ago than the night before.

Mike would play that game, too. "The same," he would say.

Then he would really be back in Gold Rock; never mind the plump blond waitress.

Mike came to the summit of the old road and stopped and looked down. For a moment he felt lost again, as he had when he'd thought about the plump blond waitress. He had expected Canyon Street to look much brighter. He had expected a lot of orange windows close together on the other side of the canyon. Instead there were only a few scattered lights across the darkness, and they were white. They made no communal glow upon the steep slope, but gave out only single white needles of light, which pierced the darkness secretly and lonesomely, as if nothing could ever pass from one house to another over there. Canyon Street was very dark, too. There it went, the street he loved, steeply down into the bottom of the canyon, and down its length there were only the few streetlights, more than a block apart, swinging in the wind and darting about that cold, small light. The snow whirled and swooped under the nearest streetlight below.

"You are getting to be an old fool," Mike Braneen said out loud to himself, and felt better. This was the way Gold Rock was now, of course, and he loved it all the better. It was a place that grew old with a man, that was going to die sometime, too. There could be an understanding with it.

He worked his way slowly down into Canyon Street, with Annie slipping and checking behind him. Slowly, with the blown snow behind them, they came to the first built-up block, and passed the first dim light showing through a smudged window under the arcade. They passed the dark places after it, and the second light. Then Mike Braneen stopped in the middle of the street, and Annie stopped beside him, pulling her rump in and turning her head away from the snow. A highway truck, coming down from the head of the canyon, had to get way over onto the wrong side of the street to pass them. The driver leaned out, and yelled, "Pull over, Pop. You're in town now."

Mike Braneen didn't hear him. He was staring at the Lucky Boy. The Lucky Boy was dark, and there were boards nailed across the big window that had shown the sign. At last Mike went over onto the boardwalk to look more closely. Annie followed him, but stopped at the edge of the walk and scratched her neck against a post of the arcade. There was the other sign, hanging crossways under the arcade, and even in that gloom Mike could see that it said Lucky Boy and had a jack of diamonds painted on it. There was no mistake. The Lucky Boy sign, and others like it under the arcade, creaked and rattled in the wind.

There were footsteps coming along the boards. The boards sounded hollow, and sometimes one of them rattled. Mike Braneen looked down slowly from the sign and peered at the approaching figure. It was a man wearing a sheepskin coat with the collar turned up around his head. He was walking quickly, like a man who knew where he was going, and why, and where he had been. Mike almost let him pass. Then he spoke.

"Say, fella—"

He even reached out a hand as if to catch hold of the man's sleeve, though he didn't touch it. The man stopped, and asked impatiently, "Yeah?" and Mike let the hand down again slowly.

"Well, what is it?" the man asked.

"I don't want anything," Mike said. "I got plenty."

"Okay, okay," the man said. "What's the matter?"

Mike moved his hand toward the Lucky Boy. "It's closed," he said.

"I see it is, Dad," the man said. He laughed a little. He didn't seem to be in quite so much of a hurry now.

"How long has it been closed?" Mike asked.

"Since about June, I guess," the man said. "Old Tom Connover, the guy that ran it, died last June."

Mike waited for a moment. "Tom died?" he asked.

"Yup. I guess he'd just kept it open out of love of the place anyway. There hasn't been any real business for years. Nobody cared to keep it open after him."

The man started to move on, but then he waited, peering, trying to see Mike better.

"This June?" Mike asked finally.

"Yup. This last June."

"Oh," Mike said. Then he just stood there. He wasn't thinking anything. There didn't seem to be anything to think.

"You knew him?" the man asked.

"Thirty years," Mike said. "No, more'n that," he said, and started to figure out how long he had known Tom Connover, but lost it, and said, as if it would do just as well, "He was a lot younger than I am, though."

"Hey," said the man, coming closer, and peering again. "You're Mike Braneen, aren't you?"

"Yes," Mike said.

"Gee, I didn't recognize you at first. I'm sorry."

"That's all right," Mike said. He didn't know who the man was, or what he was sorry about.

He turned his head slowly and looked out into the street. The snow was coming down heavily now. The street was all white. He saw Annie with her head and shoulders in under the arcade, but the snow settling on her rump.

"Well, I guess I'd better get Molly under cover," he said. He moved toward the burro a step, but then halted.

"Say, fella—"

The man had started on, but he turned back. He had to wait for Mike to speak.

"I guess this about Tom's mixed me up."

"Sure," the man said. "It's tough, an old friend like that."

"Where do I turn to get to Mrs. Wright's place?"

"Mrs. Wright?"

"Mrs. William Wright," Mike said. "Her husband used to be a foreman in the Aztec. Got killed in the fire."

"Oh," the man said. He didn't say anything more, but just stood there, looking at the shadowy bulk of old Mike.

"She's not dead, too, is she?" Mike asked slowly.

"Yeah, I'm afraid she is, Mr. Braneen," the man said. "Look," he said more cheerfully. "It's Mrs. Branley's house you want right now, isn't it? Place where you stayed last winter?"

Finally Mike said, "Yeah, I guess it is."

"I'm going up that way. I'll walk up with you," the man said.

After they had started, Mike thought that he ought to take the burro down to John Hammersmith's first, but he was afraid to ask about it. They walked on down Canyon Street, with Annie walking along beside them in the gutter. At the first side street they turned right and began to climb the steep hill toward another of the little streetlights dancing over a crossing. There was no sidewalk here, and Annie followed right at their heels. That one streetlight was the only light showing up ahead.

When they were halfway up to the light, Mike asked, "She die this summer, too?"

The man turned his body half around, so that he could hear inside his collar.

"What?"

"Did she die this summer, too?"

"Who?"

"Mrs. Wright," Mike said.

The man looked at him, trying to see his face as they came up toward the light. Then he turned back again, and his voice was muffled by the collar.

"No, she died quite a while ago, Mr. Braneen."

"Oh," Mike said finally.

They came up onto the crossing under the light, and the snow-laden wind whirled around them again. They passed under the light, and their three lengthening shadows before them were obscured by the innumerable tiny shadows of the flakes.

BIOGRAPHICAL NOTES

STEPHEN VINCENT BENÉT *1898–1943*
Prevented by poor eyesight from following in the footsteps of his father and grandfather as an army career officer, Benét was encouraged by his family to take up a literary life. A published poet while still a student at Yale University, he was awarded a Pulitzer Prize in 1929 for *John Brown's Body*, his brilliant epic poem of the Civil War. His fascination with the American character is evident in his many novels, and in his short stories, the most famous of which, "The Devil and Daniel Webster," has become almost legendary since its publication in 1936. Page 30

ALGERNON BLACKWOOD *1869–1951*
His two most absorbing passions were a love of the wilderness and a deep conviction that the average person possesses psychic powers which can surface at odd and unexpected times. Blackwood came from a prominent British family in Kent, was educated mainly in Europe, and turned to writing after disappointing ventures as a farmer, hotelkeeper and newspaperman in Canada and the United States. He achieved great fame in his later years as a teller of ghost stories on British television. Page 446

MORLEY CALLAGHAN *1903—*
Between college and law school Callaghan worked for the Toronto *Star*, where his fellow reporter Ernest Hemingway became interested in his short stories. After law school Callaghan joined Hemingway's circle of literary expatriates in Paris. He returned to Canada to practice law, but with the success of his first novel, *Strange Fugitive*, in 1928, he turned to writing as a full-time career. Since then he has written seventeen additional books, several plays, and more than one hundred short stories. Page 224

G. K. CHESTERTON *1874–1936*
In a career that spanned nearly four decades, Chesterton was a prolific writer of serious novels, essays, poetry and criticism. Yet today he is best known for his small collection of detective stories featuring the unique priest-detective, Father Brown. Born and educated in London, Chesterton first studied art, then switched to literature, launching his career with book reviews. A deeply religious man, he was formally received into the Roman Catholic Church in 1922 by his friend Father John O'Connor, who was the original inspiration for Father Brown. Page 360

ALICE CHILDRESS *1920—*
Actress, director and playwright, Childress has used her many talents to dramatize the struggle of black Americans to achieve dignity and respect in a white society. She was born in Charleston, South Carolina, and was active for many years in the American Negro Theatre in New York. Page 376

WALTER VAN TILBURG CLARK *1909–1971*
Most of Clark's early life was spent in Reno, Nevada, where his father served as president of the University of Nevada. That state also

was the setting for his best known novel, *The Ox-Bow Incident,* a masterful depiction of a western lynch mob. He wrote this while teaching in public schools in New York State; after its success he settled in the West to devote himself to writing. Page 617

JOHN COLLIER 1901–1980

British born, he began writing verse at nineteen and had his first poetry published when he was twenty. Nine years later his first book appeared, a macabre, satirical short novel called *His Monkey Wife.* In Collier's hands, witchcraft, sorcery and the wildest fantasies become almost plausible; when a major collection of stories, *The John Collier Reader,* was published in 1973, one reviewer advised that it be read only in "broad daylight." Page 609

WILKIE COLLINS 1824–1889

A master of plot and incident, Collins has been called the father of the English detective novel, a designation he earned with *The Moonstone,* published in 1868. Born in London, the eldest son of a prominent painter, he began writing while serving as an apprentice in the tea trade. The influence of his close friend Charles Dickens brought his talent to full flower, and for over three decades he produced nearly a book a year. He collaborated with Dickens on a number of works, and is credited by some with helping develop Dickens' plotting ability. Page 232

STEPHEN CRANE 1871–1900

The fourteenth child of a New Jersey Methodist minister, Crane died before his thirtieth year. Yet within that short span he produced novels, short stories and poetry that fill fourteen volumes. Best known for *The Red Badge of Courage*—a classic novel of combat experience in the Civil War that he wrote without ever having seen battle—Crane was one of the earliest and among the greatest of the realistic school of American writers. Page 66

ROALD DAHL 1916—

Born in Llandaff, South Wales, of Norwegian parents, Dahl began writing as a result of his experiences as a Royal Air Force fighter pilot in World War II. In short stories published in the 1950s and 1960s he established himself as a master of situations in which the comic and the gruesome combine with devastating results. The author, also, of many widely acclaimed children's books, Dahl is married to the American actress Patricia Neal and makes his home in Britain. Page 42

LEN DEIGHTON 1929—

The phenomenal success of Deighton's first novel, *The Ipcress File,* established him, at age thirty-three, as a master of the modern spy story. Deighton was born in London, studied art, and has worked as a pastry cook, dress-factory manager, advertising man, teacher, magazine artist and photographer, and as a steward for British Overseas Airways. In recent work, such as his novel *Bomber* and the collection from which "Winter's Morning" was taken, Deighton has shifted his attention from the spy story to the broader tapestry of modern warfare. Page 596

MERRILL DENISON 1893–1975

Denison's writing career began at the Hart House Theatre of the University of Toronto, for which he wrote a series of realistic comedies. He later became a specialist in radio drama, as well as an expert on economic history, and was the author of many books on the settling and industrialization of Canada and the United States. Page 320

CHARLES DICKENS 1812–1870

Unsurpassed as a creative genius, the author of such immortal works as *David Copperfield, Great Expectations, A Tale of Two Cities* and *A Christmas Carol* peopled his novels and stories with brilliantly original characters in all manner of situations. Indeed, ideas came to him so quickly that often, as G. K. Chesterton put it, "he wrote short stories because he had not time to write long ones." Page 102

SIR ARTHUR CONAN DOYLE 1859–1930

The creator of Sherlock Holmes was born in Edinburgh, attended university there, and later pursued the improbable career of eye doctor before taking up the pen professionally. But it was while studying medicine that Doyle met a thin, angular surgeon named Joseph Bell, whose ability to diagnose occupation and character as well as disease helped provide the model for the immortal Holmes. Knighted in 1902, Sir Arthur wrote several historical romances in addition to innumerable tales involving Holmes and Dr. Watson. "The Speckled Band" in this collection remains one of the master's most intriguing and entertaining puzzles. Page 393

MARGARET DRABBLE 1939—
The author of "The Gifts of War" has already been marked on both sides of the Atlantic as one of the most talented of the younger generation of British writers. Born in Sheffield, she graduated from Cambridge University with honors, then joined the Royal Shakespeare Company at Stratford-upon-Avon as an actress. She is married to the actor Clive Swift and lives in London. Page 291

DAPHNE DU MAURIER 1907—
Granddaughter of George du Maurier, who wrote *Trilby*, daughter of noted actor Gerald du Maurier, Daphne du Maurier was educated at home and in Paris. In 1932 she married Lieutenant Colonel F. A. M. Browning, who in 1941 became the youngest general in British Empire forces. She now lives in Cornwall, where she combines her writing with her love of gardening, sailing and walking. *Rebecca* and *My Cousin Rachel* are but two of her many haunting books, for which, in 1969, she was created a Dame of the British Empire. "The Birds," presented here, is the story on which the famous suspense film by Alfred Hitchcock was based. Page 522

WALTER D. EDMONDS 1903—
All of Edmonds' novels and most of his stories have been set in upper New York State, especially in the Erie Canal area, where he grew up. His novel *Drums Along the Mohawk*, which re-creates scenes from the Revolutionary War years, has been called "one of the best examples of the regional chronicle ever written in America." Page 564

WILLIAM FAULKNER 1897–1962
One of America's most distinguished writers, Faulkner was born and raised in Mississippi, the descendant of a once prominent family ruined by the Civil War. In a series of compelling novels set in his home countryside, fictionalized as Yoknapatawpha County, he mirrored the decline of the old South under assault by the modern world. In World War I Faulkner served with the Royal Air Force; later he worked as a newspaperman and screenwriter. He earned international fame with such novels as *The Sound and the Fury* and *Sanctuary*, and was awarded the 1949 Nobel Prize for literature. Page 342

DOROTHY CANFIELD FISHER 1879–1958
Although born in Kansas, where her father was professor of Romance languages at the University of Kansas, Fisher was descended from Vermont pioneers, and it was to this locale that she returned again and again in her life as well as in her writing. A prolific author of novels and stories, she assisted her husband in the operation of a family farm in Vermont, was the first woman to serve on the Vermont state board of education, and for twenty-five years was a member of the editorial board of the Book-of-the-Month Club. Page 215

C. S. FORESTER 1899–1966
An Englishman born in Cairo, Forester studied medicine for a time but forsook that for a career in writing, making an auspicious debut in 1926 with the widely acclaimed story of a murderer, *Payment Deferred*. However, it was not until 1937 and the appearance of the first of his Captain Horatio Hornblower stories that Forester took his place as an internationally best-selling author. His knowledge of German militarism, as echoed in "The Hostage," was obtained firsthand from assignments as a foreign correspondent in Europe on the eve of World War II. Page 130

PAUL GALLICO 1897–1976
Throughout his long and prolific career as a newspaperman, sportswriter, novelist and storyteller, it was to the "little people"—like

the charlady star of his novel *Mrs. 'Arris Goes to Paris*—that Gallico turned for his heroes and heroines. A native New Yorker who graduated from Columbia University and began as a sports reporter for the New York *Daily News*, Gallico spent most of his later years abroad, where he also established a reputation as a bon vivant, gourmet and athlete, serving as a fencing master to the French army until a year before his death.　Page 197

BRENDAN GILL *1914—*
New York, its people, and their distinctive way of living and thinking, provide much of the material for Gill's fiction. And in fact, he has been associated with *The New Yorker* magazine since graduation from Yale University in 1936; he is currently its drama critic as well as a contributor of short stories and poetry. The father of seven, Gill is active in civic affairs in New York, serving on the boards of the Film Society of Lincoln Center, the Municipal Art Society and other cultural organizations. His most recent book is a biography of Charles Lindbergh.　Page 352

NADINE GORDIMER *1923—*
Growing up in the gold-mining country of South Africa, Gordimer went on to the University of Witwatersrand in Johannesburg, where she now lives. She has written several novels, but it is her short stories on the theme of the troubled relationship between the races of her native land that have won her a wide international following.　Page 558

LAFCADIO HEARN *1850–1904*
Hearn's exotic life began, appropriately, on the Greek island of Leukas, where his father, a British surgeon major, was stationed. After failing in studies in England and France, Hearn was sent to the United States. He soon gravitated toward journalism, working as a reporter and essayist in Cincinnati and New Orleans. In 1890 he went to Japan for *Harper's Magazine*. There he married the daughter of an impoverished samurai, became a Japanese citizen, and remained in that land teaching English and writing about the Japanese scene until his death.　Page 120

PAUL HORGAN *1903—*
A perceptive writer on the American Southwest, Horgan is actually a transplanted Easterner who was born in Buffalo, New York, and taken to New Mexico as a child when the family moved because of his father's health. The winner of both the Bancroft and Pulitzer prizes for *Great River*, his monumental history of the Rio Grande, Horgan has received additional honors for his many novels and short stories, most of which are likewise set in the Southwest.　Page 458

RICHARD HUGHES *1900–1976*
Mercurial, whimsical and fantastic, novelist Hughes was one of literature's most fascinating figures. Of Welsh descent, he was educated at Oxford, where as an undergraduate he wrote his first play. International acclaim came to him following the publication in 1929 of *A High Wind in Jamaica,* which has been called "unlike any novel ever before written . . . a classic in English literature, certain of permanence."　Page 518

WASHINGTON IRVING *1783–1859*
Known for his gentle nature, charm and courtesy, Irving was a personal as well as a literary success in both the young United States and in Europe. Born in New York, he briefly practiced law and for a time represented the family mercantile business in England. But most of his life was spent in travel, in diplomatic missions, and in the writing which earned him a permanent place as America's earliest author of importance. Sunnyside, his lovely Hudson River estate not far from the locale of "Rip Van Winkle," is still preserved.　Page 149

W. W. JACOBS *1863–1943*
Chiefly a writer of humorous sea tales in which the sailors rarely leave port, Jacobs is most famous for his classic horror story, "The Monkey's Paw," which was unlike anything else he did. Despite the chilling qualities of this haunting tale, Jacobs was a quiet, gentle man, a former civil service clerk who turned to writing full time to support his wife and five children.　Page 77

HENRY JAMES *1843–1916*
Though born an American, in New York City, James's major works are set in Europe, where he lived for most of his life. Brother of William James, the psychologist and philosopher, and son of Henry James, Sr.—the eminent theologian and friend of Emerson's and Carlyle's—Henry James, Jr., was reared in privileged circumstances. Hailed for such classically probing novels as *The Portrait of a Lady* and *The Ambassadors*, he was also known for his short stories and criticism. When war broke out in 1914 he disapproved of America's neutrality, and he became a British citizen in the year before his death.   Page 112

MARY LAVIN *1912–*
In a reversal of the typical immigrant experience, Lavin was born in the United States and taken to Ireland as a young girl. She now lives on a farm in County Meath. A graduate of the National University, Dublin, she is a winner of Britain's prestigious James Tait Black prize for her book of short stories, *Tales from Bective Bridge*.   Page 547

D. H. LAWRENCE *1885–1930*
David Herbert Lawrence was the son of an English coal miner and a schoolteacher mother to whom he was devoted. One of five children, he was brought up in an atmosphere of poverty, brutality and drink, much of which is reflected in his partially autobiographical novel, *Sons and Lovers*. Enfeebled by tuberculosis and pursued by controversy, he spent much of his life wandering through Europe, Australia and the United States seeking the ideal place to live. Though some of his fiction and poetry was banned when he wrote it, he has become recognized with the passage of time as one of the major forces in English literature.   Page 261

DORIS LESSING *1919–*
Like the boy in "Sunrise on the Veld," Lessing grew up in southern Africa, in what is now Zimbabwe. Though she moved to Britain permanently when she was thirty, her African background continues to have a profound influence on her work. "The chief

gift from Africa to writers, white and black," she has said, "is the continent itself. . . . Africa gives you the knowledge that man is a small creature, among other creatures, in a large landscape."   Page 509

JACK LONDON *1876–1916*
By the age of twenty-two London had been a cannery worker in San Francisco (his birthplace), an oyster pirate, a deckhand on a sealing vessel, a hobo, a socialist agitator, a college student and finally a gold miner in the Klondike. It was this trip to the Far North that inspired his most famous novel, *The Call of the Wild*, and many of his best stories. His vivid adventure tales became so popular that by 1913 he was said to be the world's highest paid author. At forty, in despair over his health, finances and deteriorating talents, he died from an overdose of drugs.   Page 179

KATHERINE MANSFIELD *1888–1923*
She was born in Wellington, New Zealand, and educated in England. Her first story was published when she was only nine, and by the end of her brief life she was famous for inimitable short stories that capture the twists and subtleties of human relationships.   Page 432

W. SOMERSET MAUGHAM *1874–1965*
Maugham published his first novel in 1897, when he was twenty-three, and he was still writing at the time of his death, at ninety-one—a literary life span unequaled in length and productivity in modern times. An unusually astute observer of human nature, Maugham found the models for many of his most memorable characters in his travels to remote and exotic places, some of which were conducted at the behest of the British secret service in World War I. Among his most enduring works are the novels *Of Human Bondage, Cakes and Ale, The Moon and Sixpence,* and the story "Rain," better known as a powerful play and motion picture.   Page 477

LIAM O'FLAHERTY *1897–*
Ireland has been the setting of almost all of O'Flaherty's many short stories and novels; it has been said that his first and best subject

matter is "the fauna—human and otherwise—of his native place." Born in the Aran Islands, off Galway Bay, O'Flaherty studied for the priesthood but gave it up, served with the Irish Guards in World War I, then knocked about as a stoker, deckhand, beachcomber, hobo and lumberjack before beginning to write seriously. His best known novel, *The Informer*, was made into an Academy Award-winning movie by the American director John Ford in 1935. Page 210

EDGAR ALLAN POE *1809–1849*
One of America's first important writers, Poe was born in Boston. Orphaned at three, he was reared by foster parents in Richmond, Virginia. Working as an editor, critic, and writer of short stories, he first gained attention in 1833 with his tale "MS. Found in a Bottle." There followed a series of world-renowned stories, including "The Murders in the Rue Morgue," which is considered to be the first true detective story. His poem "The Raven" remains one of the most popular in American literature. Page 413.

KATHERINE ANNE PORTER *1890–1980*
The remote little town of Indian Creek, Texas, was Porter's birthplace, and many of her finest stories have been set in the American Southwest and in neighboring Mexico. Her great reputation has been achieved with a relatively small output of material, most notably short stories in two collections— *Flowering Judas* and *Pale Horse, Pale Rider*— and the novel *Ship of Fools*. Page 586

THOMAS H. RADDALL *1903—*
Raddall was ten years old when his family migrated from Britain to Nova Scotia, and he has lived there ever since, his work showing a deep affinity for the land and its people. As a historian and a writer of fiction, his unusual ability to evoke the mood of an earlier time and place has thrice earned him the silver medallion of the Governor General's Award. "The Wedding Gift," presented here, was dramatized on television by the Canadian Broadcasting Corporation in 1973. Page 378

SAKI (H. H. MUNRO) *1870–1916*
As a master of humor as well as of the chilling and macabre, Saki has few peers. Born in Burma but educated in Britain, he learned the writer's craft as a newspaper reporter and foreign correspondent in the Balkans, Russia and France. With World War I intensifying, he enlisted as a private in the Royal Fusiliers, refusing several offers of a commission. A brilliant career ended tragically with his death in battle in 1916. Page 257

IRWIN SHAW *1913—*
Shaw began his writing career in New York by doing scripts for radio serials, among them a dramatization of the "Dick Tracy" comic strip. Within two years he had established himself on the Broadway scene with his hit play, *Bury the Dead,* produced in 1936, and his many short stories. His best-selling first novel, *The Young Lions,* has been called "one of the most important American novels to come out of World War II." Page 164

G. E. M. SKUES *1858–1949*
A practicing lawyer who was admitted to the British bar in 1884, Skues's passionate interest all his long life was in trout fishing. So charmingly and knowingly did he write on this subject that such technical-sounding titles as *The Way of a Trout with a Fly* and *Minor Tactics of the Chalk Stream* created for him a popular readership far beyond the ranks of expert anglers. Page 316

ROBERT LOUIS STEVENSON *1850–1894*
The Scottish-born author of *Treasure Island, Dr. Jekyll and Mr. Hyde,* and *A Child's Garden of Verses* first studied engineering, and then law, before he became a writer. In Samoa, where he lived his last years, the natives called him Tusitala—teller of tales. And "The Bottle Imp," like many of his tales, has an exotic island setting. Page 9

ELIZABETH TAYLOR *1912–1975*
Quiet English villages, such as Penn, Buckinghamshire, where she lived for many years with her family, provided Taylor with much

of the material for her novels and stories. Though she began writing as a child, it was not until she was thirty that her work was published regularly. The short story was her specialty; in it she could best express her "warm heart, sharp claws and exceptional powers of formal balance," as a British critic once said. Page 331

GILLIAN TINDALL *1938—*
Tindall lives in London with her husband and son and is a regular contributor to the London *Observer*, the Manchester *Guardian* and the *New Statesman*. Since taking her degree at Oxford in 1959 she has written several novels, a nonfiction book entitled *A Handbook on Witchcraft*, and *Dances of Death*, a recently published short-story collection from which "The Loss" is taken. Page 244

KURT VONNEGUT, JR. *1922—*
Though first acclaimed as a new talent in the science-fiction field, Vonnegut has since reached a much wider audience with books like *Slaughterhouse-Five* and *Breakfast of Champions*, which make serious statements about many aspects of the American way of life. A native of Indiana who now lives on Cape Cod, Vonnegut served with the U.S. Army in Europe in World War II and was a newspaperman and public relations official for the General Electric Company before becoming a full-time writer. Page 88

PATRICK WADDINGTON *1912–1973*
Chief of international news for the Canadian Broadcasting Corporation at the time of his death, Waddington was born in Westmeath, Ontario, and educated in England. After graduating from the University of London he returned to Canada; he worked first for the Ottawa *Citizen*, then moved to Montreal, where he wrote for several publications prior to joining the CBC staff. Page 173

H. G. WELLS *1866–1946*
Wells was one of the best known and most prolific authors of his time. An honors graduate in science, he developed a reputation as a master of science fiction with such works as *The War of the Worlds, The Invisible Man* and *The Time Machine.* He wrote more realistic novels as well, and for many years no respectable bookcase was complete without his encyclopedic *Outline of History*. Page 274

H. H. WILSON *1902—*
The descendant of a pioneer Australian family, Helen H. Wilson was born in a remote town in Tasmania and was graduated from the University of Western Australia. In six novels, three histories and more than one hundred short stories, she has become known for her literary excursions into the dramatic and colorful history of her native land. She lives in the Sydney suburb of Manly. Page 304

P. G. WODEHOUSE *1881–1975*
"The master of those who laugh," Wodehouse has been called. His many volumes about the adventures of such lordly British boneheads as Bertie Wooster and his inimitable "gentleman's gentleman," Jeeves, have delighted millions throughout the world for more than six decades. As at home on the Continent as in Britain, Wodehouse also spent many years in the United States, where he wrote film scripts and collaborated on Broadway musicals. In the early 1950s he settled on Long Island, where he died at the age of ninety-three, shortly after being knighted by Queen Elizabeth. Page 492

ACKNOWLEDGMENTS

AN END TO DREAMS, copyright 1932 by Stephen Vincent Benét, copyright © renewed 1960 by Rosemary Carr Benét. Used by permission of Brandt & Brandt. PARSON'S PLEASURE, copyright © 1958, 1962 by Roald Dahl, is from *Kiss Kiss* by Roald Dahl, published by Alfred A. Knopf, Inc., Michael Joseph Ltd., and Penguin Books. Used by permission of Alfred A. Knopf, Inc., and of Murray Pollinger on behalf of the author. THE MONKEY'S PAW is used by permission of The Society of Authors, literary representative of the Estate of W. W. Jacobs. THE FOSTER PORTFOLIO, copyright 1951 by Kurt Vonnegut, Jr., is from *Welcome to the Monkey House* by Kurt Vonnegut, Jr., and was originally published in *Collier's*. Used by permission of Delacorte Press/Seymour Lawrence. THE HOSTAGE, copyright 1954 by C. S. Forester, copyright © 1978 by The Estate of C. S. Forester. Used by permission of Harold Matson Company, Inc., of Michael Joseph Ltd., and of A. D. Peters & Co. Ltd. THE GIRLS IN THEIR SUMMER DRESSES, copyright 1939, 1952, copyright © renewed 1967 by Irwin Shaw, is from *Selected Short Stories of Irwin Shaw* by Irwin Shaw. Used by permission of Random House, Inc., and of Hope Leresche & Sayle on behalf of the author. Originally appeared in *The New Yorker*. THE STREET THAT GOT MISLAID by Patrick Waddington is used by permission of Marcus Waddington. A PIECE OF STEAK by Jack London is used by permission of The Estate of Irving Shepard, I. Milo Shepard, Executor. THE SECRET INGREDIENT by Paul Gallico, copyright 1952 by The Curtis Publishing Company, is used by permission of Harold Ober Associates Incorporated. THE HAWK by Liam O'Flaherty is used by permission of A. D. Peters & Co. Ltd. THE APPRENTICE, copyright 1947 by The Curtis Publishing Company, is condensed from "The Apprentice" in *A Harvest of Stories* by Dorothy Canfield Fisher. Used by permission of Harcourt Brace Jovanovich, Inc. A SICK CALL, copyright © 1959 by Morley Callaghan, is used by permission of Harold Matson Company, Inc. THE LOSS, copyright © 1973 by Gillian Tindall, is from *Dances of Death: Short Stories on a Theme* by Gillian Tindall. Used by permission of the publisher, Walker and Company, and of the author. TICKETS, PLEASE, copyright 1922 by Thomas B. Seltzer, Inc., copyright 1950 by Frieda Lawrence, is from *The Complete Short Stories of D. H. Lawrence, Volume II*. Used by permission of The Viking Press and of Laurence Pollinger Ltd. and the Estate of the late Mrs. Frieda Lawrence. Page 268, line 28: excerpt from "I'm Afraid to Come Home in the Dark," copyright 1907 by Warner Bros. Inc., copyright renewed, all rights reserved, is used by permission of Warner Bros. Music. THE COUNTRY OF THE BLIND by H. G. Wells, copyright by Professor G. P. Wells, is used by permission of Professor G. P. Wells. THE GIFTS OF WAR, copyright © 1969 by Margaret Drabble, is used by permission of A. D. Peters & Co. Ltd. THE SKEDULE, copyright © H. H. Wilson, first appeared in 1956 in *Australian Signpost*, published by Cheshire Publishing Pty. Ltd. Used by permission of the author. "WELL I'M—!" by G. E. M. Skues is from *The Chalkstream Angler: Sidelines, Sidelights & Reflections*, and is used by permission of the publisher, Barry Shurlock & Co. (Publishers) Limited. THE WEATHER BREEDER by Merrill Denison is from *The Unheroic North*, copyright 1923 by McClelland & Stewart, Limited, and is used by permission of Elizabeth Denison. IN AND OUT THE HOUSES, copyright © 1971 by Elizabeth Taylor, copyright © 1972 by The Literary Estate of Elizabeth Taylor, is from *The Devastating Boys and Other Stories* by Elizabeth Taylor. Used by permission of The Viking Press, Inc., of The Literary Estate of Elizabeth Taylor, and of Chatto